A PLUME BOOK

CRUSADE

ROBYN YOUNG is the author of the internationally bestselling Brethren trilogy, which includes *Brethren*, *Crusade*, and the forthcoming *The Fall of the Templars*. She has traveled extensively in Europe and Egypt and has a Masters in Creative Writing from the University of Sussex. During an eclectic career, she has been a creative writing teacher, financial advisor, folk singer, and music festival organizer. She lives in Brighton, England.

Praise for the novels of Robyn Young

"A terrific thirteenth-century thriller."   —*Midwest Book Review*

"Intricate but wonderfully written, a romp of a read and an exhilarating ride . . . [*Crusade*] evokes the atmosphere of the times brilliantly."
                                                    —*The Birmingham Post* (UK)

"One of the best historical debuts in recent memory. Exciting and enthralling."
                        —John Connolly, bestselling author of *Bad Men*

"Swords clash in the first sentence of Young's latest and go on clashing throughout . . . Plenty of action . . . [and] attention to historical detail offset by pacey dialog."   —*The Times* (London)

"*Crusade* is a sweeping historical adventure."   —*Financial Times*

"Pacey but intricate . . . this book will not disappoint those wanting to dive into an epic story of war."   —*News of the World*

"Richly worked and captivating . . . an epic story of war, intrigue, and heroism."
                                                    —*The Good Book Guide*

"Pacey and well-written, with vivid, convincing characters, *Brethren* captures your interest until the last page. I eagerly anticipate the sequel, knowing I will not be disappointed."
                —Alison Weir, author of *Eleanor of Aquitaine* and *Henry VIII*

CRUSADE

ROBYN YOUNG

A PLUME BOOK

PLUME
Published by the Penguin Group
Penguin Group (USA) Inc., 375 Hudson Street, New York, New York 10014, U.S.A. • Penguin
Group (Canada), 90 Eglinton Avenue East, Suite 700, Toronto, Ontario, Canada M4P 2Y3 (a
division of Pearson Penguin Canada Inc.) • Penguin Books Ltd., 80 Strand, London WC2R 0RL,
England • Penguin Ireland, 25 St. Stephen's Green, Dublin 2, Ireland (a division of Penguin Books
Ltd.) • Penguin Group (Australia), 250 Camberwell Road, Camberwell, Victoria 3124, Australia (a
division of Pearson Australia Group Pty. Ltd.) • Penguin Books India Pvt. Ltd., 11 Community
Centre, Panchsheel Park, New Delhi – 110 017, India • Penguin Group (NZ), 67 Apollo Drive,
Rosedale, North Shore 0632, New Zealand (a division of Pearson New Zealand Ltd.) • Penguin Books
(South Africa) (Pty.) Ltd., 24 Sturdee Avenue, Rosebank, Johannesburg 2196, South Africa

Penguin Books Ltd., Registered Offices: 80 Strand, London WC2R 0RL, England

Published by arrangement with Hodder & Stoughton Limited.

Published by Plume, a member of Penguin Group (USA) Inc. Previously published in a Dutton
edition.

First Plume Printing, August 2008
1   3   5   7   9   10   8   6   4   2

Copyright © Robyn Young, 2007
Excerpt from *The Fall of the Templars* copyright © Robyn Young, 2008
Map © Sandra Oakins
All rights reserved

Ⓟ REGISTERED TRADEMARK—MARCA REGISTRADA

The Library of Congress has catalogued the Dutton edition as follows:
Young, Robyn, 1975–
Crusade / Robyn Young.
p. cm.
ISBN 978-0-525-95016-5 (hc.)
ISBN 978-0-452-28960-4 (pbk.)
1. Crusades—Eighth, 1270—Fiction. I. Title.
PS3625.O97C78 2007
813'.6—dc22   2007016163

Printed in the United States of America

Contents

Acknowledgments

Once again, I find myself indebted to a large number of people, without whom this book, or at least my sanity, may not have prevailed.

Love and thanks to my parents for their constant encouragement and unfailing support. Special thanks also to Sue and Dave for the roof over our heads and for finding so many excuses for celebration.

Much love to all my friends who allowed me to share this incredible journey with them. In particular I want to thank Jo, Niall, Mark, Bridie, Clare, Liz, Monica, Patrik, Becky and Charley for their generosity, both in terms of help with the creative process and their friendship. Also, hats off to Ali for being a star.

My gratitude to David Boyle for great reading suggestions, who I must also credit for the fantastic chapter on Acre in his book *Blondel's Song*, which gave me a real insight into the city. Thanks to staff at the language department of the British Library for their help with the "code" issue and to Charles Davies for checking it over. And my sincere thanks to Dr. Mark Philpott at the Centre for Medieval and Renaissance Studies and Keble College, Oxford, for casting an expert eye over the manuscript. Any mistakes remain my own.

Many, many thanks as ever to my agent, Rupert Heath, for generally being a superstar and for guiding me around the corners.

I am greatly indebted to everyone at Hodder & Stoughton for their amazing support and commitment. Special thanks go to my editor, Nick Sayers, for pearls of wisdom; his assistant, Anne Clarke, for keeping everything running smoothly; and also to Emma Knight, Kelly Edgson-Wright, Antonia Lance and Lucy Hale. But there are many others, particularly those in the art department, foreign rights, sales, marketing and publicity who I cannot fit onto this page, but whose hard work is nonetheless enormously appreciated.

Huge thanks also to my fantastic American publishers at Dutton, especially my editor, Julie Doughty, for her insightful suggestions.

Last, but in no sense least, my love goes to Lee. Without him none of this would have been possible ... or half as much fun.

CRUSADE

Black Sea

KINGDOM of CILICIA

COUNTY of EDESSA

Kayseri •

ANATOLIA

PERSIA

Taurus Mountains

• Edessa
• al-Bira

Antioch

• Aleppo

CYPRUS

PRINCIPALITY of ANTIOCH

SYRIA

Tripoli

COUNTY of TRIPOLI

Beirut

Mediterranean
Sea

• Damascus

Baghdad •

Tyre
Acre

Kabul

KINGDOM of JERUSALEM

Caesarea

R. Jordan

Alexandria

Jerusalem

Dead sea

al-salihiyya

• Cairo

Sinai
Desert

ARABIA

R. Nile

EGYPT

The Hijaz

Red Sea

• Medina

THE
HOLY LAND

• Mecca

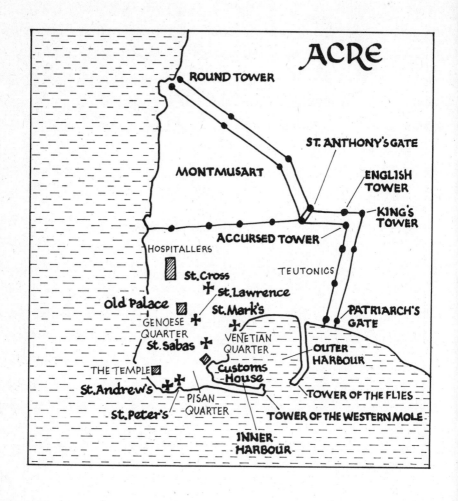

PART ONE

✝

1

The Venetian Quarter, Acre,
The Kingdom of Jerusalem

28 SEPTEMBER A.D. 1274

The swords arced, then swung in and slammed together. Steel met steel with harsh ringing clangs, again and again. Each blow was fiercer than the last, the brutal concussion almost wrenching the weapons from the hands of the wielders. The sun baked the courtyard's dusty red stones and beat down on the heads of the two men who stamped and lunged, back and forth.

The smaller of the two was sweating profusely, his white hair plastered to his head, lips curled back in fierce concentration. His shirt was drenched and stuck to his back. Neither he nor his opponent wore armor. He was initiating more of the attacks, stepping forward after several whip-quick parries to thrust a lethal jab at the other man's chest. But the strokes were becoming desperate. It was as if each one had been designed to be the last—precise, powerful—and he hadn't expected to have to force another. He couldn't keep up such a barrage. He was exhausted, and his tall, athletic opponent kept blocking, with imperturbable ease, each and every blow. And the more frustrated and frantic the small man became, the more his opponent grinned. It was the kind of grin a shark might flash when opening its razor-lined jaws for the killing bite. It was a little strained—more bared, gritted teeth than smile—but Angelo Vitturi was clearly enjoying himself.

After several more thrusts, however, which he snapped aside with savage, blocking cuts of his sword, Angelo grew bored. It was hot, and he could feel a blister forming on the ridge of his palm where his skin had rubbed against the leather grip of the slender, narrow-edged blade, the pommel of which was a chunk of translucent rock crystal. As the small man lunged in again, Angelo sidestepped him, grabbed hold of his wrist and turned his hand viciously aside, bringing the edge of his own blade up to the man's throat. The man let out a yelp, part in frustration, part at the pain in his wrist.

Angelo's face, wet with perspiration and set with boyish, scornful pleasure, hardened with contempt. "Get out." Dropping the man's wrist, he lowered his blade and leaned it against a low wall that ringed a square of grass.

The white-haired man stood there agape, sweat dripping from his nose as Angelo strode over to a servant, standing rigid as the statues that decorated the palazzo's courtyard. The servant handed Angelo a goblet of watered-down wine from the silver tray he carried. Angelo drained it, then turned to the gaping man. "I told you to leave."

The man seemed to collect himself. "My money, sir?"

"Money?"

"For my tuition, sir," said the man, unable to meet Angelo's unwavering, black-eyed stare.

Angelo laughed. "And what would I be paying for? What new skills have you taught me today? What has this lesson given me that is worth a single sequin?" He arched an eyebrow. "The amusement perhaps?" He set the goblet on the servant's tray. "Leave, before I decide to finish the duel. You'll lose more than your wages if I do." Turning his back on the instructor, he picked up a black velvet cloak trimmed with sable that was draped over the wall and shrugged it on.

The sword instructor, utterly defeated, snatched up his own coat and headed across the courtyard, his face a mottled red.

Angelo was fastening a belt of silver rings around his waist when a girl appeared through one of the doors that led into the grand building behind him. Like the other household slaves, she wore a filmy white gown, girdled at the waist with stiff gold braid. A coif covered her hair. She saw Angelo and headed over, eyes downcast, expression carefully blank.

"My lord ask me tell you his guests arrive." Her words were hard to understand, clipped and strained with the still unfamiliar language she forced her tongue around. "He asks you join them, sir."

With a forceful stab that made the girl start, Angelo sheathed his sword in the scabbard that hung from his belt. Without acknowledging her, he walked toward the palazzo, the girl flinching from him as he passed.

At twenty-eight, Angelo was the eldest son of Venerio Vitturi and heir to the family business, established prior to the Third Crusade by his great-grandfather, Vittorio. Angelo was a regular sight in Acre's slave market, where he sold off any surplus his father had acquired before helping to ship the bulk back to Venice. When the business was in its heyday, at a time when the Venetians controlled trade around the Black Sea, the Vitturi family had dominated the slave markets on the borders of the Mongol Empire. They supplied the prettiest girls to Western nobles in Outremer and Venice, and the strongest boys to the Mamluk Army in Egypt. But then Genoa, the second of the three great Italian merchant states, wrested control of the Black Sea trade and forced Venice out. The Vitturis were one of only a few Venetian families who still trafficked in humans, and they now had to rely on trade coming north from the Red Sea for their supply.

The girls Angelo's father kept for the household were always the best of the crop. Aged between eleven and sixteen, they were mostly petite Mongolians, with oval eyes and glossy black hair, and Circassians whose youthful faces already showed signs of the handsome, strong-boned lines characteristic of their race. Venerio's family had grown rapidly over the past ten years, and Angelo resented every darkly pretty sibling that was presented to the household, none of whom looked anything like his plump mother. Though the girls who bore his father's accidental offspring remained slaves, their own children were brought up as free citizens, baptized and educated. Angelo could understand his father being unable to resist the temptations of such young, exotic flesh; he himself had sampled it and had found it pleasing. But he couldn't comprehend how Venerio could raise the products of these low women in the same way he did his own. Things, Angelo had long ago decided, would change when he ran the business. If, that was, he still had a business to inherit. The way the last year had gone, it was looking increasingly uncertain. But he refused to fully consider that possibility. And if all went according to plan today, he wouldn't have to.

Angelo walked down a wide passage decorated with blue and white mosaics. As he pushed open a set of dark wood doors, four men looked up from where they were seated around a large octagonal table positioned centrally in the spacious, airy reception room.

Angelo regarded the men as he approached the table. There was the armorer, Renaud de Tours, a balding man of middle years, who had clad King Louis IX and his elite French knights during both of the sovereign's ill-fated Crusades. Beside Renaud, hands clasped tightly on the table, was Michael Pisani, a dark, slender Pisan specializing in the exportation of Damascene swords, some of the strongest blades in the known world, who also supplied nobles of the West for war. He was much feared by his competitors, whom he had been known to force out of deals, using mercenaries to intimidate his rivals into capitulating, leaving him to secure the contracts. The third man, sunburned and sandy-haired, was Conradt von Bremen, whose home city was affiliated to the Hanseatic League, the powerful confederation of German cities that ruled the Baltic Sea. Conradt's business, favored by a lucrative contract with the Teutonic

Knights, was the breeding and shipping of warhorses. The German's flat blue eyes and lazy smile concealed a potentially more sinister nature, for it was rumored he had ordered the murders of two of his own brothers to seize control of the family business, although this was perhaps malicious gossip put about by his competitors to discredit him. No one knew for sure. The bulky, sweating man trussed up in a heavy, brocaded coat despite his obvious warmth was Guido Soranzo, an affluent Genoese shipbuilder. Angelo knew them all, most merchants in Acre did, for they were four of the most successful Western traders in the Holy Land, his father excluded.

As Angelo sat, a fifth man came into view from an adjacent room, followed by three slave girls in white, who trailed him like the wispy tail of a comet. They carried silver trays on which were jugs of rose-colored wine, goblets and pewter dishes laden with black grapes, purple figs and almonds dusted white with sugar. "My son," said Venerio in greeting as he spotted Angelo. His voice was deep and gritty. Though a solidly built man, he moved with a gracefulness acquired from years of instruction with the sword. Knighted by the doge of Venice, and a former governor of the republic, Venerio was a fourth-generation noble with all the schooling and military training that went with the title. "How was your lesson?" he asked, as the girls fanned out around him, waiting until he sat before placing the platters and jugs on the table.

"I need a new instructor."

"Already? That is the second you have been through in as many days. Perhaps you no longer require training."

"Not from the dregs I have fought this week."

"Still," said Venerio, smiling a cool, expansive welcome at the silent men around the table, "these are matters for another time. We have rather more grave concerns to discuss today."

Angelo smiled to himself as he took in the merchants' expressions. Behind those carefully composed exteriors he detected confusion, impatience and, from Guido Soranzo at least, barely concealed anger. None of them knew why they had been invited here. But they were about to find out.

Wiping his brow with a crumpled silk cloth that he snatched from the sleeve of his brocaded coat, Guido was the first to speak. "And what are these grave concerns?" He fixed Venerio with a truculent stare. "Why have you called us here, Vitturi?"

"First, let us drink," replied Venerio, slipping with ease into the Genoese dialect. Two slave girls came forward at a snap of his fingers and began to pour the wine.

Guido, however, wasn't ready to dance to his host's tune. Not bothering to do Venerio the courtesy of speaking the Venetian tongue, he continued in his native Genoese. "I have no desire to drink your wine until I know why I have been summoned." He extended a meaty hand to the luxurious chamber. "Did you bring me here to gloat?"

"Nothing quite so petty, I assure you."

Guido erupted at Venerio's calm. "You sit in a palace of my kinsmen like a barbarian who wears the adornments of his victims as trophies!"

"Venice did not start the battle that resulted in Genoa's expulsion from Acre, Guido."

"The monastery of St. Sabas was rightfully ours! We were protecting our property!"

Venerio's jaw twitched with the first sign of irritation. "Is that what you were doing after you seized the monastery? When you broke into our quarter, over-ran homes, killed men and women, burned scores of our ships in the harbor? Protecting your property?" His face relaxed, his voice sinking back to its normal level. "You kept your own palace, did you not? You benefited from the war as much as I did, Guido. Unlike the majority of your people, you retained your business in Acre. Besides, the Genoese have now been allowed back into their quarter."

"Our quarter? That which the Venetians have left for us is little more than a ruin!"

"Comrades," interrupted Conradt in languid, heavily accented Italian. "The War of St. Sabas ended almost fourteen years ago. Let us leave the past where it belongs. Your wine is making my mouth water, Venerio." He gestured to the goblets, his eyes swinging to Guido. "Must we argue over old battles whilst thirsty and still sober?"

"Well said," said Michael Pisani, raising his goblet and drinking.

After a moment, Guido settled into a belligerent silence. Seizing his goblet, he gulped at the wine.

"Gentlemen," said Venerio, leaning forward, his navy silk burnous, the long Arab-style cloak with a hood worn by many settlers, straining at his broad chest, "I thank you for attending this meeting. I appreciate my invitation must have come as a surprise. None of us are friends. Indeed, at one time or another we have all been on opposite sides in conflict. But now, perhaps for the first time, we have something in common." He paused, meeting their gazes. "Our businesses are failing."

There was silence.

Michael unclasped his long-fingered hands, leaned back, then sat forward again. Conradt smiled, but his blue eyes had fixed intently on Venerio.

After a moment, Renaud spoke, in a singsong voice that was like the ringing of a tiny bell. "You are mistaken, Venerio. My business is perfectly secure." He stood. "I thank you for your hospitality, but I do not believe that I have anything further to discuss with you." He inclined his head to the others. "Good day."

"When did you last make armor for the kings of the West, Renaud?" questioned Venerio, rising to tower over the diminutive Frenchman. "How long is it since you equipped an army for battle? And you, Conradt?" He turned to the German. "How many horses have the Teutonics bought from you this year? How long is it since kings and princes bartered for consignments of your destriers?"

"That isn't your concern," murmured Conradt, his smile fading.

Venerio turned to Guido, who was staring up at him with undisguised hostility. "My sources tell me your shipyards haven't been active for months, here or in the Genoese quarter at Tyre."

"I cannot believe I am hearing this," growled Guido. "You might have stolen yourself a Genoese palace, Venerio, but I swear by God you will not have my business. Were I living in the gutter without a shirt on my back, I would not sell it to you!"

"I do not want your business. Any of them," said Venerio, looking at the others. "I am in the same position as you."

Guido snorted.

"My father speaks the truth," said Angelo grimly, his black eyes on Guido. "If our profits continue to fall the way they have these past two years, we will not be able to afford to keep this palace. We have already had to dismiss four servants. In the last twelve months we have seen a sharp decrease in revenue. In the past the Vitturi Company's most profitable contracts were with the Mamluks, but since Sultan Baybars began his campaigns against our forces in Palestine and the Mongols in Syria, he has had slaves free for the taking. In his attack on Antioch alone he is rumored to have captured more than forty thousand. That glut, coupled with the new truce, means that he doesn't currently require slaves from us as soldiers for his army."

Venerio was nodding. "Over the last century our businesses, established by our fathers and forefathers, rose to become five of the oldest and most affluent companies in the Eastern world. Now I see vendors of sugar, cloth and spices taking *our* places," Venerio jabbed the table with his finger, "*our* profits."

Renaud had now sat, but still appeared poised to leave.

"It has been a slow year for us all," said Michael Pisani. "I will admit my business is suffering. But I do not see what point there is in the frank discussion of such personal affairs. There is nothing we can do."

"There is," responded Venerio, sitting back down. "If we work together, we can turn our fortunes around. Desire for Crusade wanes in the West, and in the East the Mamluks remain bound by the truce. That is the cause of our falling capital; the peace treaty signed between Edward of England and Sultan Baybars two years ago." Venerio swept a hand through his hair, which was as clipped and neat as the rest of him, shot through with white. "Our businesses profit from war, not peace."

Guido snorted again. "And what do you propose, Venerio? That we end the peace?"

"Yes. That is exactly what I propose."

"This is preposterous!" exclaimed Guido.

The other men looked astonished.

"War is necessary to our businesses, Guido," responded Venerio calmly. "It is what we need to survive."

"It is *contracts* we need," snapped Guido.

"We deal in blood, in battle. Every one of us has been made rich through conflict. Let's not be coy about it."

Guido went to argue, but Michael interrupted him. "Wait, Guido," he said, watching Venerio, "let him speak."

"There have been periods before," continued Venerio, "when such truces have created a lull in the markets we deal in, but this year, I think you will agree, has been particularly bad. We have lost many trade lines and outposts to the Mamluks this past decade. Now that Acre, Tyre and Tripoli are the only worthwhile cities Baybars's campaign has left us with, competition for trade between us and our younger rival firms grows fierce."

Michael nodded. "And now the new grand master of the Templars has been granted consent to build a fleet to serve the eastern Mediterranean, that competition will only grow."

"The fleet will be for military use," Renaud interjected. "That is what was agreed at the Council of Lyons in May. As I heard it, the grand master wants to block merchant ships out of Egypt, weakening the Saracens' trading abilities. The pope would not have approved the motion had it been for mercantile purposes. The military orders remain the papacy's last hope for the retaking of Jerusalem and the winning back of territory lost to the Saracens. I doubt the pope would want the Templars to waste such valuable resources by lining their own pockets."

"The Temple has been lining its pockets for years." Conradt shrugged. "I would not be surprised if they used this opportunity to fill them."

Venerio interrupted. "This is not an issue we need concern ourselves with today."

"I doubt you will have to concern yourself with it at all," said Guido bitterly, draining his wine and setting his goblet down hard. "Venice and the Temple will go hand in hand as always. My business will suffer more than any of yours from the grand master's contract."

"How so," responded Venerio, "when the Knights of St. John have entered into the venture with the Templars? You have not, as far as I'm aware, lost your contracts with them. Indeed, I would expect your business to thrive with this opportunity."

"We all know how the mighty Temple works," spat Guido, pouring himself another measure of wine. Some of it sloshed onto the table. "They will take over the whole venture. I doubt the Hospitallers will build so much as an oar!"

"If that is the case, I assume you will want to find other ways of reviving your shipyards in the meantime?"

Guido glowered into his goblet, but said nothing.

Venerio looked around the table. "Do you want to see your wives in the streets begging for food?" he demanded. "Your servants gone, your finery and homes sold? Look outside your palaces. There are nobles like you who have lost everything. You'll find them rotting in Acre's gutters with the flies, the dung and the lepers. Do you know how many children I've bought from starving parents desperate to feed newborns? Do you want your own children sold in the markets to a rich amir?"

"This is distasteful, Venerio," said Renaud, frowning delicately. "None of us want that, of course."

"If we do nothing, Renaud, that might be what we face. We know full well the only reason the Saracens have kept the truce is because they have been forced to concentrate their efforts on the Mongols. When they are ready, the Mamluks will turn their eye to us again and they will destroy us. I have worked with them long enough to know how they hate our kind, how they want us gone. And until that day comes, and I assure you it will, we sit here waiting for our destruction, getting poorer by the day. We must do something now, on *our* terms, before we lose everything."

Conradt plucked a handful of grapes from a platter and rolled one into his mouth. "I am mystified by your proposal, Venerio. How do you plan on breaking the truce established between our forces and the Saracens?" He picked the seeds from his teeth. "The Christian troops are weak and divided. There is trouble over the throne. And unless we mounted a full-scale invasion against Egypt itself, I do not see what would spur the Saracens to launch any serious assault."

"What I propose will bring conflict to Palestine," responded Venerio briskly, "of that I have no doubt. To the Muslims it will be a far greater act of war than any we could perpetrate against their cities. They would rise against our forces in the thousands. And, yes, we will need military might to accomplish it, but not an army, just a small group of soldiers."

"And which tree will you pluck those from, Venerio?" said Guido cuttingly.

"We plan to have help from the Temple," answered Angelo. "The new grand master has been very vocal about the need to take back territory lost to the Saracens. From what we have been told, he intends to come to Acre to take up his position a year from now. We believe he can be persuaded to help us. We are confident he will see the benefit behind the risk."

Guido grunted, but averted his eyes as Angelo continued to look at him.

Michael was frowning. "Even if we manage to start a war, we do not have a hope of finishing one. We cannot beat the Saracens in battle. It would be over before it began."

"If our forces were defeated by the Mamluks, we would still not lose out, Michael," countered Venerio. "Indeed, we would profit from the West's expulsion from these shores. The Mamluks, if victorious, would drive out our competitors, leaving us free to dominate trade between the East and our homelands. We do not need to keep a base here in order to make money from the Saracens. They will have other battles to fight when our forces have gone, the Mongols, for instance. They will still need to be equipped for war." Venerio paused to let his words sink in. Michael and Conradt were looking thoughtful. "Ultimately, it would not matter who won, Christians or Saracens. Either way, our profits would soar."

"But what, *exactly*, will we do, Venerio?" asked Renaud. "What is your proposal?"

Venerio smiled. He had their attention, he could hear it in their voices, see it in their faces. Even Guido was listening now. He took up his goblet. "Gentlemen, we are going to change the world."

2

The Genoese Quarter, Acre

13 JANUARY A.D. 1276

"Marco, tell me! What are you going to do?"

"Let go of me, Luca," said Marco in a low voice, trying to prise the young boy's hands off his arm.

"I'm your brother! Tell me!"

There was a muffled cough from the adjacent room, and a tremulous voice floated through the limp sacking that covered the opening. "Marco? Is that you?"

"Yes, Mama," called Marco, still struggling, as quietly as possible, with his brother.

"Where have you been?"

"Working, Mama."

There was a contented sounding sigh. "You're a good man, Marco." The quivering words ended abruptly in a fit of coughing, a series of violent whooping sounds that made both brothers flinch.

Luca's brown eyes, large with fear, flicked to the opening.

"Go," urged Marco in a whisper, "get her some water. She needs you!"

Luca looked as if he were about to concede, then the coughing faded into long rattling breaths. Emboldened, he stared up at his brother. "I'll tell Father."

Marco's eyes narrowed. He jerked his arm from Luca's grip, causing the boy to stumble forward. "Tell him then," he hissed. "But you know he'll be too drunk to listen!" Marco fell silent, his gaze fixing on the object of their struggle that remained tightly grasped in his fist. The dagger's deadly sharp tip was pointed at his brother's face. Slowly, he lowered the blade, his hand white-knuckled around the hilt.

"It's Sclavo, isn't it?" said Luca in a tiny voice. "You're working for him again. You promised. You said you wouldn't do it anymore. You *promised*."

"What else can I do?" muttered Marco roughly. "We're Genoese. Do you know what that means in this city? It means we're nothing. The Venetians and the Pisans and the rest have taken everything from us. Sclavo's the only one who'll give me work."

"Father said we would go to Tyre. He'll work again and we'll help him and Mama will get well."

"He's been saying that forever," snapped Marco. "It's never going to happen."

"Maybe it will. You don't know."

"I can't believe you can still put your faith in him." Marco kept his voice low with effort. "He doesn't give a damn about anything, not since he lost the business."

"It wasn't his fault; it was the war."

"You're too young to know what you're talking about," said Marco bitterly. "I was six when the War of St. Sabas ended. I remember. Father could have left the bakehouse and gone to Tyre with the others, started again. But he was too proud, too stubborn to let the Venetians win, and so he stayed. I watched as the Genoese left our quarter and the families who bought our bread began to vanish." Marco's fierce eyes were bright. "In the end, he couldn't afford to have his crops gathered or his grain milled."

Luca was watching Marco in silence, anguished to see his older brother in such open distress. "Maybe it will get better, now the Genoese are starting to come back."

"It will take years for our people to rebuild what they had here, and Father no longer cares about the business. He doesn't care about anything except his drink and his whores!"

Luca clapped his hands over his ears, but Marco threw down the dagger and grabbed his brother's wrists, pulling his hands away. He dragged Luca to the window, away from the opening to the adjacent room, where their mother's breaths had evened out into the wheezing sighs she made when she was sleeping.

"Where do you think the money from the family who lives below us goes?" Marco demanded. "Father rented our house so he could keep visiting the taverns! When are you going to open your eyes, Luca? It's just you and me and Mama now. We have to take care of ourselves!"

"Sclavo's a bad man," sobbed Luca. "You've come back with blood on you. I've seen it on your clothes. And I've seen how people look at you, like they're scared. They say you do bad things."

"I have no *choice*, Luca. Who else will feed you or buy Mama the potions she needs?" Marco cupped his brother's chin in his hand. He licked his thumb and wiped a smudge of dirt from Luca's cheek. "This is the last time I will do anything for Sclavo, I promise."

"You said that before."

"This time it's different. Sclavo will pay me enough money that we won't have to worry about anything for the rest of this year. I can look for other work, down at the docks or collecting night soil for the market gardens, *anything.*"

Luca looked at the dagger that was lying on the floor, its blade glinting dully. "You're going to hurt someone," he murmured.

Marco's jaw tightened. "If I don't, Mama won't survive the rest of the winter. You have to let me go, Luca. And you cannot tell Father. Will you do this for me?" When Luca hesitated, Marco added, "For Mama?"

Luca gave a small nod and Marco forced a reassuring smile. Letting go of his brother, he crossed the bare boards and picked up the dagger. He snatched up a lumpy-looking sack bag and stowed the blade inside, between a coarse blanket and a loaf of hard bread.

"How long will you be gone?" asked Luca, watching him tie a knot in the sack. A chill wind that smelled of rain gusted through the window behind him, making him shudder. "What if Mama gets worse?"

Marco paused, glancing at his brother. "I'm going to the harbor. I don't know how long I'll have to wait for his ship. Maybe days, maybe longer." He sounded nervous for the first time. "It should be here soon, that's all I know."

"Whose ship?"

"You know where Mama's potion is. If she gets sick, you can give it to her." Marco went to his brother. "Tell her I'm working. You can tell Father the same, if he asks." He gave Luca a rough hug, then headed out, bundling the sack over his shoulder.

Luca crept into his mother's room. It was dominated by the straw-filled mattress on which she lay, fragile as a wounded bird, a worn-out blanket pulled up to her face. He crouched and felt her brow. It was neither too hot nor too cold. He kissed her cheek, soft as parchment, then left, closing the door quietly behind him.

THE TEMPLE, ACRE, 17 JANUARY A.D. 1276

Will Campbell planted his hands on the ledge and looked out of the narrow window. The view before him fell dizzyingly into space. Far below, waves crashed against the rocks at the base of the adjacent treasury tower that jutted from the preceptory's curtain wall. Will felt the impact vibrate in the stone. The wind coming off the blue Mediterranean was freezing, and he was glad of the thick mantle he wore over his surcoat and undershirt, the splayed red cross at his heart blood-scarlet against the white. He remembered winters in Scotland and in London and Paris, where he'd spent his adolescence, being bitterer than this. But after eight years in the Holy Land, he had grown accustomed to the warmer climate and had been surprised by the plummeting temperatures.

It had been a hard winter. The coldest, some had said, for forty years. Northerly winds raced up from the sea to be funneled through the stone maze of churches, palaces, shops and mosques of the Crusader capital, chasing rubbish into the air, snatching back hoods and flicking off caps, whipping tears from eyes. Now the ice that rich nobles paid to have brought to them from the peak of Mount Carmel in the summer sprouted freely from window ledges and door lintels for street children to snap off and suck. In the outer harbor, galleys rose and fell with the waves that curled in past the breakwater, spewing gusts of foam into the air as they struck the base of the Tower of the Flies, a sentry fort positioned on the extremity of the eastern mole. No ships had ventured out of the harbor for several weeks and none had entered. The knights of the Temple now kept constant vigil on the preceptory's seaward walls, squinting at the storm-dark horizon and cursing the weather as they waited for a glimpse of the longed-for vessel that would bear their grand master to the shore for the first time since his election over two years ago. The mood among the hundreds of knights, priests, sergeants and servants that inhabited the preceptory was one of feverish impatience.

The door opened and a man entered, joining the nine others in the chamber. Will looked around as he heard a familiar rasping cough and saw Everard de Troyes shuffling to a stool that had been left free beside the fire. The ancient priest's wrinkled face, with its ugly scar that furrowed his cheek from lip to brow, was pale against the black of his robes. A pair of spectacles was pushed high on his nose, the glass almost touching his bloodshot eyes. Fragile wisps of white hair floated around his face from beneath his cowl. "I apologize for my lateness," he said, his voice, though frail, commanding the attention of every man in the room. "But the walk here almost defeated me." He sat heavily on the stool and frowned at the strapping man with iron-black hair who sat opposite him. "I do not see why we must always meet in your quarters, Master Seneschal. Perhaps in my youth I could have bounded up a hundred steps like a mountain goat, but such a time is many winters past."

"We agreed, Brother Everard," responded the seneschal stiffly, "that this was the most appropriate setting for full assemblies of the Brethren. At least here, I can give the excuse that we are meeting to discuss Temple business. I doubt such a claim would deter interested inquirers were we to meet in your chambers. We are too large a group to gather unnoticed. We must be careful when we do that suspicions are not aroused."

"With the exception of the marshal you are currently the most senior Templar official in Outremer, Master Seneschal. I doubt anyone would dare to question your movements." Everard sighed as the seneschal's brow creased. "But I agree, we must be careful."

"Certainly we must when the grand master arrives," said the seneschal grimly. "Then the freedom we have enjoyed these past two years will be sorely restricted." He looked around the chamber at the other men. "Some of you have not yet borne the burden that others of us have endured; to live and work alongside a master to whom you have sworn allegiance, and whom you must deceive, even work directly against, each day. When you joined the Brethren, you were asked to swear new oaths, oaths that would run counter to those you swore when you were initiated into the Temple. When he comes, you will fully understand the weight of this charge. But it is something you will learn to overcome," he emphasized, covering them all with his gaze. "The secrecy of the Anima Templi must be maintained at all costs. We were almost exposed seven years ago by those who, through ignorance and malice, wished to destroy us. The simplest mistake could cost us our lives." He glanced involuntarily at Everard, who scowled, knowing that the seneschal was referring to the Book of the Grail. "Never forget," the seneschal continued, pretending not to notice Everard's discomfort, "you each believe our aims are laudable, but the Church would burn us at the stake were they to discover what we are working toward. And if they knew what we were using the Temple's coffers to achieve, the men of our own order, our brothers-in-arms, would be there to help fan the flames."

Will watched the men as they listened intently to the seneschal, who was more than twice the age of some of them and four times as imposing. The young Portuguese priest who had joined the Brethren a few years after Will, the three recently admitted knights and the sergeant, at twenty their youngest member, were transfixed. Even the two older knights who had worked alongside the seneschal for years seemed engrossed. Everard might be the head of the Anima Templi, but the seneschal was its backbone.

It was the first time in months that the ten of them had met as one. Only two of their group were missing: the knights who looked after their interests in the West and were based in London and Paris. Together, twelve for the Disciples of Christ, they formed the Anima Templi: the Soul of the Temple.

Will was not quite so enthralled by the seneschal's rousing speech. He found it hard to get on with the domineering man who, outside the Brethren, was responsible for overseeing the general administration of the Temple in the East, with particular regard to judicial proceedings within the order and the punishment of knights. The seneschal had never forgiven him for his rebellion five years ago and made it plain that he still believed Will should have been imprisoned for life for his treacherous conduct. Admittedly, it had been a grave misuse of the Anima Templi's resources that cost one man his life and almost destroyed any chance of peace between the Christians and Muslims. But Will felt he had apologized enough and had more than proved his loyalty to the Anima Templi's cause in the years since. If he were able to turn back time and undo the illegal contract made with the Order of Assassins for the murder of Sultan Baybars, an attempt that failed and resulted instead in the death of one of the sultan's officers, then he gladly would. But as such a thing was impossible, he could only hope the seneschal and the other members of the Brethren would one day forgive him. He didn't want to continue paying for his mistake for the rest of his life.

"For now, let us open this meeting," finished the seneschal, looking to Everard, who had been gazing distractedly into the fire. "We have much to discuss."

"Indeed," said the priest, seeming to come to life. His pale eyes flicked to Will. "As Brother Campbell returned to us this morning with news from Egypt, I suggest he begin."

Will stood up straight as everyone turned to him. He locked eyes with the seneschal, who stared back, hostility carved into his chiseled face. "Several months ago, Brother Everard asked me to arrange a meeting with our Mamluk ally, Amir Kalawun, to discover the Mamluks' plans for the coming year. Twelve days ago I met with Kalawun's man on the frontier of the Sinai Desert."

"Forgive my interruption, Brother Campbell," said one of the younger knights tentatively, with a glance at the seneschal, "but might I ask why you didn't speak directly with the amir?"

"Kalawun feels it is too dangerous to meet with any of us face-to-face," said Everard, before Will could answer. "That was the condition under which he agreed to work with us when James Campbell first secured his support." The priest didn't notice Will tense at the mention of his father. "It is a reasonable and prudent provision. As Baybars's chief lieutenant, Kalawun is far too conspicuous to travel abroad unnoticed, and any absences would be difficult for him to explain. He has been using this particular servant as his go-between since he became our ally. If there were to have been any breaches in this confidence,

I believe they would have occurred by now. Continue, brother," said Everard to Will.

"The Mamluk camp has been relatively quiet since Sultan Baybars signed the ten-year truce with King Edward. For the past few months, they have mostly been concerned with preparations for the forthcoming marriage of Baybars's son to Kalawun's daughter. A move," added Will, looking at the newer members, "that we and Kalawun hope will bring him closer to the heir to the throne, over whom he continues to exert his influence. From what I was told, Baybars has no immediate plans to attack our forces. He is currently more focused on the Mongols. There are reports that they are encroaching on the Mamluks' northern territories."

The younger knights and the sergeant were nodding, looking pleased.

"This is good news, brothers," said Everard, watching them, "but we must remember how fragile the balance that now exists is. Many truces have been made between our forces and the Muslims over the years. Many have also been broken. It may seem a blessing that Baybars's eye is turned from us, but any war is detrimental to our cause and we cannot allow ourselves to be thankful that his gaze has fallen upon another race. Peace, brothers, is our aim, between all nations, all people." He fixed them with his blunt stare. "Remember that."

"Brother Everard is right," said Velasco, the Portuguese priest, a nervous little man who had a habit of raising his eyebrows whenever he spoke, as if continuously startled by the words coming out of his mouth. "And it's not just the Muslims we must focus our attention on. If the peace we have helped to create is to continue, our own forces must also be enlightened."

Will found himself frowning at the use of that word. It made him uncomfortable. He believed completely in the Anima Templi's aims, but the more idealistic concepts or, at least, the language of them, still sat uneasily in him, like a heavy meal he hadn't finished digesting.

Perhaps it was because for most of his life he had been taught to hate the very people he now formed alliances, even friendships, with. Saracens and Jews were enemies of God, to be reviled and fought, so the Church and the order had taught him. He no longer adhered to that doctrine, nor did he have any interest in reclaiming Jerusalem, or in fighting the so-called infidel. He had experienced the full horror of a battlefield and witnessed the undignified, senseless deaths of soldiers from both sides; had lost his father in one such conflict. He knew these were not routes to a better life. But so did many Westerners who had settled in Outremer, the land beyond the sea. In Acre, in the midst of such diversity where so many races lived and worked together, peace was not simply an ideal;

it was a necessity. Sometimes, Will felt the world around them was moving so congruously with their own that they should just stand up and shout about it. Sometimes he hated the secrecy of it all. But he knew this was how the Brethren survived. The world might seem to be moving in the same direction, but delve a little deeper and the old hatreds and hostilities could be felt, like riptides below the surface, even in Acre; the city of sin, as the pope in Rome had declared it. The Anima Templi's secrecy was its shield, protecting it from these conflicting forces.

Will was drawn from his thoughts as he noticed Everard watching him. The priest's expression was inscrutable. Will looked away, discomforted by the intensity of Everard's stare, feeling that the priest was reading his mind.

"Half that battle has been won for us," one of the younger knights was saying in response to Velasco's comments. "Until the Church accepts there is a need to reform and addresses the corruption that riddles its entire structure, it will find it a hard task to persuade the leaders of the West, let alone the people, that Crusade is a worthy route to absolution. For too long now, it has contrived these wars for its own purposes. Its motives have become transparent. Citizens of the West have no desire to make the treacherous journey here, risking life and limb, only to fall upon their swords, now it has been revealed that those who entice them to do so do it not for the glory of God, but for their own pockets."

One of the older knights, an Englishman called Thomas, shook his head in disagreement at the younger man's impassioned speech. "There are many Christians in the West who would gladly wrench Jerusalem from the Muslims given the chance. They still believe Muslims and Jews are blasphemers and worshippers of false gods, whose presence pollutes the Holy City. They still believe that they and *only* they follow the true path. Do not be so assured that the desire to Crusade is dead. It isn't."

"But at the Council of Lyons," countered the young knight, "no great Western kings came forward at the pope's call to take the Cross. Few even attended."

"At present, the West's leaders are too embroiled in their own struggles to commit to a Crusade," responded Thomas. "But all it needs is one strong ruler to unite a determined force beneath him and the men of the West will throng here in the hope of liberating the Holy City. The men of our own order want this. Brother Everard is right. The peace we have helped create within this kingdom is fragile indeed. A tug in either direction and it will tear."

"And I fear our grand master may be one such ruler," said the seneschal, clasping his large hands. "He has made no secret of the fact that he wishes to reclaim territory we have lost to Baybars through military means. At Lyons, he was the most credible advocate of a new Crusade. He could prove to be one of the gravest threats to peace we have faced since the treaty was signed."

Thomas and the other veteran knight were nodding soberly.

"Then we will need to do all we can to persuade him down other courses of action," said Velasco, his eyebrows shooting into his fringe. "We cannot allow Baybars to be given any cause to attack us whilst we are still so weak. His forces would overwhelm us. And Acre," he looked to Everard, a little abashed, "our Camelot, would perish, along with every citizen within its walls and any hope for reconciliation between Christians, Muslims and Jews that we, and our predecessors, have been striving for almost a century to bring about. Until Baybars dies and a new sultan, one with whom we have an alliance, assumes control of Egypt and Syria, we are not safe."

Everard gave a small smile at the mention of Camelot, his name for the city, but it quickly faded. "There may well be hard times ahead," he said in his gruff tones, "but there always will be. This is not an easy task with an easy solution that we have pledged ourselves to. Nothing that is worthwhile in this world ever is. It is a slow process." His eyes swiveled to Will. "But we are making progress. Despite our concerns, we mustn't lose sight of that. We now have a powerful ally in Egypt who will have influence over the next sultan, and in Acre we have formed alliances with those who believe in our cause. It was we, through our Guardian, who brought peace to Outremer. And all the while there is peace, all the while God's children live in harmony, we triumph."

Will leaned against the wall as the men soaked up Everard's speech. He saw the priest's words fill them with hope and conviction, and found himself surprised by just how inspiring the old man could be. He had known Everard for too long to be overly awed or cowed by him anymore; had been whipped, insulted, comforted and taught by him; had seen him at his best and his worst. But every now and then he would catch something, some spark of wonder in the priest's abrasive tone, and suddenly he would be nineteen again, back in the Temple in Paris, listening to Everard telling him about the Anima Templi for the first time.

Memory, he knew, had probably colored the moment, made it more grandiose, more momentous than it actually had been. But he remembered being held, as if in a spell, by the priest's revelations of how the Brethren were formed following a war with the Muslims that all but annihilated the Christian forces in the Holy Land; a war incited by a former Templar grand master. He recalled how attentively he listened as Everard explained how the Anima Templi's initial mandate was to protect the Temple and its vast military and economic resources from the personal or political agendas of its leaders. But that in time, as other members were admitted, many of them high officials and men of learning, they brought with them their own ideas and this aim grew to encompass the preservation of peace in Outremer and among the Christian, Muslim and Jewish faiths.

At the time, Will protested hotly against such a notion, saying that they were irreconcilable; that there could be only one true God for any of them, and that none of them would bow to the beliefs of the others. Even when Everard explained that the Anima Templi didn't propose to change the faiths to suit one another, but rather a mutual truce in which people of all religions could exist together, Will hadn't believed it possible. But in the years since, he had seen with his own eyes how people of any faith could live alongside one another, benefiting from trade and from shared knowledge and experience.

Now, as he listened to Everard discuss a treatise he and Velasco had written, outlining the similarities among the three faiths, Will wondered if he could ever be so inspiring. Could he move men to give up their lives for a cause he championed, the way the priest had moved his father, the way Everard had moved him? The thought crept into his mind of what they would do when Everard died. He was approaching ninety and was older than anyone Will had known. Often he thought the sheer bloody determination to see the Anima Templi's aims consummated was what held the old man together; was the sinew and the muscle where the flesh had long since failed. Will's eyes moved to the seneschal, who was talking about how they could distribute the treatise. The seneschal would most likely be elected as their head when Everard died. And Will knew, when that day came, his place in the circle he had helped Everard rebuild, the circle his father had sacrificed himself for, would hang in the balance.

The meeting continued for another hour before the seneschal brought it to a close. Will noticed that Everard seemed increasingly impatient and kept looking over at him. As the Brethren began to disperse, agreeing to meet again after the grand master had arrived, the priest caught him on the stairs.

"I need to speak with you, William."

"What is it?"

"Not here," replied Everard quietly. "Come to my quarters."

3

The Citadel, Cairo

17 JANUARY A.D. 1276

The beast paced, hunched shoulders flexing, slabs of muscle sliding and stiffening beneath the skin. Every now and then its lips would curl back to reveal rows of tusklike teeth and it would growl, a low rumbling noise that sounded as if it came from deep within the earth, like stones grinding. Its liquid gold eyes, flecked with jet, stared out through the bars of its cage at the milling, chattering crowds as it ranged the confines of its prison, instincts screaming against the incarceration, screaming to spring forward and attack.

On the other side of the grand hall, Kalawun al-Alfi, commander of the Syrian troops, watched the lion pace. It was magnificent. All power and raw fury. Later, they would tow its cage outside the city walls to a fanfare of trumpets and kettledrums, and set the beast free. For a time it would be beautiful. Then they would hunt it. Today, though, it was all for show. It would be the privilege of the bridegroom to make the killing strike, and Kalawun knew the usual excitement of the hunt would be dulled. He liked to track and pursue his quarry, liked to work and compete for the kill. This would be too easy. The death less noble.

Kalawun took a sip of sweet sherbet, his eyes moving over the mass of royal officials, governors and soldiers who filled the hall, their voices drowning the softly plucked notes of the zithers and harps being played by the musicians. His gaze drifted over his two sons, as-Salih Ali and al-Ashraf Khalil, both born to his second wife and both dark-haired like himself, with the same strong features. Khalil, at twelve his youngest child, was picking restlessly at the stiff collar of the blue cloak the servants had gently forced him into that morning. Kalawun smiled to himself, then looked away, his gaze caught by a knot of youths partially hidden behind one of the white-and-black marble pillars that flanked the chamber. One of the youths was Baraka Khan, heir to the throne of Egypt and, from today on, his son-in-law. Mildly curious as to what had caught their attention, Kalawun rose onto the steps of the dais behind him, where the sultan's throne stood, arms capped with the heads of two lions fashioned from gold.

Standing with his back to the wall, surrounded by the knot of boys, was a slave, a little older than the youths themselves, maybe sixteen or so. His head was tilted away from the group, eyes fixed on some distant point. His expression was paralyzed in an unreadable mask, and only his unnatural, frozen posture revealed his distress. Baraka was talking animatedly to the others, his face, framed by his black curly hair, split in a broad grin. Kalawun frowned and craned his head to see above the crowds.

A commander of one of the Mamluk regiments, clad in a yellow cloak, hailed him. "Amir, it was a beautiful ceremony. You must be pleased."

Kalawun nodded distractedly. "As pleased as any father could be, Amir Mahmud."

Mahmud maneuvered himself in front of Kalawun. "Perhaps, now the festivities are over, we can begin speaking of our strategy for the coming year. I was wondering if you had talked with the sultan? Perhaps you know of his plans?"

Kalawun noted the predatory look in the young commander's eyes. "No, Mahmud. My thoughts of late," he spread a hand to take in the chamber, "have been elsewhere."

"I understand," said Mahmud, touching his heart with false sincerity, "but now there will be less to occupy your thoughts, I thought we might speak to the sultan, arrange a council for—"

"Excuse me," said Kalawun, stepping down from the dais and moving past Mahmud, who glared after him. Two of the youths with Baraka had parted. In the gap between them, Kalawun had seen that Baraka had hold of the slave's tunic. He was lifting it, revealing the scars of the boy's castration to the others. A couple of the youths were laughing along with Baraka, the rest were staring in appalled fascination at the disfigurement. The slave closed his eyes.

For men such as Kalawun, the term *slave warrior* wasn't just a name. Years ago, he, like many other Mamluks, including Baybars, had been captured by slave traders following the Mongol invasions against the Kipchak Turks around the Black Sea. They were sold in the markets to officers in the Egyptian Army and, taken as prisoners to Cairo in their thousands, were educated as devout Muslims and raised into an elite fighting corps by the former Ayyubid sultans of Egypt. The Ayyubid dynasty had ended twenty-six years ago when the slave warriors overthrew their masters and took control of Egypt.

The younger boys remembered the parents and siblings they had been separated from. But over time, toughened by the rigorous training and consoled by the camaraderie of the barracks, those memories faded. When they were freed to become soldiers and officers of the Mamluk Army, very few deserted and returned to their families. Kalawun had been twenty when he was captured, old for a slave. He remembered his wife and child, memories that were slow to dissolve. Even now, at fifty-four, with three wives, three children and another on the way, he sometimes wondered whether his first family had survived the Mongols' attack and were out there somewhere, unaware he was still alive, unaware he was now one of the most powerful men in the East. Baraka, born into a world where the slave warriors were the rulers and resided in grand palaces surrounded by finery, didn't know the chains his heritage had broken from.

Generals and officers passed by the group of tormentors, but said nothing. The household slaves who, unlike soldiers, were subjected to castration to protect the harem and to keep the slaves themselves docile, occasionally rose from lowly beginnings to fill offices of high authority under their masters, even being sent as ambassadors to foreign dignitaries or training recruits for the army. But most, although often treated better than servants in Western households, were simply part of the silent, invisible race that thronged the halls and passages of every wealthy residence in Cairo. Baraka was a prince, the eunuch just another nameless body. Kalawun, however, would not ignore such cruelty.

Passing his goblet to a servant, he started to make his way through the crowd. He had not gone far when he was greeted by the familiar face of Nasir, one of the officers of his own regiment, the Mansuriyya.

The tall, solemn young man, an olive-skinned Syrian, inclined his head respectfully as he approached his commander. "Amir, it was a truly beautiful ce—"

"A beautiful ceremony," said Kalawun, forcing a smile, "I know."

Nasir looked at him quizzically, then returned the smile, which brightened his otherwise plain face. "I'm sorry, Amir, I must be one of many to have spoken to you today without truly saying anything at all."

"As is the tradition at weddings," responded Kalawun, glancing back to the youths. As he did so, Baraka stepped away from the slave and caught his eye. For a second, there hung a look of guilty shame on the young prince's face as he realized what Kalawun had witnessed. Then, almost as quickly as it appeared, the expression was gone, replaced by one of haughty defiance. Baraka nodded curtly to Kalawun and moved off with his friends, leaving the slave huddled against the wall, near to the cage where the lion paced.

"Amir?" questioned Nasir, studying the commander's face, which was tight with concern. He followed Kalawun's stare and saw Baraka laughing with the group of boys. "He will make a fine son," he commented.

"But will he make a fine husband?" murmured Kalawun. He met Nasir's gaze. "A fine sultan? Sometimes, I think he ignores everything I have tried to teach him."

"You have guided him well, Amir. I have seen how you have instructed him so patiently, as if he were your own." Nasir lowered his voice. "You have given him more than his own father has."

"Sultan Baybars has not had the time to train him," answered Kalawun. But they both knew this wasn't true.

Baybars had ignored Baraka for most of the boy's early life, saying that he belonged with his mother in the harem until he was old enough to be trained as a warrior. When he finally felt Baraka was of an age suitable for training, he handed him over to a tutor and, for a brief time, took a real interest, even pleasure, in his eldest son. But then Omar, his closest comrade, was killed by an Assassin's blade that had been meant for him, and following that death Baybars hadn't taken much interest in anything.

Nasir shook his head. "Still, it amazes me how much you have given of yourself to the boy."

"I want him to lead his people well."

"And he will. He may have become a man today, but in his heart he is still a boy, and boys of his age sometimes believe they are better than their masters." Nasir met Kalawun's eyes. "We all have."

Kalawun put a hand on his shoulder. "You are right. It is just that sometimes I feel as if I am trying to mold clay that has already been fired. I worry, Nasir, that he is . . ." His next words were cut off as a girl's voice called across to him.

"Father!"

Kalawun turned to see Aisha, his fourteen-year-old daughter, weaving through the throng. Her black *hijab*, threaded with gold, was dangerously close to sliding off her head and uncovering her sleek dark hair. On her shoulder, its claws making little nicks in her black gown, was a tiny, amber-eyed monkey. It had a jewel-studded collar, from which hung a leather leash that Aisha had twined around one long finger. In her other hand was a fistful of dates.

"Look, Father!" she said, tossing up one of the fruits. The monkey reached out and snatched it out of the air. With little jerking movements it grasped the date and chewed, looking around inquisitively.

"I see you have been training him," said Kalawun, cupping his daughter's face in his large, callused hands and kissing her brow. He tugged her *hijab* over the line of hair that had been revealed, making her frown. "You haven't let him out of your sight." Kalawun smiled at Nasir. "If I had known such a gift would have preoccupied her so, I would have given one to her years ago."

Aisha ignored the comment. "I still cannot think what to name him."

"I thought you had called him Fakir?"

Aisha rolled her eyes. "That was last week. I don't like that name anymore. I told you that."

Kalawun touched his daughter's cheek. "I think now is not the time to concern yourself with this. It has been a long day and you must prepare yourself for the night to come." His smile faded as she shrugged away from him, obviously discomforted.

Kalawun felt a wrench in his gut at the thought that he had put his daughter's happiness in the balance to secure his position with Baraka. She felt like a sacrifice. He supposed most fathers giving away their daughters into marriage must feel something like this, but the thought didn't comfort him. He had bought her the monkey to alleviate his guilt. It had worked for a few days as he watched her delight over the creature. But after what he had witnessed with the slave, he felt troubled again. "You are a woman now, Aisha," he told her, trying to sound firm. "You must be modest in your worldly appearance and obey and support your husband. You cannot run wild around the palace halls anymore or play with the servants or wade in the fish pool. Not as a woman. Not as a wife. Do you understand?"

"Yes, Father," murmured Aisha.

"Go now, await your husband."

The part of Kalawun that wasn't bound by duty or custom, the part of him that was all father, was secretly glad to see that none of the defiant sparkle had left her eyes as she moved off.

Kalawun heard doors opening and turned to see four gold-cloaked warriors of the Bahri regiment, the Royal Guard, entering the hall. Behind, standing several inches taller than the soldiers, came Baybars Bundukdari, the Crossbow, sultan of Egypt and Syria, with whose sword the Ayyubid dynasty had ended in blood and the reign of the Mamluks had begun. He wore a heavy, fur-lined cloak of gold silk, embroidered with inscriptions from the Koran. Black bands of cloth on his upper arms displayed his rank and title. His tanned face was stony and his eyes, with the star-shaped defect in his left pupil that turned a simple gaze into a piercing glare, were as blue and fathomless as the Nile. At Baybars's side were three military governors, including Mahmud and a fifth man dressed in the violet cloak of a royal messenger, one of the men who worked the posting houses through which information was relayed by horse across the empire. The messenger's cloak was dust-stained, his face weary. It looked as if he had been on the road for some time. Baybars said something to him and he bowed and moved off. The sultan's eyes swept the crowd and came to rest on Kalawun. He beckoned sharply. Leaving Nasir with a nod, Kalawun followed as Baybars left the hall.

Together, the governors and their sultan headed up to the quieter second story of the palace, leaving the music and crowds behind. Here, the Bahris pushed open a set of ivory-paneled doors, which led out onto a wide balcony. The guards remained by the doors whilst Baybars and the governors moved out into the sunlight. It was a cool day with a strong breeze that plucked at their cloaks. The afternoon sky was a wide, flat blue without a trace of haze, and in the far distance, southwest of the city, they could see the Great Pyramids rising from the desert. The citadel, built by Saladin, was situated at the highest part of the city, just below the Muqattam Hills, and the view from the balcony was spectacular.

Below them sprawled Cairo, whose name, *al-Qahira*, meant the conqueror. Minarets spiraled into the sky over the domes of mosques and palaces adorned with glass and mother-of-pearl that glittered in the sun. Woven in between these majestic edifices was a tight jumble of houses and shops that formed a complex warren of narrow streets and covered souks, in places so dark and airless it was like passing through caves.

Camel and horse markets, madrassas and mausoleums all jostled for space in this cramped arena, where districts for the Greeks, the blacks, the Turks and others were crowded around the newer quarters of the city to the north, established by the former Fatimid dynasty. Here, the al-Azhar mosque, with its adjoining university, had stood for three centuries and was now the highest seat of learning in the Islamic world. Part of the building was still shrouded by scaffolding from the repairs Baybars had ordered begun several years earlier. The smooth white limestone that clad the new side had been taken from the Pyramids and the many Crusader castles in Palestine the sultan had spent the sixteen years of his reign demolishing. The old part of Cairo, Fustat Misr, was located south of the citadel, opposite an island in the Nile. On the island was a palace erected by the Mamluks' former Ayyubid master, the towers of which Baybars had given to Kalawun and the Mansuriyya Regiment as barracks. Between the sand-blown city and the hostile expanses of the desert, the Nile, the city's lifeblood, flowed endlessly.

Baybars turned to Kalawun with a smile, the expression not quite reflected in his wintry eyes. "We have been comrades for more than half our lives, my brother," he said, kissing the commander's cheeks. "Now we are family."

"It is an honor I cherish, my Lord Sultan," replied Kalawun.

"But now the wedding of our children is over, we must turn our eye to matters abroad." Baybars's manner was instantly all business. "A messenger has come bearing news from our northern territories. The Ilkhan has assembled an army. The Mongols are on the move."

"How large an army?" questioned Kalawun, the sultan's words causing the familiar ripple of concern to spread through him, as it always did whenever news came in to inform them that their calm was about to be shattered; that battle and death might be just around the corner.

"Thirty thousand, made up of Mongols from the Ilkhan's Anatolian garrison and Seljuk soldiers under the command of their pervaneh."

"Do we know where they are headed?" asked Kalawun, surprised that the Seljuk *pervaneh* was leading his men alongside the Mongols. It was rumored that the *pervaneh*, who acted as regent for the boy sultan of the Seljuk realm of Anatolia, was unhappy with the Mongols' occupation of his lands. His relationship with his overlord, Abaga, Ilkhan of Persia and great-grandson of Genghis Khan, was said to be strained.

"One of our patrols on the Euphrates frontier captured a Mongol scout. They were able to extract the information from him. The Mongols plan to attack al-Bira."

Kalawun, glancing at the other amirs, saw by their faces that they had already heard this news. "Do we know when, my lord?"

"Soon. That is all they were able to ascertain. But it was almost five weeks ago that our garrison at al-Bira received this information. The attack could have already occurred. The message went by way of Aleppo. My governor there was sending seven thousand troops to help fortify the city. He also planned to raise a levy of Bedouin. But we all know how unpredictable mercenaries can prove," Baybars added.

"Then we have need of haste."

Baybars gestured to one of the amirs, a dusky-skinned man of his and Kalawun's age. "Amir Ishandiyar will lead his regiment to al-Bira, along with two other commanders. They leave tomorrow. If the Mongols have not yet attacked, our forces will remain to reinforce the city. If they have ..." Baybars paused. "Ishandiyar will deal with them."

"If we ride swiftly, we can reach Aleppo within thirty-six days," said Ishandiyar. "We can collect fresh supplies and any auxiliary forces available to us, then continue to al-Bira. It is only a two-day march from there."

"We have to hope that will be enough time," said Kalawun. "The city will not keep out a determined force indefinitely. The Mongols managed to take it before."

The other governors nodded. The city of al-Bira was their first line of defense on the Euphrates frontier. If the Mongols took it, they could use it as a staging post from which to launch further attacks on Mamluk territories in Syria. Five years ago, under orders of Abaga, the Mongols had crossed the Euphrates and raided down to Aleppo, but they had caused only minimal damage. The Mamluks had been lucky. With a stronger force, they would have been deadly. The bones of eighty thousand Muslims buried beneath the dust of Baghdad were testament to that.

Baybars looked to Ishandiyar. "I am counting on you."

"I will not fail you, my lord."

"Make sure of it. I do not want the Mongols to hold any position that could threaten my rear when I continue my campaign north. Abaga is no fool. He will be aware that my raid in Cilicia last year was a prelude to an invasion of Anatolia. He knows I seek to expand my empire. And with the Seljuks reportedly growing restless with his rule, his position has weakened. I knew he would flex his muscles sooner or later. But if he takes al-Bira, my plans for expansion in Anatolia will be gravely hampered."

"My Lord Sultan," Mahmud cut in quickly, "you have not yet discussed those plans with us. Before the messenger brought this news to you, I was going to ask if we might now speak of your strategy for the coming year. As you must be aware, there is some dispute over which of our enemies requires our attention first."

"Yes, Amir Mahmud, I am well aware of what goes on within my own court." Baybars smiled humorlessly. "But perhaps you would like to inform me further?" He moved to the balcony ledge and leaned against it.

Mahmud answered, unabashed. "My lord, of all the sultans of Egypt who have warred against the Franks, you have delivered the most victories to our people. Of their once great empire, the Western Christians hold just a few scattered cities on the coast of Palestine. You have destroyed the castles of their knights, driven fat barons out of towns once inhabited by Muslims, returned to us mosques that were turned into churches, slaughtered the infidel in their thousands." Mahmud's voice rose in passion as he spoke.

Baybars didn't look impressed. "What is your point?"

"There are those within your court who believe it is time to finish what you started when you proclaimed the jihad against the Christians sixteen years ago. They believe it is time to erase the Franks in Acre and Tripoli and the other strongholds they possess, time to drive them once and for all from our shores."

"They?" said Baybars dryly.

"I will admit, my lord, this is something I personally hope for. But so do many here."

The fourth amir, an old Mamluk veteran called Yusuf, who had so far been silent, was nodding in time with Mahmud's words. Ishandiyar looked thoughtful.

"You agree with this?" Baybars asked them.

"The truce we signed with the Franks was, by your own admission, my lord, only meant to be temporary," said Yusuf in his scratchy, ancient voice. "Reports from our spies in Acre say their pope has been in council with rulers of the West to discuss a Crusade. Why give them time to launch another? I say we end them now."

"I would counsel caution," said Ishandiyar slowly. "Let us first deal with the Mongols at al-Bira before making any firm plans. We may need to put all our resources into that."

"I agree," said Mahmud swiftly as Baybars nodded, "we need to safeguard the city, of course. But if we are victorious, then let us at least speak of our concerns over the Franks before any campaign against the Mongols in Anatolia is launched."

"What do you say, Amir Kalawun?" asked Ishandiyar.

"I have already spoken to the sultan of my thoughts," replied Kalawun. He ignored the affront in Mahmud's face.

"Can you share these with the rest of us?" croaked Yusuf, looking to Baybars, who nodded to Kalawun to indicate his permission.

"I believe, as Ishandiyar does, that we should concentrate on securing our northern borders from further attack by the Mongols." Kalawun looked at Yusuf. "Only a handful of leaders attended the council you speak of. I see no great force being launched from the West in the immediate future. From what I hear, they are too busy fighting amongst themselves. The Mongols pose a real threat. The Franks, at present, can do us no harm."

Mahmud was shaking his head and staring out across the city, his jaw taut.

Baybars was quiet for a few moments, studying each of them. "Khadir tells me that the signs are auspicious for a war against the Christians." None of them looked happy at the mention of his soothsayer. "But I myself am keen to deal with the Mongols sooner rather than later. However," he said, his gaze swinging to Mahmud, "I will not make any firm decisions until I have spoken with the rest of the governors. I will arrange a council."

"My lord," called Mahmud, as Baybars moved to head back inside. "With all due respect, do not keep the governors waiting too long. Some of them grow restless." He faltered slightly under Baybars's barbed stare, but continued. "In the four years since you signed the truce, you have uncovered two conspiracies to overthrow you and survived one attempt to kill you by one of your own amirs. It is not something your men want any longer, this ..." he scowled, "this *peace* with the infidel."

"Peace, Amir Mahmud?" said Baybars, his voice low. "Is that what you believe I want with the Western pigs? Is that what you believe I was seeking when I destroyed their cities, razed their fortresses into ashes and dust, ground the bones of their soldiers beneath my feet? Peace?"

"My lord, I simply ..."

"Yes, I have fought off insurgents and murderers. But none of them sought to defeat me because they wanted to continue my noble war against the Franks. They rebelled against me because they coveted my position. Those who know me well, Mahmud, those *loyal* to me know, without question, that if there is one man in all the East who despises the Christians more than any other, it is I. But I will not rush at them blindly and put my empire in jeopardy for the sake of a few hot-blooded, impetuous youths. When I am ready, I will destroy them. But only when I am ready."

"Destroy who, Father?" Baraka Khan stood in the doorway, shielding his eyes from the sun.

"What do you want?" Baybars asked him.

"You are discussing matters of importance, obviously. I wish to join you."

"You have nothing to add to our debate that is of any value," responded Baybars shortly. "And I have neither the time nor the inclination to pander to your wishes. When I want you involved in my affairs, I will summon you, Baraka." There was no malice in Baybars's tone, but the bluntness of his words caused Baraka to blush fiercely.

The youth looked as if he were about to retort; then he turned and ran from the balcony.

"We will speak again in a full council," said Baybars to the governors, as if nothing had happened. "You are dismissed."

The governors bowed and moved through the doors, Mahmud looking stung and irritable, Ishandiyar heading off to gather his men for the march to al-Bira. Kalawun lingered.

"You have something to say?" asked Baybars.

"Is there any need to keep Baraka from our debates, my lord? He should be a part of such things if he is to learn."

"His tutors teach him well enough, and I know I can count on you to continue training him in military matters."

"Your lack of affection upsets him. He doesn't believe you think him worthy to be your son."

"He was spoiled by his mother, Kalawun," said Baybars harshly. "All the time he spent in the harem made him soft. I must be stern with him now or he will never even make it to the throne, let alone be a strong enough leader for our people." With that, Baybars headed off.

Kalawun looked out over the walls. From one of the citadel's towers, a flock of the pigeons the Mamluks used to carry messages between their troops soared into the sky. The impromptu meeting hadn't given Kalawun time to prepare his arguments, and now he had a war council to contend with. The peace he had helped bring about between his people and the Franks seemed to be slipping away, little by little. He didn't know for how long he would be able to keep the lion from the Christians' door.

4

The Temple, Acre

17 JANUARY A.D. 1276

Puzzled, Will followed Everard down through the tower and out into the courtyard, which was dusty with sand blown up from the beach. In the West, the order's preceptories were more like manor houses and weren't usually fortified, but in Acre the Temple's headquarters was an impregnable fortress. Surrounded on all sides by high walls, in places almost thirty feet thick, it perched like a stone giant above the sea on the port's western side. At the corners were massive towers, the largest of which, on the city side, straddled the main gate, capped by four turrets, each decorated by a life-size statue of a lion made of gold. The treasury tower, which formed the oldest part of the precptory, had been built by the Egyptian sultan, Saladin, a hundred years earlier.

Inside the compound it was like a miniature town, with gardens and orchards near the servants' quarters, domestic lodgings for knights and sergeants, a great hall, workshops, an infirmary, training ground, stables, an elegant church and a palace for the grand master and his staff. Unlike many of its sister preceptories, the Temple in Acre also benefited from lavatories connected to the city's complex sewerage system, which drained into the sea. Running through part of this underground labyrinth of water channels was a tunnel that led from the preceptory right under the city to the harbor, which enabled the knights to transport cargo from their ships and which could also serve as an effective escape route.

To Will, the fortress was home: familiar, ordinary. But whenever knights or sergeants arrived from the West and entered the gates for the first time he was reminded, by the amazement in their faces, just how magnificent the preceptory was.

As Everard struggled with the heavy door to the knights' quarters, Will moved to aid him. But the priest tutted him away irritably, eventually managing to push it open himself. Will followed him up to his chamber on the second floor, Everard wheezing breathlessly. "You should ask the seneschal to move you to another room," suggested Will, as they entered.

"I like the view," replied Everard testily.

Will shrugged. "What do you want to speak to me about?" he asked, moving a pile of vellum-bound books from a stool by Everard's workbench and sitting. On the bench, where the priest worked on his translations, was a large book, the pages of which flowed with delicate Arabic script. Beside it was a parchment, smoothed with pumice stone, upon which Everard was writing out a Latin translation of the text. Many people in Outremer now used paper, which was cheaper to produce, but Everard still preferred his animal skins and insisted on having parchment specially made up and delivered by a local supplier.

The priest, who hadn't answered him, was busy pouring a goblet of wine. His damaged hand with its two missing fingers, lost thirty-two years ago when Muslim forces recaptured Jerusalem, trembled. The priest drank so much these days that some knights had started to joke he must have Burgundy for blood. Will waited until Everard had taken several sips before repeating the question.

"I was going to talk to you this morning when you returned," responded the priest. "But I wanted the meeting over and done with." Curling the fingers of his good hand around the stem of the goblet, he sat on the window seat. "In the past three years since he returned to England and was crowned king, Edward has written to me three times to request funds from our coffers. He said he needed money to help him establish his position as our guardian; to pay emissaries to journey to the Mongols and other races in the hope of securing future alliances; to pay contacts to keep him informed of events in the wider world that may have an impact on us. The first time, I paid him. The sum did not seem extravagant and I had no reason to doubt his intentions. But last year, when Matthew, our brother in London, visited, he told me he had learned that Edward had been meeting with the pope to discuss the possibility of a new Crusade, following the Council of Lyons."

Will nodded. "I've heard this too. The pope has been very determined. I'm just glad so few turned up for his council, else we might have been knee-deep in blood by now."

"The pope didn't arrange the meeting," said Everard soberly. "Edward did."

Will frowned in puzzlement, but waited for the priest to continue.

"It seems he wanted to apologize for missing the council and wished the pope to know that he would make it his personal mission to lead a Crusade to the East. He said that when he had secured his own kingdom, he would take the Cross."

"That makes no sense. Edward was the one who signed the treaty with Baybars. Why would he break his own truce?"

"Perhaps because he had no intention of keeping it." Everard finished his wine and moved to pour himself another.

Will was up and taking the goblet before he could rise. He filled the vessel and returned it to Everard. "I will admit, I was never comfortable having Edward as our guardian, but I cannot believe he would go back on his pledge like this."

"You weren't comfortable with him?" said Everard, surprised. "You never told me that."

Will paused. "It wasn't something I could put into words. I just didn't trust him, but he never gave me any good reason not to. Could Brother Matthew have heard it wrong?"

"When he left for England, I asked him to look into it. I also told him about the money Edward had requested from me and had him check whether the king had sent any such emissaries. Before I heard from him again, Edward sent me a third request, asking why I hadn't answered his previous petition. This time, he asked for a much larger amount."

"Did you pay it?"

"No. But here is a letter I received from Brother Matthew shortly afterwards."

He handed Will a scroll. It was cracked and smudged, as if it had been read several times.

"Read it."

Will looked up when he had finished. "What did the others say when you showed them this?"

"You are the only one I've shown."

Will glanced at the parchment. "You've had it for a while?"

"A few months."

"Why haven't you told anyone?" said Will, incredulous. He struggled to keep his voice down. "This is evidence that the king of England, our own guardian, is working against us! I would say this is a more pressing topic to bring to a meeting than some treatise you and Velasco have written!"

"It isn't evidence," said Everard quietly. "As Matthew himself says, he cannot prove it. It is speculation."

Will read it again. "He says he has learned that Edward is planning an attack on Wales, that he believes the king wishes to use the requested money to fund the early stages of his campaign." He looked up. "That seems fairly certain to me."

"He is certain about the attack, yes, but not that we will be funding it."

"Does it really matter what he would be using the money for?" said Will, shaking his head. "Edward is planning to attack another country. The man you made ..." Will stopped himself. "The guardian of a group whose sole purpose is peace is about to start a war, and not only in his own kingdom so it would appear. Matthew says people in England are calling him the *Crusader King*. They believe he will be the one to deliver Jerusalem."

"He can have no immediate plans for that," said Everard, "not if he is planning on attacking Wales."

"But if he's already met with the pope to discuss it, it seems clear that he intends to in the future." Will rolled up the parchment and stuffed it roughly into its case. "Part of me isn't surprised."

Everard's lip curled in a scowl. "Well I'm glad you saw it coming. Perhaps you might have been so gracious as to let us lesser mortals in on your divine knowledge before now?"

"What has he done in the years since you appointed him, Everard? Since he signed the truce with Baybars, what has Edward actually done as our guardian? As far as I'm aware, he's done nothing to help us continue to secure the peace, reconcile the faiths or open lines of trade and communication between East and West."

"Those aren't his duties," corrected Everard. "When our founder, Grand Master Robert de Sablé, chose Richard the Lionheart to be the first guardian, it was because he wanted a trusted man from outside the Temple who could mediate in disputes between the Brethren and offer advice or financial and military aid."

"Whatever his duty is, I don't think it's to steal money from us for a war," responded Will.

Everard stared into his goblet. "Brother Thomas spoke of how it would only need one strong ruler to unite a force under him for a Crusade. King Edward

could be such a man. He is young and popular and powerful. He knows how
to lead and inspire men." Everard shook his head. "I was impressed by him because of those very things. I thought his authority would be an asset. Richard
the Lionheart was his great uncle, for the sake of Christ! How did I let a wolf
into the fold?" he murmured into the goblet's red depths. "How could I have
been so eager? So foolish?"

"Why haven't you told the others? The seneschal at least?" As he asked the
question, Will felt a small surge of triumph that Everard had confided in him,
not the seneschal.

"It was my fault we were almost destroyed seven years ago. I can hardly bear
to tell them that we may face an even worse threat now because of me."

"What happened with the Book of the Grail wasn't your fault."

"When Grand Master Armand de Périgord died, I should have burned the
damn thing, not left it lying around for the Knights of St. John to steal. Of
course it's my fault. If you hadn't retrieved the book for me, the Anima Templi,
perhaps even the Temple itself would have been destroyed. And they all
know it," Everard muttered. "I saw Master Seneschal give me that look in the
meeting."

"Why tell me?"

Everard raised an eyebrow. "You've made mistakes too, William. I thought
you might understand. After all, when you used the Anima Templi's money to
try and have Sultan Baybars killed, you almost caused a war."

A hot rush of anger and shame colored Will's cheeks. He stood. "I've paid
for that mistake, Everard, with interest. You know why I contracted the Assassins, why I wanted Baybars dead. No, it didn't bring my father back, and yes,
it was senseless and wrong. But how many more times must I do penance before
you will forgive me? I'm sick of being reminded about it."

Everard waved his hand. "I'm sorry. Please, sit down. I trust you, William.
That is why I came to you before the others."

Will had never heard Everard say that before. He wanted to be trusted. After
his father died, Everard was the only one who could offer the pride Will had
craved since he was a boy, since he caused the death of his sister, Mary. It was
an accident, but the grief tore his family apart and drove a wedge between him
and his father. It was what had caused James to join the Temple as a fully pro-
fessed knight, relinquishing Will's mother and his other three sisters to a nunnery outside Edinburgh. "What can we do?" Will murmured, sitting back
down.

"We must tread very carefully. Pope Gregory is a close friend of Edward's.

We risk exposing ourselves if we anger the king. He could inform the pope of our aims, and I do not need to tell you what that would mean."

Will didn't speak. He knew full well what the consequences of any exposure of the Brethren's aims would be. It was how he was able to live with their secrecy, how he bore their silence.

The foundations of the West, of their entire society, were built upon the rock of the Church. Any threat to that edifice could bring the whole structure tumbling down, which was why the Church took heresy so seriously. It wasn't only Muslims and Jews, Will knew, who had felt the Church's wrath in the form of a Crusade. Everard had told him of the Cathars: men and women from the south of France who were slaughtered in their thousands by the Church's soldiers because they opposed orthodox doctrine and preached ideals that ran counter to those of Roman Christianity. What the Anima Templi proposed in the reconciliation of the faiths was anathema, was heresy. Were their aims to be discovered, the Church would destroy them and possibly the Temple if they believed the corruption had spread within its ranks. It wasn't just a matter of religion; it was also a matter of geography. The Church, and many in the West, wanted to liberate Jerusalem from those they deemed the nonbelievers, a wish that had led Pope Urban II to preach the First Crusade two hundred years earlier. If Muslims and Jews were to become allies, Christendom would be forced to relinquish its desire to rule the Holy City. And, as Everard had once put it, there was room for only one faith in the Holy Land until such a time when more men embraced the Brethren's ideals.

Everard slumped forward, looking suddenly exhausted. "I cannot believe that I have just finished reforming the Anima Templi after the schism that broke us apart, only to be faced with another menace. It seems that in each generation something rises up and threatens us: Armand de Périgord, the Knights of St. John and now possibly our own guardian."

"Perhaps we are meant to face such threats," said Will, after a pause. "The Anima Templi was born out of blood and strife. That was why Robert de Sablé created it." He fought to recall how Everard once put it. "When Grand Master Gérard de Ridefort caused the Battle of Hattin through his own greed, de Sablé knew that the Temple had become too powerful. As an order we were beyond secular laws, we made and deposed kings, answered only to the pope and even to annoy us was an offense punishable by excommunication. We traded in the East and West, built castles and fleets, bought estates, towns even. As you once said, the Temple is Heaven's sword and the grand master is the hand that wields it. De Sablé created the Anima Templi to safeguard that power, to hold that sword in check. Perhaps, in each generation, God needs to test us to make sure we don't grow weak, unable to wield it."

Everard chuckled softly, but it wasn't a mocking laugh. "I've not often heard you speak so poetically, William."

Will returned the smile, then sighed. "Listen, don't pay Edward until we know for certain that he intends to launch a Crusade, which we obviously won't want to fund if he does. Write and tell him you don't have the funds at present. By the time the letter reaches him and he has a chance to reply, we may have found out more."

"How can we find out more when he is all the way over in England?" Everard shrugged wearily. "I suppose Brother Matthew may be able to get closer to him somehow."

"Why use Matthew when we already have an ally in Edward's staff?"

Everard frowned. "Who do you ...?" Understanding dawned on his face. "No," he said vehemently, "I'll not have that ... *traitor* involved in this."

"Garin was served his justice in our cells for four years, Everard. And he was never a willing traitor. Rook forced him to steal the Book of the Grail. It wasn't his fault."

"How you can forgive that wretch for what he did astonishes me." Everard fixed Will with a provocative stare. "It wasn't too long ago that you wanted to see him hang."

Will tried not to rise to the bait, but stagnant memories he had tried to bury seeped into his mind at the comment. Everard was right; it wasn't so long ago that he had wanted his former best friend dead.

When Will had joined the Temple in London, aged eleven, Garin de Lyons had been assigned as his partner-in-training. For two years, they were inseperable, sharing triumphs and torments, Will struggling through his father's departure to the Holy Land, Garin suffering at the hands of his abusive uncle. Then, on a mission to escort the English crown jewels to France, everything changed. Their company was attacked by mercenaries and Will's master was killed, along with Garin's uncle. When Will was apprenticed to Everard in Paris and Garin returned to London alone, their friendship faded. Years later, reunited, they found themselves enemies when Garin became involved in a plot to steal the Book of the Grail. Eventually, he was imprisoned, but although he paid for his crimes against the Brethren, his betrayal of Will had cut much deeper and, for that, he had never been charged.

But this, Will reminded himself, was all in the past. He had forgiven Garin for what had happened in Paris. He shouldn't dwell. Ignoring Everard's shrewd stare, he spoke. "Garin knows about the Brethren and that Edward is our guardian. He can help us. Wasn't the reason you released him so that he could prove himself useful?"

"If Edward has done nothing to help the Anima Templi, then I cannot see what use de Lyons has been at all," growled Everard.

"Then let him start now. I'll write and ask him about Edward. I don't have to mention our suspicions. Just let me get a gauge of things there."

As Everard was deciding, a bell began to clang. He frowned. "It cannot be Vespers yet surely?"

"It isn't Vespers," said Will, rising.

Hearing voices and footsteps in the passage outside, Will opened the door to see several knights hurrying past. Others were opening doors, looking out in confusion.

"What's happening?" Will called to one of the passing knights.

"The grand master's ship has been sighted in the bay," responded the knight, his eyes shining. "He has come at last!"

THE CITADEL, CAIRO, 17 JANUARY A.D. 1276

Baraka Khan leaned against the cool marble wall of the passage and wiped his nose with the sleeve of his wedding robe. He could hear music and laughter continuing in the grand hall without him, as if his absence hadn't even been noticed. He knew Aisha would soon go to his private room that had been readied for their wedding night. But the thought of entering the place made him feel sick. Although she had been promised to him five years ago, he had never grown accustomed to the idea, or to her. She had teased him in their younger years and had ignored him since early adolescence. Aisha made Baraka uncomfortable: her quickness; her girlishness; those mystifying giggles and scornful looks. He felt tongue-tied and awkward around her, and for all the bravado he had displayed to his friends, the idea of spending a night with her secretly terrified him.

His father's words echoed back to him, distorted with a cruelty that had not been there when uttered, but which now seeped through the memory, wounding him. All day, he had felt so powerful. Everyone's attention had been focused on him and he had basked in their flattery. For the first time in his life, he had felt like the son of a sovereign, had felt like a man. But with a few words, his father had wiped all that away and now he just felt like a scolded child.

Baraka pushed himself from the wall and paced the passage, glaring at a servant who passed, carrying a tray of peeled fruits. He wanted to pummel the wall, but was afraid it would hurt and, instead, settled for slapping it hard with his palm.

"What is wrong, my prince?"

Baraka whipped round at the whispery voice. Before him stood a hunched, wizened old man. His hair was so matted it had formed into clumped coils that twisted like fat worms down his back. His creased, weathered skin was dark with sun and dirt, and his eyes, white with cataracts, looked almost pupil-less. He wore a threadbare gray robe and his bare feet were caked with dust.

"Where have you been?" demanded Baraka. "You said you would be at the ceremony." He folded his arms across his chest. "My father isn't pleased, Khadir. He wanted you to make a favorable augury of the marriage."

Khadir grinned, showing a couple of yellow-brown stumps in an otherwise toothless mouth. He proffered a cloth doll that was gripped in his fist. "*Look!*" he hissed in a furtive whisper. "I've given her a heart."

Baraka watched with mounting disgust as Khadir opened up the back of the filthy doll, which had been cut open, then crudely sewn back together. A fetid smell drifted out, and Baraka saw a small piece of flesh inside, surrounded by the cloth stuffing. It was slippery-looking and liver-colored, possibly the heart of a rabbit or some other vermin. Baraka recoiled, utterly repulsed.

Khadir chuckled and laced the doll back up, pulling the stitches tight. "She needs a heart, if she's to feel," he chanted in a singsong voice. "She does. She does."

"Why do you carry that foul thing around with you?" said Baraka, grimacing. "You've had it since we took Antioch."

"She was a gift from your father," said Khadir, frowning as he threaded the doll through the leather belt that was looped around his scrawny waist, on the other side of which hung a gold-handled dagger, its hilt embedding a plump, glossy ruby. "Would you abandon the things he gives you?"

"My father gives me nothing," replied Baraka moodily.

"That will change," said Khadir, giving the boy his full attention now the doll was safely stowed.

"No, it won't. I tried to join in one of his discussions, like you told me to," said Baraka, lowering his voice as two courtiers passed them. "But he ..." Baraka felt his face grow hot. "He dismissed me like I was nothing! Like I was a silly child." He jabbed at his chest. "I'm fifteen, Khadir. I have a wife. I'm *not* a child!"

"No, no," said Khadir softly, "you are not."

"He'll never take me into his trust."

Khadir's mouth split in a wide grin.

"What is funny?" snapped Baraka.

Khadir's smile vanished, his white eyes narrowing to slits. It was like a candle being blown out. "Change is nigh. I see it on the horizon, like storm clouds gathering. War will come again."

Baraka shook his head, ignoring the shiver the shift in the old man's manner sent up his spine. "How will that help me?"

Khadir giggled like a little boy and his solemnity dissolved. "Because *you* will start it."

"What are you talking about?" Baraka's tone was scathing, but he was intrigued by the prediction.

"Your father has not yet fulfilled his destiny, the destiny I told him was his before he killed Sultan Kutuz and took the throne. Nations will fall," murmured Khadir, "kings will perish. And he will stand above them all on a bridge of skulls that spans a river of blood. Your father's destiny is to drive the Christians from these lands. This he must do. But I fear there are those in his court who will persuade him otherwise." Khadir's eyes flashed with some hidden anger. "Since Omar died, he has lost his way. We must set him back on his true path." Khadir leaned in close and touched Baraka's arm. "Together, we will help him. And when he sees what you have done for him, he will see you for who you are: a man and a sultan in waiting." He stroked Baraka's arm fondly. "Then you will sit at his right hand until the day when you take the throne and Khadir will use his sight to see for you."

"I don't understand," said Baraka, shaking his head.

"You will," replied Khadir.

5

The Docks, Acre

17 JANUARY A.D. 1276

"Can you see him? Can anybody see him yet?"

As the galley drew closer to the docks, the men at the back of the assembled company of one hundred or so knights craned their necks, trying to see over the heads of their fellows for a view of the vessel's eminent passenger.

Robert de Paris rolled his eyes at Will, who smiled. Robert leaned in close to the knight who had spoken. "You'll see him soon enough, Brother Albert," he murmured. "Although you should probably hope he doesn't see you."

"What do you mean?" said Albert, frowning at the fair-haired knight.

Robert's usual roguish grin and laughing gray eyes were hidden behind a convincing solemnity. "Your surcoat, brother," he said in a delicate whisper.

Albert looked down perplexed, then tutted as he spotted several brown droplets marking the white cloth.

"Last night's supper?" inquired Robert sympathetically.

"I didn't notice," said Albert, licking his thumb and rubbing vigorously at the stains. "Thank you, Brother. Thank you."

Robert straightened as Albert cursed and fretted. Will was shaking his head, trying not to laugh. "Anyone would think God was arriving in that boat the way they're acting," said Robert derisively. But he kept his voice low as he said it.

"It's been over two years since we've had a master with us," responded Will. "You cannot deny it has raised morale."

"But do they have to fuss so?" Robert, who was always impeccably neat, eyed his eager companions scornfully. "You would think the grand master has never seen dirt before. I mean, look at you." He gestured at Will. "You haven't combed your hair in weeks and your mantle's blacker than a wolf's mouth, but is he really going to care so long as you're a good soldier?"

Will glanced down at himself as Robert looked away.

Tall and rather lanky as a boy, Will had filled out during his youth, until now, at twenty-nine, his chest was broader, his arms and shoulders more muscular and he moved with greater ease and confidence, as if he had finally grown into his skin. Like all Templar Knights, he was forbidden from shaving his beard, although he wore it clipped as short as he could get away with. After a month on the road, however, it was a little bushy. His hair was perhaps a bit unkempt, with black strands falling in his eyes and curling untidily around his ears. And Robert was right; his mantle really was filthy. Will went to brush at a smear of dust, then stopped himself as he caught his friend's impish smirk. Folding his arms, he scanned the harbor.

The area was bustling as usual, although nowhere near as busy as it would be by Easter, when ships sheltering in ports all around the Mediterranean, Adriatic and Atlantic coasts would set out for the East, laden with pilgrims, soldiers and cargoes of wine and wool. The knights stood in neat formation on the dock wall, just in front of a wide stone jetty that sloped down to the water, where smaller boats could off-load cargo and passengers. Acre's inner harbor was protected by a heavy iron chain, which could be raised to block the approach of enemy ships and was suspended across the water between a tower on the end of the western mole and the Court of the Chain on the harbor. The inner harbor was always crowded with the vessels of local merchants and fishermen, the larger ships having to moor in the outer harbor just off the crumbling eastern mole. In the distance, near the Tower of the Flies, which rose from the end of the mole, the Templar warship the galley had sailed from surged in the choppy waters. The white mainsail with its red cross had been lowered, but the Temple's black-and-white banner fluttered madly from the mast.

The marshal, Peter de Sevrey, the Temple's chief military official, left in charge during the grand master's absence, was waiting in front of the company of knights. He was deep in conversation with one of the customs officers and Theobald Gaudin, the Temple's grand commander. The seneschal was also there. Will made out his stiff, upright form. Behind the customs building, which dominated the dockside, the city walls stretched right and left; the massive iron gates that led into the city were open on the busy Pisan market. A confusion of sounds and smells drifted from the market to mingle with the shouts of fishermen hauling nets engorged with fish onto the harbor wall and the thick smell of pitch from a boat repairer's. Seeing the Templar warship out in the bay and the knights arranged in stately formation, a small crowd had gathered, filtering through the city gates.

As Will's eyes roved over the onlookers, his gaze was caught by a young girl. Uninterested in the approaching galley, she was playing with a ball, tossing it into the air and catching it. She was walking slowly, coming toward the knights. Will's breath caught in his throat. He turned away sharply.

"What's wrong?" asked Robert.

"Nothing." Will glanced surreptitiously over his shoulder to check where she was. His heart stopped. The girl was looking straight at him.

Her eyes lit up and she grinned widely. "Weel!" She skipped over, the skirts of her yellow dress trailing over the damp stones, silvery with fish scales.

"Who the hell is that?" murmured Robert.

"Cover for me," Will urged quietly, then stepped out of formation and went to meet her.

"She must be lost," he heard Robert saying cheerily to the curious knights in their row. "Don't worry, he'll help her find her parents. Ever the good Samaritan, Will."

The girl bounced up, her unruly hair flopping in her eyes. She flicked it back with a careless toss of her head and grinned. "Where you been? I'm not seeing you for weeks!" Her lilting Italian accent made her English sound foreign.

"What are you doing here, Catarina?" Will asked, steering her gently away from the knights. He looked worriedly over at the marshal and grand commander, but they were still talking with the customs officer and hadn't noticed his departure from the ranks. Will led Catarina behind a stack of crates that were being loaded onto a merchant galley. The crewmen were stamping up and down the gangplanks. "Are you here on your own?" Will repeated the question slowly when Catarina frowned blankly.

"My sister," Catarina said after a moment. "I here with Elisabetta." She giggled and then dissolved into a stream of rapid Italian, which Will didn't understand a word of.

"You should go to Elisabetta," Will told her. "I have to get back." He pointed to the knights.

Catarina pouted and flipped her ball into the air, catching it deftly. "You no come to my house? Elwen no working today."

Will shook his head. "I cannot. Not now." He bent so that he was eye level with Catarina. "Will Elwen be at home tomorrow?"

Catarina nodded after a pause. "Night." She grinned slyly. "You kith her?" She frowned intently. *"Kiss."*

Will gave an embarrassed laugh. "Elwen's taught you another new word, has she? Never mind," he said as Catarina looked puzzled. "Tell Elwen I'll come to her after Vespers tomorrow. Do you understand? After Vespers."

"I tell her," Catarina said solemnly. "I go now." She threw a hand in the vague direction of the city wall.

Will saw a slender, raven-haired girl standing just inside the gates, talking with a woman. He recognized Elisabetta, the eldest daughter of the Venetian silk merchant, Andreas di Paolo. "Don't tell your sister," he reminded Catarina. "Or your father." He watched as Catarina skipped off.

"Excuse me, sir." A crewmen from the ship was wanting to get at one of the crates. He ducked his head, eyeing with a mixture of respect and fear Will's mantle with its red cross.

"Sorry," said Will, moving out of the way.

The crewman looked taken aback by the apology, then hauled a crate from the pile, swung it onto his shoulder and tramped up the gangplank.

Will never failed to be surprised or discomfited by the deferential attention his status attracted. On the inside, he was simply himself, the person he had always been. He sometimes forgot that to the outside world he was one of the noble elite, a warrior of Christ, who lived beyond secular laws and temporal desires, guarding the treasuries of kings and answering to the pope alone. But the world had no idea that behind that stainless visage, personified by the white mantle, he was as deceitful and weak as the rest of mankind when it came to certain matters. Will's eyes followed Catarina as she disappeared through the gates. Matters of the heart, for instance.

He was about to head back to the company, when he saw that the marshal had turned in his direction. Will recoiled behind the crates with a curse. Between him and the knights were a few fishermen, the men loading the merchant vessel and a young man watching the galley approach. None of them would give him any substantial cover and in his uniform he stood out a mile. Will tried to think of a suitable excuse he could give for deserting the ranks. He looked over at Robert, who beckoned urgently. The galley had reached the jetty.

Two of the oarsmen leapt ashore to hold her steady as a man, who looked to be in his late thirties, jumped agilely out, declining their offered hands. Beneath his white mantle, he wore a surcoat, sectioned by a belt from which hung a broad-bladed sword in an ornate scabbard. His hair, which he wore in a tail, was long and dark, and a black beard framed his jaw. Will was too far away to see his face properly, but the cross on his mantle, outlined in gold, clearly marked his elevated status. He was Guillaume de Beaujeu, grand master of the Temple.

Related by birth to the royal house of France, Guillaume had been a member of the order since he was thirteen. During the past decade, he had been master of the Kingdom of Sicily, where his cousin, Charles d'Anjou, brother of the late French monarch, Louis IX, was king. The government of Acre had been awaiting Guillaume's arrival with mixed emotions, for although he had a reputation as a shrewd military strategist and a dynamic leader, he was also one of Charles's staunchest supporters. And the last thing the city needed, fractured as it was by the internecine wars of the past, was any furtherance in influence of the ambitious Sicilian king, whose current bid for the throne of Acre was already causing old rifts to widen.

Will lost sight of the grand master as the young man lingering on the dock wall moved into his line of vision. Four knights were dragging chests from the galley. Noticing someone come up alongside him, Will glanced around. A small boy was standing a few feet to his right, seemingly transfixed by the grand master. Will, deciding he could risk moving now everyone's attention was on Guillaume de Beaujeu, was about to head across, when he noticed the young boy's face. It was a mask of terror. His skin was ashen, his eyes large and unblinking. His hands were bunched into fists at his sides and he was quivering like a leaf in a storm. Will was stopped in his tracks. He looked to where the boy was staring, wondering what on earth could have frightened him so. But there was just the grand master, now striding up the jetty toward Peter de Sevrey, a couple of burly fishermen and the young man.

And then he saw it.

The young man's right arm was pressed stiffly to his side, much like the boy's, his hand covered with the sleeve of a shabby cloak. Protruding from the sleeve's edge was the tip of something hard and silvery.

Will felt shock tighten the skin on his face as all his instincts sang out. The man's position near the point where the jetty met the harbor wall between the waiting knights and the approaching grand master; his out-of-place look; the object concealed in his hand; the boy's terror—all were wrong. In one moment, Will took this in, and then he was out from behind the crates and shouting at the marshal. The calls of the merchant vessel's crew drowned out his words. Will began to run as the young man's hand slipped from beneath the cloak's sleeve, revealing a dagger. The grand master was almost at the wall.

Will knew he wasn't going to make it. All eyes were on Guillaume de Beaujeu, apart from Robert's, and he watched in amazement as Will ran across the dock, yelling. Wrenching his falchion from its scabbard, Will did the only thing he could. Halting to take aim, he flung the blade at the young man, who was darting forward. He heard a high-pitched scream somewhere behind him as the short blade went sailing out of his hand and flew, five, ten, fifteen feet.

The weapon landed with a ringing clang and skidded across the wall a few feet behind the heels of the young man. Will had missed. The man's arm was coming up, the dagger a slice of silver cutting air. But the sword had caught the attention of the knights and they all now realized the danger. The face of the grand master changed as he saw the man bearing down on him. He reached for his weapon.

Two seconds later, just feet from the grand master, the young man was cut down by the marshal, who leapt forward, swinging his sword in a mighty stroke. The force of the blow, combined with the young man's momentum, which drove him onto the razor edge of the arcing blade, almost cleaved him in two.

The knights were shouting, drawing swords, scanning the dockside for other attackers. The marshal wrenched his sword from the young man, who crumpled to the dockside like a string-cut puppet. There were screams as the onlookers on the harbor wall saw him go down, blood and ropes of intestines gushing free from the gaping wound in his stomach. The grand master's guards had dropped the chests and now raced to surround him, and the grand commander was barking orders. By the time the young man's life had drained, the grand master was being hastened across the harbor to where the entrance to the knights' underground tunnel lay.

"I want witnesses questioned!" Peter de Sevrey shouted, bending down to rifle through the young man's tatty cloak that was fanned out around him, sodden with blood.

Within moments, the dockside dissolved into chaos as knights moved to question the crowd. Some people tried to leave, not wanting to get involved. Others tried to get closer to see the body, and there was soon a crush at the city gates. The crew of the merchant's vessel had stopped working and were watching on, and customs officers were running from their building.

Will turned to the boy by the crates. His gaze was still transfixed by the young man, but his expression was no longer one of terror. Tears were rolling down his cheeks, making tracks through dirt. He looked up and started as he saw Will staring at him, and then he was off. Shouting for him to stop, Will chased him, but the boy dove into the excited, babbling crowd and was gone. Will forced his way to the gates, where rumor of an attack on the grand master and a death on the dockside had whipped the crowd into a frenzy. He tried to get into the marketplace, but although his mantle would usually be enough to clear a respectful path, the area was so packed that even if the citizens wanted to get out of his way, they couldn't. By the time Will squeezed through, the boy was nowhere to be seen.

6

The Temple, Acre

17 JANUARY A.D. 1276

It was approaching dusk when Will returned to the preceptory. The wind had blown tattered gaps in the clouds, and sky had appeared, pale blue in the east, bronze and vermilion in the west. Will stepped through the gates and entered the main quadrant to find the place buzzing with talk of the attack. Knights had gathered outside the officials' building, behind which rose the white towers of the grand master's palace. They were speaking in fast, if decorously hushed voices, those who had been on the dockside describing what had happened to absent comrades. The sergeants, particularly the younger ones, were milling about in an agitated group outside the great hall gabbling loudly. As Will walked across the yard, a knight strode over and ordered them to return to their duties. With just a few snapped commands, the group disbanded, the sergeants hurrying off to see to horses or help prepare supper in the kitchens, or to light candles in the chapel for the evening office of Vespers.

Will caught sight of the silvery hair and rangy form of Theobald Gaudin in the group outside the officials' building and headed over. Having returned to the dockside to collect his sword, he had found that the marshal and the grand commander had gone, and he'd been unable to inform anyone about the boy. Before he could reach Theobald, however, he saw the squat, barrel-chested form of Simon Tanner jogging over.

Simon's broad, square face, with its slightly bulbous nose and ruddy cheeks, was tense with concern. "Will?" he puffed. "Are you all right? What happened?"

"I'm fine." Will looked over at the grand commander, who was heading into the officials' building. "Simon, I've got to—"

"Everyone's talking about you," Simon cut across him.

"They are?" said Will, surprised.

Simon stuck a hand through his thatch of brown hair. A few twigs of hay were dislodged by the movement. "I thought you'd been hurt trying to protect the grand master. The reports were confused."

"You should know not to listen to stable gossip."

"I couldn't help it. I was worried."

"There was no need to be," said Will a little abruptly. Simon had been one of his closest friends since they were boys in the London preceptory, but even after eighteen years the groom's almost motherly concern for him still made him uncomfortable. He wasn't sure why. Maybe because it reminded him of the way Elwen sometimes worried over him—and thus seemed more befitting a woman's nature than that of a brawny thirty-year-old man. But then Simon was a groom, not a warrior. He hadn't been toughened by training or taught to hold his emotions in check for the brutal reality of battle.

"Well, you know I'm as daft as a brush." Simon shrugged, then smiled and immediately looked like his normal, easygoing self.

"Dafter," said Will, returning the smile.

"Brother Campbell," came a stern voice behind them. It was Peter de Severy.

"Sir Marshal," said Will in greeting, inclining his head. Simon also bowed.

"Have you just returned, Campbell?"

"Yes, sir. I was on my way to speak with Grand Commander Gaudin to report what I saw at the harbor."

"You can report it to the grand master," replied the marshal. "He wants to see you in his quarters."

"Now, sir?"

De Sevrey, a tight-lipped man with a long, waxy face that remained pale even through the torrid summer months, gave a thin, rare smile. "You saved his life, Brother. I expect he wants to show his gratitude."

Moving off with the marshal, Will gave Simon a brief nod.

Simon understood and headed for the stables, knowing they would finish the conversation later.

The grand master's palace was the tallest building in the preceptory, its towers competing with the chapel's elegant spire and winning by a few meters. Will had never been inside, although he passed the entrance every day on his way from the knights' quarters to the great hall.

The porch led through doors reinforced with iron rivets into a chilly stone corridor. There were no windows, and even in daylight it would be dark if not for the torches set at intervals along the passage wall, the flames throwing a warm glow across the stones. The marshal approached some narrow steps winding up. Will climbed them behind him, and they came out in a busy area, where Templar officials were working, some talking quietly with fellows, others moving with purpose in or out of the doors that lined the passage. One set of doors at the end was larger than the others. They were open, and as he followed the marshal toward them, Will could hear a man's voice issuing from within. It was a deep, resonant voice, all confidence and strength.

"I thank you for your concern, but I assure you my person is perfectly sound. I need neither your pills nor your prodding."

"But, my lord," came a clipped, quieter voice, "you have had a shock. At least let me have a servant bring you a cup of wine. A good red will serve to bring the color to your cheeks."

"I have been in more battles than I have seen summers, have been captured and imprisoned by the Saracens, survived torture and disease. If my attacker's blade had pierced my flesh, then I may have had need of your services, but it will take more than the sight of a kitchen knife in the hand of an angry young man to put me out of humor, Master Infirmarer."

Will reached the doors with the marshal and saw Guillaume de Beaujeu standing in the center of a spacious, well-appointed solar. There was a desk and a cushioned chair beneath a narrow, pointed window that looked out over the darkening courtyard. A silk rug was laid in front of a massive hearth where a merry fire was leaping high into the soot-blackened chimney, roaring now and then in the gusts of wind that echoed down. To either side of the hearth were two couches, draped with embroidered throws, and the walls were strung with tapestries which portrayed Christ's journey from the hall of judgment to Calvary. Standing in front of the grand master was a short man with a shock of white hair, the Temple's chief physician.

Guillaume de Beaujeu looked around as the marshal rapped on the opened door. "Ah, Marshal de Sevrey," he greeted. "Come in. And this, I take it, is the man I am to thank for my continued existence?"

As Will bowed and came forward, Guillaume extended a hand. When Will offered his own, the grand master took it in the warriors' grip: a firm grasp of the wrist that Will had always found strangely more intimate than a shake of the hand. Up close, he saw that the grand master looked younger than he had first thought, early or mid-thirties perhaps, although he had heard one knight say that he was at least forty. Despite the infirmarer's insistence, there seemed to be no lack of color in his cheeks. Indeed, he looked the peak of health. Tanned and hale, he had a strong, angular face, the hardness of which was softened by an easy smile. Will was immediately aware that they looked alike, a realization that struck the master at the same time.

"We could be brothers, could we not?" said Guillaume with a short laugh, stepping back. "And I am told we also share the same name." He nodded to the marshal. "You may leave us." As the marshal bowed, the grand master turned to the infirmarer. "I will drink wine with my supper if it will put you at ease."

The infirmarer heard the dismissal in the grand master's tone. "As you wish, my lord," he conceded, following the marshal out of the room.

"You would think they would be thankful I had survived the attack," Guillaume said to Will. "But I have never seen such solemn faces."

"They are just worried, my lord," said Will, not sure what else to say. The grand master had an energy about him that unnerved him, a crackling intensity that fizzled beneath that unruffled exterior.

"Well, I myself am deeply grateful for what you did. I am in your debt, William Campbell."

"It was nothing, my lord."

"Nonsense. If not for you, I would have most likely died today." Guillaume studied Will. "But I wonder," he continued, moving over to the table, which he leaned against, folding his arms across his chest. "How, out of one hundred and twenty knights, were you the only one to see the danger?"

Will averted his eyes. In all the excitement, he had forgotten that he had deserted the ranks without permission and the reason for it. He searched for an answer, but only Catarina's face came into his mind. He decided something near the truth was better than an outright lie. "I was helping a young girl, my lord. She had lost her parents in the crowd and was upset. I found them for her and was heading back when I saw the man who attacked you." He paused. "I'm sorry I broke rank."

"I see," said the grand master. His face was unreadable. "And what alerted you to this man? What was he doing that caught your attention?"

"At first, nothing. It was a boy who signaled me to the danger."

"How so?"

Will explained what he had seen and how he had pursued and lost the boy.

The grand master looked thoughtful. "What would be your assessment of this? Who do you believe this child was?"

"Family perhaps? Their ages were too different for them to be likely comrades. He almost certainly knew the attacker and seemed, I would say, to know what was about to happen. As I said, he was terrified."

"Would you recognize him if you saw him again?"

"Yes."

"Good," said Guillaume. He breathed in deeply through his nostrils, unfolded his arms and perched on the edge of the table, his mantle settling around him. "Tell me about the mood here, William."

Will was disconcerted by the shift in conversation. "My lord?"

"I need to better understand this place if I am to command it. I spent half my life in this preceptory, but the view from this position is somewhat different to that which I am used to and I have been away from the Holy Land for some time. Grand Commander Gaudin and Marshal de Sevrey sent reports to me in France and Sicily during my absence, but they too see things from an elevated place. For a more general picture I need to speak with the men of the barracks, the soldiers of the front lines. I want to know how they feel." Guillaume cocked his head. "How you feel, William."

Will was silent, uncertain how best to respond. He knew the answer, but wasn't sure he wanted to give it. "Obviously," he began slowly, "we are pleased to have you here. We have been subdued by your absence. But the mood is mostly good. The peace is holding strong."

"Ah, yes," said Guillaume, "the peace." He fixed Will with a shrewd stare. "Interestingly, yours is somewhat sunnier than earlier reports I received." He gave a slight smile. "You need not worry about telling the truth to me. I am aware of how despondent the men have been. I only needed to look into their eyes as I entered this place to see that. It is *because* of the peace that they are dispirited." Will went to speak, but the grand master continued over him.

"How many holdings have we lost to the Saracens these past decades? Almost thirty. How many men? Well," he finished quietly, "they are countless."

"It is true," agreed Will, "we have all suffered hardships during the wars, but—"

"And you, William? Have you lost anyone dear to you? Comrades? Masters?"

Will faltered. But the grand master was looking at him intently. "I lost my father."

"How?"

"At Safed."

The grand master's hard face thawed in sympathy. "I was in Acre when the massacre happened. I was deeply affected by the courage our men showed, choosing death over conversion to the Saracens' faith. I heard too of Baybars's brutality and his defilement of their bodies. It sickened me to the core. You, however, must live with that hurt even now. How you must despise his killers."

Will felt a pain and realized he had clenched his fists so tightly, the nails had bitten his skin. "I did once," he said, struggling to keep his voice measured. "But not anymore. I forgave the sultan when he allowed me to bury my father." The words were flame to a wick, and as Will spoke them, memory flared.

After handing Prince Edward's peace treaty to Baybars at Caesarea, Will had journeyed to Safed with two Bahri warriors the sultan had ordered to escort him. The huge fortress that dominated the Galilee, standing sentry over the River Jordan, was broken and scarred, its sides pitted with the marks of boulders hurled against the walls from siege engines, blackened by Greek fire and stained with oil. A squadron of Baybars's Mamluks garrisoned the stronghold, and goats and chickens were scattered about the outer enceinte, where children, sons and daughters of the soldiers and their wives, played in the dust. Despite the inhabitation, it was a desolate place. Too big to be filled by a mere hundred or so men, its halls and passageways were echoing, empty. Will felt the sadness that lingered there, seeped like water that leaves behind a stain, in the deserted courtyards and the gutted interior of the chapel, where a statue of St. George, the Temple's patron saint, had been pulled from its plinth and shattered with some blunt weapon. On one wall near the barbican, he found several Latin words scrawled in a dark substance that looked like pitch.

Non nobis, Domine, non nobis, sed nomini tuo da gloriam. Not unto us, O Lord, not unto us, but unto Thy name the glory.

It was the psalm the knights said before they went into battle. Will had passed his fingers across the black letters, wondering who had written them.

Had it been before the men had left the fortress under Baybars's promise of amnesty, just before they were led unaware to their executioners? Or was it older? Had they seen it as they had passed out of the gate and been comforted by the familiar markings?

When Will stumbled over the rocky, scrubby ground at the base of Safed's hill, the sight of the eighty or so heads stuck on pikes shocked him more than he had been able to prepare for. He had sunk to his knees and stayed there, staring at them for some time, before he was able to rise and do what needed to be done. After six years exposed to the elements, they were mostly skulls, with very little flesh or indication of who they had been or what they had looked like in life. A few had fallen off their pikes or slipped down, the iron tips protruding from repulsively huge eye-sockets. Two were missing. Will had been mortified to learn that the bodies of the knights had been burned after the executions; that only their heads remained in this world. But he still felt that if he could lay a part of the form that had once been his father beneath the ground, then both of them could rest.

The identity of his father's head, however, had not yielded to his inspection, and by the time he had gone down the whole line twice, he had given up. In the end, the Bahri warriors watching on in silence, he returned to the fortress and took a shovel from one of the animal pens. Unhindered by anyone, having, after all, the sultan's permission to be there, he worked his way through the scorching afternoon digging a grave for all of the skulls, until the sweat and the thirst and the pain in his arms left him delirious. Finally, as the sun had gone down behind the distant pink mountains, throwing the wide plain and the river into hazy shadows, redolent with the scent of the warm grass that hummed with mosquitoes, he turned the last of the earth over the grave. Then he had sat heavily on the ground beside it, too exhausted to think of any prayer to say.

Will looked up at the grand master. "My hatred toward those who killed my father almost consumed me. If I had let it, I would have lost myself to that darkness. I had to forgive them."

"I understand," said Guillaume. "But that doesn't change the simple fact that this peace is crippling us. Baybars and his people want us gone. The peace will not last. I can say that as certainly as I can say the sun will rise tomorrow. We need to pull ourselves back from the brink of our own extinction." His voice was calm, sincere. "If we do not, it will be the end of a Christian Holy Land. And your father and all those brave men before him will have died in vain. I know you do not want that."

"No, my lord," murmured Will. What else could he say? The grand master expected him to hate the Saracens, expected him to want to fight for the Temple's possessions and for Christendom's dream. It was the view of most good Christians, all good knights.

For two centuries they had come, those the Muslims called *al-Firinjah*: the Franks. After they invaded the great cities of Antioch, Tripoli and Jerusalem, wresting them bloodily from the Muslim, Jewish and native Christian inhabitants, the First Crusaders settled, establishing four Latin states. Here, they gave birth to generations who would never know the rolling hills of England or the verdant forests of France and Germany, but whose vistas would be the endless, timeless deserts of Syria and Palestine.

Crusade after Crusade swept out from the West, men and women seeking riches in wealthy Eastern cities and absolution for their sins. But over time, their numbers diminished. Weakened, the Franks tired of the constant struggle to defend Jerusalem from the infidel. The city that had called so many with its siren song to dash themselves against its walls had been back in the Muslims' possession for thirty-two years. Of the four Latin states established by the First Crusaders, only the County of Tripoli and the Kingdom of Jerusalem, of which Acre was now the capital, were still in Christian hands. The County of Edessa was gone, and of the former Principality of Antioch only a port remained. The vessels that glided into Acre's harbor were mostly half-empty, filled with mercenaries and straggling lines of pilgrims, those running from poverty and crimes committed, those running to a new life.

Will knew the grand master was right. Many of the men were despondent, bitter over what they had lost in Baybars's campaigns. Despite the Anima Templi's efforts for peace, the Templars and others still watched the horizon for those kingly ships that would herald a new Crusade and the return of Jerusalem to Christian hands. For the Franks were being forced closer and closer to the sea with every year that passed, their settlements eroded by the Mamluks, and no one knew how long they could remain, teetering on the edge of the Mediterranean's green-blue line.

As the grand master began to speak of how he intended to restore their position within the Holy Land, the words of the seneschal came back to Will, heavy with gravity. *He could prove to be one of the gravest threats to peace we have faced since the treaty was signed.*

"We must work to unify the territories Baybars has left us with. We are fractured, unwilling to pool resources, weakened. Acre is ...," Guillaume searched intently for the words, "... a plump worm that wiggles on the end of a hook." His gaze focused on Will, who had been starting to feel as if he weren't even in the room; the grand master seemed to be speaking to some larger, invisible audience. "Most of us are too preoccupied with our own internal convulsions to notice the predator that lurks in the water beneath us, waiting to open its jaw and snap," Guillaume closed his fist, "one last time." He rose and took a candle and taper to the fire. "We must work together if we are to survive the peril that will inevitably come our way again." Bending down, he held the taper in the flames. "The enthronement of my cousin should help in this matter. In time, I am confident he will help to unite us."

As the grand master lit the candle, Will realized how dark it had become since they had been talking. Soon the bells would ring for Vespers, calling them to chapel. "Is that definitely going to happen, my lord?" he asked carefully. "Will Charles d'Anjou take the throne?"

"It is my hope, yes. At the Council of Lyons, Pope Gregory arranged for Maria of Antioch to sell her rights to Jerusalem's crown to Charles. When the sale is completed, which I expect it will be within the year, he will be able to make his claim against King Hugh. And we will be governed once more by a *capable* ruler."

Will didn't miss the disdain in Guillaume's tone. He had heard much talk of these matters since word reached Acre of events at Lyons. The current king of Jerusalem was Hugh III, who was also king of Cyprus. The position was obsolete, Jerusalem having been lost to the Muslims, but the title remained and gave the bearer authority over Acre and what was left of the Franks' lands in Outremer. Rather than remain in Cyprus and let a regent control Acre, as many of his predecessors had, Hugh decided to exercise his authority. Will had noticed increasing complaints about the young king's interference; the government of Acre, made up of knight-masters, nobles, merchants, the commune of burghers and officials from the High Court, had successfully resisted royal rule for decades and had grown used to their autonomy. Another person opposed to Hugh's rule was his cousin, Maria, a princess of the vanquished city of Antioch, who believed she held the rightful claim to the throne. Such conflicts had split Outremer apart before, and the lawyers of Acre, aware of the danger the schism posed, had decreed that Hugh should take the crown. Will could understand their decision: the young king of Cyprus was a much surer candidate than an old, unmarried princess, but Maria had reportedly turned up at the Council of Lyons to complain, and the pope had convinced her to sell her rights to Charles d'Anjou.

Will had heard the seneschal remark that Pope Gregory wasn't impressed by Hugh and sought the elevation of a stronger leader. But he couldn't see how Charles, the powerful king of Sicily, could unify things. Hugh was unlikely to yield his throne without a fight, and with the grand master and d'Anjou arrayed against him, old battle lines would surely be drawn up: the Temple and the

Venetians banding together under Charles, the Hospitallers and the Genoese under Hugh. Will had the distinct impression that if things did go the way the grand master hoped, they would get bloodier before they got better.

"Still," said Guillaume brusquely, seeming to realize he had said more than he should, "such matters should be discussed when there are others present to hear them." He stood. "I summoned you here to thank you and instead I have talked you deaf." He spread his hands apologetically and gave Will a charmingly boyish smile. "It was a long journey. I was alone with my thoughts for quite some time. You must forgive me."

"There is nothing to forgive, my lord."

"There is one last thing." The grand master clasped his hands behind his back. "I would like you to find out who wanted me dead. My attacker was not an experienced killer, of that I am certain, and as I know of no reason why a young peasant should wish me harm, it is entirely possible that he was acting under the orders of another. Having inspected the body, Marshal de Sevrey believes him to have been an Italian. That and this boy you pursued are the only trails I can see to be followed. But I want you to look."

"Perhaps, my lord," began Will, "the marshal, or the grand commander, might be better suited to organizing such a task?"

"You are the only one who was aware of my attacker and the only one who saw the boy. I cannot think of anyone better suited."

Outside, a hollow clanging informed them that it was time for Vespers. The grand master didn't take his eyes off Will.

Will was filled with a sinking feeling. He had more than enough work to do for the Anima Templi. But the grand master was waiting for a response. "Yes, my lord, of course."

Later that evening, Guillaume sat at his desk in his chambers. In front of him he placed a prayer book, bound in leather-covered boards and closed with an ornate gold clasp, that he had just removed from his traveling chest.

For a moment, he didn't open it, but simply ran his fingers down the cover, feeling the cracks in the leather. He was tired and his head ached. He was rarely ill, and the unusual pain was distracting. He had given a speech in the chapel after the evening office, which had been gratefully received by the men, who were eager to welcome him. Afterward he shared a meal with them in the great hall, but he had wanted to speak with his officials before retiring and his headache had prevented him. Still, it was only his first day. Any discussions could wait for tomorrow. He unsnapped the book's clasp and opened a dog-eared page.

Our Father, which art in heaven, hallowed be thy name. Thy kingdom come. Thy will be done in earth, as it is in heaven. Give us this day our daily bread. And forgive us our debts, as we forgive our debtors. And lead us not into temptation, but deliver us . . .

There was a rap at the door. It opened, and one of Guillaume's personal guards, a Sicilian with short white-gray hair that made his tanned face appear even darker, entered.

"What is it, Zaccaria?"

"I'm sorry to disturb you, my lord, but there is a man at the gates asking to speak with you. He swears he knows you."

"Did he give a name?"

"Angelo."

Guillaume's face changed, subtly, but just enough that Zaccaria, who had worked under him in Sicily for five years, noticed something was wrong. "My lord?"

Guillaume gestured at the knight. "Bring him to me."

When Zaccaria left, the grand master made himself finish the Paternoster, then closed the prayer book. As he was setting it back inside the chest, the door was knocked on again, and this time, Zaccaria had another man with him. At a nod from Guillaume, the knight closed the door, leaving the two men alone in the solar.

"My lord," greeted Angelo Vitturi. His dark, handsome face was arrogantly impassive. "I wasn't sure you would be taking visitors, after your unfortunate welcome on the dockside."

"I forgot how fast news travels in this city," responded Guillaume wryly.

"It is good that it did, for it alerted us to your arrival."

"I'm sure our discussion could have waited a day or two," responded Guillaume, heading to a table where a servant had placed a jug of wine.

"Actually, it couldn't. I am leaving for Egypt." Angelo shook his head as Guillaume offered him a goblet. "The contact I told you about when we spoke in France, I am meeting him."

"Then he agreed to aid you?" said Guillaume, sipping his wine. "I must say I am surprised. I did not think you would be able to turn one of them so easily."

"He doesn't much care for the situation he finds himself in. It was not so hard."

"What are you doing here, Vitturi?"

Angelo frowned at the bluntness in the grand master's tone. "We wanted to make sure you are set and that nothing has changed." He gave a small shrug. "Your mind perhaps?"

Guillaume smiled, as if he found the game amusing. "I would be careful about questioning my word. It is a precious thing. Do not treat it lightly."

Angelo noted the danger behind that smile, but it didn't faze him. "My father and I are simply concerned that everything runs as smoothly as possible. We only have one chance to do this. Have you thought about who you will use to accomplish the theft?"

"I cannot do that until my position here is established and I have formed relationships with men I can trust. From what you told me, I presumed I had time in which to do this. Is that no longer the case?"

"The theft itself will not occur for some while yet. You will have plenty of time."

Guillaume looked into the Venetian's eyes, black and predatory as a shark's, and touched his brow, the ache making his thoughts muddled. "Then we are finished here for now. I will keep my end of the bargain, Vitturi, if you keep yours."

Angelo bowed stiffly and left the chamber, to be escorted back to the gate by Zaccaria.

Guillaume moved to the window. He had disliked the young man on their first meeting, and a second had done nothing to change that. He was angry that he was working with these merchants; his pride fought against the alliance, knowing they were using him for his resources. He believed their plan could work, where nothing else had. But it was a dangerous game and, not for the first time, Guillaume felt the weight of doubt pressing down on him. He pushed it aside. He had strong allies: King Edward, King Charles, Pope Gregory. They wouldn't let the Holy Land fall. When the time came, they would rouse the West. He was sure of it.

Guillaume looked over the courtyard beyond the walls to the scattered glitter of a thousand torches that lit the sleeping city like stars cast from heaven. If all went according to plan, they would soon be at war with the Muslims. "We do what we must," he said quietly. And then, quieter still. "God forgive me."

7

Al-Bira, Northern Syria

26 FEBRUARY A.D. 1276

A howled cry rose on the air, shattering the quiet dawn. Clouds of birds soared into the sky from thickets on the riverbanks, as seventy catapults lined up in formation around al-Bira were fired in succession. Giant boulders went spinning from the siege engines' slings to smash into dust and debris as they struck the city walls. As soon as the load was fired, one of the Chinese engineers who manned the catapults would winch down the sling, suspended from a long arm pivoted on the crossbar of the engine's wooden frame. His comrades would then position another stone in the leather cradle. Every now and then, the sky lit up as the engineers substituted barrels of flaming pitch for the stones, which left trails of black vapor in their wake as they streaked up to explode across the fortifications.

Under cover of the relentless bombardment, three towering monstrosities rolled cumbersomely toward the city. Within the lurching wooden structures, mounted on wheeled platforms, were four floors reached by internal ladders, on which groups of Seljuk archers knelt before arrow slits, bows primed. On the top floor of each tower, cramped beneath a heavy wooden hatch, were ten Mongol warriors. They were clad in lamellar battle armor, maces and swords ready in their fists. Behind the siege towers, lines of infantry marched in formation carrying long ladders. These men wore a lighter armor made from varnished oxhide, with shields slung over their shoulders and swords at their hips. Clothes hung loose on forms they had fitted snugly just three weeks earlier. A sickness causing violent bouts of vomiting and diarrhea had ravaged the army over the past few days, killing several hundred. But still they came, dogged, determined, the colorful cloaks and turbans of Seljuk and Iraqi troops garish amidst the brown leather armor of the Mongols.

Shortly after the initial crashes and thuds of rocks and barrels, the first screams went up from the walls, as the Mamluk soldiers manning them were wounded by flying shards of stone or crushed by boulders that smashed through the ramparts. Mamluk archers answered their enemy with arrows that sprang in wide sheets that turned the sky dark before arcing in a lethal volley into the advancing troops, thumping into shields, mud and men. Within the city itself, citizens crowded nervously into the mosques, men praying, mothers trying to quiet infants who wailed at the booming sounds of battle and the strained dread they sensed in their parents.

The Mamluk garrison Baybars had set in al-Bira, following an attack by the Mongols eleven years ago, were no strangers to sieges. Baybars had wrested the city from the occupying Mongol forces shortly after his accession to the throne, and the Mamluks had been involved in a tug-of-war with them over possession of it ever since. But this time was different. The Mongols knew the weak spots and were concentrating all their efforts on them. Even with the extra troops that had come up from Aleppo two weeks earlier, the assault was taking its toll.

Mamluk soldiers primed *mandjaniks* and *'arradas* mounted on the tower platforms that buttressed the walls, letting loose a barrage of stones and javelins into the approaching engines and troops. One javelin, four feet long, went shooting from an *'arrada* into a line of Mongols who were carrying one of the ladders. The first man didn't even see it coming. It plunged into him, driving clean through his hide armor, barreling through him like he was made of water, not flesh and bone. The impact picked him off his feet and drove him backward, where the javelin continued its deadly trajectory into three more men, impaling them like pigs on a spit. Four soldiers raced out from the lines of infantry that waited just out of range of the arrows, picked up the fallen ladder and continued the march. As more fell, others were there to take their places, leaving the dead to cover the ground behind them.

Stones from the Mamluks' *mandjaniks*, which were launched at the siege towers, had less effect than the javelins, as each of the wooden structures was covered with a deadening shield of cloth, hay and sacking. They did, however, shudder and sway ominously as the missiles struck them. Heavy rainfall had turned parts of the plain into a slimy mire, making further work for the rope pullers. Feet slipping, legs coated in gray, stinking mud, teeth gritted against the pain in their stretched muscles, they heaved and hauled the siege towers awkwardly, but steadily, toward al-Bira.

Ishandiyar was less than a quarter of a mile away when the first of the siege towers reached the walls. Dimly, through the clouds of smoke and dust that hung like a shroud in front of the city, he saw the hatch of the tower flip down onto the wall. Figures leapt out into the Mamluk lines waiting on the ramparts. Moments later, two of the ladders were hoisted against the walls. From his vantage point, on a slight incline beside the Euphrates, Ishandiyar saw Mongol warriors begin to climb. A barrel of pitch flew up from a catapult and erupted across a corner tower. Men burned like phoenixes as they fell from the heights, clothes and hair flaming. Their screams came to him; then a tattered veil of smoke swirled in to obscure his vision.

Ishandiyar turned to the two military governors beside him. "Ready the men."

"Should we reveal ourselves to the enemy so soon?" said one of the amirs doubtfully.

"We cannot stay hidden for much longer." Ishandiyar motioned along the river. For several miles the broad, sloping banks had shielded them. Ishandiyar had sent out soldiers to find and kill any Mongol scouts in the area, so that no one would be warned of their approach. Ahead, however, the bank leveled out, and within a hundred or so yards, the Mongol Army would see them. Ishandiyar looked down the slope behind him to the line of troops that stretched into the distance. It was as if a brightly colored forest had sprung up out of the desert, bristling with bows and spears. Men waited, calming horses, drinking water from skins, tightening armor. As well as his own regiment of four thousand, there were the regiments of the two amirs and the auxiliary forces they had gathered at Aleppo. They were twenty thousand in total. But that matched only two-thirds of the Mongols' force. "If we move now, whilst they are concentrating on the walls, we may be afforded some measure of surprise. Either way, we cannot linger."

"I agree," said the second governor.

"I will lead a charge against the troops at the walls. You and your men will focus on the soldiers behind the siege lines, and on the engines." Ishandiyar nodded to them. "Allah be with you."

The amirs turned their horses. Kicking up dust, they sped down the bank and galloped along the line of waiting soldiers, past infantry, cavalry, Bedouin tribesmen and men carrying pots of naphtha. They barked orders as they went, their silk surcoats flying out behind them to reveal glittering coats of mail beneath. Ishandiyar steered his horse over to the officers of his regiment. After a few brief commands, they were ready. All along the line, men moved into position, infantry jostling to move out of the way of cavalry, as the distant thuds and screams at the city walls continued.

Ishandiyar raised his sabre. *"Allahu akbar!"*

His officers answered his cry, and together, the first cavalry of the Mamluk elite charged their horses up the sloping, sandy banks, like a wave curling over a shore.

Within moments of the Mamluks' appearance, the horns blared an alarm

from the Mongol camp that was stretched along the plain between the city and
the river. Mongol cavalry, watching the battle from behind the lines, rushed to
their mounts, grabbing spears and helmets as the dust cloud churned up by the
Mamluk charge grew, thickening the air.

The other siege towers had now reached the walls. Warriors spewed forth
from the towers' tops, whirling maces and swords. Six ladders had gone up, the
Seljuk archers inside the siege towers shooting at Mamluks on the walls who
were attempting to cast them down. More Mongol warriors were scrabbling up
through the siege towers to join their comrades fighting fiercely on the ramparts, trying to punch through the lines of Mamluks. Men shoved and snarled
and spat as they fought one another in the cramped space, eyes stinging with
dust and sweat, feet catching on bodies, tripping on rubble.

The Bedouin tribesmen were the first of Ishandiyar's troops to reach the
Mongol camp. Their cloaks and kaffiyehs flying like ragged shadows around
them, they swarmed in under command of their sheikhs like a plague of wasps.
Arrows, knives and stones whipped from bows and hands and slingshots, and
several catapults went still as the Chinese engineers manning them were viciously cut down. Ishandiyar had worried about the Bedouin; he had known
them to desert to the enemy side when their own faltered, offering their allegiance in return for a share of any plunder. But as he glimpsed their lightning
raid on the camp, he was glad they were with him. They were canny fighters,
swift on their light horses, and for now at least, the Mongols were feeling the
full force of their skill. The wounded and the sick were given no mercy as
whooping tribesmen tossed flaming brands into tents, which caught and flared
like paper. Here, disease had done its work and many of the men were simply
too weak to fight. Despite the rallying shouts of their commanders, some began
to flee.

Ishandiyar saw a line of Mongol heavy cavalry approaching to his right, and
shouting for his men to follow, he bore down on the sprawl of soldiers at the
foot of the walls as the right flank of his regiment broke away to engage the
cavalry. The mass of troops scrambled into lines ahead of him that tightened as
he closed the distance, shields and spears going up. One of the ladders fell back,
pushed from the wall by the Mamluks on the ramparts. Men clung to the rungs,
shrieking as it plunged to earth. Others jumped free, only to be crushed moments later by their comrades as the ladder crashed into the ground.

Ishandiyar launched himself into the fray, slicing his sword in a sweeping arc
then stabbing backward as he barreled through the first lines of infantry, killing
indiscriminately. One man leapt at him, grabbing his horse's neck. His face,
beneath the streaks of dust and mud, was ugly with battle rage. Snarling, he

stabbed at the commander with a dagger. Ishandiyar kicked out, catching the man in the jaw and snapping his head back. Deftly, he turned his horse with his knees. The beast, which was well trained, knocked the man aside, sending him sprawling to the ground, then reared up and stamped down, the impact of its hooves crushing his skull.

In the first seconds, the Mamluk cavalry sheared through the tangle of men that choked the foot of the walls, like a scythe through corn. But the cramped space quickly became treacherous. The slimy ground, littered with rocks and bodies, caused men and horses to slip and stumble. Some Mamluks were pulled from their mounts and butchered by Mongol warriors; others fell dying with a Seljuk arrow in the neck or were thrown from their saddles as their horses were slashed by stray blades. Blood turned the air and the boggy ground red as men cut and thrust, and struck one another.

Ishandiyar managed to stay in his saddle and relentlessly blocked and delivered blows. His face a mask of concentration, he grunted with effort as the long march and the fierce charge quickly caught up with him, locking in his limbs. He hacked a man down, then turned to face another. Two more of the ladders had toppled and the boulders had ceased to fall. But the battlefield was chaos. Ishandiyar had no idea what was happening around the rest of the city. Thick smoke was rising from the Mongols' camp, but the enemy had rallied and were pouring into the melee to aid their comrades. His soldiers were falling. He could hear them dying around him. Panic rose in him. But he forced it down ruthlessly. His conviction lent strength to his arms and he hammered at the Mongols. If his death was required today, so be it. He would face it as a warrior and as a Muslim. He would face it with his men.

For some moments, Ishandiyar, caught up in the fury of battle, didn't hear the horns, and when eventually he did, he couldn't discern where the sound was coming from. Then he saw one of his officers thrusting a saber to the sky, jubilation plain in his face. Turning his horse, Ishandiyar saw Mamluks riding onto the plain in their hundreds. He thought for a second that they were his own troops, but then he realized that they weren't clad in the colors of any of the regiments he had led to the city. They wore the uniform of the regiment of the amir of Aleppo. The gates of al-Bira had opened. The city's garrison was riding to their aid.

And within moments, the battle turned.

The Mongols around al-Bira, seeing the reinforcements pouring from the city, began to rout. Their camp was in flames, their forces divided. Some men, locked in combat or too hemmed in to escape, fought on to the death. Most fled, running to the river, where they swam to the other side, arrows from the

Mamluks who pursued them darting into the water around them. Others charged weary horses toward the ford they had crossed by. After a siege that had lasted almost two weeks, with victory in sight, the Mongols and their Seljuk allies were driven back across the Euphrates a weaker, smaller force, leaving a trail of dead and wounded behind them.

Ishandiyar met with one of his officers after the fighting had ended, the last few pockets of resistance having been swiftly dispatched. A knife wound in his leg had been hastily bound by one of his physicians and stung like fire. He sucked water from a skin, swilled it around his mouth, then spat dust and blood into the sand.

"Take this to Aleppo," he said, handing a scroll to the officer. "Give it to the amir and have him send it by post-horse to Sultan Baybars. Cairo will be keen to learn of our victory."

The officer bowed and left.

Ishandiyar winced as he put weight on his leg and limped toward the gates, where wounded men were being carried into the city. The battle had ended in triumph. They had defeated the Mongols. But now it was time to count the dead.

THE CITADEL, CAIRO, 1 MARCH A.D. 1276

The sound of gruff voices was a dull drone in Baybars's ears as he looked down on the assembled company of governors, seated cross-legged on carpets and cushions before the dais. Resisting the urge to yawn, he pushed himself straighter and grasped the lions' heads that capped the throne's arms, feeling the metal solid and cold beneath his hands. "Enough, Mahmud. I think we are all familiar with your position on this matter now."

Mahmud bowed, but his face clearly displayed his gall at the brusque chastisement.

"Amir Kalawun," said Baybars. "You have kept very quiet. What do you say to this?"

Kalawun felt the attention of the fifteen men in the throne room turn on him. He took a sip of cordial from the goblet he held, so as to allow himself a moment to collect his thoughts. The younger men, like Mahmud, fidgeted impatiently. The war council had been tense and animated since it started, with arguments and counterarguments clashing into one another without resolution for over an hour. When he was ready, Kalawun set the goblet on one of the low tables arranged on the carpets and met Baybars's waiting gaze. "As I have stated before, my lord, I see no point in wasting precious resources attacking a people that are no threat to us at present."

"No threat?" voiced a haughty youth, a close comrade of Mahmud's. "Until they launch another of their Crusades that is. Every day we give them peace allows them to get stronger, allows their rulers in the West to build ships and gather forces to attack us. We cannot give them that chance!"

"Our economy is flourishing through our trade with the Franks," responded Kalawun. "And there is no evidence to suggest that there will be a Crusade in the near future. Indeed, our reports indicate a lack of enthusiasm for the continuation of the war."

"The traders will still come, even if we destroy the Franks' bases. They rely on us. We do not need them to occupy our lands to make money from them. Why leave ourselves open to attack, whether it comes next week or in another ten years?" The young governor looked for support around the company. Some nodded at his words. "Every day the Franks spend on these shores is an insult."

"It is a foolish man who goes to war on an insult," answered Kalawun calmly.

The governor gave a curt laugh, piqued by the comment. "You might appear Muslim on the outside, Amir Kalawun, but I think inside you're starting to look more like a Christian!"

There was an eruption of angry voices in the chamber.

"Silence!" barked Baybars. His eyes glittered with anger. "You will apologize to Amir Kalawun," he ordered the governor. "He is an honorable general and as devout a Muslim as I. Insult him and you insult me."

"Forgive me, Amir," the governor murmured to Kalawun. "My tongue ran away with me."

"Any effective commitment to war must be concentrated on one enemy at a time," said an older Mamluk, coming to Kalawun's defense. "The Mongols are actively aggressive toward us. Therefore, I agree with Amir Kalawun. Our next move is apparent."

"We are dealing with the situation in al-Bira," voiced Mahmud, unable to help himself. "It is not the first time the Mongols have attacked one of our holdings and I doubt it will be the last." He became emboldened when Baybars said nothing. "Let our forces in Syria concentrate on keeping the Mongols behind the Euphrates, whilst our forces here focus on the Franks. Then, once we have taken Palestine and erased the infidels' last vestiges of power, we can march as one army, vast and mighty, into Anatolia. We can defeat the Mongols if we are united, without fear of invasion or attack from the rear by the Franks. We cannot defeat them if we are divided." He spoke passionately, and Kalawun noted sourly that the young governor could be an inspiring orator. "Let us turn our full attention to the Mongols when we have it to spare. First let us drive out the Franks and set Palestine back in the hands of the righteous. The Mongols are a distraction we must not allow ourselves to be diverted by."

"A distraction?" questioned Kalawun. "Is that what you would call a force that has destroyed nations and erased whole tribes? Who now has half the world in its possession and who controls the supply roads in and out of the East?" A few of the other governors murmured their agreement, but more were frowning. Kalawun's face hardened as he saw their contention. "I did not lead my regiment into Cilicia ten years ago, see them haul themselves over miles of desert and mountain passes to fall on Armenian swords just so we could now leave the territories we secured in that struggle open to the Mongols. We took Cilicia so that we could take Anatolia. We cannot give way now. Today, it might be a city they are attacking, but if we give them one inch of territory, the Mongols will sweep down on us with all the force they can muster and everything we have done, everything we have built since Ayn Jalut will have been for nothing."

Baybars stirred at the mention of that battle.

It had been the first defeat of a Mongol force the world had ever known. And it had been his doing. That day had been sweet with triumph. Retribution for the Mongols' attack on his tribe, which had seen his delivery into slavery, it heralded the end of an old life, begun in chains, and the beginnings of his rise to power. The memory made him feel young again. He felt anticipation bubble up inside him, felt his assurance grow. For too long, the Franks had been a bitter taste in his mouth. He didn't have the stomach to swallow the dregs of them yet, not when a force that made his heart sing with that youthful, strident battle song was out there. The Franks were locked away in impregnable cities. The Mongols waited on the edges of his empire, daring him to meet them. He wanted the feel of a sword in his hands, the dry breath of the desert on his face again.

"I have made my decision," he said, his voice cutting through the murmurs of the men.

The governors fell silent. Kalawun's face was a placid mask, but inside his heart was thudding painfully fast.

"We will march on Anatolia."

Mahmud and several of his young companions looked furious, but were careful to keep their emotions unspoken. Kalawun felt a surge of relief, but immediately afterward felt hollow. The outcome was still war. Before he died and gave up his realm to his son, Baybars was going to create another storm. There was nothing Kalawun could do about it, and even if there was, he wouldn't. He wanted peace, but the Mongols didn't. He would protect his people.

"I will use the truce I have with the Franks to concentrate on the Mongols," said Baybars. "I do not believe they will break it. They are too fearful of losing their last territories to enter into a fight they cannot hope to win. When we have taken Anatolia and the Mongols are driven out, I will deal with the Franks." He rose. "When I receive word on what has happened at al-Bira, I will summon you to discuss our strategy."

As the governors filed out of the throne room conversing in low tones, Kalawun slipped past them, not wanting to be cornered. He'd had enough debates for one day. He moved down a vaulted passage, where the breeze coming through the windows tousled the leaves of ornamental plants and whispered of summer. He had almost reached the end when a gray figure slunk into his path. Kalawun's brow knotted in dislike as Khadir grinned at him.

"Amir Kalawun," greeted the soothsayer, giving an exaggerated bow.

"What do you want?"

"The outcome of the war council," said Khadir, "what was it?"

"Ask your master," replied Kalawun. He continued down the passage.

Khadir's white eyes narrowed, but he followed, scurrying to keep up with Kalawun's long-legged stride. "Where is it, Kalawun, that you steer my master?"

"Steer him?"

Khadir stepped into his path. As Kalawun went to go around, the soothsayer darted in to block him. He giggled. "See how we dance?" He did a graceful twirl. "Like you danced in the council? Danced around my master until he was so dizzy with your voice he did not know his direction."

"You were spying again?" As Khadir smiled, Kalawun reminded himself to have the wall passage that ran alongside the throne room blocked up. He had seen Khadir crawling into it before. "If you know the outcome of the meeting, then you have no need to ask me."

Khadir hopped nimbly out of his way as he moved off. "I want to understand why you turn his eye from the Christians, Amir."

"It is our sultan's decision to attack the Mongols."

"No!" snapped Khadir, looking suddenly furious. "Not his. You've been whispering in his ear for months. Don't fight the Franks! Don't fight the Franks!"

"I don't have to explain my reasons to you."

"Truces can be broken, Amir. There are those in the West who threaten us:

the king of Sicily and Edward of England. The Templars have a new master, a
strong one. If any of these men rise against us, legions will follow. We both
know how our master changed after Omar's death." He snatched at the air with
his fist. "Gone! Just like that. And with him, our master's destiny. I have seen,
Kalawun. I have *seen* how we will lose this land."

Kalawun came to a stop. The old man's eyes were wild and wide.

"Yes," murmured Khadir, as Kalawun's expression shifted slightly. "We
must save it, you and I."

"I will not change my mind, Khadir," said Kalawun, starting to shake his
head. "I will not persuade Baybars to attack the Franks when I do not believe
in that course of action."

"Not that," snapped Khadir irritably, "not that."

"Then what are you asking me to do?"

"For our master to return to his former glory, he must exact blood vengeance
on those who turned him from his path." Khadir's face contorted in anger.
"The *Hashishim* have paid." He nodded vigorously. "They have. But not those
who hired them." He absently began to finger the gold-handled dagger that
hung from his belt as he spoke of the Assassins, the order he had been exiled
from. "Our sources believed Franks organized the killing." He hissed like a
snake at Kalawun's nonplussed expression. "We must find the Franks who
wanted our master dead! Only when vengeance is served, will he be able to return to his true path and defeat the Christians."

Kalawun shook his head. "The past is dead, Khadir. Let it stay that way. It
is a fool's errand you suggest. It could take months to discover who contracted
the Assassins. Indeed, it may never be discovered."

"Our governors control the Assassins' strongholds now," responded Khadir.
"It will be easy to question the *Hashishim*. Send Nasir. He is a Syrian. He knows
the regions they reside in."

"No," said Kalawun, heading off.

"I see what you are doing with Baraka," Khadir called at his back.

Kalawun turned, careful to disguise the worry the words had caused. "What
do you mean?"

"Your influence over the boy grows stronger every day. You married your
own daughter to him! Only a blind man or a trusting fool wouldn't see that you
are trying to gain his trust for something." Khadir moved toward Kalawun.
"You dislike the child, I know you do. And yet you spend your days teaching
and training him. He has tutors for such things."

"Is it wrong to take an interest in my own son-in-law?"

The soothsayer's face contorted with contempt. "Bah! You persevere beyond the duties of father or friend. You want power over the throne, Kalawun. I *see* that too."

Kalawun laughed. "But of course I do."

Khadir's eyes squinted in suspicion and puzzlement.

"Any man close to a throne seeks to be bathed in its light," said Kalawun. "I do not dismiss your claim, but neither would any governor, wife or advisor if they answered truthfully. I do not seek the throne for myself; I seek a secure position for my masters from which they, in turn, may favor me." Kalawun's face hardened. "Before you play games with me, Khadir, I suggest you look into your own future, for it will be neither long nor happy if you test my patience." He strode off, feeling the soothsayer's stare like a dagger in his back.

It was approaching evening in Cairo. Darkness crept across buildings colored orange by the setting sun as Angelo made his way to the meeting place. The trees in the orchard below the citadel's wall swayed hypnotically in a breeze that bore the smells of smoke, dung and food from the city that was tumbled down the hill below him. Beyond the walls, the Nile was jet black against the soft shadows of the desert. Angelo, who had left his horse at his lodgings, wrapped his cloak tighter about him.

Over the years, he had been to Cairo on a number of occasions to do business with the Mamluks, bringing them cages of boys for their army in return for bags of bright Saracen gold. But his business today was more delicate, and he had been careful to remain hidden in his lodgings until it was time. When he had sought out his contact on his arrival, paying a street child to deliver a message to the citadel, he had been told to meet him here.

Angelo paused. At the far end of the orchard was an old cistern with a crumbled ledge. There, in the shadows of the tangled trees, a figure was waiting. "You have it?" said Angelo in Arabic as he approached.

The figure wore a long black cloak and a kaffiyeh covering his head and face. Only his eyes were visible as he rose from where he had been sitting on the cistern. He reached into his cloak and pulled out a silver scroll case, ornately filigreed with patterns of lotus flowers.

Angelo took it. Opening the top, he pulled a scroll from the case, which he unfurled. He glanced at the page, then at the man who had given it to him. "It says exactly what I asked for?"

"Yes."

"I presume only Kaysan will be able to read it?" asked Angelo, stowing the case in the pouch that hung from his belt. "If it fell into the wrong hands, it would be bad for us all."

"Can you read it?" said the man curtly.

Angelo ignored his tone. "And your brother will do as you ask? He will take our men into Mecca when the time comes?"

"Yes."

Angelo stared hard at him. "Remember what is at stake. If you betray me, if there is *anything* in that letter that damages my plans at all, I will see that you and your brother suffer for it. You owe me. Do not forget that."

"How could I?" murmured the man. As Angelo went to leave, he called out. "You will give me what I asked for?"

Angelo looked back. "When the Stone is taken, you will have everything you wanted."

The man watched him walk away. "It has been a long time coming," he whispered.

8

The Venetian Quarter, Acre

12 MARCH A.D. 1276

The door creaked open, intrusively loud. Will glanced over the gallery to the deserted entrance hall. He could hear faint voices from the kitchen, as Elwen entered the solar and ushered him in.

The solar was yellow with sun, the whitewashed walls and several oval mirrors of beaten silver reflecting the light into every corner. In the main chamber a table and bench stood close to a hearth. The table was scattered with papers, and from a clothes perch behind it hung a blue silk robe and cap. As he saw the robe, Will thought for a second that it was someone standing there, and his stomach, already tight with unease, lurched. A door led through to another room, dominated by a bed. The bedcover was of an extravagant material and design; plum-colored damask with gold threads woven through it. The fabrics in the rest of the solar were no less sumptuous; the drapery at the windows, the cushions on the couch, a hanging fixed above the hearth, all lent a majestic, sensuous air to rooms that would have otherwise been sparse and plain. A delicate smell of flowers came to Will, and he noticed a bowl filled with dried petals on a table by the couch. No doubt put there by Andreas's wife. Apart from the papers on the desk, the solar had a woman's tidiness, a delicate order that was far less austere than the military neatness he was used to. Despite his unease, he found it comforting. He had a memory of his mother arranging flowers in the kitchen of his boyhood home in Scotland, his baby sister, Ysenda, perched on her hip.

Elwen crossed to the window seat. She looked back when Will didn't follow. "What is it?"

"Can we not go to your room?"

"Not unless you want to share it with a sick maid." Removing the white coif that covered her hair, Elwen shook free a tumbling mass of copper-gold curls. As she sat and leaned over to slip off her felt shoes, her white linen gown dipped into a V at the neck, offering Will a tantalizing view of the pale skin between her breasts. Sun-bronzed and freckled in the summer months, she was white as marble in winter. "Don't worry," she assured him with a smile, lifting her long legs up under her.

"Andreas is at the warehouse?"

Elwen rolled her eyes and patted the cushions beside her.

"And Besina and the girls are at the market?"

"You know they are." Elwen studied him quizzically. "Why are you so worried all of a sudden? Is it the room?" She looked around. "You've been in here before."

"And I was worried then," replied Will pointedly. Heading over, he unfastened his black cloak, which concealed the white surcoat he wore beneath. Laying it on the seat, he sat beside her, noticing how sheer her dress became in the sunlight. "It's risky."

"It's been risky since we were sixteen, Will." Elwen frowned. "What *is* wrong?"

"Nothing. Honestly," he added, as she continued to frown at him, her pale green eyes webbing slightly at the corners. He wanted to reach out and smooth away the lines with his thumb. In them, he saw time passing. "It's just since the grand master arrived, we've all been making sure we do everything by the book. Everyone's keen to impress him." Will grinned. "You should see some of the suppers the cooks have prepared. Wild boar baked with apples, saffron rice, sweets spun out of sugar and honey."

"I thought you were looking a little broader," Elwen answered dryly. But she smiled. "He is keeping you busy then?"

"Very. That's why I haven't been by for so long. I haven't had time."

"In truth, neither have I," said Elwen, sleeking down her dress self-consciously. "I've been promoted."

"Promoted?"

"Since the doge in Venice became one of Andreas's patrons, the demand for his silks has risen and Tusco has to spend most of his time in Venice at the warehouse or organizing transportation. Andreas is training Niccolò to take over the shipping."

Will hadn't met Andreas's sons, or the rest of family he had heard so much about, apart from Catarina, which had been an accident. He did know, however, that Niccolò was interested in Elwen. She once told him, laughingly, that the young Venetian had come to her room in secret, with flowers and a proposal. Will knew why she had done it: to remind him that she was an attractive woman that he hadn't claimed for his own yet. It had worked. Now, whenever she mentioned Niccolò, he would feel a tiny bee sting of jealousy that occasionally swelled to plague him long after the initial stab.

"It means Andreas will have fewer hands to help him in the warehouse," Elwen was saying. "He needs someone to aid him with the accounts and Elisabetta and Donata aren't interested in the business. Anyway, he already has a suitor in mind for Elisabetta, and Donata is fast approaching fourteen." Elwen smiled. "He said he thinks of me as family and that I do so much for the business already I was the natural choice."

"I'm pleased for you." Will knew how hard she worked for the Venetian.

Back in the royal palace in Paris, as handmaiden to the queen of France, Elwen hadn't had to worry about her place in the world as an unmarried woman; she had lodgings and was paid well. Now that that net had been taken from under her and she was living an independent life, the pitfalls were that much greater. Very few industries approved the direct involvement of women, mostly just cloth manufacturing, brewing and more menial work such as laundering and cleaning. The promotion proved that she had started to become invaluable to Andreas and his business, and made her footing that much surer. Without him, her existence in Acre would be a lot less comfortable. It was no real surprise, from all the women who came to the East in search of freedom and independence, away from the trappings of forced marriage, that for every five men in the city there was one whore.

"Thank you," said Elwen, twisting the coif in her lap. "It will mean that I have to work harder though." She glanced at him. "That we will have even less time together."

"I don't mind, as long as you're happy."

Her brow creased and she looked away.

Will chewed his lip, wondering what he had said. He inhaled deeply. "Well,

I've had a promotion myself since I saw you last. The grand master has made me a commander."

Elwen stared at him. "A commander?"

"It came as a surprise to me too. I was summoned two weeks ago to give him a report on what I'd found out about the attack. He told me afterwards."

"Must have been a good report," said Elwen a little sardonically. "Did you find out who wanted him killed?"

"Not yet. We only knew that the attacker was Italian, so all I could do was speak with the consuls of Venice, Pisa and Genoa and ask them to conduct their own investigations. The Venetian consul was more helpful than the others, but even he couldn't find anything on the dead man." Will shrugged wearily. "The trouble is they are all suspicious of anyone from outside their own quarters. We might live in the same city, but for all the walls we put up to keep each other out we might as well reside in different countries. I told the grand master to offer a reward for any information that led to our discovering who tried to kill him. He agreed. We sent criers around the city."

"I heard Niccolò saying something about that the other day."

"Good," said Will, relieved. "At least word is getting out." He rubbed at his beard, a habit he had recently formed when preoccupied. "I just hope someone comes forward soon. I have no other ideas and I don't want the grand master to think he made a mistake promoting me."

Elwen reached out and took his hand, drawing it from his chin. "You'll rub it bald," she said softly. "You did your best and he rewarded you for it." She shook her head. "You always do this, Will. As soon as something good happens, you immediately wonder when it will be taken away from you." As Will looked at her, Elwen guessed what he was thinking. On the day he had gained his knighthood, he had lost both his father and her. Cursing herself inwardly, she pushed on. "You cannot do everything right all the time. You try to please everyone and that's commendable, but you also need to know when to let go."

"Look," said Will tiredly, squeezing her hand, "I came here to see you, not to talk about my frustrations." He threaded his fingers through hers until their hands were locked, pushed palm to palm. "Can we start again?"

Elwen moved closer. "Let's not start at all."

Will closed his eyes as she leaned to kiss him. He felt her lips brush his, so softly it was almost painful. Then their mouths were pressing together. Reaching out, he caught her by the waist and guided her onto him until she was straddling his lap, her white gown riding up to expose her thighs. God, but it had been a long time since they had been together. They came apart and she stared down into his eyes, her fingers tracing tingling lines through his hair, across his scalp, down to his neck, where a blue vein pulsed.

"I've missed you," she whispered, then kissed him again to conceal the brightness that came into her eyes.

Will trailed his hands up the outside of her thighs, then over the folds of the dress to grip her waist again. But Elwen took one of them, led it back down to her thigh, and under the folds of material. Both their heartbeats quickened. Will pressed his hand into the small of her back, crushing her to him, as she bent to kiss his neck. Her skin was hot. Dizzy with pleasure, he half-opened his eyes. Over Elwen's shoulder, he saw a figure in the doorway, watching them. It was as if someone had thrown a bucket of ice water over him.

"Jesus!"

"What?" said Elwen, straightening abruptly. She followed his gaze and saw Catarina standing there.

Hopping off Will, Elwen pushed down her dress. Her cheeks felt as if they were on fire as she padded barefoot to the girl. She said something in Italian, which Will didn't understand, then shooed her out of the room.

Will had stood and was rearranging his crumpled surcoat. He heard Catarina giggle and the word *kiss*.

A moment later, Elwen reappeared. "What are you doing?" she asked, watching him pick up his cloak.

"Getting out of your master's bedchamber before his wife finds me here, you lose your job and I lose my mantle," he muttered, swinging the cloak around his shoulders.

"Will, calm down," said Elwen, crossing to him. "Besina isn't back. Catarina didn't go with them to market today. I told her to play upstairs, but she must have seen you come in."

"What if she tells her father?" said Will, unwilling to be placated by her easy tone. "It was all right before she found out. But now? If anyone in the Temple learns of this, I'll—"

"They won't," Elwen cut across him. "And it isn't as if no one there knows about us."

"Robert and Simon know," responded Will shortly, "but they have for years and neither of them is going to inform on me."

"And Everard."

"Everard wouldn't notice if you turned up at the preceptory and walked naked through the courtyard. He only cares about his work."

Elwen grinned impishly at the image. "I'll wager he would."

"Elwen, this is serious. With Catarina following us around, we've no privacy anymore."

"If we were married and living in our own home, we'd have privacy," she responded. "We wouldn't have to meet on set days when everyone else is out. I wouldn't have to sweeten the maids with presents for their silence and leave a cloth outside my window to warn you when someone's here, or wonder what has happened when you don't come at all."

Will sighed. "You know that isn't possible."

They stared at each other in silence.

Elwen pressed her lips together, then shook her head. "This isn't how I wanted today to be." Will watched as she moved to the table and opened one of the drawers. She took out a leather pouch. "Open your hand."

"Elwen . . ."

"Do it," she insisted.

As he did so, Elwen shook the pouch over his palm. A thin silver chain coiled out with a small disc attached to it. Will pushed the disc over with the tip of his finger. On it was embossed an image of a man with his foot on a serpent.

"It's Saint George," she told him, as he raised it to the light to see the detail.

"It's beautiful." Will looked at her. "What have I done to deserve this?"

"I saw it and wanted to give it to you." She shrugged. "To celebrate my promotion."

"I don't have anything to give you."

"That isn't the purpose of a gift." Elwen took the chain and undid the clasp.

Will stood still as she draped it around his neck and stood on her toes to fasten it. The metal disc was cold against his chest.

"It was to remind you that he's still there, protecting you. It's just a little thing."

For Will, the sweetness of the gift was soured by guilt. It wasn't just a little thing. Elwen knew the significance of it. He had told her how he had found the statue of the Temple's patron saint shattered in Safed's chapel and how that had come to symbolize his father's burial; something broken, ended. He wanted a gift to offer her in return, something more than this frantic lovemaking whenever they had the chance. But he was scared anything he gave her would feel too much like payment. "Thank you," he murmured.

She kissed his mouth gently, the passion gone, replaced by tenderness.

Will gave her a brief, hard hug. "Next time will be better," he said, releasing her. "I promise."

After leaving Elwen, Will headed onto the Street of the Vintners that led to the western gates of the quarter. The street was barely wide enough for him to pass through, clogged as it was with traders and impatient men leading braying donkeys and pulling handcarts piled with barrels and food. Toothless women and dirty-faced children held out begging hands to the endless stream of passersby and men gathered in doorways to discuss wares and deals and prices. Washing hung from hemp lines stretched between the houses like banners at a festival, whilst pigs rooted in the rubbish and excrement that carpeted the street below. The comforting smell of fresh bread from a communal oven mingled with the cloying scent of hashish and the sharp aromas from the vintners'. It was like moving through a wall of sound and smell that invited, intoxicated and repelled at once.

As he walked, Will mulled over the things he needed to do that afternoon. It was a blessing in one sense that his meeting with Elwen had been cut short. Before Vespers, he had to check with the criers who had been sent out with news of the reward, to see that all the quarters had been reached. He would then have to file a report with the marshal and the grand commander, and he should try to see Everard. He hadn't spoken to the priest for several days, having been kept busy for the grand master. When he had last seen him, Everard had been preoccupied with his concerns over King Edward. Will hadn't been able to offer much comfort, except to assure the priest that he had written to Garin. There wasn't much else they could do. It would be months before the letter even reached England.

Will was almost at the end of the street, when he felt a tug on his cloak. He spun around, thinking it was a pickpocket, and grabbed hold of a small boy behind him. The boy let out a cry as Will took a fistful of his threadbare tunic and almost lifted him off his feet. Will was about to shove him away, when he realized, with a jolt, that he recognized him. "You were on the dockside," he exclaimed, keeping a tight hold on the boy. "The day the grand master was attacked." Will ignored the annoyed calls and grumbles of the crowd, now having to pass around him. Someone told him to leave the child alone, but whoever it was kept on walking, pressed on by the tide.

"Let me down," cried the boy in garbled Latin. "You're hurting!"

"Not a chance. You'll run again."

"I won't! I *want* to speak to you. I've been following you for hours."

Will stared at him, then took hold of the boy's arm and led him down the street, forcing him through the mob. Before reaching the gates, he squeezed into a narrow alley. It was deserted. Beyond the alley mouth, the stream of people continued on. "What were you doing that day on the dockside?" asked Will, turning the boy to face him.

The boy hung his head miserably.

Will studied him. He was a scrawny thing, with bruised circles under his eyes. He looked half-starved and his clothes seemed barely held together by their frayed threads; one good gust of wind and they'd be off. "What's your name?" he said, more gently.

"Luca," replied the boy, sniffing and wiping his nose.

"Why were you following me, Luca?"

"I was outside the Temple this morning. I was going to go in, but then I saw you, so I followed. When you went into that house, I waited. I ..." Luca faltered, then pushed on quickly. "I wanted to tell you something."

"About the man who tried to kill the grand master?"

Luca looked up. "It wasn't his fault. He didn't have a choice." His eyes flooded with tears.

"Who?"

"My brother, Marco. He wanted to take care of me and our mother. But now he's dead and Sclavo hasn't paid and Mama's worse than before. I told her he's gone away to look for work. I cannot tell her he's dead."

"Who is Sclavo?" said Will intently.

"He's a bad man." Luca gave an angry sob. "I wish he had been killed too, for making him do it."

"This Sclavo paid your brother to attack the grand master?"

Luca nodded.

"Why did you decide to come to the preceptory to tell us now?" asked Will, already guessing the answer.

"I heard about the reward," said Luca in a quiet voice. Through his tears his expression was defiant. "I have to buy potions for my mother."

"I understand." Will paused, studying the boy. "How do you know Latin?" he asked, still undecided as to what he should do.

"Marco taught me," muttered Luca. "He said I should learn it so I could find better work than him, maybe become a clerk or someone important."

Will gave a small smile, then nodded. "I will give you the reward if you can tell me where to find Sclavo."

"Oh," said Luca, taken aback. He hadn't imagined it would be so easy. "He's in the old part of the Genoese quarter. He runs a tavern there. Everyone calls it the Saracen."

9

The Citadel, Cairo

12 MARCH A.D. 1276

Baraka climbed over the blocks of fallen masonry and entered the tower's lowest chamber, his nose itchy with the shifting layers of dust that cloaked the air. An earthquake the day before had caused the upper part of the corner tower, already pronounced unstable by the stonemasons, to topple in on itself. Rubble had tumbled down the stairs from the level above and lay strewn across the floor, blocking an opening on the other side. The quake had caused little other damage in the citadel, although some houses in Fustat Misr had collapsed, killing at least fifty people. The stonemasons would be coming later that day to inspect the damage and begin repairs. Baraka scanned the empty chamber, then glanced back through the partially obstructed archway he had entered through. It led into a narrow passage that cut through the outer walls, scored with arrow slits. The passage stretched into a gloom his eyes couldn't penetrate. Hearing shouting outside, Baraka went cautiously to the tower's entrance and peered out, blinking at the sunlight.

Near the tower on the opposite corner of the wall, behind a line of trees, two Mamluk guards were dragging a man across the scrubby ground. He was shrieking, trying to twist away. He was rewarded with a punch in his side from one of the soldiers. After that he slumped in their arms as they hauled him toward a large wooden grate set into the ground. There were two other Mamluk guards here, who bent down and pulled on an iron chain attached to the grate. It opened like a maw, revealing a square of darkness. The man was roused as he saw it and cried fiercely at the guards, his head thrown back. "Innocent! I'm *innocent*!"

The two soldiers holding him tossed him unceremoniously into the hole, where he disappeared, his scream fading like an echo. The Mamluks gripping the chain let go and the grate banged shut.

In the cool shadows of the tower, Baraka shivered. He used to have nightmares about the citadel's dungeon. The grate opening and his feet, unable to stop, taking him closer and closer, until at last there was no more earth beneath him and he was falling, endlessly. One of his friends, having learned of his fear, had delighted in describing the conditions inside the prison, a cavernous pit cut into the bedrock, which went down thirty feet. It was a place of nightmares, crawling with lunatics and murderers, thieves and rapists. They clotted up the darkness, preying on the young or the weak who were hurled into their dank lair of slime and mud and unimaginable filth, where bats clustered in soft, twitching clumps on the cavern roof. Baraka's friend spoke of a boy, imprisoned for stealing bread, who had been eaten alive by some of the starving captives.

Baraka was brought sharply out of his private horror as he heard a noise behind him. Khadir was slinking into the chamber, stepping lightly over the broken stones. Baraka crossed his arms, his emerald- and jet-colored surcoat, which matched his turban, tightening across his chest. "I didn't think you were coming."

"Please forgive me, my prince," said Khadir fawningly, "my legs do not carry me as fast as yours."

"I've been waiting ages."

"It is but minutes since we spoke and arranged to meet here."

"Not since we spoke," snapped Baraka. "I've been waiting ages for you to tell me about your plan. It's been almost two months. You said you would make my father take notice of me. That I was going to start a war."

"Ahh, yes," said Khadir, nodding sagely. "But we must wait for another first."

Baraka scowled as Khadir grinned secretively. He began to pace and cursed as he stumbled on a loose rock. Moments later, a man appeared in the archway. Baraka stared at him in alarm, guilt rising red in his cheeks, his mind struggling to think of some explanation as to what he was doing in the deserted tower with the soothsayer. "Amir Mahmud," he stammered, as the young governor strode in.

"Now we can begin," came Khadir's voice, and Baraka realized that Mahmud was whom the soothsayer had been waiting for.

"I cannot stay for long," said Mahmud, glancing outside to check the courtyard.

"What's happening?" asked Baraka, nervous in the presence of the forceful military governor.

Mahmud looked to Khadir. "You haven't told him?"

Khadir was about two feet shorter than the governor, but Mahmud took a step back as the old man came toward him. "I wanted to be certain I had your support before I spoke to the boy."

Baraka was irritated at being spoken of as if he weren't there, but he held his tongue, impatient to know what the two men were talking about.

"Amir Mahmud has agreed to assist us," said Khadir, turning to Baraka. "He too sees our master has lost his way."

"I will help you," said Mahmud to Baraka, "but my part in this is to be kept secret. Do you understand?"

"Of course he understands," hissed Khadir. "He is not a child. He will one day be your sultan!"

Baraka's cheeks reddened again, this time with pride. Emboldened, he looked Mahmud in the eye. "I think what Khadir is saying is that I am deserving of a little more respect, Amir."

"My sincere apologies, my prince," murmured Mahmud, shooting a black look at Khadir.

"Your impudence is forgiven," said Baraka, the sudden authority giving him a strange thrill of pleasure. He wanted to say more, perhaps make the governor kneel, but Khadir started speaking before he could.

"In Palestine, close to the city of Acre, lies a village, my prince," said the soothsayer. "There are Frankish spies there. They trail our soldiers and notify the infidel leaders in Acre of their movements."

Baraka shrugged carelessly. "It happens all the time. We have spies and emissaries in Acre who report the Christians' doings to us, don't we?"

"We have," said Khadir, nodding keenly. "We have indeed."

"Your father has been given a report of this," said Mahmud, interrupting Khadir. "But he refuses to deal with the matter, saying he wishes to concentrate on his plans for Anatolia before he makes any move against the Christians. Under the peace agreement, we agreed to let the Franks keep what possessions they still owned. This village is under that agreement. To attack it would be an act of war." Mahmud's face twitched with impatience at Baraka's blank expression. "If their village was sacked, the Franks would be forced to retaliate."

"Not just sacked," Khadir corrected Mahmud, "it must be enough to fire the Christians into a holy rage. It must be a *massacre*." He said the word tenderly, as if it were the name of a loved one. "Their men must be butchered, their women defiled and their children enslaved. We must *provoke* them."

Realization dawned across Baraka's face, but he shook his head. "The Christians won't attack us whatever we do to them. They cannot. Their forces are nothing compared to ours. Even if you could get my father to storm the village, it wouldn't start a war."

"Clever boy," said Khadir, grinning at him. "You are right. But we do not expect the Christians to attack us. We expect them to react in kind. An eye for an eye," he chuckled. "That is what they'll want."

"They will most likely turn on our own emissaries in Acre," Mahmud explained to Baraka, "behind their walls where we cannot go. They will demand some form of compensation from Baybars, probably the release of Christian prisoners, maybe even the return of territory, and will use our people as hostages for their demands. The sultan will refuse and the Christians, in their arrogance and rage, will most likely kill our men."

"How can you be sure my father will refuse?"

"Rarely has he given way to any of their demands in the past," answered Mahmud before Khadir could speak. "And he will be even less likely to if the attack on the village was not of his doing. For he will not order the attack himself. He has already made it plain he won't do this. We have to arrange it for him."

"But only my father or one of his amirs can . . ." Baraka frowned at Mahmud. "You will order the attack?"

"No," said Mahmud quickly. "As I said, my part is to be kept secret."

"Our soldiers will *think* our master has ordered it," said Khadir. "A message will be sent in Baybars's name, with his seal stamped upon it." His white eyes fixed on Mahmud. "You will make sure of it?"

"It will be done tonight."

Khadir clapped his hands gleefully. "We will make the crossbow fly!" He looked at Baraka. "And *you* will drive the bolt home."

"What do you mean?"

"When the sultan hears that an order was sent in his name, using his seal, he will demand an investigation," said Mahmud calmly. "Neither Khadir nor myself can be found to be involved. In all likelihood we would be imprisoned, or executed."

"You must tell him you did it," said Khadir, heading to Baraka.

Baraka was flooded with fear at the mere thought of it. "I couldn't! He would be so *angry!*"

"You will explain your reasons," said Khadir softly, insistently. "You will tell him how you have been studying well, learning all that you can about his victories over the Franks. You will tell him how you heard reports of the spies and wanted to help. You will say you knew he was burdened by other matters and that you wanted to aid him, that you wanted to show him you are no longer a little boy."

"I couldn't," repeated Baraka. His eyes drifted toward the tower's entrance, beyond the line of trees to the grate that led down into the dungeon. "I *couldn't.*"

"Then he'll never take notice of you!" snapped Khadir, making Baraka start. His tone softened. "I have *seen* it. If you do not do this, he will never take you into his trust, and when you become sultan, not a man here will respect or follow you."

Baraka swallowed dryly at these words, so similar to words his own mind had mocked and troubled him with. "I . . ."

"You are his heir," said Mahmud firmly. "Only you would be able to bear his anger without retribution. It is the only way. When the Christians retaliate for the attack, after Baybars refuses their demands, the sultan will be forced to move against them. I and other governors here will make certain of that. Whilst the Franks cause us no trouble, the sultan can forget them, but when that balance shifts, he and others of his government will no longer be able to use the excuse that the Franks pose no threat to placate the rest of us. Surely you must see this is the best way?" Mahmud's tone was incisive. "Khadir told me you understood the need to remove the infidel from our lands."

Baraka stared at the two men, two sets of eyes, one white, one dark, boring into him. He felt himself grow small beneath their adult gaze, felt his newfound power slipping. We knew you didn't have the courage to do this, their faces said. You are just a child after all. "I do understand," he told them in a rush, desperate to cling to that vanishing authority, frantic for their favor. "I'll do it."

Mahmud studied him, then nodded, satisfied. He turned to Khadir. "I will prepare the order to attack."

As Mahmud left through the archway, Khadir smiled at Baraka. "You have made an ally today. A powerful ally. But you must faithfully keep your silence, until the time is right."

"When will I know the time is right?"

"When we are at war with the Christians," answered Khadir with a chuckle. He grew solemn. "I will guide you. For now, we shall wait and see what fruits *all* our little trees bear for us." He smiled as Baraka frowned in incomprehension, and put a finger to his lips. "All in good, good time."

Aisha flitted like a shadow through the corridors, bowing her head until her chin almost touched her drab robe as she passed Mamluk guards in their bright cloaks, officials, governors and slaves. She clutched a wooden pail, surreptitiously placing her palm over it whenever the bundle of cloth inside began to squirm. Some of the guards' eyes followed her, but no one called out, demanding to know what she was doing, and she made it to the quieter areas of the citadel unhindered.

Here, the solitude was a balm after the constant noise of the harem. Heading through passages cut through the outer walls, intersected by towers, Aisha came to a small recess, a guard post or a disused food store she had thought when she first found it. Crouching in the cool gloom, she set the pail down and gently unfolded the bundle. A tiny, wrinkled brown face looked up at her accusingly as the cloth fell away. "I'm sorry," she whispered, letting the monkey climb her arm to her shoulder, where it perched and shrieked softly until she gave it a fig.

Sitting with her back to the wall, Aisha felt herself relax as she watched the monkey eat. She still hadn't given him a name. It had bothered her for a time, as if it might mean that he didn't belong with her or that she didn't really know him. But now she liked his namelessness. It gave him autonomy. He was his own free self and didn't need a mark of ownership. The monkey made a warbling noise and she stroked his head. The earthquake had made him anxious. To her mother-in-law Nizam's deep disgust, Aisha had kept him in her bed last night.

"You share a bed with my son," Nizam had snapped, when she had seen the monkey crawling out from under the covers that morning, "not *vermin!*"

When she had first moved into the royal harem shortly after her marriage to Baraka, leaving her mother and the quiet harem that belonged to her father, Aisha had been grateful to Nizam. Baraka's mother, an imperiously statuesque woman with sleek black hair and fierce eyes, ruled the harem and had taken Aisha into her care in the palace, where more than one hundred women lived together, some wives and concubines, most of them slaves. It was a place of rumors and vicious intrigue, where cliques and factions reigned and where, Aisha discovered through the gossiping of the younger girls, murders were not uncommon. The sultan's four wives had personal food tasters to guard against poison. Baybars was not a particularly amorous sultan and many of the girls, gifts from various princes and governors who wanted to impress or please their ruler, had never even seen his bed. Competition for his affections between the wives and those women who wanted to elevate their status, perhaps becoming a favorite lover, even a wife when one of the four died, was brutal.

At first, Aisha, in a high position as wife of the future sultan, who was too young to have his own harem, elicited suspicious resentment from the younger women. She wore the most beautiful gowns made by the slaves, as instructed by Nizam. She was given two black eunuchs who were responsible for her daily needs: escorting her to the communal baths, fetching food and drinks and sweets whenever she desired. She was bathed and massaged daily by female slaves, as ordered by Nizam; her body hair, which had only recently started to appear and had caused her enormous embarrassment, was removed, painfully, with tweezers, and her skin was pumiced until it glowed. The attention made her feel awkward initially. She giggled uncontrollably during massages and protested vocally through the long plucking sessions. But eventually it had just grown tedious, and now it was simply excruciating.

Nizam had taken to overseeing her grooming, telling the slaves to use more soap, which stung her eyes, and to brush her hair until her scalp was raw. Since her wedding day, Aisha had been in Baraka's bed only once, and she was well aware Nizam thought it her fault her *sweet* little son hadn't summoned her again. The only blessing was that since she was no longer Nizam's favorite, a few of the other girls had warmed to her. Only these blossoming friendships, her monkey and some of the lessons, namely poetry and dancing—she hated embroidery—kept her from despair. That and the private walks she took when Nizam was busy, managing to escape through a loose grille in one of the bathhouses.

Sometimes, she thought she might venture farther: leave the citadel, go down into the city. But she would be in such trouble if she were caught, and would bring such disgrace down upon her father, that she hadn't dared to. She was also terrified of the chief eunuch, a colossal Nubian with ebony skin responsible for punishing the girls, by the whip or by execution, depending on the severity of the crime. Most of the male slaves were slow and stupid, castration causing their voices to be as high as a girl's, their chins to be beardless and their bodies to grow flabby and lethargic. Aisha found them utterly intriguing and viscerally repulsive. They were not men, or women. In some ways they weren't even people, just things that had been made, out of butter or soap, or something else soft and malleable that did what it was told. The chief eunuch was another matter. Perhaps his position gave him greater occasion to exercise his mind, or maybe his castration had been different—Aisha didn't know. But he was quick and dangerous as a snake, and woebetide any girl who angered or insulted him.

Aisha rested her head against the wall, relishing the sense of freedom the silence gave her. At first she had been grateful when Baraka hadn't called her back to his chambers, but recently she had found herself wondering why he hadn't summoned her. Admittedly, the wedding night had been an ordeal that she didn't think either of them would want to repeat, but she didn't think that was her fault.

She had gone to him dressed in a gown of the barest silk, her face painted, jewels and gold clustering at her neck and wrists, leaving a trail of perfume behind her. She had been told what to do by Nizam and the women, and although her heart was thumping and her hands were clumsy and trembling, she tried. Baraka sat there for what seemed an age after she entered, not saying a word, pale-faced and sullen. They perched, side by side, on the foot of the bed, which was strewn with petals, in a silence so unbearable that Aisha finally turned to kiss him in desperation. Their teeth banged together as they opened their mouths, and she fought off an urge to giggle. The feel of his tongue in her mouth was strange, like a wet, wiggling fish, slimy and unpleasant. There was a brief moment of inept fumbling on his part, until, frustrated by his awkwardness, she lay back on the bed and pulled him onto her. He had lain torpidly on top of her for several long minutes, before finally rolling off and striding from the room, slamming the door behind him.

Aisha sighed and opened her eyes, wondering if she should send Baraka a message. They could just talk. Nizam wouldn't know that they were just talking; she would be pleased, would stop crowding her. Maybe Baraka wanted a friend more than he wanted a wife? If it meant she could regularly escape the harem without fear of being caught, she could force herself to like him. She stiffened, hearing footsteps coming out of the gloom toward her. Holding the monkey's leash tight in her fingers, she slid into the shadows, pulling her knees to her chest. The footsteps grew louder. Aisha froze, willing herself to become one with the darkness, as a tall figure swept past. He wore the uniform of a commander. She recognized him from her wedding day. Aisha loosened her hold on the monkey's leash as the footsteps faded. She was about to move, when she heard another noise, this one, a soft *pad, pad*. She'd barely had time to register it before another man passed by. This one she knew by name, and reputation. Her breath caught in her throat as Khadir sloped past the recess, eyes glinting in the blue-gray light slanting through an arrow slit farther down.

Aisha waited a few moments, then rose to her feet and grabbed the pail. The passage had always been deserted, and she didn't know why the two men had come through it, but she obviously couldn't risk staying any longer. She was about to slip out, when she heard yet more footfalls, these ones heavy, stamping. Aisha recoiled against the wall of the recess, but, in doing so, she trapped the monkey's tail. He let out a high-pitched cry. The footfalls stopped. Aisha stood stock-still, holding the leash as firmly as she could as the monkey scrabbled angrily at her shoulder. The footsteps came closer, slowly now. She wanted to run, but was too scared to move. The owner of the footsteps appeared. Aisha, who half-expected the chief eunuch, Baybars or Nizam to emerge, let out a small gasp of relief as she saw Baraka. The prince, for his part, looked more terrified than she did, his dark eyes widening under his thick fringe of curly hair. For a few seconds, they stared at each other.

Then, Aisha managed to summon a smile. "Hello."

Baraka's eyes narrowed in suspicion. "What are you doing here?"

"I went for a walk. Your mother knows I'm here," she added, then cursed herself for being so stupid; he only had to ask Nizam to find out it wasn't true. He appeared even more suspicious now. She started to feel annoyance bubbling up inside her just looking at his brooding face. "What are *you* doing here?" she retorted.

"None of your business."

Aisha heard a note of fear in his voice. "Were you with Khadir?" she asked, intrigued as to what had worried him.

"Why? What did you hear?" he demanded, coming toward her.

"What . . . ?"

Baraka grabbed hold of Aisha's arm. "What did you hear?"

"Let go of me!" Aisha struggled to free herself from his painful grip. The monkey screeched and darted from her shoulder, the leash slipping through her fingers into air. "I didn't hear anything!" she shouted at Baraka, as the monkey raced out of the recess and away down the corridor. "Let me *go!*"

Baraka held her a few seconds longer, his fingers pinching cruelly into her skin. Then he released her and turned away.

Aisha glared after him, rubbing her arm, which would be bruised tomorrow. "Foolish boy," she said beneath her breath.

Baraka whipped around and slapped her across the face, putting all his strength behind it.

Aisha stumbled into the wall with the shocking force of it and stayed there, unable to do anything but clutch her cheek and stare, unable even to stop the tears welling and falling. The small smile that curled up the corners of Baraka's mouth as he saw them hurt her even more than the slap, hurt her deep down inside like a knife turning. Baraka walked out of the recess, leaving her alone.

Kalawun headed through the palace corridors, sifting through the papers he held. He greeted a man he passed by. "Amir Kamal, have you seen the sultan this afternoon?"

"He is visiting the al-Azhar mosque," replied the governor. "He was worried that yesterday's earthquake had damaged it."

"Then I will find him on his return. Thank you." Kalawun paused in the passage as the amir moved off, looking at the papers. The scouts in Cilicia had sent a fresh report that he was impatient to discuss with Baybars. The reports from the borders were good. It was timely news. The balance of power within the court was still unstable following the fraught war council. The sooner the Anatolian campaign was under way, the sooner the more rebellious governors would be compelled to fall in line. But if Baybars was at the mosque, he might be gone for some time.

Just recently, Baybars seemed to have become obsessed with the repairs. Kalawun thought he understood why. Rebuilding the mosque was simple. Up it went, brick by brick, until it became a complete structure. Building territory wasn't so tangible. It was all points on a map, boundaries that moved and changed. The mosque just became. It was something Baybars could look at every morning and know he had helped create. His frequent visits had, however, attracted unwelcome attention. Only last week, he was attacked by a Shia Muslim: the opponents of the Sunni majority. The man flung stones at him, shouting the name of Ali, before running off into the crowds. Baybars wasn't hurt and the Shia was caught shortly afterward and crucified. But the assault had unsettled the sultan. He had tried to conceal it, but Kalawun had known him for too long not to see it. It was one of many attacks on his person and position over the past months, and it was unlikely to be the last.

Kalawun was about to move off toward the officials' quarters, when a gray shape came flying down the corridor. He gave a grunt of surprise as Aisha barreled into his arms. She was shaking, her whole body wracked with sobs. His surprise turned instantly to concern. Gripping her shoulders, he pushed her away from him so that he could look at her. Her eyes were red and swollen. Strands of hair had twisted free of her *hijab* and clung to her face, sticky with tears. Kalawun frowned and pushed them aside, seeing a scarlet mark on her cheek.

"What is this?" he asked her. "Aisha? Talk to me. What has happened?" The firmness of his tone seemed to settle her.

"I've lost him, F-father," she stammered.

"Lost who?"

"My monkey. He ran away."

"Does Nizam know that you are out of the harem?"

Aisha couldn't meet his gaze.

Kalawun sighed sharply. "You must not leave it without her permission, Aisha. How many times must I tell you?" He escorted her through a door that led into a deserted chamber. Kalawun turned to face her, but his expression softened as he saw another tear slide down her cheek. He touched the red mark imprinted there. "What happened?"

"Baraka," she said fiercely. "He *hit* me!"

"He did what?" said Kalawun, feeling something shoot through him, a cold, iron something that made his whole body rigid.

"He was in one of the passages at the northern enclosure's walls. The ones near the broken tower."

"You were together?"

Aisha shook her head. "He was there with Khadir, I think. There was a commander there too. I thought it was deserted." She looked up at him miserably. "I only went there to play."

Kalawun didn't answer. He trolled quickly through the reasons Khadir and Baraka might be together. As far as he was aware, they rarely spoke. Khadir's threats and insinuations from the other week came back to him, and he worried. "This commander? Do you know who it was?"

"He was wearing a yellow cloak. I saw him talking with you at the wedding, before I came to speak with you."

"Mahmud," said Kalawun at once, his frown deepening. "Come. I'll escort you back to the harem, where you will apologize to Nizam." Kalawun spoke on before Aisha could protest. "And then I am going to have some of my men find Fakir for you."

Her eyes registered watery gratitude. "Thank you, Father," she said, not bothering to remind him that Fakir wasn't the monkey's name anymore.

But there was no need for any search party, for when Aisha and Kalawun arrived at the harem palace they found the monkey sitting on Aisha's bed, much to Nizam's annoyance.

Leaving his daughter, Kalawun headed back toward the main buildings, his mind clouded with the image of that handprint on Aisha's cheek. Forcing himself to focus, he raked over the reasons Baraka, Khadir and Mahmud might have for being in a deserted part of the palace, together or alone. He found no answers and didn't like the uneasy feeling it gave him.

"Amir Kalawun."

Kalawun saw Baybars crossing the courtyard, followed by two Bahri. For a moment, he wondered about mentioning it to the sultan, but a little voice stopped him. There was really nothing to talk to him about yet. "My Lord Sultan, I was looking for you. I've received reports from Cilicia that we should go over."

Baybars nodded. "We can do that now." He slipped off his kid riding gloves. "There is one thing first, Kalawun. I meant to speak of it to you yesterday, but the earthquake distracted me. I was talking with Khadir and he suggested that I send someone to interrogate the Assassins, now that they are under my control, in order to discover who it was that contracted them to kill me."

"My lord," said Kalawun, furious that Khadir had gone over his head with this, "is this wise? Surely we have more than enough to concentrate on, without wasting men or resources on what could prove to be a fruitless search?"

"Khadir thought Nasir would be good for this task," said Baybars, and Kalawun heard the finality of his decision in his tone. "I take it you can spare him?"

"My lord," said Kalawun in a low voice, nodding.

Baybars studied him for a moment. "I wouldn't ask you to do this if I did not believe it necessary." He faltered and looked away. "Omar's death was always too raw for me to want to look. I served vengeance by assuming control of the Assassins and taking their territory. I thought that would be enough." His gaze flicked back to Kalawun, his blue eyes as flat and uncompromising as the desert sky. "But Khadir's words awakened in me a desire that I have harbored for some time. I want to know who is responsible, Kalawun. I want to know who killed Omar. Tell Nasir to find me their names." He smiled coolly. "Now, let us discuss these reports."

Kalawun walked in silence at Baybars's side, his thoughts racing, sharpened by anger. Khadir was more of a viper than he had thought. He had never trusted the soothsayer. But the old man was becoming more and more meddlesome. And what, Kalawun wondered, was his interest in Baraka?

Later that evening, Kalawun left the citadel and returned to al-Rawda, the island in the Nile where he lived with his family and regiment. During the meeting with Baybars, his mind had been too preoccupied with details of the campaign to think of anything else. But on the journey to the island, his thoughts had once again become plagued with images of his daughter's bruised cheek and Khadir's sly smile.

He crossed the bridge over the river, the water flowing slow and black beneath him. Reaching the banks, he spurred the beast along the tree-lined path that sloped up to the palace. The huge structure rose dark against the purple sky, the towers, where the men of the Mansuriyya were barracked, rising like two horns from the head of stone. The guards at the gates stood straighter as they saw him approach. In the courtyard, Kalawun slipped down from the saddle. An attendant was there immediately to lead the beast to the stables.

Kalawun could hear the chime of iron before he reached the inner courtyard, the sound carrying through the vaulted passageway toward him. Out in the yard, two youths were fighting. Around them other boys, ranged between nine and sixteen, had formed a circle. All of them wore leather jerkins over short woolen tunics, with *tahfifas*: neat, round turbans, covering their heads. Their faces were a mix of colors, but most were ruddy-skinned Turks. In their midst stood the tall, slender form of Nasir. He was wearing the blue silk cloak of the Mansuriyya, the bands of material on his upper arms displaying his name and rank. The younger boys around him were the newest slaves he had bought for the regiment, although even they were already two years into their training. Following the destruction of so many Christian strongholds, the Mamluks had found themselves with a surplus of slaves, and the subsequent peace had continued to keep these soldiers alive. The younger they were when taken, the better. Boys were easier to train than a broken man wrenched from his family after a siege. They were impressionable, quicker at submitting to the strict military regime and to full conversion to Islam, easier to mold into steel.

The courtyard was chilly in the shadow of the walls that surrounded it, the windows and entranceways like a hundred dark eyes looking down on the boys as the two at their center battled. There was a harsh *crack* as one of the youths hacked into the other's polished wooden shield, which was large and round, the shield of the infantry.

"Halt." The two youths fell apart, panting, as Nasir stepped forward. "That was a good block, Shiban," he said to the youth, whose shield had a new score across the center. Nasir glanced around as Kalawun approached. He bowed to the commander and barked an order at the youths, who all did the same, heads dipping in unison. Nasir pointed at two. "Begin your stretches." He went to Kalawun, who had stopped a short distance away. "Amir."

Kalawun made himself smile at the officer. "Their training is going well? They seem stronger."

Nasir looked at the boys. "The younger ones are coming on." He lowered his voice. "But some of the older boys are restless. One here is almost seventeen. I think it might be good to place him in the regiment. I feel he is ready."

Kalawun nodded. "Certainly. I will arrange it." He paused, the silence broken by the sound of the youths limbering up for the fight. "There is something I need you to do, Nasir." He explained what Baybars had commanded.

Nasir remained silent for some moments after Kalawun had finished. "Can I ask why I have been chosen for this task, Amir?" He shook his head, frowning. "Why not one of the Bahri?"

"Baybars requested you specifically. You know the area where the Assassins live."

Nasir looked away. There was a hardness in his gaze that Kalawun hadn't seen for a long time. "What about them, Amir?" Nasir asked, gesturing at the boys. "I bought and trained them. They are accustomed to me and to my methods."

"Another officer will continue your work whilst you are gone." Kalawun was quiet for a moment. "I am sorry, Nasir. If I could, I would send someone else. I know it will be difficult for you to return to that place."

Nasir's gaze swung back to Kalawun. "That is in the past, Amir." He gave a small smile, but the flint in his eyes remained. "I will do my duty."

Kalawun put a hand on the officer's shoulder. "I know you will, my friend."

10

The Genoese Quarter, Acre

12 MARCH A.D. 1276

The sun was starting to dip in the west as Will steered his horse through the busy streets of the Genoese quarter. Above several palazzos, warehouses and shops the flags of San Marco, the patron saint of Venice, still fluttered. The Genoese might be trickling back into their vanquished quarter, but Venice, it appeared, would be slow to relinquish her hold. Beside Will rode Robert and bringing up the rear were four more Templars. It was Will's first assignment in charge of other knights, and he'd felt a little self-conscious summoning them to follow him into the city.

"I suppose you'll expect me to call you sir," Robert had complained, grinning as Will muttered something in reply. "Maybe you'll get another promotion if this Sclavo turns out to be the one who ordered the attack? You'll be grand master by next year if you keep this up."

The others, seasoned knights whom Will had trained with for several years, accepted his authority without question, and by the time they entered the old quarter he was feeling surer.

"How are we going to find the tavern? This place is a warren."

Will glanced at Robert. "The boy said it was behind the soap maker's."

"The Saracen," said Robert thoughtfully. "Is it supposed to be a joke?"

Will didn't answer. He was frowning at the streets ahead, trying to get his bearings. He had rarely passed through this quarter, and the winding alleys were confusing. Fixing on the spire of the Church of San Lorenzo, which thrust loftily above the disorder of rooftops, he pointed at a narrow street leading off the main thoroughfare between a tangle of shops. "I think this will take us to the church. We should be able to find the market square from there. The soap maker's is just beyond that."

The way became tighter the farther in they went. For much of the route, Will had heard the Venetian dialect being spoken by the crowds, but as they moved past a large factory that had once been the prosperous Genoese soap maker's, since abandoned, the accents began to change. In the old part of the quarter, a rundown and derelict district, the Genoese who hadn't been able to afford to leave with their kinsmen in the exodus to Tyre remained. Here, children went about barefoot and half-naked. Alleys, coated with night slops thrown from windows, teemed with rats and overflowed with piles of stinking rubbish, alive with flies. Mistrustful faces looked out from doorways as the knights passed, whole families living together in rooms meant for two. It was a desperate place, and Will was glad when, after a few wrong turns, they finally came upon the tavern.

The Saracen formed the dead end of a wider road near the walls, a broad stone building straddling the street that looked more like a warehouse than an inn. There was no sign on or above the door, and it was only by asking a passerby that they found it at all.

Will led the knights back to an alley farther up the street. "We shouldn't make ourselves too obvious," he said, handing the reins of his mount to one of the men. "Wait for me here." He pulled the black cloak he had worn to Elwen's from his saddlebag and drew it over his mantle. The cloak was long and covered his uniform and falchion, but even so he still looked conspicuously out of place in comparison to the shabby, underfed citizens.

"You're going alone?" murmured Robert, catching his arm.

Will hung back. "Let me scout first. I'll probably have more luck finding Sclavo myself than if we all go in swords drawn. I'll come back if I find him and we'll go in together to make the arrest." He set off down the street, leaving the knights to crowd into the alley with their horses. Dusk had fallen, shrouding the city in a pallid half-light. He had almost reached the tavern when he heard a loud cheer rise from somewhere behind the building. Will glanced up, but the blank facade of stone stared back impassively, offering no clue as to what the noise might mean.

The door had warped in its frame and he had to force it with his shoulder. It opened halfway then stuck on the floor. A curtain of warm, moldy air blew against him as he entered. The interior was hot and dark, clouded with smoke from a dying fire. Something large brushed against Will's leg and he saw a shaggy hound lope off toward the back of the room. The chamber was long and low, with crooked beams protruding from the ceiling like ribs. Benches and boards were arranged in two lines down the center, and as he walked the aisle between them, Will could see figures slumped around the murky glow of oil lanterns. The floor was sticky underfoot and the smell of old ale filled his nostrils. Through a set of doors at the back of the chamber came a muffled din. As Will reached the doors, they opened, throwing light and noise across him. Two men reeled past, clutching tankards, and stepping forward, Will found himself on the edge of a wall of men.

The tavern backed onto a wide courtyard, surrounded by dilapidated buildings, a cavernous barn and the wall that separated the Genoese quarter from the grand enclosure of the Knights of St. John. Torches had been lit around the quadrant, spilling brightness across stacked barrels and crates and the faces of the crowd who formed a ring, leaving a wide space at their center. A few men glanced at Will as he closed the tavern doors and slipped in alongside them, holding his cloak shut, but most of the mob's attention was on the empty space before them, which after a moment, Will saw wasn't empty at all.

In the center were two men. Both, by their appearance, were Arabs, although neither wore the robes or turbans donned by most of their people, but rather the short, coarse tunics and hose of any Western peasant, their heads bare, hair unkempt. One was taller and stockier than the other, his face grim in the torchlight, which pushed back the deepening blue of evening. He held a battered-looking saber in his left hand, while his right hung limp at his side. As the man paced the ring, Will saw a horrific scar running from his elbow down his forearm to his hand. The flesh was knotted pink and white where it had healed, the arm deformed and useless. His wary pacing was measured, however, and he gripped the weapon comfortably in his left hand. The smaller man was far less composed, the sword in his hand held rigidly in front of him, his body locked, awkward with tension. As the scarred man advanced, he backed away, sweat glistening wetly on his face in the flame light. Will, who had heard of men fighting for sport, was wondering why the terrified-looking Arab was in the ring at all, when suddenly, the man darted toward the wall of onlookers. They fell back in a wave, but two powerfully built men wielding clubs and swords stepped out to face the Arab and, with weapons raised, forced him back into the ring to a chorus of jeers from the restless crowd. Immediately it became clear to Will what he was witnessing and the name of the tavern made horrible sense.

The small man shouted something in Arabic, a prayer Will thought, then flung himself at his waiting opponent, the sword thrust before him like a lance. Will, appalled, saw what was coming. The stocky Arab sidestepped the clumsy charge, bringing his saber around in a mighty arc. The blade sailed into the back of the man's head with a sickening *crunch*. The blade was yanked free, and there was a halfhearted cheer from the spectators as the small Arab folded.

Revolted by the display, Will watched as three armed men, Italians by the looks of them, walked out, one gesturing for the scarred Arab to put down his weapon. He did as he was told with the all resigned compliance of a slave, and they escorted him toward the barn as two other men dragged the dead man away, leaving a wide smear of blood in the dust. Around the yard, money changed hands. Will took the opportunity to move farther in, squeezing through the press. There were four more armed men by the barn where the Arab had been taken. Will saw, in what would have once been stalls for horses—now covered with heavy wooden gates—a straggling bunch of what could only be described as prisoners. There were Arabs, a few Mongols and others, Circassians perhaps. The guards opened one of the gates and dragged out a thin youth who must have been no more than sixteen. Will had seen enough.

He turned to a man beside him, who had a tankard in one hand and a money pouch in the other. By the cut of his clothes Will guessed he was a merchant, but not a particularly affluent one. "Do you know Sclavo?" he asked in Latin.

The man focused on Will with difficulty, then shoved his tankard in the direction of the barn. "There," he slurred.

Following the merchant's unsteady gesture, Will picked out a group of men seated on benches away from the press of the crowd. One, at their center, was better dressed than the others in a floppy green silk cloak that ill-fitted his scrawny frame. He had pale wispy hair and a patchy beard, and his face was lumpy with the scabs of some disease. At his feet were two huge hounds. As one of the armed men crossed to him, leaned in close and said something, the dogs raised their huge heads and snarled uneasily.

Will questioned the drunk man. "The one in green?"

The merchant nodded and staggered against him. "That's him."

Will pushed his way back through the crowd as the thin youth was led into the yard, compelled by the swords of Sclavo's men.

"They're doing what?" said Robert, when Will returned to the alley and told the knights what he had seen. His nose creased in disgust. "Animals."

One of the other knights, a stoic, middle-aged man called Paul, gave a shrug. "This isn't our business." He looked at Will. "If you want my opinion, Commander, I think we should concentrate on what we came for."

"I agree," responded Will. He went on as Robert started to protest. "There's over one hundred men in there and at least nine armed guards. We would need a stronger force to deal with what's happening here tonight. And, however much I want to intervene, it isn't our place. When we've got Sclavo, we'll report it to the Genoese consul. He must be the one to close it down."

"If he'll do anything," said another of the knights, called Laurent. "If Sclavo's bought them, then they're his slaves to do with as he will. There's nothing anyone can do about that."

"There is if the Temple puts pressure on the consul," said Will firmly. He looked at Robert. "And I'll make sure we do. If Baybars found out about this outrage, he would demand retribution. The peace is weak enough without dogs like Sclavo tearing at it."

Robert conceded after a pause. "How should we proceed?"

"From what I could see, other than through the tavern itself, the only obvious exit from the yard is down an alley that leads between a barn on the left-hand side and the wall. Robert, you and Laurent will cover that alley in case Sclavo tries to run." Will described the landlord.

"Green cloak, lumpy face," said Robert, nodding. "I'm sure we'll recognize him."

"I'll lead the others through the tavern."

"Are we going in disguise?"

Will pulled off his black cloak and stuffed it into his saddlebag. "No. I want them to see us for who we are."

Robert grinned wolfishly. "That should put the fear of God in them."

"Exactly. Most of them will be lower-class merchants and laborers. I doubt they'll give us any trouble."

"And the guards?" asked Paul.

"They look like thugs, not warriors, and their weapons are pretty basic. It's death to any who wounds a Templar. They know that as well as we do. I think we can handle them."

With that settled, Will let Robert and Laurent go first to reach the alley, before leading the other three knights to the tavern. He worried about leaving their mounts untended, but he needed the men with him. All that mattered was that they got Sclavo.

He shoved at the Saracen's door and entered the thick gloom of the chamber, hearing the sounds of cheering again. "He has dogs," he murmured to the knights.

Paul nodded and reached for his sword.

The scattered occupants of the room were either too drunk or too shocked to react as the four Templars strode through their midst and thrust open the doors to the courtyard.

For a few seconds, the men in the yard, their attention fixed on the fight in the center, didn't notice what was happening. Then, as Will and the knights began to push through, they started to realize that all was not right. The knights' coming caused a ripple effect through the crowd. The ones closest to the doors saw them first. Gazes that had been locked eagerly on the combat ground swiveled around in surprise. Men who were snarling cheers and shouts grew silent, fearful, as Will and the knights drew their swords and advanced. Those near the front of the ring shouted as they were pushed further into the yard, where the thin youth Will had seen being dragged out earlier was locked in a vicious, desperate fight with a Mongol boy. A shout went up: *Templars!* Men jostled and shoved one another to get out of the way, some already heading for the doors, streaming around the knights. The fight in the center was continuing, but the armed guards were now coming over to see what the commotion was.

"Hey!" barked one, shoving his way through. "What's happening here?" The guard paused in his stride as he saw Will move out of the fretful crowd, followed by Paul and the others. Then he steeled himself and came forward to meet them. "What do you want?" His words ended in a yelp as Paul elbowed him savagely in the face. The other guards hung back, seeing their comrade reel away, blood gushing from his broken nose.

But the disturbance had reached Sclavo's attention, and he was crossing the yard with more guards and his two hounds that strained at their leashes and growled thunder. The fight had stopped, the youths falling back from each other, looking around in fearful confusion.

"What is the meaning of this?" demanded Sclavo. His voice was gritty and coarse, like sand scratched over paper. He eyed the knights warily, but stood his ground. Five of his guards moved in around him, forming a protective ring. "This is a private house. The Temple has no jurisdiction here."

"Tonight we do, Sclavo," responded Will coldly. "We're here to arrest you."

More men were melting from the yard, slipping down the alley by the barn.

Will's eyes moved to the guards surrounding the scrawny landlord. "You should stand down. Unless you plan on fighting us?" There was a natural power in his voice, but the words resonated all the more strongly coming, as they did, from a man dressed in that white mantle. Two of the guards lowered their weapons and began to back away.

Sclavo turned on them. "Stay where you are, you rats!" he snapped. His gaze flicked to Will. "Arrest me for what? What charge do you lay on me?" His dogs were hauling desperately at their leashes and Will wondered how he had the strength to hold them. "This is my property," Sclavo went on. "Everything here belongs to me." He jerked his head toward the youths in the ring. "Them too."

"Your property doesn't concern us," answered Will. "We are here to arrest you for the attempted murder of the grand master of the Temple. That is the charge we lay on you."

Sclavo's eyes widened. Instantly, he released the dogs' leashes and fled. This seemed to signal the last of the crowd that it was time to leave, and a final stampede began. Will whipped his falchion at one of the hounds as it leapt at him. The blade opened a red streak through the dog's flank and it fell writhing to the ground. "Get Sclavo!" he shouted to the other knights as the mob surged. Three of the guards protecting Sclavo had fled with him, but two remained. Paul advanced on one, who, after a moment, dropped his club and ran. Will went for the other, a colossal Italian with a hefty-looking blade, expecting him to do the same, and was brought up sharp when the man came at him.

Will dropped into a fighting stance, but barely had time to gain his footing before the Italian lunged at him. The blow was forceful. The man had been trained well and, despite his size, was quick and light on his feet. Will himself was a fast fighter, but he was wearing chain mail and the extra weight hampered him. The Italian, by comparison, wore only a leather jerkin and woolen hose. The man's brazen courage was disturbing: he had no need to fight. But perhaps it wasn't need that was driving him. Indeed, by the eager look in his eyes, it seemed he wanted this. Will locked his concentration on his opponent, letting everything around him fade away. He was a little out of shape. He had spent so much time trying to track down those behind the attack on the grand master that he'd forsaken some of his routine training. But the sword in his hand soon found its familiar rhythm and he was cutting and thrusting back and forth across the bloodstained yard.

The two youths had gone, vanished with the spectators, and the prisoners left in the barn were shaking their cages, yelling in different tongues for the knights to free them. Will skidded in the dust and the man stepped in and slashed at his chest. The chain mail deflected the blow and the blade only succeeded in tearing Will's surcoat. It was a shock nonetheless, and Will, galvanized by the rush of fear that shot through him, stepped up his attack. The man's face changed subtly, the first signs of concern showing through his grimace. Their swords clanged together, flew apart, came in again. Will pushed him back toward a pile of crates to hamper his movements. The Italian tried to force him off, but couldn't. His growing fear was now apparent. Will's sword was whirling in his hands. He was grinning, green eyes shining in the torch flames, heart racing.

"Pax!" shouted the man suddenly. "Pax!" He dodged Will's blade and flung his own to the floor, holding up his hands. *"Pax!"*

Will came to a stop, his blade inches from the man's side. He was breathing heavily, sweat beading his forehead.

"Will!"

Will glanced around to see Robert and Laurent coming across the yard with Paul and the others. Between them, they were dragging a bloody-faced Sclavo. Robert's own face was bruised and he was looking murderous. He went to call something, then his expression changed to one of alarm.

At the same moment, Will sensed movement behind him. He whipped around as the Italian grabbed the fallen sword and jabbed it at him. He got his falchion in the way, barely, and the blades screeched together. Pushing the sword aside and down with a chopping cut that left the man's defenses open, Will brought the falchion back in a fierce arc that struck the man in his exposed shoulder. The blade sheared through flesh, to bone. The Italian howled, his weapon falling from his useless hand, nerves severed. Will kicked the sword away and staggered back as his comrades came running.

"My God," said Robert, eyeing the screaming man. "I distracted you."

"I'm fine," panted Will, looking at Sclavo, who was staring agape at his shrieking guard. "I'm just glad you got him."

"He put up a fight though," responded Robert grimly. He poked his tongue gingerly into his bruised, puffy cheek. "I think the bastard knocked a tooth loose."

Sclavo's eyes went to Will. "You've got the wrong man," he hissed.

"That can be decided back at the Temple." Will nodded to Paul. "Open those cages. Tell the prisoners they are free to go. Robert, Laurent and I will escort Sclavo to the Temple. I want the rest of you to go to the Genoese consul and tell him what has happened here. I'll speak to the grand master myself, see if we can't have this place closed down by morning."

"That shouldn't be too hard," said Robert, looking at Sclavo.

"I hired the man who attacked your grand master for someone else," growled Sclavo. "If you give me clemency I'll tell you who."

"Let's take him back," said Will to Robert.

"It's my only offer," shouted Sclavo. There was fear in his face, but his tone was obstinate. "I'll tell you here and now who wanted him dead if you spare my life."

Will hesitated. It wasn't his decision to make; that would rest with the grand master or the seneschal. But it was his task to find out who wanted the grand master killed, and if it wasn't Sclavo, then his job here wasn't done. "Who was it?" he said finally.

"Swear you'll spare me," demanded Sclavo.

"I swear," said Will. "Tell me."

"A Genoese merchant," replied Sclavo instantly, "called Guido Soranzo."

THE TEMPLE, ACRE, 12 MARCH A.D. 1276

Angelo pushed down his animosity with effort as the door to the solar opened to reveal the imperious figure of Guillaume de Beaujeu. As the eldest son, favored by his father, Angelo had rarely been in a position of subservience to anyone, and it didn't come easily to him, especially when angry. Nonetheless, he made himself bow to the grand master.

"Thank you, Zaccaria," said Guillaume, ignoring Angelo and nodding to the Sicilian.

Zaccaria inclined his head, then moved away and stood to attention a little way down the passage.

Leaving the door open, Guillaume headed back into the chamber.

Gritting his teeth, Angelo entered. "My lord," he said, pushing the door to. "I am somewhat surprised by your summons, given our strict agreement that I would be the one to contact you, and only when absolutely necessary." He followed Guillaume into the solar, which was stiflingly warm, illuminated by the blaze of a fire in the hearth and the hazy shimmer of candles. "I was planning on coming to you later this week. I have the message from Cairo that your knights are to deliver." His voice hardened, losing some of its taut courtesy. "But your man gave me no chance to collect it, insisting, on your orders, that I come straight here. I will have to return with the scroll later, and every time we meet poses a risk to our secrecy. My lord?" he demanded, his black eyes fixed belligerently on the grand master, who was pouring a goblet of wine. "Are you not concerned by this?"

"Why would Guido Soranzo want me dead?" questioned Guillaume calmly, turning to Angelo, goblet in hand.

Angelo stared at the grand master. "Where did you hear this?"

"Here, an hour ago, from the man Guido hired to find someone willing to murder me." Guillaume took a sip of wine. "One of my knights arrested this man earlier this evening. I have since questioned him myself and it is clear he is telling the truth." The grand master's eyes bored into Angelo. "I take it you know nothing of this?"

For the first time, Angelo felt a twinge of concern. "No, my lord," he said quickly. "I have no idea why Soranzo would do this." He shook his head, thinking furiously. "He made it plain that he wasn't happy working with us when my father first revealed our intentions to him, but since then he has been aiding us willingly. His business stands to gain as much as any of ours from this strategy." Angelo spread a hand to Guillaume. "I do not see why he would remove our best chance of achieving it."

"His business?" Guillaume's reserve fell away at these words. "I am not doing this to help any of your *businesses*, Vitturi. Remember that." He drained his wine and swung away from the Venetian.

"Of course, my lord, of course," said Angelo with mock gravity, claiming back some of his authority as the grand master's poise slipped. "I was just trying to divine his possible motives." He watched Guillaume pace the chamber. "The most important thing now is to discover what damage has been done. We need to know if Soranzo has betrayed us all. If he has exposed our plan."

"What do you suggest?"

"I will go to his house immediately and speak with him."

Guillaume stopped pacing. He looked at Angelo derisively, his composure returning. "You expect him just to offer up this information to you? No, I do not think so. And he will have personal guards, will he not? If he is the one responsible for my attack, he will know that his death will be required as punishment. I doubt you would have much opportunity to question him with a sword in the gullet."

Angelo drew himself up. "Then let me lead a company of your knights and I will arrest him by force."

"A merchant lead a company of Templars?" Guillaume went to the door. "I will send them myself."

"I know Guido, my lord," called Angelo at his back. "He won't speak to your knights. We are not the same as you. We deal in money, commodities, not swords and battle lines. I understand him. I can make him talk." Guillaume halted at the door. "It is not just you who has been affected by his betrayal," continued Angelo. "Indeed, if we have been exposed, out of all of us, you stand to lose the least. We came to you with this plan, my father and I. Let me deal with Soranzo in my own way."

"No Templar would ever be led by you," said Guillaume, turning back to him.

"They would if you ordered it," countered Angelo. "Tell them I'm a former associate of Soranzo's, brought in by you to interrogate him. Put one of your men in charge, by all means, but let me question Soranzo. You know I'm right," he added. As Guillaume's eyes flashed with anger, Angelo thought he had gone too far. He was searching for some way of retracting his words when Guillaume opened the door. "My lord," said Angelo, worriedly.

"Zaccaria."

There came the sound of footsteps.

"Yes, sir?"

"Gather the others." Guillaume paused. "And find Commander Campbell. He will escort Angelo Vitturi to Soranzo's house."

Angelo felt a surge of triumph. A moment later it faded into a simmering rage. For months he had been forced to put up with Guido Soranzo's snide comments and foul temper, and now it seemed that all the while he had been plotting against them. How much damage had been done to their plans for war, and, ultimately, to his plans to salvage the Vitturi business, he did not know. But one thing he was certain of was that Guido would pay for this. And pay dear.

11

The Genoese Quarter, Acre

12 MARCH A.D. 1276

"Secure the gates. Don't let anybody through."

"Yes, sir."

Guido Soranzo watched the guard head down the corridor, sword in hand, but felt no reassurance. He jumped as a hand touched his shoulder. His wife was behind him, her face filled with confusion and worry. She was wearing a richly embroidered cloak over a white silk nightshift that ballooned around her ample middle.

"What is happening, Guido? My maid has just woken me and told me that you want us to leave?"

Guido grasped her firmly, making her gasp. "I need you to rouse the children and pack as many belongings as you can. Take only things we can carry to the harbor." He stared around the wide corridor at the ornate tapestries and life-size statues, torchlight reflected in the marble surfaces. "We'll just have to leave the rest."

"Guido, you're scaring me."

"Do you trust me?" he said urgently.

She nodded tentatively.

"Then do this for me. I will explain everything later, but we need to get to a ship as soon as possible. I want to sail for Genoa tonight."

Dazed, but compliant, his wife allowed him to press her in the direction of their children's bedchambers.

When she had gone, Guido hurried to his study. In the crisp air, he could smell his own sweat. Entering, he went to a chest behind his desk. He paused before he reached it, his eyes drawn by a leather ball on the floor. For a second, he felt annoyance; how many times had he told his son not to play in here? Then reality crashed in and he had to fight back an urge to sob. He had put them all in peril. And for what? More gold? No, he told himself savagely, *not* for gold. He had done it because it had been the right thing to do. The grand master and the others had to be stopped: they were going to destroy everything. But deep down inside him a sad little voice disagreed.

He had been in the church of San Lorenzo for Vespers when he'd heard about the raid on the Saracen. Templars, people were saying, had arrested the landlord and freed Muslim slaves. Unable to glean any clear information from their whisperings, Guido slipped out of the aisles and left the church. His mind spinning, he hastened to the tavern, skidding through the dirty streets, his velvet hose soon caked with mud and excrement. He was followed by a company of ragged Genoese children who started clamoring for money, then chased the panting, sweating man for the fun of it, laughing and whooping. By the time he reached the Saracen, Guido was drenched and gasping. Seeing a Templar coming out of the tavern with several men wearing the colors of the Genoese guard, he decided to go no closer. It hadn't taken him long to find someone willing tell him what had happened: the whole district was buzzing with the news. For a couple of coins, several eager informants were tripping over themselves to tell him how Templars had arrested Sclavo for the attempted murder of their grand master.

On hearing those words, Guido returned home as if the Devil himself was at his heels. But he had approached the palazzo with caution, dreading to see Templars moving inside the grounds. His fear for his own life initially overtook his concern for his family, and for a few moments, he thought of running to the docks. Then, sickened by his own weakness and inspired by guilt, he had been filled with an almost valiant desire to defend them and had stridden determinedly inside, ready to fight all comers.

Now, as he opened the chest to reveal an ornate silver dagger, he realized how violently he was shaking. But surely having a weapon in his hands had to feel better than this cringing helplessness? Through the windows came the sound of hoofbeats, shattering the quiet night. Guido curled a meaty hand around the hilt. He heard shouts from his guards, then an agonized cry. The gates of the palazzo clanged harshly as they were flung open.

THE TEMPLE, ACRE, 12 MARCH A.D. 1276

King Hugh III of Cyprus sat easily in his saddle, head held high, as he steered his white mare down the Street of St. Anne, past the convent of the same name, whose lofty bell tower disappeared in darkness. The area was hushed, with most of the citizens now in their homes for the night. Hugh and his entourage, made up of royal guards and his solemn advisor, Guy, moved in a glowing amber sphere cast by the torches three of the guards held. The flames shone on the outer walls of the Temple that rose up to their right, where creepers trailed green fingers across the stonework and tiny black lizards darted away as the light passed over them. After a few more yards they could see the massive tower that straddled the Temple's gates, the four gold lions that capped its turrets visible as patches of glittery brightness far above. The gates were shut.

Hugh caught his advisor looking at him. "What is it, Guy?"

Guy seemed hesitant to speak, but did so. "Are you certain you wish to do this now, my liege? Would it not be better to wait until morning?"

"If I come in the morning, he will be in chapel or eating or in a chapter meeting, or doing something else that *regretfully* cannot be interrupted." Hugh's tone was caustic. "At this time of night, I defy him to think of any such excuse."

Guy nodded, but didn't looked convinced.

"I will go in alone."

"My liege . . ."

Hugh raised a gloved hand. "I wish to speak with him in private, one man to another. Perhaps then he will afford me the respect he has so far withheld."

The company reached the gates, and Hugh swung himself easily from the saddle, straightening his gold cloak that snugly fitted his lean frame. One of the guards took the reins of the mare; another jumped down and approached the door cut into the huge wooden gates, crisscrossed with bands of iron. He banged on it with a mailed fist as Hugh slipped off his gloves and passed a hand through his dark, curly hair. His olive-skinned face was taut with anticipation.

A bolt slid back on the other side of the door. Torchlight spilled out and a man appeared, clad in the black tunic of a Templar sergeant. He wore a helmet and had a short sword strapped to his hip. "Yes?"

"My liege lord, Hugh III, king of Cyprus and Jerusalem, demands a meeting with Grand Master de Beaujeu." The guard spoke loud and clear, as if addressing a much larger audience.

The sergeant looked a little surprised. "I'm afraid Grand Master de Beaujeu is seeing no visitors."

"Then he will tell me that himself," said Hugh, stepping forward, so the guard could see him.

"Your Majesty." Looking discomforted, the guard offered Hugh a bow. "I have been given strict instructions not to—"

"I am a king," said Hugh patiently, as if the guard hadn't spoken at all. "King, indeed, of this whole region." He swept a slender, ring-encrusted hand out behind him. "It is my privilege to go where I will, man. Your grand master is well aware that I wish to speak with him. And have for some time." His calm began to slide away. "Thrice, I have invited him to an audience and thrice I have been refused. You will let me in or I swear Master de Beaujeu will know my anger!" He spoke these last words with such vehemence that the sergeant took a step back.

"I will tell him, Your Majesty, but I cannot guarantee a favorable response." The sergeant opened the gate wider. "Bring your men inside. You can wait in the guardhouse if you wish. We have a fire there."

Hugh settled a little at this. "Thank you," he said cordially, stepping through the gate, followed by his men, who led the horses in one by one.

The sergeant spoke quickly to his comrades in the guardhouse, then set off across the yard toward the grand master's palace. The royal company filed awkwardly into the cramped, stuffy chamber at the bottom of the gate tower, eyed by the Templar sergeants. Hugh stood in the doorway brooding, his eyes passing over the expansive courtyard, bordered by impressive buildings. He resented the preceptory's high walls that shut him out; resented that the Templars were untouchable inside them, locked away in their own sacred space. The rest of the city was much the same in its divisions, but at least he always felt he had authority in the other quarters. People listened to him there, treated him like a king. Here, he felt as if he were imposing, as if he should apologize for intruding. And he hated that feeling. Raising his shoulders, he made himself stand erect. He didn't care who the knights thought they were or how favored they were by the pope in Rome. He might not be able to touch them here, but back in Cyprus their holdings weren't fortresses like this. Back in Cyprus they were vulnerable.

He had power over them. And if they pushed him too far, by God he would use it. The thought lent him renewed confidence, and by the time the sergeant returned with the news that the grand master would see him briefly, Hugh felt almost cocksure.

Five minutes later, he entered the grand master's solar. Guillaume turned from the window as the sergeant shut the door. His face was half in shadow, his expression unreadable. The two men faced each other across the room. Hugh was shorter, slender rather than muscular, and at twenty-six he was fourteen years Guillaume's junior, but he maintained his erect pose in the presence of the grand master. There was a long moment of silence as neither man moved, both expecting the other to bow first.

Finally, Hugh, clasped his hands behind his back. "I am glad that you acceded to see me, Master de Beaujeu."

"It seemed I had no choice," answered Guillaume. "It is late, my lord. What is so important that you needed to see me at this hour?"

"It is not yet Compline," retorted Hugh, irritated by Guillaume's aplomb. "And I believed that this must be the best time to see you, being that I have summoned you at other hours of the day and have been told that you are occupied with some business or other." He fixed the grand master with a glare. "I would like to know exactly what business has kept you from addressing me since your arrival in my lands. It is customary for dignitaries to pay homage to their king. Or were you simply unaware of this etiquette?"

Guillaume's eyes narrowed, but his tone, when he spoke, remained flat and low. "I did pay homage to my king. Back in Sicily."

Hugh wanted to explode at this comment, but with Herculean effort he managed to dampen down his fury, Guy's advice from earlier sounding in his mind. *You must try to turn the grand master to your side. I'm afraid it may be your best chance of keeping Charles d'Anjou from your throne.*

"Charles may be your king in Sicily, Master de Beaujeu," said Hugh, pushing the words through clenched teeth. "But in Outremer I am sovereign. The High Court has decreed it. I have the greater claim to the throne. According to the law I, not Maria, hold the right to Jerusalem's crown. It has been settled."

"Not as far as the pope is concerned. Not as far as I am concerned."

"Why do you dispute my right?" demanded Hugh. "Because Charles is your cousin? I thought you above petty nepotism."

"It has nothing to do with blood and everything to do with power," replied Guillaume. "Charles has the power to raise armies and lead a Crusade. He has the power to turn the tide that threatens to drown us. You do not and have shown no willingness to take back our lost territories. Indeed you pandered to

Baybars's demands at Beirut rather than risk any hurt to your position. I have been told you even pay him a tribute now. Twenty thousand dinars a year?" Before Hugh could answer, Guillaume continued. "The pope knows this, which is why he advised Maria to sell her rights to Charles." His tone was forthright rather than malicious. "You should stand down, Hugh, let Charles do for us all what you will not."

"You are mad!" spat Hugh. "Would *you* step down from your position if I asked you to?"

"If it were for the good of Outremer, then yes," said Guillaume easily. His tone intensified. "I would do anything to bring God's land back to us."

Hugh shook his head adamantly. "You think Charles cares what happens here? He got his own brother killed when he advised him to invade Tunis rather than come to Palestine, where he was needed."

"King Louis died of a fever."

"Charles has never got his hands dirty. He is more interested in adding Byzantium to his empire than winning back territory in Outremer. You will be on your own if you rely on him." Hugh touched his hand to his chest. "I will fight with you if you pledge your fealty to me." His voice softened. "Stand with me, Guillaume, and we will take back the Holy Land together. Speak to the pope; help me call off this sale of rights, and let Charles aid us where he will." Hugh held out his jeweled hand for the grand master to kiss. "Come now."

Guillaume regarded the king for a long moment. "Your concern is for your crown," he said finally. "Not the Holy Land."

Hugh's outstretched hand wavered then fell. This time, no subtle words could allay his rage. "How dare you!" he spat. "You are a fool, de Beaujeu. A holy fool! I will keep my throne with or without your help, and when Charles is forced back to Sicily with his tail between his legs, you need not look for aid or friendship from me." He raised his hand again, his finger directed at Guillaume. "We are now enemies, you and I."

Once at the gates, Hugh didn't bother to collect his horse, but strode past his waiting men and headed out of the preceptory before the sergeants could open the door for him.

Guy hastened to follow after ordering the guards to bring their mounts. "My liege!"

Hugh halted abruptly and turned.

Guy was startled by the violence in his eyes. "My liege?" he repeated tentatively.

"I want you to write to King Edward of England."

"I already did, months ago." Guy's voice was wary.

"Then write to him again," snapped Hugh. "Why hasn't he replied, for God's sake?"

"I take it the meeting didn't go well?"

"King Edward is Charles d'Anjou's nephew and a close friend of the pope," said Hugh, ignoring the question. "Maybe we will have more luck with him." He went to turn away, then whipped around, fist clenched. "We have to do something, Guy. I will not lose my throne to that *bastard* and his puppet knights!"

THE GENOESE QUARTER, ACRE, 12 MARCH A.D. 1276

Will grabbed Angelo's arm as the guard sprawled to the ground in front of the gates, clutching his chest. "What the hell are you doing? We're here to arrest Soranzo, not kill his men!"

Angelo pulled his arm from Will's grip as the four Sicilian knights, led by Zaccaria, rounded up the other three guards. "He came at me with a sword," he replied coldly. "What was I supposed to do? . . . Sir Knight?" he added, after a mocking pause.

Will checked the guard's wound. It was only superficial, but he knew it probably felt a great deal worse than it was. "He's going to be fine," he told the guard's comrades. Straightening, he gestured to one of them. "Help him up." The man, who had been disarmed by Zaccaria, came forward warily and pulled the groaning guard to his feet.

Angelo began to walk toward the house that rose up in front of them. Torch-light flickered in the upper windows, and Will saw a shadow move quickly across one of them. "I'll go first."

Angelo hesitated, then gestured to the house with an unfriendly smile. "Be my guest."

As he approached the door, Will heard a baby crying in a room upstairs. He didn't like this. The guards seemed to be expecting them; the palazzo's gates barred, their weapons drawn.

When he had returned to the preceptory with Sclavo, the grand master had been oddly indecisive, wanting to wait rather than send him to arrest Soranzo immediately. After interrogating Sclavo, he dismissed Will, who, before leaving the dungeon, asked de Beaujeu about the reward, neglecting to mention that Luca had been the brother of his attacker. The grand master distractedly told him that the funds would be available by morning. Planning to send Simon to deliver the money to Luca, Will returned to his quarters and was reading a translation Everard had asked him to look at weeks ago, when he had been summoned to the yard. There he found de Beaujeu's four personal guards and a man of about his age waiting with horses. Zaccaria introduced the stranger, explaining that Will had been put in charge of escorting him to the Genoese palazzo, where the Venetian would interrogate Guido Soranzo, a former business associate. Will was puzzled by this. For the grand master to call upon an associate of Soranzo's, he must have known the Genoese in the first instance, although he had given no indication of this when Will had relayed his report.

That puzzlement had since turned to unease. He couldn't understand why the grand master would send a merchant to question Soranzo, whatever their past relationship, when he could easily call upon Angelo's aid after the Genoese was locked in one of the cells. Will didn't trust the Venetian. There was something personal about this assignment for him. Something Will hadn't been told. Now, as he pushed open the doors of the palazzo, he felt a growing sense of danger, not only from the dark house before him, but from the black-cloaked Venetian behind him, who had cut down that guard before Will had been able to reach for his sword.

Beyond the door, a passage stretched into shadow, the only light a flickering glow that spilled down a set of stone steps off to the right. Gripping his falchion, Will moved in, his boots loud on the tiles. He looked up, hearing the creak of floorboards above, and headed for the stairs.

"Commander Campbell."

Will turned at the hushed voice to see Zaccaria.

The Sicilian's eyes gleamed in the half-light. "What do you plan to do with the guards?"

Will glanced back to see Francesco and Alessandro, two of the Sicilian knights, in the doorway training swords on the palazzo's guards, the wounded one holding a bloodstained rag to his chest. He realized it would be foolish to bring the guards inside; they might alert the rest of the house. He cursed himself for overlooking this and felt uncomfortable under Zaccaria's calm gaze. The Sicilian, who was at least ten years his senior, was beneath him in rank, yet probably closer to the grand master than anyone and would no doubt give a full report of Will's command as soon as he returned. Will was used to thinking for himself. He hadn't realized how complicated things could become when you had to organize everyone else as well. He pointed to Alessandro and Francesco. "Remain here with the guards," he murmured. "Keep watch in case Soranzo tries to escape." As they moved into position, Will climbed the stairs, Zaccaria, Angelo and Carlo, the fourth Sicilian, close behind.

At the top was a long corridor, lit by torches, the flames shifting, erratic.

There were three doors set into the right-hand wall and four on the left, with one at the end of the corridor. All were shut. Will moved slowly to the first, then halted, hearing the baby's cry again. It was muffled, but Will thought it had come from farther down, possibly the second on the right. He turned to Zaccaria and motioned. The Sicilian nodded, and together they approached the door, weapons ready. As Will shoved open the door, there were screams from inside the room, where twelve or so people were clustered behind two terrified guards. There were three men who looked like servants, four women, six children, and, clutched tightly in the arms of a plump woman in an embroidered cloak, a baby. The two guards had swords drawn, but made no move.

"It's all right," Will told them. "We're not here to hurt you."

"What do you want?" demanded the plump woman, her voice shrill with fear.

"We need to speak with Guido Soranzo," said Will, lowering his sword, his gaze on the skittish guards.

"He's not here," she said in a rush, but her eyes flicked away from Will as she said it and he knew she was lying.

Will was about to ask her again, when Angelo's voice snapped out behind him.

"Where is Guido? Tell me before I come in there and rip out your tongue."

The woman flinched, and one of the children grabbed her cloak and began to cry. Will was about to order Angelo back, when he heard a loud clatter and a yell from farther down the passage. Angelo sprinted for the last door.

"Guard them!" Will ordered Zaccaria, racing after the Venetian.

"Help me!" came a strangled cry from inside the room.

"Open the door, Guido," barked Angelo. Swearing, he stepped back and gave it a mighty kick. The latch shattered and the door burst open. Angelo entered, flicking his long sword, with its rock crystal pommel, out in front of him.

As Will stepped in, he thought that the room, a bedchamber, was empty and was surprised to hear another yell, until he realized it was coming from the window. Beneath the ledge was a box which had smashed open, spilling a few glittery trinkets. On the ledge itself were two meaty hands, clinging desperately to the smooth stone. Dropping his sword, Will ran to the window and just managed to grab one of them as they began to slide off the ledge.

"God in Heaven, save me!" came a wail from below.

"Help me," gasped Will at Angelo, as the sweaty hand began to slip through his.

Angelo, having paused to sheathe his own sword, came forward. Between them, they managed to haul up a panting, sweating man, who slithered over the ledge into a heap at their feet.

Angelo glanced contemptuously out of the window to the stone courtyard, two stories below. "Did you suddenly imagine you could fly, Guido?" He kicked at the merchant. "Get up."

"Please, Angelo," begged Guido, holding up his hands and staring at the young Venetian. "Please don't hurt my family."

"No one will be hurt if you tell us what we want to know," said Will, retrieving his falchion.

Angelo rounded on Will. "I will take it from here, Commander Campbell."

"I am in charge," said Will, disliking the arrogant Venetian more and more.

"And your grand master charged you with escorting me here to question this man," responded Angelo tautly. "You have played your part. Now let me do mine."

Will heard a polite cough from the doorway and saw Zaccaria standing there.

"Might I have a word, Commander?"

Zaccaria pulled the door to as Will headed out. "The grand master told us that Vitturi has full authority within this house, Commander. He will expect his orders to be carried out exactly."

Will heard no criticism in the Sicilian's words, only frankness. "He's a liability."

Angelo's voice rose through the wood. "Answer me, you wretch!"

Zaccaria glanced at the door. "That he might be. But it is not for us to question or condemn. We must only obey. Must we not, sir?"

Will nodded after a pause. "Are the family secure?" He could see Carlo standing outside the room where the women and children were huddled.

"We've disarmed the guards and calmed them as much as we can."

"Go and wait for me there," Will told him.

Zaccaria looked as if he might say something further, then seemed to think better of it and inclined his head. "Yes, Commander."

Will stood outside the bedchamber and waited. The minutes crawled by, the night silence broken only by the baby's crying and the voice of Angelo behind the door. The Venetian was speaking in a low tone, and Will could only hear snatches of the conversation.

"Did you tell anyone?" The question was repeated several times.

Will heard Guido's voice.

"It was the contract! I swear! I wanted the shipping contract! That's all!"

There was a hissed response to this.

Will wanted to go closer, but Zaccaria was watching him, and even though he was the ranking officer he knew that any interruption of the task at hand would be reported to Guillaume. He didn't relish the thought of losing his commandership as soon as he had been granted it. He heard shouting again, then a harsh cry, followed by a scream.

The door was yanked open and Angelo appeared, holding one hand to his cheek, where a red line had been scored. The blade of his sword was bloody. Beyond, Will could see Guido on the floor, clutching his hand, his face screwed up in pain.

"The bastard had a dagger," said Angelo, brushing past Will and striding down the passage into the room where Guido's family waited. There was a wail and Angelo reappeared dragging a young boy.

"What are you doing?" demanded Will, as Angelo marched the screaming child down the passage.

"I told him what the consequences would be if he didn't talk."

"No," said Will flatly, planting himself in front of the Venetian. "I'm not going to let you hurt a child to force Soranzo to talk. I don't give a damn what the grand master ordered."

"Move aside, Commander," growled Angelo, brandishing the struggling boy.

Just then, the two unarmed guards barreled out of the room where the family was gathered. Several servants came rushing out to help them, and Zaccaria shouted at Will. Cursing, Will ran to aid his men, leaving Angelo to haul the boy into the room where Guido was still prostrate on the floor. Will ducked in past Zaccaria, who had pinned one of the guards against the wall, and tackled the other. Together, he and Carlo got the man to the ground. There was a scream from down the passage. Will whipped around in time to see Angelo stab down at Guido with his sword. "No!" he shouted, running back to the bed-chamber.

The scream was continuing, one strident note like a trumpet sounding an alarm. Will thought it was coming from Guido, until he entered and saw the boy had been thrown to the floor and was staring at his father, lips peeled back. The sound was coming from him.

Angelo turned to Will. "It is done. I got what I came for." Will went to push past him, but Angelo caught his arm. "I said it is done, Commander."

Zaccaria was shouting again. Guido's wife, on hearing that scream, had launched herself at the Sicilian. She was a big woman, and the knight, who was still holding the guard against the wall, couldn't restrain her.

Will wrenched his arm from Angelo's grip and went to Guido as she raced down the passage.

"My husband!" she was screaming. "My God, *what have you done!*" She flew at Angelo, who caught her by the wrists and turned her expertly, pinning her arms remorselessly behind her back.

Will crouched beside Guido. There was a neat, bloody hole in his chest. Will was about to rise, when the merchant's eyes opened. He gurgled blood down his chin. He was groaning, his eyes wide, bulging. No, not groaning, Will realized. Guido was speaking, trying to form words. His wife's shrieks and Angelo's curses echoed around the chamber, drowning him out. Will put his head closer.

"You and your grand master will burn," came the words, forced through Guido's lips. "The Black Stone will be your downfall, not your salvation. I swear it. I *swear it!*" He dragged in a whistling breath, then slumped and lay still.

Will sat back on his heels, as Guido's wife collapsed in Angelo's grip and began to sob. Angelo let go of her and she slid to the floor.

The Venetian turned to Will. "Escort me back to your grand master, Commander Campbell. I have the information he wanted. We are finished here."

Ignoring Angelo, Will went to Guido's wife and helped her to her feet. Her face crumpled as she saw her dead husband. "I'm sorry," Will told her quietly. "This wasn't supposed to happen."

She pursed up her lips and spat in his face. Throwing herself down by her husband, she cradled his face in her hands.

As Will wiped the warm wad of spit from his cheek, he met the black eyes of Angelo Vitturi. The Venetian stared at him for a moment, before heading from the room. Will let him go, then followed, leaving the Soranzo family with the dead body and their grief. Walking numbly into the night air, Guido's final words echoed back to him.

The Black Stone will be your downfall, not your salvation.

12

The Venetian Quarter, Acre

The warehouse on Silk Street was cool and dark. It always was, even at the height of summer, the shutter closed over the window to protect the rows of fabric from fading in the light. Elwen breathed in the familiar smell of the place. The warehouse had a rich, almost sweet odor. Hundreds of bolts of cloth lined the shelves, ready for transportation to Venice and from there to cities across the West. Elwen walked the rows, counting the bolts, a last check before they were secured for shipping. She ran her hand over a roll of luxurious samite, a favorite of her former mistress, the queen of France, who for years had been one of Andreas's best customers.

Elwen looked round as Andreas muttered something. He was shuffling through a pile of papers on the workbench that she had tidied earlier.

"Where is the ledger for the stock?"

Elwen moved over to the shelf behind the bench, stood on her toes and pulled down a thick leather-bound book.

Andreas smiled as she handed it to him. He was a large man, not fat, but broad around the shoulders, with big hands and a long face, framed with hair the color of tarnished metal. "I do not know how I managed before you came," he told her, licking his thumb and flicking through the ledger. The early pages were filled with his careless scrawl, the later ones with rows of orderly numbers printed in Elwen's neat script. He ran a finger down the list on the last page. "You checked each bolt is recorded?"

"Twice."

Andreas nodded, pleased. "I will take this to Niccolò so that he can oversee the loading tomorrow." He shut the book. "We should do well with this shipment."

Elwen smiled to herself as he stowed the ledger in a bag and began to whistle a tune. She liked to see him happy, liked that things were going well for him and his family.

Andreas was a first-generation mercer, who had started in the trade twenty-five years ago. He had spoken of how hard it had been to build the business, setting himself against already established and powerful Venetian families. His father had instructed him in accounting, expecting him to follow in his footsteps, but Andreas, an unwilling pupil, was captivated by tales of distant kingdoms told by the merchants whose books his father kept. He had listened in awe to hear them speak of slaves who dove for pearls off the Arabian coast, rising out of incandescent blue waters with fistfuls of coarse gray shells to buy their freedom. He hung on every word as they told stories of strange beasts and blue mountains, a red moon rising over a desert, whispered tales of perfumed, ebony women. Elwen, listening to Andreas speak of his early life, had recognized that lure.

For years she had wanted to travel, restless wherever she had lived, whether the cramped two-roomed hut in Powys she had shared with her silent mother or the echoing gray halls of the royal palace in Paris. Once, she had asked Andreas whether he found the reality to be as good as the dream.

"Better," he had replied. "For in the dream I did not have such a beautiful wife and children."

Elwen had nodded, but kept silent. Her own reality was somewhat different to how she had imagined.

Andreas set the bag on the table. "I know it has been busy of late and that I haven't shown you how to keep the accounts, as I promised." He held up a hand as Elwen started to speak. "But I do have something I want you to do for me in the meantime. The spring fair in Kabul, I need you to go in my place. Niccolò is going to Venice, the Easter market will soon be upon us, and with Besina about to give birth I simply cannot leave her, not even for a day." He smiled at Elwen's expression. "You are surprised?"

"I've never bought before."

"Of course you have."

"With you," she responded.

Andreas shook his head. "You do not know your own talents, Elwen. I have watched you." He tapped the corner of his eye. "I see how good you are." He regarded her as she frowned thoughtfully, appraising the situation. He had not made the decision lightly, and she would not accept it lightly.

Elwen had a quick mind and a desire to learn, but that wasn't what made a merchant rich. You had to know how to charm, to barter, to sell, and at these she was a natural. The local suppliers in Acre's market loved her. When he had taken her there for the first time to show her how to judge the quality of the cloth, Andreas had been astonished to see the prices falling when she tried, with a sweetly embarrassed laugh, to ask her questions of the sellers in the few words of Arabic she knew. Afterward, when she confessed that she had often been sent into the markets in Paris to buy little luxuries for the queen, Andreas had seen an opportunity.

"Is it safe?" Elwen asked him. "On the roads?"

"I wouldn't send you if it wasn't," Andreas replied. "The treaty that was signed with Sultan Baybars grants us all safe passage on the pilgrim roads in Palestine. Kabul is less than a day's ride from here and you will have Giorgio and Taqsu with you."

The men were Andreas's escorts, who drove the wagon when he traveled to suppliers to buy the silks. Giorgio was a retired Venetian soldier, once a member of the city guard, and Taqsu was a former Bedouin slave whom Andreas had bought in Acre's market fifteen years ago. He had freed the young Bedouin the day after and had offered to pay him a wage. Taqsu had been with him ever since and acted as guide and interpreter. Elwen knew and liked both men.

"You can take Catarina," Andreas added, seeing that she was going to accept. "Besina needs her rest. Besides, I take Catarina every year and she'll be disappointed if I don't let her go."

"All right," said Elwen, now smiling. "Thank you," she added. She gestured at the shelves. "Everything is ready. Do you need me to do anything else?"

"We are finished with work for today. But I need to talk to you about one last thing." Andreas leaned against the workbench. "This man you see, Elwen. Who is he?"

The words shocked her as much as if Andreas had just slapped her. There was no time to hide her guilt or fear; they were etched into her face in her flushed cheeks and open mouth, in her startled green eyes.

"Catarina told me," he said.

Elwen hung her head. "Andreas. I am sorry. I ..."

"You are not in trouble. Indeed, I am pleased."

"Pleased?"

"You are a beautiful woman, Elwen. But you are almost thirty. You've been alone too long. Besina was married to me when she was fourteen and she has brought the greatest joy to my life." Andreas shook his head. "At least now I understand why you spurned Niccolò's advances."

Elwen flushed even hotter. "It wasn't that I didn't ..." She paused, struggling to find the Italian. Sometimes the language flowed like water; at other times, particularly when she was flustered, it felt slow, clumsy. "I was flattered. I just ..."

"You don't have to explain it to me. But I do need to know, when you marry, will you still work for me? Will your husband allow this?"

Elwen dropped her eyes. "He is a Knight of the Temple, Andreas."

Andreas looked shocked. "A Templar? Catarina did not tell me this." He blew through his cheeks. "Now I am not so pleased for you. This is no life. To live in sin, in secret? Do you want to lose your chance at children? At a family?" His voice softened. "I think of you as a daughter, Elwen. I want you to be happy. If this man cannot offer you that, then I pray you find someone who will."

"I can't help the way I feel." Elwen's eyes were fierce and bright. "I wish I could, but I've loved him since we were children. We grew up together in France. We were betrothed once."

"Before he was a knight?"

"He asked me to marry him on the day he took his vows. I know," she said ruefully at his incredulous expression. "We were going to do it in secret."

"What happened?"

She sighed heavily. "It is a long story. It is enough to say that he was betrayed by a friend and did something that hurt me very deeply. It wasn't really his fault, but we ended that day and he came here to Acre and I stayed in Paris."

"And now you are back where you started?"

Elwen gave a humorless laugh. "Except with more lines on my face."

"Will he not leave the order for you?"

Elwen was quiet for a pause. "No," she said finally. "I thought he might for a while, but not anymore. He is a commander now. He waited to become a knight for so long. It was what he always wanted. I think …" Her brow furrowed. "I think if you took away the mantle, you would take away part of him. If he wasn't a knight, he wouldn't be Will anymore." She shrugged. "Surely, if I love him, I should love every part? I should want him to be happy, shouldn't I?"

"But where does that leave you?"

Elwen pushed off her coif and ran a hand through her hair, tousling it.

Andreas was looking thoughtful. "I have heard of men joining the Temple with their wives."

"Only if they are already wed," Elwen corrected. "They can join the order, but cannot wear the white mantle, and if they take the vow of chastity they cannot share a bed with their wives. If any of the masters knew Will was visiting me, he would be stripped of his mantle and expelled. And anyway," she added resolutely, "I have no desire to join the Temple. Life as a nun in a monastery is no life for me."

"And a secular life is not for him. So what do you do?"

Elwen twisted the coif absently around her finger. "I don't know, Andreas."
She closed her eyes. "I really don't know."

THE TEMPLE, ACRE, 16 MARCH A.D. 1276

"You seen Elwen recently?"

"Keep your voice down," murmured Will, hopping down from the bench
where he'd been sitting.

Simon's head appeared from around the horse he was grooming. "Sorry."
He went back to rubbing the brush down the beast's flanks. "There's no one
who can hear though."

Will glanced along the vaulted stone stables. The stalls here were for destriers: the massive war chargers, ridden by the knights, that in battle would be
armored just as their riders. The palfreys and packhorses used by the sergeants
and for light riding were housed in an adjacent stable. "All the same," he said,
looking back at Simon, "I'd rather not speak of it." He adopted a smile. "I came
to see you. I haven't had much time for friends of late. Now I have a spare minute, I don't want to spend it talking about me."

Simon pulled a face. "I wish you would. It's not like I've much to tell you
stuck in here all day." He straightened and wiped his forehead with his arm,
smudging dirt across his brow. "Though I was speaking to Everard yesterday."

"Oh?"

"He seemed vexed. More so than usual."

"What did he say?"

"Nothing much, he just wondered if I'd spoken to you. He wanted to know
where you were."

Will frowned. "He hasn't come to see me."

"You know Everard. I reckon he just wanted me to tell you, you know, so
he didn't have to summon you himself. Wanted you to go to him."

Will rubbed absently at his chin, his beard grazing his fingertips. "I haven't
had time to see him, not since we found the grand master's attacker."

"No?" Simon cocked his head. "Yet you're hanging about in here, not wanting to talk about anything?"

Will didn't answer. It was true; he had been avoiding the priest. Everard
would want to know what happened at Guido Soranzo's house; would have
heard the rumors, may have even heard, through the seneschal, that a man
named Sclavo was being held in the dungeon in connection with the assault on

the grand master. Will had never been any good at fooling the priest. Everard would know he was hiding something.

Since he had returned from Guido's, Will had thought, several times, of going to the priest and telling him everything: about Sclavo, about the grand master's decision to send a noncombatant to interrogate their suspect, about Guido's final words. But concern for the old man stopped him. Everard was frail, unwell and already burdened with worry over the possibility that King Edward might be working against them. The prospect of the grand master being involved in something underhand might push him to the edge. And for what? All Will had to go on were the cryptic words of a dying man. Before he faced Everard, he wanted more.

He had scoured his mind for any meaning behind Guido's oath, but was none the wiser. He had never heard of any black stone, nor did he understand why the grand master would burn because of it. There was only one person, other than Everard, he could think of to ask—Elias, an old rabbi who owned a bookshop in the Jewish quarter. He and Everard had been friends for years. Elias knew of the Anima Templi and had helped them find rare treatises for translation, on occasion using his shop to disseminate knowledge that the Brethren wanted spread. He dealt in books on everything from history to medicine, from astrology to strange magic practiced by tattooed desert men. He seemed to know a little something about most things. Will just needed to think of a way to ask him without it getting back to the priest.

"I'm sure I'll see Everard at supper," he told Simon, who shrugged.

"Sir Campbell."

Will looked round to see Zaccaria in the stable's entrance.

The Sicilian nodded to him. "Grand Master de Beaujeu wishes to see you in his quarters."

As Will entered the grand master's solar, he saw Guillaume seated at his desk. Sunlight threw a wide square of brightness across the papers spread in front of him. In his hand he held a quill.

"Commander," he said in greeting, not looking up. "Close the door behind you." He dipped the quill into an inkpot and continued writing on a sheet, tutting as the ink blotted.

"You wanted to see me, my lord?"

After three more lines, Guillaume set down the quill. "You did well the other night," he said, sitting back. "I haven't had a proper chance to thank you since you gave me your report. Once again, I find myself in your debt. Because of you, the man who wished me dead has been brought to justice."

Will didn't speak for a pause, then found he couldn't hold it in any longer. "I would have preferred to see Guido Soranzo served his justice in our cells, my lord, rather than on the floor of his home in front of his children."

Guillaume studied Will, his expression revealing nothing of his thoughts. "It wasn't the most conventional of trials, certainly. But Angelo Vitturi informed me that he had no choice. Soranzo attacked him. The death occurred in self-defense."

"I feel it could have been prevented had we arrested Soranzo and brought him here for questioning, my lord."

"Had we done so, Soranzo would have had time to put up his guard. Vitturi had the best chance of getting answers from him when he was at his most vulnerable." The grand master's tone was patient, but there was a low undercurrent to it that suggested Will was on dangerous ground.

"And did you find your answers, my lord?" Will knew he was pushing his luck, but he couldn't help himself. He realized he was angry at the grand master; angry that Guillaume had sent him on an assignment with the unpredictable Angelo without any reasonable explanation; angry that he now had this ambiguous mistrust.

Guillaume, however, leaned back, his manner changing, becoming lighter. "It seems Soranzo wanted to exchange me for a shipping contract."

"A shipping contract?"

"At the Council of Lyons I was granted consent by the pope to build a fleet of ships that would serve the eastern Mediterranean. Work for this has already begun back in France. Soranzo was a shipbuilder whose business was failing. Had I died, the building of the fleet would have become the responsibility of the Knights of St. John, with whom Soranzo had contracts."

"Oh," said Will, his brow furrowing.

Guillaume laughed. His face became instantly younger, the frown lines disappearing. "You sound almost disappointed. Were you expecting some higher motive from this man to account for his actions, William? Something grander? More noble?"

"No," said Will quickly.

"To tell you the truth I was disappointed myself," said the grand master, his smile fading. "To know how low someone will stoop to pluck the coins from a dead man's hand."

Will didn't respond. Was he wrong? Did the grand master really know nothing more than this? He sounded so sincere. As Will thought this, he had a sudden wish for it to be true. He wanted to trust Guillaume. There was something satisfyingly direct about the grand master, something solid, dependable.

"Still," said Guillaume, rising and heading over to an ornate armoire, "it is done, and perhaps now we can all return to our duties." Opening the doors, he reached inside and pulled out a slender tube. As he moved back to the desk, Will saw that it was a scroll case, delicately filigreed in silver. "I have a new assignment for you."

Will took the case as Guillaume handed it to him.

"I need you to convey this to a man named Kaysan. He is one of our spies. The scroll inside contains highly sensitive information about our Saracen enemies which we need him to verify." Guillaume returned to his chair. "Kaysan belongs to a group of Shia mercenaries who work the pilgrim roads from Syria and Iraq into Arabia. They are paid to protect traders and those traveling to Mecca from desert tribes who attack the caravans and demand illegal taxes from pilgrims. Kaysan lives in a village called Ula, three days north of Medina, the Saracens' holy site, where the bones of their Prophet are interred. I am sending you with Zaccaria, Carlo and Alessandro. Francesco is ill. What is the name of that comrade of yours? The one who helped you bring in Sclavo?"

"Robert de Paris?"

Guillaume nodded. "Take him also. As I said, Kaysan works the pilgrim roads. He is often on the move, so you may have to wait awhile before he returns to the village. Syrian Christians trade on these routes, selling provisions to pilgrims, so you will travel there as merchants. One of the Temple's guides will lead you. Ula is the last village in Arabia any Christian may enter. Beyond that, on the road to Medina and Mecca, only Saracens are permitted. Give Kaysan's name when you arrive. People there will know him. You leave tomorrow."

Will felt the silver case growing warm in his grip. "Sensitive information, my lord?"

"Highly sensitive," Guillaume emphasized. "Be on your guard, William. There are many perils on those roads. Make sure you keep it safe."

"Yes, my lord."

Guillaume picked up his quill. He frowned when Will didn't move. "Was there something else?"

Will shook his head. If there were answers to his questions, he did not think he would find them here. "No, my lord."

13

The Docks, Acre

Seabirds wheeled and shrieked, their spiraling forms dark against the dawn. The first rays of sun blazed in the east, painting the spires, domes and towers that rose within Acre's walls a soft gold. Garin de Lyons shielded his eyes as he stood at the galley's side, the light touching his face.

Acre.

He had spent almost five years of his life in this place, yet it seemed as unfamiliar to him as any foreign city. The lack of recognition was hardly surprising. When he had first come to the Holy Land, he had been stationed in Jaffa and Antioch. Following the fall of both cities to Baybars's forces, he had returned to Acre, where he had spent only two weeks before being imprisoned in the Temple's dungeon for four years. His memories of the city were comprised of smells and sounds that had existed as faint ghosts beyond the confines of his prison: the vibration of waves, the odor of salt and dampness, bird cries. Since boarding the galley in London six months earlier, he had been waiting for Acre to appear on the horizon with all the strained hostility of a man about to face an old enemy. The slight swell of excitement he now experienced as the city grew larger surprised him. Maybe it was because he had spent so long at sea and was just pleased to see land, or maybe it was the prospect of freedom that the city offered. Either way, he found himself restless with it as they approached the harbor wall.

He grabbed his bag from the corner of the deck that had been his home for the voyage. Other royal messengers got robes of office and passage on stately ships, but King Edward had said it was necessary that he travel unobserved for the assignment, and so he wore no garments of velvet, just a plain cotton shirt and hose and a scratchy woolen cloak. The vessel that had conveyed him was a wool-carrier filled with rough London men. At first, Garin had been quietly incensed. But halfway down the coast of France, he had discovered that his mean surroundings offered certain pleasures in which he could indulge to pass the time, namely drinking and gambling.

As soon as the gangplanks were thrown across, the crew began moving their cargo. The captain disembarked and headed across the dockside to the customs house. Garin glanced at the crew, but they were busy with the crates and he had nothing to say to any of them anyway. With the sun in his eyes and the calls of fishermen loud in his ears, he stepped down the planks onto the bustling dockside. The solidity of the stone beneath his feet was a shock after so long on the water, and he swayed with the dizzying sensation of abrupt inertia. After a few tentative steps, however, he found he could manage a straight enough line if he focused on something static. With his gaze on the huge iron gates of the city that rose ahead, Garin slung his bag over his shoulder and crossed the harbor wall.

Passing the round towers of the sugar mills and rows of warehouses and taverns that lined the docks, he entered the city proper. Traders were already setting up their pitches in the Pisan market, which was covered by a giant canopy of heavy cloth painted blue and green, designed to keep the sun off the heads of the sellers. Garin's stomach growled hollowly as he saw a brown-skinned man emptying a basket of pomegranates onto a stall, beside bunches of greenish-yellow curved fruit that he remembered were called apples of paradise. Garin opened his bag and pulled out a leather pouch fat with coins. He approached the man and pointed to the pomegranates, holding up two fingers.

The man grinned, showing blackened teeth, and plucked two from the stall. "You just come?" he asked in heavily accented French, jerking his head toward the docks.

Garin nodded as he handed over the money.

"Welcome to Heaven," said the man with a chuckle, passing him the fruit.

Walking away, Garin stowed the pouch and one of the pomegranates in his bag. He pulled a thin dagger from a sheath attached to his belt and sliced open the fruit, revealing its dark, seeded flesh. He looked around as he ate, trying to get his bearings. He knew that the Temple lay to his left; he could see the walls in the distance, but he wasn't going there yet. First, he had other business.

Garin had never had the chance to explore the city, but he knew roughly the direction he needed to take. Moving north, he left the Pisan market and entered an alley. He had only gone a little way, when he heard his name being called. Behind him were two men, stocky and muscled. One was bald, his head sunburned and peeling; the other had wiry hair that covered his head and most of his face.

"You've taken something that's not yours, de Lyons," said the bald one gruffly. He was sweating and breathless as if he had been running.

Garin exhaled wearily. "I won it fairly, Walter."

"You tricked us," said Walter, jabbing a stubby finger at Garin. "All these months you've been losing. Then, on our last night on board, you win it all back? You was planning that all along."

"It made for an interesting game," said Garin, still in that weary tone, although he had discarded the pomegranate and had one thumb hooked through his belt, close to the dagger.

"We want it back, runt," growled Walter's hairy companion. "All of it."

Garin's face showed the first sign of anger in the faint flush rising in his cheeks. "Runt?" He laughed, although there was no mirth in the sound. "You think to intimidate me with insults, John?" The laughter died away. Garin dropped his sack and walked toward them. "There was a time when I could have had you hung, drawn and quartered just for speaking to me this way. Things have changed since then; I no longer wear the mantle. But I haven't forgotten the things they taught me."

Walter pushed John back. "He's mine."

Garin continued walking slowly, almost strolling, as Walter came at him, fists raised. As the thick-set sailor swung the first punch, Garin ducked gracefully out of the way and slammed an elbow up under Walter's jaw. The man's head was snapped back, and he staggered away with a shout of pain, blood spilling from his mouth where he had bitten his tongue.

"*Bastard,*" he hissed, coming in again.

Garin feinted left as a second punch was launched at him, and, again, he slipped in past Walter's defenses. This time, he caught the sailor in the eye and was rewarded with a singing pain in his knuckles that told him the blow had been a good one. Walter reeled away, clutching his face, and John shoved past him. Garin held up his fists, but he wasn't expecting such a lightning charge from the stocky man and found himself being pushed back, trying to block and avoid a series of rapid jabs. One got in, and Garin felt his nose crunch as John's fist connected with his face. Blood filled the back of his throat, thick and sour, and tears blinded his eyes as pain roared through him. Spitting blood onto the ground, he moved in, his anger now piqued. Ignoring the blows that rained in on him, Garin managed to grab hold of John's wiry hair and yanked the sailor's head down, at the same time bringing up his knee. John's nose broke and his lower lip was ripped open on his teeth. Garin shoved him roughly back, and the sailor went down hard, cracking his head on the alley floor. He didn't get up. Wiping the blood from his face, Garin stepped over John and crossed to Walter, who was staring in disbelief at his fallen comrade. The sailor backed away as Garin drew his dagger. Then he turned and fled.

Garin watched him go, then sheathed the dagger and bent down over

John to inspect the man's belt. There was a small money pouch hanging from it, beside a leather flask. Garin yanked off the pouch and stowing the money bag in his sack, took a swig from the flask. Cheap wine stung the back of his throat and he grimaced. Swilling it round his mouth, he used it to rid himself of the taste of blood, then tossed the empty flask at the unconscious John.

Men like them had no idea. When they looked at him, they saw a quiet man in his late twenties, with no apparent trade or status, a well-spoken, handsome man; someone soft whom they could make fun of or milk for a bit of coin; perhaps a scholar of some sort. Not a man worth worrying about, who would cheat at dice or steal your woman, or slit your throat in the middle of the night. They hadn't noticed the scars he bore, carefully disguised by the golden hair that hung in a curtain over his face and the dark blond beard that framed his jaw. They hadn't noticed the way he moved, fluid, graceful, like one who has been trained with the sword, or the way he hadn't ever slept with his back turned to any of them, as a man who never expected to be attacked would do. No. They hadn't any idea at all.

Swinging his bag over his shoulder, Garin left the alley and moved onto the Street of the Three Magi, heading for Acre's royal palace.

KABUL, THE KINGDOM OF JERUSALEM, 15 APRIL A.D. 1276

Elwen turned the cloth over in her hands, checking the weave. "It's beautiful," she said, glancing at the seller.

"I do good price," said the Arab, smiling.

A middle-aged man beside Elwen pointed to a glistening length of samite, asking how much it was, and the seller moved away to answer him. Elwen felt someone bump against her and looked around to see a woman smile apologetically as she tried to get past. Even though it had been going since dawn, the market was still packed. People were jostling one another, sellers calling out prices, buyers poring over the wares spread out on stalls, bartering for a bargain. It was mostly cloth vendors at Kabul's spring fair, but a few merchants sold spices, dyes and incense. The smell of peppery meat and smoke from fires hung in the warm, yellow air, and the hauntingly beautiful sound of a lyre drifted above the noise of the crowds. In the shadow of a stone church, the largest building in the village, the lyre player had attracted a gathering and was singing songs in a language Elwen hadn't been able to place.

"Is that the last of it, miss?"

Elwen turned to see Giorgio. His face was ruddy from the sun, now high in the sky.

"Taqsu's almost finished loading the wagon."

"I might buy some of this," Elwen told him, threading the cloth through her fingers. "I think Andreas would love it." She showed it to the Venetian. "What do you think?"

Giorgio held up his hands. "What I know about cloth, miss, you could write on the head of a pin. All I can say is Andreas trusted you enough to let you come here on his behalf, so I guess you might as well trust yourself to do what you think best."

Elwen returned his smile. "You're right." She peered over the heads of the slow-moving crowds to an area where wagons and handcarts were stationed. Squires and drivers of all nationalities were packing stock into leather bags strapped to camels. There were sellers from Damascus, Mosul, even Arabia here. Baybars's twelve-year war against the Franks had swept virtually all Christian settlements from Palestine and Syria, leaving only a few cities on the coast and a smattering of villages in the Galilee region, mostly inhabited by native Christians. Local merchants now had fewer opportunities to sell their goods to Western traders, and as a result, fairs like this one and the established markets at Acre, Tripoli and Tyre were becoming busier with every season. There were many Westerners here, as well as Arabs. "Is Catarina with Taqsu?" Elwen asked Giorgio.

"Yes, she's helping him load the last of the cloth."

"Let me finish up and I'll join you." As Giorgio moved off, Elwen turned to the seller and passed him back the sample cloth. "How much per yard?"

She had felt nervous when they had arrived just before dawn, having traveled through the night from Acre, unsure of herself and the faith Andreas had placed in her. But after her first purchase, Elwen had grown more confident, occasionally relying on Taqsu to interpret for her. Now she found herself enjoying bartering with the seller. She was agreeing on a final cost when she felt a tug on her sleeve. Catarina was at her side looking hot and restless, black bangs flopping in her eyes. "I thought you were helping Taqsu," Elwen said, brushing the girl's hair back from her face.

"I'm bored," Catarina told her with a deliberate sigh. "When are we leaving?"

"Soon. I'm almost finished. Why don't you wait in the wagon?"

"Can I go and listen to the man with the music?"

Elwen glanced over at the lyre player. It was some distance to the church, and the crowds were still dense. "I think you should stay with me."

"You have money?" asked the seller expectantly.

"Father would let me," said Catarina, pouting.

"All right," said Elwen distractedly, opening her money pouch. "But stay by the church, where I can see you."

Catarina grinned and skipped off.

"Your daughter very beautiful," said the seller.

Elwen laughed. "Oh, she isn't mine." Her smile disappeared as the seller took her coins and began to fold the cloth. The words were loaded with unexpected emotion, and she found herself suddenly close to tears. She blinked them away, annoyed at herself.

For several weeks, she had been weighed down with a sense of sadness. She had even started to think of her mother and father, ghosts who rarely entered her thoughts. Her father had died shortly after she was born, and her mother had been lost to her for years. Elwen had written to her each season in Paris, but had never heard anything back. She no longer knew if her mother was still alive. There was pain in that, but not for the loss; it was pain for something she had never known: family. It was the talk with Andreas that had caused it. Now that her relationship with Will was out in the open, Andreas would bring up the subject whilst they were working, telling her she should find a husband who would care for her properly. Elwen knew he just wanted what was best for her, but the constant reminder of the lack in her life was wearing her down.

The seller handed her the heavy bundle of cloth.

"Thank you," said Elwen. Just then, she felt a faint tremor in the earth beneath her feet. It grew stronger. The seller was staring around him, and other people were looking up, halting in mid-conversation. Elwen heard a Frenchman say, "Is it an earthquake?"

No one answered him. The stall in front of Elwen was now trembling, a china cup that the seller had filled with spiced tea was clinking, the black liquid rippling.

"Catarina!" Elwen shouted, her gaze snapping to the church, where the musician had stopped playing. Elwen caught sight of Catarina's black head, then a scream tore through the air. A woman ran into the market square, shouting. Elwen didn't understand what she was saying, but the woman's terror was evident in the pitch of her voice and her wild expression. Her shout was taken up by others. Suddenly, the market was chaos. People started running, knocking into one another, banging against stalls.

"Catarina!" Elwen yelled, causing people to look round, wide-eyed. She stood on her toes to see over the crush, but a heavyset man knocked into her and she fell back against the stall, cracking her hip. The seller was grabbing at his merchandise, frantically scooping bundles of cloth into his arms. *"Catarina!"*

There was a churning sea of people between her and the church, racing for the wagons and horses, snatching up money pouches, grabbing children. An elderly woman fell and disappeared beneath the tide of running feet. The rumbling was louder.

"What's happening?" shouted one man, in bewildered Latin.

Elwen dropped the cloth and went to force her way through the press, but felt a strong grip on her arm. Giorgio was behind her.

"Mamluks," he told her, over the din. "We've got to go. Now."

Elwen stared up at him, the words skittering across the surface of her thoughts, refusing to sink in.

"Taqsu's at the wagon. Come on!"

As Giorgio tugged at her, Elwen felt reality crash in around her. "I've got to get Catarina!" she shouted, trying to pull away. She could hear more screaming. People were funneling out of the wide street that led past the church, racing into the square. Pouring in behind them were riders. Elwen went still as she saw them. Some had swords in their hands; others carried bows. The blades and arrowheads were points of sharp brightness in the sunlight. These men were yelling fiercely as they came, charging up behind the fleeing fairgoers in a shuddering rush of steel and jangling bridles, pounding hooves and bared teeth. Elwen caught two words. *Allahu akbar!* Then the tension in her body was released in a cry as a Mamluk's sword curved down at a sprinting man whose head was ripped from his body in a shower of blood that splattered those running alongside him. A young boy went down, arms flailing. Then, Giorgio was pulling her and she was moving.

As the Venetian dragged her through a sea of faces, each a mask of terror, Elwen screamed Catarina's name until her throat burned, hoping against hope that the girl would hear and know to run toward her. The crowd was pushing them away from the wagons, where squires, unable to force the horses through the crush, were jumping down and fleeing. A row of mud-brick houses and a barn loomed up ahead. People were flowing between them. Elwen heard someone behind her utter a hideous, gurgling shriek, then she felt herself falling as Giorgio went down, hauling her with him. Someone tripped over her legs, half fell on her, then rolled away. Elwen lay winded for a second, then pushed herself onto her hands.

"Giorgio!"

She grabbed his arm, then saw something protruding from his back. The arrow was embedded deeply, almost bloodlessly. She gave a cry as something whistled past her face. There was a *thump* as another arrow sunk into the side of the barn, inches from her head. Elwen threw herself forward on her hands and knees, scraping skin, snapping back a fingernail, not noticing. She was panting with fear, her whole body buzzing with expectation, waiting for the arrow that would bury itself in her back. She scrabbled headlong into the barn, kicking up hay and dust, until she was in darkness and there was a ladder before her. Gasping now, she grabbed at the rungs and hauled herself up. She lost a shoe, ripped her dress, kept going. She scrambled into the hayloft, into piles of warm, pungent straw. She heard a shout below, followed by hoofbeats. She lay flat as a young man came running into the barn, followed by a Mamluk rider. The man fell with a harsh cry as the rider cut him down with a chop of his saber. Elwen shut her eyes tightly and pushed herself into the hay.

She didn't know how long she lay there, eyes closed, ears ringing with the screams outside. After a time, the screams became less frequent, until she mostly just heard the clattering of hooves and the calls of the Mamluks, who shouted to one another in Arabic. At one point the voices were very close and she heard someone moving below, but whoever it was left after a few moments.

Eventually, Elwen opened her eyes and, slowly, lifted her head. She felt unspeakably tired and her body was cramped and weak. Her skin was hot and damp, yet she felt cold and shivery. She raised herself onto her palms and looked down from the hayloft. She averted her eyes quickly as she saw the dead man sprawled in the entrance. Blood was a red fan around him, lurid in the sunshine. Someone shouted outside. Elwen ducked down, heart thumping, but no one appeared. She crawled to the edge of the loft and began to climb down the ladder. Her hands were so weak they could hardly grip the rungs. Halfway down she slipped and simply hung there limply for a minute before she could continue.

Finally, she reached the bottom and slipped along the side of the barn. When she came to the entrance, Elwen crouched down, careful to keep out of sight. She heard the buzzing of flies around the dead man and felt bile rise in her throat. Closing her eyes and taking steady breaths, she fought it down. Several shrieks rent the air and her eyes snapped open. Peering out, she saw two women and a boy being dragged from a mud-brick house by three Mamluks. One of the soldiers picked up the boy and carried him down the street toward the market square, as the other two hauled the women after him. Craning her head, Elwen could just make out the square behind a line of wagons, some of which had been overturned, horses lying dead beside them. She caught glimpses of people, mostly women and children, sitting on the ground. Standing over them were Mamluk soldiers. Others moved about on their mounts. It was where the concentration of sound was greatest. The survivors were being rounded up. Taken prisoner, Elwen realized, with dread.

There was a girl's scream and Elwen pressed herself back as a soldier passed by, dragging a wounded man whom she recognized as the lyre player. The lyre player struggled, but a second soldier appeared and cuffed him viciously about the head. The lyre player slumped and was dragged away, his feet making lines in the dust. The scream came again, and she saw another Mamluk holding onto a girl, who was kicking and yelling. Elwen went cold as the girl threw back her head and her hair fell away from her face. It was Catarina. A small gasp of fear escaped her lips as Catarina screamed her name. But she realized after a second that the girl hadn't seen her: she was simply crying for help. In that instant, Elwen's terror faded, obscured by an immediate, powerful sense of responsibility. Her mind cleared as her gaze focused on an arrow that was lying outside the barn, beside the fallen figure of Giorgio. Her heart beating a steady rhythm in her chest, she crawled toward it.

ULA, ARABIA, 15 APRIL A.D. 1276

Will swatted at a swollen bee that droned around his head as he entered the grove of palms. Sunlight sliced through the branches, stabbing down. He went deeper, dry foliage crackling under his feet, until he had left the sounds of the village behind him. He had told the others he was going to fetch water. It was partly true, or, at least, he had brought skins for the purpose, but water was the last thing on his mind. Against Will's lower back, held in place by his belt and hidden by his shirt, was the silver scroll case Guillaume had given to him. It had been burning a hole in his pocket since he had left Acre, and the urgency was that much greater now. Kaysan, they had been told, was due to return any day.

Finding a grassy rock between two palms, Will set the skins down and drew the case from his hose. The metal was warm from where it had lain against his skin. Sitting, he turned it over in his hands. The grand master hadn't told Will not to open it; he hadn't needed to—it was implicit. He had been tasked with delivering the scroll, and its contents were none of his business. If he read it and Guillaume found out, he might be expelled, possibly even imprisoned.

Above him, the palm trees rustled, their jagged-edged fronds sharp as sword blades. Everything in this country was harsh: the rocky wastelands of sand and emptiness where water had to be dug from deep within the hard ground; the savage sun, blinding and blistering at midday; the freezing nights where the stars in the blackness were hard and bright as cracked diamonds. For twenty-six days Will had traveled through it, and the dusty plains of Palestine had come to seem like verdant oases in comparison. When they left the last town in Syria behind them, their guide, a quiet Arab who had been in the employ of the Temple for nineteen years, told him that Muslims believed when you entered the Hijaz you lost yourself and when you departed you were reborn. Will understood why. The region was the most desolate he had ever experienced, and the journey through it had weighed heavily on him and his comrades, their conversation drying up along with their skins, until they had ridden through the days in parched silence.

From Acre, they journeyed through the Galilee, passing painfully close to Safed, then crossing the Jordan at Jacob's Ford. Here they entered the Hauran district and joined the pilgrim road that led down from Damascus into Arabia. The route was busy. It wasn't yet the month of the Hajj, the great annual pilgrimage to Mecca, but many Muslims, the guide told Will, performed something called the Umra, a more personal journey, which could be undertaken at any time. As well as pilgrims, many of whom traveled together in caravans of camels that carried provisions and water, there were traders who hawked milk and fruit to the thirsty faithful. Guillaume had been right: Will and the knights had not seemed out of place, clad in simple merchants' clothing, their weapons concealed in bags. But there were other, less peaceful travelers on these roads. Mounted bandits from rival tribes roamed the region, drawn by the promise of plunder from the pilgrim lines like wasps to honey, and it soon became clear why men like Kaysan were paid for protection. Will and the others were stopped no less than five times on their journey south by companies of men carrying bows or knives, who demanded a tax. These men, who would target anyone no matter whether Shia, Sunni or Christian, backed down when the knights drew their swords. But, even so, it had been exhausting to keep alert as they rode slowly through stony passes, not knowing whether the rocks around them shielded archers who might not ask for money first; who might just shoot to kill.

Finally, after a journey of almost eight hundred miles, they reached Ula, and the little green village with its cool springs and palm groves welcomed them like Paradise. The houses were of stone and mud, and there were inns for travelers. Will and the knights had gone to the largest. The landlord seemed suspicious when Will had asked after Kaysan. He wanted to know why he had never seen them before if, as they claimed, they peddled goods on these roads. But he eventually told them that Kaysan should return within a few days.

"He'll not work for you," the landlord added, when Will thanked him. "Kaysan works only for the Shias. Not Sunnis. Not white men. Not Christians."

He had led them to a shelter erected on the inn's flat roof, made out of dried, woven palm fronds, with rush mats on the floor to serve as beds. That had been four days ago.

Will's fingers passed down the scroll case, over the patterns traced in silver. There was nothing stopping him from looking inside; the grand master would never find out. Yet still, he hesitated, an old obedience staying his hand. On the journey, Will had asked Robert whether he thought the assignment unusual. The knight had looked at him perplexed, wanting to know what he meant. None of the others had questioned the mission. Why should they? The grand master commanded and they obeyed. But they hadn't been given cause to doubt his motives, hadn't had Guido Soranzo's last words repeating in their minds. Will reached inside resolutely and pulled out the rolled parchment within. Sunlight played across him as he opened it. He let out a sharp sigh of annoyance as his eyes skimmed the black text. It wasn't in any language he recognized: not Latin, French or Greek. It looked a little like Arabic, but he quickly realized that it wasn't. He stared at it for a few moments longer, then rolled it up irritably and stuffed it inside the case.

He was making his way back through the trees when he heard the shouts. After a moment, he recognized Robert's voice. The knight sounded alarmed. Stuffing the scroll case back inside his hose, Will began to run. When he reached the tree line, he came to a halt. He could see Robert, Zaccaria and the others. They were being marched out of the inn, along with their terrified-looking guard, by twelve men dressed in black robes and kaffiyehs that covered their faces. Eight of them had crossbows trained on the knights; the others had swords. Bringing up the rear came the landlord, looking pleased with himself. Will crouched down in the undergrowth.

"They are Western spies," the landlord said in Arabic to one of the black-robed figures, a tall, slender man who bore a band of scarlet cloth on his upper arm. "I looked through their belongings when they were sleeping. They have no wares to sell, only swords. They are not merchants. What they want with you I do not know. But I thought you would want to be warned."

"You were right," said the slender figure. His voice was flat, cold. "Take them," he said to his black-robed companions.

Robert tried to protest as one of the men pushed him forward, but he fell silent as a sword was put to his back. Will watched as his comrades were led away. He heard the cracking of dry leaves behind him. Turning, he found

himself looking at the gleaming tip of a crossbow bolt. The man holding the
weapon was clad in a black robe and kaffiyeh. Will could only see his brown
eyes as the man gestured, with a nod of his head, for him to stand.

14

Kabul, The Kingdom of Jerusalem

15 APRIL A.D. 1276

Elwen's fingers closed around the arrow. The sun was blinding after the
darkness of the barn, and it hurt her eyes. Ahead, his back to her, the
Mamluk soldier was struggling with Catarina. The two soldiers hauling
the lyre player had passed the wagons and were entering the market square. To
the left and right the street was empty. Elwen hunkered in the dust, the arrow
shaft clenched in her fist. It was about thirty inches in length, with gray and
white speckled flight feathers, perhaps from an eagle. The tip was barbed. Terror had quickened her heart. She couldn't move. Her instincts were roaring at
her to go back into the barn, to hide in the darkness. She stiffened as the Mamluk gave a shout. Catarina had bitten him. He wrenched his hand from her
mouth and it came away bloody. Spitting words through his teeth, he back-
handed her across the face. As Catarina crumpled, Elwen began to run.

A cry loosed itself from her lips as she plunged the arrow into the man's
neck, pushing as hard as she could. It was a cry of horror and anger and revul-
sion. The iron tip sunk into the soft skin, then caught on the tougher muscle
within. Blood welled instantly. The soldier yelled in pain and shock. As he
turned to see Elwen, he reached for her, hands wrapping around her throat.
Elwen gasped and tried to prise him off. Panic rose, obscuring her thoughts,
smothering her like his hands. The soldier continued to squeeze. Then he
coughed abruptly. Blood spilled from his mouth and his breaths rattled wetly
in his throat. As his grip slackened, Elwen's mind cleared and she slammed her
knee into his groin. The soldier sank to the ground and curled over, the arrow
still protruding from his neck. Elwen reached for Catarina and hauled her to her
feet. Dragging the girl beside her, Elwen sprinted down the street. They had only
gone a short distance when they heard hoofbeats coming toward them from be-

yond a cluster of mud-brick homes. Elwen threw herself into the shadow of a
low doorway, pulling Catarina in after her, as two soldiers galloped by outside.

There was a smell of blood in the gloom, dark and metallic. Elwen picked
Catarina up and held the trembling girl to her. Catarina's lips were flecked with
red where she had bitten the Mamluk. Her dress was wet at the back and Elwen
realized the girl had wet herself. She went forward cautiously. On the floor behind a table a man lay on his stomach. His throat had been cut. Elwen put her
hand gently on the back of Catarina's head, to make sure she didn't turn around,
as she crossed to a window, where a piece of sacking was blowing in the breeze.
Through it, she could hear incoherent sobs and whimpers, angry shouts, gruff
commands. Her breathing slowed. With something to focus on other than her
own fear, she felt oddly calm. She was responsible for Catarina. The girl needed
her. She parted the curtain slightly and felt Catarina's arms tighten around her
neck as a scream sounded outside.

The little window looked out on Kabul's market square, where it seemed all
the people left alive following the attack had now been gathered, some sitting,
some kneeling, others lying wounded on the ground. For a moment, Elwen
could only see women in this group, and she wondered what had happened to
all the men. Then, as her gaze moved toward the church, she saw they had been
corraled in a separate group, of about one hundred or so, and were lined up on
their knees, their backs to the women. Some of them were Westerners who had
been at the market; others were merchants, and quite a few were locals. Around
the square on foot or on horseback, the Mamluks waited, swords and bows
trained on the crowd. There was another scream, and as Elwen watched, two
soldiers dragged a young boy from the group of women. He must have been no
more than ten. One woman, presumably his mother, was shrieking as the Mamluks tried to pull him from her arms. Elwen averted her eyes as one of the Mamluks clubbed the woman in the face with the hilt of his sword. When Elwen
looked back, the boy had been freed and was being carried off. The woman was
on the ground.

Elwen scanned the men, but couldn't see Taqsu. There were, however, many
bodies around the square, where people had died in the first few minutes of the
attack. Perhaps Taqsu was dead, or perhaps he had fled. Either way, she couldn't
think about him now. One Mamluk on horseback near the church raised his
hand, and a line of soldiers moved toward the kneeling men. This mounted
Mamluk seemed better dressed than the others. A long coat of mail glimmered
beneath his jade-colored silk cloak, and golden feathers flew from the crown of
the helmet that covered his face, with shadowy slits for his eyes and mouth. For

a moment there was silence, broken by sobs and whimpers; then the first of the Mamluks reached the men. Before any of the shocked crowd realized what was happening, one Mamluk had grabbed the hair of a youth in front of him, yanked back his head and wrenched his sword across the boy's throat. Elwen flinched and dropped the sacking. It fell across her view as a chorus of screams and cries tore through the air, and the butchery began.

"What's happening?"

Elwen glanced down as Catarina whispered the words into her neck. "We have to leave," she said quietly, moving from the window and stepping over the dead man. She set Catarina down near the door. "I need you to stand here while I find food."

Catarina's eyes were dazed and glassy. "I'm not hungry."

"You might be later. Can you do as I ask and be a good girl?" Elwen murmured. After a moment, Catarina nodded and let Elwen turn her gently toward the wall, away from the corpse.

Elwen looked around the room, trying to block out the screams from outside that were pushing maddeningly into her mind, setting all her senses on edge. There was a hunk of bread that she whipped from the tabletop and four wrinkled oranges in a bowl. She couldn't see any water, but Acre wasn't much more than a day or two's walk and she thought the fruit would quench their thirst. She was about to head back to Catarina when she realized that she still only had one shoe. She had lost the other in the barn. Steeling herself, she removed the hide shoes from the dead man's feet. They were far too big for her and so she ripped a few strips of cloth from her torn skirts and stuffed the material inside, padding them out. Her hands were shaking again now. Ripping another length from her dress, she bundled up the oranges and bread in it and went to Catarina. The girl let Elwen lead her to the doorway, but there she halted. "Come on," Elwen coaxed her.

Catarina shook her head.

"We have to go, Catarina, whilst the soldiers are ..." Elwen swallowed back the dryness in her throat. "Whilst they are busy."

With Catarina clinging numbly to her hand, Elwen led them out of the house. Keeping close to the buildings, they slipped unseen toward the road that led from the village. Behind them, the sounds of slaughter and terror spiraled into the air like ragged birds, clawing fear into every part of them.

As the Mamluks began the executions, their commander, a middle-aged man named Usamah, watched on, his sight channeled into a direct line by the slits in his visor. It was bloody work. Some of the men tried to run, but were cut down or shot by waiting archers. There was nowhere to go to avoid this death. For each of these men and boys it was inevitable. Some, realizing this, simply knelt in silence, others prayed as the blades of the Mamluks rose and fell, cutting throats, hacking into necks like axes into firewood. Women tried to help their husbands and sons, throwing themselves at the soldiers. But the Mamluks held them back.

Behind his helmet, Usamah's face was grim. He had patrolled this region for the past six years and had never been asked to do work like this. He had seen plenty of battles as a slave warrior, but sending men to fight for their country against enemy soldiers was a different matter than sending them against unarmed men, women and children. Already, he had seen one of his soldiers, fresh from training, wheel away from the massacre to vomit. Others were blank, holding back emotions as they killed on his orders.

When he had received the scroll from Cairo two weeks ago, Usamah had been surprised. Kabul had been ceded to the Franks when the peace had been signed and was under the protection of the treaty. He had known that there were rumored to be spies in the village, but, even so, the orders from Cairo had been exceptionally aggressive, instructing him to leave no man or boy alive. He had also been commanded to undertake the attack during the spring fair, presumably when the most damage could be done. Usamah had guessed that an example was being made. He had not liked it, but he had not questioned the order that had come direct from Sultan Baybars. It was not his place to do so.

ULA, ARABIA, 15 APRIL A.D. 1276

"I thought this Kaysan was one of ours," said Robert in a low voice, crossing to the door of their prison to test the sturdiness of the slender wooden poles that were latticed together to form a cage. The poles flexed as he shook them, but showed no signs of breaking.

Will looked up from the bundle of hay where he had been sitting since the black-robed men had ushered them into the cage, some kind of animal pen, several hours ago. It stank of dung and straw. "He's one of our spies. It doesn't necessarily mean he's a friend."

"But you would think he might be expecting us, or at least not entirely surprised that a group of Westerners would show up asking for him?"

Will glanced at Zaccaria, who was standing at the back of the cage with

Alessandro, Carlo and their nervous-looking guide. Zaccaria appeared as calm as ever. He met Will's questioning gaze. "I cannot offer any advice. I have never dealt with this man, nor any spy in this region before."

Will wondered, by the Sicilian's tone, whether that meant Zaccaria thought the assignment unusual. But before he could think of a neutral way to ask the question, he heard voices outside in the yard. They sounded angry.

Robert stepped away from the entrance as a figure appeared. It was the man with the scarlet band on his arm. He had removed his kaffiyeh, revealing his face. He was in his mid-forties, deeply tanned, with a black beard and dark eyes that held a watchful intensity. An old scar drew a thin white line down the side of his face. "Where did you get this?" he asked in Arabic, looking at Will. He held up the scroll case.

Will understood what he said, but something stopped him from answering. He had presumed this man was Kaysan from what the landlord had said outside the inn, but before he gave away anything of himself, he wanted to be certain. Will rose and went to the pen's door. "We came here looking for Kaysan," he said slowly in Latin. He pointed to the scroll case. "That is for him."

The figure's eyes narrowed as he studied Will. "As was I told," he replied after a moment, in hesitant Latin. "I am Kaysan." He raised the scroll case again. "Where you getting this?" His voice was hard.

"From the grand master of the Order of the Temple. We were told to deliver it to you."

"Templars?" questioned Kaysan, gesturing to Will, who nodded. Kaysan looked around as another man appeared outside the cage. "What is it?" he asked, switching into his native tongue.

"The others are concerned, Kaysan. They want to know who these men are. And what the scroll says."

"I am questioning them now," replied Kaysan gruffly. "They are Templars."

"Then our friend at the inn was right," said the second man, his gaze flicking to Will, who had adopted a frown to disguise his comprehension of their conversation. "Western spies."

"No."

"How can you be sure?"

"This." Kaysan showed him the scroll. "I know who wrote it." He glanced at Will, then walked away from the pen into the sunlit yard. His comrade followed. They began speaking in hushed voices. Will turned away from them, but stepped closer to the pen's door, trying to hear what they were saying.

Robert crossed to him. "What's happening? Can you not understand him?"

Will gave a small nod of his head. The knight looked puzzled, then seemed to understand. As Robert moved away, Will heard Kaysan's comrade utter two words in Arabic in a tone of stunned disbelief. Two words that carried to the cage.

"*Al-Hajar al-Aswad?*"

Will looked around sharply, forgetting to conceal his awareness of their language. But Kaysan and his comrade were so engrossed in their conversation they didn't notice. Their voices were low again, low and urgent. Will strained to hear them.

"They are mad," Kaysan's comrade said fiercely. He continued in a quick stream of words, of which Will only caught a few: death, hell, destruction.

Kaysan said something about a reward, then looked over at Will. His expression subtly changed from one of cold intensity to one, Will thought, of hope. After a moment, he walked away, followed by his comrade.

"What now?" said Robert, looking at Will. "What were they saying?"

"I don't know. I only caught a few words and they didn't make much sense."

Robert frowned at their guide. "What about you? Did you understand any of it?"

"I am sorry, sir." The guide rose. "I was too far." He sat back down as Robert swore.

"We could probably break down the door if we all put our weight to it, Sir Campbell." It was Alessandro who had spoken.

Will noticed irritably that he half-looked at Zaccaria as he said it, as if he were really asking the question of the Sicilian. "No," he told the knight. "I do not believe they intend to harm us."

"But this makes no sense. We were told the scroll contains information Kaysan must verify. Why does he not just do that and let us leave?"

"The grand master knew what he was doing when he sent us here," replied Will. "We wait until the assignment is complete."

"Or until we are turned into camel food," muttered Alessandro.

Zaccaria stirred, his blue eyes moving to the knight. "Our commander is right, Brother. We should wait." His tone was quiet, yet absolutely implacable.

Alessandro bowed his head, chastised.

The knights waited as the minutes turned into hours and the sun moved gradually around. They were all tired, thirsty and uneasy when at last, almost three hours later, Kaysan returned. With him were five of his black-robed companions, all with crossbows in their hands. The knights rose, their expressions tense.

Kaysan raised the beam that locked the pen's door in place and opened it. "Out," he said.

The knights filed from the pen, followed by their guide, the crossbows of Kaysan's comrades trained on them.

Kaysan moved to Will and held out the silver scroll case. "For your grand master."

Shadowed by the black-robed men, the knights were led across the yard. At the front of the mud-brick house, where skinny children were playing in the dirt, they found their horses waiting. The sun was red and low in the sky, and the warm air buzzed with insects. Will stowed the scroll case in his saddlebag, dug his foot into the stirrup and mounted.

Kaysan pointed along a track bordered by palm trees. "Leave that way."

With a tug of the reins, Will headed out of the yard, followed by the others. As the sun melted behind the rocky hills to their left, throwing the desert plain and the road ahead into gray-pink shadows, he eased himself into the rhythm of his horse. When night fell and they stopped to rest, he would open the scroll. As he rode, he tried to piece together the fragments of conversation he had overheard between Kaysan and his comrade. Most of it made no sense, out of context as it was, but those two words Kaysan's comrade had uttered in that stunned tone rolled over and over in his mind.

"*Al-Hajar al-Aswad.*"

The Black Stone.

THE ROYAL PALACE, ACRE, 15 APRIL A.D. 1276

There was a sticky smell of incense in the chamber. Cloying, overpowering, it reminded Garin of his mother. When he was a boy and she was in a rare good humor, she would sometimes play a game with him, where he would have to guess the names of spices she kept in a locked box. Closing his eyes, he drew in a draft of the incense. "Sandalwood," he murmured, then opened his eyes, hearing a bolt rattle on the other side of the door.

A servant clad in an embroidered tunic appeared, looking sartorially superior to Garin, still in his shabby cloak and bloodstained shirt. "His Royal Highness, the esteemed king of Jerusalem and Cyprus, will permit you an audience."

"It's about time," said Garin tautly, his voice sounding slightly nasal from the punches to the nose he'd sustained in the fight with the sailors. "I've been waiting almost nine hours." The servant didn't respond, but ushered him into the passage. Pushing back his irritation, Garin followed.

He had seen little of the palace when he had passed through the heavily guarded gate that morning, the letter with King Edward's seal on it granting him entrance. From the outside, it looked the same as any Western castle: high curtain walls with corner and flanking towers and a prominent keep. Inside, however, it was very different. Garin remembered the Temple in Acre being grand, but sparse, military order and fortifications being of greater importance to the knights than worldly comfort. This palace extended into its interior the Eastern grandiosity that existed in its dimensions. The vaulted corridors were tiled with intricate mosaics, there was glass in many of the windows, and rich hangings lined the walls, which were smooth with plaster and whitewashed. The surroundings were a far cry from Garin's chambers in the Tower of London: a dark, cramped room that was always chilly, with a pallet for his bed and a slit window that looked onto the leaden Thames where the Tower's sewage was discharged.

Edward had kept his word, in part, and had given Garin an estate for his mother. Granted, it wasn't any bigger than Lady Cecilia's former home in Rochester, but it was closer to London and slightly less damp. The rest of the promises given in the early years of his service to Edward—the lordship, the gold, the grand manor—had slipped quietly away, with Edward reminding Garin that he was the one who had secured his release from prison. And this after Garin had betrayed him, killing Rook, his manservant, and forsaking the Anima Templi's Book of the Grail, which Edward had desired to blackmail them with in return for money for the planned expansion of his kingdom.

It was shortly after his return to England that Garin realized he had simply exchanged one prison for another. There were no iron shackles, no walls or bars to hold him. Edward was much cleverer than that. In his rush to please his bitter, ailing mother, Garin hadn't stopped to think of the vulnerable position he was putting both of them in by allowing Edward to house her in an estate owned by the crown. Now Edward only had to threaten to evict her, and Garin was compelled to obey. His duties were simple. He was Edward's eyes, and Edward's fist. He blackmailed recalcitrant barons into submitting to unpopular laws the king wanted to pass through parliament, extorted money from rich magnates, conveyed sensitive information across the kingdom and spied on the royal staff. He had taken on the mantle of Edward's former manservant and, in so doing, had become the very man he had despised. Sometimes, in the gray, sepulchral hours before dawn, when he had drunk himself into a fitful half sleep, self-loathing would rise sour inside him, leaving him ashen-faced and trembling, sweat pouring off him to soak the sheets.

Garin followed the servant into a spacious hall, where marble pillars rose to support the painted ceiling. At the far end, carpeted steps led up to a high-backed throne, with curved legs that ended in claws. A burnished copper sunset flooded through the arched windows. Seated on the throne was a young man of around Garin's age, wearing a gold silk burnous and a haughty expression. Beside him was an older man, with short white hair and a solemn face. To the sides of the chamber slaves stood to abrupt attention.

"Garin de Lyons, my liege," called the servant, bowing.

Garin approached the throne. "My Lord Hugh," he said, inclining his head, "my master, King Edward of England, sends his greetings."

Hugh studied Garin, one elbow balanced on the throne's arm, his jeweled hand propped against his face. "Greetings are all well and good. But I had hoped for something a little more useful." The king held up his free hand, and in it Garin saw the letter he had passed to the guards, complete with Edward's seal. "Perhaps you can explain what your master means by this, for aside from a few pleasantries he says nothing at all. There is no mention of the aid I requested. No mention, indeed, of any help he can offer me with regard to the position I find myself in. And yet he sends you, his man, all the way here with a scrap of parchment?" Hugh dropped the letter back into his lap. "I must say I am mystified."

"My Lord Edward wished me to convey his terms to you directly, rather than in an impersonal note."

"His terms?" questioned Hugh, his eyes boring into Garin.

"My lord expresses his deep regret for your current position and believes he may be of assistance. As you are aware, he is a close friend and confidant of Pope Gregory and nephew of the king of Sicily, Charles d'Anjou."

"Of course I am aware," snapped Hugh. "This is why I asked for his help! I need him to go to the pope and call off this ridiculous sale of my cousin Maria's rights to d'Anjou."

"That is within his power," replied Garin carefully. "Although my lord is currently experiencing difficulties of his own, forced to confront rebels on the borders of his kingdom. For him to act quickly upon your request, he will need certain favors in return."

"What favors?" It was the man with white hair standing beside Hugh who had spoken.

Hugh glanced at him. "Peace, Guy." His gaze flicked back to Garin. "I am sure we can oblige the Lord Edward, if his aid secures us our throne. What, exactly, does he want?"

"A monetary donation and an assurance from you, Your Majesty, that he will be allowed to use Cyprus as a base from which to launch a new Crusade."

"Edward intends to take the Cross again?"

"In time."

Hugh sat back in his throne. "What sort of donation are we talking about?"

"I will certainly discuss that with you, Your Majesty. But first I would appreciate a good meal and a room where I might wash."

"Indeed," said Hugh, disdainfully, "it looks as if you have been in a fight."

"A simple misunderstanding."

Hugh looked to Guy, then back at Garin. "And if I agree to this donation, Edward will see to my request?"

"I have other business in the city. Once it is completed and we have come to an agreement, I shall return to the Lord Edward with all speed and he will endeavor to do what he can for you. In the meantime, Your Majesty, I presume I can call upon you to lodge me for my stay?"

"You presume a great deal," retorted Hugh. He waved his hand irritably as Garin began to speak. "Yes, yes, you may have a room. But we will talk of this again tomorrow, first thing." Hugh snapped his fingers, and the servant who had led Garin to the throne room came forward. "Show our guest to quarters."

Guy waited until the servant had led Garin from the hall. "I am not happy about this, my liege."

Hugh massaged his brow delicately. "We have hundreds of rooms, Guy. It is no great trouble for us to lodge him."

"It is not our lodging him that troubles me, my liege, it is these demands King Edward seems to be laying down before he has even agreed to help you, or proven that he can." Guy flung a hand at the doors. "And he sends little more than a commoner to treat with the king of Jerusalem? It is an insult, my liege."

Hugh shook his head, his dark gaze fixed on the closed doors. "Whoever he is, he is not a commoner. He speaks as one who has been educated, and he has the bearing of a nobleman. Unless Edward's demands are wholly unacceptable, I am inclined to give in to them. He is my best hope of securing my throne from that crow, d'Anjou. There is no one else who can intervene in this affair."

"There is one," murmured Guy.

"No," said Hugh flatly.

"We may have to consider the possibility, my liege."

"I will not ask the Saracens for help," snapped Hugh. "I simply will not!"

"They have intervened before in Christian affairs and matters of state."

"I am well aware of that fact, Guy," said Hugh, rising from his throne. "If not for Baybars meddling in my affairs, I would still have Beirut!" Hugh clasped his hands behind his back and stared out of the high windows, which framed a sky streaked gold and purple.

Oh, he remembered Baybars's meddling all too well. Three years ago, the fief of Beirut had passed to the widowed daughter of its former lord. She remarried, offering herself and the fief, which under feudal law was Hugh's by rights, to an English nobleman, who the year after had also passed away. Knowing death was upon him and fearing Hugh would take control of his bride's territory, the nobleman placed his wife and Beirut under the protection of Baybars. When Hugh sent men to bring the widow forcibly to Cyprus so that she might be married to one of his vassals, the sultan intervened. According to Acre's High Court, the nobleman's contract with Baybars was binding, and without their backing, Hugh had been powerless to do anything but send the widow back to Beirut. Now both she and the fief were lost to him, protected by Baybars's Mamluks. The Saracens might be the enemies of God, but it seemed to Hugh that contracts drawn up by Christian lawyers were more binding than even *His* will in some matters.

Hugh turned back to Guy. "I dislike and distrust Baybars as much as I dislike and distrust Charles d'Anjou. I refuse to go crawling to him for help."

"But he is on cordial terms with d'Anjou, my liege. They have negotiated in the past. When the treaty between Edward and Baybars was signed, it was sent through d'Anjou. Baybars might be able to put pressure on him to relinquish his rights to the throne. You pay the sultan a tribute. I doubt he would want to lose that."

Hugh's jaw tensed. "Let us not speak of this any longer, Guy. I am tired. We will see what Edward's man says tomorrow. I am hoping we do not have to look any further for aid."

Garin couldn't help but smile as he entered the room behind the servant. A wide window looked out over Acre, fronted with a snug, cushioned seat. Against the chamber's back wall was the largest, most sumptuous bed he had ever seen. Ethereal curtains were draped from a frame suspended above a thick mattress, held aloft by four intricately carved wooden posts. The mattress itself was almost certainly filled with feathers, not straw, and covered with silk-covered pillows, plump and soft as clouds. There were elegant furnishings, damask hangings, a rug over the tiles, and two braziers filled with charcoals.

"You may wash there," said the servant, pointing to a porcelain basin and jug. "The bathhouse will be made available to you tomorrow, should you require it. I will have food sent up shortly."

"Wait," Garin told the man as he made to leave. "Fetch me some wine first."

The servant, who appeared to be one of Hugh's personal valets, looked affronted by the command. But he forced a bow. "Of course."

When the door was shut, Garin tossed his bag on the bed and crossed to the window. He shook his head and grinned as he looked out over the city. He was thousands of miles away from his master, from cold nights, drafty halls and stale beer. He had two simple jobs to do, neither of which would demand much of his time, and he had a whole city to explore in the meantime, a city whose whispered delights he had never had the chance to sample. This was not the Acre he had resented for all those years. This room, this view, this sense of freedom and slow-rising excitement—these were the things he had been waiting for.

15

The Venetian Market, Acre

14 MAY A.D. 1276

"I should have been there."

Elwen glanced at Will and saw the anguish in his face. Inwardly, through her weariness, she felt a certain satisfaction: he realized how close he had come to losing her; he knew how much he cared for her now. But the feeling lasted only a moment. He carried enough guilt as it was; she didn't want him burdened with more for her. "I can take care of myself," she assured him, "and I did." She shrugged her shoulders as if to pitch away the problem. "It happened a month ago, I'll have forgotten all about it soon."

As she went back to studying the rows of bread set out on the stall in front of them, Will watched her. She wasn't fooling him. She was pale and drawn, and looked as if she hadn't slept or eaten properly in weeks. Around them, the Venetian market bustled, traders shouting, coins being exchanged at the many stalls where pastries, jewels, daggers and purses were all out on display, shaded from the sun by the huge canopy. It was impossible to talk in the clamor, and despite the black cloak he wore over his uniform, Will was on edge at the prospect of someone from the Temple seeing him with Elwen. Threading his fingers through hers, he led her away from the baker's.

"Will," she protested, hanging back, "I have to buy bread and—"

"And you will," he cut across her. Weaving his way through the crowds, he guided her to a secluded street behind the square, where a sweep of green stretched between rows of two-story houses. The fruit trees in the market gardens were pink and brown with dying blossom that cascaded around them like snow as they walked. Finding a secluded spot of grass away from the workers who were tending the gardens, they sat.

Elwen drew her legs up to her chest, her emerald green gown, girdled by a twisted gold belt, settling in folds around her. She wrapped her arms around her knees and let out a long sigh. "In truth, I'm just glad to leave the house." She rested her head on her arms and looked at Will sideways. "Everything has been so strained. Andreas is blaming himself, Catarina isn't sleeping, and when she does she has nightmares and wakes us with her screams, and with Besina up at all hours with the baby there's no peace for any of us. And I can't help feeling it's my fault."

"You cannot possibly think that. How could you have prevented the attack? Of course it wasn't your fault." Will averted his gaze, his eyes squinting against the sunlight as he stared out across the gardens. If the attack on Kabul had been anyone's fault, it was his. He hadn't heard any word of it before it had happened. Perhaps, if he had been concentrating more on his duties for the Anima Templi and less on finding the grand master's attacker, he would have. The information might have filtered through to him and he could have prevented it; warned the village or sent word to Kalawun to stop it. Something. Having only returned the day before, he was still reeling with the news of the attack. He just thanked God that Elwen had been so lucky. She could be lying dead in a mass grave, or in some prison or harem in Egypt. Will closed his eyes and tried to block out these thoughts. "It's not your fault," he repeated.

"Maybe if I had kept Catarina with me ...?" Elwen's brow furrowed. "She must have been so frightened."

"You saved her. Remember that."

"I wish I could have saved more of them. All those young girls taken from their families. Taken into slavery. I don't know how to understand it. I start to think about it and it just fills me up. I feel so ..." She searched for the words.

"Guilty," he said quietly.

Elwen looked at him quickly. "Why do you say that?" She faltered. "But you're right. That is how I feel."

"I felt the same," Will explained. "After Antioch. Thousands of people died in the siege, and tens of thousands more were taken prisoner. For months I wondered why I had been spared and they hadn't. I felt I didn't deserve to be alive and free, that I had somehow cheated death and that all the others had accepted their fate as they were supposed to. But they hadn't accepted it at all. They just hadn't been as lucky as I had."

"Only seven people escaped from Kabul, me and Catarina included. There must have been hundreds there." A tear slipped down Elwen's cheek.

Will moved his hand to rest on hers. "It will get better, I promise."

She wiped her cheek. "The worst of it was telling it all to the High Court when I returned. I had to live the whole thing over again in front of these lawyers and noblemen, who just seemed to care about the fact that their precious treaty had been broken, not about all the lives lost, the families destroyed. At least Andreas came with me. If he hadn't been there, I don't think I would have been able to go through with it."

"What did the High Court decide to do?" asked Will, trying to make the question sound less important than it was. This was a volatile situation indeed. If the government of Acre were out for blood, as well they might be for the unprovoked attack, measures would need to be put in place to prevent this from getting out of control.

"They sent knights to Kabul to search for survivors, and to bury the dead. From what I heard, they were set to scour Acre for any Muslims who would be able to explain why this happened, interrogate spies they said. Andreas thinks they will contact Baybars to demand compensation." She looked over at the workers in the gardens. "He found out about us."

Will, engrossed in his thoughts about the High Court's reaction, didn't understand the random comment.

"Andreas," said Elwen, taking in his blank expression. "He knows about us. Catarina told him."

"My God," said Will, sitting up straight.

"Don't fret," she said dryly, "he isn't going to inform the Temple."

"That isn't what I meant. I was thinking about you ... your position?"

"Andreas doesn't mind. He would like it if I married, as long as I kept working for him."

"Married?"

"Yes, Will," Elwen shot back, not missing the alarm in his tone, "married. That's what normal people who love each other do. They protect each other, have families, that's what they do."

"Not knights," Will responded quietly.

"Why can't we do it in secret?" she asked him, hating the pleading tone that was creeping into her voice, but unable to stop it. "You asked me once to be your wife and I said yes."

Will felt frustration rise in him. Yes, he had asked her to be his wife. But it seemed like a lifetime ago now; the two of them standing together in that cold, dim passage in the French royal palace, him holding onto her as if he were drowning. Hours before, he had learned of his father's execution at Safed. He was overwhelmed with grief, feverish in mind and body, and the words just came, without thought. But everything changed that evening, in a Paris brothel, and things had been done that could not be undone, or forgotten. Love then was vanquished by a burning need for revenge, and all his plans, and hers, had been consumed by that fire. How could they return to that moment? So much had gone wrong after that one innocent proposal, spoken in heartache, that he did not dare make the same mistake again. It had been too soon, too sudden. If he were to propose again, it had to be for the right reasons, in the right moment. With uncertainty over the grand master's integrity hanging over him, how could he commit to her wholeheartedly? He had sworn an oath to the Anima Templi to work for peace and to safeguard the Temple from enemies within and without. If either were in danger, he could not, in good conscience, promise himself to anything else. For now, his commitment to his duty had to come first, before his needs, or hers.

Will turned to Elwen and spoke gently, but determinedly, not wanting to hurt her, but needing her to listen. "Our being married will not change anything, not really."

"It's a pledge, Will," Elwen answered, feeling herself close to tears. "It's proof that you love me as much as that mantle you wear." She looked away. "And maybe I wouldn't feel so empty each time you leave my bed, like I'm just any woman you might lay with, just any common ..." She didn't continue, her words tumbling into silence.

"You're not just any woman," Will said, his voice gruff with emotion. "You know that. You *have* to know that. I've never been with anyone but you."

Placing her palms on the grass, Elwen pushed herself up and stood. "Well, that isn't exactly true, is it?"

Will rose too, anger turning his voice to flint. "What happened in Paris wasn't my fault." He sighed roughly as she turned away. "Elwen, I love you. But there are things I need to do in the Temple, important things. Everard turns a blind eye to our relationship because he knows I can still do my work, but I cannot commit any more to you than I do already. Not now, not yet."

"Maybe if you explained what these important things are I would understand, Will. But you never do. Don't you trust me?"

"It isn't that."

"I know you do work for Everard that is beyond your duties in the Temple."

Elwen raised an eyebrow as a look of concern spread across his face. "You forget that I was the one who stole the Book of the Grail for Everard. I don't know why he wanted it; he never did explain it. But it was clear it was something unusual. Why else would a Templar priest ask a woman to steal a heretical book from under the noses of the inquisitors? You're always off on some errand that you never tell me about." Her voice was strained. "You don't know what it's like to not know where the person closest to you is for weeks at a time, not knowing if they're in trouble, or hurt."

"I can't tell you what I do."

"I can keep a secret."

Will stared into the sky. "It isn't my secret to tell."

For a long moment, neither of them spoke, both fighting against their emotions, struggling to hold back a flood of love, anger, frustration and fear.

Finally, Elwen nodded, as if some question had been answered. "I have to go," she said wearily.

"I'll walk you back."

"There's no need."

Will caught her arm as she moved off. "I want to."

Elwen searched his eyes. "All right."

Together, they walked away across the gardens, the fallen blossom scattering in the breeze, carpeting the grass with wilted petals.

When they returned to Andreas's home, they found Simon looking agitatedly up at the house. His face was blotchy, his hair plastered to his forehead. He had a fistful of what looked like gritty road dust in his hand, and as they approached, he drew back his arm as if to launch it, his gaze fixed on the upper-floor windows.

"Simon?" called Will sharply.

"Thank the Lord," said the groom, flinging the grit away and going to them.

"Why are you here?" demanded Will. "I told you never to come unless it was urgent."

"And it is," responded Simon. "You have to come to the preceptory. Now."

"What is it?" asked Elwen, looking at Simon questioningly. He gave her a faint nod, which she replied to with an equally faint smile, their acknowledgment of each other concealing a far deeper well of shared empathy and rivalry than Will, standing between them, could know.

"It's Everard," said Simon to Will.

"What about him?"

Simon took a breath. "He's dying."

"Go," said Elwen, as Will turned to her.

He needed no more encouragement. With Simon panting behind him, struggling to keep up, Will sprinted down the street. He shrugged off his cloak as he reentered the marketplace, to show the people who he was so they would move out of his way. But even so, it was slow going through the crush. Using his hands and arms to funnel his way through the press, ignoring the murmured grumbles of those he barged past, Will had almost reached the other side, when a golden-haired man stepped out in front of him.

"William Campbell?" said the man, with an astonished laugh.

Will's eyes focused on him, the recognition a shock. "Garin?"

Garin reached out and grasped Will's hand in a firm grip as Simon came puffing up behind. "How in God's name are you?"

"I'm ..." Will shook his head. "What are you doing in Acre? Did you get my letter?"

"What letter?"

"De Lyons."

Garin looked past Will at the gruff voice, to see Simon standing there, glaring at him. "Ah, Simon Tanner," he said, with a small smile. "How good it is to see you again."

"The feeling isn't shared."

Garin's smile wavered, then he switched his attention back to Will. "I received no letter. When did you send it?"

"A few months ago now. Listen, I ..."

"Well, that explains it. I had already left London. What did it say?"

"I need to talk to you. I want to," Will added, forcing a brief smile. "But right now I have to get to the preceptory."

"I need to speak with you also. It is one of the reasons I came."

"You can speak with *Commander* Campbell, when he has finished with more important business," growled Simon, stepping up to Garin.

"Commander?" murmured Garin, his blue eyes on Will. For a split second, there hung a look of bitter envy on his handsome features. But it vanished so quickly that Will, who had turned to give Simon a warning look, didn't notice it.

"Where are you staying?" Will asked him.

"The royal palace. I'm there on business for King Edward."

"Then I will send word to you as soon as I am able."

Garin clasped Will's shoulder. "It is good to see you again, Campbell."

Will nodded after a pause. "And you."

As Will and Simon hastened away through the crowd, Garin stood and watched them. The first meeting hadn't exactly gone as planned, but at least now he had established contact with Will.

After discovering, through one of the Temple's servants, that the knight was away on business for the new grand master, Garin had been kicking his heels for almost a month. Hugh and his troublesome advisor had become increasingly impatient, with Hugh refusing to agree to Edward's request, protesting that the donation was more than he could afford, but yet allowing Garin to remain in the palace, seemingly unwilling to dismiss his one hope of securing his throne. The Temple's servant, true to his word, came to the palace late the evening before to tell Garin that Will had returned. Having spent all morning in a tavern across from the Temple's gates, Garin was rewarded, shortly after the office of Nones, when he saw Will head out. He was pleased, having thought he would have to wait longer for the knight to leave the preceptory. But the reason Will had been drawn from the fortress so soon after his travels quickly became clear when he arrived at a house in the Venetian quarter and the door was opened by Elwen.

Garin had followed the couple at a discreet distance as they moved through the market into the gardens. Spying on them as they sat and talked gave him a certain perverse satisfaction, as if the fact that he knew something they didn't made him greater than them. But watching the old affection between them, his smugness soon turned into a sense of detachment from the world, from anyone.

So Will was a commander? Well, that would just make it easier for the knight to get him inside the Temple, from which he had been banished. Then, Garin only needed to get to Everard and squeeze some money out of the old man and his duty here would be done. Acre was starting to lose its appeal.

THE TEMPLE, ACRE, 14 MAY A.D. 1276

Will rushed into the dim chamber, not bothering to knock. His lungs burned and he could scarcely talk. As his eyes grew accustomed to the gloom, he saw Everard, hunched over his worktable. Will was surprised to see no one else in the room: he had expected physicians, perhaps another priest. He crossed to Everard. "What's wrong?"

Everard's face was pallid, puckered with deep lines. His skin had sagged on his cheeks, drawing them down into gaunt hollows, making the twisted scar that carved its way up the side of his face even more prominent. He looked frail, certainly, but not much more so than usual. He was holding a quill in his good hand, which hovered over the pages of a large, well-worn book, which Will recognized as the chronicle the priest had started to keep the year before. "I feel I must record evidence of my life," he had told Will, "before I pass into anonymity. Other people have children. I have words." Will stared at him. "What is it?"

"What is what?" responded Everard in his papery voice.

Will paused to let his breath catch up with him. "Simon told me you were dying."

"We are all dying," responded Everard tartly, setting down his quill and rising stiffly. "Little by little each day."

Will watched as the priest hobbled to an armoire, into which he carefully pressed the tome. "You lied to Simon," he murmured. "You tricked me."

Everard glanced at him as he returned to the table. "At least you came quickly." He sat with a wince. "Now I know I can still command your attention, perhaps even your concern."

"How could you do that?" Will demanded. "*Why* would you do that?"

"I will die soon, William," responded Everard brusquely. "And will you be ready then? I have to say, for some months now I have not been sure. The legacy of Robert de Sablé must be passed on. It is the duty of all the Brethren to ensure that. And, at the last count, you were one of them."

"And I will. If the seneschal will let me."

Everard's pale eyes narrowed. "The question of my successor hasn't yet been decided. Do not be so quick to presume."

"What do you want, Everard? I don't have time for this."

"Oh, indeed!" said Everard. "And so it would seem! You have little time for anything these days. You're either out on business for the grand master," Everard's voice hardened, "or with her."

Will avoided his accusatory stare. "I might have sworn oaths to the Anima Templi, Everard, but that doesn't mean I'm not still beholden to the Temple's Rule. If the grand master orders me to do something, I cannot well refuse."

"Obeying orders is different to reveling in them. Now you are de Beaujeu's commander, it seems that you have little care for your other commitments. Even when you have been here, you have been avoiding the Brethren. The seneschal believes you are becoming disloyal and untrustworthy again. Some of the others agree."

"You've been talking about me behind my back?"

"You cannot blame them for their mistrust. You betrayed us once before."

Will stared at the priest, then looked away. "I'm never going to finish paying for that mistake, am I? How many times must I tell you I am sorry? I tried to have Baybars killed, yes. But there were reasons for it." He turned on Everard. "As well you know, since it was you who sent my father here to his death in the first place!"

Everard rose, jabbing a finger at Will. "Your father died in *loyal* service to the Anima Templi. If you want to continue his work, as you're always telling me you do, you should take a leaf out of his book."

"You want my life, Everard? My blood? How many more sacrifices must you make for your peace? Were Hasan and my father not enough?" Will's words rang into silence.

"My peace?" questioned Everard finally.

"That isn't what I meant," murmured Will. He looked around for a stool and sat opposite the priest. "I am loyal to you, Everard. I know I could have made more time to see you and I'm sorry I haven't, but I don't think you are aware of just how busy Grand Master de Beaujeu has been keeping me."

"And Elwen? Just because I allow you a certain measure of freedom, beyond that which the Temple itself allows you, it doesn't mean you can take my lenience for granted. You should have come to me immediately when you returned from Arabia. That you saw the grand master first, I can accept, but that you went to Elwen before you even had the decency to announce your return to me is simply unacceptable."

"She was at Kabul," said Will quietly.

Everard was silent for a pause. "I didn't know that. She is unharmed?"

Will nodded, grateful, and a little surprised that Everard had asked. "Are the Brethren going to intervene? From what she said it sounds as if the High Court are after retribution."

"The Brethren have been debating what the best intervention will be," answered Everard. He drew in a breath. "But before I discuss any of that with you, I must know that you are with me, William, with *us*, that your heart is still in this. Because, if it isn't ..." Everard didn't finish.

"I am. It is." Will saw in the priest's ancient, wizened face a desire to believe, but the mistrust hadn't left his eyes. He hesitated for a moment, then reached into the leather pouch that hung from his belt beside his falchion and pulled out a piece of paper. "Here."

Everard took it. "What is it?"

"I'm not sure." Will had copied the scroll Kaysan had given him, having opened it in the desert only to discover that he couldn't read it. Yesterday, on his return, he had handed the original to de Beaujeu. He had kept the copied text in his pouch when he had left to see Elwen, planning on taking it to the rabbi, Elias, to see if the old man might know what language it was in.

Everard opened the folded paper and pushed his spectacles higher on his nose to read it.

"Do you know what it says?" asked Will, leaning over.

"What is this about?"

"It's a mystery I have been trying to solve, without success. Do you think you can decipher it?"

Everard turned his attention back to the paper. "Perhaps. But ..."

"Do you trust me?" Will cut across him. "Truthfully?"

Everard exhaled slowly. "You wear me down, William, and you aggravate me on an almost daily basis." He shook his head. "Yes, I do trust you. But sometimes I question your judgment."

"Then help me decipher this and perhaps both of us will find answers to our questions."

16

The Citadel, Cairo

25 MAY A.D. 1276

Aisha sank back into the water, feeling it glide over her scalp. Her fingertips had turned wrinkled and spongy, like the skin of overripe fruit. The bathhouse, which had been golden in the late afternoon light pouring in through the high windows, had grown shaded and chilly. Most of the women had gone; just a few were left at the sides of the pool, drying themselves off with scented linen towels.

"You'll miss salat if you stay in there much longer," warned one woman, looking down at Aisha.

Aisha smiled nonchalantly. "There's an hour left till prayers. I've plenty of time."

A few minutes later, the rest of the women moved off, leaving Aisha alone in the bathhouse with her two slaves.

"Leave me," Aisha told them.

She watched them go, then climbed out and picked up a towel. She needed to hurry or she would miss him.

The bathhouse was eerily quiet, the water in the pool, dark blue in the fading light, occasionally rippling as moisture dripped from the painted ceiling to disturb its surface. The air was stale with smoke and perfume, old gossip, left-over fruit. After drying herself off, Aisha pulled on her gown, dragged an ivory comb perfunctorily through her hair and draped her pale gold *hijab* over her head. Moving swiftly, she hauled a low couch to the window. It was made of wood and heavy, the legs screeching on the tiles. She paused to catch her breath, silence falling densely back around her, then stepped nimbly onto the back of the couch, grabbing hold of the window ledge to steady herself.

The iron grille was supposed to be fixed in place, but Aisha, climbing up to let her monkey peer through it, had discovered that the nails were rusty and loose. She wondered if any of the other women knew of it; whether any of them left the harem compound in secret to explore the outside world like she did.

Almost two months ago, she had been sitting hunched on the window ledge, just before evening prayers, when she saw Baraka passing through the gardens at the back of the harem compound. He was moving quickly, keeping close to the hibiscus bushes and palm trees that bordered the walkways, where narrow water channels led to a dark pool at the garden's heart. She was startled to see him. As a young boy, Baraka had lived in the compound with his mother. But now that he was a man, he was forbidden from entering unannounced: that privilege belonged to Baybars and the eunuchs alone. If he wanted to see her or his mother, Baraka would have to come to the main entrance of the palace and summon them. Aisha had watched him until he passed out of sight, disappear-ing beyond the fruit trees that led to the kitchen garden.

Baraka had been in her mind more than usual since she had seen him in the passage. Her father's reaction, when she revealed that he, Mahmud and Khadir had been in the deserted part of the palace together, intrigued her. He had been concerned: more so than perhaps was normal for such an ambiguous incident, and that was without the obvious fear Baraka had shown on finding her there. She had sent several messages to her husband, telling him she needed to talk. Nizam was initially pleased at the effort she was making, but the lack of any reply from Baraka simply drew more venom from the woman, as if his unre-sponsiveness was Aisha's fault.

The next few weeks in the harem had been truly miserable. Then, almost a month later, she had spied Baraka again. Intrigued by his presence in the forbid-den place, she wanted to know what he was doing, especially when she realized he had returned on the same day at the same time, just before prayers. During the next week she kept watch from the bathhouse, and sure enough, seven days later as the sun was slipping beyond the Citadel's walls, Baraka had come slink-ing through the gardens.

Now she was ready for him.

Her fingers working quickly, ears strained for any creak of the bathhouse door, Aisha drew the long nails from their holes at the bottom of the grille. Carefully, she inched out the top two, but didn't remove them, allowing the grille to be swung inward. Now for the tricky part. A larger woman wouldn't be able to do it, but Aisha was slim and supple, and pulling herself onto the ledge until she was sitting sideways, knees against her chest, she pulled the grille toward her. The bars were heavy and the muscles in her thin arms tightened with the weight as she slid her legs round through the gap. The bottom of the grille was now resting on her thighs, her bare feet dangling above a hibiscus bush below the window. Inching forward, she carefully turned onto her front and slithered the rest of the way through, until her head was out and she could drop down into the bushes, leaving the grille to clang shut above her. Beads of sweat glistened on her forehead and upper lip as she squatted in the undergrowth. The mud was cool beneath her feet, the scent of flowers heady.

She was just in time. The gardens were enclosed on one side by a high wall covered with creeping green plants and on the other by the bathhouse buildings. The only access to them was through the kitchen gardens or a door in the main harem building which was always guarded. Aisha realized how Baraka was getting inside, when, minutes later, she caught him shinning down the wall by an overgrown palm tree. She watched through the bushes as he moved past. Then, keeping low, she hastened down one of the walkways on the opposite side. When she came to the fruit trees that bordered the kitchen garden, Aisha dropped down. Baraka was heading for the door that led into the kitchens. Aisha ducked lower as he glanced around. He knocked, two short raps. The door opened and a eunuch appeared, his skin blacker than the shadows. Baraka said something that Aisha couldn't hear, then reached into his silk tunic. Something was exchanged and the eunuch disappeared, pushing the door to. Baraka turned and looked out over the gardens. Through the green web of leaves, Aisha thought he looked nervous, yet still defiant. The moments crawled by, until the door opened again. This time, there was a girl with the eunuch. Aisha recognized her as one of the harem slaves, a skinny girl of about nineteen, who had been captured in a raid on a Christian village. She was white as blossom, with pale yellow hair and a subdued expression. As the kitchen door was shut, Baraka gestured sharply and the girl trudged in front of him, away through the gardens.

Her heart thumping hollowly in her chest, Aisha followed them at a discreet distance, until they reached the fruit store at the back of the gardens. Baraka opened the door, but the girl hung back. He took her arm and led her inside, closing the door behind them. Pulled by a sickening impulse, Aisha crept to the store, both dreading and needing to see inside. There were tiny square apertures set in the walls. They were too high for her to look through, but slipping around the back, she found a wooden pail. Setting it upside down, she stepped onto it and peered in. The space was draped with cobwebs, the interior deep in shadow. She heard Baraka's voice. Rising onto her toes, her eyes following the sound, Aisha made out his form. The girl was standing before him. She heard Baraka's voice again.

"Do it."

There was a faint sniffing sound and Aisha realized that the girl was crying.

"Do it!" repeated Baraka fiercely. "Or you'll be punished." His voice sounded shaky, with nerves, or excitement—Aisha couldn't tell.

Slowly, the girl knelt in front of him, her shoulders making little jerking movements, as if she was trying to quell her sobs. Baraka placed his palms on a shelf behind him as the girl reached out and lifted his tunic. Her head and shoulders were blocking Aisha's view, but it was obvious what she was doing as she leaned in close. Baraka closed his eyes, his face strained.

Aisha's legs gave way and she half-jumped, half-stumbled from the pail onto the warm stones. Her whole body shaking with disgust and rage, she turned and fled.

THE CITADEL, CAIRO, 26 MAY A.D. 1276

Blood dribbled thickly from the lion's mouth as it swung to and fro from the pole, legs trussed together over the beam, great head lolling. Flies, drawn to the bloody puncture in its side, buzzed in an agitated cloud. The servants swatted them away every so often, but the flies kept returning in lazy, ever decreasing circles.

Kalawun relaxed in his saddle, holding the reins with one hand, feeling the horse's muscles shift and slide beneath him as the beast moved slowly up the sandy path toward the citadel. Behind him came a company of courtiers, including his sons, Ali and Khalil, and bringing up the rear were squires and the servants with the lion.

"You've been quiet since we left the plain," said Kalawun, glancing at Baraka, who rode beside him on a jet-colored gelding. "Is there something wrong?"

"No," murmured Baraka, staring straight ahead.

"It was a fine kill."

Baraka's eyes narrowed. "No, it wasn't. You were there first. The kill was yours to take. Instead, you let me have it. I don't need your help. I can do things for myself."

Kalawun was quiet for a moment. "I'm sorry, my prince. You are right, of course."

Silence descended, punctuated by the conversation of the courtiers behind them and a burst of laughter from Ali as his younger brother, Khalil, said something that amused him. Kalawun's smile faded, the brief pleasure he had found in the hunt gone. In trying to please Baraka, he had only succeeded in alienating him further. Things were not going as planned.

For the past two months, he had been kept busy with the organization of the forthcoming Anatolian campaign, especially so since Baybars had been absent for several weeks, having marched on Karak, a stronghold in the Sinai Desert where the Mamluk garrison were reported to have rebelled against him. Baybars returned several days ago, the horses of his Bahri officers dragging the mutilated corpses of the ringleaders behind them, the rest of the dissenters having been banished from the kingdom and a new company installed. Baybars was in a foul rage. The only good news that had come in over the past month was in Ishandiyar's victorious return from al-Bira. Baybars had declared an evening of feasting and a polo tournament to celebrate their victory over the Ilkhan and the Mongols. Kalawun, listening to Ishandiyar speak of his Syrian venture, had wondered how Nasir was faring in his hunt for the Assassins. He was used to having the officer around and missed his solid company.

Since Aisha had told him Baraka may have been meeting with Khadir and Mahmud, Kalawun had been locked between his private concern over the youth, who seemed to be becoming increasingly withdrawn and volatile, and an inability to do anything about it. The hunt that morning had been the first real opportunity he'd had to speak with the youth, but Baraka had been sullen and pensive and all of Kalawun's efforts to draw him from his mood had been in vain.

Up ahead, a black snake emerged from the bushes, its thick body glistening as it waved back and forth across the path, making a twisting pattern through the sand. Kalawun's horse snorted uneasily, and he slowed the beast with a squeeze of his knees, waiting until the snake disappeared. "Have you seen Aisha of late?" he asked Baraka, with feigned lightness, as they continued on up the hill, joining the main path to the citadel, which Kalawun noticed was marked with many hoofprints and lines drawn by wagon wheels.

Baraka glanced at him. "I do not wish to speak of her."

"Does my daughter not please you, Baraka?"

Baraka mumbled something that Kalawun didn't catch.

"We all have duties to our wives," Kalawun went on gently. "To our positions. When you are sultan, you will need an heir. I know your mother is concerned about this. Is there anything you wish to discuss?"

"I said no."

"Very well. I just want you to know that I am here. I would like to think you would come to me if you needed me. Although you have your friends, of course, and your father and Khadir."

Baraka's head jerked up. His eyes flashed with suspicion. "Khadir? He is my father's companion. Why would you think I would talk to him?"

"I know he is fond of you," responded Kalawun carefully.

Baraka continued to stare at him, then turned back to the road, his face troubled. The walls of the citadel loomed ahead, white against the turquoise sky. A group of ragged children, playing on the verge, ran alongside the stately procession, calling out to the company. Baraka ignored them, but Kalawun reached into the pouch at his belt and pulled out a handful of silver coins, which he tossed to the children, who dove on them, shouting delightedly.

"Why did you do that?" asked Baraka moodily, after they had left the children behind.

"They are poor, and I am not. Would you not do the same for your citizens?"

"They aren't my citizens."

"One day they will be. Those same children might be grown when you come to power. Would it not be good for them to remember your benevolence, your charity?"

"My father doesn't throw coins to peasants, yet they admire and fear him. People respect strength, not pity."

"You are not your father, Baraka."

"No," said the prince in a low voice. "I am not."

"Besides," said Kalawun, keen to keep the conversation going, "Sultan Baybars helps his people in other ways. He builds them schools and hospitals, great places of worship, cisterns for fresh ..." He stopped, hearing shouting ahead. As they rounded a bend in the path al-Mudarraj, the citadel's gate, rose before them. The portcullis was raised and a train of wagons, horses and people were filing in. As Kalawun and Baraka approached, they realized that the train had halted halfway, the back of the procession stalled outside the gates. The shouting was joined by children wailing. Kalawun's brow furrowed as he saw lines of women and girls between the wagons. They were a bedraggled company, their faces drawn with exhaustion and shock. Guarding them were Mamluk soldiers on horseback and on foot. The shouting was coming from deeper within the citadel.

"What is it, Father?"

Kalawun glanced around to see Ali and Khalil craning their heads to look. He raised his palm, signaling for his sons to hang back with the rest of the hunting party.

"Wait here, my prince," he told Baraka.

The Mamluks guarding the women and children moved aside as Kalawun passed through the gate. Riding into the courtyard, he saw Baybars. The sultan was looming over a Mamluk soldier clad in jade-colored robes, who was holding a mail helmet under one arm. Baybars's face was thunderous. He turned as he saw Kalawun and strode toward him, leaving the beleaguered soldier behind him, whom Kalawun now recognized as an amir named Usamah.

"Do you know anything of this?" Baybars demanded.

Kalawun swung a leg over his saddle and jumped down. "Anything of what, my Lord Sultan?"

Baybars was pacing like a cornered lion, watchful, wrathful.

Kalawun looked to Usamah, who came forward cautiously when Baybars didn't answer. "Amir Kalawun, we have returned from Palestine, following our assault on Kabul, to deliver the captives we took in the raid."

"An assault?" demanded Kalawun. "On whose orders was this executed?"

Baybars turned on Usamah. "If you say once more that the order came from me, Amir, I will gut you where you stand."

Usamah was pale beneath his tan, but he continued speaking. "It seems the order we received did not come from Lord Baybars," he explained to Kalawun. "It was, however, marked with his seal." He reached into his robe and drew out a scroll.

Kalawun inspected it. "He is right," he said, looking at Baybars.

"I sent no such order, Kalawun," responded Baybars in a voice like steel.

Kalawun glanced at the terrified women and children. He expected very few of them, if any, could understand what was being said. For all they knew, Baybars and Usamah might be arguing over the best way to kill them. "Then it would appear that someone has been using your name to do their own work, my lord."

"It was me."

Kalawun, Baybars and Usamah turned.

Baraka had entered the courtyard. He had dismounted his horse.

"What did you say?" murmured Baybars.

Baraka tried to speak again, but his voice cracked. He cleared his throat, then pulled himself up straighter and looked his father in the eye. "I wanted to help you, Father. I heard reports of spies in this village and I knew you were too busy planning the campaign to deal with them and so I took it upon myself to act. I sent the order in your name."

Usamah was looking stunned. Kalawun's face was stony, yet thoughtful. Baybars moved away from his son.

"I thought you would be pleased," continued Baraka, taking a tentative step toward him. "I wanted to help." His voice was growing weaker, becoming more beseeching. "I did it for you, Father."

Baybars whirled on him. Striding to the youth, he took a fistful of his tunic, which tore as he hauled Baraka up. Raising his hand, Baybars cuffed him brutally across the face with the back of his closed fist. Still holding onto him, he struck him again. Baraka cried out, trying to fend off the blows, struggling in his father's grip. But Baybars refused to relinquish his hold. Blood started to pour from Baraka's nose with a third blow, and a crimson gash opened above his eye as one of Baybars's rings snagged on the soft skin and tore it.

"My lord!" Kalawun managed to grab hold of Baybars's arm as the sultan went to strike again.

"Let go of me!" Baybars hissed into Kalawun's face, blue eyes blazing.

"I don't believe this was all your son's doing," said Kalawun quickly.

Baraka was hanging like a rag in his father's grasp.

"I think he was coerced into it," continued Kalawun, still holding Baybars's arm. He looked at Baraka, whose face was a mess of blood and snot. "Weren't you?"

Baraka let out a throaty sob and closed his eyes.

"Answer him, you whelp," barked Baybars, "or by Allah I will finish you!"

"My lord!" A gray shape came scurrying out through one of the doors leading into the palace. It was Khadir. He dropped at Baybars's feet, staring aghast at the frozen tableau. "He is your son, my lord!" exclaimed the soothsayer. "Your heir!"

"Stay out of this," said Baybars fiercely.

Kalawun watched Baraka's eyes swivel pleadingly, hopefully, toward the soothsayer. The look told him everything. "It was you, wasn't it?"

Ignoring Kalawun, Khadir reached out and stroked Baybars's booted foot with a skeletal, liver-spotted hand. "Let your son go, Master," he pleaded. "What can he have done to displease you so?"

Baybars wasn't listening. "What did you say, Kalawun?" he asked in a dangerous tone.

"You planned this, didn't you, Khadir?" said Kalawun, looking down at the cringing soothsayer. "And you had Baraka help you."

Khadir hissed at him.

Baybars jerked Baraka up to face him. "Is this true?"

Baraka sobbed something unintelligible.

"Is it?"

"Yes!" wailed Baraka. "It wasn't my fault!" He was yelling now, his voice carrying in the utter silence that had descended on the courtyard. "It was Khadir, Father! Khadir and Mahmud! They made me do it! They *made* me!"

Baybars quickly dropped his hold on his son, as if he had realized he was holding something disgusting. Baraka slumped to the ground crying, dribbling blood into the sand. He stared up at his father, then at the ranks of Mamluk guards watching on. Scrabbling to his feet, he fled.

There was a rasp of steel on leather as Baybars drew one of his sabers from its scabbard. Khadir shrieked and threw himself flat as Baybars turned the blade on him. "Do *not* strike Allah's messenger!"

His cry stayed Baybars's hand.

"Kill me, Master, and you will kill yourself," breathed Khadir. "Our fates are bound, yours and mine."

The sultan stood there, breathing hard, then kicked out at the soothsayer. "Get out of my sight. I will deal with you later." As Khadir cowered in the sand, Baybars barked at two Bahri soldiers standing nearby. "Bring me Amir Mahmud." He whirled on the men who waited by the wagons. "Does anyone else want to betray me?" His voice cracked across them. *"Do you?"*

The guards fell back from his fury.

Suddenly Baybars slumped, his saber dropping to his side. "They are all against me, Kalawun. All of them."

"No, my lord," said Kalawun, going to him. "Just a few rotten apples spoiling the barrel."

Baybars looked at him. "What do I do? The treaty has been broken. The Franks will demand retribution for this act against them." He raised his head to the sky. "All my plans for Anatolia will be in ruins if I am forced to deal with them. I may not get another chance. Ilkhan Abaga will move on me again in time. I must be ready, Kalawun. I *must!*"

"And you will be," said Kalawun calmly. "All is not lost. Send an apology to the Christians. Send it today, with an explanation of what happened. Tell them that you were betrayed but you dealt with the traitors severely. Send them compensation. One dinar for every citizen killed at Kabul. Release twenty Christians from the dungeon and send them back to Acre along with these women and children." Kalawun gestured at the line of bedraggled captives. "We might be able to mend this before it is broken any further."

After a moment, Baybars nodded. "Make sure it is done," he said, tight-lipped.

As Kalawun moved off toward the wagons, ordering the men to fetch the women and children water and fruit, Khadir crouched in the dust and watched him, hatred smoldering in his white eyes.

Baraka ran through the palace corridors, trailing splashes of blood. His face felt oddly numb, although there was a humming sensation building in his skin that told him that pain was on its way. Soon it would scream. At first, he had wanted to go to his mother, but the thought of the harem guards seeing him like this had pulled him up short. Weeping with humiliation, he had swerved away down the passage that led to his rooms, images of the soldiers and Kalawun and his father all staring at him, beaten and cowed, burning in his mind.

He arrived at his chamber and was reaching for the door when a figure appeared, swathed in a black robe and veil. Baraka stumbled to a halt as Aisha dragged the veil from her face. When she spoke, her voice was marble. "I saw you."

Baraka hardly heard what she said. "You told your father that you saw me that day in the broken tower, didn't you?" His voice shook, muffled through his swollen mouth and nose. "That's why he kept asking me those questions. That's how he knew about Khadir."

"Yes, I saw you!" Aisha shouted again, making him flinch. "I saw you with that *slave*! Last night!"

Baraka stared at her in horror, then grabbed at his door, fumbling with the latch.

Aisha flew at him, her hands curling into claws. "I'll tell everyone! I'll tell them all how you can't even bed your *wife*! How you need to steal one of your father's slaves to do it!" She struck at his face. "You let your mother think it was my fault! Let her think I wasn't good enough for you!" Baraka cried out as she caught his swollen lip with her nails. "It's you who's no good! It's *you*!"

Baraka managed to shove her away, then yanked open his door and slammed it shut. He could hear Aisha on the other side, yelling curses at him as he sank to the floor.

17

The Pisan Quarter, Acre

26 MAY A.D. 1276

The tavern was hot and dingy. Flies circled listlessly over the sticky tables, where laborers sheltered from the midday heat. Two of them got up to leave, letting in a brief sigh of air as they opened the tavern's door and Will sat back, relishing the faint breath of it on his face. Every year, he forgot just how uncomfortable the summers in Acre could be. The annual reminder was never pleasant. The stink of dung, human and animal, that clung to the dead air by midday; the way even the thinnest linen felt like a heavy woollen cloak; the stench of sweat, spoiling meat and animals in the crowded markets.

"Here," said Garin, placing a cracked cup of wine in front of Will. He sat, taking a sip from his own, and grimaced. His hair had lightened in the sun and his skin was tanned. He looked the picture of health, except for the faint shadows under his eyes. Will envied the loose cotton shirt he wore. It looked wonderfully cool and light in comparison to the shirt, surcoat and mantle he was forced to wear. He wondered if Garin missed being a knight, then looked away and drank as Garin met his gaze. The wine was sour.

"Well," said Garin with a half smile, "we finally meet."

"I'm sorry I couldn't see you sooner."

"I expect you must be preoccupied most of the time, now you're a commander."

Will gave a noncommittal nod, uninterested in small talk. When he had first met Garin in the market, part of him had been pleased to see his old comrade. He had envisioned them reacquainting, talking about old times and old masters in the London Temple. But, now, sitting opposite him in the stuffy tavern, Will realized that the two of them had nothing left between them except the stale reticence of long-stifled resentment.

It had been different when Garin was chained in his Temple cell, dependent on Will for small comforts and news of the world beyond his walls. Will had felt able to forgive him, because every time he saw him he saw the evidence that Garin was paying for his betrayal. With him sitting here, sipping wine, tanned, healthy and confident, Will felt an old anger stir. An image of another tavern crawled into his mind. He was tied to a bed, bruised and beaten. Garin was standing over him holding his mouth open, forcing a thick, gritty liquid down his throat. A moment later, other memories came: a girl with golden curls moving over him; a soiled mattress; the shock in Elwen's voice.

"So," said Garin, into the silence, "how is Elwen? I take it she's still here with you?"

Will's jaw locked tight as he looked at Garin. "She's fine. But what of England? Your mother?"

Garin looked surprised at the question, surprised and pleased. "She's a little frailer. But as whip-tongued as ever." He picked at a smear of grime on his cup. "I don't see her as much as I should. King Edward keeps me busy."

"What do you do for him?"

Garin looked up, hearing the sharp note of inquiry in Will's tone. "I run errands mostly. Send messages." He shrugged. "Nothing exciting. Anyway, you still haven't told me about this letter. What was it?"

"Everard was worried about the requests for funds Edward sent him. I hoped to get your view on the matter."

Garin leaned forward. "Good. This is what I wanted to talk to you about." He extended a hand to Will. "You speak first."

"These funds. Everard needs to know for certain that they are being used for what the king states they are. He has heard that Edward is planning a war on Wales and might be using the Anima Templi's resources for the expansion of his own kingdom."

Garin was surprised. "You are well informed. Very few people know about those plans."

"We have allies in London."

Garin took his time answering. When he did, his voice was slow, deliberate. "You are right."

Will sat up, a look of triumph on his face.

"Edward is planning on mounting a military expedition in Wales. But he is not intending to use Anima Templi funds to do it. He doesn't need to. He has plenty of other resources to call upon. That is partly why I am here, visiting King Hugh."

"Then what does he want the money for?"

"A new peace mission to Abaga, the Ilkhan of Persia. He wants to send emissaries to reestablish contact with the Mongols of the ilkhan's garrison in Anatolia and to make sure the alliance he formed with them four years ago is still holding strong. Edward believes that if each side is as powerful as the other, ourselves and the Mongols standing jointly against the Mamluks, then no side will attempt to attack the other; a stalemate. He believes it is the best way he can continue to secure the peace he made with Baybars."

"But he is planning on attacking Wales?"

"His hand has been forced. Llewelyn, the prince of the northern territory of Gwynedd, has been a thorn in the English side for some time. For years his people have raided into English lands, stealing livestock, abducting children, raping women, and Llewelyn has done nothing to stop them. Indeed, he has actively encouraged it. Now Edward feels enough is enough. He must deal with these barbarians once and for all."

Will listened in silence. Garin sounded like one of Edward's speechmakers. His tone was sincere, but his eyes held little emotion, and Will knew it was just words. It was what Edward would want him to say. Whether it bore any relation to truth was another matter. Will knew well enough from his years in the Holy Land that when a ruler wished to invade another kingdom for territory or power, he would plant propaganda justifying his reasons. If the nation he was intending to invade was perceived as posing a threat, the populace would be far less likely to protest against the decision. It was part of the age-old process of waging war, as necessary and commonplace as the weapons used to fight it. "What about his meeting with Pope Gregory?" he asked. "Everard heard that the king is intending to launch a Crusade."

This time, if Garin was surprised by their knowledge, he didn't show it. "Of course. Edward has to make the pope believe that he is planning on taking the Cross. Gregory is a friend of his and a staunch advocator of a new Crusade. When Edward didn't attend the Council of Lyons, the pope was displeased and called upon him to explain his reasons. Edward was simply keeping him appeased."

Will was unconvinced, but seeing he wouldn't get any useful information from Garin, he changed the subject. "What did you want to discuss?" he asked.

"Edward wanted me to appeal to Everard in person regarding the requested funds. If he is to undertake this mission to the ilkhan, he will need them as soon as possible. Obviously, you and the other Brethren cannot easily leave the Temple on such a journey, and Edward has already established a relationship with Abaga." He shrugged mildly. "He says this is, after all, one of the reasons you appointed him: that he might help the peace process."

It all sounded so reasonable, yet still mistrust clung to Will's mind. "I will speak to Everard, but I cannot promise that he will agree to Edward's request. The Anima Templi has many plans. We cannot fund all of them at once. We only receive so many donations and we need to be careful about how much gold we siphon from the Temple's coffers."

"I understand," said Garin, nodding. "But if I can speak with Everard, or at the very least get an answer as soon as possible, I would be grateful. I cannot stay here much longer. The hospitality of my royal host only extends so far."

"I will speak to Everard tonight and meet you here tomorrow at the same time with whatever answer I have." Will stood, leaving his wine almost untouched. "I'm afraid I must go. I have things I need to do."

"Tomorrow then."

Garin watched Will head out, a few laborers glancing up as the knight passed them, a look of respect in their faces. Once, people had looked at him that way. Now he was just another face in the crowd. He reached for Will's cup and drained the bitter wine, then headed into the white blaze of the afternoon.

The dusty walls of shops, houses and churches crowded in around him as he walked the narrow streets to the market, moving in a sluggish tide of merchants, donkeys and carts. Passing through the market square, he entered the covered street: a vaulted stone passageway with arched openings running its length, where merchants displayed their wares. These openings led into cramped stores, which sold anything from porcelain to poison. Garin kept his hand on his money pouch, close to his dagger, as he headed deeper in, past men drinking spiced tea and playing chess, past a woman who beckoned to him, her body a gauzy shadow behind a silk drape which led into a smoky darkness that smelled of sin and cinnamon.

Garin was fascinated by how quickly the alien became familiar. He had come to the covered street just over a fortnight ago and had been back five times already. The same men played chess, the same woman beckoned to him. The same smell of oranges and lemons greeted him as he passed a fruit seller's and came to the store where the Arab outside saw him and smiled.

Garin nodded in return, unsmiling. *"Qannob."*

But the Arab was already disappearing into the store, knowing what he wanted. He reappeared through the curtain and handed Garin a small parcel of dark green leaves, bound with twine. "You sleep well now?" he asked, taking the coins Garin handed to him.

"Better."

"I see you again soon," the Arab called as Garin moved off.

When he reached the royal palace, he went straight to his room. The drapes were closed to keep out the heat, and the chamber was cool. He had told the servants not to come in, and his bed was crumpled and unmade, the silk sheets damp from another fitful night. Cushions were scattered on the floor in front of a low table on which stood a pair of iron tongs and a clay censer, its bowl blackened. Empty stone pots once filled with wine were amassing in a gray congregation under his bed.

Closing and bolting the door, he kicked off his boots and walked barefoot to the table, where he took the leaf parcel from his pouch. Taking the tongs, he dug them into the brazier, the white ashy charcoal flaking and disintegrating. As the top layer was disturbed, an amber glow was revealed. Carefully, Garin caught one of the smoldering lumps in the grip of the tongs. Placing the charcoal in the censer's bowl, he sat cross-legged on the cushions and opened the parcel. The sticky, sharp smell that leapt out at him filled him with the thrill of anticipation. Taking a small amount of the dried, pale green flower heads, ground up with hard, brown seeds between thumb and forefinger, he moved his hand over the censer, leaned forward and dropped the mixture in.

Hemp, cultivated from the stalks of the plant, was used throughout the Eastern and Western worlds for rope, twine, paper and cloth. But the leaves, resin and flowers were used for other purposes: as medicine; incense; drug. Years ago, in Paris, Garin had spent several months in the company of the mistress of a brothel in the Latin Quarter. Adela was a healer and had told him of people who ate the leaves of the hemp plant, who would have beautiful dreams and fabulous visions, how it made a man more virile, how it soothed and calmed the most restless spirit. Garin had never tried it, until seventeen days ago, when he had been searching the Pisan market for a potion to help him sleep through the hot nights and had been pointed to the Arab's store. Sultan Baybars had banished the use of the plant for all Muslims, although the Sufi mystics still ingested it during their religious ceremonies. Now the men who grew it were forced to sell it, more and more, to Westerners and other nonbelievers.

That first day, Garin had been given several round, pale brown sweetmeats, which smelled deliciously of honey, nutmeg and something he didn't recognize. He ate one that evening and waited for the promised sleep to claim him. When nothing happened, he finished the rest of them, disappointed. Almost an hour later, he was lying facedown on the rug in his chamber shaking with uncontrollable laughter, so violent that he was hardly able to force air into his lungs. He lay there, thinking he was going to die and finding it hilarious for some thirty or so minutes, before collapsing into a sleep, the like of which he had never known. Four days later, he returned to the store. Telling the Arab he found the sweetmeats too potent and asking if there was a subtler dose that would only induce the sleep he craved, he had been sold the censer and the dried flower mixture and told what to do.

As the mixture hit the hot charcoal, it burned instantly, the seeds crackling and popping, a plume of bluish smoke curling into the air. Garin leaned over the table, like a priest at an altar, and drew the smoke into his mouth, then on into his lungs. The first few times had made him cough horribly, but he had quickly grown used to it and had learned how much to imbibe. He took long breaths as the chamber filled with the smell of the plant and his vision grew hazy. Just a little of the mixture and he would experience the kind of calm he could never find at the bottom of a jug of wine. It felt like being caressed. A little more and he would find sleep.

As the last of the flowers burned up and turned to ash, Garin leaned back against the cushions, eyes half-lidded. He had run out of the *qannob* two days ago and had slept badly without it. The meeting with Will had further drained him. Will's self-righteous aloofness had made him want to throw himself across the table and slam a fist into his face, and it had been an effort to keep that pleasant, asinine smile on his face through the probing questions.

Garin recalled Will as a wet-nosed boy back in New Temple, crying over how his father blamed him for his sister's death, and took some small satisfaction from the image. Will had been a good swordsman, but a poor sergeant, flouting the Rule on an almost daily basis and yet somehow always managing to get away with it. Indeed, when Will had misbehaved, it had often been he, Garin, who had taken the blame and the beatings, a pattern that continued when he had rescued Everard's Book of the Grail and was given four years in a cell as a reward. Will, who betrayed the Brethren when he attempted to have Baybars murdered, had been forgiven. Garin's satisfaction faded into sour self-pity. Now Will had a place in the secret brotherhood he was supposed to have been a part of, and a commandership. No matter what he seemed to do wrong, he always came out on top. But the thing that really stuck in Garin's throat was the fact that when all was said and done Will was nothing but a commoner, only a few generations removed from hill-dwelling barbarians, whatever he now wore to disguise it. His father might have been a Templar, but his mother was little more than a peasant and his grandfather had been a wine merchant! It made Garin itch with fury to think of it. He was a de Lyons, the last of a noble line that stretched back to the glory days of Emperor Charlemagne. His father and brothers had died fighting for King Louis, and his uncle had been one of the Brethren. Now he was a nobody. No, worse, a *dogsbody* that Edward, Will, Everard and the rest of them thought they could order around as they saw fit.

What they all seemed to have overlooked was the fact that he was the one man standing between the Anima Templi and their guardian: the one man who knew the secrets and weaknesses of both sides. There was power in that. He just had to work out how to use it. At least Will seemed to believe the answers he had given. Fool that he was. Garin's eyes closed, his hand falling limply into his lap.

The sound of someone hammering relentlessly on his chamber door woke him. He came awake with a jerk, then rose stiffly. As he slid back the bolt and opened the door, he was startled to see King Hugh glaring at him.

"Your Majesty," Garin said, recovering his composure and covering his surprise.

Hugh pushed into the chamber, forcing Garin to move aside. The king's eyes were angry slits as he surveyed the room, still hazy with smoke. "I have seen pigs living in better order," he remarked, stepping over Garin's discarded boots. "Tell me, does King Edward let you treat his castle so?" He didn't wait for an answer. "You were supposed to come to me this afternoon, de Lyons. Why did you disregard our appointment?"

"I'm sorry, Your Majesty, I fell asleep."

"Perhaps from the effects of too much wine," muttered Hugh, looking balefully at the stone jugs peeping out from under the bed. He gave the air a keen sniff. "I presume you have been burning that incense to cover the filth in here. The servants could smell it down the hall." He sniffed again.

"What did you wish to see me about, Your Majesty?" Garin asked quickly. "If you give me a moment to dress, I will follow you to the throne room, surely a more seemly environment for you to discuss your affairs in."

"I will decide where is seemly for me to discuss my affairs," said Hugh, turning to him. "We will talk here. I am impatient and will wait no longer. You said that you would conduct your other business here in the city and return forthwith to England. Edward must intervene before d'Anjou buys the rights to my throne from my dried-up hag of a cousin, Maria, or I will loss my crown!"

"My other business is almost concluded, Your Majesty," Garin replied. "But before I leave, I still have need of your agreement. You have signed the document?"

"No," snapped Hugh. "I have told you, Edward demands too much. He can have the use of my lands in Cyprus as a base for a new Crusade. But I will not pay him the sum he has asked for. Just for him to speak with the pope?" Hugh shook his head adamantly. "It is outrageous. How do I know that Edward will even succeed?"

"If he cannot, Your Majesty, then no one can. But I do believe Edward will be able to help you in this matter."

"No," said Hugh again, shaking his head. "No, it is too much."

Garin nodded. "Then I will leave today."

"What do you mean? You will not speak with Edward?"

"I will, of course, tell him what you have told me, but as I explained, Edward has difficulties of his own. For him to take the time to help you with yours, he must be compensated adequately."

Hugh turned away, his frame tense. "I would pay it if I knew it would work."

Garin gave a sympathetic shrug. "It is a risk. But what else can you do, Your Majesty? How much is your throne worth to you? What lengths are you willing to go to, to keep it from your enemies?"

Hugh's gaze was fierce. For some time, he didn't answer. When eventually he did, his voice was low. "I will sign the document," he said through gritted teeth. "It will be my heirs, *my* sons, who will rule Outremer, not d'Anjou's. I will give Edward what he wants."

"Then my business here is almost done," said Garin, his smile lost in the chamber's smoky shadows.

THE JEWISH QUARTER, ACRE, 26 MAY A.D. 1276

A line of golden bells that hung from a nail on the back of the door tinkled delicately as Will stepped inside the bookshop. The musty interior offered a welcome respite from the feverish heat. It was a fair walk from the Pisa Road to the Jewish Quarter, and sweat trickled down his back beneath his thick garments.

At the sound of the bells, a man appeared from a doorway at the back of the cramped store, the walls of which were lined with books. There were books of all sizes on shelves, covering the top of a counter, rising in teetering piles like haphazard towers from the tiled floor. The man was in his late sixties and was short and stooped with wavy, grayish-black hair and a wiry beard. His skin was weathered and brown, and his eyes squinted keenly at Will. "Sir William. I was wondering when you would return."

"How are you, Elias?"

Elias chuckled and waved his hand. "Pleasantries are for the young, William, and for those who have time to spare. I know what you have come for." Before Will could answer, he went to the counter and bent down. He rose with a wince, clutching his back and a thin book, bound in faded red leather. "Here."

Will took the book. It looked old and the bindings were loose. Inside, he saw that most of the pages were filled with a faint Latin script.

"A traveler from Rome wrote it years ago," said Elias, peering over Will's shoulder. "It isn't any great work, a rather flaccid treatise commenting on the customs of the people of Syria. But it does contain what you need." He held out his hand. "May I?"

Will returned the book, watching as Elias thumbed through the pages, his brow creasing as he struggled to read the text in the dim light.

"Ah, here we are. This should help you."

On the page Elias had opened were two blocks of text, one on either side. One was Latin and the other was a language that looked a little like Arabic, but wasn't. Will recognized it. It was the language from the scroll. "This is it," he said, a note of excitement in his voice.

Elias nodded. "Everard was almost right. It is Syriac, although it is the Jacobite rather than the Nestorian form. But both are very similar and it was an easy mistake to make."

"The language of the Syrian Christians," said Will, glancing at him.

"Yes, although it was derived from Aramaic, the ancient language of my people. The dialect branched in two when a schism occurred within the Eastern Christian church, which formed into two sects under Nestorius of Persia and Jacob of Edessa."

Will nodded. "Hence the names."

"It took me a little while to find this, but as you can see the writer has translated the Jacobite script from a simple poem into Latin." Elias leaned over and turned the page for Will. "He also notes the letters of the Jacobite alphabet and the corresponding letters in Latin, where applicable. Within Syriac there exist no actual numerals, so wherever numbers are used in your scroll they will show as letters, each of which has its own numerical value."

Will looked up from the book. "Thank you."

Elias smiled. "Oh, yes," he said suddenly, bustling back to the counter and fishing a piece of paper out from under a pile of books. "You'll be wanting this back."

The paper had a few lines of text from the copy of the scroll that Will had given Elias to check against a source book, after Everard had concluded what language it was written in.

"What is it that has you and Everard so excited?" asked Elias, watching Will slip the paper inside the book to mark the page.

Will hesitated.

Elias laughed and shook his head. "Perhaps it is better that I do not ask, yes? Then you will not be betraying any confidences and I will most likely sleep better at night." He smiled. "Just tell the old devil to visit soon. I have plenty of new books that I am sure he would be very interested in, that may help your cause." He paused, then added, "*Our* cause," in a quiet, earnest tone. "Tell him, William, that I have a drop of Gascony left in my cellar and the need of good company to share it with."

Will smiled slightly. "I will."

THE TEMPLE, ACRE, 26 MAY A.D. 1276

"Is it done?"

Everard didn't look up, but frowned and pushed his spectacles up his nose. "If you stop interrupting it will be. Tell me what de Lyons said," he murmured, as he copied out another line of text, checking both the poem and the alphabet, then transferring it painstakingly into Latin.

"I already have," said Will impatiently. He felt incredibly on edge, unable to sit or stand still. Everard had no idea where the scroll had come from, and Will wasn't sure how he was going to explain himself when its contents, whatever they might be, were revealed.

"Tell me again."

Will forced down his restlessness and sat on the edge of Everard's bed. In a few moments, he had recounted what Garin had said.

"And you do not believe him?"

"I do not believe Edward. Whether Garin thought he was telling the truth or whether he was knowingly covering for Edward, I'm not sure."

Everard sighed heavily. "Then we are back where we started." He glanced at Will. "Unless he is speaking the truth and our suspicions have no basis in reality."

Will shrugged. "That is possible, of course, but I'm not convinced."

"Why did you say you would give de Lyons an answer so swiftly?" asked Everard irritably. "I must think carefully about this matter before I act."

Will didn't tell Everard that he had wanted his business with Garin over and done with as soon as possible. "To be honest, I assumed your answer would be the same. We cannot afford to send Edward these funds at present. That is all we need to say."

"And if he retaliates by going to Pope Gregory and telling him our secrets? What then?"

"He cannot reasonably do that without implicating himself. He is our guardian. He can be accused of heresy as much as we can."

Everard shook his head. "Edward could say he only joined our organization to spy on us and learn our secrets that he might aid in our downfall."

Will exhaled sharply. "Well, then he'll never get his money. You cannot give in to him, Everard." He rose. "If you do, we might end up funding Edward's wars for the next decade."

Everard nodded after a pause. "You are right, I know. I just wish I had never put us in this position. Tell de Lyons to convey the message to Edward that we regretfully cannot assist him at present, but that we will review the situation again in due course." He sat back, holding up the parchment, the black ink glossy and wet. "Your scroll makes no sense, William."

"What?" Will crossed to him. He took the parchment carefully from the priest, so as not to smudge it. His eyes scanned the Latin text. Everard was right. It was just a series of letters and jumbled words that seemed to contain no discernible meaning whatsoever. "Elias said the Syriac alphabet doesn't have numbers. Could you have put letters in places where the scroll has numerals?"

Everard shook his head. "Even if I had done, the rest of the words would make some sense at least. I can see no pattern, numerical or otherwise here. I admit, in places the scroll is hard to decipher and some of these words cannot be transliterated exactly into Latin. But even so, this should give us the gist. The only thing I can think is that it is in code."

"What sort of code?"

"Without more information on this scroll, where it came from for instance, I have no way of guessing."

Will met his gaze. "All right," he said quietly. He sat and began to speak, telling Everard about the grand master's decision to send Angelo to interrogate Soranzo and that the Venetian had murdered the Genoese merchant. He also recounted Soranzo's dying words.

"The Black Stone?" said Everard sharply.

"That's what he said. The Black Stone will be your downfall, not your salvation."

"Go on," said the priest urgently. "Tell me the rest."

When Will had finished explaining about Kaysan and the Shia mercenaries in Arabia, Everard's expression was grim. He didn't say anything, but turned back to the scroll and snatched up his quill. Starting again on the lower half of the parchment, he began to write fresh lines of text.

"What are you doing?"

"I've seen it used before, once or twice. A message in one language is written using the alphabet of another to disguise it. To anyone looking at it, this message appears to be Syriac, but really it is something else."

"What?" asked Will, watching as Everard wrote.

"If this Kaysan is a Shia, the obvious choice is Arabic." Everard nodded as he finished the first line, using the Syriac alphabet from Elias's book and his knowledge of the Arabic alphabet to swap the letters round. "Yes," he said eagerly, "see here. Our Shia friend has used the Jacobite script to encode an Arabic message. For every letter in Arabic, he has used the corresponding letter in Syriac. Translated literally, it means nothing, but reverse each letter back into Arabic and you have your message."

"That seems pretty easy," said Will, watching as the Arabic text flowed from right to left, across the page. Everard made it look simple.

"No, no," said Everard, sounding pleased with himself, despite his concern, "it is quite a clever disguise. Only if you knew who the sender and the recipient were, or what language they would be likely to speak, could you break the code. If the letter had fallen into just anyone's hands, how would they know what language to reverse it back into to get the meaning of the text? Presumably sending this *sensitive* information, as you say our grand master called it, with a company of illiterates wasn't much of a danger anyhow. You are, after all, a minority. Most men in this preceptory can't even write their own names, and I expect the grand master didn't think anyone would either dare read it, or be at all inclined to. Your suspicious mind is a great asset, William. Never let anyone tell you otherwise." He turned his attention back to his writing. "Now, again, some letters of these alphabets do not match up exactly, but we should get an accurate enough interpretation."

Will went to the window and looked out across the busy, sunlit courtyard, trying to contain his renewed impatience, as Everard continued to write, the quill scratching ferociously across the parchment. After a while, the scratching ceased.

"Dear God."

Will turned. "What is it? Everard?" When the priest didn't reply, Will snatched up the parchment and began to read, slowly translating the Arabic. Some of the letters, as Everard had said, had been lost in the translation, but it was nonetheless decipherable. His mind filled in the blanks.

So long it is since I have heard from you, my brother, I had begun to fear that perhaps you had traveled from this world. The Sinai that separates us might as well run to the ends of this Earth, for you are so close and yet so far from me, trapped within their Babylon. To see your words brought joy to my soul and eased a fearful heart. But let me speak no more of this now. My men are restless. Some among them do not agree with this plan, and I must send the knights who conveyed this message away from here with all speed. They are my men and will follow my lead, but I am asking much of them. Indeed, my brother, you are asking much of me. In truth, I am afraid. But I will do this, that you might escape your bonds and return to me.

Next year, in the week before the first day of Muharram, we will be waiting for the Western knights at Ula. Tell them to come to the mosque and give my name. We will take the Christians down the forbidden road to the Holy City. We will help them enter the holy place. But not a man among us will touch the Stone. Not even I. The Western knights must do this alone.

I trust, Brother, that your reward is as great as you say, for when we have done this, every one of our kin, be they the righteous, or our enemies, will revile us forever. And there will be no home for us in these lands. I only pray that God will forgive us, knowing that no ill to His Temple exists in our hearts and that it is for love that we do this.

Will looked up at Everard. "I don't understand what this means."

"They are planning to steal the Black Stone."

When Will didn't respond, the priest sighed roughly. "It is a rock." He spread his hands apart roughly twelve inches. "About this big. Said to have been brought from Heaven by the Angel Gabriel. You have heard of the Ka'ba?"

"The Muslims' sacred shrine at Mecca?"

Everard nodded. "The Ka'ba, which means *cube,* is a temple, which Muslims believe was built by Abraham with the aid of his son, Ishmael, who built it brick upon brick and dedicated it to God. Others believe it was a site of worship for the Arab tribes who existed before the birth of Islam. It is said by some that when Muhammad came to unite the tribes under one God, he destroyed the idols the tribes had housed within the Ka'ba and rededicated the temple to Allah. The only object the Prophet did not destroy was the Black Stone, which is believed to have been a relic of Abraham. It is said Muhammad kissed it and set it within the wall of the Ka'ba, where it was held in place with a band of silver and came to symbolize the oneness and unity of Islam. Muhammad decreed that pilgrimage to Mecca, the Hajj, was one of the most important duties for every Muslim and that the Black Stone should be revered during this journey. Now, each year, Shias and Sunnis unite and travel the many miles to Mecca, where, following in the footsteps of the Prophet, they walk around the Ka'ba and kiss the Stone. Some say the Stone was once as white as snow, but has turned black with the sins of mankind and that on the Day of Judgment it will testify before Allah in favor of the faithful who have kissed it." Everard fixed his bloodshot gaze on Will. "It is the Muslims' most important relic. It is forbidden for any nonbeliever to even approach the holy city. To enter Mecca and steal the Stone from its sacred resting place would be an insult beyond all insults."

Will was listening intently, growing more and more sober with every word Everard spoke. "What are you saying?"

"I am saying that if Western knights are to do this, as the message states, then every Muslim in the known world would rise against us. It would be war on a scale that has not been seen since the First Crusade. Perhaps greater."

"But surely Kaysan wouldn't do this? He is a Muslim."

"As, by the sounds of it, is this brother he addresses. But it is not without precedent. There is written a tale of a company of Shia Muslims of the Ismaili sect who did just this, centuries ago. They sacked Mecca and carried off the Stone, which remained in their possession, as a ransom, for twenty years. When they finally restored it, they began to profit from the revenue generated by pilgrims returning to Mecca. Other Muslim rulers have taken control of the city, sometimes by force, for their own purposes since that time." Everard rose and went to a table where a jug and goblet stood. He poured himself a large measure of wine. "Even our own people have tried something similar. A French knight, whose attack on a Muslim caravan traveling to Mecca led to the Battle of Hattin, planned to do this. It happened shortly before the Anima Templi was formed. He wanted to mount a raid into Arabia, intending to demolish the tomb of Muhammad at Medina and to sack Mecca and burn the Ka'ba to the ground. Three hundred Christians followed him to this end and with them a similar number of Muslim outlaws. They didn't succeed in entering either holy place, but they laid waste to a number of caravans, including one in which Saladin's aunt was traveling. The knight paid with death for his disgraceful crimes." Everard drank deep from his goblet. "But it seems," he murmured, "that the lessons of the past have been forgotten. I must think about this," he said quietly. "What it means. What can be done. We must call a meeting of the Brethren immediately."

"Why would Grand Master de Beaujeu be involved in this?" asked Will, watching as Everard sat, fear and exhaustion showing in his lined face. "It makes no sense. Why would he want to start such a war?"

"I do not know. I have many questions myself. Who is this brother Kaysan mentions? Is he blood kin or a fellow member of an order? The message certainly doesn't seem to have been intended for the grand master, as it sets Kaysan and his brother apart from the *Western knights*, so how did de Beaujeu come to send the original message? Did he know what it contained? And how did Soranzo know of the plan?" Everard took the scroll from Will and glanced over it again. "Sinai," he murmured, "trapped in their Babylon." He looked up at

Will. "At least we know where this brother of his is based. Babylon-Fort was the ancient name for Cairo, when the Romans lived there."

"Why *their* Babylon?" asked Will.

"The Sunni's control Cairo. Kaysan is a Shia, which probably means his brother is also. Kaysan speaks of the month of Muharram, a significant time for Shias." Everard frowned thoughtfully. "I would have to do the proper lunar calculations, but I believe Muharram will fall in April next year."

"So the grand master is working with someone in Cairo to do this?"

Everard inhaled deeply. "We cannot be certain of anything; we have too little information. But one thing we can be sure of is that any chance of peace between ourselves and the Muslims would be shattered irrevocably if such an abhorrent act were to happen. The truce would be utterly destroyed and most likely all that remains of a Christian presence in the Holy Land. Acre would burn and with it the dreams of us all. It cannot happen, William," he said, his voice changing, becoming stone. "It *cannot.*"

18

The Citadel, Cairo

26 MAY A.D. 1276

Mahmud's expression was rigid as he was marched through the palace by four silent Bahri warriors. His turban was damp and slightly lopsided where he had wound it hastily over his hair, still wet from his afternoon bath. The grim-faced Bahri had refused to answer his questions or tell him where they were taking him. But deep down, he thought he knew. Deep down, a worm of fear uncoiled in his gut.

As he passed into the unforgiving glare of the afternoon, Mahmud saw Baybars standing in the center of the northern enclosure's courtyard. On his hips, hanging from his ornate black and silver sword belt, were two sabers. With him were two Bahri and fifteen Mamluk governors, all commanders of regiments. Ishandiyar was there, as were Yusuf and Kalawun, and several of Mahmud's comrades. Only a few of them met his gaze, Kalawun among them. Baybars's face was a mask. The only emotion showed in his blue eyes. There, the intensity of the anger emanating from his stare was terrifying, the white star in his left pupil seeming to focus all that rage into a single point of fierce brightness.

Mahmud's eyes flicked to a granite stone that rose like a tombstone out of the dust beside the sultan. He knew that up close the stone would be stained brown, from all the heads that had been severed upon it. And fear squirmed in his insides and rose into his throat, constricting him. He wanted to speak, to cover his fear with indignation and feigned confusion. For a moment, he couldn't. But then, as the warriors beside him melted away, leaving him standing alone before Baybars and the hushed company of governors, he found his voice. "My Lord Sultan?"

"Do not call me that." Baybars's voice was whip-sharp. "I am not he."

Mahmud faltered. "My lord?"

"I cannot be he. The man you pledged your allegiance to in the sight of God. To you I am not lord, or sultan. To you I am ... what? A simple fool? A child? Someone you think to beguile, someone witless, artless?"

"No, my lord, I ..."

"Why have you betrayed me, Mahmud? I have heard it from my son's mouth. Now I want to hear it from yours. Why did you send the order to attack Kabul in my name? Why did you corrupt my son?"

"I do not understand," Mahmud repeated, hesitant.

Immediately, Baybars gestured at two of the Bahri. "Bring him," he barked.

Mahmud cried out as the warriors grabbed hold of his arms and marched him toward the stone. As he was forced to his knees and his head was pushed roughly onto the cold granite, he cried out again. "I am not the only one of your people who wants to see your eye turned first to the Christians! There have been others who have spoken against you, who to your face have smiled and agreed with your plans for the Mongols, but who in private have questioned your judgment."

The governors shifted uncomfortably, their eyes lowering as Baybars turned his violent gaze on them.

"But I have never hidden my mind from you!" Mahmud continued in a rush. "You have always known what I thought." He swiveled his eyes upward to look at Baybars, the palm of one of the Bahri still pressed firmly to his head, holding him down on the stone. "Surely that is worth some scrap of mercy, my lord?"

"I see a serpent," murmured Baybars, "a serpent who has slithered its way into my house, wrapping its coils around those close to me, those less cunning than itself."

"That was not the way of it!"

Baybars continued as if Mahmud hadn't spoken. "I see a creature whose poison has infected my family, whose flicking tongue whispers untruths. I see my betrayer. And like the serpent you are, Mahmud, you will crawl on your belly from this day forth." Baybars issued a command to the Bahri warrior holding Mahmud's head, who now released him and grabbed his shoulders, pulling him back. The other warrior took his arm and forced Mahmud's hand, palm down, on the stone.

"My lord! I beg you!" shouted Mahmud, as a third Bahri came into view. The gold-cloaked warrior held an axe.

"Wait," snapped Baybars as the warrior walked toward the stone.

Mahmud looked imploringly up at the sultan. Then, all hope faded as Baybars took the weapon and turned his pitiless blue eyes on him.

"I will do it."

Mahmud screamed as Baybars raised the axe and brought it down in a furious arc. The blade cut through the wrist, through flesh and bone, to ring like a harsh bell on the stone beneath. Mahmud screamed again, this time a strangled shriek. He arched back against the soldiers holding him, blood spurting over his yellow cloak and the dust around him. His severed hand lay on the stone, pale and obscene like a bloated spider.

But Mahmud's ordeal was only just beginning.

He was almost delirious by the time Baybars hacked his other hand from his body.

"Now his feet," said Baybars grimly. His blood-spattered hands were white-knuckled, gripping the axe's shaft. As the two Bahri let Mahmud slump to the floor and placed one of his legs awkwardly on the stone, holding the ankle joint flat, Baybars looked at the governors. Most of them were looking elsewhere, at the ground, the sky, anywhere but at the squirming, bloodied thing over by the stone that had once been a man, a comrade. "You will watch this," Baybars commanded them. "Too long have my own people whispered in secret against me, against my rule and my decisions. You will see with your own eyes the price of such betrayal." Baybars waited until their gazes were turned to him, then raised the blade. He was breathing hard and sweat had broken out across his brow. "This mutiny stops *now*, or by Allah this will be the fate of you all!"

The axe fell again.

Baraka was sitting slumped against his chamber's door when he heard the screams. They were faint, yet so piercing that they jolted him from his torpor. He struggled to his feet and went to the window. They sounded as if they had come from somewhere near the northern enclosure. He wondered at their source and trembled as he thought of his father's murderous rage. His face was throbbing, the skin taut over his eye, sticky with blood. His reflection in the mirror on his table stared up at him, distorted. He hardly looked like himself. His father's fists had reshaped his face. *You're not his son anymore.*

Baraka reached numbly for the basin of water that stood beside the mirror, then stopped. There was something gratifying about keeping the injuries un-washed and undressed, something defiant, accusatory. But the pain in his face was hot and intense. It galvanized him. After listening at the door, he opened it. There was no sign of Aisha. Her words blasted into his mind again. Gingerly, he touched his lip, where her nails had torn his skin. As the cuts stung, he felt the liquid fear that swirled in his belly harden into anger, like wax when the air hits it. How dare she spy on him? Threaten him! She was his *wife*! She should obey him. Instead, she had informed on him to her father, telling Kalawun she had seen him with Mahmud and Khadir that day; for how else would Kalawun have known of the soothsayer's involvement? It didn't matter to him: he had admitted the deed to his father, as had been the plan, and either way he would have been beaten. What Aisha had told her father only mattered to Khadir and Mahmud. But it was the fact that she had betrayed him that galled him. That and her threats about the slave girl. How he hated that she had watched him in his most private moment. How he now burned with the shame of that secret, opened like a wound.

For months, his mother had begged him to see Aisha, imploring him to overlook whatever flaws he saw in the girl for the sake of his position. He needed an heir, she told him. But he hadn't been able to bring himself to do it. Aisha scared him. She always had. The night of their marriage simply com-pounded those fears. She made him feel like a failure. But yet he was left curious after the event. Aisha's body, smooth and scented, revealed to him that one night had plagued his mind, even as the girl herself repelled him. He had known some of the eunuchs in the harem palace since he was an infant, and it wasn't hard to bribe one of them. With the slave girl, he was the one in control, the one who held the power, and his impotence had vanished in the face of her ter-ror. But now that control had gone. Aisha knew what he had been doing. And if his father found out that he had defiled his harem? Well, these bruises would feel like kisses in comparison.

Shutting the door behind him, Baraka moved along the marble corridors, making his way down into the lower levels, where the air was warm from the kitchens and the rooms, mostly servants' quarters and stores, became smaller and darker. No one stopped him or asked him where he was going. No one dared. He was heir to the throne of Egypt and Syria, above them all in rank and status. Too often he had forgotten that, cowed by his father's harsh words and strict discipline. Too long now, had he let himself be broken down.

Shortly, Baraka came to a cobwebbed storeroom, near to the kitchens, where behind several sacks of corn, stacked one upon the other, he found Khadir. The soothsayer had set up home in a space between the sacks and the wall. There was a pile of soiled blankets, tarnished goblets, a bucket encrusted with some foul matter and, placed along a rotten timber beam, an array of bizarre objects. A pile of dried rushes had been woven into some kind of nest beside a collection of tiny skulls. There were smooth round stones with holes in them; little jars of colored substances—red, brown, black and gold—that looked like spices; several coins—sequins, florins and bezants; a few tattered parchments and the flaky, mottled skin of a snake. An oil lamp smoked in one corner of the den and gave off a pallid glow, casting more shadows than it dispelled, and the whole place stank of mice and sweat.

Khadir was sitting cross-legged on the blankets, his gray robe rucked up over his knees, exposing his scrawny legs, marked with weeping red sores, possibly from insect bites or some disease of the flesh. He was rocking back and forth, his white eyes staring. He looked like a frightened child, not an ancient Assassin.

"Khadir," said Baraka, when the soothsayer didn't acknowledge his presence. He squeezed through the tight gap in the sacks. Although Baybars had given Khadir a lavish property of his own years before, he rarely used it and could more often than not be found in this warm recess beneath the throne room. "Khadir?"

The soothsayer's gaze swiveled to Baraka. He carried on rocking.

Baraka crouched down before him. Seeing the old man like this made him feel oddly grown up. "What is it?"

"Do you hear the screams?" murmured Khadir.

Baraka frowned. "Screams?" He understood the reference after a moment and nodded. "I heard something earlier."

"Your father takes his revenge personally. Mahmud is no more. He has been sliced up like fruit and thrown into the dungeon. I expect he has bled his last now, down in that darkness."

Baraka paled as his mind turned the words into pictures. He felt nothing for Mahmud, but he was sickened by the thought that such a fate might have been his if Kalawun hadn't intervened.

"It is your fault."

"What?" Baraka rose as Khadir glared at him balefully. "How was it my fault?"

"It was Khadir, Father! Khadir and Mahmud! They made me do it! They made me!"

Baraka cringed at the hideous mimicry of his own voice. "They knew anyway," he responded quickly, though he was unable to meet Khadir's accusing stare. "Aisha told my father."

Khadir's eyes narrowed. He was on his feet in an instant. "And how did she find out?" he demanded, hooking a bony finger cruelly under Baraka's chin. "Did you tell her? Did you?"

Baraka pushed Khadir's hand away. "No," he said forcefully, taking the soothsayer by surprise with the challenge in his tone. "The day we met in the tower to discuss our plan, she saw us leave. I confronted her, but she must have told her father. That was how Kalawun knew you were involved. If he hadn't known, I would have kept quiet. I would have taken the beating for you. But it was pointless to deny it. Kalawun *knew*."

The soothsayer wheeled away. *"Kalawun,"* he spat viciously. "How cunningly that spider weaves his webs. I underestimated him and his hold on our master. My plan should have worked!" He dropped to the blankets and drew his knees up to his chest. "All the signs were right," he murmured. "It should have worked. Now we have nothing but our master's mistrust." Putting his filthy hands over his eyes, he breathed words. "I am sorry, my master. Your servant is sorry."

Disgusted, Baraka grabbed one of Khadir's arms and wrenched his hand away from his face with a force that caused the soothsayer to shriek. "You forget, Khadir, that my father isn't the only sultan. I am his heir, and when he dies, I will take his place. I have just as much authority, or I will soon. Then *your* place will be at my side, as you said before." Khadir's wide eyes focused on the youth's bruised and brazen face. "Soon," continued Baraka, "he will have forgotten his rage. All we need do is keep out of his way. Then things will go back to how they were."

Khadir reached out and touched Baraka's cheek. "You are wounded, my prince."

"That is why I came. I need you to make me a poultice."

"I will need cloth and warm water."

"I can have the servants fetch those," said Baraka, as Khadir turned to his shelf and began selecting jars from the collection arrayed there. Baraka's mouth felt dry and there was a churning in the pit of his stomach. He went to speak, but the words wouldn't come. He licked his swollen lips, tasted blood and tried again. "I also came because I want you to do something else." He watched Khadir set the jars on the floor.

"What is it, my prince?" muttered the soothsayer distractedly.

"I want you to make a poison for Aisha."

Khadir's head snapped round. "What?"

Baraka's voice was still low, but now it was firmer. It hadn't been so bad, saying the words. In fact, it had been easy. "It is her fault Kalawun found out about you and Mahmud. Don't you want her to pay?"

"She is your wife."

"In name alone. I feel nothing for her."

"What has she done, Baraka, to deserve such a punishment? Surely you cannot want her to die just because of the trouble she has caused for me, for Mahmud? Her telling Kalawun did not affect you. And besides, it is not the girl who deserves our wrath; it is that interfering wretch of a father." Khadir clenched his fists. "He is the one who should die!"

"And don't you think he will, in spirit at least, if his daughter dies?" Baraka shook his head. "You do not need to know my reasons and I do not need to tell you. All I need from you is your help, the kind of help a faithful servant would willingly give his master."

Khadir sat back on his haunches at Baraka's words, a strange expression upon his wizened face, almost a smile. After a pause, he reached into the folds of his blankets and drew out the ragged doll he had once shown Baraka, the doll Baybars had given to him at the fall of Antioch. He held it close, stroking its dirty face.

"Didn't you hear me?" demanded Baraka impatiently. "What is your answer?"

Khadir immediately put a finger to the boy's lips and made a shushing sound. Baraka drew back, but Khadir moved away and sat. Carefully, he pushed up the doll's torn and faded dress, exposing her gray, lumpy stomach. Like her back, into which Khadir had once inserted an animal's heart, her front had been cut open and sewn back together. There was a stench about her; decayed flesh and spices. Laying her lovingly across his knee, Khadir took the ends of her silk stitches and began to untie them, opening her up. With his forefingers he prised apart her insides. In the hole was nestled a black glass phial.

"What is it?" murmured Baraka, frowning.

Khadir delved in and withdrew the tiny phial. His eyes fixed on Baraka's. "How quickly the cub becomes a lion," he whispered.

"What does that mean?" asked Baraka sharply, suspecting some offense.

As Khadir passed it across the oil lamp, Baraka saw that the phial was filled with liquid. "It means you are right," said the soothsayer.

It was late afternoon, just before salat, when one of the eunuchs from the harem kitchen came to Aisha's room with a tray of food and a goblet of warm, black tea. She turned over on her bed to face the wall as the eunuch entered and set the tray on the floor; she guessed that Fatima had ordered it to be sent. Earlier on, she'd excused herself, complaining that she was feeling unwell. Fatima, who was Baybar's second wife, wanted the physicians to check her, but Aisha convinced her it wasn't serious. She just wanted to sleep and be left alone.

Since confronting Baraka, she had wrestled with what to do. Part of her had wanted to rush into Nizam's room and tell her what she had witnessed with the slave girl, but Nizam would protect her son. She guessed the best person to tell would be her father, but she was mortified by the thought of repeating to him what she had seen. Now she just wanted the whole sordid thing forgotten. At least if Baraka was seeing slave girls, she wouldn't have to be the one to go to his bed. She despised him so much that even Nizam's wrath seemed bearable when faced with the alternative. No. She would leave it be.

As the eunuch's footsteps faded and the door closed, Aisha rolled over and sat on the edge of the bed. Her monkey crawled out from under the cover, where he had been curled asleep. The food smelled good. Slipping off the bed, she sat cross-legged and took a handful of yellow, spiced rice, mixed up with raisins and apricots. Her stomach growled appreciatively. She smiled as the monkey climbed onto her shoulder, his tail brushing her cheek, and she handed him a few grains of rice, which he chewed thoughtfully. Aisha ate a little more herself, then reached for the goblet. The rice was salty and made her thirsty. She took a sip, then another. The tea was dark and heavily-spiced. It tasted a little pungent, but she finished it all the same.

After a minute or so, Aisha set the goblet down and leaned against the bed, idly stroking her monkey's back and feeling sleepy. Her eyes began to feel heavy after a time, as, she realized, did her arm. She could hardly move her fingers. She flexed them, but found them stiff and immovable, like blocks of wood. She dropped her arm to her side. Her limbs were leaden and her throat felt tight, restricted. The room looked odd, or rather her eyesight felt wrong. As she tried to stand, she found that her legs and arms weren't working properly. She stumbled onto her knees, knocking over the goblet, which clanged on the tiles. She felt suddenly scared. Her monkey had grabbed a handful of rice and was perched on the bed watching her with his tiny amber eyes. Her throat closed even further, muffling her cry as she collapsed forward onto her rigid hands. Aisha was

gasping for breath now, from fear and from the feeling of suffocation that was
growing in her throat. There was a cold numbness spreading through her. The
door seemed a hundred miles away.

19

Assassins' Stronghold, Northern Syria

26 MAY A.D. 1276

Nasir hunkered down, his back to the rock. He unhooked his waterskin
from his belt and slapped at a mosquito that landed on his neck. The
air in the mountains was blessedly cool in comparison to the savage
heat of the desert plains, but the slopes were hazy with insects. Behind the rock,
a track twisted around the mountainside, heading right, down the mountainside, and left up to the fortress above, the walls of which were scarred and
cracked.

Nasir took a drink from the skin. Through the spindly trees that covered the
slopes, he could see the plains stretched out below, the endless rise and fall of
yellow emptiness a dead place where nothing grew, yet beautiful for all its dead-
ness, a land pinned under vast skies where the shadows of clouds raced for miles.
This place was timeless. It looked the same as it had when he was a boy, living
in one of the villages scattered around the foothills. The closer he had come to
the Jabal Bahra mountains, hunting for the Assassins who had been involved in
the attempted murder of Baybars, the clearer old memories became, until now
they clung thickly around him, visible in every scrubby slope, palpable in every
gust of wind that smelled of wildflowers and heat. He had passed through this
region many times since he had left it, but always on campaign, the pounding
of soldiers' feet dulling his thoughts. But now, surrounded by silence, he only
had to close his eyes and he would hear the ring of swords and smell the smoke
as into the darkness of his mind came men with wild eyes and lunatic grins,
faces red in the swirling light of the torches they held. Women screamed and
his village burned.

At a shift in the undergrowth, Nasir's eyes opened. He reached for his sword,
but relaxed when he saw a familiar face. It was one of the four soldiers of the

Mansuriyya regiment Kalawun had sent with him from Cairo. The soldier was staying low behind the line of rocks and bushes that bordered the track.

"There's riders coming down, sir," he murmured, as he reached Nasir. "Three of them."

Nasir frowned. "Show me."

The soldier led him a short distance down the track where the slopes above dipped into a crescent, offering a clearer view of the scarred fortress. After a moment, Nasir caught sight of three horsemen on a high ridge, riding in single file.

"Do you think it's him?" asked the soldier.

"We've no way of knowing," replied Nasir. "Are the others in place?"

"Yes. But what do we do? There are three of them."

"If I verify the identity of our man, I will give the signal and we will proceed as planned."

"And the other two?"

"We will have to kill them," said Nasir grimly. "We cannot hold all three."

The soldier looked worried. For centuries, the Syrian Assassins had struck terror into the hearts of men, be they Christian, Sunni or Mongol. Fanatical followers of the Ismaili branch of the Shia faith, they were silent killers whose feats of cunning and daring were legendary. Many a leader who had opposed them or their beliefs had felt an Assassin's dagger slip between his ribs. Until five years ago, they had controlled the region from a network of strongholds, established in Saladin's time by their most famous leader, Sinan, the Old Man of the Mountain. Even now, although most of the brothers, or *fidais* as they were called, had been reduced to little more than hired killers under the control of Baybars, their name still held a vestige of that dread.

"We have the advantage of surprise," said Nasir, seeing the soldier's concern.

"I've heard it said they can't be killed by normal means," muttered the soldier.

"If they are made of flesh and blood, they can be. Let the others know. Await my signal." With that, Nasir moved back through the undergrowth to his position by the rock, where he waited, eyes on the track. The riders had gone from view, but as he heard the harsh warning cry of an eagle and the sound of loose rocks skittering down the slopes somewhere above him, he guessed they weren't far. He gripped the hilt of his sword. He wanted to draw it, but resisted the urge. It had to look as though he came in peace.

This fortress was the last stronghold in the Assassins' control. It, like all of the others, had been subsumed into Baybars's territories five years ago, after the sultan was attacked by two of their order. Mamluk officers and garrisons were installed, with the fidais kept firmly under their yoke. But the Assassins here had rebelled the previous winter and killed their new overlords, regaining possession of the fortress. At Qadamus, the last Assassin stronghold he had visited, Nasir was told that the Mamluks had attempted to retake it several times and were now awaiting fresh troops from Baybars's garrison at the nearby city of Aleppo before they tried again. It was at Qadamus that Nasir found a name. Idris al-Rashid. He had interrogated several fidais in his search for those who had been involved in Baybars's attack, but they had refused to inform on their brothers and were subsequently executed by their Mamluk masters: disloyalty to the new regime wasn't to be tolerated. One fidai, however, was more forthcoming and offered up the name and Idris's likely location at the rebel fortress.

Nasir crouched lower, hearing the hoofbeats grow louder. He looked at the trees on the other side of the track. A slight movement in the brush told him his men were in place. A few moments later, the three riders appeared around a bend in the hillside. They looked watchful as they came; two held bows in their hands. The man in front was olive-skinned like his comrades, but stockier in build and older. After they had passed by, Nasir stepped out from behind his hiding place. "Idris," he called.

Instantly, the three men wheeled their horses around. The nearest to Nasir dropped his reins, snatched an arrow from the quiver on his back and fitted it to his bow in a matter of seconds.

Nasir held up his hands as the weapon was pointed at him. "I am here to see Idris. I mean you no harm."

The older man jumped lightly down from his horse and approached Nasir. "I am Idris," he said calmly.

"I sent the message to you," replied Nasir. "I have information on the forthcoming attack the Mamluks at Qadamus are planning against you."

"You are the deserter?"

Nasir glanced at the younger men, who both had bows trained on him. "I asked you to come alone."

"And you said you wished to meet me in the village," responded Idris, still in that calm tone. "So we have both broken our word."

"It was too open in the village. I don't want anyone to see me talking to you. I cannot risk being found by the Mamluks. They crucify deserters. I just want money and then I can disappear. That's why I came to you."

"Who gave you my name?"

"A friend."

"I have no friends."

Nasir didn't reply. He raised his hand. Two arrows shot out of the trees on the opposite side of the track and slammed into the mounted men. One was shot in the neck, the other in the back. Both dropped their holds on their weapons, one slipping from his saddle, the other slumping forward. Idris's horse reared in fright and took off down the track, swiftly followed by the other two, one dragging the fallen Assassin, whose foot had caught in the stirrup, the other still bearing its slumped rider. Within moments of the first arrow being shot, Idris had wrenched a gold-handled dagger from his belt, but Nasir had drawn his sword and two Mamluk soldiers were now darting from the brush to aid him. Idris managed to stab one of the soldiers in the thigh, before a hood was thrown over his head and the three Mamluks grappled him to the ground. He struggled wildly, his bulky body almost throwing them off. Then Nasir slammed the hilt of his sword into the base of his skull and the Assassin slumped in their grasp.

"Are you all right?" Nasir asked the soldier who had been wounded.

The soldier was breathing hard through gritted teeth, and blood had stained his blue robes, but he nodded. "Yes, sir."

Nasir gestured to the other soldiers who had emerged from the brush, bows in hands. "Find the horses and the bodies, and bring them to the cave. We must dispose of them. Quickly."

The soldiers headed off, keeping close to the bushes.

"Help me with him," said Nasir to the others, gripping Idris under the arms.

Together, they carried the unconscious Assassin away from the track, down through a tree-tangled gully. The way was steep, and they had to scramble over rocks and avoid sudden fissures that yawned to either side. Eventually, they reached the cave where they had set up camp four days ago. The two squires who had come with them from Cairo were there, along with their horses. "Get me rope," gasped Nasir, hauling Idris into the cave. The squires obliged, and soon Idris was propped upright on the damp ground inside, his back against a stout pillar of rock to which he was bound by his stomach and neck. His hands were tied behind him, his feet secured at the ankles. Nasir took the hood from Idris's head. Blood had stained the material. He checked the wound his sword hilt had made, but it was only superficial. Idris groaned groggily. Taking his skin, Nasir poured water into his palm and splashed it over the Assassin's face. After a moment, Idris's gaze focused. Nasir stooped before him. "I have been sent by Sultan Baybars to find those who were contracted to kill him five years ago."

"Those men are dead. You have wasted your time."

"Only two were killed that day. From what I have been told, there were others involved in the plot. I have heard that you are the one who ordered the death. I want to know who contracted you. Sultan Baybars believes it was the Franks. He wishes to know the names of those who paid you for your service."

"You will not get that information from me. Again, I say, you have wasted your time." Idris met Nasir's gaze. "You should kill me. I will not betray my oaths to my order or dishonor private agreements."

"There are worse things than death, Idris," said Nasir. He rose. "I used to live close by to this place when I was a boy, until my village was attacked and I was forced to flee. Eight years later, I was at Baghdad when the Mongols stormed the city. I escaped the butchery, only to be sold into slavery. I was bought by the Mamluks. The first thing they taught me was how to be a good Muslim."

Idris spat on the ground. "They taught you to be a Sunni. It is not the same thing."

"The second thing they taught me was how to kill," continued Nasir. "And the third thing." He crouched again before Idris. "The third thing they taught me, when I became an officer, was how to inflict pain. How to keep a man alive for weeks, yet in agony. Which wounds will hurt and which will kill. I am sure you are very strong, Idris, steadfast in your faith. But I will take what I need from you."

THE CHURCH OF SAN MARCO, THE VENETIAN QUARTER, ACRE, 26 MAY A.D. 1276

The voices of the congregation joined in song as the priest closed the breviary and the choir led the last hymn of the Vespers service. Besina rocked her baby in her arms, making shushing sounds as the singing woke him with a start and he began to cry. Beside her, Andreas put his arm around Catarina, who yawned widely. Andreas leaned over to Elwen as the rows of people at the back of the church began to file out, the song drifting to an end. "Here," he said, handing her a small pouch, "for the alms box. I'm going to take the girls outside."

Elwen took the pouch and waited until the people beside her had shuffled out of their places before making her way down the crowded aisle to where the priest was talking with several members of the congregation. One of his acolytes held a wooden box with a hole cut into the top. He nodded quiet thanks to those

who paused to place a few pennies inside, charitable donations for the poor. Elwen shook three gold coins into her hand, noting Andreas's generosity.

The acolyte's eyes widened a little when she dropped them in. "Thank you,"
he said earnestly.

"They're from my master, Andreas di Paolo."

"He will be remembered in our prayers."

Elwen crossed to one of the side aisles where the crowds were thinner.
She had to pause behind a group of people as the last of the congregation
trickled out into the amber evening. Someone grabbed her arm. Turning,
startled, she found herself staring at Will. He wore the cowl of his black cloak
pulled over his head and his face was shadowed. "What are you doing here?"
she whispered.

"I had to see you." His expression was tense.

"What is it? What has happened? Is it Everard?"

Will realized that the last Elwen knew was that the priest was dying. He
hadn't seen her since that day in the market, almost two weeks ago. "Everard's
fine. He lied about being ill." He shook his head impatiently as she frowned
questioningly. "I'll explain another time. It isn't important now. Listen, Elwen,
I have to leave Acre for a while."

"Where are you going?"

"That doesn't matter. I just needed you to know."

Elwen stared at him for a long moment, then removed her arm from his
grip. "No, Will, that isn't good enough. You cannot come in here like this, tell
me you're leaving and expect me just to nod and smile and bid you good-bye
without being told anything of where you're going or why, or for how long."

"I don't know that."

"You don't know where you're going?" she said bitingly.

"For how long. I don't know for how long. Maybe a few weeks, maybe
longer."

"No," she repeated, louder now. An acolyte looked reprovingly over at her
and began to head in their direction. "You're not going to keep doing this!"

"Elwen," Will hissed as she pulled away and headed for the doors. He tried
to grab her, but she had gone. Pushing his way through the last few stragglers,
Will followed her out into the balmy air, down the steps into the street.
"Elwen!"

She turned on him, stopping him in his tracks with the anger in her green
eyes. "I cannot do this anymore, Will. I *cannot*."

People were glancing curiously at them.

"Elwen."

They both turned at the voice to see Andreas standing there with his family. Catarina waved at Will, who avoided the Venetian mercer's stern gaze.

"Andreas," said Elwen, falteringly.

"We'll meet you back at the house," Andreas told her, taking his wife's arm.

Besina, who had been frowning at Elwen, looked inquiringly at her husband, but let herself be led off.

Elwen watched them go, her cheeks flushed. Her anger seemed to drain from her, her shoulders slumping. "Why are you doing this to me?" she said tiredly, looking back at Will.

As he saw the hurt in her face, Will wanted nothing more than to sweep her into his arms and hold her there until that pain was driven out. But he refused to allow himself to give in to that. He had to be stone and steel. He had pledged himself to the Anima Templi, to the work his father had begun. He couldn't turn his back on that, not when he knew what was at stake. He was the one who had discovered the truth about the Stone. He was the one who would stop the theft from happening. "I didn't want to leave without telling you. I didn't want you to wonder where I was. But also I need you to know that I cannot tell you more than that."

"And I need you to know that I do not accept that." Elwen drew in a rapid breath, then let it out slowly. "I'm leaving you, Will."

Will stood there, stunned, and watched her walk away.

Then, his feet were taking him forward and he was racing toward her, not caring that his cloak had come open and the white of his surcoat was revealed beneath. "I'm doing this for you!" She kept on walking, but he grasped her and turned her forcibly to face him. "I'm doing this so that we *have* a future. If I don't ..." He lowered his voice. "If I don't, then none of us will. Acre is in danger, Elwen, great danger. I have to go for all our sakes."

Elwen searched his eyes for a lie, but found only the intensity of truth. "What danger? And why you?" she demanded. "Why not someone else? I need a reason to stay, Will. So far all you've done is scare me." Her brow was furrowed. "*Tell* me."

Will looked at her desperately, then his jaw tightened and he led her into an alleyway close by. "You cannot speak of this to anyone else. I mean it. If you do, you could jeopardize everything."

"I give you my word."

Elwen remained silent as Will told her that men, the grand master possibly among them, were planning to steal the Black Stone of the Ka'ba, a plan which, if accomplished, would plunge them all into the bloodiest war they had ever known. He told her how he had discovered this plan, aided by Everard and, without mentioning anything of the Anima Templi or Kalawun, explained how he had formed a relationship with a Mamluk high up in the Egyptian Army, whom he needed to warn.

When he had finished, Elwen's face was grave with concern. "You're going to Cairo?" she murmured. "Alone?"

"I leave tonight. These people need to be stopped. They cannot be allowed to do this. It will be the end of everything if they do."

Elwen was shocked to feel a sudden hope for this. If the Mamluks came for Acre, the Christians wouldn't stand a chance. They would all be forced to return to the West and then the knights, *Will*, would have nothing left to fight for. It would be over. All of it. But she pushed the foolish hope aside, knowing that it wouldn't be like that. The Christians wouldn't just give Acre up; they would fight tooth and nail to the death for it. They would die by the thousands. "I don't want you to go," she whispered.

Will drew her into his arms. She tensed for a second, resisting, then softened in his embrace. Raising her head, her lips found his and they kissed, lightly at first, then more ardently. As she opened her mouth over his, their tongues moving together, Elwen pushed back his cowl with her hands until she reached the nape of his neck, where his black hair was curled and damp from the heat. When she grabbed at him, her nails scraping skin, she heard a strained, almost animal noise come from deep within his throat. Lifting her up, Will pushed her against the alley wall. His black cloak fell from his shoulders to pool like a puddle around his feet as she wrapped her legs about his waist, her skirts slipping up. She held on tight.

"Do you love me?" she whispered fiercely.

He dragged off her coif to release her hair. "Yes."

As the bells of San Marco began to toll the hour, they made desperate love in the alleyway, where rats scurried in the rubbish heaps and shadows closed around them like a veil.

THE CITADEL, CAIRO, 26 MAY A.D. 1276

"Where is she? *Where?*"

Kalawun pushed past the guards who had escorted him into the harem palace and sprinted down the passage, sending servants scuttling out of his way. Seeing a knot of people clustered outside a chamber, the door of which was open, he barged through. Baybars's wives, Nizam and Fatima, were by a bed with one of the palace physicians. Nizam turned as he came forward. Her expression was as hard as ever. "Amir," she began.

Kalawun took no notice, but rushed to the bed, where a body was lying. He looked down upon his daughter's face and shock twisted freezing hands around his heart. Aisha's brown eyes were wide and staring. Her skin was waxy in the light of the oil lanterns, cast with a bluish tinge. His gaze traveled the length of her, taking in the stiffness in her limbs, the hands locked in clawed fists. Then he returned to her contorted face, her open mouth, the tongue protruding, purple and swollen. His first thought, which followed the initial shock with an odd detachment, was that she had been strangled. But there were no marks on her neck. He reached for her, then drew back with a jolt as his fingertips brushed her skin. She was cold.

"Did you say the Shahada?" he whispered, not looking round.

"We only found her a short while ago," replied Nizam.

The physician took a step forward. "I would estimate, Amir Kalawun, that she has been dead for some time, perhaps as long as four hours. I'm afraid it would appear that your daughter choked on her food."

Kalawun paid him no heed, but leaned forward and breathed words into his daughter's ear. *"Ashadu an la ilaha illa-llah. Wa ashhadu anna Muhammadan rasul-Ullah."*

"Where is my son?" Nizam demanded of someone behind him. "Have the servants not found him yet? Baraka should be here."

Beyond the voices of Nizam and the other women, Kalawun could hear shrieking, but his mind was now collapsing in on itself, folding down in anguish, and he neither knew nor cared where it was coming from as he gathered his daughter's lifeless body into his arms. His cries felt as though they were being wrenched from him, each one containing the rawest grief and the purest loss, painful in the extreme as they were torn from his throat. Tears blinded him as he rocked with her. The shrieking continued. Dimly, he heard Nizam's sharp voice.

"Remove it!" she was shouting. "Get that thing out of here!"

Through his streaming eyes, Kalawun saw a tiny brown shape hunched on the chamber's window ledge. The monkey's whole body was quivering, its amber eyes wide and terror-stricken. It was screaming. A eunuch approached and tried to reach up, but the monkey leapt backward and jumped onto the window grille, where it clung wretchedly. As Kalawun's gaze moved away, he caught sight of a platter of food and a goblet on a tray near the head of the bed. It looked like it had been pushed hastily aside, the goblet lying on a half-eaten pile of dry, yellow rice. The eunuch was still trying to capture the monkey. Something brushed through Kalawun's mind, a pale ghost of a thought. It formed into a specter, rising dark before him. Abruptly, he let Aisha down on the bed and stood. "Who brought her the food?" His voice was weak and at first didn't carry above the monkey's cries and Nizam's harsh orders. "Who?" he demanded when no one answered. He turned to them as they fell silent. "Who brought her this?"

"One of the palace servants," replied Nizam, "before salat. She had asked to be left alone. One of the girls came in to clear the tray and found her on the floor."

"She retired early to her bed," added Fatima, unable to meet Kalawun's intense gaze, "saying that she wasn't feeling well."

"Before she ate the food or after?"

Nizam frowned. "I do not understand what you—"

"Tell me!" raged Kalawun, making her start and step back a pace. "Did she say she was unwell before or after she had eaten?"

"Before," said Fatima.

Kalawun faltered, but he shook his head. "Find me the eunuch who brought her the food. I want to question him." He turned to the physician. "You will check it for poison."

"Poison?" began the physician.

"It cannot be," said Nizam firmly, recovering her poise. "When I came in, I found that vermin eating the food." She gestured at the monkey, which the eunuch had given up attempting to grab. "It would be dead by now if the food was poisoned."

"What about the drink?" Kalawun stooped and snatched up the empty goblet, he sniffed inside, then passed it to the physician. "I want this checked. Now!"

"Amir, with all due respect, without the presence of any liquid, no tests can be accurately performed."

But Kalawun was already pushing his way out of the room. The nervous women thronging the doorway fell fearfully back. His face was murderous as he made his way out of the harem and across the courtyard into the main palace buildings. His suspicion had become certainty, and his grief now towered like a vast wall of water behind a dam of rage. He walked swiftly, running when he reached the stairs, heading down into the lower levels. Kalawun found Khadir curled on a filthy blanket in his den, snoring. He woke the soothsayer with a kick. "Get up!"

Khadir leapt to his feet. He hissed, then yelled as Kalawun slammed him against the wall.

"What did you do to her? *Tell me!*"

Khadir screeched, his white eyes huge with fear, thin arms flailing, struggling vainly to push against Kalawun's muscular form. Outside in the passage, a servant, hearing the commotion, looked inside the storeroom. Seeing Kalawun attacking the soothsayer, he rushed off. Kalawun's eyes alighted on the timber shelf, lined with strange objects and jars of colored powders. Pushing Khadir roughly to the floor, he dropped down and began grabbing at jars, pulling off their cloth coverings. Khadir wailed in protest as Kalawun held each to his nose, before throwing them aside, sending golden and rust-colored dust across the floor and blankets. Glass shattered as, one by one, he discarded cinnamon, clove, cardamom, ginger. He then swiped at the other objects lining the shelves, sweeping them all off, the fragile skulls breaking, glass beads cascading. As Khadir fell on him, Kalawun threw him off and pinned him down on the blankets, his hands wrapping around the old man's scrawny neck.

Kalawun didn't hear the shouts in the passage outside, or the running footsteps; he only heard Khadir's choking, rasping noises as he tried futilely to breathe. Hands gripped his arms. He felt himself being hauled backward. "No!" he shouted, his hands still squeezing Khadir's neck. The soothsayer's face was purple and his eyes were bulging. Kalawun felt a muscular arm lock around his own neck, tightening his airway, stopping up breath. Instinctively, he let go of Khadir, who flopped back on the blankets, gasping desperately. Grabbing at the arm around his neck, Kalawun just managed to turn his head enough to see that it was Baybars who had hold of him.

"Enough, Kalawun," said the sultan.

"He killed her," panted Kalawun, his eyes alight. "My daughter's dead and he killed her!"

"I came to the harem palace moments after you left," said Baybars. "Nizam told me your daughter choked on her food."

Kalawun shook his head. "It was him. I found Baraka out and made your son admit who helped him. I uncovered this traitor. Khadir was an Assassin, Baybars. He knows how to use poisons. It was him."

Khadir was rolling around on the floor, choking and retching.

"And he will be punished for his part in that plan," said Baybars firmly, "but not for something he did not do."

"I want the food checked. Every last scrap of it. I want it checked."

"And it will be. But even if poison is found, and I do not believe it will be, it would be more likely to have come from within the harem. Aisha was the first wife of my son, the bride of the heir to the kingdom. Women, in my experience, can be as hungry for power as men and sometimes more ruthless in the pursuit of it. It would not be the first murder within those walls." Kalawun was starting to shake, high keening sounds building in the back of his throat. Baybars put his other arm around the trembling commander and held him. "I am sorry, my friend," he murmured. "Truly I am. We have both lost a daughter today. The kingdom will mourn her."

At those last words, the dam inside Kalawun broke and his grief engulfed him in a rushing, tumbling torrent. Khadir crawled limply to the wall, where he hunched, bitterly savoring every one of the commander's wrenching sobs.

Baraka Khan walked unsteadily into the night, dazedly passing the harem guards. The wind had picked up and blew hot and dusty around him, drying the sweat on his face. An image of Aisha lying stiff on the bed jumped into his mind: her pallid, twisted face and her tongue poking hideously from between her teeth. Baraka paused by one of the palm trees that bordered the courtyard, pressing his hand against the solid, rough bark. He retched, doubled over and vomited. His eyes watered as he retched again. Then, slowly, he straightened and walked on. Now he was purged, he felt better.

20

The Street of St. Anne, Acre

27 MAY A.D. 1276

"Well, find me someone who does know where he is. I'll not give you money for nothing." Garin gritted his teeth as the young servant scuttled across the street and back through the preceptory's gates.

He leaned against the wall of the shop behind him and tried to rein in his anger. It was more than two hours past the time that Will had promised to meet him in the tavern. Now King Hugh had signed the document promising to let Edward use Cyprus as a base for a holy war and to deliver a substantial sum of money—half now and half when Edward had spoken to the pope had been his condition—Garin was almost ready to return to England. He just needed to collect the gold from Everard, and then his business here would finally be done.

He looked up as the small door in the preceptory's massive gates opened again and tutted irritably as he saw a familiar, barrel-chested figure striding across the road toward him. There was no sign of the servant.

Simon's broad face was set with anger. "What do you want?"

With massive effort, Garin managed to force a smile. "Simon."

"Save the horseshit. I'm not here to make conversation with you. Leave the servants alone. They're not yours to command and they aren't allowed to accept bribes. That boy would've been beaten if you'd paid him and he'd been found out."

"I'm sorry," said Garin contritely, "I forgot. Well, maybe you can help. Will was supposed to meet me this afternoon, but he hasn't, and as he was well aware of the importance of our engagement, I can only assume something very serious must have delayed him. Perhaps you could tell me where I might find him?"

Simon stepped closer to Garin. "Will might have forgotten what you did to him back in Paris, but I haven't. You're a dog and if I had my way you'd have been put down years ago. There's no good in you, and all your pretty smiles won't fool me otherwise. I see through you. Whatever you want with Will, you'll not get it. I'll make certain of it."

Garin's smile faded. "I think that's up to Will, don't you?" he murmured. "You're not his nursemaid, Tanner, nor his commander. You're a lowborn stable hand. You should leave the big decisions to men of rank and keep to what you know best. Shit and straw."

"I'll keep to mine if you keep to yours. And at the last look that was ale and whores." Turning, Simon headed back across the street.

"You're not the only one in the Temple," called Garin, stalking after him. "I'll pay a dozen servants if I have to. I'm not leaving until I see Will."

"You'll have a long wait then," retorted Simon, glancing back before he reached the gates. "Commander Campbell is away on business. And will be for weeks, months maybe." He paused before opening the door. "Whatever it is you were after, you can forget it. Will's gone. Go back to England. You're not wanted here." With that, Simon entered the preceptory and shut the gate.

Garin stood in the street, trembling with rage. As he turned to move off, a young woman clutching a basket filled with fruit got in his way and he pushed her roughly aside. She stumbled with a cry, dropping her basket, sending the fruit spilling. A man shouted at Garin and jogged over to help her, but Garin was already walking away. He kept going for several minutes, before swerving abruptly into a narrow pathway between two bakers' shops. With a harsh cry, he slammed his fist into the wall. The skin across his knuckles tore and pain shot through him, but he punched it again, a second time, almost relishing the agony. He put his palms flat against the wall and rested his head on it. After a few moments, he pushed himself upright. If Simon wouldn't speak to him, there was one other who might.

THE TEMPLE, ACRE, 27 MAY A.D. 1276

"Enter," called Everard tiredly at a rap at the door. He set down his quill on his chronicle. His memory wasn't what it used to be, and he had come to fear that if he didn't write things down he would forget them. He wouldn't have the others questioning his judgment. He had made enough mistakes.

The seneschal strode in. "What have you done, Everard?"

Everard looked up with a frown.

"Brother Thomas has just told me everything." The seneschal's brow was knotted. "Why didn't you wait for me? I should have been part of this."

"You weren't here, my friend," replied Everard matter-of-factly. "I had to make the decision. There was no time to lose."

"So you sent Campbell to Cairo on his own? Into the lion's den, where God only knows what trouble he'll get into? Are you forgetting, Everard, that he betrayed us once before? I never would have sanctioned such a move had I been here."

"Campbell has dealt with Kalawun in the past. The two met face-to-face when he delivered the peace treaty to Baybars. De Beaujeu has been informed that he is securing a valuable treatise in Syria that will greatly benefit the Temple, so his absence will not arouse suspicions. If not for him, Brother, we wouldn't know that any of this was happening."

"From what Brother Thomas told me, Campbell might not have informed us at all if not for the fact that he couldn't decipher the message and needed you to do it for him."

"But he did tell us," replied Everard wearily, "and now we know. We must put our differences aside. This overshadows all else. Nothing can matter except that we stop it."

The seneschal said nothing for a moment, then pulled up a stool and sat. "Sclavo is dead," he said gruffly. "It happened shortly after he was brought in."

"What? Why did none of us hear of this?"

"There was little to report. All the attention had shifted to Soranzo by that point and no one cared about some petty criminal."

"How did he die?"

"It isn't known. He collapsed after breaking his fast one morning. The physician said his heart had given out."

"Poisoned?" asked Everard quickly.

"At the time, I did not think it suspicious, but from what Brother Thomas has told me it would seem that maybe there was a reason for his death. Maybe someone did not want him talking. Why did you wish to speak with him anyway?"

"He dealt with Soranzo, who knew the grand master was involved in the proposed theft of the Black Stone. It is possible he knew more about the plot itself. I had hoped to interrogate him."

"I think we should concentrate on the grand master," responded the seneschal after a pause. "He is obviously at the center of this."

"We do not know for certain that de Beaujeu knows of the plan, Brother. The message from Kaysan doesn't seem to be addressing him."

"Soranzo told Campbell that the grand master would burn because of the Stone; de Beaujeu gave Campbell the scroll and told him to meet this Kaysan, and this scroll apparently speaks of Western knights who will enter Mecca with these Shias and steal it. I would, in truth, be very surprised if he didn't know anything of it."

"I agree, but we must have more facts before we can proceed."

"What about this man, Angelo Vitturi? Could he have been involved? It was unorthodox that the grand master should send a merchant to interrogate Soranzo. Perhaps we should look into him, his business here in the city, his connections with de Beaujeu?"

"Not yet. Not until we know more. If he is involved, then I do not wish to alert him to the fact that we know anything. For the moment, we would appear to have time on our side. From what the scroll says, the theft will not occur until during the month of Muharram, which would put it sometime during April next year." He clasped his hands on the table. "I am convinced that will give us enough chance to act."

The seneschal shook his head. "We had better hope so, Everard. Or God help us all."

THE VENETIAN MARKET, ACRE, 27 MAY A.D. 1276

Elwen closed the blue door behind her and moved listlessly into the street. She had a leather bag over her shoulder with the ledgers in that Andreas had asked her to bring to the warehouse. A young man and woman passed her, their arms linked. The man bent down and whispered something and the woman laughed. As the woman locked eyes with her, Elwen averted her gaze, realizing she had been staring. She continued walking, head down.

The brief euphoria she had experienced last night with Will had faded quickly. It followed the same pattern it always had. They made love and he left. There were no languid, tender moments, no comfortable silences or shared laughter, just frantic passion, soon spent, and a feeling of emptiness that lingered long after he slipped from her. He had been honest with her this time; had let her in for once, and that at least was something, but even so, nothing had really changed. She felt as though she had been fooled.

Elwen was roused from her thoughts by someone calling her name. For a moment, she thought it was Will, and she turned, hopeful and uplifted. But there was no sign of him, only a tall, blond-haired man who smiled as he approached her.

"Elwen," he said again.

She stared at him, then recognition dawned. "Garin," she murmured.

"How are you? It's been ... how long?"

Elwen's initial shock quickly turned to hostility. "What are you doing here?"

Garin looked surprised. "Will didn't tell you I was in Acre?"

"No. What do you want?"

"I wanted to see you actually."

Elwen looked around. "How did you know where I would be?"

"Will told me where you lived," Garin replied offhand. "I saw you come out."

"I'm busy," said Elwen, moving off, confused and unsettled as to why Will had given this information to him.

"I do not wish to keep you," said Garin, following her. "I just want to know where Will is. He promised to meet me earlier, but he never showed up."

"He promises a great many things."

Garin caught the anger in her words. "But you know where he is?"

"No."

Garin heard the lie in her voice. "Elwen, this is important. Please. I know we've never been good friends, but you do know me. Surely you can tell me this?"

Elwen came to a halt. "Yes, I know you," she said frigidly. "I know you lured Will to that brothel in Paris with a message you pretended was from me. I know you watched as he was bound and beaten, and then forced him to tell you what you wanted to know by saying you had captured me and would hurt me if he didn't comply. I know you drugged him and tied him to a bed, and let that woman—" Elwen stopped abruptly. "I have nothing to say to you."

"Did he tell you why?" Garin demanded, before she could walk away. "Did he tell you that I was being threatened by someone? That this man, Rook, made me do these things with the promise that if I didn't he would kill my mother. And before he did that, that he would *rape* her?" He emphasized that word to provoke her womanly fear of such an act and was satisfied with the appalled look that flashed across Elwen's face. "I didn't leave him in bed with anyone, Elwen," he continued quietly. "What happened with the woman was a mistake. I thought I was saving his life by drugging him. Rook wanted to kill him." Garin ran a hand through his hair. "I'm sorry, I truly am. I wish I could change it."

Elwen winced as she caught sight of his torn and bloodied knuckles. "What did you do?"

Garin glanced at his hand and tried to hide it behind his back. "It's nothing." He shrugged, then laughed self-consciously. "I punched a wall."

Elwen went to say something, then shook her head. "I have to go."

"Listen, I was about to buy myself a drink. Why don't you join me?" Garin pointed down the street. "There's a tavern just over there."

Now it was Elwen's turn to laugh, in astonishment. "Even if I wanted to drink with you, which I don't, do you honestly think it would be seemly for a woman like myself to share wine in some common tavern with a man?"

"This coming from a woman who once stowed away on board a Templar ship?" Garin shot back.

Elwen smiled slightly at the memory, then looked away. "That was a long time ago." She started walking again.

Garin went after her, his mind locking desperately on one last idea. He had to know if Will really was gone or if Simon had been lying to him. "Just tell me one thing," he implored. "Does Will's absence have anything to do with Everard and the Anima Templi?" He fought back an urge to grin as a frown creased her brow.

"The what?"

"Oh," he said quickly, "nothing." Garin backed away. "Look, if Will comes back anytime soon, just tell him to find me."

"Wait," said Elwen. "Explain what you said."

Garin came to a stop. "All right. But not in the street. And you didn't hear this from me." He gestured to the tavern. "In there."

He opened the door for her as they reached the building. Elwen halted, looking up and down the street, terrified that someone she knew would see her. But Garin was at her back, ushering her inside, and so she stepped quickly, nervously over the threshold. Elwen kept her head down as Garin motioned her to a table.

He bought two cups of wine before returning to sit with her. "Drink this," he said, pushing a cup across the table.

She took several sips. "Talk to me."

Elwen was silent as he leaned across the table and told her in hushed tones of a secret organization within the Temple, known as the Anima Templi. The Soul of the Temple had been established almost a century ago, and many men had pledged themselves to its cause. At its heart it was dedicated to the reconciliation of Muslims, Christians and Jews, and formed relationships with men from different backgrounds and faiths to further this idealistic cause, all the while in secrecy, without the knowledge of the members' brothers in the Temple. He told her how Will's father had been a member, as had his own uncle, Jacques, who had been killed in France along with Elwen's uncle, Owein, in an attack by mercenaries years before. He told her how Will had been initiated into this group back in Paris by Everard, their head, and how he now worked against his own masters, breaking the oaths he took when he became a knight—to fulfill the Brethren's ultimate aim. And he told her how Will, after the death of his father, had gone behind even Everard's back to pay the Order of Assassins to murder Baybars in retribution for James's execution.

By the time he had finished, Elwen's face was taut and pale. She sat back, knocking over her wine. She hardly noticed. She tried to conjure an image of Will, but what came was clouded and obscure. She knew that he and Everard were involved in something. But this? This was more than she could comprehend. This changed him as a person, as the man she thought she knew. He had paid to have someone murdered. How could he have kept that from her? And if he lied so easily, every day, to his masters and his friends in the Temple, how easy must it be for him to lie to her? All those promises that he loved her; were they real, or did he just want a faithful whore for free? Was that why he wouldn't marry her? *You don't know him,* said a voice inside. *You never have.*

"I cannot believe he hasn't told you any of this," said Garin.

"Was it all a lie?" she asked him numbly. "Were the things he said about the Stone and the war just made up? Did he tell me those things so I wouldn't leave him?"

"Stone?"

"The Black Stone of Mecca," Elwen snapped at him. "He said the grand master is involved in a plot to steal it, that it's the holiest relic of the

Saracens and that if it is stolen there will be war. Do you know about it?" she demanded.

"I …"

"He said he was the only one who could stop it," Elwen cut across him, "that he was going to warn a contact in the Mamluks in Cairo and save us all." She laughed bitterly. "Just how much of a fool have I been? I need to know." Her face hardened. "Was any of it true? Any of it at all?" She rose. "Or did he just say it so that I would …" But she couldn't finish. She felt sick.

"I don't know," said Garin distractedly. He glanced up at her. "I know he has to lie sometimes to cover things he is doing, although I cannot offer you an answer about this. But I guess I now know why he didn't meet me."

Elwen went to speak, then shook her head and pulled off the table her leather bag with Andreas's ledgers in it. It caught the fallen cup, which rolled off and shattered on the stone floor.

Garin watched as she fled the tavern. He drained the rest of his wine as a servant girl came to gather up the broken pieces of the cup, his mind picking over Elwen's words like a crow with a carcass.

21

The Royal Palace, Acre

27 MAY A.D. 1276

It was late in the evening when Garin returned to the royal palace. He had spent several hours in the tavern after Elwen had left, then several more walking off the alcohol he had consumed, until his thoughts, moving in slow, determined circles, had finally come to a point of clarity. He found King Hugh alone in the throne room, checking through a pile of papers on the desk where his clerk would usually sit. One of the servants admitted him.

"Well?" said Hugh, glancing at Garin as he approached, then turning his attention back to the papers. "Is it done, your other business? Guy has found you a place on a ship that is due to leave for England in two days."

"I'm afraid I could not meet the man I went to see."

Hugh's eyes narrowed. He set down the sheets. "What?"

"My business has not finished here."

Anger built in the young king's face. "I have had enough of your excuses. I signed that damn document and I demand that you return to Edward with it at once. De Beaujeu has begun a campaign of hatred against me, and my subjects no longer show me the respect I deserve," Hugh's voice snapped out. "He may not have my throne yet, but d'Anjou's minions work swiftly to secure support for him. I am running out of time." He threw some of the papers on the floor and stalked to his throne, where he sat, his head in his hand. "I cannot do this alone, by God! Why are they all against me? What did I do to deserve their betrayal?"

"I might be able to help, Your Majesty."

Hugh looked at Garin as if he had forgotten he was there. He waved a tired hand. "Begone."

"I have discovered that one of your enemies is involved in something that you may be able to turn to your advantage."

"Just go."

Garin moved closer to the throne. "De Beaujeu is planning to steal the Black Stone of Mecca."

Hugh dropped his hand to the throne's arm and pushed himself up. "What did you say?"

"The Black Stone of Mecca. It is apparently a relic that the Saracen's—"

"I know what it is," said Hugh swiftly. "Tell me where you heard this."

"The man I was going to meet today has gone to Cairo to warn the Mamluks of this plan. That's why I couldn't see him."

"This man? He is a Saracen?"

"No, he's a Templar. His identity isn't relevant at the moment," Garin continued, seeing Hugh's confusion. "All you need to know is that he has allies within the Mamluk Army. My guess is he will attempt to stop this from happening."

"As well he should," said Hugh, "for such an act could devastate us all." He rose from his throne. "Why would de Beaujeu do this? It makes no sense. He must know we could not hold back a determined Saracen force."

"I don't know. But I believe this could benefit you."

Hugh was shaking his head, not listening. "I have nowhere near enough men to fight a war; even if all my vassals from Cyprus were to come to our aid, it would not be enough. Baybars would have thousands, *hundreds* of thousands. And if they would not all fight for the man, they would certainly fight for his cause. We would be devastated. The Saracens would *erase* us from this Earth."

"Not necessarily," said Garin. Hugh looked at him. "What if de Beaujeu stole the Stone, Your Majesty, then we, in turn, took it from him and offered it back to Baybars?" Hugh was frowning, but his dark eyes followed Garin, who began to pace. Garin's face was animated, his hands moving as he talked. He had worked this through during the long afternoon, going over and over it, until his mind was feverish. "We find out more about this plan, when it will occur and who will be involved. We take the Stone for ourselves and we tell Baybars that we have saved the Muslims' relic and are willing to bring it safely to him in return for certain favors."

"What favors?"

"Whatever we want. Your throne, for instance?"

Hugh was quiet for some moments. "Baybars could intervene in this matter," he said slowly. "But it does not mean that d'Anjou will listen to him."

"He might if Baybars threatened to destroy us all, which, as you say, the sultan would if the Stone was stolen. D'Anjou would not want to rule over a kingdom in ruins. It would be in his best interests to comply. And it is not simply your throne we could save," continued Garin, when Hugh didn't speak. "How would it be if you were the king who took back Jerusalem?" As Hugh's hands tightened on the arms of his throne, Garin nodded, noting his interest. "We would tell Baybars that we wanted the Holy City in return for the Stone. Your throne, my lord, would once again stand in its rightful place. I would imagine your subjects would quickly be shown the error of their judgment were that to happen. I doubt even d'Anjou would dare to challenge you if you secured Jerusalem. And the pope?" Garin's smile widened. "I expect you wouldn't be able to prise his grateful lips from your hand long enough for him to congratulate you."

Hugh's expression was intent. But he shook his head. "Baybars could come anyway. He could take the Stone for himself and kill us all. He would be capable of it."

"Baybars isn't a fool, my lord. It would take time, money and effort to capture Acre. And we could destroy the Stone before he did. It would be much simpler and safer for him to give in to our demands. I'm sure the Saracens would attempt to take back Jerusalem in time, but our chances of holding the city are much greater than our chances of retaking it. Then, my Lord Edward could return to these shores at the head of an army and begin a new Crusade against the infidel, with your help, from out of the gates of the Holy City itself. It would be like the First Crusade. Men would flock to your banners. No more tributes, my lord," said Garin. "No more bowing to the infidels' demands."

As Hugh took in these words, Garin watched him. He had to see what an audacious plan this was. What did it matter that Will was a commander in the Temple? He, Garin, was going to save Jerusalem. The troubadours would sing songs about him. His name would go down in history. And Edward? Well, there would be no more broken promises, no more dingy towers, no more veiled threats. Edward would give him that lordship and that grand estate if he made this happen. He was certain of it.

Hugh was speaking. "How would it work?"

Garin looked up, distracted from his thoughts. "First, we need to find out more. The details."

"And how will we do this?"

"I think I've found someone who will be able to help us. I'm just going to have to work on her a little more."

The doors opened and a figure hurried toward the throne. It was Guy. "My lord," he said in greeting, casting a suspicious look at Garin.

"Do we no longer knock, Guy?" demanded Hugh.

"It is important, my lord." Guy looked again at Garin, who stared back.

"Go on," said Hugh impatiently. "Speak."

Guy faltered, then focused on the king. "I have received news, my lord, from one of the men we sent to watch de Beaujeu. There was a meeting yesterday, held between the grand master of the Temple and several of your vassals. Our man managed to find out about it and had one of the servants present tell him what transpired. De Beaujeu has arranged to buy La Fauconnerie from its lord. They did the deal yesterday. The Temple now owns the village."

"What?"

"When the lord asked de Beaujeu whether or not he had gained your permission for the sale, the property being in your domain and under your control, the grand master said that he had consent from the true king, Charles d'Anjou." Guy was incensed. "They are mocking you, my lord. All of them! You must act at once. Demand that the passing over of the village be stopped, until your permission is granted or denied. Or demand severe punishment for their insolence if they refuse." With effort, Guy got his anger under control. "I beseech you, my lord, do this at once, or you will lose the respect of those who still support you. They want a strong leader. They need to see that you are better than d'Anjou, that they should continue to support you whatever venom the Templars' master whispers in their ears on behalf of his cousin."

Hugh rose from the throne and stepped down the dais. He went to the desk, where papers were still scattered on the floor. "I try my best," he murmured, planting his hands on the table. "I read their pleas and requests and act upon them swiftly. I administer justice fairly and do my best for the city and my people." He picked up several sheets. "What more do they want from me? Do they want a tyrant on their throne?" His hands whitened as he crushed the papers in his fists. "Then let them have one!" he roared, grasping the edge of the heavy table and pulling it over, sending scrolls, quills and ink pots flying. His voice dropped to a whisper. "I will not stay where I am not wanted. I will not rule where I am ridiculed." He drew his gold robe tighter and strode toward the doors. "You will pack my belongings, Guy. We leave for Cyprus. I will return to my people. They have been without their king for too long." He paused. "But the Templars will no longer be welcome in my lands. De Beaujeu thinks to steal my property?" He let out a bark of bitter laughter. "We shall see how he feels when I take his. The Templars in Cyprus will be driven out, their estates burned to the ground, their livestock destroyed. Gone," he said in a flat tone.

Guy was standing there, mouth open as the king uttered these words.

Garin was quicker to act. "My lord," he said swiftly, seeing his plan falling away from him just as he had made it. He went to the king, out of earshot of Guy. "Do not do this," he whispered. "Not when you have hope. Our plan can work."

Hugh shook his head. "I will not stay." He walked toward the doors. Before he reached them, he stopped abruptly and turned back. "Act on your plan, de Lyons. Do what you suggest. If you succeed, I will return to make terms with Baybars. But not before."

"I cannot do this alone, my lord, without men, money or a place to stay."

"This palace still belongs to me. You may stay here. I will put some of my men at your disposal, but I will have no more to do with this place."

Garin watched the king head for the doors.

Guy rushed after him. "My lord, please, listen to reason."

"No, Guy. I have had enough of this land. I want to go home."

"At least remain in the city until you have chosen a suitable bailli to govern in your absence. The merchant states and the knights and the Commune of Burghers will fight over who is to rule in your stead. They will all try to put themselves in your place. It will be chaos!"

"Maybe then they will see the error of their ways," said Hugh, sweeping out through the doors, leaving Garin standing alone in the throne room.

22

Fustat-Misr, Cairo

17 JUNE A.D. 1276

After tethering his horse in a cramped square in the old part of Cairo, Will wandered over to the steps outside a tiny Coptic church. When he had happened upon this place earlier, there had been a busy market going in the square. Now it was almost deserted, just a few children playing around a well. It was early evening and most people were home preparing for evening prayers. As he sat on the church steps, Will wondered what life was like for the native Christians who lived in the heart of the Muslims' empire, men and women who had been here for generations, long before the Mamluks had come to power. Were they part of the community, as Muslims and Jews were in Acre under the Franks, or were they ostracized, ill-treated?

The church was dwarfed by the six-story buildings that rose around it, painted with blue, pink and yellow stripes. Arabic inscriptions flowed across the walls within the bands of color, each one a message of devotion to Allah. Will had been told about Cairo and had read descriptions of it in books, but nothing had prepared him for its enormity and elegance: the citadel flying high above the walled quarters; the broad blue Nile; mosques crowned with domes of silver and blue; spiraling minarets. And, in the distance, visible as he had ridden down from the hills, the Pyramids, rising strange and gigantic from the desert floor, like ancient, alien gods.

Will stretched out his legs with a wince. He had been riding for twenty days and his muscles were sore. The last part of the journey, across the Sinai, had been the hardest. The white robe and turban he wore helped to keep him cool, but the sun still managed to burn him. Reaching into the bag he had dumped on the steps beside him, he brought out a thin linen shirt, which he unwrapped to reveal two segments of watermelon. He had bought it the day before from a boy on the side of the road who had a pile of the swollen, luminous green fruits and who, for a few pennies, had hacked one of them into four pink smiles. Will had finished the fruit and was readjusting his kaffiyeh when he saw someone enter the square. It was a tall, well-built man dressed in blue robes, his lower face covered, as Will's was, by a strip of cloth that hung down from his turban from ear to ear. As he approached, Will stood warily.

The man's hand was curled around the hilt of a sword that hung from his belt. "Who are you?" he asked in Arabic.

It had been four years since he had met him, but Will recognized that strong, self-possessed voice immediately. "Amir," he greeted, pulling down the folds of cloth that covered his face.

Kalawun's eyes widened in recognition, then narrowed. He went closer, taking his hand from his sword. His voice was low with caution and anger. "You should not have come. We had an agreement. Your master gave his word that neither he nor his followers would seek me out. We cannot be seen together. It would be death for us both."

"It was imperative that I talk to you."

"You should have followed the procedures that were agreed upon. You should have contacted my servant and arranged a meeting."

"There was no time." Will gestured to the church. "Come. Please. You will understand when I tell you why I am here." Picking up his bag, he climbed the steps.

Kalawun hesitated, looking at the cross nailed above the door, then checked the square and followed him inside. "What are we doing here?" he asked, as Will pushed the door closed.

"It's somewhere we can talk in private." Will went to one of the rickety benches at the back.

Kalawun stared about him as he seated himself on the bench beside Will. Satisfied that they were alone, he drew down the cloth that covered his face. Will was shocked to see how old the commander had grown. His face was wan and haggard, and an air of sadness and despondency hung about him like a veil. His brown eyes were empty. "Is this to do with the attack on Kabul?" Kalawun asked. "The Franks at Acre should have received our compensation by now."

Will faltered for a moment, staring into those hollow eyes; then he began to speak, his voice whispering around the deserted church.

Kalawun listened, without interrupting. By the time Will had finished, Kalawun's face had changed. Color had returned to his cheeks and his expression was alert, alive. He looked like a man who has awoken from a deep sleep. He shook his head and looked toward the altar. He said nothing.

Will could feel the anger coming from him, saw the tension in his body and the strain in his face as he struggled to restrain his emotions.

When Kalawun did speak, his voice was composed, but rigid. "You say the message was written by this man, Kaysan, for someone in Cairo? A Shia?"

"It is what Everard believes, yes."

"But you have no name?"

"No. The message wasn't addressed to anyone."

Kalawun fixed his gaze on Will. "And your knights are to do this? It is they who will take the Stone?"

"The message just says Western knights, but as it would appear that our grand master is involved in this, then it is likely that Templars will execute the theft. From what the message says, the knights will meet Kaysan at the village of Ula sometime in the last week of March, before Muharram, and he and his men will take them down to Mecca."

"This cannot be allowed to happen. I cannot convey to you the severity of this."

"We know," replied Will.

"No. You don't. For a Christian to even touch the Stone would be an outrage, desecration of the highest order. My people would slaughter you. And not just knights, or the Franks in Acre, *all* of your people, *all* Christians would suffer." Kalawun spread a hand to take in the church. "Innocents everywhere would die and, with them, all hope for peace. For the moment, Baybars has no interest in dealing with your forces. If this were to happen, that would change in an instant. He would *annihilate* you." Kalawun was silent for a moment, then he looked at Will, his eyes hard. "And what is more, I would help him." He took in Will's expression and nodded. "I would not wish to, but if your people destroy the Stone of Mecca, I will help to destroy them. In the face of such action, I could no longer be a part of your brotherhood, could no longer work with you for reconciliation."

Will gave a small nod. "I understand. That is why we must stop this from happening."

"What do you propose?"

"The Anima Templi are all involved in this now and are working to find more details on the plan and who, exactly, is part of it. When we know this we can start to work out ways to stop it. We are confident that we will be able to. But Everard and I wanted you to know that only a few people are involved in this. Not our order as a whole, or the government at Acre."

"I realize that," said Kalawun. "But that doesn't change the fact that all of your people would suffer because of it. These men are obviously intent on starting a war, for whatever reason. If they do this, they will get one. I cannot help that."

"Perhaps not," said Will, "but you might be able to help us now, before this goes too far. As I said, it seems likely that someone in Cairo is working with these men. If you could find any connections to this Shia, Kaysan, here in the city?" Will shrugged. "I know it isn't much to go on, but it is worth a try."

"I already have some ideas," said Kalawun flatly.

Will was surprised. "You do?" When Kalawun didn't answer, Will nodded. "Then if you concentrate your efforts on finding this connection here in Cairo, I will concentrate on making sure the theft is stopped."

"I would ask an officer of mine to aid me in this matter," murmured Kalawun distractedly. "The importance of this, I feel, outweighs our contract of secrecy, and I know I can trust him to keep silent. But he has been sent to look for the Assassins who tried to murder Sultan Baybars and may be gone for some time yet." Kalawun sighed roughly. "It will be difficult for me to do this alone."

Will had looked up sharply. "The Assassins? I thought ... We heard that they were killed in the attempt on Baybars's life."

"They were," replied Kalawun grimly, "but those who ordered the killing remain free, or so it is believed. Baybars wishes to know the names of the Franks who contracted the Assassins. After all this time, he wants revenge." Kalawun, staring at the altar, didn't notice how still Will had gone. Finally he turned. "Is that all? I cannot linger. I have things I must do, things I must look into in light of this."

"Yes," said Will thickly. "That is it."

Kalawun rose and pulled the cloth of his turban back over his face. "Then I will take my leave." He held out his hand. "I thank you for warning me of this."

Will took the commander's hand. Kalawun's grip was firm.

"If there is any further news, follow our arranged procedure and send for my servant immediately. He will get the message to me." Kalawun paused. "Peace be with you."

Will watched Kalawun stride out of the church, then sat heavily on the bench.

THE VENETIAN QUARTER, ACRE, 17 JUNE A.D. 1276

Elwen was halfway down the stairs, a bundle of dirty laundry in her arms, when she heard the knock at the front door.

"I'll go! I'll go!" came a singsong voice. Catarina raced for the door.

"Wait, Catarina," called Elwen, stepping quickly down the last few stairs.

The girl came to a stop and turned, rolling her eyes. "I only want to open the door."

"You heard what your father said. We have to be careful."

Catarina hung back, adopting a pout.

Elwen was still amazed by how swiftly the girl had come to terms with her ordeal. Only two months had gone by since the attack on Kabul and already she seemed to have forgotten just how close she had come to being captured or killed, and was back to her carefree self. Elwen still had nightmares about it; still saw the look in the Mamluk's eyes as she drove the arrowhead into his neck. She felt alone in this, however. It was not only Catarina who had forgotten about the attack. So, it seemed, had Acre.

Two days ago, the women and children who had been taken prisoner in the raid had returned to the city, along with twenty Christians released from the dungeon in Cairo, a personal apology from Baybars and several bags of dinars. Andreas had come home last night with the news, having heard through one of his customers. But although the families of those returned were surely over-joyed, the city itself had hardly noticed. Despite the government's initial out-rage at the attack, all the attention had since shifted to the unexpected departure of King Hugh, which had left an empty throne in Outremer, causing confusion and power shifts within Acre's already fractured governing body of noblemen. The Temple and the Venetians were, according to Andreas, maneuvering them-selves into the space left by Hugh's exit, with the Hospitallers, Genoese and Teutonics trying to stop them. Groups and factions—landlords, guilds, mer-chants, religious orders—were choosing sides, looking for ways to put them-selves in the best political position. Messages had been sent to Cyprus, begging Hugh to return, or to at least instate a steward. But there had been no reply. Unrest was growing. Last night, a Venetian youth, whose father was secretary to the Venetian consul, had been brutally murdered by three Genoese. There was talk of a curfew being imposed.

Concerned by the escalating disquiet and with the death and disappearance of Giorgio and Taqsu at Kabul still painfully raw, Andreas had spoken to his family, telling them not to venture out of the quarter until things had calmed, and that the girls weren't to leave the house alone. Thus, it was with a certain amount of trepidation that Elwen, still holding the bundle of laundry balanced in one arm, opened the front door. They weren't expecting visitors.

On the step stood Garin. Elwen felt a flush color her cheeks as she saw him, a mixture of surprise, annoyance and shame rising in her. "What are you doing here?"

"I wanted to see you," said Garin.

"Who is it?" Catarina asked, trying to look around the door.

Elwen turned. "Go back inside," she told the girl, switching to Italian. "And take this to the kitchen for me." She passed her the laundry.

"That's not fair!"

"Catarina."

Taking the dirty sheets and turning on her heel, Catarina flounced off.

Elwen stepped into the hot afternoon, pulling the door closed behind her. The street was busy. "You shouldn't have come. My master isn't particularly fond of strange men turning up to see his female staff."

"Does he not mind about Will then?"

Elwen's eyes glittered at the remark. "That's hardly your concern."

"I'm sorry," said Garin. "That was a foolish thing to say. But it is partly why I'm here. Will, I mean."

"You've seen him?" asked Elwen quickly. The urgency of her tone surprised her.

At first, on learning of Will's deceit, Elwen's anger had been a raging fire, consuming all sense of love she felt for him. But with no fuel to keep it burning these past weeks, it had started to dim, turning into hurt, confusion, then a desire to see him and to hear for herself, in his words, that it was true: that he had lied to her all this time. There was also an element of doubt that had crept in, leaving her wondering whether Garin had embellished the facts, or even fabricated the whole thing, although there seemed no reason for him to have done so.

Garin shook his head. "I wanted to ask you the same thing."

Elwen's face fell. "No," she said, deflated. "I haven't seen him."

"I didn't think you would have, to be honest. If he's gone to Cairo, he'll most likely be away for a few weeks yet. But I thought I'd best check, in case his plans had changed."

"You seem to know more about his plans than I," responded Elwen defensively.

"About that, I'm sorry. I shouldn't have told you. I do think Will is a fool for having kept it from you. But, still, it wasn't my place to say anything."

Elwen blushed again, the initial shame she had felt on seeing Garin returning. "You're not the only one to betray a confidence," she said quietly. "I wasn't supposed to tell anyone where Will was going, or why." She looked at the ground. "I just felt as if all of you, Will, Everard, his friends in the Temple, were laughing at me because I didn't know. I was angry. It seemed everything he had ever told me was a lie." She looked up at Garin. "And maybe it was. Maybe he isn't in Cairo at all. But I shouldn't have told you."

Garin cocked her a sudden, boyish smile. "Well, I can keep a secret if you can."

Elwen gave him a small smile in return, which quickly vanished. "I appreciate that." She glanced at the sky, sunlight filling her eyes. "I should get back to work."

Garin nodded. He moved closer and held out his hand.

Elwen laughed a little mockingly at the formal, masculine gesture, but took it all the same. His hand was cool. She could smell drink on his breath and something else, something sweeter, smoky.

Garin let go of her hand and stepped away. "When Will returns, could you tell him to come to me? I'm staying at the royal palace."

"The palace? But the king has gone."

"He told me I could remain in his absence." Garin moved into the street, then turned back. "Just so you know, I'm not laughing at you."

Elwen stood in the doorway and watched him go, before heading back inside.

THE ASSASSINS' STRONGHOLD, NORTHERN SYRIA,
18 JUNE A.D. 1276

Nasir crouched beside the stream. The water ran fast and white, foaming over rocks that protruded from the stream's bed like broken teeth. Nasir thrust his hands in. It was achingly cold. There was a swirl of redness as the blood was washed away. He closed his eyes and felt the cold sink deeper.

"Sir?"

Nasir looked round. One of his soldiers was standing behind him. He had been so lost in his thoughts, he hadn't heard him approach. He'd had two of his men on scouting duty for the past three weeks, keeping an eye on the Assassins up in their mountain fastness. They had seen fidais scouring the hillside for several days after they had taken Idris, but no one had disturbed their hiding place. Still, he needed to be careful. Trouble was, he was tired, worn down by the childhood memories that choked him here, sick of the smell of blood on his skin. "What is it?"

"I think he's ready to talk." The soldier jerked his head toward the cave.

Nasir's hands tingled as he shook the water from them. He took his time.

Idris had said this before and nothing had come of it. The man's stamina was truly incredible.

Nasir had known it wouldn't be easy; the Assassins' capacity for the endurance of pain was well known. But still, to have spent so long working on Idris and to have got nothing more than blood out of him was almost unnatural, frightening even. Twice, Nasir had almost lost him. And once, Idris tried to take his own life by smashing his head back against the pillar of rock he was bound to. Fortunately, he only succeeded in wounding himself, but even so it unnerved Nasir, who had one of his squires secure a pad of cloth to Idris's skull to prevent him from doing it again. After the first week beating and cutting him, Nasir resorted to other measures: starving Idris to weaken him and then force-feeding him poisonous plants to make him violently sick. He hoped, by this method, to make the Assassin so delirious that he would talk without realizing what he was doing. But Idris, although feverish and insensible, gave him nothing. In the end, Nasir was forced to leave him for several days to let him recover, until this morning, when he had begun again, this time, grimly removing three of Idris's fingers, stuffing a filthy, bloody wad of linen into his mouth to stop up his screams.

Making his way back through the undergrowth, Nasir entered the cave. Idris was hanging limply in his bonds. His maimed hand had been bound, but the dressing had already turned red. His skin was gray and lifeless, except where there were cuts and bruises, and there it was a mixture of dull browns, livid purples and dark yellows. "Idris."

Idris's breaths were erratic. At the sound of his name, his good eye flickered open and focused on Nasir.

"My soldier tells me you want to talk," said Nasir.

Idris looked at him, but said nothing.

"You must talk to me, Idris," continued Nasir, after a long pause. "You and I, we are both running out of time. I have to return to my masters. They want this name. I must give it to them." He sighed roughly. "I do not want to do this, Idris. It sickens me." He swept a hand around the cave. "This place. Your suffering. They sicken me."

Idris grunted.

"Tell me the name and I will leave," said Nasir quietly. "I will let you live." His voice hardened. "I can make it worse for you yet." He gripped Idris's injured hand and began to squeeze.

Idris let out a high, breathless cry.

Nasir reached out and with his free hand gripped the man's chin. "I am out of time, Idris. I must return to Cairo. I *must*!"

Idris's mouth moved slightly. Nasir leaned closer. He could hear a throaty whisper coming from the Assassin. Idris's lips moved again. This time, they contained a name. Nasir dropped his hold on the Assassin and rose. "We have it," he called, hearing someone enter the cave.

"Step away from him," an unfamiliar voice commanded.

Whipping round, Nasir found himself staring at a man dressed in black. As his hand was falling to his sword, two other men appeared in the cave entrance. They wore the same black robes as the first: the robes of the fidais. They both held daggers, one of which, Nasir just had time to notice, was bloodstained. The man who had spoken raised a crossbow and fired, before Nasir could even touch his sword hilt. The bolt slammed into his shoulder. Pain drove through him as he hit the ground, cracking his head on the cave floor. Dimly, he saw Idris being untied and helped up by the fidais. Another two entered the cave, dragging the dead bodies of the Mamluks and the squires. A booted foot came down on his chest, pushing the breath out of him and making the pain in his shoulder sing. Looking up, he saw a crossbow bolt pointed at his face. Beyond it, the man who was holding the weapon was staring down at him.

"Sunni filth," spat the Assassin.

"Wait," came a croaking voice.

Nasir recognized it as Idris's.

There was a feeble cough. "Wait, Brother," came Idris's voice again, this time stronger. "Let him live."

"What do you owe this animal, Brother?" asked the Assassin with the crossbow. "Look at what he has done to you. The Mamluk cowards dare not attack us again openly, so they used you to get to us."

"No," said Idris weakly. "They didn't come here for us, or the fortress. This one is an officer from Cairo. He was sent here by Baybars to find the name of the Frank who contracted the sultan's murder. We can use him to get what we want. If we are to continue to survive out here, we need fresh supplies. He will fetch a good ransom."

Nasir felt the pressure leave his chest as the Assassin removed his foot. The crossbow stayed trained on him, however. After a barked command, Nasir was hauled roughly to his feet. His sword was removed, his hands bound. Every movement caused the bolt in his shoulder to shift and a fresh wave of agony to wash over him. Sweat stood out on his face and his eyes stung as he was dragged out of the cave into the blinding sun. In his mind, the name whispered by Idris swirled, nebulous at first, unfamiliar in sound and shape. Then, clearer, more defined and finally coming sharply into focus.

William Campbell.

23

The Temple, Acre

8 JULY A.D. 1276

The city was burning. A veil of smoke hung in the gritty air over the Venetian quarter as a row of houses in the merchant district burned, flames flickering madly within the billowing vapors, devouring timbers, blackening stone. Children screamed in their mothers' arms as desperate men formed a line along the street, hauling buckets of water from the cisterns to throw futilely over the conflagration. In the Muslim quarter other, smaller fires burned unchecked in a market square, consuming stalls and wagons. The ground was littered with rocks and broken glass. Men ranged the streets, their faces covered, clubs and torches in their fists. Some of them chanted as they walked, moving together in a pack, hatred in their eyes. People watched fearfully from nearby windows as a second company slipped out from behind a wagon that blocked one street and ran, yelling, into the square to face the masked men. The two groups met and blood was spilled.

All across Acre, makeshift barricades had gone up around the streets, erected two weeks earlier when the tension and random acts of violence that had been growing steadily worse since King Hugh's departure had finally erupted into open hostilities. The gates of various quarters were now closed from dusk till dawn, and curfews had been imposed. Guards roamed each district, but with so wide an area to cover and with so many factions involved, fires, robberies and skirmishes between rival groups were springing up unchecked, almost daily.

The descent into chaos had begun when a group of Nestorian merchants from Mosul had rioted against Muslim merchants from Bethlehem in one of the markets. The Templars, who protected the Bethlehem merchants, had forced their way into the fray, and in their attempts to quash the violence several Nestorians had been killed. The Knights of St. John, who protected the Nestorians, had intervened and a Templar had been wounded, provoking a furious argument between the grand master of the Hospitallers and Guillaume de Beaujeu that had rocked Acre's High Court. After this, the violence had continued to grow as the fragile peace between rival communities dissolved. Templar was set against Hospitaller, Venetian against Pisan and Genoese, Christian against Jew, Shia against Sunni. Even where these hostilities didn't erupt into open conflict, relations between the various leaders were so strained that any chance at reconciling their divided citizens remained impossible.

And so it was to the smell of smoke and a pervasive sense of anarchy that Will returned. The Temple's gate was shut and barred, and it was several moments before someone answered his repeated knocks. "What's going on in the city?" Will demanded of the sergeant who finally let him through.

"It's been like this since the king left, Sir Campbell," replied the man, snapping his fingers at a younger sergeant in the guardhouse, who hurried to take Will's horse.

"Since he left?" Will untied his pack from the horse's saddle as the sergeant took the reins. "What do you mean left? Where has he gone?"

"Back to Cyprus, sir. The High Court has written to request that he appoint someone to govern in his stead, but no one has come."

"What happened? Why did he leave?"

The sergeant looked uncomfortable. He lowered his voice. "Rumor has it that he and our grand master had words the night before."

Will's face was troubled. "Thank you," he said distractedly.

"Sir," said the sergeant quickly as Will turned away, "I was told to look out for you and that on your return I was to send you immediately to the grand master."

Will frowned. "Very well. I'll go when I've deposited my bag and washed."

"Begging your pardon, sir," said the sergeant, "but he said you must be sent to him at once, no matter the hour of day or night."

His concern growing, Will made his way across the courtyard toward the grand master's palace.

He found Guillaume in a meeting with the seneschal and Grand Commander Theobald Gaudin, and was told by a solemn official to wait outside. He sat on a bench in the passage, dumping his bag on the floor. His mind was filled with disquieting thoughts: the grand master's urgent need to see him; the smoke hanging over the city and the empty streets; the news that the king had left Acre. But behind these another darker fear lurked, a fear that had plagued him since his meeting with Kalawun, trailing him like a shadow back across the desert. *They are searching for you. What happens when they find you?* The words had become exhausting in their persistency. He leaned forward and put his head in his hands.

"Sir Campbell?"

Will jumped as he felt someone touch his shoulder. He realized he had almost fallen asleep. He looked up as the seneschal and the grand commander headed down the passage. The solemn official was standing over him. Will rose in time to see the seneschal throw him a black look, then picked up his bag and followed the official into the solar.

Guillaume was seated at his desk. He gestured to a stool in front of the table as Will entered. "Sit."

The official closed the doors, leaving him alone with de Beaujeu. Will's eyes darted to the window as he approached the desk. The sky in the south, over the Venetian quarter, was gray with smoke.

Guillaume caught his look. "You have returned to ill times, Brother."

"What is happening, sir? I was told that King Hugh returned to Cyprus without appointing anyone in his stead?"

"You heard right. But peace will be restored soon, when Charles d'Anjou fills our empty throne. Then, everything will finally be well within this kingdom. For now," said Guillaume briskly, "there are other matters I wish to discuss. I wanted to speak to you of this some weeks ago. But, of course, you were not here. I take it you found this treatise Brother Everard de Troyes sent you to acquire in Syria? That your journey was fruitful?"

Will lied with a nod.

"Everard was fortunate to have you at his command," said Guillaume after a moment. "His role here is an important one. I have been told how much he has accomplished for the order in his search for knowledge. Tell me, William, how long have you known him?"

Will's mind was working furiously. What was the grand master implying? Did de Beaujeu know that he hadn't gone to Syria? Was this a trap? "For sixteen years, my lord," he answered, keeping the concern from his voice. "Everard took me on as his apprentice when I first went to Paris."

"Why did he do this?"

"My master, Owein, had just been killed, following an attack by mercenaries on our company at Honfleur in France. We had been escorting the English crown jewels to the Paris preceptory and these men tried to take them. Everard needed a scribe. I could read and write, and I had lost my master." Will shrugged. "I suppose I was a natural choice for the role."

"So you would say you know him well?"

"Yes."

"Do you trust him?"

Will was thrown by the comment. "Yes," he said, falteringly, then, more strongly, "with my life."

Guillaume picked up something from the desk. It was a rolled piece of parchment. He handed it to Will. As Will opened it, he recognized it immediately.

"It is the scroll you brought back from Arabia," said Guillaume. "I need it translated."

Will, his heart thumping, chose his words carefully. "I thought Kaysan was one of our spies?"

"That is correct."

"Then forgive me, my lord, but how is it that we cannot read his message? Why would he send something we couldn't understand?"

"The man I was assured could translate it for us is unavailable to do so at present. I, however, cannot wait. Everard's skills are legendary in this precept-ory. If any man here can decipher this message it is him." Guillaume stood and stared out of the window. "But I have a problem." He said nothing for a long time. Finally, he turned back. "These past few months you have proven yourself an asset to the order, and to me. If not for your keen perception and quick ac-tions, I may have been killed by Soranzo's man at the docks. You discovered the identity of my enemy and helped bring him to justice, even though you did not agree with my methods, and you executed an important mission for me in Ara-bia, leading my own men with authority and skill. For some weeks now, I have been wondering whether to involve you in something that was set in motion almost two years ago. I have now made my decision. We are failing, William," said the grand master softly, "little by little every day. We quarrel, we fight, and we ignore the threat that creeps steadily upon us. For whether today, tomorrow or in five years hence, the Mamluks will come for us again. And when that hap-pens, none of us will be able to stop them. Few in the West have the stomach for Crusade. Our list of allies grows thin. But we have a chance to change this. *One* chance." Guillaume clenched his hand in a fist. As he spoke, his voice be-came deeper, stronger. "Imagine the men of the West rising up to take the Cross in their thousands. Imagine our soldiers making their way across the seas to aid us, we, their brothers, who have toiled for so long to keep the dream of Chris-tendom alive in these lands. We have come too far to let all those before us down. Men like your father, who died for our cause.

"Baybars and his Mamluks fight to reclaim their land. But it *isn't* theirs to claim! All of them were born hundreds of miles beyond Palestine. They say they are fighting to win back what we took, but they took it too. And if it isn't theirs by rights, by God, I say that it is ours. Our Holy Land. So much Christian blood has been spilled on these sands, so much we have lost. We cannot let it be in vain. We *cannot.*" Guillaume was pacing now. Will watched him in si-lence. "I am involved in a plan to take back what is ours. At the Battle of Hattin, the Saracens stole one of our holiest relics: part of the True Cross on which Christ was crucified. Christendom has mourned that theft for almost a hundred years. Imagine her jubilation were we to take something of theirs."

"What?" said Will thickly. "What would we take?"

"The Black Stone of Mecca," replied Guillaume. "Their holiest relic. It would be seen across the Western world as retribution. Our forces here and in the West would rally around such a victory, of this I am certain. It would give them hope, renew their hunger to finish what they started two centuries ago. I have already been in contact with leaders of the West, men like King Edward and King Charles d'Anjou. For months now I have been seeking support for a new Crusade in secret, promising these leaders that a change is coming, that all of them must be ready for it. I have even sent word to the Mongols."

"The Mamluks will destroy us."

"No," said Guillaume firmly, "not immediately. Even through his rage, Baybars would be aware of the need to properly plan any campaign against us. Using the Stone as a symbol of triumph, of God's will for us to reclaim what is ours, we can build a new Crusade, whilst he is building his own army against us. There is a chance, a *good* chance that we would meet on an even field. If we do not do this, William, we will simply fade quietly away, eroded at last by the Saracens. This is the only way to convince the West that there is still hope, that we can hurt the enemy, that we can take from them what they have taken from us." Guillaume sat. His eyes were bright, but it seemed more with sadness than fervor. He waited until his voice was steady, then spoke again. "I need you to help me, William. Firstly, by taking this scroll to Everard and asking him to decipher its message. Whatever contents are revealed, I will need you to make certain that the priest never speaks of it to anyone. I would not do this, but I have no other choice."

"You said we. Are there others helping you?"

"Yes. But they do not matter at this moment. If Everard manages to decipher this, I will tell you more. The theft of the Stone will occur in the spring of next year. I have been choosing a small group of men to carry it out. I would like you to lead them."

"This is it. This is our chance to stop him!"

Everard glanced up, his gaze following Will, who was stalking around his chamber. In his hand, the priest held the scroll the grand master had given to Will.

"You should have heard him," continued Will angrily. "He is so convinced that he is doing God's work. *Our Holy Land,* he kept saying. He has no concept of peace!"

"Did you?" asked Everard softly. "Before you were shown a different way? Before you were inducted into the Anima Templi?" Will stared at him. "I rather think you didn't," Everard went on. "Indeed, even after you learned that peace between our peoples was possible, that men from different religions and cultures were working toward this end, you balked against it and tried to murder our so-called enemy. Was that peace?"

Will swallowed dryly at the reminder, fear stabbing at the center of his stomach. For a brief moment, he wanted to tell Everard what Kalawun had said in Cairo. He opened his mouth to say it, then Everard spoke again and the moment vanished.

"Do not be so hard on him, William. Understanding is necessary for change to occur. You need to realize that de Beaujeu, like many others, has been brought up to believe he is better than Muslims, Jews, and anyone else who doesn't follow the Christian law. They were taught this by their fathers, by their priests, by their fellows and their masters. Is it any wonder they believe it? Change, as I so often have told you, happens slowly, over years. One man today might read one of our treatises and find something in it that might make him think, that might make him realize that we are all children of God, whatever name we choose for Him. He may tell his sons and daughters of this and they may carry less hatred in their hearts as they grow. The Anima Templi are physicians, William, drawing poison out of each generation. But it must be done slowly, with care, or we risk losing our patients. Had your father been anyone but James, you might now feel very different. You might agree entirely with everything de Beaujeu just told you."

"I don't understand," said Will, sitting on the window seat opposite the priest. "De Beaujeu keeps Arab clerks and I know he treats them as well as he treats his Christian staff. And after we caught Sclavo, he made sure the tavern was closed down and that the slaves used in the arena were cared for."

"Yes, and de Beaujeu has even been criticized for his lenient treatment of Muslims and Jews by some since his arrival in the city. He isn't a monster, or a fool. For him it isn't about the people. It is about the place. God's land, *our* Holy Land, as he calls it. He wants Jerusalem back, William. As do so many of our people. He believes it belongs to Christians and that we are its rightful keepers. He doesn't see that we all have an equal claim to the city, that it is the heritage of all peoples of the Books: Old and New Testaments and the Koran. For Jews it encompasses the site where God commanded Abraham to sacrifice

Isaac and is where the Temple of Solomon was built and housed the Ark of the Covenant, containing the laws given to Moses on Mount Sinai. For Christians it is the place where Jesus lived, died and rose again. For Muslims it is the place from which Muhammad ascended to Heaven." Everard's gaze grew sad and distant. "This ground is holy to us all. But somehow we seem unable to rejoice in this commonality and instead block up our ears and cover our eyes, stamp our feet like angry children and demand *this is ours, and ours alone.*"

"We have a chance to stop this, Everard," said Will, gesturing to the scroll in the priest's hand. "All you have to do is tell de Beaujeu that you couldn't decipher it."

Everard looked at him. "No," he said eventually, "that is not the right course of action." His eyes hardened with authority. "You will take him my translation and do exactly as he says."

"Why?" said Will incredulously.

"What do you suppose will happen if I fail to decipher it?" demanded Everard, rising and looking down on Will. "This contact of theirs," he shook the scroll, "which is presumably the man this letter is addressed to, could reappear at any time. Either that or they'll find someone else to translate it for them. I am not the only man capable of it."

"But it could delay them, perhaps even ruin their plans."

"If the grand master has been planning this for two years and has already gone to this much trouble to make sure it happens, he will not let this problem stand in his way. He will find some other way to execute it. And if he is delayed and the details we have already taken from the scroll—the time and place—change, we may end up knowing less than we do now."

"It is too dangerous," said Will, shaking his head. "We have to stop it before it starts."

"And we will," said Everard firmly. "You have been invited into de Beaujeu's circle. You will stand at the heart of this. More than anyone else, you have a chance to stop it. De Beaujeu isn't alone in this. It is no use cutting out the rotten part of the apple, but leaving the worm inside. We need to find out who these others are, who de Beaujeu is working with, who this man in Cairo is. Soranzo knew of it; potentially Angelo Vitturi knows of it also." Everard held Will in his stare. "You must find out."

Through his concern and disbelief, Will felt something stir. Pride. It was what he craved, from his father, from Everard and the Anima Templi, even, to some extent, from de Beaujeu: their pride in him. Now he had the chance to play the hero, to be the one who stopped this from happening. As Will felt these thoughts take him over, he tried to ignore them, telling himself that he would do this because it was his duty and the necessary thing to do. But a little voice called to him, sweet and seductive, saying he could be the one to save them all.

THE VENETIAN QUARTER, ACRE, 8 JULY A.D. 1276

Elwen hastened through the quarter. She could smell smoke on the air and heard the distant shouts of men as they tried to put out the fires, just streets from Andreas's home. At Vespers several men had stood up in the service when the priest had asked them to pray for those who had lost property in the blaze. These men had demanded retribution, saying that they all knew who had started the fire. That it was the Genoese. That it was time to drive them out again, this time for good. It had taken all of the priest's skills of diplomacy to prevent a mob from forming.

The strap of the leather bag Elwen had hung over her shoulder pinched at her skin as she hurried toward the warehouse on Silk Street. The bag was filled with samples. Andreas, preoccupied with the troubles, had left it on the kitchen table. He was due to meet with a customer and would need them. Besina had told her not to go: that Andreas could come back for it. But Elwen knew that it would be a waste of his precious time. Evening was drawing in and the streets were rapidly emptying of people. The heat was stifling, oppressive.

As Elwen turned a corner onto Silk Street, two men emerged from an alley and began making their way toward her They were moving slowly, erratic in their steps. Elwen guessed that they were drunk. One of them spotted her and patted his companion's shoulder. The other man looked up and laughed as his comrade said something that Elwen didn't catch. She moved into the street to avoid them.

"Good evening, my lady," one of the men called. He spoke Latin, rather than the Venetian dialect, but his voice was so slurred she could hardly understand him.

Elwen kept on walking, quicker now.

"I said, good *evening*, my lady," repeated the man, stepping into the street. Elwen flashed him a cool smile, then continued on, passing him.

"I got a smile!" crowed the man to his companion.

"I think she likes you," said the other, staggering out and blocking Elwen's path, so that she was caught between them. They were both red in the face. "Hey, girlie, you got one for me?"

"I'm in a hurry," said Elwen. Her heart was beginning to thump. "Please, just let me pass."

"Where are you going?" asked the first man. He was broad in the shoulders and had a long black beard. "There's a curfew on."

"I'm aware of that," said Elwen, becoming annoyed by the interruption despite her anxiety. She tried to move around the other man in front of her, who was bigger than his friend, with a belly that hung over his belt and ale stains marking his shirt. He had lank black hair and a greasy face that seemed to slide about as he spoke, his two chins wobbling.

"Not so fast," he said, stepping in front of her.

Elwen realized that there was no one else in the street. As the leering, fat man reached for her, all her bravado vanished. She did the only thing she could think of. Opening her mouth, she screamed. She just had time to see the fat man's expression change from drunken lechery to one of alert concern. *He isn't drunk at all,* a voice inside her said. Then, the words were forgotten as a hand curled around her mouth from behind, shutting off the noise. She felt herself pinned against the broad chest of the bearded man and hauled into an alley between two warehouses. Fear came down over her like a suffocating cloud as she felt the bag ripped from her shoulder, the strap snapping painfully apart.

"What's in it?" demanded the bearded man, who had hold of her, one hand clamped over her mouth, the other arm wrapped around her chest, pinning her arms to her sides. She was struggling madly, but he was too strong. Her energy, already sapped by the heat, was disappearing with every move. She got her mouth free and managed to let out another cry, but the bearded man quickly tightened his grip on her.

The fat man was opening the bag. "Silks!" he exclaimed. His drunken slur was back. "These'll fetch us a few coins." He chuckled at his companion. "She must like us after all."

"I don't know," said the bearded man. "I think she could be a bit nicer."

The fat man's lips split apart.

Elwen gasped in horror as she felt the hand of the man who had hold of her slide over her breasts. Her whole being screamed against the trespass. She writhed and pulled against him, but now the fat man was reaching for her and she didn't have the strength to stop them.

"Get away from her."

The fat man glanced around at the cold voice that seemed to come out of nowhere. Elwen thought she recognized it, but her terrified mind refused to place it. She couldn't turn her head against the bearded man's grip, but she watched as the fat man's expression became one of disdain.

"Stay out of this."

"I said, get away from her."

The fat man laughed. "This won't take long, girlie," he murmured, moving out of view. Elwen heard a wet, thudding sound, followed by a howl.

"Jesus!" the bearded man hissed.

Elwen was shoved roughly aside. She went down, throwing out her hands to break her fall as, behind her, there was another yell and a crash. Elwen felt someone grabbing her under the arms, hauling her up. She lashed out wildly and heard a grunt of pain as her hand connected with flesh.

"Elwen, it's me!"

She whipped around and found herself face-to-face with Garin. Looking past him, she saw two bodies lying on the alley floor. "Are they dead?" Her voice was strained, high-pitched.

"Come on," said Garin, taking her by the arm.

Elwen let herself be led by him for several streets, before she halted. "No," she said breathlessly, "wait." She looked down at her hands, specked with blood where grit from the alley had cut her. Tears sprang into her eyes, the trauma of her ordeal finally reaching her.

"It's all right," said Garin, touching her shoulder. "You're safe."

Without meaning to, she moved in at his touch, burying her face in his shirt, her hands splayed on his chest. Garin stood still. She could hear his heart beating fast against her ear. Then she felt his hand move awkwardly onto her back to give her a brief pat.

"It's all right," he said again. He sounded embarrassed.

Elwen pulled back from him suddenly. "How did you know?"

"Sorry?"

"How did you know I was in the alley? Why were you there?"

"I came to see you. I was worried when I saw the smoke. I went to your home and was informed that you had gone to the warehouse. A little girl told me where to find it."

"Catarina?" said Elwen, faintly.

Garin looked a little sheepish. "I told her I had come from the Temple with a message from Will. I was entering Silk Street when I heard a scream come from the alley. That's when I saw you with those men. Come on, let's get you home." He guided her along the street toward Andreas's house, his hand on her shoulder again.

Elwen paused at the front door. "Thank you," she said. Her eyes were red and several strands of hair had come free of her coif.

Garin stepped back as she slipped inside and closed the door. After waiting a few moments, he headed off. When he turned a corner and was out of sight of the house, he moved quickly, retracing his steps.

He found the two men waiting for him in the alley. The bearded man was sitting on a pile of crates, holding a bloodstained rag to his nose. Gone was any sign of his feigned inebriation; his eyes were clear and hard. "You didn't have to hit me so hard," he growled nasally.

"I had to make it look real, Bertrand," replied Garin.

"Then that gold you promised had better look real too," replied Bertrand, holding out his hand.

Garin reached into his pouch and pulled out a handful of bezants. He counted them out reluctantly. "I thought you were helping me because your liege lord ordered it," he said cuttingly.

"King Hugh ordered me to help you take the Stone, not molest maidens in alleyways." Bertrand grinned as he said it. "Not that I didn't enjoy it." His smile faded. "But, still, I'm only doing what was commanded of me for free. The rest, you pay for."

"I think we should get extra," complained the fat man, who was sporting a black eye. "What if she informs on us?" he said, looking at Bertrand.

"She won't," said Garin gruffly, annoyed that Hugh had left him Bertrand and his soldiers. They might be competent fighters, but they weren't the subtlest of men. "Just keep out of this district for a while." Garin pointed to the leather bag the fat man was clutching. "Is that what she had on her?"

The man clutched it tighter and looked to Bertrand, who took his time, but eventually nodded. "Give it to him, Amaury."

Garin caught the bag as Amaury tossed it to him. Looking inside, he saw several shimmering lengths of silk. He took out two pieces, leaving three inside. "Here," he said, holding them out to Bertrand. "Your compensation."

Bertrand took the silk and passed it to Amaury. "Did she believe you?"

Garin nodded as he tied the bag's broken strap. Even if Elwen asked Catarina if he had come to the house with an urgent message from Will, his story would be corroborated.

"What now?" growled Bertrand, as they moved out. "Do you really think she's going to come running as soon as her sweetheart returns and tell you everything she knows?"

"No," said Garin calmly, slinging the leather bag over his shoulder. "But she trusts me now. And that's all I need."

Kalawun stifled a yawn. The air in the throne room was muggy and they had been in council for several hours now, poring over maps of Anatolia and her borders.

"This is a weak spot," Baybars was saying to Ishandiyar. He pointed at a section of the map that was spread out on the table. He put a finger in the north beyond the city of Aleppo, marked out in black ink. "We can leave our heavy equipment in Aleppo and make a strike into the Ilkhan's lands. Once we have secured a base in his territory, our infantry can follow with our supplies. We need to work in stages or we risk being cut off."

Ishandiyar nodded, and several other advisors added their agreement.

Kalawun reached for a goblet of cordial and raised it to his lips, the sweet liquid refreshing him. He watched Baybars and the men talk. Following the brutal execution of Mahmud, things in the Mamluk court had changed dramatically. There had been no further attacks on the sultan, and all those who had previously opposed his decision to focus on the Mongols rather than the Franks had immediately fallen into line. With the campaign now fully under way and all obstacles removed, Baybars had calmed and stepped firmly and confidently into the role of strategist, a role he always played extremely well.

As Kalawun set the goblet on the table, he caught a brief flicker of something on the wall behind the throne. Had his gaze not been focused in that direction, he wouldn't have seen it, so tiny was the movement: just the barest shift of a shadow. His eyes picked out a thin crack in the whitewashed wall, with a darker section where the crack widened. The flicker came again. As he stared at the hole, Kalawun could almost feel Khadir's eyes upon him.

After his involvement in Mahmud's plot, Khadir had lost Baybars's trust. He now spent most of his time hiding in the wall, listening to their war councils, Kalawun guessed so that he could try to tempt Baybars back to him by offering him information and advice that he couldn't know unless he was prophesying. Baybars hadn't been fooled.

Whilst Khadir had been fixated on worming his way back into the sultan's favor, Kalawun had been doing a little digging of his own. As soon as William Campbell had told him of the involvement of a Shia in Cairo, Kalawun had been certain that he had found the traitor. Khadir had been an Assassin; an Ismaili Shia, whose background and family were unknown, and who, by his own admission, had already been involved in one plot to start a war between their forces and the Christians.

And, of course, there was Aisha.

Since the death of his daughter, Kalawun had felt as if a hole had been torn out of him. The only thing that served to fill this aching gulf was his desire for revenge. An investigation into her death had come to nothing, and for everyone else, life had returned to normal. Kalawun had even heard that Nizam was pressing Baybars to find another bride for their son. Baybars, to Kalawun's gratitude, had refused to consider it until after the Anatolian campaign, when a suitable period of mourning would have passed. Kalawun had begun looking into Khadir's background the day after Campbell had gone, but had found little. After his expulsion from the Assassins, it was rumored that Khadir had spent time as a hermit, living in a cave in the Sinai, but there were no references to any relatives he might have. His past remained shrouded in mystery. Kalawun, however, refused to be defeated. Somewhere there were answers.

"My Lord Sultan." A Mamluk official appeared in the doorway.

"What is it?" said Baybars. "I told you we were not to be disturbed."

"I beg your pardon, my lord, but I felt it was important. There is someone here to see you, a messenger from Jabal Bahra. He says he has come on behalf of the Assassins."

Baybars frowned. "Send him in," he said after a pause.

The official disappeared.

"My lord," said one of the governors, "is this wise? An Assassin?"

Baybars ignored the warning and watched as a man in a travel-soiled cloak was led into the room. Some of the governors had risen and had their hands on their swords. Four of the Bahri, who had been standing silently at the sides of the throne room, stepped forward, crossbows raised.

The messenger glanced at them, then around the room until his gaze fixed on Baybars. "My Lord Sultan?" he asked. When he didn't get a response, he held out a scroll. "I have a message from the Assassins."

"Why didn't it come through my lieutenants?" demanded Baybars, his voice commanding.

"It is from the Assassins in the fortress beyond Qadamus, who still oppose you," said the messenger.

Baybars scowled at this. "Read what it says."

The messenger broke the wax on the scroll. "You have taken the lives of our men, Sultan Baybars of Egypt. Now we take one of yours. The officer, Nasir, whom you sent to interrogate us, has been captured, his men killed. In return for his release we demand ten thousand bezants. Half to be given to the man who delivers this message, half to be given on the return of your officer. If you do not accept these terms, your man will die."

"Ten thousand!" exclaimed Yusuf in his croaking voice. "That is ridiculous." The aged governor rose. "My lord, you cannot seriously consider paying this sum. What was this officer doing in this place? Who was he interrogating?"

Baybars looked at Kalawun. "He was there for me." After a moment, he turned back to the messenger. "I accept these terms."

Inaudible to the men in the chamber, through the crack in the wall behind the throne, came an eager hiss of breath.

PART TWO

✠

24

The Royal Palace, Acre

Garin's eyes were closed. Sweat ran off him, spreading dampness across the sheet. The charcoals in the braziers were smoldering and the window drapes shut out sun and air. Garin's bare chest glistened in the dull glow coming off the coals, his eyelids fluttering as he slept. The sweet smell of the *qannob* he had imbibed earlier permeated the chamber's stagnant air, mixed in with the scents of ambergris and aloe, which he now habitually, though pointlessly, burned in an effort to disguise the drug's telltale odor.

He was sitting with his mother on the lawn outside their old home in Rochester. It was summer and the ground was parched and brown. Grasshoppers hummed and clicked in the hedgerows. The heat was a solid, sticky mass, pushing into him, trapping him like an insect in amber. His mother was speaking. In her hands, Cecilia held a vellum-bound book open on her knees. Her silvery blond hair was like water down her back, impossibly smooth as it flowed over her, following the curve of her thin, bony shoulders. Her lips moved, but no sound came. As he watched, a translucent bead of sweat ran slowly down her pale white neck. He followed it with his eyes as it slid between her breasts and disappeared behind the collar of her cream-colored gown. In his sleep, Garin groaned and clutched at the bedsheet.

The sunlight faded and shadows closed in. Garin turned to see clouds rising in dark towers on the eastern skyline. The hedgerows had gone and the land stretched before him all the way to the horizon. There was nothing between him and the storm. It was moving quickly, picking up speed. He could feel lightning charging the air around him, smelled metal and destruction. He turned to his mother, calling out to her. She was gone. In her place stood Elwen. Her green eyes fixed on him and filled with darkness as the storm reared up to engulf them.

Garin surfaced from the terror of the dream to a persistent banging sound. Disoriented, he pushed himself up, his vision focusing slowly. His head was pounding and there was an unpleasant taste in his mouth. The banging sound was coming from the door. Swinging his legs over the bed, he stood, swaying. The tiles were like ice beneath his bare feet as he staggered across the chamber and opened the door. Beyond it stood two men. One was a palace guard, but Garin hardly glanced at him, all his attention fixing on the second man, the sight of whom caused his drug-induced daze to vanish in a jolt of uneasy surprise. The man wore a blue and russet striped cloak; the livery of King Edward's personal messengers. In his hand was a scroll.

"This man came to the gates asking for you, de Lyons." The guard gave the messenger a surly look, which he then turned on Garin. "Said he had an urgent message from England that he must place directly into your hands. Refused to leave until he'd done so."

The messenger, ignoring the guard's irritation at the imposition, held out the scroll to Garin, who took it with a rising sense of apprehension. Without a word, the messenger turned to let the guard escort him away. Garin shut the door and leaned against it, the wood cold against his sweat-oiled skin. His heart beating uncomfortably fast, he broke the wax seal. His eyes glossed impatiently over the terse greeting and moved to the first line.

> *It was with anticipation that I received your letter at the Tower in the month of October, but upon reading it my expectation proved premature and I was left sorely disappointed by its contents.*

Garin went to his table and took up a half-empty cup of wine. He drained it quickly, but the stale liquid did nothing for his nausea and he forced his eyes back to the letter.

> *I was certain that I sent you to Acre with clear and simple instructions. But it seems my faith in you was ill-judged. In your letter you make repeated references to the fact that you have secured consent for the use of the Kingdom of Cyprus as a base for my intended Crusade, I presume in an effort to turn my notice from your failures. The primary reason for your journey was to procure that which I have a current need for; not a base for a future war, but funds to fight more immediate battles. You say you have acquired only half of that which the king has promised to deliver and if I am to see the rest of his generosity I must beseech the pope to revoke the planned sale of the rights to Jerusalem's crown. I did not expect to have to do quite so much for my money, when I have not yet seen a penny of it. Now I am forced to send an emissary to Rome and all because you have lost your powers of persuasion. King Hugh has great need of my aid, which is why*

*he begged for my help in the first place. I am certain that a little more en-
thusiasm on your part would have yielded up his full gratitude. Nor is this
the only assignment entrusted to you in which you have let me down. On
the matter of our friends in the Temple and their refusal to agree to my
repeated requests for funds, I find myself further dissatisfied.*

*On receipt of this letter, you will inform King Hugh that I have dis-
patched a trusted envoy to the pope and then you will convince him to deliver the remainder of his promise. Following this, you will turn your
attention on Everard and his misguided disciples. If they still refuse to comply with my demands, you will remind them that the crime of heresy is
punishable by death and that if by some unfortunate design their blasphe-
mous secrets were divulged to the wider world, I myself would make sure to
reserve a front row seat for their trial and execution. The time for subtlety
is passed. I will not let my plans be hampered by fools and fantastists.*

*Once you are in possession of these monies you will return to me imme-
diately, whereupon you will be rewarded, as ever you shall, for your faithful
service, or else punished for your lack of it.*

Garin swallowed down the sick feeling in the back of his throat and crossed
to the bed, where he tossed the letter, smudged by his sweaty hand, onto the
damp sheet. Planting his palms on the mattress, he closed his eyes, his emotions
clashing within him, first fear, then fury, then helplessness. He had almost
heard Edward speaking the words in those cold, disdainful tones that always
made him feel stupid and worthless. So wrapped up in his thoughts was he that
Garin didn't hear the door open behind him. It was only when a heavy hand
came down on his shoulder that he was brought sharply into the present. He
turned, startled, to see Bertrand's grim, bearded face. "What are you doing in
here?" he snapped, his anger at the intrusion forcing away his shock. "This is
my private room."

"It's the Lord *Hugh's* private room," corrected Bertrand gruffly. He hooked
his thumbs into his belt, the stance making him look even broader and brawn-
ier. "We need to talk."

"About what?"

Bertrand's eyebrows knotted. "It's been weeks since we got the news and
you've done nothing." His scowl deepened as Garin sighed and closed his eyes.
"You gave my lord your word. Are you breaking it?"

Garin's eyes opened at the threat in Bertrand's tone. "I gave King Hugh my
word that I would secure the Stone so that he could offer it back to the Saracens
and that is what I am working toward. Nothing has changed."

"Nothing's changed?" Bertrand laughed harshly. "That shit you've been choking yourself with has addled your brain." The laughter vanished. "The sale is complete. Don't you know what this means?"

Garin closed his eyes again. He could feel a pressure building behind them. The message from King Hugh had arrived a month ago, warning that Charles d'Anjou had bought the rights to the throne. It had been delivered to the bailli Hugh eventually and reluctantly put in place as his representative in Acre after the repeated pleas of nobles from Acre's High Court following the violence of the year before. The bailli, a man named Lord Balian of Ibelin, announced the black news to his court. Two days later, Garin received a personal message from Hugh, saying he was relying on him to help win back his crown and, if he did so, that he promised to honor the agreement made with Edward. As he saw Bertrand looking at it, Garin took Edward's letter from the bed and crumpled it in his fists. Edward's emissary had either not been able to persuade the pope, or else had arrived too late to stop the sale. Either way, it didn't matter now. If his plan for the Stone worked, he could deliver Edward a lot more than mere bags of gold; he could deliver him the Holy City. "I'm not in control of the theft," he said, turning back to Bertrand. "We cannot make our move until it occurs. When it does, we will be ready. What else do you want me to say? You know the plan."

"All I know is you've spent the past eight months trailing after that maid. And for what?"

"As I keep telling you," Garin said slowly, deliberately, as if he were explaining something complex to a child, "Elwen is the best way of gathering the information we need." He went to one of the braziers and dropped Edward's letter into the coals, where it flared brightly.

"Why is it taking so long?" growled Bertrand, not in the least placated. "After we had her in the alley, you said she trusted you, you said she'd talk. That was seven months ago. We haven't got time for this."

"I can't risk making her suspicious, and I don't want to attract Will's attention. He thinks I've remained in Acre on business for King Edward, but he isn't pleased about it and I know he's tried to persuade her not to speak with me. Fortunately, she hasn't listened to him, but the more inconspicuous I keep myself where he is concerned the better, which means choosing when I see Elwen and what I try to prise from her very carefully." Garin exhaled wearily as Bertrand continued to stare at him. The man was a soldier through and through. Point him in the direction of a battle or set him at a guard post and the job would get done, but if you wanted cunning and subtlety you'd best look elsewhere. Garin had quickly become frustrated by the man's lack of imagination and now only told him the barest details that he and his men needed to know. The rest, the plotting and the strategizing, he had done by himself; consulting maps of the Hijaz and routes to Mecca, securing a guide. It was how he preferred things. And, so far, everything had gone as planned.

When Will returned from Cairo the previous summer, he and Elwen had eventually made their peace. Garin, who initially worried that she wouldn't forgive the knight for his deception, helped to encourage the reconciliation by gently persuading Elwen that Will might have been trying to protect her by keeping the details of the Anima Templi from her. The two of them seemed to fall swiftly back into old patterns, with the difference that Will, to Garin's satisfaction, talked to Elwen more openly now that she knew his real business in the Temple. His own reunion with Will had been somewhat less harmonious.

A few days after the knight's return to Acre, having discovered what Elwen had learned in his absence, a furious Will had sought Garin out, demanding to know why he had told her of the Anima Templi and his attempted assassination of Baybars. Garin feigned remorse, then wounded indignation, saying he wouldn't have told her anything if Will had shown up for their arranged meeting as promised. As no one had been forthcoming about his whereabouts, he'd had no choice but to be a little more direct in trying to ascertain the reason for his disappearance. And how was he to know that Will had never told Elwen about what he really did in the Temple? The conversation ended abruptly with Will telling him coldly that Everard had denied Edward's request for further funds and that he was advised to return to London as soon as possible with Everard's apology.

"Don't worry," Garin told Bertrand. "We'll get all we need from Elwen when the time comes. Already we've learned when the theft will occur and when the raiding party is due to leave."

"We've also learned this former friend of yours, Campbell, is going to be in that party and, as you've told me, he might even try to stop the theft. How are you going to deal with him? And what about details? Numbers of those involved? Their actual plans?"

"We don't know Will is going to attempt to stop it," said Garin, growing increasingly irritable. He felt hemmed in on all sides, by Edward, by Hugh and Bertrand. "Quite frankly I don't see how he will be able to if everyone else de Beaujeu is sending is under orders to steal it. If I know Will, he'll most likely try and give the Stone back to the Saracens himself." Garin's lip twisted sourly. "Just so he can be the hero. But we're going to make sure he doesn't get the chance. As for the details, we just have to be patient." He pushed his toilet bucket out from under the bed with his foot. "Now leave me. I want to dress."

Anger flared in Bertrand's eyes. "I've had enough of you thinking you're lord of this castle," he snarled. "Living here like a pig in shit, giving me orders like some little king. You're here to do a job like the rest of us. And by God I'll make sure you pissing well do it." He reached for Garin, meaning to turn him to face him. But he didn't get the chance. Garin spun and grabbed his wrist in midair. His free hand came up in the same instant and clutched his throat. As he propelled the soldier into the wall, Bertrand gave a winded grunt.

"Don't *ever* touch me," said Garin in a dead voice.

Bertrand stared into Garin's dark blue eyes and saw something deep within them, something ferocious, feral. It was as if he were looking into the eyes of an animal who had been beaten and cowed one too many times and had turned savage. "All right," he said, his voice coming out strangled from the crushing grip on his throat. "All right."

Garin eased his hand away and stepped back, but he was poised to attack again should the need arise.

A clanging sound rose in the silence, fast and urgent. Bertrand broke from Garin's gaze, his expression changing. He strode to the window, knocking over an empty cup, and whipped aside the drapes.

Garin shielded his eyes with a wince as vivid daylight flooded the chamber. "What is it?"

"The barbican bell," muttered Bertrand, leaning out of the window and peering in the direction of the palace's entrance.

Now, beyond the clanging, Garin could hear shouts and the chime of swords.

Bertrand straightened and drew back from the window. Ignoring Garin, he marched to the door and flung it open, pulling his sword from its scabbard as he went.

Garin moved to the window. The curtain walls swept vertiginously to the moat that surrounded the royal stronghold. Because of the line of the fortress, he couldn't get a view of the barbican or the drawbridge below it, but the sounds of shouting and fighting were intensifying. Throwing on a creased tunic, he forced his feet into his boots, then snatched his sword from the floor beside his bed. Unsheathing it, he followed Bertrand. He had no idea who would dare assault the royal palace, but he wasn't going to sit and wait for the marauders to come to him.

The palace corridors were filling with soldiers as more men heard the call of alarm and raced toward the castle entrance. Courtiers and servants were standing in groups or hurrying in the opposite direction to the soldiers, looking anxious and confused. Garin heard Bertrand's gruff voice farther down the passage and moved in his direction. The soldier was in the corridor with Amaury and five other men from his company.

"Get the Lord Balian," Bertrand barked at one of the guards. To me," he told his men, stamping off.

Garin went after them, keeping a short distance behind. He wasn't going to fight if he didn't have to, but he did want to know what was happening.

They neared the entrance that led onto the drawbridge, spanning the moat between the castle and the double-towered barbican, Bertrand shouting at any stray soldiers they passed to fall in behind him. A stone passage, wide enough for a wagon to pass through, led to the main entrance from the corridor. The fortress's doors were open and the drawbridge was down, as it usually was. Just as Bertrand and his company were marching toward them, a group of palace guards fled in through the doors, weapons drawn. Two of them were wounded and were being supported by comrades. "Raise the drawbridge!" Garin heard one of them shout, a well-built Cypriot with graying hair whom he recognized as the captain of the guard. Three men ran to the winch at the side of the doors.

Bertrand called out to the captain. "Sir! What's happening?"

"They've taken the barbican," shouted the captain. "We tried to hold them off, but they broke through. They captured eight men." He looked to the entrance. His face filled with alarm. "Back! *Back!*" he shouted. "Close the doors!"

"The doors close and your men die," came a loud, clear voice from outside. "Stand down."

The captain seemed to hesitate, then slowly stepped away, but he kept his sword raised, trained on someone only he could see. He kept moving, the palace guard and Bertrand and the others falling back behind him, the soldiers who had been at the winch moving uncertainly with them.

As the press of men pushed toward him, Garin ducked into a narrow staircase and stood on the first step to see over the heads of the soldiers. He watched them fan out into the main corridor and saw the captain emerge from the passage, still holding point with his sword out. Several seconds later about fifteen men in a livery Garin didn't recognize appeared. Among them were the eight palace guards they had captured from the barbican, blades trained on them. Behind the armed company came seven other figures, clad in stately apparel. One in their center was particularly well groomed, standing erect and self-assured, wearing a crimson velvet cloak over a gold surcoat and matching hose. A velvet hat adorned with a swan's feather covered his head. He had a delicately trimmed beard and a youthful face, which would have been hand-some if not for the arrogant expression that soured it.

Garin looked on in surprise as a further ten men marched in behind this man. Five of them were Venetian city guards, recognizable by their uniform. The others were Templars. The last to enter were two banner bearers, holding aloft a broad standard, on which was painted a shield bearing a coat of arms Garin hadn't seen before. Or, at least, he had seen both arms separately, but never together. One half of the shield was decorated with a gold cross in the center and four smaller crosses surrounding it on argent, the royal arms of the Kingdom of Jerusalem. The other half was made up of gold fleurs-de-lys on an azure background, the arms of France.

"Stand down," said the man in the crimson cloak, looking at the captain.

Garin glanced out of the stairwell as he heard footsteps in the main corridor. A portly man with mousy-brown hair and a paunch appeared, flanked protec-tively by several advisors and palace guards. It was Lord Balian, Hugh's repre-sentative in Acre.

Balian halted when he saw the intruders. His eyes locked on the banner, then on the man in crimson beneath it. "What is the meaning of this?" His usu-ally soft voice was raised in anger. His gaze alighted on the stony-faced Templar Knights.

"You are the lord of Ibelin?" inquired the man in crimson.

"I am. This castle and this city are under my command. Who are you, who dares to trespass here and assault my men?"

"I am Roger de San Severino, Count of Marsico. I have come on behalf of his majesty, Charles d'Anjou, King of Sicily and Jerusalem. I am here to take your place as lawful bailli of this city and this state, until King Charles takes up his throne."

Murmurs of shock and anger rippled through the guards and the advisors standing with Lord Balian. Bertrand looked black as thunder.

Roger de San Severino gestured to one of the men with him, who reached into a bag and pulled out a scroll. "I have here a statement signed by my lord, King Charles, the new pope, John XXI, and Maria of Antioch, relinquishing her rights to the throne."

Balian shook his head. "Maria of Antioch was never the rightful heir to this kingdom. The High Court in Acre agreed that my lord, King Hugh of Cyprus, should take the throne over her. The rights that your lord has bought are obso-lete."

"That decision is obsolete," retorted de San Severino, his haughty voice filling the corridor. "The pope in Rome overruled it. Stand aside and let me take control, or face the consequences." He motioned to the Venetian guards and the Templars. "The Venetian consul supports this decision as does the Temple. They have pledged their allegiance to me as King Charles's man and will help me achieve my rightful place by any means."

Balian looked at the Templars. "Grand Master de Beaujeu would raise arms against me? Against the bailli of this city?"

De San Severino answered for them. "He would."

Balian looked to his advisors. A few of them shook their heads. Bertrand and his company were staring rigidly at him, but Balian's gaze moved over them, unseeing, and returned to de San Severino. "Then it would appear that I have no choice," he said in a quiet voice. He took in the shock in the faces of the men around him. "What else can I do?" he asked helplessly. But none had an answer. "Stand down," he ordered the guards faintly. "Obey your new master."

Bertrand was the last to lower his sword. As Count Roger de San Severino moved in, his men disarming the captain and the rest of the palace guards, Bertrand's gaze swept the stunned crowd and came to rest on Garin. He gave him a fierce look, before relinquishing his sword and marching off down the corridor, Amaury following. Garin watched them go, then slipped into the staircase and disappeared, before de San Severino's men tried to disarm him.

Less than half an hour later, Count Roger's banner bearers climbed the stairs to the roof of the palace's highest tower, where the flag of King Hugh billowed from a pole. Between them they pulled the pole from its iron stand and laid it carelessly on the ground, where the flag trailed in a puddle. After they had hoisted Charles d'Anjou's banner in its place, they headed back down through the tower, dragging Hugh's limp flag behind them. The banner with the gold crosses and fleurs-de-lys fluttered proudly, defiantly above the city of Acre. Charles d'Anjou, the Temple's greatest ally, now had Outremer in his grasp. The balance of power had shifted again.

THE TEMPLE, ACRE, 20 FEBRUARY A.D. 1277

Will watched as Guillaume de Beaujeu unrolled the map across the table. Zaccaria, standing to the grand master's left, set a goblet on the parchment to stop it springing back.

"This is the only map Zaccaria has been able to locate which shows the environs of the Hijaz and the city of Mecca itself." Guillaume pointed to the right-hand edge. "This is Ula, where you will meet with Kaysan at the mosque as arranged. You will leave your guide at the village and continue to Mecca with the Shias."

Will glanced around the table as the grand master continued to speak. The faces of Zaccaria, Carlo, Alessandro and Francesco were somber, their gazes fixed on the map as Guillaume pointed out the landmarks. The only man not focused on what the grand master was saying was Robert de Paris. As Will locked eyes with him, Robert gave him an intent look. Will averted his gaze as Guillaume continued.

"From what we have been able to ascertain, the journey from Ula to Mecca may take as long as a fortnight, possibly longer. We cannot know how Kaysan plans to lead you into the city and under what disguise you will enter, but we have to hope that it will be effective enough to fool the Mamluk guards that are known to line this route. The month before the Saracens' Great Pilgrimage has been chosen for the theft because the roads and the city itself will be quieter, with less trade and fewer pilgrims, many choosing to wait for the Hajj by that point. It will also serve to create a greater impact among their people, their pilgrimage ruined." Guillaume's voice thickened. He cleared his throat and reached for the goblet placed on the table in front of him. "But this also means that any company traveling these routes will be more conspicuous and may be subject to more thorough checks."

As the grand master spoke, Will thought of the message winging its way down the coast. It should, he guessed, reach Cairo in a matter of days. Keeping the details secret, not willing to risk exposing them in a letter, he had written to reassure Kalawun that their plans were in motion and the theft would be prevented. But listening to the grand master, he felt his own private doubts begin to close in and his assurances now seemed hollow in the face of the trial they were about to endure.

Guillaume, however, didn't seem to share the same misgivings. He finished speaking and looked at Zaccaria and Will. "But I have faith, brothers, in your abilities to overcome any difficulties that may arise." He moved his finger to a large circle at the bottom left of the map, ringed with Arabic inscriptions. Will, reading them, saw they were praises to Allah. It was a depiction of the holy city of Mecca. A circle with a black dot at its center showed the Haram Mosque and the Ka'ba.

"The Black Stone is embedded in the wall of the temple. As far as we know it is only held in place with a band of silver, so it shouldn't prove too difficult to remove."

"Will we have a container for it?" asked Will.

"On your journey to Ula you will once again be disguised as Christian merchants. This time you will carry supplies. You will have spices in panniers on your horses. One of these panniers will be large enough to contain it." Guillaume studied each of them, his gaze lingering longest on Will. His eyes, Will noticed, were tired and flat. "Do you have any questions?" When no one spoke, Guillaume nodded. "Very well. You leave in five days. Until then, get as much rest as you can. You have a grueling journey ahead of you."

Will, Zaccaria and the others bowed and moved toward the door.

"Men," called Guillaume. The six knights turned and looked back at him. "You are aware of why you are doing this?"

Zaccaria glanced at Will, allowing him to answer for them.

Will met the grand master's questioning gaze. "To save Christendom, my lord."

"To save Christendom," echoed Guillaume. "Remember that upon your journey, whatever you face. Remember your oaths to me, to the Temple." The lines in his brow deepened. "May God be with you all. His blessings upon you."

Will was the last to leave the solar. As he shut the door, he saw Robert in the passage ahead, hanging back.

The knight moved into step beside him. "We need to talk."

Will nodded. "We'll go to my chambers. It's almost supper. It should be empty."

Together, they moved through the preceptory grounds to the knights' quarters. The dormitory Will shared with four knights, each of them commanders like himself, was on the top level and was larger than most of the other rooms in the domestic complex. It was, as Will had hoped, deserted.

Robert turned as he closed the door. "I cannot believe this is happening. *How* is this happening?"

Will watched him stride to the window. The knight planted his hands on the ledge. His usually humorous demeanor had vanished. In its place was a grave anxiety Will had never seen before. He felt an unwelcome sense of responsibility for putting his friend in this position and wondered whether he had done the right thing.

It had been his idea, his and Everard's. Their plan would be difficult enough to accomplish as it was, with Zaccaria and the Sicilians looking over Will's shoulder, harder still if he had to do it alone. Eventually, after much debate, they had brought Robert into it. After they explained to the stunned knight what the grand master was planning and that they proposed to stop it, it was up to Will to persuade de Beaujeu to let him join their company. It wasn't difficult. Robert had been involved to some extent already, with the capture of Sclavo and the delivery of the message to Kaysan, and Will had told de Beaujeu he had known the knight since he was fourteen and there was no one he would trust more to watch his back.

"I still don't understand why the grand master would do this," continued Robert. "He has effectively just signed our death warrants." He threw a hand toward the window. "A death warrant for every Christian in Outremer."

"He believes it is the only way we can save ourselves now." Will joined Robert at the window. "He knows the West won't support a new Crusade unless they are given good reason. The old propaganda doesn't work. The people need something more definite to rally around. De Beaujeu sees the taking of the Black Stone as retribution for the theft of the True Cross. He thinks the West will see this also."

"Do you really think our leaders would launch a Crusade if we do this?"

Will sighed sharply. "I don't know. Maybe. De Beaujeu, because of his position and his links to the French royal house, commands a great deal of support. I know he has been in talks with King Edward and, of course, there is Charles d'Anjou. Now he has taken control of Outremer, he may play a more active role in its liberation from the Mamluks." As Robert hung his head and shook it, Will placed a hand on his shoulder. "I'm sorry. Maybe I shouldn't have involved you in this."

Robert looked at him. "I'm just reeling a little, Will. You've had months to think this through. I've had three days." He gave a short laugh. "One minute I'm minding my own business, my only worry whether to have the kid or the boar for supper. The next I'm being sent a thousand miles through hostile desert to steal the holiest relic imaginable from under the noses of our enemy in a city which Christians are forbidden to even set foot in." He blew through his cheeks. "I think I'll choose the kid."

"I would have told you sooner, but Everard and I wanted to keep it to ourselves for as long as possible. The fewer people that know, the better."

"I understand that, but the time for ambiguity is passed. I'm in this now, under the grand master's orders no less. I need to know everything. You can start by telling me how on earth you and Everard came to be involved in this ..." Robert paused. "This treason." He shook his head as Will went to speak. "For that's what it is. And it'll be treason's punishment for us if we're caught betraying the grand master. I know I might buck the Rule here and there, maybe not say *all* my Paternosters, see a girl in the market and find myself thinking about her through a sermon, cut my cheese a little too thickly at supper. But I've never disobeyed a direct order from any of my superiors, no matter how much I disagreed with it. You're going up against the grand master of the Temple and you're asking me to go with you."

"You know what the consequences will be if we don't do this. You said it yourself. The death of every Christian in Outremer. I can't tell you everything, at least not about how Everard and I became involved. Not yet. There isn't time and it isn't important right now. But I can tell you how we will stop it."

"How?"

"With a copy of the Stone."

Robert frowned questioningly. "Copy?"

"Since we learned of the proposed theft, Everard has studied every text, every drawing, every description possible both of the Ka'ba and the Black Stone itself. Under the pretense that he is writing a treatise on holy relics, he has even spoken to Muslims who have been on the Hajj and who have seen it for themselves." Will shrugged. "After that it was simply a question of finding a rock that fitted its rough dimensions. It isn't that large so it won't be too difficult for us to conceal on the journey. It's been painted with pitch and lacquered to produce the right effect. Apparently, the real relic looks more like black glass than stone."

Robert was looking incredulous. "A *fake* Stone?"

"We enter the Haram Mosque," Will went on, "just as de Beaujeu intends. I will order Zaccaria and his men to keep watch whilst you and I go alone to the Ka'ba. Here, we will pretend to perform the rituals of pilgrimage, which Everard has explained to me, during which time we will be expected to execute the theft. When we return to the others, they will think we have it. But, in truth, what we bring back to de Beaujeu will be no more holy than a lump of quartz from the beach."

"So the Black Stone will never leave its place?"

"We won't even touch it."

Robert fell silent for a moment. "What happens when there is no war? Won't the grand master know we tricked him?"

"How would he?" said Will. "Why would he even suspect it? He'll have his Stone."

"What's to stop him using it to rally our troops as he intends?"

"He cannot very well brandish a relic of the Muslims to any great effect when, as far as they're concerned, he has nothing of the sort. It may cause tensions to rise in the short term, yes, but as soon as the Muslims start saying the Stone hasn't left Mecca, he'll just end up looking foolish."

"And that's when he'll come after us," muttered Robert.

Will shook his head. "We brought him his Stone as ordered. It isn't our fault it didn't go according to plan. Perhaps the rulers at Mecca were too embarrassed to admit their relic was stolen from under them, we'll say. Perhaps they kept it quiet? Covered it up?" He sighed roughly. "It's the best plan we've been able to come up with and the one most likely to succeed."

Robert gave a snort. "I'd hate to hear your worst."

"We kill Zaccaria, Carlo, Alessandro and Francesco, and return empty-handed saying we were caught stealing it."

Will spoke these words so coldly, so flatly and so seriously, that Robert could hardly believe that they had come from his friend. He stared at Will in silence and saw something in his eyes that surprised him, something determined, almost fervent. Will was deeply, personally involved in this, much more so than he had realized. It sobered him. "That's not much of a second option."

"No," said Will, breaking eye contact with Robert, which dispelled the tension that had risen. "Believe me, Everard and I have been through it, over and over. The only way we can do this without resorting to murder, whilst not forfeiting our own lives or positions in the Temple, is to make everyone involved think that we did exactly as ordered."

"It's not going to be easy," said Robert, turning his gaze to the darkening courtyard.

"No," agreed Will. "But we have to try."

Guillaume took his time rolling up the map, smoothing out the creases in the parchment. Outside, evening was encroaching, filling the room with shadows. The grand master didn't bother to light any fresh candles. His eyes were accustomed to the darkness, and the flames in the hearth were bright enough to see by. Just before he folded up the last section of the map, his eyes caught the circle that was the city of Mecca. His gaze lingered on the black dot at its center, his mind plagued with a sense of foreboding.

It was a feeling that started months ago. But he had been too preoccupied to fully acknowledge it and had put his tiredness and unease down to the difficulties faced in the wake of King Hugh's departure the previous summer: first the riots, then the news that Hugh had confiscated several Templar holdings on Cyprus in retaliation. But with Count Roger de San Severino now in place as bailli and Charles having made his claim on the throne, as yet unchallenged by

Hugh's supporters or the High Court, Guillaume thought his troubles would have eased. Instead they had grown worse, and with nothing but the plan for the Stone to focus his attention on he had finally come to realize the cause.

It was the theft itself.

In the beginning, his convictions were cast-iron. He was adamant that he was doing what was best for Christendom, unlike the Vitturis and the other merchants who were doing it for the benefit of their own pockets. He still believed in the righteousness of his cause. But something had changed. Doubt, at first buried, had begun to rise in him, moving to the surface like a sunken ship pulled up by a storm tide. With every month that passed in which he received no word from the West, it grew clearer, larger, until now it was before him, unmistakable and ugly. There was no message from King Edward with tidings of busy shipyards, or from the pope of legates sent to preach holy war in crowded market squares, or from Charles promising troops and arms, no word even from his own order, reporting on the fleet being built in La Rochelle. There was only silence and his own nagging thoughts. Without a Crusade, they could not hope to beat back a united Muslim force. Without a Crusade, they were doomed.

Guillaume forced his eyes from the map, rolled it brusquely in his hands and twisted a piece of twine around it to hold it shut. He crossed to the window and gripped the frame, feeling the evening breeze wash over him, cool and calming. Four days ago, Angelo Vitturi had come, wanting to know if everything was set. Guillaume had hidden his doubts from the Venetian. Now he had to hide them from himself, had to hold to his convictions. Had to trust to himself, to God. He had known this course of action to be a dangerous one, reckless even. But not to act would be just as dire. At least this way they had a chance. No word did not necessarily mean that the men who had promised to bring fresh aid to the Holy Land had reneged on their pledge. He had to have faith.

Guillaume turned from the window and looked at the great tapestry on the wall of his solar. His eyes lingered on the white silk Christ hanging from the cross, head down, hands and feet pierced.

"You faltered once," murmured Guillaume. "You faltered and were saved."

Dropping to his knees in front of the tapestry, Guillaume clasped his hands, pressing his palms together as firmly as he could, as if by doing so he could make his prayers that much stronger, that much surer. He stayed there for a long time, the darkness growing around him as the fire died down.

25

The Docks, Acre

"You're not really here, are you?"

Will's thoughts were broken by the voice. He turned, surprised by the question, and saw the weary resignation in Elwen's face.

They were sitting together on one of the stone benches outside the customs house, their eyes blinded by the stark morning sun. The water in the harbor was lucent green, the distant waves that broke against the western mole tipped with glittery gold. Around them, dockworkers and fishermen were going noisily about their daily business. But Will, all his attention focused inward, had hardly noticed them.

He took Elwen's hand, clasping it firmly. "I *am* here, I promise. I'm just preoccupied."

"Are you thinking about Arabia?"

Will missed the anxiety in Elwen's tone. "The journey itself will be hard enough, without what we've got to do at the end of it." His gaze became distant again and his brow creased. "There are so many things that could go wrong."

"Don't say that, Will," she said in a quiet tone. "Please."

Will looked at her. "Perhaps I shouldn't speak of it at all." He sounded sharper than he'd meant to.

"You cannot blame me for being worried," said Elwen, removing her hand from his. "And as for speaking of it, you've hardly told me anything. Not recently."

"Because when I do you always become upset, and I don't want you involved in this." He sought her eyes, and when she didn't look at him, he put a finger to her cheek and moved her gently to face him. "You know where I'm going and why. You don't need to know the details."

Elwen looked across the water at the rows of ships swaying like old, drunk men. She hadn't told Will, but in reality knowing a little was worse than knowing nothing at all. It was like trying to look out of a dirty window, tantalizing and frustrating her that she couldn't see the whole picture.

Will sucked his lip, then stretched out his legs. "So," he said, trying to sound light, "what are you going to be doing for the next few weeks? The Easter fair is coming up soon. I expect Andreas will be keeping you busy."

Elwen gave a small nod.

Will hesitated, then steeled himself. "Do you think you'll see Garin?"

Elwen felt a shock of blood rise to her cheeks, hot and prickling. She averted her face, pretending to watch a group of fishermen hauling a net full of fish from a boat, in an effort to hide the blush. "I've no idea," she said airily, keeping her tone noncommittal. "If we happen to meet one another, then I suppose I might."

"Or if he comes to the house?"

Elwen turned quickly, guiltily. "The house?"

"Catarina told me a while ago," said Will quietly, noting the color that had risen in her cheeks and fearing it. "She was asking me who he was."

Elwen's heart was thudding so fiercely that she thought Will must be able to feel it. She uneasily recalled all the times Garin had sought her out. Only last week he had come, bringing her a book, a romance she had been wanting to read. She had forgotten mentioning it to him and the surprise was all the sweeter for his remembering. They stood on the step in the chilly shadow of the house, talking. He made her laugh and she found herself opening up to him in ways she rarely did with anyone else. It was because he knew about the Anima Templi and she could talk freely about her worries for Will with him. He understood and sympathized, made her feel less alone. At least this was what she had told herself.

Will was still looking at her.

"I didn't tell you because I knew you'd be upset," Elwen said, after a long pause. She shrugged crossly. "I've never invited him. What can I do if he seeks me out?"

"You could tell him to leave you alone."

"No." Elwen stood. "You don't get to tell me who I can and cannot see when I have absolutely no say in your life. I'll speak to whom I want, including Garin de Lyons."

Will rose and moved in front of her. "He's not a good person to be around, Elwen. I don't trust him."

"I do," she replied simply.

"Why?" demanded Will. "I thought you hated him because of what he did to us in Paris. What has changed?"

"He has." Elwen glared at him as he rolled his eyes. "Garin told me why he did what he did, Will. I don't blame him. He's been a good friend to me recently when ..." She stopped herself, but it was too late.

Will nodded bitterly. "When I haven't."

"Can we not do this," Elwen murmured. "You're going tomorrow." She met his gaze. "I don't want us to fight. Not now."

"Neither do I," said Will quietly. He took her hand again. "Let's walk back."

Elwen let herself be led across the dockside. She walked in a daze at Will's side, both of them silent, distracted.

When Will had returned from Cairo the previous summer, he had bowed to her furious demands and admitted his deception. He had spoken openly about his work in the Temple and the reasons he had kept it from her, which, just as Garin said, had been for her own protection. He had explained why he had organized the murder of Sultan Baybars after the death of his father, and eventually, unable to stand his pain or guilt any longer, she had forgiven him.

For the next few months, things between them were better than they had been in years, perhaps ever. He visited her more frequently and was more attentive, bringing her gifts: wildflowers from the preceptory's gardens; a pot of thick, amber honey from the stores, which they shared from each other's fingers until they were almost sick with sweetness. In those last days of summer, Elwen felt a sense of belonging unlike anything she had ever experienced, a warm encircling of love that remained with her even when they were apart. But as autumn had drawn on and the year turned, that feeling had begun to fade.

In the past few months, the visits had become shorter and less frequent, and Will had grown more distracted. She told herself that his work for Everard and the Anima Templi was more important; that he needed to be focused on stopping what could end in a terrible war, and once that was done he would return to her. But she couldn't fool herself, or deny the separation widening between them. She had come, finally and painfully, to the stark realization that she would always be second to his duty, that this danger or that crisis would be followed by something else that would take him away from her. She had pledged herself to him. But he had pledged himself to something greater. Will needed to be the champion. He needed to rescue the world in order to feel part of it. As long as she was safe and protected in Acre, he was comforted. He didn't see that she needed saving too. Or, and this was a hard thing to admit, he did see it, but chose to ignore it because to save the world would mean approval from others. To save her would mean exclusion.

But instead of becoming angry or upset as he withdrew and grew more distant, she too had begun to drift.

The first sign of that drift had been a shock. It was just after the Christ Mass and Andreas was away buying silks in Damascus. Will had come to the warehouse. They had argued about something, she couldn't recall what; then, forgiving each other, they had made love. There, as she lay beneath him, her back against the cold floor, an image of Garin entered Elwen's mind. It was so unexpected she opened her eyes. The surprise must have registered on her face, for Will slowed and looked down at her searchingly. She smiled and cupped her hand to the back of his neck, bringing him down and kissing him until he found his rhythm again. But it had left her unsettled.

The next time she saw Garin, she had felt herself color and something had leapt in her stomach. She kept it like a secret, a pearl or a coin, a treasure in a box that only she had the key to. Now and then she opened that box and looked inside, and took pleasure in the looking. But she hadn't thought anyone had noticed her private absorption. Least of all Will.

She glanced at him as he walked beside her, his eyes on the crowds. Did he know? Or was it simply, as he had said, that he didn't trust Garin? Until now, she had absolved herself by calling her interest harmless curiosity, but faced with the possibility of discovery, her own defensiveness had shown her just how important that secret had become. She felt as though she had been torn in two. The man beside her, whose hand was warm and firm around hers, one half of her loved immeasurably. This half was crumpled and distraught at the thought of the danger he would soon be walking into, desperate to hold onto him, to stop him from going. The other half was cool and aloof, telling her he had made his choice and that she would never find what she wanted here, only more of this suffering. It was this half that had opened that box.

All too soon, they were standing outside Andreas's house and he was kissing her good-bye, telling her not to worry. As Will walked away down the street, a lone figure in his black cloak, his stride purposeful, taking him away from her, Elwen was filled with the sudden, crushing feeling that she would never see him again. And the pain and relief that clashed in her at the thought was unbearable.

THE CITADEL, CAIRO, 25 FEBRUARY A.D. 1277

From a covered walkway that straddled the gate between two towers, a hunched figure watched the Mamluk Army make its last preparations. Khadir's face was a sour mask of vitriolic contempt as he surveyed the gathering men beneath him. The vanguard, headed by the Bahri, would be the first to leave, with

Kalawun's Mansuriyya and two other regiments. The middle section and rear guard, which would follow later that day when the van had moved out, would be composed of two further Mamluk regiments, creating a force, when combined with the slaves and servants who would accompany the army on its long march north, of more than eight thousand. It was an impressive display. But this just made Khadir seethe all the more, knowing that it would not be the Christians in Palestine who would feel its might.

Seventeen years had passed with him watching Baybars smite down the infidel that plagued their lands. His master had come so close to destroying the Franks once and for all; that Baybars had cast his eye elsewhere when he had so nearly consummated this aim was incomprehensible to Khadir. But it was not his master's fault. No. It was the fault of those who had led him astray, turning him from his true path. The rot had set in with Omar's death and had spread like a festering cancer with the influence of Kalawun. But there was still time for Baybars to fulfill his destiny. All he needed was a cure for his disease, and Khadir believed he had found it.

Nasir was alive. When the Assassins were paid their ransom, he would be returned, and if he had the names of those responsible for Omar's murder, Baybars could exact his revenge. Once Baybars had fresh Christian blood on his hands, that old scent would be reawoken, and then let the Franks' final days begin. That was one cure. The other, something he had planned for Kalawun, was altogether simpler.

Since Aisha's death, the commander had become his shadow, paying spies to tail him and search his house in the city. Khadir wasn't bothered by Kalawun's suspicions of his involvement in Aisha's demise; indeed he took pleasure in the fact that Kalawun *knew* that he was responsible, but could do nothing to prove it, reveling in the amir's silent desperation. But he was troubled by the investigations Kalawun seemed to be conducting into his past. He wasn't sure what the commander expected to find there, but it disturbed him.

Khadir looked down upon the soldiers, his white gaze crawling slowly over the heads of the Mansuriyya. He couldn't see Kalawun among them, but he picked out the amir's two sons, Ali and Khalil, mounted on horses and clad in new cloaks of royal blue. The boys, aged fifteen and thirteen, would not be engaged in any fighting, but would travel with the main force to Aleppo, from where the cavalry, led by Baybars, would go on to Anatolia to face the Mongols. Movement at the main palace entrance caught Khadir's attention. Out of the doors, accompanied by the call of horns and flanked by officers of the Bahri, strode Baybars, magnificent in battle gear. His head was covered with a black turban, banded with gold, and his long mail coat shimmered as he walked to a black charger adorned with golden trappings. Some distance behind came Baraka Khan, his face pensive and unreadable. Khadir had been pleased when Baybars had conceded to allow his son to join him on campaign. It was a sign that relations between them were finally beginning to mend. A thin smile of pride crept onto Khadir's face as he watched Baraka climb into his saddle amongst the Bahri warriors. This past year, the boy had truly become a man, and he had no doubt that all his efforts to turn Baraka to his side would be rewarded when the prince took the throne.

Seeing that the army was almost ready to leave, Khadir scuttled across the walkway and down through the tower. He was making his way along the passage, heading for the main doors, when he heard low, urgent voices ahead. He turned a corner and saw Kalawun and Ishandiyar. Kalawun was dressed for battle, but Ishandiyar, whose regiment would remain in Cairo, was clad in a loose robe. Both men had their backs to him and were standing close together. Khadir took a step back, out of sight.

"But you say he promised to stop this, Amir?" came Ishandiyar's voice.

"This is too serious to rely on a promise," replied Kalawun. "However much I trust him, he isn't one of us."

Outside, the horns began to sound the army's departure, cutting across their voices. Dimly, between the calls, Khadir heard footsteps fading. Glancing around the corner, he saw Ishandiyar heading through a door. Kalawun reached the end of the passage and disappeared into the sunlit courtyard. His brow kinked in suspicion, Khadir hastened down the passage and into the yard to take up his place in the vanguard. Baybars gave him a cool nod as he was helped into the saddle of a tan mare by a squire, his scrawny legs gripping the beast's flanks. Khadir bowed regally to his master, then scanned the crowds for Kalawun, wondering what the rat was up to. Whatever it was mattered little. As al-Mudarraj rolled ponderously open and the first lines of the Mamluk Army began to move out, Khadir dropped his hand to the faded silk pouch hanging from his belt. The darkness inside concealed a collection of coins, tiny animal skulls and dried herbs, and his cloth doll with her deadly secret. Khadir would see the father follow the daughter into hell. If nothing else, this northern campaign would grant him that.

26

The Royal Palace, Acre

Her head bowed, Elwen moved through the palace corridors. Having spent most of her adolescence as a handmaiden in the French royal household, she knew how to go unnoticed in such a place. As a servant you were invisible. She had thought she might have encountered more difficulty entering the palace, but the sullen-looking guards at the gates hadn't even glanced at her as she had trailed in like a shadow behind two finely dressed women.

Elwen counted the doors in the dim light. She could smell incense. Her breaths were erratic and her face felt hot. A voice was shouting inside her, demanding to know what she thought she was doing. But she was at the ninth door now and didn't know how to turn back. Didn't want to. There was defiance inside her, borne out of anger and frustration. But, more than that, there was need.

She reached out, closing her hand into a fist to knock, then froze, hearing voices on the other side, coming closer. Immediately, she moved off down the corridor. Behind her, the door opened and a wave of incense washed out.

"This had better work," came a gruff voice that sounded oddly familiar, although she couldn't place it. "Our lord is counting on us. He is finished in these lands unless we help him."

"It will work," said a second voice. It was Garin's.

Elwen risked a glance over her shoulder and saw a heavyset man dressed in the livery of the palace guard striding off down the gloomy passage. Garin was standing there, his back to her, watching the man head off. As he turned to go back inside, his eyes fixed on her.

His annoyed expression switched to one of shock. "My God." His gaze flicked down the passage to where the guard had now vanished, then to Elwen, who stood rooted to the spot. He went to her and took hold of her upper arm, firmly guiding her into the room. "What are you doing here?" His tone was urgent, commanding, and his grip was verging on painful.

"I'm sorry," said Elwen, as he shut the door behind her. "I . . ." She turned to him, her eyes desperate. "I needed a friend."

Garin was still looking surprised, fearful even. But at these words, the sharpness with which he had ushered her into his chamber seemed to melt away. "What is it?" he asked, putting his hands on her shoulders, gentle now.

At the comforting gesture, Elwen's grief overflowed. "Will's gone," she said, pushing the words through a harsh sob.

"To Mecca?"

Elwen nodded, her hands rising to her face, trying uselessly to cover her distress. Garin wrapped his arms around her and pulled her to him. She felt the tension in his muscles and the solidity of his frame against hers. The black linen tunic he wore smelled strongly of the incense that filled the room. Beneath that there was a smell of sweat on him, but it had a sweetness to it that was not unpleasant.

"When did he leave?"

"Yesterday," she murmured, her voice muffled against his chest.

Garin thought quickly. Only a day's head start. He could catch Will easily. It was still early. If their guide was willing, they should be able to leave that evening, dawn tomorrow at the latest. He had made sure that Bertrand and the others were ready a fortnight ago. Supplies were gathered, horses secured. With so much upheaval taking place in the palace, the organization had been simple. The only thing he worried about was how he would find out when Will left. He expected to have to go to Elwen at some point. He certainly hadn't expected her to come to him. He let out a quiet breath, thinking how close his plans had just come to being ruined. But it all seemed fine; she couldn't have recognized Bertrand.

Garin thought of Edward's letter, with its demands that he obtain the funds from the Anima Templi. He had ignored the king's order, wanting to stay out of Will's way as he formulated his plan to take the Stone. His confidence that he could deliver Edward so much more than gold had kept him from worrying about his disobedience. But now, after the shock of Elwen's arrival, he felt the first doubts begin to prickle at the back of his mind. What if he failed? How could he return to Edward empty-handed? "You don't need to worry," he said, as much to himself as to Elwen, stroking her hair distractedly and thinking through the arrangements he had made for the journey. "Will won't be gone for long."

"You don't know that." Elwen lifted her head from his chest. "You know what he's going there to do. If he steals the Stone, he could be killed."

"I know Will," said Garin, summoning a smile as he wiped a tear from Elwen's cheek with his thumb. "He's good at what he does. He'll be fine."

"Don't coddle me," she muttered tautly, disentangling herself from him and stepping away, closing her arms about her. She looked thin and tall in her white gown, girdled at her waist with a loop of red-and-gold braid. In the half-light filtering through the gap in the window drapes, her cheeks appeared sharper, more defined than usual, the outline of her mouth like the smooth twin curves of a bow. Her eyes moved over the disorder of his chamber: forsaken wine cups, discarded clothes, a blackened censer on the table, crumpled sheets on the bed. To Garin, she seemed at once rebellious and lost as she turned back to him. "I shouldn't be here."

"Of course you should," he said soothingly. "Come, have some wine." He crossed to the table, his bare feet making no sound on the rug. Seizing a cup, he poured out a measure, sloshing a little over the rim.

Elwen went to take it. As she did so, her fingers brushed against his. She started at the intimacy of the contact. His skin felt soft. Forbidden. Suddenly emboldened, she moved her hand over his, her fingers tightening. Rising onto her toes, her mouth sought his. Her lips parted.

His didn't.

Elwen rested against Garin for a heartbeat, feeling the whole of him go still, then stepped back as quickly as if she had been bitten. She took in his shock, and shame burned itself into her cheeks. She opened her mouth to say something. Then, Garin's expression changed. He dropped the goblet, casting a crimson fan of wine across the rug, and took her face in his hands, clasping it as his mouth found hers. Greedily, he kissed her, greedily and hard, in a way that Will had never done, and her desire, so abruptly extinguished, flared again.

Still holding her face in his hands, still kissing her, Garin forced Elwen back. Their feet tangled in scattered clothes and bumped against wine jugs, sending them rolling across the floor, until, in just a few strides, they reached the bed. Garin pushed her down onto the mattress, throwing a hand onto the bed to stop himself from crushing her as he collapsed on top of her. With his free hand, he tore the coif from her head, letting her hair loose of its starched, stainless covering, setting free the gold within. He moved his lips from hers to look at it for a moment, realizing that it wasn't just gold. The light that shot through the drapes caught in the strands, turning them shades of copper, amber, scarlet. He was astonished that he had never noticed it before, then realized that he hadn't ever seen Elwen without the cap modestly perched on her head. She was watching him, her green eyes intense. Her lips were red where he had kissed her too roughly, and her chest was rising and falling. Propping himself up on his elbow, he placed a finger lightly on her chin and ran it down her neck to the line of her gown. He wondered what other delights were concealed, and couldn't help the smile that raised his lips as his hand moved impatiently to her waist where the ties of her dress were tightly crisscrossed.

Elwen closed her eyes whilst Garin's fingers worked the knots of her dress. Her mind conjured an image of Will to accuse her with. But she pushed it aside ruthlessly, angrily. Will wasn't here. He was off saving the world. Oh, the irony of that pendant she had presented him with. How well he played his part, the part of a saint, and now she would play hers: the mortal, the sinner. She wanted the earthly; things she could hold and touch. Will wanted an ideal. She admired him for that, loved him for it. But love demanded more than that. She didn't want to be second to the world, always the mistress, never the wife. Love was fire and physical and total surrender. And those things she wanted now.

Once the ties were undone, the gown came away from her like peel from fruit. Beneath it was a plain white shift. Garin sat upright on the bed beside her, his throat now dry, constricted. She was watching him again as he reached down and slid the material upward. She shivered as the air touched her bare skin and put her arms above her head, allowing him to push the shift from her. He took in her nakedness: her arms dappled with goosebumps from the cold; a ring of pale freckles on one of her thighs; the sudden curve and swell of her breasts, nipples pink and raised. He leaned over her and caught one of them in his mouth, hearing a hiss of breath escape her as his teeth bit down. Her hands came up and tangled in his hair.

"I want you," he heard her say, strain catching in her voice. "I *want* you."

Garin's mouth came away, leaving her glistening. He tugged his tunic viciously over his head and dragged open the laces at the front of his hose. Then he was on her again and, then, in her. He felt himself encompassed, caught by her. Her legs came up over his hips and he went deeper, hardly hearing as she cried out. As his body gave itself up to sensation and his eyes closed, his mind was flooded with a torrent of images.

He saw Elwen at thirteen as she knelt beside the body of her uncle, Owein, on the dockside at Honfleur. Her screams rent the night, and when she raised her hands to her face, they were wet with blood. He saw the black-robed mercenaries Edward had sent to get the crown jewels from the knights fleeing, their mission failed, but not without a price. And the blood on Elwen's hands was now on his. For it was he who had betrayed the knights to Edward and had given the information necessary for the attack. And the faces of her dead uncle and his were staring up at him, white like skulls, accusing him. He saw her as a woman, sitting beside Will in the market gardens, her face sad and drawn, the sunlight unkind on her delicate features. He saw her in the alleyway with Bertrand and Amaury, her terror transformed to utter relief as she turned to face him. Then, at the last, he opened his eyes and saw her under him, skin flushed, lips parted, her fingers digging into his back. Garin kept his eyes on her until he shuddered inside her and grew still.

As he lay slumped on her, the familiar languid drowsiness enfolding him warmly, comfortingly, he felt Elwen's chest spasm beneath him. He pushed himself up on his hands, hearing a muffled breath and thinking she was laughing. Elwen's head was turned to one side, her hair clinging limply to her face. The rush of breath came again. Garin smiled tentatively, wondering what the joke was, and brushed her hair aside to see. Elwen didn't stir at his touch. Her eyes were open and tears were streaming from them.

THE ROAD TO MECCA, ARABIA, 14 APRIL A.D. 1277

A thin line of smoke hung suspended in the distance, a white exclamation over the next point of civilization or, for the party of sixteen men on the road, the next point of danger. Their scattered moments of laconic conversation faded into nothing and the tension grew. Soon, all that could be heard was the endless crunching of feet and hooves in the gritty sand and the continuous *swish* and *thwack* of sticks as the two men in front beat the ground to ward off snakes and scorpions. The air was baked, and every breath the men took parched their mouths and throats a little more, as if the desert was trying to enter them, to make them part of itself.

Will, rocked from side to side in one of the seats of the wooden *shugduf* that straddled the camel, steeled himself. This would be the tenth guard post they had passed through in fifteen days, but their frequency hadn't lessened the anxiety that built in him each time they approached one. A fresh rivulet of sweat wormed its way down his spine and soaked into the tunic he wore beneath the black, voluminous burka, the Muslim woman's garment that covered the whole of his body and face with the exception of his eyes. He met Robert's gaze. The knight, also shrouded and masked, was wedged in the seat on the other side of the lurching camel, with a cloth canopy that floated above their heads to keep off the heat. Robert gave Will a nod, then lowered his head.

It had been a brutal journey, worse for Zaccaria and Alessandro, the only two of the Templar party on foot. Arriving in Ula, which they reached with little incident, the six knights had gone to the mosque as instructed by the message. Here, they gave Kaysan's name and were taken to the same house they had been held captive at the year before. They were given one night to rest, then, their horses replaced with camels and their merchant garb discarded, they were on the road again. Zaccaria and Alessandro were handed men's clothing and were forced to walk with Kaysan and the Shias, leading camels that bore supplies and the other knights, who masqueraded as their wives. The Mamluks were used to seeing Muslims of varying shades of skin, themselves originating from so many different regions. Will had doubted the adequacy of the disguises when he had first seen them. But so far they had worked.

They could smell the smoke now, and a cluster of huts appeared, with the figures of men, distorted by the heat haze, moving between them. As their party approached the guard post, four Mamluk soldiers came out to greet them, others watching from the shelter of the huts. Will was careful not to look any of the guards in the eye as they moved past, checking over the company. Two soldiers headed for the camel in front of his, and Will's hand reached instinctively to his side, seeking the falchion that wasn't there. One of the guards lifted the lid of a pannier. He dipped a finger in and it came out covered in powdered nutmeg. He licked it, shut the lid and moved to the next. Will's hand drifted slowly from his hip as the guard continued down the line, oblivious of the pannier's true contents, which lay swaddled in cloth beneath the false tray of spices, a smooth, black secret, known only to himself and Robert.

Satisfied, the Mamluk guards waved them on, and several hours later, as evening shadows were creeping across the valley floor, the company reached the last settlement, where they would leave their supplies and head into Mecca.

"It looks busy," murmured Robert to Will as they entered the jumbled array of mosques, houses and tented stalls that had sprung up out of the valley. Torches were burning, orange stars floating in the growing darkness. The sounds of music and laughter came to them.

Will was troubled by the sudden appearance of humanity in the wasteland. They had passed pilgrims on the road, although according to Kaysan they were mere drops of water in the face of the flood that would inundate this valley in a month's time when the Hajj began and the caravans from Damascus, Cairo and Baghdad moved sinuously through the desert. Will had grown used to the solitude, had been relying on it.

Kaysan glanced round at Robert's voice. "We have friends here," he said in halting Latin. "We will be safe. Do not speak now."

Will and Robert fell silent as they reached the settlement and headed through a lively bazaar. Beyond the stalls, a series of wooden poles, just visible in the torch flames, rose from the sands like strange naked trees. Will realized that each had ribbons tied to it, hundreds of fluttering strands of color, then the poles were swallowed by darkness and the party moved toward a row of houses, opposite a mosque. After leading them into an enclosed courtyard at the back of one of the buildings, Kaysan pointed to a stone bench on the other side of the courtyard. "You will wait here," he told Will and the knights. "In six hours we leave."

Will stood alone for a while as the knights stretched their stiff limbs and talked amongst themselves, away from the Arabs. The stars in the black were like dust on velvet. He had never felt so far from home. The desert's empty hostility was soul crushing, and the feeling of trespass weighed heavily on his heart. Closing his eyes, he murmured the Lord's Prayer, feeling the chant of words flow from him, familiar, comforting.

THE HIJAZ, ARABIA, 14 APRIL A.D. 1277

It was late afternoon when the company of eight halted and looked down from the foothills over the settlement two miles north of Mecca.

"We should send someone to see if they've arrived."

Garin didn't look around as Bertrand moved up behind him. The soldier's voice had roughened over the course of the journey. "Send Amaury," said Garin, moving his gaze along the road, which wound out of sight between the mountains. "But tell him to be careful." He turned to Bertrand to emphasize this point and saw, now that the Cypriot had removed the kaffiyeh he had been wearing, the journey's affects in his face. Bertrand had lost weight and his skin sagged loosely around his jaw. His beard was dusty and unkempt, and his eyes had a new hardness to them, along with a subtle desperation. Garin knew that he looked much the same, as did the rest of the men. Those who had survived.

Ten of them had set out from Acre with their guide, two days behind the Templar party. Riding hard, they caught them quickly, sending one man ahead to scout. Garin, who had been unable to get details of their numbers from Elwen, had been secretly relieved that he hadn't been wrong in his estimations, and that his own company outnumbered Will's party almost two to one. Against Templars, the Cypriot soldiers would need every advantage they could get. In Ula it hadn't been hard to keep track of the knights. Garin, concealed in oversize robes and a kaffiyeh, followed them to the mosque and then to a rundown house. His earlier satisfaction was cut short by the appearance of a group of

Arabs, which more than doubled the Templar party. But concern over this was rapidly replaced with a more pressing problem.

In Acre, their guide, who had been only too keen to lead them to Ula for money, had brushed over the issue of how they would proceed to Mecca along the guarded road, by telling them that there would be plenty of people willing to take them. This, as it turned out, wasn't true, and it seemed, as the Templars set out the next morning in their disguises, Garin and Amaury watching them go, that their plan would be over before it had begun. Finally, after a few threatening words from Bertrand, their guide suggested that they ask the local Bedouin. At first, the desert nomads wouldn't even speak to Garin. Then, later that evening, a young, whip-lean man had sought him out and offered to be their *khafir*.

All the way down through the Hijaz and on, beyond Mecca, the Bedouin owned grazing lands where their animals were pastured. Each tribe owned its own territory and no one was allowed to enter without permission. A *khafir* was a member of the tribe who agreed to act as guardian for those wanting to cross the territory. At the point where one tribe's lands ended and another's began, a new *khafir* would be summoned to continue the guardianship. The Bedouin didn't use the main roads, negating the danger posed by the Mamluk guards. And so Garin and the soldiers, leaving Ula and civilization behind them, headed into the wilderness, following their barefoot, solemn guide. Each time they had been passed on to another *khafir*, Garin had handed out more gold, like he was scattering bread crumbs to mark a trail, hoping against hope that they would lead them home again. Some of these tribes would attack pilgrims in the Hijaz, stealing their money and even their clothes and food, leaving them to the mercy of the vicious elements, but there seemed to be a certain honor amongst them that prevented them from stealing from their guests. But even though the people were relatively clement, the land itself was anything but.

The first death occurred in the first few days. One of the Cypriots rolled onto a snake in his sleep and was bitten. He died vomiting and foaming at the mouth. The second came four days later. They were trudging across a high ridge, the sun in their eyes, when one man slipped. He slid down a scree-covered slope, taking half the skin off his back and breaking both his legs. Amidst his anguished cries when they reached him, the other soldiers spent some time arguing as to what they should do, before Bertrand ended his suffering with a fast slash across the throat.

Traveling through the foothills of the mountains, moving parallel to the road that wound through the valley, it had been relatively easy to keep track of the Templar party, quiet as the roads were. Sometimes, they hadn't seen them for days, and Garin would grow pensive and irritable, until they picked them up again. The *khafirs* didn't know why they wished to track the men on the road, nor did they seem particularly to care. If the gold kept flowing, their feet kept moving.

"Where were you planning on setting the trap?" Bertrand asked Garin. "The village won't work."

Garin agreed. There were too many places for them to scatter. "We need to catch them on the road." He pointed down the valley to where the road narrowed and the mountains pressed close on both sides. "That's where we'll wait. It should allow us to keep hidden whilst still being able to watch the road."

"And the Arabs? How do we deal with them as well as the Templars?"

"We have bows," answered Garin. "We can take out the Arabs before we tackle the knights."

Bertrand nodded, pleased. "So you've decided then? We use any force necessary against them?"

Garin looked away. Bertrand had been asking him this question for weeks, and for weeks he had avoided it. An image of Elwen drifted into his mind. He saw her lying beneath him, that change in her face from ecstasy to despair, the way she had continued crying those silent tears as she dressed and left his chamber. "Yes," he murmured coldly. "Any force necessary."

MECCA, ARABIA, 15 APRIL A.D. 1277

Mecca remained hidden until the last moment, encircled by the mountains. Then, all of a sudden, it was before them, stretched across a dusty plain within a formidable ring of rock. The sky was changing from black to blue with the approach of dawn, and the slender columns of minarets rose pale against it. South of the city, a domed hill dominated the view, whilst to the east sprawled an extensive bazaar. The roads, lined with sturdy houses, public baths, barbershops and apothecaries, were like strands of a giant spider's web, at the center of which lay the Haram Mosque, or Noble Sanctuary.

Approaching from the north, Will and the others saw the mosque rising before them, radiant against the darkness, torches burning around the walls, illuminating the flowing Arabic script that adorned it. A set of arched wooden gates lay open. They were guarded. As Kaysan hung back and removed his shoes, preparing to enter the sacred place, Will caught Zaccaria's eye. The Sicilian unfastened the straps that held the panniers in place, whilst Will and the others followed Kaysan's lead. Two of the Shias gathered up the shoes and headed off, leading the camel.

"They will meet us at the gate," Kaysan explained to Will.

As they walked barefoot toward the Haram Mosque, Zaccaria and Alessandro each bearing one of the panniers, the tension rose to a new pitch. Kaysan was the first to enter. He nodded respectfully to the guards as they passed through. Will's heart was a fierce drumbeat. He leaned in close to Robert as they approached the gates. "This is it," he murmured. "Are you ready?"

Robert inclined his head and they passed beneath the shadow of the gate, heads bowed. They had only taken a few steps, when there was a shout behind them. Will froze. Zaccaria and Alessandro had been stopped. One of the guards was speaking, pointing to the panniers. Quickly, Kaysan moved past Will and began answering the guard in rapid Arabic. He opened the lid of one of the baskets and pointed at the contents. After a moment, the guard waved them on with a brusque gesture and Will felt the relief in every nerve inside him.

Once through the gates, they found themselves passing through an arcade into an expansive courtyard. There were pavilions erected within it, all encircling a squat, cube-shaped building, two stories high, at the courtyard's center: the Ka'ba. The temple was covered, as Everard had told him it would be, with a vast black and gold brocade cloth, called the kiswa, which each year was replaced during the Hajj. The words of the Shahada were woven through it and seemed to shimmer in the light of the torches that were placed around the compound. The place was neither as dark nor as empty as Will had been hoping. Around the courtyard were little pockets of people, who had bedded down for the night under blankets. There were even a few fires, burning low. Other figures wandered through the arcade that ringed the courtyard, some of them guards, others pilgrims.

As arranged, Kaysan and the Shias moved off, melting into the shadows between the arches of the arcades, from where they would keep watch. Will and Robert took the pannier from Zaccaria. Between them, the two knights lifted it easily and headed for the Ka'ba, the hems of their burkas trailing across the sand, whilst the Sicilians moved toward the western gate. Will and Robert advanced on the temple, moving silently past groups of sleeping pilgrims. The area around the Ka'ba was paved with black tiles, painfully cold beneath their bare feet. As Will approached, he could see the relic.

The Black Stone was a smooth, glossy orb, encircled within a band of silver set at chest height in the wall of the temple. It had a strange sheen to it that was quite unlike anything he had ever seen before, similar to glass, but deeper and darker, with concealed depths. A shiver ran through him as he recalled Everard telling him how the Muslims believed the Stone recorded the sins of mankind, which it would repeat on Judgment Day. He almost felt it watching him, a single, silver-rimmed eye, and had to look away.

The plan was for Robert to wait with the pannier whilst Will began the circumambulation of the Ka'ba, which was to be done seven times, each circle of the temple marked by kissing the Stone. On the last pass, he was supposed to stop before it. To any of the guards it would look like he was taking his time honoring the relic, to Zaccaria and the rest of the party, it would look like he was stealing it. When he returned to Robert, who would open the pannier for him, he would simply lean over it, pretending to put something into it, and the ruse would be complete. The rest of their party was too far away, lingering near the western gate, to see that the Stone would remain in its place as they left the compound.

About ten paces from the temple, Will and Robert set down the pannier, facing the corner where the Black Stone was embedded. Will took a step toward the Ka'ba. At once, a barked command rent the air. All around the shrine, the sleeping pilgrims rose, the coarse blankets that covered them falling away to reveal silver chain mail and scarlet robes, with black bands on the arms. The one who had shouted the command was a powerfully built, dusky-skinned man, whose armband was embroidered with gold. As the others fanned out, he unsheathed a sword and went straight for Will.

27

The Plain of Albistan, Anatolia

15 APRIL A.D. 1277

On the towering heights of the Taurus Mountains, the winter snows remained, clinging stubbornly to jagged peaks, frozen hard in the shadowed depths of plunging ravines. In the deep blue of dawn, the icy peaks, marching east and west, were stark and infinite. Kalawun, looking out across them, felt diminished in their presence. The air was wintry and sharp, and his breath misted before him. He wrapped his cloak, lined with rabbit fur, tighter and headed through the awakening encampment.

The Mamluk Army had set up a temporary base on a plateau. Horses grazed the scrubby grass close to a large circle of tents. Between the structures, fires were points of brightness in the purple gloom. Men stirred, woken by their officers, and the hum of conversation punctuated the stillness. Kalawun nodded to the men of his regiment, who greeted him with respectful salutes. He paused, speaking briefly with some of his officers, then moved on, passing the infirmary tent. Nearby were several fresh graves. So far, they had lost twenty-eight men on this campaign, and five of those had been to the mountains.

Passing through Damascus, where they had gathered the Syrian troops under Kalawun's command, the Mamluks had entered Aleppo. Baybars, until then resolute and assured, was subdued in the city. He visited Omar's grave as soon as they arrived, and Kalawun later heard, from one of the amirs who had accompanied the sultan, that he had also spent some considerable time standing in silence outside a burned-out structure in the city. The amir hadn't been able to guess the significance of it, although Kalawun knew that Baybars had spent his first year in slavery in Aleppo, and privately he wondered if the ghosts of the past had not yet been laid to rest there for the sultan. Whatever haunted him seemed to find no purchase outside the city walls, however, for when they left the following day, Baybars's spirits had risen as dramatically as the mountains before them.

Dispatching one of his amirs with a regiment to the Euphrates frontier to prevent the Mongols from attacking his rear, Baybars had led the Mamluk cavalry north into Anatolia, leaving the infantry, heavy equipment and siege engines in Aleppo, along with Baraka, Khadir and Kalawun's sons. Scouts had delivered reports that Abaga, the Ilkhan of Persia, having learned through his own spies of Baybars's arrival, had amassed an impressive force. It was under the control of a formidable Mongol commander, Tatawun, and augmented by Seljuks led by their *pervaneh*. They were thought to be camped out on the Plain of Albistan, beyond the broad Jayhan River. Baybars's plan was to take out this force, before he attempted to capture any strongholds or towns. The route he would be taking was too treacherous for anything other than mounted men, but even they were at its mercy.

The defile through the Taurus had claimed the lives of many since the First Crusaders, having sailed across the Bosphorus from Constantinople, were faced with the awesome mountain barrier that lay between them and Syria. The narrow pass stretched dizzyingly through craggy limestone peaks, in places clad with ice and dark pine forests. Now and then, the track would wind around the mountains, and chasms, thousands of feet deep, would yawn beside it. In the mist one morning, after a cramped, freezing night in the pass, one man's horse lost its footing and plunged into one of these chasms, taking its rider and another Mamluk with it. Another three were riding close to the edge when part of the track disintegrated, hauling them screaming into the abyss. The army was still in the defile when a scout returned to tell them that a company of Mongols, two thousand strong, was waiting for them beyond the pass. Baybars sent one of his amirs ahead with a regiment bolstered by Bedouin troops to deal with them. By the time he led the rest of the army down from the heights of the Taurus, the Mongol dead were already bloated and flyblown in the field where they had been cut down.

Kalawun found Baybars standing at the edge of the encampment, looking down on the Plain of Albistan. Several Bahri were close by. "My lord? You wished to see me?"

Baybars didn't look round. "Are the men ready?"

"The officers have begun rousing them. They will be fit to leave within the hour."

"Good."

Kalawun followed Baybars's intense gaze. In the somber half-light, the land stretched away, folded and creased like crumpled cloth. A wide, pale strip flowed like a hem of silk through it. The Jayhan. Beyond the river, visible by the fires they had lit, was the Mongol camp. Kalawun made out faint movement, as riders rode between the tents, probably waking their men. He always found the mirror armies made of each other disturbing. This far, unable to see faces or hear voices, he might as well have been looking at his own soldiers. But then he made himself focus on who they were, and the impatient glint he saw in Baybars's blue eyes became reflected in his own. For it had been Mongol swords that had cut down their families and the families of so many others during raids into the lands of the Kipchak Turks, destroying lives and condemning the survivors to slavery. It was years ago now, but the old memories were like dry wood, the merest spark setting a fire within him. The Mongols had paid the price for those attacks seventeen years ago at Ayn Jalut. Now they would pay again.

"You've been quiet on this campaign, Amir. What is troubling you?"

Kalawun tore his gaze from the Mongol encampment to see Baybars watching him. It was true, he had been preoccupied, but he couldn't very well tell the sultan why. Forcing aside the troubling image of the Ka'ba in Mecca that sprung into his mind at the question, he answered. "I am concerned for Nasir, my lord. I have been wondering when he will be returned to us. It has been months since we heard from the Assassins."

"They would not have known we were leaving Cairo. I imagine that when we return we shall find him waiting for us there. Come, let us prepare for the battle."

Together, Baybars and Kalawun headed across the grass to their camp, two old warriors walking in silence, the gray in their beards made silver by the advance of dawn.

MECCA, ARABIA, 15 APRIL A.D. 1277

Will, only a few yards from the Ka'ba, barely had time to draw his falchion from beneath the burka's folds, before the scarlet-robed man was on him. A word leapt into his mind. *Betrayed!* Then he was lashing out with his sword to deflect the blow the dusky-skinned man cast at him. Their swords met with shocking force, almost threatening to buckle the blades. Will clenched his jaw with the impact of it and heard Robert, a few paces behind him, fighting with another of the men who had risen from what had, now so obviously, been a protective circle around the temple. As he lunged at his attacker, Will glimpsed a word inscribed on the man's armband, the gold thread picked out by the torchlight. *Amir.* The only time he had seen that title displayed in such a way was on Kalawun's uniform. This was no ordinary guard and no mere soldier. The man he was fighting was a Mamluk commander.

Within moments, the courtyard surrounding the Ka'ba was filled with the hollow ring of steel and shouts as the Templars and Shias raced to help Will and Robert. The Egyptians spread out to meet them, aided by the mosque's guards. One of the Shias fell at a thrust from a Mamluk sword, and Carlo let out an anguished howl as a blade punched through his side and was ripped out again, blood spraying as he collapsed to his knees. A second thrust punctured him in the stomach, killing him. Francesco went down a few moments later, a Mamluk sword through his throat. Zaccaria had felled one soldier, but two more were circling him, and the powerful Sicilian, already wearied by the journey, was feeling the uncustomary bite of fear.

Will heard Robert cry out, and he stabbed desperately at the Mamluk amir in front of him. He wanted to yell at the man that he had no intention of stealing the Stone, but he had no words, only breaths, ragged and desperate, that were ripped from him as he fought for his life.

Suddenly, something solid connected with the back of his legs and he fell back, landing with a shout on the black tiles, his sword jolting from his hand to clatter away behind him. He had tripped over the pannier. It toppled, dislodging the tray of spices fitted inside, which fell out as the lid came away, spilling powdered nutmeg. And something else. The stone, which had been nestled at the bottom of the pannier covered in cloth, rolled out beside Will. The triumph that flared in the Mamluk commander's eyes as he bore down on Will vanished. He faltered, staring in shock at the oval-shaped black stone, which had come free of its coverings. His gaze flicked to the true relic that was still safely embedded in the wall of the Ka'ba. Confusion spread through his face, and the few seconds' pause was all Will needed. Grabbing for his sword, he brought the blade round, lunging toward the Mamluk. The amir saw it coming and just managed to get his own weapon in the way, but he wasn't quite quick enough to avoid the strike. Will's falchion, although deflected from its trajectory toward his groin, slipped past the outside of his leg, below the point where his mail coat extended, slicing flesh. The amir cried out and stumbled, dropping to one knee. Will was up a second later. The Mamluk raised his head, seeming to brace himself. But Will didn't strike a second time. Instead, he turned and fled.

Robert was close to the Ka'ba, fighting vainly. There was a rip in his burka, and Will could see a nasty slash through his upper arm, a fold of skin flapping loose, blood flowing thickly. His eyes were slits of pain and he didn't see Will racing toward him. Neither did his attacker. Will whipped his sword brutally across the back of the Mamluk's knee, hamstringing him. As he fell with a howl, Will grabbed Robert and propelled him toward the west gate. A shout went up. Zaccaria and Alessandro were close to the gate. Four Mamluks and two guards were down, as were three of the Shias, Carlo and Francesco. Will glimpsed Kaysan fighting savagely with two soldiers, drenched in sweat, a ferocious grin twisting his face, then he and Robert were at the gate. Two guards were there, fighting with two Shias who, Will realized, were those left in charge of the camel. "Get out of here!" he shouted at Zaccaria. Pulling Robert with him, Will ducked a stray sword blow that arced in his direction and raced through the shadows of the arcade and out of the gate.

"I can't," gasped Robert, as they stumbled into the deserted street, the sounds of fighting behind them muted by the mosque's high walls. He collapsed, dropping his sword.

Will caught hold of him and hauled him roughly to his feet. "Yes, you can," he said fiercely. "Pick up your damn sword." As Robert lifted the weapon with a groan, Will's eyes darted left and right until he found what he was looking for. Their camel was tied to a post a short distance down the street. Will's arm around Robert's waist, almost dragging him, they staggered toward the beast as the eastern sky took on a bloody hue and day began to break.

THE PLAIN OF ALBISTAN, ANATOLIA, 15 APRIL A.D. 1277

The dawn stretched bright fingers across the land, stirring gold into the currents of the broad river, brushing the tips of the tall grasses of the plain, turning them crimson. In the tatters of mist that still clung to depressions in the ridges and folds of the earth, thousands of shapes were moving phantomlike through the milky air. The Mongols had crossed the Jayhan.

On the other side of the plain, following a steep trail down from the plateau, the Mamluks advanced to meet them. The kettledrummers kept up a steady, monotonous beat, conducted by the officers known as lords of the drums. The sound rolled over the grasses, low and ominous, giving the fields a heartbeat, out of time to the slow-thudding hooves of horses and camels.

Less than a mile away from each other, the two armies halted. In the empty expanse between them wind rustled and insects hummed. Both forces spread out on the plain, drawing quickly into practiced lines and sections at the calls of officers. Viewed from above, the armies made huge patterns on the ground, each a single mass of men, moving in formation. The wings were limbs stretching out from the torso that was the center, the extremities of each like talons, bristling with thousands of lances and spears, ready to curl out and lash at their enemy, ready to tear red rents through it.

Baybars, mounted on his black warhorse, was poised on the crest of a shallow hill, slightly back and to the left of his army, with a company of one thousand Bahri. He watched Kalawun and the commander of his own regiment riding along the front lines, arranging the golden and blue center that was made up of Bahri and Mansuriyya troops, the strongest section of the Mamluk force. The right and left wings were composed of the remaining regiments, the Syrian troops and soldiers under the prince of Hamah, whom he had called to arms on the journey north, and Bedouin light cavalry. Pleased with the calm efficiency of his troops, Baybars turned his judging gaze on the enemy.

It was a larger army than the one he had faced at Ayn Jalut seventeen years ago, and back then he'd had the advantage of surprise, the trap he had sprung for the Mongols in the hills proving lethally perfect. Now, the two titans faced each other on open ground, with little visible advantage to either side: the Mongols, born in the blood of conquest, sons of Genghis Khan, terror of nations and scourge of the Eastern world, against the slave warriors of Egypt, who had built their dynasty upon the bones of their masters and who, under Baybars, now commanded territory from Alexandria to Aleppo, the banks of the Nile to the Euphrates. But although the terrain did not favor the Mamluks today, something else did. Baybars could see it in the eyes of his men, could feel it in the drums' determined rhythm.

At Ayn Jalut, the Mongols had been invincible, undefeated in battle, unrivaled, unmatched. But no longer. The one man who had vanquished them now stood before them on the plain, brazen in their territory, a song in his heart and the blaze of ambition in his aging blue eyes. Furthermore, Baybars had heard word of trouble between the Seljuks and Mongols, who stood apart from each other on the field. His spies had informed him that the ilkhan no longer trusted his subjects, and it was rumored that the Seljuk *pervaneh* might not even fight. Baybars felt the wind tug at his cloak, and his horse stamped the ground, sensing his strained anticipation, but outwardly Baybars remained calm, giving no word of attack to his men. He would let the Mongols come to them.

Shortly, a blare of horns ripped through the stillness. As it died away, the rumble of hooves took its place and the left wing of the Mongol force set out, moving in five lines, two composed of heavy cavalry bearing swords and lances, the other three made up of light horsemen, who wielded javelins and carried bows. The iron of their round, onion-shaped helmets and the tips of their spears reflected the smoldering sun, now rising, a ball of fire throwing its brilliance across the Plain of Albistan, from the river to the mountains. As they neared the Mamluk center, the Mongol light horsemen rode swiftly between the lines of the heavy cavalry and let loose arrows and javelins into their enemy. They were a swarm of mosquitoes who would strike then dart back behind the protective line of the cavalry, who were advancing on the Mamluks like prowling tigers. Their sting was lethal, and within moments, scores of Mamluk soldiers had fallen, javelins and arrows finding targets across the field, sweeping in past shields and armor to strike the exposed flesh of horses and men.

Baybars, tension a hard knot inside him, gripped his reins and watched intently as his commanders shouted orders and the ranks closed tighter, shields clanking against one another to form a protective wall as the deadly rain continued. Within a short while, a thicket of arrow shafts and javelins had sprung up across the grass in front of the Mamluks. The Mongol light horsemen were called back by their officers, their job done, and now it was the turn of the heavy cavalry. The voices of Kalawun and the amir of the Bahri rose above the din, and with a cry of horns the two Mamluk regiments, the best of the best, went forward to meet the Mongols, hooves sending shudders through the earth. Lances were raised on both sides and locked under arms. Eyes found a target and fixed upon it, and prayers were chanted in the minds of five thousand men as the Mongol left wing charged into the belly of the Mamluk center, punching straight through it in a shock of iron, bared teeth and howls.

Within moments, the air turned red around the tangle of men and the fighting grew savage. Horses screamed as lances plunged into them, tearing skin and sinew. Men stabbed and hacked at one another, were thrown from their saddles, died in the churned up earth, trampled and crushed. Quickly, the numbers of dead mounted and slowly, the Mamluks were pressed back, their ranks breaking up as the howling Mongols forced their way through in a bloody barrage of whirling swords and thrusting lances.

On the hill, Baybars rose in his saddle, his sharp gaze picking out the pattern in the Mongols' attack. The heavy cavalry were pressing deep into his own troops, and he saw the danger to his weaker right wing, a short distance behind on the field. Immediately, he drew one of his sabers and lifted it high. "To me!" he roared.

And with that call, the sultan swept down from the hillside, followed by the Mamluk elite, as another blare of horns rose from the Mongol lines and their right wing advanced to meet the Mamluk left.

Baybars and the Bahri were a scythe through the Mongols as they entered the fight, refreshing the troops already engaged, breathing new fire into their spirits. Kalawun and the sultan met in the fray as the rest of the Bahri and Mansuriyya came together, tightening the ranks. The sultan and the commander were pushed together and fought side by side, swords hammering at the enemy, faces grim and bloodstained in the morning light. All sections of each army were soon in the fight, with the exception of the Seljuk force, who seemed to be guarding the back of the Mongols' lines, preventing the Mamluks from sweeping around and attacking them from the rear.

The battle was brutal and bitterly fought. The Mamluk center buckled, threatened to scatter, then pulled tight again. Gradually, painfully, the Mongols were repelled. Tatawun, a huge figure in the midst of his men, arms lathered in gore up to his elbows and a gash on his forehead streaming blood into his eye, roared a new command across the heads of his soldiers. One by one, the scattered Mongol cavalry began to dismount and closed into knotted groups, forcing the Mamluks to do the same and to fight them one on one. Lances were cast aside and swords were drawn, and the piles of the dead rose around the living.

But the Mamluks refused to give quarter, and despair gradually began to muddy the determination in the eyes of the Mongol soldiers.

After almost three hours of intense fighting, it was over. Tatawun, captured and defeated, gave the call of surrender, and all around the field exhausted Mongol survivors laid down their arms, vanquished once again by the might of

Baybars and the Mamluks. The *pervaneh* and his Seljuk troops didn't heed the order and fled the field before the Mamluks could reach them.

More than nine thousand corpses, at least seven thousand of them Mongols, littered the Plain of Albistan. Men—brothers, sons and fathers—were reduced to a bloodied mass of meat in the fields. And as Baybars surveyed the devastation he had wrought upon his enemy, the battle lust faded from his eyes and the knot of tense anticipation inside him disappeared, leaving a hollow space that wasn't filled by the victory spread redly before him.

28

The Road Outside Mecca, Arabia

15 APRIL A.D. 1277

A whistle sounded on the air. Garin stared up at the rocks above him and saw one of the Cypriot soldiers pointing east toward Mecca.

"Someone's coming," said Amaury, behind him.

Garin moved cautiously around until he could see the road ahead, keeping close to the rock face that jutted into the track, forming a bottleneck in the valley. Sure enough, in the distance, partially obscured by the rising sun, was a single point of motion. After a few moments, he realized that it was a camel, being ridden fast along the road.

"Is it them?" called Bertrand, crouched behind rocks on the opposite side of the track. With him was another of the Cypriots. Two more were stationed on a ridge above, bows primed. Lying like a dead snake across the track, camouflaged against the sand, was a twisted length of hemp, bartered from the Bedouin camp their *khafir* had taken them to last night.

Garin shielded his eyes. "There's only one ... No wait, I can see two riders."

"But is it them?"

"How can it be, if there's only two?" replied Garin shortly. He frowned at the beast, which was getting closer. Rapidly. It was moving at a terrifying pace, making great, lolloping strides, throwing dust into the air behind it, the riders on top seeming to lurch and roll, as if they were clinging on for dear life. Garin strained his eyes against the glare. Both riders were wearing black robes, but the head of the one in front was bare. Garin began to pick out features. "I think it's Will," he called to the others, slipping out of sight before he was spotted.

"Where are the rest of them?" asked Amaury.

"I don't know." Garin shook his head, troubled. "Something must have gone wrong."

"It doesn't matter," said Bertrand sharply. "We do it anyway. Whatever's happened we'll get answers from them."

Garin looked over at him. One end of the hemp rope, which was looped slackly around a jagged pillar of rock before him, was curled through his fists. Garin nodded.

Bertrand met Amaury's gaze as hoofbeats began to drum the air and the two of them gripped the rope, easing off the slack.

The hoofbeats grew louder, echoing off the rocks that closed in on both sides. An arrow thumped into the sand behind Garin. The signal from the scout above.

"Now!" hissed Bertrand.

Together, he and Amaury wrenched on the rope, which snapped taut around the rocks and became a stiff line, a foot above the ground. The Cypriots braced themselves. Barely seconds later, the camel thundered through the bottleneck, straight into the waiting rope. Its front legs hit the barrier at tremendous speed, throwing it forward and hurling the two riders from the saddle.

Will was the first to hit the ground, throwing out his hands as he landed hard, sending up a shower of dust and grit. Robert crashed down a second later, rolled over and over, then lay still. The camel collapsed, its saddle torn off by the impact. Dazedly, it tried to sit up, but its legs buckled beneath it. Will lay stunned, the impact reverberating through him like a bell, summoning little knots of pain that flared when he tried to move. He cried out as hands gripped his arms and hauled him up. He tasted blood and sand. Slowly, his eyes focused and he saw four men in a circle around him. A fifth was holding him up. All of them wore Bedouin robes and kaffiyehs. What he wasn't expecting was the clear, precise Latin that issued through the black mask of one of them, a brawny figure.

"Where is the Stone?"

Will blinked. For a moment, he could say nothing and the question came again. Finally he shook his head. "I don't know what you're talking about."

The brawny man strode forward and slammed a fist into Will's stomach. Will gasped and tried to double over the pain, but the man holding him wouldn't let him. He coughed out the blood that was in his mouth and hung there weakly, trying to force air into his lungs, a feeling of solid constriction running through his stomach all the way up into his throat.

"Where is it?" repeated the man.

Will dragged in a breath, then met the man's fierce gaze. He shook his head. "I ... don't ... know," he breathed, forcefully.

The man came in again, anger lending more power to his punch.

This time, Will took longer to recover. Through his streaming eyes, he glimpsed one of the figures moving over to another, a short, fat man. Leaning in, the figure whispered something.

"Wait," the fat man called as the brawny man drew back his arm for a third strike. "Use his friend." The fat man pointed at Robert who was lying motionless.

Will struggled vainly as the brawny man went to Robert and kicked him onto his back. Robert's arm was bleeding heavily, clotting the sand around him. His burka had slipped from his head in the fall, uncovering his face, which was ashen and slack. Will felt a stab of horror as he saw him, thinking he was dead; then he was flooded with relief when Robert's chest heaved. His relief was short-lived as the brawny man drew a sword from the belt slung around his hip.

"Tell me where the Stone is, or I'll kill him."

The words were spoken coldly, bluntly and without any shred of a lie.

Will knew that he was beaten. "We were caught," he said through gritted teeth, "in Mecca. We had no chance to take it."

"Where are the others from your party?" asked the fat man.

"Dead," replied Will in a low voice, not taking his eyes off the brawny man, who still had the tip of his sword poised over Robert's shuddering chest. "Or they soon will be."

"We've got to get it," said the brawny man, turning to his companions. "We've not come all this way for nothing. I'll not leave without it. We go into Mecca and we take it ourselves!" He lifted his head as a whistle came from the rocks above the track.

Will saw three more figures scrabbling down from a ridge.

"What is it?" shouted the fat man.

"Riders coming out of the city," panted one of the men, as he jumped the last few feet. "Fast."

The brawny man swore bitterly. He looked at Will. "Who are they?"

"Mamluks. They are coming for us. If you know about the Stone then you'll know why. You'll also know what they'll do to us, and to you, when they get here."

The man swore again.

"We have to leave," said the fat man, going to him. "It's over."

The brawny man flicked his sword at Will, who stiffened. His eyes were filled with defeated rage. He swept it back as if to strike.

"Don't!"

Will looked to the source of the muffled shout and saw that one of the figures had stepped forward. The brawny man glanced around and the figure shook his head. Hissing through his mask, the brawny man sheathed his sword, then turned and ran.

Will slumped to his knees as the man holding him let go and followed the others across the track and up a slope where the mountains sucked themselves back from the road. The men reached a series of stony columns that protruded from the rock face with some sort of trail, just visible, leading behind them. Within a moment, they vanished from sight.

Scrabbling over to Robert, Will touched his clammy brow. "Robert?"

Robert's eyes drifted open. He groaned through bloodied, swollen lips. To their left, the camel lay snorting in pain. Will staggered to the bottleneck. He could hear hoofbeats. There was nowhere to hide. Two riders were approaching fast. Behind them, in the distance, there were more, dust clouds rising thick around them. Will drew his falchion in desperation. "God, give me strength."

The first of the riders emerged from the bottleneck. Will stared in disbelief. It was Zaccaria, his face and clothing blood-spattered. Behind him came one of the Shias.

Zaccaria pulled his horse up roughly as he saw Will. "Get on!" he shouted, as the beast reared.

Sheathing his sword, Will ran to Robert and hefted him up. Zaccaria grabbed the half-unconscious knight by his clothes and hauled him over the saddle in front of him, then kicked the beast away as Will vaulted up behind the Shia.

"Kaysan?" shouted Will, grabbing the back of the saddle.

"Dead," replied the Shia bitterly, slamming his heels into the beast's flanks. "All dead."

MECCA, ARABIA, 15 APRIL A.D. 1277

Ishandiyar winced, the sword cut on his leg, close to the old wound he had sustained at al-Bira, stinging hotly. "Well?" he asked of the two Mamluk soldiers who rode up to him.

One of them shook his head. "I'm sorry, Amir, we couldn't catch them. I left several men in the village searching for them in case they tried to hide there, but I think they must have fled into the hills."

Ishandiyar's voice was gruff. "Well, they are dead anyway. If the desert doesn't kill them, the Bedouin will. Call the others back. We will stay here tonight. But I believe the immediate danger has passed."

The soldiers bowed and turned their horses away down the street, which was busy with morning traders and workers, many of whom were looking curiously at the group of Mamluks outside the Haram Mosque. Ishandiyar limped back inside the building, away from their inquisitive stares.

The courtyard of the mosque was bathed in sunlight. The sharif of Mecca was there, talking somberly with some of his guards. The bodies of three dead guards and five dead Mamluks were laid carefully in the shadows of the arcade. Close by, unceremoniously dumped, were the corpses of eight of the attackers. Already, flies were making interested passes over the bodies. Ishandiyar looked over at the Ka'ba. Servants were on their hands and knees around the temple, scrubbing blood from the tiles. His eyes moved to the Black Stone, sitting darkly, silently in its place, and he felt relief like sweetness inside him. He had fulfilled his promise to Kalawun, and to Allah. The Stone remained unharmed. It had been a hard journey and a tense wait, and he and his men had accosted several groups of pilgrims over the last few days in the mosque. But when he had seen the two figures, tall for women, move up to the temple with that pannier, he had known they were the ones.

He crossed to where the pannier stood. The stone that had been inside it was on the ground, being studied by two of the mosque's mullahs. "What is it?" he asked. "Do you know yet?"

One of the mullahs looked up. "A copy, we believe, Amir. Nothing more. Perhaps they planned to put this in place of the real relic that they might escape unnoticed?"

Ishandiyar remained silent. Kalawun had said that the Christian knight who warned him of the theft also had a plan to prevent it. He wondered for a moment if some of the men he had killed were allies, but he didn't dwell on this. Kalawun was right; it was their responsibility to keep the Stone safe. That they had done so was all that mattered.

Ishandiyar moved over to speak with the sharif, leaving the mullahs to finish their investigations and the servants to wash the rest of the blood from the stones.

After a while, the bodies were taken for burial and the last sign that anything at all had happened disappeared. An hour later, as the chanting calls of the muezzins lifted from the city's minarets, the gates of the Haram Mosque rolled open and pilgrims, waiting patiently outside, filed in, their faces filled with wonder.

29

Damascus, Syria

9 JUNE A.D. 1277

The growing tremor of the kettledrums could be heard in Damascus sometime before the Mamluks reached it, a thudding wave of sound rolling across the boiling desert to lap against the city walls.

At the head of the army rode Baybars, the Bahri shouting his title in fierce celebration.

"*Al-Malik al-Zahir!*" Victorious King.

The blood-red banner with its yellow lion sailed boldly above the vanguard.

Kalawun, riding beside the sultan, felt the soldiers' roars pounding in his ears. They, at least, were pleased.

A few days after the victory at Albistan, the Mamluks had entered Kayseri, the capital of the Seljuks' realm, as liberators of the Seljuks' lands and vanquishers of the Mongol garrison placed over them against their will. In Kayseri, the Muslim Seljuks praised Baybars, minted a new coin in his name and made him heir to the throne of their kingdom. The Mamluks lounged in luxury for several weeks, before Baybars decided to return to Syria. To the soldiers, this was fortunate news. They had fought the Mongols and had beaten them once again, with comparably little loss of life. Their task done, they could return to the comfort of Damascus, where the sultan would no doubt reward them, in plunder and slaves taken from the battlefield. Some of the generals and advisors, however, had taken a different view.

Why, they demanded, as strongly as they dared in the face of the stony-eyed sultan, were they leaving, having only just captured the territory? They should remain behind, strengthen their position, bring in more forces. Hadn't this been what he wanted? To expand the Mamluk frontier and defeat the Mongols? Baybars countered their arguments staunchly. Scouts had informed him that Abaga, roused by the defeat of his garrison, was leading an army of more than thirty thousand Mongols from Persia into the Seljuk realm to avenge their loss and reclaim the country. Baybars did not have men enough to meet this challenge, nor time to summon more forces, and he told the generals that they were at risk of being cut off from the rest of the army, still in Aleppo, if they remained.

Kalawun, who agreed with the decision, had noticed that Baybars had been growing increasingly weary since they had entered the Seljuk capital. The victory over the Mongols at Albistan appeared to deliver him no real satisfaction; indeed, Kalawun might have said, if it hadn't sounded so unlikely, that the sultan almost seemed to regret it. It was as if something inside him, which had been withering for some time, had finally died. All the way back from Kayseri to Aleppo, the sultan had hardly uttered a word.

Kalawun glanced at Baybars, whose stare was fixed on the walls of Damascus, getting larger ahead, beyond a fringe of lush orchards. Looking past the sultan, he met the gaze of Khadir. The soothsayer had somehow managed to maneuver himself so that he was riding at Baybars's left hand, even though he had been specifically positioned several rows behind with Baraka Khan. Khadir had, over the past few weeks, wormed his way back into Baybars's inner circle, through his persistent forewarnings of a coming lunar eclipse, a bad omen said to herald the death of a great ruler. This prediction had caused the soothsayer to fret and fawn over Baybars, pleading with him to take extra precautions when the time came, warnings Baybars had listened to carefully, though not with undue concern. As Kalawun locked eyes with Khadir, he saw that his ancient face was contorted with hatred and suspicion. The commander had felt that vicious gaze upon him for most of the journey. He was tired of it and, in truth, a little unnerved. It was as if the soothsayer were trying to work some black spell upon him with that constant, hooded glare. Kalawun, his mind on other things, had tried to push his personal feud with Khadir aside during the campaign. But it was almost impossible to forget about him, for he was always there, a malevolent presence on the edge of his vision.

Heralds had been sent to warn Damascus of the army's arrival and to make sure rooms in the palace were prepared for Baybars and his amirs. The main streets had been cleared for the approaching troops, and citizens lined the route to the palace, eager to welcome their sultan. Flowers were thrown as Baybars and the Mamluks entered, covering the street in a fluttering carpet of color, and the kettledrums' thunder made babies cry and dogs howl in houses all across the city. Whilst the bulk of the army set up camp on a plain outside the walls, Baybars and the vanguard made their way to the citadel, where they were met by the governor of Damascus.

Kalawun was handing the reins of his horse to one of his squires when a man dressed in the violet livery of a royal messenger approached him.

"Amir Kalawun?"

Kalawun looked around. "Yes?"

The messenger bowed and handed him a scroll. "This arrived at my post five days ago. When I learned that the army was headed for Damascus, I came straight here."

Kalawun took the scroll and broke the wax seal. He unfurled it to reveal three words in a hand he recognized.

It is safe.

As he saw Ishandiyar's message, Kalawun felt relief rise like a spring inside him, washing away the troubles that had been clouding his mind since he had left Cairo. But hardly had his worry for the safety of the Stone faded, when he felt a new twinge of concern, as he wondered whether any of Campbell's men, or even Campbell himself, had been hurt by his actions. Had he been rash to send Ishandiyar? No, he told himself firmly. Campbell's letter revealed none of his intentions, and all his assurances counted for little in Kalawun's mind when faced with the possibility of failure. Not only could he allow no harm to come to the Stone, but the threat of war behind the theft had simply been too great for him not to act. But still he remained discomforted by the feeling of betrayal that darkened his mind and the thought that he might have stained his hands with yet more blood in his pursuit of peace.

THE CITADEL, DAMASCUS, II JUNE A.D. 1277

After only two days' rest, the Mamluks gathered to discuss their plans, following the news that Abaga had entered the Seljuks' realm with his three *toumans* and had set about making swift reprisals upon the Muslims in Anatolia who had welcomed Baybars. Some indication of the ilkhan's wrath and his capacity for vengeance could be gauged by rumors that the Seljuk *pervaneh*, who fled the battlefield at Albistan after his lackluster involvement, was killed and served up in a stew at a state banquet. Abaga himself was said to have accepted a healthy portion. The ilkhan was now camped out in the realm, glaring at Syria across the Taurus divide. But word was that he had no plans to enter his enemy's territory, lacking the manpower to attack Baybars on his own ground. The two lions, their prides gathered around them, could only watch each other from afar, both grudgingly accepting of the fact that neither, for the moment, was strong enough to defeat the other.

During the debate, which centered around what the Mamluks' next move should be, a Bahri warrior entered and crossed to Baybars.

Kalawun glanced over, seeing the sultan lower his head as the soldier moved in close and murmured something.

"Bring him in," said Baybars, his deep voice cutting across the amirs who were speaking.

"My lord?" questioned Kalawun, as the amirs looked around, wondering who would dare to interrupt their council.

Baybars didn't respond and, instead, rose to his feet. A few moments later, the Bahri soldier returned, with two others flanking a young man in dirty black robes. The man carried his head high as he entered, his arrogance evident in his bold stance and his keen eyes, which met the sultan's gaze unflinchingly.

"Sultan Baybars," he said, not bothering to bow. "I have come to collect the remainder of the money promised to my order for the ransom of your officer, Nasir. We would have delivered him sooner, only we did not realize you had left Cairo. We have been tracking you for some time."

Kalawun looked to the side of the chamber, hearing an eager noise come from Khadir, who was seated there, cross-legged in a patch of sunlight. The soothsayer moved into a crablike crouch, his white eyes shimmering as he studied the young Assassin.

The rest of the chamber was hushed.

"Where is he?" demanded Baybars.

"Nearby," responded the Assassin carefully. "Two of my brothers are with him. When I have received the rest of the ransom, I will go to them immediately and order him to be released."

"Those terms are unacceptable. I will pay no ransom until I know the officer is safe."

The young Assassin didn't falter. "Then you will not see him again. My brothers have been given instructions to kill Nasir if I do not return within the hour."

Baybars's jaw twitched. For some moments, he didn't speak, then he gestured to one of the Bahri. "Summon the treasurer," he said, not taking his eyes off the Assassin.

Once the Assassin had been handed a bag of gold and had left the chamber, Baybars called four of the Bahri to him.

"Follow him," he told the soldiers. "Don't lose him. His brothers cannot be far if he is to return to them within the hour. Secure Officer Nasir, if he is with them, then kill the fidais and bring me back my gold."

The Bahri warriors saluted him.

When they had gone, Baybars turned to Kalawun. "I want the rest of these insurgents destroyed, Amir. Send a battalion of Syrian troops to Qadamus.

They will join forces with my lieutenants and proceed to the rebel fortress from there. I want this business ended."

"Yes, my lord," murmured Kalawun. He saw it in the sultan's eyes, heard it in his harsh voice: that old spark of rage, which had guttered and winked out these past months, had flared again. Khadir, too, seemed to have noticed it, for he was staring at Baybars, a look of triumph in his face. Seeing that look, Kalawun thought of the soothsayer's desire to set Baybars back on the path to war against the Christians and his plan to start a conflict with the attack on Kabul. He recalled too that it had been Khadir who had wanted someone to be sent to look for the Assassins, and he thought of his own, private suspicion that the former Shia had been somehow involved in the plot to steal the Stone. Kalawun felt unease stir. If Nasir had proof that it had been Franks who had wanted Baybars dead, what then would be the outcome? The Mamluks and Mongols had reached a stalemate, and Baybars's army, victorious and rested, was stationed in Damascus. Only three days' march from Acre.

THE DOCKS, ACRE, 11 JUNE A.D. 1277

Garin tossed his bag onto a bench at the stern and planted his hands on the ship's side, looking down at the green water eddying beneath. The sun needled the back of his neck, irritating the dark red patch it had already burned into his skin. His hair was a bleached, silvery-white against it. Behind him, the crew's voices were coarse and loud as the ship prepared to leave Acre's harbor, carrying a cargo of sugar to France. For Garin, their departure could not be swift enough.

He had returned to the city three days ago. Arriving at the royal palace, exhausted and embittered, he and the Cypriots had discovered that they were no longer welcome. Whilst they had been away, Count Roger had ejected the last of Hugh's staff from the fortress, and they were only admitted briefly to collect their belongings. Bertrand and his men, as defeated as their usurped master, had departed the next day on a ship bound for Cyprus. Garin had been left alone in a tavern on the harbor to brood over his misfortunes. Not only had he failed completely in his plan, but he had also been forced to relinquish every last gold coin he'd had on him to get himself and the Cypriots out of the desert. He had been using part of the money King Hugh had given him for Edward after signing the agreement, now useless since King Charles had eased himself onto the throne. A fair amount had now been eaten away out of the pile. Not only had he wasted a year, using Edward's money on his *qannob* and his whores and his stupid, useless idea, but he hadn't even managed to force out of Everard and the Anima Templi the funds the king had

demanded he secure. His only hope was that the members of the sugar vessel's crew
were partial to the dice and he might win back some of the lost profit, or he might
as well throw himself overboard now and save Edward the job.

He had nothing. And he was nothing.

The words held a sour echo of his uncle, Jacques, and his mother, and Edward. He tried to push them out, squeezing his eyes shut against their stinging
tones, but they just assailed him all the more, telling him he never did anything
right, that he was useless and would never be good enough, good as his dead
father and brothers, good as Will. That name entered his mind with the force
of a knife stab. Almost as frustrating as the failure of the mission was his failure
to remove, when he'd had the chance, that one galling thorn that had been
stuck in him since childhood. He needn't have done anything; only let that
sword in Bertrand's hand fall when it wanted to. It would have been over
quickly, quietly, with no blood or blame on him. He didn't understand why he
had shouted. Why he had stayed Bertrand's hand. All the way back through the
desert, Garin had recalled that moment, over and over, without ever coming to
any conclusion as to why he had saved Will's life when he could have so easily
let it be snuffed out. He had no feelings for Will, other than anger and dislike
and envy. Everything the knight had should have been his. The commandership, the place in the Anima Templi, the respect and friendship of his fellows,
the family who loved him whatever he had done wrong, the woman who wanted
him. Even as she had given herself so freely to him that day in the palace, Elwen
hadn't really wanted him, Garin knew. If she had, she wouldn't have cried so
bitterly afterward. The only pleasure he could now find in that sullied memory
was that he, at least, had taken something from Will, if only for a moment.
Something precious that could never be returned.

As the mooring ropes were loosed and the crew dug the oars into the water,
Garin put his head in his hands and, with numb detachment, felt wetness pressing against his fingers. He didn't look back as the vessel pulled out of the harbor
and Acre slid slowly away behind him, the empty sea swelling ahead.

THE CITADEL, DAMASCUS, 11 JUNE A.D. 1277

The minutes dragged into hours as Baybars sat, rigid and pensive. The council
had been brought to an abrupt close with the arrival of the Assassin, and only
Khadir and Kalawun remained in the chamber, Kalawun having been asked to
stay and Khadir having been forgotten, huddled in the corner.

Finally, after three tense hours, there came a knock at the doors and four figures entered. Three of them were the Bahri soldiers Baybars had set in pursuit of the Assassins. The fourth was Nasir. Kalawun rose as he saw the officer. Nasir was thin to the point of emaciation, his hair and beard filthy and matted, his olive skin pale and bruised. He was a husk of the man he had been. Guilt took a stab at Kalawun for being the one who had ordered his officer and friend into such danger and degradation, and struck him hard in the center of his chest. He took a step toward Nasir.

Baybars stopped him with a raised hand. "Is it done?" he asked the Bahri.

One of the soldiers came forward and handed him the leather bag the Assassin had been given, filled with gold. The bag was splattered with some dark matter. Blood, Kalawun thought. There was more of it on the uniforms of the Bahri, and one of them appeared to be wounded.

"It is, my lord. But we lost one man."

Baybars nodded whilst he weighed the bag in his hands, as if the loss was acceptable, then turned his attention on the wasted figure of Nasir, who hardly seemed able to support himself. "Do you have what you were sent to find?"

Nasir nodded wearily and opened his mouth to speak. His voice came out as insubstantial as a breeze, just the faintest breath of sound. He coughed weakly and tried again.

Baybars reached for one of the goblets of cordial left on the table. He strode to Nasir and put it into his hand. "Drink."

Nasir took the goblet and put it to his cracked, yellowed lips. After a moment, he handed the goblet back to Baybars. "Yes, my lord," he murmured roughly. "I have it."

Baybars's voice shook a little as he spoke. "Who was it? Who hired the Assassins to murder me?"

"A Frank, my lord, as you thought. A Templar, called William Campbell."

Baybars looked around as Kalawun let out a shocked noise. "What is it, Kalawun?"

Kalawun felt words gluing up in his throat. He didn't know what to say to cover the exclamation. He was saved, unexpectedly, by Khadir, who leapt to his feet.

"You know him, my lord!" the soothsayer gurgled. "You know him!"

Baybars started to shake his head.

"That was the name of the man who bore the treaty!" Khadir's voice climbed to a feverish pitch. "He bore the Franks' peace treaty five years ago!"

Baybars saw himself amidst the ruins of Caesarea, sitting on his throne in the center of the broken cathedral. He recalled the young Christian knight, a Templar, who had handed him the truce signed by Edward of England. He remembered that he had dark hair and spoke Arabic and remembered the knight asking to be allowed to go to Safed. Then, at the last, Baybars recalled his name and knew Khadir was right.

"You let him bury his father," said Khadir, almost crowing now.

"Be quiet," murmured Baybars, his hand tightening around the goblet, fingers pressing into the soft metal.

"You let him cross your lands with an escort of your own men!"

"I said be quiet!" roared Baybars, flinging the goblet against the wall, where it rang like a bell and sprayed scarlet across the whitewash.

Khadir dropped to the floor, cringing from the sultan's wrath. The soldiers and Nasir said nothing, but judiciously avoided Baybars's ruinous stare.

"My lord . . . ," began Kalawun.

"I want you to find him," said Baybars, cutting across Kalawun and looking at the Bahri. "Find him and bring him to me."

"Where do you propose we begin our search, my lord?" asked one of the Bahri, still keeping his head lowered.

"The Temple in Acre. If he is not there, they will know where he is."

"My lord," Kalawun said again, more forcefully now.

Baybars looked at him.

"How do you know it is the same knight who delivered the treaty to you? William is a common Frankish name. Maybe there is more than one who goes by the name of Campbell?"

"Then I will kill every Christian of this name that I find," said Baybars in an iron voice, resolute, unyielding, "until I am certain that I have erased from this earth the man who hired killers to attack me at the betrothal feast of my son and heir. Killers whose blades did not find me, but the heart of the one man who loved me as a brother, unconditionally, without fear or doubt." Baybars's voice broke as he said these words. He stared at Kalawun a moment longer, then turned and swept out of the room. "You have your orders," he said to the soldiers in passing.

Khadir scuttled out after the sultan, leaving Kalawun alone with Nasir as the tired Bahri returned obediently to the citadel's stables to fetch their horses.

Kalawun went to Nasir and embraced him. "I was certain you were dead."

Nasir managed a small smile. "So was I."

"I feel ashamed," Kalawun began, falteringly, keeping a hand on Nasir's shoulder.

"You mustn't, Amir. I was doing my duty."

Kalawun shook his head. He stayed quiet for a moment, unsure of whether to continue. If he opened this box, he would not be able to shut it again. But the opportunity to make amends for his betrayal of Will filled him with a sense of urgency and he could keep it in no longer. "No, Nasir. I feel ashamed for what I am about to ask you." He sighed roughly. "I do not know what to do. There is no one else I can ask. I would go myself, only I would be missed, and the only other man I trust enough with this information is in Cairo."

"What is it, Amir?"

Kalawun crossed to the doors, pressed them to make sure they were shut, then moved to a tapestry on one of the walls, which showed a garden scene. He lifted it to check that the hidden door behind it was locked. The citadel in Damascus, like the one in Cairo, was riddled with servants' passages. Satisfied that they were alone, he went back to Nasir. "This knight whose name you have delivered to our master, I know him."

Nasir remained silent as the commander explained that the knight had warned him of a Western plot to steal the Black Stone from Mecca. "You stopped it from happening?" he asked quickly when Kalawun had finished.

"The knight swore that he would prevent it, but when it came to it I simply couldn't bring myself to entrust such a mission to a non-Muslim, however good his intentions. I sent Amir Ishandiyar. I have just received word from him that the Stone is safe."

"That is good," murmured Nasir.

"I do not know if this knight was in Mecca himself or, if he was, whether he made it out unharmed. But if he did, he must be warned. I need you to find him before the Bahri do."

Nasir stared at him.

"I know this is asking much of you," said Kalawun, "perhaps too much. But I owe this knight, Nasir. We all do. If not for him, we might now be at war, a war that would be detrimental to us all. Believe me, my friend, I would not ask such a thing of you were it not for the greater good. You have to trust me. I will explain everything when you return, but right now, I need you to find him and warn him. Tell him to leave this land and never return."

30

The Temple, Acre

14 JUNE A.D. 1277

Will started as someone grabbed his shoulder. He saw Simon behind him.

The groom smiled broadly. "It's good to see you back." He looked Will up and down. "God, but you're as dark as a Saracen. I came to see you earlier in your quarters, but they told me you was meeting with the grand master."

"I was giving my report."

"How was the assignment?"

Will shrugged. "Mostly uneventful. We spoke with the Mongols, were entertained in their court and reaffirmed our pledge to continue our friendship with their people."

Simon gave him a pointed look. "Come on," he said seriously. "I've heard the rumors. Some of your company didn't return and it's been said Robert de Paris was wounded." He lowered his voice further. "Was it the Mongols? I've heard they . . . *do* things to their foes. Terrible things."

Will was surprised. They had only arrived in Acre the day before, and he hadn't expected the rumors to start flying so quickly. "Your imagination is as active as ever." His expression grew solemn. "No, it wasn't the Mongols. There was an accident when we were coming back through the mountains, a riding accident. We lost three men and Robert was only just saved."

"What happened?"

"I'd rather not talk about it."

Simon nodded. "Course not. Sorry."

Will smiled his thanks, feeling like a traitor. "Listen, we'll talk soon. But right now, I've got to see Robert in the infirmary."

"There's something you should know first, Will. Elwen's been coming to the preceptory for the past few weeks."

"Coming here?" said Will, troubled.

"Don't worry, she was discreet and only spoke to me. She was wanting to know if you'd returned."

Will sighed quietly. He had a lot of amends to make now he was back. "I'll see her later."

Simon sucked at his lip. "I'd go and see her now if I was you. She didn't look ..." He shook his head. "Well, she looked ill."

"Ill?" said Will quickly.

"She was distressed too." Simon gave an awkward shrug. "Crying and the like. I didn't know what to say, to be frank."

Will glanced at the infirmary. He had to speak with Robert as soon as possible to brief the knight on the lie he and the grand master had agreed upon to explain the deaths of Carlo, Franscesco and Alessandro. But if Elwen needed him? "I'll go now," he said.

"I'll ready you a horse."

Will remained in the courtyard whilst Simon hastened to the stables. His mind was filled with worry. It wasn't like Elwen to cry in front of others, or to risk coming to the Temple for that matter. He was distracted from his concern by the stooped figure of Everard, crossing the yard toward him. The priest was terribly pale, and every step seemed to pain him.

"William," he croaked in greeting. "Too busy to see me again?" Everard held up a hand as Will went to speak. "We must talk."

"I was going to see you later," Will explained. "I returned late last night and didn't want to wake you."

"And you were, what? Out here catching a little rest? Sunning yourself?"

"I was ..." Will faltered, staring in the direction of the stables. He met the priest's unyielding gaze with a gritted jaw. "It doesn't matter. It can wait for a moment." He followed Everard reluctantly across the courtyard and into the knights' quarters.

"I planned to summon the Brethren as soon as I heard you had returned," said Everard, closing the door behind them as they entered his solar. "But I wanted to talk to you first. I take it you were successful?" His eyes were keen, but the anxiety in them was plain.

Will accepted the goblet of wine Everard handed to him. "It depends what you would define as a success. If you mean did we stop the theft, then yes."

Everard sat with a nod.

"If you mean did we do it without loss of life," continued Will, "or the notice of anyone, then no."

"I heard three of de Beaujeu's men died," said Everard, sipping his wine. "Tell me what happened."

Will recounted it bluntly.

Everard waited until Will had finished, then rose to refill his goblet. He stumbled as he stood, only just managing to catch himself from falling. Will was up in an instant, steadying him, but Everard brushed him away. "Don't fuss, don't fuss!"

"Are you all right?"

Everard tutted. "I'm just old, William." He let out a wheezy sigh. "Just old." He hobbled the last few feet to the wine jug. "Those who ambushed you outside Mecca. You say they knew Latin?"

"Not just knew it. They were fluent and had Western accents."

"French? English?"

"I'm not sure." Will struggled to remember. "I was dazed from the fall." He shook his head. "I don't know."

"And you believe the men who attacked you in the Haram Mosque were Mamluks?"

"I'm positive. I think Kalawun must have sent them."

"Without warning us?"

"Perhaps he didn't get my message telling him that we were set."

"Or he did, but didn't trust us to see it through."

Will nodded grimly. "It's possible."

"Well, all that matters is that the Stone is safe." Everard caught Will's eye. "And that you are," he added. "You were lucky to return at all. I would have thought, with Kaysan gone, that the Shias would have left you in the desert."

"They were wanted men as much as we were. They knew it was safer to travel back to Ula with us than to try it alone."

"All the same, you were fortunate. I hear Robert de Paris was injured?"

"He should be fine in a few weeks," said Will, staring tensely into his goblet.

"Don't shoulder any guilt for him, William," said Everard, shrewdly. "In the end, Robert made his decision based on what he thought was right."

Will finished his wine, rather than respond. "I suppose it is over now anyway."

"Not entirely. There is still the matter of the grand master's involvement and the identity of those he has been working with. As you know, I had two of the Brethren investigate Angelo Vitturi last year. We discovered that he was heir to a powerful slave-trading business, run by his father, Venerio, a business that has declined in recent years. We also discovered that Guido Soranzo was in a similar position as a shipbuilder, formerly affluent but affected by falling profits."

"I remember."

"Whilst you were away we found out that the Vitturis have had contracts

with the Mamluks to ship them boys for the army. This may be where the connection in Cairo stems from: Kaysan's brother."

"It is possible," ventured Will. "But we have no proof that Angelo Vitturi
even knew what the grand master was planning. Soranzo was the only real link
to the Stone."

"And therein lies our problem. The grand master has admitted to you that
there were others involved, but has given you no indication of whom."

"Is it really that important? We stopped it."

"For now, yes. But these men, whoever they are, are obviously determined.
To go to such lengths? To take such risks? I cannot believe this will truly be the
end of it. The Brethren and I spoke whilst you were away," continued Everard,
slowly. "We feel, William, considering your position with the grand master,
that you should attempt to retrieve this information from him."

Guillaume de Beaujeu turned back to the window as the scribe finished the last
line of the letter, his quill flicking across the paper, the goose feather twitching
with every stroke. "Say that I will be in contact again soon and end it with my
regards. You can leave when you are done."

The scribe looked up from the desk. "My lord?" He glanced at the blank
sheets beside him. "Did you not require me to write several messages today? I
thought ...?"

"Later," Guillaume cut across him. "We will finish them later. Go."

"As you wish, my lord," said the scribe, hastily penning the final words and
gathering up his writing tools and the completed letter. Bowing to the grand
master's back, he left the chamber.

Guillaume closed his eyes as the door shut, the sunlight coming through the
window leaving a red imprint behind his eyelids. Beneath his thick mantle, he
was sweating. His head throbbed and his stomach churned. He reached out and
clutched the window frame, gripping the cold stone.

After hearing Will's report, Guillaume had immediately summoned the
scribe. The messages he had been sending Charles, Edward and the pope all
these months, telling them to prepare for a new war in Outremer, were no longer relevant and he needed to retract and amend his former requests. But it
wasn't until he had begun dictating the first message that the reality of what had
happened had struck him. *Stricken* him.

They had failed.

There would be no Stone for Christendom to rally around, no relic of the
infidel to wield in triumph. The Muslims would not rise against them in rage,

necessitating an immediate response from the West. The Mamluks would continue their war against the Mongols; then, when they were ready, Baybars and his slave warriors would simply sweep away the few remaining fragmented Frankish cities and all dreams for a Christian Holy Land would finally come to an end. Guillaume had come with grand plans and a fiery determination, resolved to take back that which had been lost to them, to work God's will, to deliver Jerusalem. Everything he had done since he had arrived in Acre had been to this end: his support of his cousin Charles; his personal battle against the weak King Hugh; his secret involvement with the merchants' plot. All had been for nothing.

But even through the gravity of defeat, he felt relief as the worry he had failed to extinguish these past few months finally went out. They could have lost everything, had they succeeded. Guillaume had already been informed by the visitor, Hugues de Pairaud, in Paris, that the Temple was encountering significant delays in the building of the planned fleet. The rulers of the West might not have come to their aid in time, and even though he had secured his throne in Outremer, Charles had shown no sign that he would take up his seat in Acre anytime soon. Guillaume's jaw tightened. But perhaps it would have been better to fall in battle with honor, a battle chosen on their terms, rather than lie here supine, waiting for the axe to fall.

There was a rap at the door. Guillaume turned, angered by the interruption.

The door opened and Zaccaria appeared, his face wearied and sun-dark. "My lord, you have a visitor."

"I told you that I wasn't to be ..." Guillaume stopped as he saw a figure dressed in black behind the knight. It was Angelo Vitturi. Guillaume bit back his irritation. He had told Zaccaria to bring the Venetian straight to him whenever he came to the Temple. The Sicilian was just following orders.

"Good day to you, my lord," said Angelo, as Zaccaria closed the door, leaving them alone.

The young man's swarthy, handsome face was set and inexpressive, but Guillaume caught something inimical in his greeting, something contemptuous in the way Angelo had spoken his title, *my lord*, as if it were an insult rather than an honor. "Why are you here?" he demanded, his voice forceful.

"You know why," spat Angelo, firing the words at the grand master as if they were arrows.

Guillaume instantly understood. "You have heard."

"That our plan has failed? Yes, I have heard," Angelo replied harshly.

"How?"

"Tell me what happened," said Angelo, ignoring the question. "My father demands an explanation."

Guillaume's manner sharpened, his voice whipping out. "You would do well to keep civil with me, Vitturi. Do not forget to whom you are speaking."

Angelo paused, his stare like ice, then forced back some of his enmity. It looked as if it were an effort. "I apologize, my lord. But my father and his associates are most aggrieved by this news. We wish to know, in your words, the reason for the failure."

Guillaume threw a hand at one of the stools in front of his desk. "Sit."

Angelo seemed reluctant to comply, but did so after a moment. Guillaume remained standing as he told the merchant what Will had told him: that the knights had made it to Mecca with Kaysan and the Shias, but had been attacked inside the mosque by guards and were unable to take the Stone.

When he had finished, Angelo remained seated for a few seconds, saying nothing. Then he rose, his face displaying an almost triumphant vehemence. "We know that isn't true," he snapped, all pretense at civility falling away. "Your men didn't fail; they sabotaged the mission." Guillaume almost laughed, so great was his surprise at the accusation, but before he could speak, Angelo continued. "We have received information that one of your men has been in secret talks with Amir Kalawun al-Alfi, Baybars's chief lieutenant, working with him to thwart our plan. He warned Kalawun of it months ago."

"What man?" retorted Guillaume incredulously.

"The very same man you placed in charge of the mission. Commander William Campbell."

Now Guillaume did laugh. "This is preposterous!" His laughter faded abruptly. "Where did you get this 'information'?" He searched Angelo's face, but could see no lie. Doubt rose inside him, clouding his convictions.

"What we really want to know, my lord," continued Angelo, his voice baleful, "is how a mere knight managed to come into contact with one of the most powerful men in the Mamluk Army. He could not have done it alone."

"What are you suggesting?" said Guillaume in a dangerous tone.

"You put him in charge of the assignment and chose the men who would accompany him."

"And three of my knights died in the attempt! Men who have been with me for years. Brave souls all three."

"An acceptable sacrifice, I'm sure. You weren't comfortable with this from the start; that much was obvious. You have been working against us, making sure we would fail."

"Get out of my sight," growled Guillaume, striding around the desk to the door. "Leave and take your fantasies with you, or by God I will make you sorry. Tell your father and his associates that this matter is ended." He reached for the door handle. "It is over."

"Not quite," replied Angelo. He let the dagger he had been holding, concealed by the wide sleeve of his brocaded coat, drop down into his hand.

Guillaume caught a flash of metal as Angelo came at him, swift and determined, black eyes filled with venom. There was a second or two of motionless shock, before his mind snapped into focus and then Angelo was on him, punching the blade toward his side. Guillaume twisted at the last moment and grabbed at Angelo's shoulders, trying to force him away. As he did so, he felt a bolt of pain in his side, a slipping, slicing motion, followed by wetness, hot and sudden. There was horror, as he realized he had been stabbed. Then fury. His hands wrapped around Angelo's neck. The Venetian dropped the blade, which clattered to the tiles, and wrestled with him. The grand master was the stronger and bigger of the two, and even through his blinding pain, he pushed Angelo back, slamming him into the edge of the desk, forcing him down until he was almost bent over him.

Angelo jammed his fingers into Guillaume's wrists, pressing desperately into the flesh. He struggled and gasped, writhing on the desk as the grand master, his face white and contorted, continued to strangle him. Through his dimming gaze Angelo saw a stain growing on Guillaume's mantle, red as the cross on his chest. The grand master's eyes flickered. He reeled, almost falling onto Angelo. In the swoon, his grip loosened, and Angelo managed to prise his hands off and slide out from under him. He lurched away, choking, as Guillaume clutched the desk and stumbled round it, pressing his hand to his side, where the redness was spreading. Angelo, breathing harshly, looked around for the dagger. He saw it lying on the tiles and went for it. He spun, hearing a rasping sound, and saw that the grand master had found and drawn a sword. Guillaume's face was ashen and sweat had made a filmy sheen of his skin, but despite his obvious agony, his expression was grimly resolved as he staggered toward him. Angelo took a brief measure of the situation; then, slipping the dagger back into his sleeve, he reached for the door and opened it. As the door slammed shut, Guillaume felt another faint overcome him, and he dropped the sword and fell to his knees, streams of sickening pain coursing through him. He thought that he was dying and pushed a prayer through his clenched teeth. But shortly the dizziness passed and his vision began to clear. Now the pain was a rod of iron, a single, solid block. Forcing himself to his knees, he grasped the corner of his desk and hauled himself up, groaning as the wound in his side seared and throbbed. He made it to the door and wrenched it open.

"Zaccaria!" he shouted, his voice sounding frail in his ears.

After a moment, two knights appeared through one of the doors leading off along the stone passage. "He isn't here, my lord," said one, walking toward him. "He left to escort someone to the gates, barely minutes ago."

"God damn it," breathed Guillaume.

"My lord . . . ?" The knight stopped, his eyes falling to Guillaume's side, and the dark red stain. His mouth opened in shock. "Fetch the physicians," he barked at his companion, stepping toward the grand master.

"No," said Guillaume gruffly. "First, make sure the man Zaccaria is with does not leave this preceptory. *Go!*" he roared, when the knight didn't move.

The knight turned on his heel and sprinted down the passage.

"You," breathed the grand master to the one who remained, "find William Campbell. I want him arrested." He clutched the door tightly, holding himself upright. "Then fetch me the infirmarer."

Simon stood in the center of the courtyard, staring around him. The horse he had saddled, a swift piebald gelding, nudged him in the back and snorted. Simon stroked its nose absently. "Where is he then?" he murmured, turning in a slow circle. There were several knights over by the officials' building and a few sergeants, practice swords in hands, heading across the yard in the direction of the training ground. But no sign of Will.

After a moment, Simon walked toward the gate, leading the gelding behind him. He had been delayed, the stable master insisting that he prepare two horses for the marshal, and he guessed that Will must have grown impatient and left. But if he had only been gone a few minutes, Simon could probably catch him up. It seemed daft that he should walk all the way to Elwen's house when there was a perfectly good horse saddled and ready. Simon was setting off across the yard, when a sergeant came jogging over. It was Paul, one of the guards whose post was at the gates.

He hailed Simon. "Have you seen Commander Campbell?"

"I was looking for him myself. I thought he might have left the preceptory." Simon glanced past Paul, toward the main gate. "You haven't seen him?"

Paul shook his head. "No. But Richard and I have only just come on duty. There's a man here wanting to talk to him. Says it's urgent."

"Who is it?"

"Won't give a name. Says Commander Campbell will know what it's about and he should come immediately."

Simon frowned indecisively; then puffing a sigh through his cheeks, he walked the horse to a hobbling post. "You go and ask the guards who were on the shift before you if they saw the commander leave," he said to Paul, slinging the reins over the post. "I'll see what this man wants."

Paul looked a little unsure. "I don't mean to be rude, but I'm not certain you should be getting involved in the commander's business."

"He's my friend, Paul. He won't mind. If it's that important, he'll most likely thank me for it."

"On your head be it," said Paul, heading for the guardhouse.

Simon made his way to the gate tower, nodded to Paul's comrade, Richard, who was standing guard, then stepped through the door cut into the massive gates. He came out on the street and pulled the door closed behind him, scanning the people moving past. His eyes drifted over the buildings on the other side of the street and came to rest on a lone man, swaddled in a gray burnous, his face partially hidden by the cowl. He was the only person in the street who didn't look as if he were passing through on some business or other. The figure was staring at him, but made no move to cross the street. Simon went cautiously over, avoiding two men pushing a handcart filled with the velvet globes of peaches.

"Good day," he called tentatively, approaching the man. "Are you waiting for Commander Campbell?"

The man didn't move. "I am."

Although he spoke Latin, Simon recognized his accent as Arabic. "Can I give him a message?"

"I talk with him, very importantly. Where is him?"

"I think he's gone into the city," said Simon, speaking slowly so the man could understand him. "But if you tell me why you wish to speak with him, I can tell him when he returns."

The man frowned as he listened to Simon's words. "Where in city?"

"I ..." Simon faltered. The man's unwavering stare was making him nervous. Perhaps Paul was right; this wasn't his business. "You should wait here," he said, taking a step back. "Commander Campbell will return soon I'm sure."

The man's hand shot out and grasped Simon's arm, hard. *"Where?"* he hissed.

Simon tried to pull away, but the man, although much slighter of build, was incredibly strong and held him tightly. "Hey! Let go of me!"

The man pursed his lips and whistled. Instantly, two other figures, dressed in the same drab cloaks, emerged from the mouth of an alley a few paces away.

Simon didn't even notice. He was standing stock-still, all his attention focused on the vicious-looking dagger that the man holding him had drawn, which was now pointed toward his stomach.

"You take us to Campbell, or we killing you," murmured the man.

His legs shaking uncontrollably, his bladder bloated with fear, Simon let himself be led by the three figures down the alley, where they met a fourth man who was waiting with horses.

31

The Temple, Acre

14 JUNE A.D. 1277

"I'm not convinced it will work," said Will, placing his empty goblet on the table.

"You agreed," said Everard sharply. "You just said you would talk to him."

Will glanced round. "I said I would try. But I have to be careful. The mission failed and I was in charge. The grand master isn't particularly pleased with me at present. The last thing I should be doing is arousing his suspicions and making him think that I was in any way responsible for the failure. When I attempted before to ask him who he was working with, he brushed the issue aside, clearly unwilling to talk about it. Now the whole thing is ended, I think it will look strange me trying to find out things that are no longer relevant."

"What are you saying?"

Will flicked aside the heavy drape that covered the window, letting light rush into the solar. "I'm saying I'll talk to him, but that I don't think we should place all our hopes on finding information on those involved through de Beaujeu himself." He caught sight of a stocky figure in black in the courtyard below, leading a horse by its reins. It was Simon. He sighed roughly, realizing that he had been delayed far too long. "Everard, I have to go. We'll talk more later. Summon the Brethren. I will see what I can do to convince the Grand Master to …"

His words disappeared as the door banged open and a knight entered. His gaze fixed straight on Will. "He's here!" he shouted over his shoulder.

Everard rose and Will stared at the intruder in confusion as footsteps came pounding down the passage and two more knights burst in, swords in their hands.

"What is the meaning of this?" questioned the priest, his washed-out eyes animated with anger.

"Commander Campbell," said the first knight. "You are to come with us at once."

"Where?"

"To the cells. You are under arrest."

"What charge do you lay on him?" demanded Everard, but there was a note of alarm in his voice.

"We are here on the orders of Grand Master de Beaujeu," said the knight, ignoring the priest and heading to Will. "Put down your sword."

Will hesitated, looking from Everard to the grim-faced knights; then he drew his falchion, slowly. The armed knights tensed. But Will laid the sword on Everard's table and let them come forward and take him. He caught Everard's frightened gaze as they marched him from the solar. "Don't worry," he murmured.

Four hours later, Will was sitting slumped against the wall in one of the cells beneath the treasury tower, listening to the waves pounding the rocks outside. It had been with a horrible sense of familiarity that he had been led down into the prison, memories of his visits to Garin years earlier returning to haunt him, reminding him how terrible a fate it had seemed; how cramped the cells were; how the air seemed heavier in the dank darkness, harder to breathe. His mind reeled with the implications of his arrest. The knights had given no reason for it, but only one conclusion kept returning to him. The grand master knew. Somehow, he knew. After a while, Will had started to become maddened by the waiting, by the constant muffled rush and thump of the waves, by the thoughts in his head, unanswered, going round and round, tormenting him.

Hearing the sound of voices in the passage, Will looked up. Footsteps came closer and he rose to his feet, blood shooting back into his cramped legs. There was a clinking of keys, the rattle and clack of a bolt being drawn back. The cell door opened. Torchlight blasted into his eyes and he raised an arm to cover his face. Squinting out, Will saw Guillaume de Beaujeu ducking awkwardly through the low entrance behind a guard who inserted the crackling torch into a bracket on the wall and then left. The cell was small enough with just Will inside; with the grand master's huge frame now filling it, it seemed to shrink even further. Will blinked, trying to let his eyes settle. The first thing he noticed was how different the grand master appeared to how he had looked just hours earlier when Will had given his report. His skin was gray, and his usually composed expression had been replaced by one of pain. He had a stick in one hand, which he was leaning heavily on, and as he shifted his weight to his other foot, he flinched. Will was shocked by the transformation, wondering if some sickness had come upon him. "My lord," he began, then fell silent as Guillaume leveled him with a damning stare.

"Did you do it?" Guillaume's voice was husky, with pain or emotion Will wasn't sure.

"My lord, if I may ask, why am I here?"

"Did you betray me?" murmured the grand master. "Did you meet with Amir Kalawun and warn him of our plan?" His face changed when Will didn't respond, rage causing color to leap into his waxy cheeks. "*Did you?*"

Will let out a small breath, and with it a word. "Yes."

Guillaume looked taken aback, as if he hadn't been expecting this response or, at any rate, the swiftness of it. But his fury quickly returned. "Explain yourself."

Will looked at the floor. He felt the stone wall at his back and the vibration of the sea shuddering through him. He wavered, wondering how he could admit to the head of the Temple that he had disobeyed his orders and, worse, had actively worked against him. *You face a traitor's death,* a voice whispered warningly inside him. But he was exhausted from his journey, exhausted by the lies and the questions, the uncertainty and secrecy. Touching the wall with his fingertips as if its substantiality would somehow imbue him with the strength he needed, he raised his head and met the grand master's stare. "I believed that if we took the Stone we would be destroyed: the Temple, Acre." He spread his hands. "Every one of us. I couldn't see how we could hope to withstand the Muslims' fury over such an act. I felt it would be the end of us."

"You felt?" said Guillaume, his voice shaking with pent-up violence. He took a step toward Will, whipping up the stick and brandishing it. "I do not care what you felt! You are a knight! A commander, yes, but under me, subject to my wishes, my orders. Whether you thought them right or wrong you should have obeyed them. Without question. Without *fail!*" Guillaume paused to draw breath, but he wasn't finished. "I was elected by the council of thirteen to this position. I took a vow to lead this order, to do what is best for us, for Christendom. And to this end, my word is law."

"I took a vow also, my lord," said Will, anger jolting unexpectedly through him, making his own voice rise. "I pledged obedience to you and to all those above me at my inception, but I also swore an oath to keep safe the Kingdom of Jerusalem. In doing what you asked, I had to break one of those vows." His words rang in the tiny chamber. "The only choice I had was which."

Guillaume stared at Will in what looked like shock. His lips parted and his eyes glittered in the torch flames.

"I did what I believed was right, my lord," continued Will, quieter now. "And I thought that perhaps you ..." He faltered, then steeled himself. "I thought you weren't acting entirely under your own volition. You told me there were others involved in this. I guessed they weren't from our order."

Guillaume's free hand drifted to his side and he looked pained again. He took a few paces back and leaned against the damp wall opposite Will. "No, they weren't," he muttered. "How did you meet with Amir Kalawun?" he said suddenly. "Why would he even speak with you?"

"I was introduced to him through my father," replied Will. It was partly true. It had been James Campbell who first made contact with Kalawun on behalf of the Anima Templi.

"Your father ...?" said Guillaume, shaking his head in confusion.

"Kalawun desires peace, my lord," explained Will quickly. "He sees the benefit in it to both our peoples. The Mamluks rely on us for trade. Kalawun is on our side. He doesn't want to destroy us."

Guillaume gave a bark of scornful laughter. "It does not well matter what he wants when Baybars is the Mamluks' lord and master. The sultan wants us gone from these lands. His people will follow him to that end."

"Baybars won't be sultan forever, my lord. Kalawun has influence over his heir, Baraka Khan. He believes he can bring the boy round to his way of thinking and that when he takes the throne, Baraka will be more amenable to our occupancy of these lands than his father." Will pushed himself from the wall. "We have a chance, my lord," he said earnestly, "to save Christendom in the East *without* bloodshed. But if the Stone had been stolen, that chance would have been dashed."

"I am not a fool," responded Guillaume harshly. "I wouldn't have gone through with the plan had I not believed it could work. The Stone would have been used to gather support for a new Crusade. The West would have come to our aid if Baybars had risen against us." But his words sounded hollow. He seemed to realize this, for his face crumpled in consternation. "I could see no other way," he murmured. "I couldn't sit here doing nothing, waiting for Baybars to end us. I was trying to protect us," he finished defiantly.

Will took a chance. "What about the men you were working with, my lord? Why did they want to take the Stone?"

Guillaume glanced at him. "For the money," he said bitterly. "Not for Jerusalem." He seemed to debate whether or not to continue, then sighed gruffly. "What does it matter now?" He touched his hand lightly to his side again. "One of them tried to kill me. According to the infirmarer, he almost did. If the blade had cut any deeper ..." He didn't finish.

Will was stunned.

"He believed that you were following my orders," Guillaume went on. "That I tried to sabotage their plan. He told me of your involvement with Kalawun."

"How did he know? Who is he?"

"Angelo Vitturi. You've met him."

Will nodded slowly.

"As to how he knew, he would not say," continued Guillaume. "But he has a contact in the Mamluk camp, the man who introduced us to Kaysan. Perhaps you were seen meeting with Kalawun? Or perhaps Kalawun himself let the information out."

"I would be surprised if it were either. Do you know the identity of this contact, my lord?"

"Vitturi never told me. He and his associates were very guarded. They simply wanted me to choose men able to enter Arabia, make contact with Kaysan and attempt the theft." Guillaume nodded at Will's expression. "They were using me, of course. But I thought I could use them. I did not agree with their motives. A group of powerful merchants whose business lay in war, trying to revive their flagging profits at any cost, was abhorrent to me. But I believed I could make their plan work for us."

Both of them lapsed into silence.

Eventually, Will spoke. "What are you going to do, my lord?"

Guillaume's face hardened; then he let a long breath whisper through his lips. "I had thought to have you executed, William. I came here to try you myself, and had I found you guilty of what Vitturi accused you of, I was to have you hanged this very evening."

Will tensed and had to clear his throat before he could speak. "And what is your decision, my lord?"

"You are guilty," said Guillaume, after a moment. "Guilty of disobeying my orders, guilty of consorting with our enemy and responsible for the deaths of three of my men. Good men," he added, nodding as Will hung his head. "But your motives were not self-serving. You did not seek to gain by your actions, nor did you intend harm against your brothers, or the Temple." He crossed to the door using his stick and took hold of the handle. "The theft was not without grave risk; I always knew that, but with no other option that I could see, I would not let myself give in to that fear. But had we succeeded ..." He trailed off and looked at Will. "Perhaps God has been trying to tell me something? I refused to listen to my worries, but I cannot ignore two attempts on my life from the men I was involved with." He opened the door and gestured through it.

"I'm free to go?" murmured Will, fearing to hope.

"I want a full report of what happened at Mecca," said Guillaume harshly. "This time the truth. And you will be punished for your actions, William. I cannot ignore your gross insubordination, however noble you thought your cause." He paused. "But not today and not with a hanging."

"I thank you, my lord, for your mercy," said Will, stepping, utterly grateful, into the briny underground air of the prison passage.

Guillaume said nothing, but gave a curt nod.

"What will happen to Vitturi?" asked Will, as they moved off.

"It is being dealt with."

THE CHURCH OF ST. NICHOLAS, OUTSIDE ACRE,
14 JUNE A.D. 1277

The settlement outside Acre's walls was a ruin. It had been for eight years, ever since Baybars had last appeared before the city with six thousand troops, planning to mount an assault. Unable, once again, to break Acre's indomitable defenses, he had contented himself with the ambush and slaughter of a large battalion of Frankish knights, returning from a raid on a Muslim stronghold, and the destruction of the settlement. All that remained were a few rugged walls and crumbled foundations of houses, covered with tufts of scrubby grass, and the desolate skeleton of what had once been the Church of St. Nicholas. Children sometimes played in the ruins, although most were warned away by their parents, following a partial collapse inside the church a year ago, which had claimed the lives of two boys. The place was tainted with the stale air of decay and forlorn abandonment, the naked timbers that remained on part of the roof split and shriveled after a decade under the Palestinian sun. Scorpions, black and slick, scuttled over fallen masonry outside and disappeared into cracks in the stones as the church door, warped and stiff, groaned open.

"You took your time."

Conradt von Bremen heard the voice before he saw the speaker, who loomed out of the shadows a second later, his black silk burnous making him one with the darkness.

"I was in urgent talks with a business associate of mine, Venerio," replied Conradt, in his lazy, heavily accented Italian. "I left as soon as I could. But this place was difficult to find."

Venerio swept past him and pulled at the door. It screeched over the uneven floor of the porch, was reluctant to close, then boomed shut. "Come," he said gruffly, "the others are here."

Striding around a latticed barrier of fallen beams, feet crunching on crumbled masonry, making prints in the layers of dust on the floor, Venerio led the German into what would have been the choir aisle. More beams littered the ground inside, some having shattered into dry shards and splinters, others leaning at uncomfortable angles against sagging pillars. Half of the west wall had come down, leaving a jagged silhouette against the blue backdrop of evening. The remaining timbers on the roof were steepled like bony fingers, large gaps between them revealing more sky. The sun had set an hour ago, slipping like a circle of butter into the horizon, and a single star, blunt and brilliant, had appeared in the vault of the roof.

In a space clear of much debris, in the center of the aisle, were three men. Two were sitting on blocks of fallen masonry and the third was pacing the floor. They all looked round as Venerio and Conradt appeared.

"We've been waiting hours," snapped Angelo, halting his restless stalking, his gaze fixing belligerently on the German. "Where have you been?"

Conradt languidly brushed the flop of sandy hair from his brow. His flat blue eyes met Angelo's. "I have explained my lateness to your father." The rebuke was plain.

His pride prickling, Angelo started forward, but Venerio placed a hand on his son's shoulder.

"Enough. We are here now."

"Then let us begin," came a singsong voice, as Renaud de Tours rose from the stone he had been perched upon. His small, round face looked up at the massive Venetian, his trimmed and neat hair blue-white in the dusk.

"Sit, gentlemen," said Venerio, gesturing at the blocks of stone tumbled irregularly around the center of the aisle.

Michael Pisani stood gracefully, his lean face pinched with concern. "We have done enough sitting, Venerio." He glanced at Conradt. "He would not tell us why he had brought us to this godforsaken place until you were here." The sharpness with which he spoke the words couldn't disguise the alarm that lay beneath them. "Explain yourself, Venerio," he demanded. "Obviously all did not go well." He gestured at Angelo. "The bruises on your son's neck, the urgent summons, the fear that's been coming off you both like a stench. What happened at the Temple? Is de Beaujeu dead?"

Venerio glanced at his son. There was a look of rancor in his face, unseen by the others but caught by Angelo, who scowled sullenly. "We aren't sure."

"What do you mean?" questioned Renaud quickly. "How can you not be sure?"

"Let him speak," said Conradt, his usually torpid voice quickened by the news.

"Angelo stabbed de Beaujeu, but the grand master attacked him and he had to flee."

"I do not think he would have survived," Angelo said, looking at the men, whose faces were grim in the gloom. "He looked as if he were dying when I left him."

"Looked as if?" murmured Michael, dangerously. "If there is even a possibility he survived ..." He trailed off.

"Angelo believes the wound to have been fatal," said Venerio. "He is competent enough to know."

"You aren't certain though, Venerio," Michael shot back, "or you wouldn't have brought us to this place. What are you saying? That we cannot return home?"

"This is why we are here," responded the Venetian. "To decide what to do."

Conradt had been quiet for some moments, his sun-red face pensive. He now turned his ice-blue eyes on Venerio. "I gave you my decision when we met last night, after you told us of the knights' failure to take the Stone."

"You were outvoted," snapped Angelo before his father could speak. "The others agreed that we had to kill de Beaujeu."

"There was no proof that he was working against us, that this knight, Campbell, was acting under his orders by warning the Mamluks of our plan." Conradt shook his head. "Why would de Beaujeu send his own men to Mecca if he knew the Mamluks would be there to stop them?"

"He would have had to make it look as though he were working with us," said Venerio, coming to his son's aid. "Or we would have known of his treachery when his knights failed to meet with Kaysan."

"It is true," said Renaud quietly. "We could not take the chance, Conradt. If the grand master was working against us, he could have ruined us. If the High Court discovered what we were planning and our reasons for it, we would have been finished, our property and estates confiscated, ourselves imprisoned, or worse."

Venerio scanned them all with his imperious gaze. "What is done is done. If de Beaujeu is dead, the only one of us implicated will be Angelo. He is ready to leave, as was arranged." He glanced at his son, who nodded.

"And what about the rest of us?" asked Michael. "We cannot all hide out in

Venice under the protection of the doge, waiting for this to blow over. God damn it!"

Conradt's growled response was drowned by an echoing *bang* that resounded around the church. All five men started at the sound. It was quickly followed by two other muffled thumps.

"What in hell's name was that?" murmured Michael.

"Children?" said Renaud hopefully.

Venerio drew his sword and strode to the doors, which were obscured from view by fallen timbers. Angelo drew his own blade and made as if to follow, but he had only taken a few paces when the air was filled with faint hissing sounds. The church grew suddenly bright and the shadows were thrown back as four yellow balls of flame soared in through the gaps in the roof.

"Fire!" shouted Michael, staggering back as one of the missiles dropped toward him. It was a clay bottle, flaming from the top, which exploded in a liquid burst of fire as it impacted with the floor. A fiery substance spattered out around it, some of it spitting onto Michael's robe. The Pisan shouted as the robe caught alight, the silk shriveling instantly. He tore the garment frantically from his shoulders, whilst around him the other missiles exploded, showering more of the flaming substance around the men and the debris-strewn church. It was Greek fire.

The broken beams on the floor were the first to ignite, blossoming into flame, crackling and splitting as the fire worked through them, spreading rapidly. The five men fell back shouting in alarm.

"The doors!" ordered Venerio.

"No!" yelled Michael, who had ripped off his robe. "They're trying to drive us out. That's what they want!"

"Who?" demanded Conradt.

But they all knew the answer. The Temple had found them.

Any argument over whether they should leave or not was cut short as two more missiles shattered into the aisle, whipping the blaze higher and wider. Seconds later, three flaming arrows thumped into the roof timbers high above them. The parched wood caught and flared.

"We'll fight them," said Venerio, through gritted teeth, heading for the doors.

But when they reached the exit, the thumping sounds they had heard only moments before became clear as the doors refused to budge. Someone had wedged the other side with something heavy. Try as they might, the men could not move them.

There was a *whump* as more of the timbers behind them caught alight. The interior of the church was now bright as day. A cloud of white smoke was rising, billowing to the roof, where a second fire had started, the brittle beams above turning black and cracking apart, sending showers of embers like glowing rain into the church below.

"We'll climb the wall," shouted Angelo, sheathing his sword and darting back around the lattice of timbers by the doors, which hadn't yet caught. The heat took his breath away and seared his throat, and he halted, confronted with the roaring conflagration. He picked out a route to the side of the aisle and began climbing over the piles of shifting stones. There was a cracking sound and a gust of fire and sparks as one of the roof timbers collapsed. As the flames were fanned toward him, Angelo threw himself flat and screamed at the impossible heat of them. His cloak caught and began to burn. Scrabbling over the rest of the stones, he made it to the crumbled back wall and slammed into it, beating furiously at the flames.

The other men had left the doors and were now scaling the treacherous pile of rubble following Angelo, who had put out the last of the flames on his cloak and was slumped against the wall, whimpering and clutching his blistered and burned hands between his legs. There was another creaking, cracking noise from above. All of the men looked up. Michael cried out as another of the beams crashed down. One end of it came down on Renaud's back, smashing him into the rubble, crushing him.

Angelo screamed as the pile of masonry collapsed and his father was swept into the inferno in the center of the church, Michael following him a second later. Two more roof timbers fell and Conradt was swallowed by fire. The smoke swirled thickly. Angelo sank to his knees as flames devoured the world around him.

THE TEMPLE, ACRE, 14 JUNE A.D. 1277

"Are you certain?" demanded Everard insistently. "De Beaujeu knows nothing of us? Of the Brethren?"

"I'm certain," replied Will. He looked into the sky and took a draft of the fresh evening air, feeling the dampness and claustrophobia of the prison cell fading from him. The moon was yellow, almost full. He had heard one of the guards say there was going to be an eclipse in three days. Will felt his fear draining in shuddery bursts. Now he had been released, he realized how close he had come to never seeing daylight again. The thought made him weak. He and Everard were standing on the deserted battlements beside the treasury tower.

When he had climbed out of the underground cells, he had found the priest lingering in the courtyard.

"And the merchants? The Vitturis and the others? What will happen to them?"

"De Beaujeu said it was being dealt with," said Will, glancing at Everard. "I don't think we'll have to worry about them."

Everard rested his arms on the parapets. "I'm getting too old for this," he wheezed. "I thought we were done for." He turned back to Will. "By God and the saints, I swear you have more lives than a damn cat!"

Will laughed breathlessly in agreement. "When de Beaujeu knew I had betrayed him, I thought he was going to string me up himself that instant."

"You did well, William," said the priest seriously. He reached up and placed his bony, two-fingered hand on Will's shoulder. "A lesser man may have broken, may have given up our secrets through fear or thoughtlessness. You kept your calm and thought on your feet." A rare smile lit his face. "I feared as you left my chamber that it would be the last time I ever saw you."

Will was about to respond when he saw a figure running across the courtyard toward the treasury tower. He recognized Simon and called down. Simon came to a halt, his head snapping up. In the yellow torch glare his face, white and wretched, was starkly revealed.

"Will!" he called hoarsely, racing to the stone steps that climbed to the ramparts and rushing headlong up them. He tripped, fell forward and almost threw himself at Will, who had gone quickly down to meet him, alarm filling him at the sight of Simon's face.

"What is it?" demanded Will, catching Simon by the arms.

"Dear God," breathed the groom, "dear God." He dragged in several pained breaths and tried to speak, but only a high sobbing noise came out. "I'm sorry," he cried, sweat dripping from his nose. His black tunic was soaked and stank. He collapsed to the steps, almost pulling Will down with him. "Will, I'm so sorry!"

Will crouched beside him, grasping his shoulders. "What is it?"

Everard had hobbled down the steps and was standing behind them.

"Elwen," groaned Simon.

Will felt his alarm explode into a thousand stabbing shards of fear. "What about Elwen? Tell me!"

The power in his voice seemed to shake Simon from his hysteria. He raised his head. "They've taken her."

"Who?"

"I couldn't find you," said Simon, shaking his head wildly. "I had your horse but you wasn't there. I thought you'd gone, to Elwen like you said. I was going to go after you, but Paul said a man was here to see you and so I went out to meet him. I thought I was helping." Simon dragged in a breath. "But he didn't want to see you, Will. I ... I think he wanted to capture you."

"The merchants?" said Everard quickly. "Vitturi?"

Will glanced at him, then back at Simon, who didn't seem to have heard the priest. "Who was he? Did he give a name?"

"No. But I know who he was," said Simon bitterly. "He made sure of that. He was a Mamluk. One of Sultan Baybars's men. A Bahri."

"What has this got to do with Elwen?" urged Will.

Simon wiped his dripping nose roughly with the back of his tunic sleeve. "There were others with him and they made me take them to you, Will." He looked up quickly. "They had daggers. They said they would kill me. I should have let them," he whispered, unable to meet Will's commanding gaze. "But I was scared. I couldn't think. I thought you would know what to do and so I ..." He couldn't finish, but he didn't need to.

Will let go of Simon's shoulders and slipped back onto the step, his whole body going limp. "You took them to Elwen," he breathed.

"I thought you were there! I thought you could fight them!"

"Why did the Mamluks take her?"

Simon looked up at Everard's stern voice, seeming to see the priest for the first time. "They found out that she ..." He looked back at Will. "When they realized you weren't there, they thought I had led them falsely. There was no one in the house to help us, just servants, and the Mamluks locked them upstairs. They wanted to know who Elwen was, and when neither of us would answer, they threatened to kill us. They would have done, Will, I swear they would. Elwen told them she was your wife. They took her," said Simon exhaustedly, now resigned to the confession. "And they said I was to tell you what had happened. They said if you wanted her to live, you must come to Damascus and face trial for your crime against their sultan." He shook his head. "I didn't know what they meant. But that's what they said."

Everard had drawn in a hiss of breath at this, but Will said nothing. Simon's words echoed through his mind, blasting into all the dark places where he had plotted and planned Baybars's death, all the hidden corners where he had tormented himself after the failure of the Assassination, places haunted with guilt and sorrow, bitterness and disappointment. Finally, they erupted in the deepest part of him, where for months fear had been gnawing, ever since he had learned that the Mamluks were searching for those who had contracted the Assassins, searching for *him*. Having heard no word from Kalawun and with the theft of the Stone taking up most of his waking thoughts, Will had tried to convince himself that nothing would come of it, that no one would find the Assassins and his guilt would never surface. Now there was nowhere left for his fears to hide. Revenge had come, sharp and sudden. And it had struck at the weakest, most vulnerable part of him.

Will's hand went to the St. George's pendant around his neck. "Is the horse you readied still saddled?"

"I ... I'm not sure. It might be."

"Go and fetch it," said Will, in a flat tone.

"I'm sorry," whispered Simon, rising to face him.

Will met his gaze. "I don't blame you," he said tightly, after a moment. "You did what you had to."

Simon shook his head sadly as if he didn't agree, then hastened down the steps, making for the stables.

"What are you doing?" said Everard, clutching Will's arm as he made to follow the groom.

"What *I* have to."

32

The Citadel, Damascus

17 JUNE A.D. 1277

Kalawun was in his chambers, in talks with two officers from the Syrian regiment, when word came that the Bahri soldiers Baybars had sent to find William Campbell had returned. Having dismissed his men, he was making his way to the throne room, near to his own chambers, when he met Nasir coming the other way. The officer's face was still pallid with exhaustion and scarred with faded bruises, but he seemed more solid than the wisp of a man he had been six days ago.

"Amir, I was on my way to see you."

"What happened?" Kalawun asked, scanning the passage to make sure they were alone. "Did you find Campbell?"

Nasir hung his head. "I did not even reach Acre, Amir. My horse was injured on the second day. I made it to one of our outposts, where I secured another, but I was too late. I saw the Bahri returning on the road and so I hid and trailed them back. I came as fast as I could to warn you."

"Do they have him?"

"They have someone. I was some distance away when they passed me, but I believe it was a woman, not a man."

"A woman?" Kalawun frowned. "I will see for myself. Thank you, Nasir."

"Do not thank me. I failed in my task."

"You did what you could and that is all I asked. Go now and rest. You have done enough." Kalawun moved swiftly to the throne room, where he could hear Baybars's voice issuing from within. The sultan sounded incensed. Kalawun pushed open the doors.

In the lofty, sun-filled chamber, Baybars was in mid-stride, face ruddy with rage. He was sweeping the marble floor in front of four weary-looking Bahri. Towering over them in his black robes edged with gold, he was as menacing as a thunderhead.

Lining the walls of the throne room were a customary accompaniment of eunuchs, all with heads bowed, waiting only to be summoned or dismissed. Several governors, who had obviously been in council with Baybars, were seated around a table near the window looking perplexed. With them, to Kalawun's surprise, was Baraka Khan, and hunched like a withered old vulture on the top step of the dais beside the throne was Khadir. There was one other figure in the chamber, and despite Nasir's warning, she looked so out of place that for a moment Kalawun could only stand in the doorway and stare. As Baybars's ferocious gaze fell on him, however, he quickly collected himself.

"My lord, I was informed that your men had returned," Kalawun said, closing the doors. His eyes drifted back to the woman who was caught between two of the Bahri. She was tall and slim with a blaze of copper-gold curls that hung limp and disheveled around her shoulders. Her face, stiff with shock, was stark white against the flames of her hair. She was trembling like a colt. Kalawun noticed that Baraka Khan also seemed transfixed by the woman, his narrow eyes intent.

Baybars checked himself at Kalawun's arrival, then flung a hand toward the woman. "They brought me his wife!"

"His wife?"

"Campbell's," snapped Baybars. His gaze swiveled belligerently to the four Bahri. "And what good will she do me?" His voice grew bitter. "He will know now that I am seeking him. He will run and I will never ..." He pointed at the soldiers. "You failed me."

"We beg your forgiveness, my lord," murmured one of the Bahri, looking from Baybars to his comrades. "But we could do nothing more. We were told that Campbell would be with this woman."

"You should have killed her and everyone in that house and waited for him."

"My lord, we did not know that he would come."

"By Allah, she was his wife!" roared Baybars. "Of course he would come!"

"We left a message . . . ," began one of the other soldiers.

"As you said before," growled Baybars. "A message?" He shook his head and laughed fiercely. "And the Christian will ride here alone? To face death for her!"

"Yes," came a hissed response.

Baybars looked round as Khadir scuttled down the steps and perched, looking keenly at the woman, who shrank back from his scrutiny, but was stopped from moving by the Bahri to either side of her, gripping her arms.

"He will come," murmured Khadir, studying her with his head cocked to one side. "By their law, Knights of the Temple cannot marry. If he is wed, it was done in secret and he has risked much. He'll risk more for her yet."

"When will he come?" asked Baybars, his voice draining of some of its ferocity.

"Soon," responded Khadir. He looked at Kalawun. "And then you will see to it that the infidel bleeds and suffers as he should. As they all should." His eyes flicked back to Baybars. "As was your pledge when you ascended the throne, Master."

Kalawun felt a surge of concern as he saw Baybars's expression grow taut and thoughtful with the soothsayer's bold words. Only the other week, he would have refused to even listen to Khadir's counsel. "My lord, if Campbell comes, you should try him, certainly, and if his guilt is proven, the necessary action must be taken. But I would caution against making any hasty decisions in your anger toward one man."

"This isn't your business!" spat Khadir with naked hatred at Kalawun.

"The sultan can make up his own mind," said Kalawun calmly, although the animosity in his tone was undeniable.

"Leave me." Baybars raised his head when no one moved. "Leave me!" he shouted, stalking toward the Bahri soldiers, who stepped back from him. "And you!" He turned on the governors and his son, waiting, astonished, at the table. *"Leave!"*

Khadir shrieked as Baybars whirled on him. He scurried down the dais and fled behind Baraka and the governors.

"All of you!" Baybars yelled at the eunuchs, who hurried out, heads still bowed. "Wait!" he demanded, as the Bahri soldiers hastened to leave. "Not her." He pointed at the woman. "She will stay. And you," he barked, snapping his fingers at one of the eunuchs.

"My lord," began Kalawun, as the servants jostled through the doors. He looked at the woman quivering in the center of the room. Now that the soldiers had let go of her, she looked as if she hardly had the strength to hold herself up. But somehow she managed it, and despite her obvious terror, there was something steadfast, bold even, in her large green eyes. Kalawun, staring at her, was reminded of his daughter. "What will you do?"

"Go, Kalawun," said Baybars, shaking his head. "Just leave me."

Backing away, Kalawun reached the doorway. He took one last look at Baybars and the woman, then shut the doors.

As their closing echoed through the cavernous throne room, Elwen started. But through her dread, which had assailed her ever since the door to Andreas's house had burst open and the soldiers had entered, she felt a jolt of hope. Kalawun, the sultan had called the tall man in the blue cloak. Elwen knew that name. It was the name of Will's ally in Egypt. She hadn't missed the worried, almost pained way he had looked at her either. Her gaze lingered on the doors, until she sensed movement and realized Sultan Baybars was standing before her.

Elwen turned her eyes on his huge frame, and as they traveled upward, she saw his hard, lined face and the white star gleaming in his pupil. At once, she recalled all the times she had heard people speak of this man, always in grave or frightened tones. The man they called Crossbow, the Lion of the East. And he was as imposing and terrifying in real life as she had imagined from those stories. Elwen's hope left her, and she dropped her gaze, expecting him at any second to wrench one of the sabers he wore slung from his belt and strike her down where she stood. She didn't want to see the end coming, and so she clenched her eyes shut and gritted her teeth.

"Ismik eh?"

The words filtered through her numb shock, alien at first, then suddenly familiar. *He asked my name?* Wonderingly, she raised her head and swallowed thickly. *"Ismi Elwen, Malik,"* she managed to breathe, then bowed her head again.

Baybars's mouth twitched as she called him king. He lifted his trailing robes and strode up the dais steps to where he sat on his throne, staring down at her. "You will translate for me," he told the eunuch he had ordered to stay, not taking his eyes off Elwen.

"How long have you been Campbell's wife?"

As he spoke in Arabic, Elwen bit her lip, failing to understand. But it was repeated in stuttering French a moment later by the eunuch and she realized why he had been made to stay. For a moment, she wondered what she should say; then she decided to keep up the pretense. Just as many Christians would wholly disapprove of her illicit relationship with Will, so too would most Muslims. "Eleven years," she said, choosing the year Will had proposed to her and glancing at the eunuch, who dutifully repeated her words in Arabic.

"How did he marry you, when he is a Templar?"

This time, after the sultan's words had been translated, Elwen didn't look at the eunuch when she replied. "The Temple doesn't know that we are married."

"He risked his knighthood for you?"

"Yes," she murmured.

"He must love you."

Elwen didn't reply. She thought of Garin, and the pain of regret, still so fresh, engulfed her. She couldn't speak for the intensity of it.

Baybars, however, didn't need an answer. "Then I expect you know why he went to the Assassins," he said, his voice at once harsh and commanding. "Why he wanted me dead." He stood, looming over her on the dais steps as the eunuch spoke his words. "I want you to tell me these things. Tell me what he told you!"

Finally, Elwen understood why she was here, why the Mamluks had come for Will and had taken her in his place. So far, the shock of it had clouded any serious search for motives for her capture. She didn't know what to say for the best, but she had no time to falter here. Baybars wanted an answer and he wanted to be satisfied with it. "You killed his father, my Lord Sultan," she told him, slowly, so the eunuch would be sure to understand her. "At Safed. James Campbell was one of the knights you ordered executed after the siege. That is why he went to the Assassins."

Baybars frowned, listening to the eunuch, then grew still. Different emotions played across his face. Cognition, anger, triumph. Then, just a profound weariness. He slumped in his throne, his callused hands wrapping around the lions' heads, grasping them tightly as if they were posts on a quay and he a ship desperate to moor.

He had thought all these years that the attempt on his life had been orchestrated by Frankish rulers in Acre; barons or kings who had wanted him gone to save their territories and positions. It had never entered his head that one man would have come looking for revenge out of the countless thousands he had sent to their deaths, fortress by fortress, city by city. It was vengeance that had ruled Campbell to this end, had led him to the Assassins. And Baybars knew that silvery, incessant call. He knew it well. Many times, its siren song had kept him awake at night. It had sung to him down the years, out of time and memory. Each life he took, each town, each army had been to satisfy that call, to fill the void inside him where it echoed ceaselessly. But nothing ever had.

After Omar, that space had simply widened, opening him up to the hollowness of a constant appetite that was never sated no matter what he did. He always imagined that the call had begun with her, a slave girl, brutally raped then murdered before him by their master, a former Templar Knight, another life ago in Aleppo. But her violent passing had only stretched the hole already torn when the Mongols invaded his lands, causing his delivery into the hands of the slave traders, changing the course of his entire life. And now vengeance had claimed another victim. But this time, it was him. Under his orders, the Christian's father had died and to balance those scales, Omar had been taken. All at once, Baybars understood, with absolute clarity, that he would never find retribution for that which had been taken from him. He had been looking for it in all the wrong places. "Allah help me," he whispered, closing his eyes and gripping the lions as he felt himself swallowed by the emptiness within. "Help me."

The eunuch decided that he wasn't supposed to translate this, and the chamber grew silent, the only sounds the whispering of three sets of breaths, Elwen's fast and shallow, the eunuch's low and strained, the sultan's drawn out and trembling.

Finally, Baybars opened his eyes. They were moist and distant, and he didn't look at Elwen or the eunuch as he moved down the steps of the dais and out of the throne room.

OUTSIDE THE WALLS OF DAMASCUS, SYRIA, 17 JUNE A.D. 1277

Sweat trickled in persistent lines from Will's brow as he lay flat on a ridge of sand and looked down over the city of Damascus. It was late morning and although there was a haze, the sun's strength was not diminished. If anything it was fiercer than usual, the world sprawled listlessly beneath it. From the ridge, Will had a good vantage over the city and the surrounding land, with the main road that led west to Acre snaking from the city's gates. On one side, Damascus was bordered by a broad river, lined with verdant orchards and gardens. In front of the eastern walls, another city, this one composed entirely of tents, covered a large open plain in a riot of color. Squinting into its midst, Will could make out siege engines, and guessed that it must be the camp of the Mamluk Army.

He had been watching the road for almost half an hour and had seen a steady stream of people, camels and carts coming and going through the city gates. Satisfied that he would be able to enter without too much difficulty, he rose and hastened back down to the narrow track where he had left his horse. Mounting, he made his way out of the hills to join the road to the city.

It had been a hard ride from Acre. His plain tunic, which he'd had just enough foresight to exchange his mantle for, was damp and dirty, and there were bluish-gray circles under his eyes from lack of sleep and a merciless anxiety. Back at the preceptory, Simon, his face drawn with guilt, had gathered him an unnecessarily full pack of supplies. But Will had barely eaten a thing. He knew that he should; that he needed all his strength, but the mere sight of food had made him feel sick to his stomach and it had been all he could do to chew a few strips of salted meat the evening before. Images and memories of Elwen, brighter, sweeter than they had ever been in reality, swirled through every waking thought, until he was saturated with her. Thrumming, maddening fear beat within him, constant as a heartbeat.

Will's eyes traveled over Damascus's sheer walls, the tilted angles of hundreds of rooftops softened here and there by the globular domes of mosques, all marching upward, street by twisted street, to the crowning citadel, rising solid against the pearlescent sky, topped with banners that hung limp in the heavy air. The sight of it gave his determination a blow. Somewhere in that stone jungle was Elwen. But although he guessed the citadel to be where she would be held, he couldn't see how on earth he could hope to find her in that giant's castle, let alone rescue her. Would she even be alive? Was he foolish to hope? He shook his head as if to clear it. He had to hope. It was the only thing keeping him going. His plan was simple. He would find Kalawun, if the commander were here, and beg for his help.

Passing several traders with carts of goods, two women with water jugs poised on their heads and soldiers in chain mail, Will entered the city. Once inside, he was forced to lead his horse through the busy streets. As a major trading city and stop-off point on the pilgrim route to Mecca, Damascus had a population that was as diverse as Acre's, and as many of the Mamluks themselves were white, Will didn't look too conspicuous. But he knew he would only be able to rely on this fact for so long. Once in the citadel itself, he would be immediately out of place in his travel-soiled clothes and in danger of being recognized. He needed a disguise.

As he walked, Will's eyes drifted over the people he passed: merchants, laborers, children, beggars. His gaze lingered longest on two Bahri warriors in their distinctive robes, but he stopped himself from following, knowing that he couldn't overpower both of them. He walked for some time, going deeper into the city, becoming increasingly impatient, until at last he came to a shaded market, where he slumped against a wall. He straightened after a moment and was about to lead his horse to a busy water trough in one corner of the square when his eyes fell on a lone man coming out of a building on the western edge of the market. He was clad in a violet cloak, trimmed with black and gold braid, with a matching turban wound around his head. Will had seen such garments before. It was the uniform of the Mamluk royal messengers. The man had gone to a horse that was tethered near the mouth of a street winding off from the square and was knelt down, tightening his mount's girth. Will headed toward him.

THE CITADEL, DAMASCUS, 17 JUNE A.D. 1277

With a frustrated hiss, Khadir crouched, panting, in the middle of the chamber, surrounded by a tangle of silk cushions, overturned furniture and disheveled rugs. It was no use. However much he willed it otherwise, she wasn't here. He had searched every room, every corner he had occupied since their return, to no avail. The doll was gone. Snatching up a cushion and kneading it between his hands, Khadir squeezed his eyes shut and tried to remember when he had last seen her. But only a mocking blackness greeted him. He made a high, keening noise.

For several years, he had struggled with his memory, able in one instant to recall events from his childhood, yet unable to summon to whom he had been speaking just hours earlier. There were holes in his mind, missing days, empty moments. And it was getting worse. Struggle as he might, he could not remember whether he had brought the doll with him on the campaign. Was she still in the grain store back in Cairo, sitting pretty and useless five hundred miles away?

Khadir had planned to do the deed in Aleppo, months ago. Baybars had held a banquet the night before the cavalry had left for Anatolia, and he had thought to slip a few lethal drops into Kalawun's drink, until he had discovered that the doll was missing. That night he had searched the camp frantically, but there was still no sign of her by the time dawn broke, and an embittered Khadir had been forced to watch from Aleppo's ramparts as Kalawun and Baybars rode out of the gates at the vanguard. Deciding he must have left the doll in Damascus, he had called upon all the curses he could think of, spitting them over and over into his fists each night Kalawun was gone, demanding death by a stray Mongol arrow, a slip on a mountain pass, a snake coiling from the undergrowth. But the commander had returned with the army, alive and well.

As they had set out for Damascus, Khadir had gradually brought himself round to the conclusion that it was better this way. An unfortunate accident was too random, too purposeless. He wanted to witness Kalawun's death: to be the master of the end of the man who had so consistently ruined all his plans. Then he would truly be able to savor it as a victory. But all his fevered scheming had come to nothing when he had returned to Damascus to find that his memory had failed him yet again and the doll was simply nowhere to be found. A vague sense of worry had begun to creep in through his frustration. It was one thing to be thwarted in his attempt to murder Kalawun, but to have the only piece of evidence that could connect him to Aisha's death, which her father still believed to be his doing, go missing was another.

Abruptly, Khadir rose. None of this mattered. It was all noise in his head, confusing, pointless noise. There was only one thing he needed to do and quickly. Baybars had been stirred by the proof that the Franks had indeed tried to kill him, but Kalawun was already disrupting things and the soothsayer knew that Baybars would listen, as always, to the commander's cautious, measured response. Khadir could do it without the use of poison. His hand went to the gold-handled dagger, embedded with its blood-red ruby. A true Assassin's death. The murder would be apparent and an investigation launched, but it would keep Baybars in Damascus for longer, and with Kalawun gone, Khadir could make sure the sultan wouldn't head for Cairo when their time here was done, but would turn the full might of his army on Acre. Khadir did not mind that the finger of blame for Kalawun's murder might be laid on him. Baybars would never kill him; he was too afraid of putting his own life in danger by doing so. Khadir had long ago sown the seeds of fear in the sultan that their lives were irrevocably connected and that what affected one would affect the other. He might imprison him, but that thought did not concern Khadir overtly. After months of subtle pushing on both their parts, Baraka had finally pressed his way back into his father's trust and would, Khadir was sure, be able to secure his release. Not only that, but the youth's ambition had been awoken this past year and Khadir knew he was now ready to help steer his father in the right direction.

Khadir looked to the window, where delicate muslin drapes undulated in the hot wind, framing a blue sky. Soon that blue would fade to black and the moon would rise. Tonight was the eclipse. He had been worrying about it for weeks and earlier had insisted that Baybars double his guard for the night and avoid certain foods. But, as Baybars himself had pointed out, the death of a great ruler didn't have to mean him. The sultan had speculated that it could be an augury for the Ilkhan, Abaga, or any number of rulers: a Frankish king, a prince. Or a high commander. Khadir smiled at the symmetry of it. If the stars demanded blood tonight, then he would give it to them.

Feeling certainty surge through him, he left his room and padded down the corridor. Halfway along, he paused, looking around, then slipped into a narrow archway that led up a flight of steps into a dark riddle of servants' passages.

It was with trepidation and a quiet thrill that Baraka Khan opened the doors to the throne room, having told the citadel guards outside that his father had ordered him to collect some papers he had left behind. The guards, having been given no command since Baybars had left, almost an hour earlier, let the prince pass without a word.

The two occupants of the airy throne room started as the doors opened. Baraka's eyes went first to the woman, who was standing in the window, her gold hair, lit from behind by the early afternoon sun, luminous as a halo. Her face was pinched and pale, and her eyes were unblinking as she stared at him. They were an incredible shade of green, which made him think of water, a slow summer river or a mountain lake. Baraka swallowed thickly. Barely glancing at the room's other inhabitant, he passed an indifferent hand in his direction. "Leave," he told the eunuch imperiously.

The eunuch hesitated, but his nerves, already set on edge by Baybars's erratic behavior, got the better of him and he headed quickly for the door. The woman watched him go, then turned her eyes back to Baraka. There was strength in that stare, he now realized, where before he had only seen fear. It checked him and he felt his confidence slip a little. To cover his nervousness, he snapped the door's bolt into place and crossed to the table where he had been sitting with the governors when the woman was brought in. The surface was littered with papers. He pretended to rustle through them, all the while feeling the woman's gaze burning into him, making his neck itch and tingle and his face grow warm.

Baraka had no idea what the woman and his father had spoken about, or why she was even still alive. But he had been deeply intrigued when his father had left the throne room, his face wet with tears. Baraka, lingering in the passageway he had slipped into when Baybars had ordered everyone out, had watched his father pass in stunned silence, those tears impossible on his cheeks. Never once, in all his years, had he seen his father cry. Never once had he imagined he would. At first bemused and astonished, he had hunkered down in the passage, trying to guess what could have happened. And the more he thought, the more his mind had returned to the gold-haired woman. When she was brought in by the soldiers, he had been gripped by the look of her and by the animal fear coming off her. But that she had made his father cry? Well, now she had aroused his curiosity also.

Emboldened after Aisha's death, by his part in it and by the fact that his dalliances were once again safe, Baraka had continued his weekly trysts with the slave girls in earnest, growing all the more brazen in his pursuit of gratification. But just recently he had begun to find himself unsatisfied. The slaves had grown used to his demands, had become docile and compliant. He felt starved of the physical sense of power the act had initially granted him, when the girls were scared and unwilling. He felt the lack like a heat inside him. His wanting made him ache with restless urgency and turned him more bad-tempered and impatient than usual. He had, however, found some moments of satisfaction. Baraka didn't know why, exactly, he had taken the doll, only that to have it gave him a certain gratifying omnipotence. He wielded his lethal treasure secretly, not only over Khadir, but over every man in his father's army. At banquets, he had watched them, the phial hot and sweaty in his hand beneath the table, taking greedy delight in the knowledge that they were at his mercy and that, like some unkind god, he could, whenever he wished it, strike down any one of them.

There was a voice behind him and Baraka whipped round. The woman had spoken. But he didn't understand what she had said.

She spoke again, this time in hesitant Arabic. "Who are you?"

Baraka sucked in a breath. Here was a Christian woman, a prisoner, speaking to him bold as day, *questioning* him indeed in his own tongue! He couldn't believe her audacity. "Silence!" he snapped, angered by her unwavering stare, and was gratified when she flinched. She was only pretending to be unafraid. In truth, he guessed, she was terrified. The realization gave him a sudden rush and he went toward her, every step thrilling him more and more as she backed away, looking around for escape.

Finally, he caught her by the window. Her ashen face was now flushed, hectic with alarm. She spoke rapidly in a language he did not understand. He caught a few words of Arabic mixed within it. But he wasn't listening anymore. Her nearness, her dread, filled him like a drug, blocking out his own concern that he might be caught, blurring his vision of all else except her. He no longer cared what she had done to his father or why he had kept her alive. There was just one thing Baraka wanted.

33

The Citadel, Damascus

B ack in his chambers, Kalawun poured water into a goblet. Freshly drawn from the citadel's well, it had a brittle, mineral taste. It was freezing. He drank too quickly, causing a needle stab of pain to shoot through his forehead. He closed his eyes to let it pass and saw again the woman standing alone in the throne room, staring after him as he quietly backed away. With the image came a voice, telling him to go back. He had the sultan's ear. He could save her. But in truth, he was scared. Scared of angering Baybars and jeopardizing his position, scared of arousing suspicions as to why he wanted her to live. But most of all, scared of the pain the unexpected reminder of his daughter had brought him.

Opening his eyes, Kalawun poured another measure and brought the goblet up to drink, but before it touched his lips, he put it down. On the table beside the water jug was a silver tray of fruit: peaches, grapes, bananas, carved up and sweating in the room's heat. He glanced at it, wondering if he were hungry, but his pain wouldn't be ignored or denied so easily, and all of a sudden the fruit was just another expression of a life that was ended. Aisha would never again perch on his knee, her fingers sticky with peach juice, and tell him in swift, intense tones about her day. Kalawun planted his palms on the table, digging his fingers into the wood until they turned white, then with a single, brutal motion, swept the tray and the jug away, sending water and fruit cascading. As the jug smashed and a green hail of grapes hit the floor, Kalawun felt someone at his back. He went to turn. Too late. An arm snaked into view, coming around from behind him in a flash of gold and red. There was a dagger thrust at his throat, a rank smell of dampness and rot.

"*Serpent!*" came Khadir's voice, seething in his ear. "I've caught you!"

Kalawun, his eyes flicking left to the closed door of his chambers, realized that Khadir must have come in through the servants' passage in his bedchamber. He tried to turn his head, but felt a sting as Khadir pressed the blade against his throat, tearing his skin. He stood still. "What are you doing, Khadir?" he murmured, trying to keep his voice calm.

Khadir took no notice of his reasonable tone. "For so long have I waited for this. For so long! Now the bridle you have placed around my master will slacken. He will destroy the infidel Franks as I have foretold and you shall not stop him!"

"Baybars is his own master, Khadir. He made the decision to concentrate on the Mongols rather than the Franks. In the end, it did not matter what I said."

"Lies!" hissed Khadir. "It *is* your doing. Your actions and words, oh so many, *many* words, led my master from his path. I do not know the reason, but the truth is clear as water. You blinded him, deafened him, turned him to your will, turned him from the Christians. You speak now to save your own skin. All lies!"

"No, Khadir, I—"

"I was planning to poison you," Khadir cut across him, almost wonderingly, "like I did your daughter."

Kalawun went rigid. A breath shot through his lips.

"But this way I get to see your fear," continued Khadir. He inhaled through flared nostrils. "Get to *smell* it." So absorbed was he in his relish that he didn't notice the chamber's main door glide silently open behind him. "This way, *Amir Kalawun*, when you die, I get to feel your soul slip through my fingers!"

"Let him go."

Khadir's head snapped around at the voice, his eyes growing huge as he saw a man behind him, brandishing a short sword. The man wore the garments of a royal messenger and had a scroll bag slung over his shoulder, but when he spoke, his Arabic was awkward. A moment after his gaze alighted on the man's face, Khadir recognized him. He let loose an outraged cry, which quickly became a shriek as Kalawun twisted violently in his grip, throwing him off balance. Khadir flailed, his hand with the dagger in it going wide. Kalawun wrenched himself free. The soothsayer was swift to react, however, and lashed determinedly out. The ruby flashed, catching the light, as the blade sliced across Kalawun's arm, which he just managed to bring up in defense. There was a ripping of cloth and Kalawun's face contorted. Khadir uttered another cry of rage and came in again, but this time Kalawun managed to grab hold of his wrist.

Will moved in to help.

"No!" shouted Kalawun. "He is mine!" There was a tear in his sleeve and blood was pumping steadily from somewhere within, but even though the effort caused him obvious agony, he seized the soothsayer in a savage grip. His face apoplectic, spittle flecking white from his mouth, he turned Khadir's wrist around until the dagger's tip was pointed inward.

Khadir, his own face bulging with the strain, tried to fight him. But although the former Assassin was agile for his years, he was no match for Kalawun's strength. Slowly but surely, the dagger tip edged toward him, inch by inch. Khadir gasped, his face going purple and veins standing out like cords on his neck. He kicked out ruthlessly with his bare feet, but Kalawun's hold didn't falter. All of a sudden, Khadir's strength failed. His jaw went slack with shock. With the soothsayer's skeletal, liver-spotted hand still wrapped around the hilt, Kalawun slammed the blade home with a yell. It punched into Khadir's throat and drove right through, on up to the base of his skull, where it emerged in shining silver victory. Blood sprayed from the old man's mouth, splattering Kalawun's face. The soothsayer gurgled, choked, reared back in Kalawun's grip. His eyes were twin moons of horror as he fought against the death. A foul stench rose as his bladder and bowels gave way and voided themselves in a fetid rush. Then his spasms ceased and he collapsed.

Kalawun let go of him and slumped against the table, straining for breath and clutching his forearm, which was bleeding profusely. He looked at Will, who met his gaze in silence, then back at Khadir, sprawled crookedly amidst the debris of blood-splattered fruit and splinters of clay. The soothsayer's eyes were open and his mouth and his chest and the floor around him were awash with blood. The ruby in the dagger was glazed with it. "He's dead," said Kalawun flatly; then he staggered.

Will went forward and caught him. "Your wound is serious."

"I will live." Kalawun wiped a hand across his mouth, smearing into thin red lines droplets of the soothsayer's blood. He looked at Will. "You shouldn't have come. They will kill you."

"I had to come."

Kalawun sighed roughly and pressed his hand tighter to his wound, grimacing with pain. "I sent an officer of mine to warn you, but he did not reach you in time." He paused. "Despite the circumstances, I am glad to see you. I wasn't sure what happened at Mecca, or whether you . . ." He trailed off, looking down at Khadir's body.

"Why didn't you warn us that you were sending your own forces to protect the Stone?" Will asked him, unable to keep the anger from his tone. "Did you not think you might endanger the lives of me and my men?"

"You told me nothing of your plans in your message. I did not know what you were doing to stop it."

"I couldn't risk exposing that information in a letter. I had to—"

"I realize that," Kalawun cut across him, "and did not wish to deceive you, truly. But you have to understand that I couldn't rely on your promise alone, not for the holiest relic of my people. Any risk to your men, even to you, was outweighed by the need to keep it safe, for your people as well as mine. I am sorry, William. It was just one more sacrifice." He leaned heavily against the table, feeling the blood trickling hotly down his arm. "You understand?"

Will nodded after a moment. He did.

Kalawun laughed suddenly, a pained, breathless sound. "I sometimes wonder if any of this is worth what we pay for it, you and I. I sometimes think ..." He fell silent as faint but clear through the open door came a woman's screams. "Your wife," he said quickly.

Baybars was making his way to the throne room, pensive and preoccupied, when he heard the screams. His head jerked up and he strode down the passage, breaking into a run as he saw the palace guards he had left outside hammering on the doors. "Open them!" he barked as he reached them.

"They're locked, my lord," said one guard, stepping away at his approach. From inside came another scream, which was quickly cut off, then followed by the sound of things falling, a muffled thud and a tinkling of glass.

"Move," snapped Baybars, ramming the doors with his shoulder. The stout wood shuddered but didn't budge. "Who locked them?" he demanded, bracing himself and trying again.

"Your son, my lord," said one of the guards fearfully.

Baybars brow furrowed. "My son?" He looked at the doors, stepped away, then gave them an almighty kick. On the other side, the bolt's fixings sprang apart, tearing themselves from the wood. The doors flew inward.

Over by the window a small table had toppled, dislodging the jug that had been placed on it, which had exploded into tiny fragments. Two figures were on the floor. One was Baraka Khan. He was on top of the woman prisoner, one hand grappling with hers, trying to pin it down, the other partially clamped over her mouth. Her hair was splayed across her face and her white gown was ripped at the front, exposing a slice of pale skin, from her throat to her breast. In Baybars's mind there was a flash of memory, a grainy scene from long ago. Then he was striding forward, his rage mounting with every step.

Baraka pushed himself off the woman as his father came toward him. "She tried to escape!" he blurted. Before he could even stand, Baybars was reaching down and hauling him up by the back of his silk tunic, which tore under the arms with the violence of the motion. "Father! Please! I was trying to stop her from—"

"I know what you were doing!" Baybars stormed at him, pulling his son toward him. There was a resounding *crack* as he slapped Baraka across the face, causing the youth's head to be flung to one side. A mark, for one second white, bloomed scarlet on his cheek. Baybars shoved him violently in the chest.

Baraka staggered back, tripped over the legs of the fallen table and sprawled on the floor, crying out as his head banged against the tiles and needle-sharp specks of glass embedded themselves in his skull. "Please, Father!" he cried desperately, trying to push himself up.

The woman was on her feet, clutching her ripped gown to her chest, but neither of them were looking at her anymore.

"Do you think that I don't know?" demanded Baybars, stalking toward Baraka, the hems of his robes catching shards of glass and trailing them across the floor with a sound like the scratching of fingernails. "Do you think me blind? *Stupid?*"

"What do ...?"

"*I know!*" shouted Baybars hoarsely. "I know what you've been doing with my slaves!"

Baraka went still, his throat constricting. He couldn't speak.

"Why do you think I brought you on this campaign?" demanded Baybars, towering over his prostrate son. "Did you think it was for your counsel? Your wits?" He gave a hard bray of laughter that ceased as abruptly as it was vented. "I brought you with me so that I could get you away from my harem!" He shook his head. "For a time I thought your quietness, your newfound desire of solitude away from the disruptive influence of your friends some sign that you were ready to settle down and work, ready to become the man I hoped you would. But I should have known better. Those girls were mine, gifts to me. Some I may have taken as wives! That you went behind my back to slake your lust on them like a rutting dog disgusts me. You *disgust* me!" He kicked out in rage, catching Baraka in the side.

Baraka curled away from the kick, gasping as it jabbed into him. He groped at the floor, pulling himself from his father's wrath. But Baybars came after him, reaching down to drag him up. As he felt his father grasp the collar of his tunic, Baraka's hand shot out, looking for purchase, for something to cling to. His fingers found a shard of the broken jug, and as Baybars hauled him upright, he thrust it toward his father's face. He stopped, just short of him. The two of them stood frozen, the jagged fragment of glass occupying the space between them, a thin red line staining one edge where Baraka had cut himself picking it up. Outside the throne room came sounds of a disturbance, but neither of them looked round. All of their attention was fixed on each other, hatred, disgust, disappointment, years of it, seeping from each of their stares. Their breaths caused mist to bloom on the glass.

Baraka's nose was dripping and sweat stood out on his brow, dampening his curly hair. His narrow eyes were slits, but there were no tears in them. "I may have defiled your harem, Father," he said, in a voice that sounded utterly alien to Baybars, devoid of love, or respect, even of fear, "but you have defiled your position. Khadir, Mahmud, Yusuf, so many in your court have entreated you to keep your pledge and destroy the Christians, but you haven't listened. Do you know how many of your own men are against you now? How many want to see you dead? But I am ready and willing to do what you will not. You're a *coward*, Father."

Baybars's blue eyes widened. He tore the fragment of glass from Baraka's grasp, gashing himself as he did so. Tossing it away, he shook the youth as if he were a rag doll. "You're ready, are you? Well, let us see how ready you are without a *kingdom*!" He stopped shaking his son and resorted to his fists, pummeling and punching Baraka until his knuckles were blotchy with blood. Finally he stopped, his breaths strained. "You'll not take my throne when I am gone, Baraka," he breathed. "You're not fit to lead our people. Your brother, Salamish, will be my heir." Baybars backed away from the bloodied, half-conscious form of his son, lying small and fetal on the tiles. I tried," he whispered, "to make you ..." His shoulders sagged. "I tried."

As Will was running down the passage after Kalawun, he saw someone dash out of the throne room, through the open doors of which he could hear a fierce argument. "Elwen!"

One of the palace guards reached for her quickly; the other turned at Will's call. The guard's eyes went large with bewilderment as he saw Kalawun and a royal messenger charging toward him. Elwen cried out as the other guard caught her arm and spun her into the wall, pinning her against it. Will was on him before his companion had even had chance to call a warning, elbowing him viciously in the face and hauling him away from Elwen, then grabbing his hair and cracking his head back against the wall. Kalawun tackled the other guard, knocking him unconscious with the hilt of his sword. Elwen screamed again as Will took hold of her.

"Elwen!"

Her eyes focused on him in stunned confusion.

"Return to my rooms," said Kalawun quickly, sheathing his sword. Teeth barred in pain, he clutched his wounded arm. "Behind a tapestry in my bed-chamber there is a passage. Follow it until you reach a set of steps going down. At the base of these, turn right and you will find yourself near the kitchens."

"Kalawun ...," began Will.

There was more shouting coming from the throne room.

"Listen!" hissed Kalawun, grasping Will's shoulder and steering him in the direction of his chambers. "Beyond the kitchens is a servants' passage that leads outside the walls by a small gate and down into the city. There is a mosque, near to a cattle market in the main square. Go there and find somewhere to hide. I will send men with horses. They will leave them at the mosque's entrance." He let go of Will, leaving a bloody handprint on his shoulder. *"Go!"*

34

The Road from Damascus, Syria

17 JUNE A.D. 1277

After checking on the horses, Will took a waterskin from one of the packs, then returned to where Elwen was sitting on a rocky outcrop. She was swaddled in a blanket, knees drawn up to her chest, her gaze on the road that dropped down the ridge and wound away behind them, grow-ing thinner and fainter with distance. The moon was low and swollen, turning night to ghostly day. The tops of trees in the valley below them, which faithfully chased the curve and sweep of a river, were clouds in its light; and the desert snow, powdery and infinite.

Elwen's teeth were chattering and her warm breath fogged the air in rapid plumes. Will climbed up to where she was sitting and handed her the skin. She took it, but didn't drink.

"I should have found wood for a fire," he murmured, shrugging off his own blanket and placing it around her shoulders. Over her ripped gown, she was wearing the silk cloak he had stolen from the royal messenger. Its vibrant violet was blanched gray in the moonlight and glimmered like water around her feet. "You need it more," he said, when she started to protest. He stood on the ridge, feeling the cold settle around him.

"Are you still worried they'll come for us?"

As Elwen spoke, Will looked around and shook his head, but his eyes crept back to the road and the heavy tension he had felt since they had fled the citadel didn't vanish with his assurance.

After an agonizing wait near the city mosque, Kalawun's men had come, leaving two fine Arab horses loaded with supplies outside the mosque's entrance. Will and Elwen had ridden furiously out of the city, Will wanting to put as much distance between them and Damascus as possible. But other than the usual travelers, merchants and farmers for the most part, they had seen no one else on the road, and although Will had watched for it, there had been no sign of pursuit. They had spoken little, both of them too pensive to make conversation.

"Sit with me?"

Will forced his gaze from the road. Elwen was looking up at him. The hollows of her cheeks were rendered even deeper in this light, her face gaunt, almost haggard. Out of Damascus, noticing how thin and drawn she looked, Will had remembered what Simon had told him back at the preceptory and had questioned her about her apparent affliction. But she had brushed it aside, telling him it didn't matter. He hadn't asked her again, just as she hadn't asked him about Mecca. It was as if too much had happened in the time between for either of them to relate those things to each other. They were awkward in each other's company, strangers after all the months apart. Now, looking at her, he was struck by the realization of just how lucky he was to have saved her, and his discomfort vanished. He went to her and sat, taking her hands in his. They were smooth and cold. God, but he had almost lost her. He closed his eyes and murmured a fervent prayer that she had been spared. "Elwen," he began, then stopped, emotion sticking in his throat.

She stared at him, her eyes growing bright. "I'm so sorry."

"For what?" he asked thickly.

Elwen paused, then spoke haltingly. "For ... putting you in danger. It's my fault. I shouldn't have told those soldiers that I was your wife. I should have lied, but I didn't know what to ..." She looked suddenly stricken. "Simon?"

"He is fine," said Will, watching her close her eyes in relief. "But I don't see how you can think this is your fault."

She hung her head. "It's not just that," she whispered faintly, "it's ..."

"If I hadn't tried to have Baybars killed, none of this would have happened," Will continued, not hearing her. "That's why you were taken. Because of me."

"No, Will, I ... There are other things, things I have to tell you that—"

"Let me speak. Please," he cut across her. "I need to say this. I should have said it earlier, but ..." He halted. "No. I should have said it *years* ago. There's just always been some excuse, some distraction. I thought I knew what I wanted, but I didn't. When I came back from Mecca, I was glad that I had stopped the theft, truly, but that feeling was nothing in comparison to what I felt when I was riding to Damascus, knowing that you might be ..." He took a breath. "That you might be dead. I realized that you were more important to me than ..."

To Elwen's dismay, Will's voice cracked and he began to cry, great choking sobs that came from the very center of him. She put her arms around him, the blanket falling from her shoulders.

After a time, the grief drained from him. He raised his head to look at her. "Do you still want to marry me?"

Elwen gave a startled laugh, then saw that he was serious. Her laughter vanished and she stared at him, stunned. As she did so, it seemed he had grown somehow dimmer in her vision. Glancing up, she gave a small gasp. There was a shadow on the moon, a dark arc around its edge.

Will followed her gaze. "The eclipse," he murmured.

Together they stood and watched it for a time, his question hanging unanswered in the air between them, as slowly, almost imperceptibly, the shadow spread like a creeping stain. At some point in their muted silence, Will felt Elwen take his hand.

"I'm pregnant."

A jolt went through him, of what he wasn't sure, and then he felt a change inside. The heavy tension faded. He felt lighter, calmer. Was it the baby? He had never given much thought to having one before. Why would he? If marriage was impossible as a knight, that was nothing when compared to having a child. No. It wasn't so much the thought of the child itself; it was the realization that it *was* possible. He had thought that he couldn't be with Elwen, but he had been, for years. He heard a rush of breath and she spoke again in a whisper.

"Yes. My answer is yes."

Will squeezed her hand tightly, and a smile crept across his face as above them the moon was gradually devoured. His gaze fixed on the sky, he didn't notice that Elwen's eyes were closed.

THE CITADEL, DAMASCUS, 17 JUNE A.D. 1277

Kalawun was on his hands and knees, scrubbing at the tiles. The water in the pail beside him was dark with blood, as was the cloth. It was everywhere. He could taste its sourness each time he swallowed. Muted moonlight cast a fan across the chamber, making eerie shapes of the familiar. The eclipse had begun some time ago and was now approaching totality. The moon was dull copper-red. It looked like a bloated, diseased eye. Sitting back on his heels, Kalawun squeezed the cloth into the pail and wiped his brow with the back of his arm. His gaze was dragged, unavoidably, to the form of Khadir, wrapped in silk sheets, like a bug in a cocoon, propped against the wall by the door.

Leaving Will sprinting down the passage, Kalawun had entered the throne room to find Baraka on the floor, with Baybars standing over him, fists bruised, eyes vacant. The sultan, seeing him, left the room without a word, and Kalawun helped Baraka to his feet. But when he tried to take him to the citadel's physicians, the youth pulled away, telling him in a chillingly emotionless voice that he was to be left alone. Kalawun, aware that he had to get the horses to Will, let him go. By this point, he was almost faint with the blood loss from his own injury. Before he had been able to find two officers to take the horses and supplies to the mosque, however, he was faced with the problem of the unconscious guards, still lying outside the throne room. Baybars had passed them by without care, but Kalawun knew it wouldn't be long before somebody started asking questions about the woman's escape.

In the end, he had both men moved to the citadel's infirmary, telling the governor of Damascus, who had heard word of the disturbance, that an unknown man had forced entry into the citadel and attacked his men. Whilst his arm was stitched by the citadel's physician, Kalawun explained to the governor that he had been in pursuit of the trespasser, but that before he could intercept him the man reached the guards and assaulted them, then fled with a prisoner. He tried to stop the man leaving, but was injured when the assailant pulled a blade on him. Kalawun thought he had managed to convince the governor, but was left to wait anxiously for the two guards to come round. Both men, in awe of the Mamluk commander, and listening groggily to his version of events, appeared convinced that he had in fact been chasing their attacker. But Kalawun guessed uneasily that only time would tell if they started to remember something different. Having sent his men to the mosque, he was then left to mediate between the governor, who wanted to send soldiers after the attacker, and a silent Baybars, who had at first refused to see him at all, then eventually told him to halt any search for the woman and her rescuer. That it no longer mattered.

Kalawun dropped the cloth into the pail and stood, wincing as his muscles stretched. His arm was throbbing, and beads of fresh blood had welled up between the neat stitches the physician had made. He was beyond the point of exhaustion, his body moving almost of its own will, as if his mind were already asleep and his body had forgotten to do the same. He walked in a daze to the shrouded corpse and was dragging it along the wet floor toward his bedchamber, when there was a knock at his door. Shock went through him, firing his deadened senses. Kalawun hauled Khadir the rest of the way into his bedchamber before opening the door a crack.

In the passage, one of Baybars's eunuchs was waiting. He bowed. "Amir Kalawun. The sultan requests your presence in the throne room."

Kalawun cleared his throat. "I'll be there in a minute."

The eunuch waited outside, leaving Kalawun to hurriedly change his soiled cloak and wash Khadir's blood off his hands. When he was done, he followed the eunuch warily to the throne room. Had the soothsayer been missed already?

The sultan was standing in front of the windows, bathed in the moon's fainted red light. The throne room was surprisingly empty, the servants suddenly noticeable by their absence. The mess had been cleaned away, and only the splinters around the door bolt revealed any sign of the violence that had taken place.

Baybars looked around as Kalawun entered. "Amir. I need you to do something for me."

"My lord?"

"I want you to call a meeting with my chief of staff. Do it quietly. I do not want anyone else to hear of this yet."

"Hear of what, my lord?"

The sultan moved from the window and climbed the dais. He took a gem-encrusted goblet of kumiz from the table by his throne.

Kalawun glanced around the shadowy chamber as Baybars's drank pensively. "It is dark in here, my lord. Shall I have the servants light some lanterns?"

"No," said Baybars, sitting. "I want to watch the eclipse." He smiled dryly. "I would have thought Khadir would be here to witness it. Or at least to tell me I do not have enough guards. Have you seen him?"

"No," said Kalawun, a little too quickly.

Baybars didn't seem to notice. He took several more sips of the fermented mare's milk. "Things have changed, Kalawun. And I feel better for it. I know, now, what I must do. Too long have I surrounded myself with men who fear, rather than respect, me. I would prefer to have a few loyal advisors than many who secretly despise me."

"Your men do not despise you," countered Kalawun.

Baybars held up his hand. "Their dissatisfaction is plain. I dealt with

Mahmud, but I didn't realize how far the infection had spread. It is time to cut out the rest of the corruption." He paused. "Starting with my son."

Kalawun was silent.

"I do not want Baraka Khan to take my place when I am gone. I have decided that Salamish will be my heir." Baybars shook his head sourly. "Nizam will hate me for an eternity, but that bed has been cold for years if the truth be told."

Kalawun found his voice. "My lord, you should think carefully about—"

"He is not fit to rule, Kalawun," said Baybars flatly. "I've known it for a while now, but I think I was still hoping that he would change. He will not. I see that now. There is weakness inside him that I fear will only grow worse with time. If I had been a better father, then maybe ..." He wiped his forehead, where a sheen of sweat had appeared, and shook his head. "But I wasn't."

Kalawun's mind was whirling. He knew Baybars was right. He had known for a long time that his efforts to influence Baraka weren't working. It felt as if he had been trying to bail water from a boat that had gone beyond the point of buoyancy and would, inevitably, sink. But Salamish? He was only seven years old, and Kalawun hardly knew him at all. As he was staring at the floor, his thoughts racing, he heard a clanging sound. Baybars had dropped the goblet of kumiz. The goblet tumbled down the steps, splashing droplets of milk and ringing hollowing as it went. Baybars's hand was stretched out, his face a mask of confusion. Suddenly, he lurched forward, as if pushed by an invisible hand.

"My lord!" Kalawun raced toward the throne. He sprinted up the steps as Baybars collapsed. "Physicians!" he yelled at the top of his lungs. *"Physicians!"*

The throne room doors burst open and two Bahri guards appeared. One of them ran into the room; the other left instantly on seeing the sultan on the floor. Kalawun heard his footsteps echoing in the passage.

"What's wrong with him, Amir?" said the other soldier, running up to crouch beside the sultan.

"I don't know," said Kalawun, holding Baybars's head. The sultan looked as if he were trying desperately to breathe, as if someone or something had wrapped its hands around his throat and were squeezing the air from him. His eyes were wild, panicked in the last of the dim moonlight bleeding through the windows.

Minutes later, a physician arrived, panting and disheveled. He was followed by servants bearing warm water, knives, cloths, drugs. Right away, the physician ordered lanterns to be lit and the throne room flared into light. Kalawun was pushed aside. The sultan was gasping vainly for breath now, a fish out of water, mouth opening and closing uselessly.

"Did he swallow anything?" the physician called to Kalawun.

"Only kumiz," said Kalawun. "What can I do?"

"Let me work" was all the physician said.

Kalawun moved away and stood by the window, helpless. Outside, the city was bathed in a strange half-light. He felt someone beside him and turned to see Baraka. The prince's face was horribly bruised and puffy from the beating Baybars had given him. His eyes were locked on the choking, convulsing form of his father.

"Baraka," said Kalawun, grasping the youth's arm. "What are you doing here?"

"Is he dead yet?" said Baraka. His voice was distorted from the swelling in his face, but other than that it was eerily calm. Kalawun started at the question. He stared blankly at Baraka, who seemed to realize that he had said something odd. He shook his head. "What happened?"

"Your father collapsed," said Kalawun, after a long pause.

"Oh," said Baraka, in that same placid, emotionless tone.

As Baybars writhed beneath the throne, Kalawun's gaze fixed in dawning, appalled understanding on Baraka Khan.

35

The Temple, Acre

10 JULY A.D. 1277

The streets of Acre rang with laughter and music. Children, dressed in their feast-day clothes, skipped and played, chasing one another between the legs of the adults who stood in groups outside churches talking animatedly, gathered in market squares to sip spiced tea and share gossip, or sang songs of dead emperors inside packed taverns. Strung on hemp lines between buildings, triangles of sun-faded silk flapped and twisted in the oven-hot wind. Masons' lodges stood empty, shops were shuttered, fires burned low in the forges of smiths. Only in the Muslim quarter did people go about their normal business. For everyone else in the city, it was a holiday. But not a normal feast day, celebrating the life of a saint, or a festival from the Bible. No. Today, the people of Acre were celebrating death.

Baybars Bundukdari, the man who had herded them like sheep to this little strip of coastline, ravaging their numbers, diminishing their power in the Holy Land, was gone.

Rumor had it that he had been poisoned, some said by his own soothsayer, but no one much cared how it had happened. All that mattered was that the greatest threat the Franks had faced since the days of Saladin had died, and his heir, a mere youth of sixteen, was known to be weak-willed and directionless. And so they rejoiced and laughed, told stories and jokes, and, in one square, someone had made an unflattering effigy of the sultan which was thrown onto a hastily constructed pyre to exuberant cheering.

The news of Baybars's passing had come almost a week ago and was announced by the bailli, Count Roger de San Severino, at an emergency meeting of Acre's High Court, after which the count had cemented his favorable position in public opinion by declaring a holiday to celebrate the event. The people liked Roger. As did Acre's oligarchic government. Not for his rule, but for the lack of it.

Following the upheaval of the previous year, Acre had finally settled into its old routines. Business was back to normal, the uneasy peace between the divided quarters had returned, and worry over whether Charles d'Anjou would arrive to upset the balance was starting to dissipate. It was well known that the monarch was too busy struggling to create yet another empire for himself in Byzantium to bother about taking his now established seat in Acre. Some joked that the ambitious king simply had too many thrones and not enough asses to fill them. The people here liked their kings at one remove; the absence of visible rule was what maintained the Crusader capital's delicate equilibrium. It left the Commune of Burghers, Italian merchant states, masters of the military orders, the patriarch and others all free to rule their little pieces of the city's pie without too much interference from above, which in turn left Count Roger free to organize jousts and feasts for his noble friends, meaning that, in general, everyone was happy.

Will, standing at the window, looking out over the preceptory, could hear the drunken merrymaking of a group of revelers beyond the Temple's walls.

"Close the curtains."

He looked round to see Everard blinking painfully at him. He let go of the drape, which swished back into place with a swirl of glittery dust motes, shutting out the afternoon and throwing the chamber into a depressing dusk. He crossed to the priest, who was lying huddled on his narrow bed. "I'm sorry, I didn't realize you were awake."

"For some time now," said Everard with a drawn-out sigh, laying his head

back on his pillow as Will sat on a stool beside him. "The singing woke me."
His bloodshot eyes fixed on Will. "Is it for him?" He sighed again at Will's nod,
this time with sadness in his face. "Like scavengers, picking at the bones of a
fallen lion. Crowing as if they killed him indeed!" Everard broke from his indignation as a coughing fit took hold.

Will slid a practiced hand under his head as the priest hacked relentlessly,
then, with an enormous effort, finally brought up a glob of discolored, bloody
phlegm, which he spat into the cloth Will held in front of his mouth.

"You cannot blame them for their joy, Everard," murmured Will, handing
the priest a cup of water, which was brushed away disdainfully. "During Baybars's campaign against us, many of them lost loved ones, homes, businesses.
This is their justice."

"Justice?" scoffed Everard. "Were the Muslims offered justice when we came
here and invaded their lands? Slaughtered their families?"

"I'm only saying ..."

"I know," murmured the priest, closing his eyes, "I know."

"At least now, we have a better chance for peace, *sustainable* peace. Bàraka
Khan will take the throne and Kalawun will be able to work more freely with
us to renegotiate the treaty and to continue building relations between our
people. Baybars's dying is for the best."

Everard opened one eye a crack and studied him intently.

"And I'm not saying that for me, or out of any sense of vengeance," said
Will, seeing the look.

"In truth, I wouldn't blame you if you did. He ordered the execution of your
father and kidnapped your beloved. You have your own cause to wish him
dead."

"Maybe once. But now he is gone, I find no pleasure in it." Will frowned.
"I'm not sure why. Perhaps because he kept Elwen alive when he could have
killed her? I don't know. I just feel ..." He shrugged. "I feel nothing."

"I know why," said Everard sagely.

Will waited for an answer. For some moments, the priest was silent, his eyes
closed, ribs rising and falling erratically beneath the blanket. His skin was almost translucent, and stretched thinly over his face, as if there were not quite
enough left to cover him. But he was still holding on with every breath. He had
been for over three weeks now, far beyond the point where the Temple's infirmarer believed any man could live. "He is what?" the infirmarer had said to
Will. "Ninety years old? He should have passed long ago. I expect this fever will
take him very soon." But that had been a fortnight ago, and even though the
last rites had been said over him three times now, Everard was still clinging

grimly to life. Will reached out to lay a hand on his forehead, wondering if the priest had fallen asleep. But then Everard spoke.

"You've grown up, William."

Will smiled a little sardonically. "I'm thirty, Everard. I would hope I had grown up sometime ago."

"For a knight, yes," said Everard, nodding, "for a commander in the Temple. But not for one of the Brethren, not fully, or to the extent that I knew you could." Will started to protest, but Everard spoke over him. "For all the years I have known you, William, you have been ruled by passion. A passion to reacquaint yourself with your father and to atone for sins of the past, passion for a woman, for your friends, for revenge. But a man of the Brethren cannot let himself be ruled by personal desires and battles. He has a greater war to fight, above the petty squabbles and toilings of most other men: a war for the future, beyond the immediacy of a battlefield. It is the hardest war: to change the world for the good, not of himself, of politics or of a nation, but of all. You feel nothing for Baybars's death because you view it now, not in any personal sense, but as one of the Brethren. Perhaps even more so than I do."

"I wish I could take your praise, Everard. It's not exactly often that you offer it. But I cannot."

"Why?"

Will slipped a hand inside the collar of his white mantle and lifted free a long silver chain. Dangling beside the St. George pendant was a delicate gold ring. "I'm still ruled by passion."

Everard smiled and shook his head. "No, William. You *have* passion. And that is very different to being ruled by it." He shifted in the blanket, coughed a little, then settled. "How is she?"

"You don't have to ask. I know you don't approve."

"Nonsense," retorted Everard abruptly. "She sent me pomegranates."

Will laughed despite himself. Returning from Damascus to find Everard ill, he had kept an almost ceaseless vigil at the priest's bedside, leaving the preceptory only once, to marry Elwen. Andreas had arranged it in secret for them. It had been a brief, simple ceremony, just the two of them and a priest. Afterward, Will had returned to Everard. Since then, he and Elwen had communicated in messages, passed through Simon, and along with her words, Elwen had sent a basket of fruit for Everard. "She is fine. Better than."

"And she is eating again? She will need to keep up her strength."

Will leaned forward, elbows on his knees, and put his head in his hands, grinning in amused disbelief.

"What?" demanded Everard.

"I just never imagined that I would one day be sitting with you discussing the eating habits of my wife and our unborn child."

"Well, in my experience, William," said Everard with a long, wheezy breath, "nothing in life is ever quite what you expect." He closed his eyes again. They remained closed this time, and soon his breaths leveled out, growing slower and fainter, until Will was sitting poised on his stool, straining to hear the next one.

An hour later, Will was drifting into sleep, his chin resting in his cupped hand, when Everard's eyes lids flickered and his desiccated lips cracked apart. "I think Rabbi Elias still has that book I lent him. Would you ask him for it the next time you see him?"

Will stirred. "Of course," he said groggily.

Everard's papery brow furrowed questioningly. "I wonder if Hasan will know."

"Know what?" Will was awake now. "Everard? Know what?"

But although Everard's mouth hung open, as if to say something else, there were no more words. Will touched the side of his neck and felt the last faint flutters of the vein. Then nothing. Slowly, Will drew his hand away and sat back, staring at Everard's lifeless form. He was fragile, almost childlike, under the folds of the blanket. Will knew he should get a priest and the infirmarer. But instead he rose and walked over to the window. For a moment, he hesitated to draw back the drapes. Then he pulled them apart, flooding the solar with golden light. When he turned back to Everard, he saw that the old man was bathed in it, his transparent skin seeming to glow from within.

That evening, after Everard's body had been dressed for burial and prayers said for him at Vespers, Will was called to the seneschal. He had been numb since the death, numb and dazed. But as he climbed the stairs to the seneschal's chambers, alertness returned to awaken his mind. For years, he had known this day would come, but even though it had always been certain, he was still filled with an ominous sense of trepidation. Now that Everard had gone, another would have to be chosen as head of the Anima Templi. Will had no doubt in his mind of who that other would be, and although he tried to convince himself otherwise, he felt he also knew what this meeting would be about. It was time, he told himself, to face his final punishment for the attempted murder of Baybars and his betrayal of the Brethren.

The seneschal glared at him over the top of a sheet of paper as he entered. Lit from behind by the evening sunlight, he seemed larger than usual, a hulking silhouette of a man, his iron-dark hair cropped close to his square, brutish head. "Sit down," he said, not bothering with a formal title or greeting.

Will steeled himself, then crossed determinedly to the stool set in front of the table, where he sat, wryly aware of how much lower the seat was than the seneschal's own chair. He felt like a naughty schoolboy in front of a master, which, he supposed, was just what the seneschal intended. He sighed quietly to himself, wondering why, when so much had passed, the seneschal could not forgive him. He had risked his life to safeguard the Black Stone, had brought the grand master back from the brink of corruption and had stopped a war. What else could he possibly do to make amends in the eyes of this man?

The seneschal said nothing, but continued reading the sheet of paper he had been studying. The silence dragged on, the seconds turning into minutes. Will fidgeted on his stool. Finally, he could bear it no longer. He stood. "Sir, I should like to spend the evening mourning our master and offering prayers for him in chapel, rather than sitting here waiting for you to expel me. So please have done with it so that we can both go about our business."

The seneschal's eyes snapped up. "*Sit* down!" he bellowed, slamming the paper on the table in front of him.

"Sir, I ..."

"You are not being expelled."

The seneschal had spoken quietly. Will wasn't sure he had heard him. "Sir?"

"Sit, Campbell," repeated the seneschal gruffly. He paused for a long moment as Will sank onto the stool; then, with a rapid exhalation, he spoke. "When you were in Arabia, Brother Everard called a meeting of the Brethren. He knew that he didn't have long left in this world. He wanted to be there himself to arrange his replacement. The Brethren voted on his recommendation. They agreed with his choice."

"And?" said Will, shaking his head in confusion.

"And they chose you," said the seneschal roughly.

"What ...?"

"They chose you," repeated the seneschal. "To be the head of the Anima Templi."

Will felt something nervous and shivery bubble up through him. He realized it was laughter, and he had to fight it back. It turned into a cough. "The Brethren voted for me?"

"Not all of us," said the seneschal sourly.

Will placed his hands on his thighs, elbows out, and rocked back on the stool. "Why didn't he tell me?" he murmured.

The seneschal gave a shrug. "Everard was never one for displays of emotion or gratitude. I expect he was too embarrassed to tell you. As well he should have been," he added beneath his breath.

Will caught the words, but refrained from saying anything. He watched as the seneschal leaned down behind the table and brought out a large, well-worn book, the edges of the pages, sandwiched between the leather-bound boards, frayed with handling. Will recognized it as Everard's chronicle.

The seneschal passed it over. "He wanted you to have this. He thought you might continue it. Personally, I think you should destroy it. We had a difficult enough time when the Book of the Grail went missing. We cannot afford any such blunders again. But that is my opinion. You're the head now. It is up to you to do with as you wish."

"I'll look through it, then decide."

The seneschal nodded. It was as much of a sign of reconciliation that he would get right now, Will realized. He nodded in return and headed for the door. Tomorrow, he could think about what this meant, about what would happen next. For now, he wanted to be alone. After shutting the door, he paused before descending the stairs, hugging the large book to his chest. A pungent, animal smell rose from the yellowed sheaves of parchment, which Everard, ever the traditionalist, still favored over paper. Had still favored over paper, Will corrected himself. *Had.*

And that's when the grief finally came.

THE CITADEL, DAMASCUS, 10 JULY A.D. 1277

Baraka Khan sat on the throne, his eyes fixed contemptuously on the gathering of men below him, as the Mamluk chief of staff droned through a lengthy legal speech.

Kalawun was struck by how small the prince seemed in comparison to the colossus of a man who had occupied that seat only three weeks earlier, smaller in presence as well as size, dwarfed by the ornate gold throne and by the distinguished men around him. Kalawun's fists clenched. Baybars was barely cold in the ground and already his place had been taken. Kalawun might not have agreed with the sultan's policies, but on many levels, despite his flaws, Baybars had been someone he respected. He had tried to make the sultan's son into a better man than Baybars had been, but the sullen, malicious youth didn't even come close. All those years had been wasted, the sacrifices he had made, greater than he could have imagined.

Three days after Baybars's death, a cloth doll had been found, bloated and sodden, caught in reeds in the river outside Damascus. The fisherman who found it had been going to throw it back when he saw a jagged cut sewn into its stomach, which had been partially open. Intrigued, he had prised the doll apart and had found a tiny glass phial. Fearing sorcery or foul play, he had taken it to a local guard, who, not knowing what to do with it, had passed it to the Mamluks. The doll had been recognized, two days later, as belonging to Khadir, who had been pronounced missing. The physician, who had tried in vain to save Baybars, had suspected poison, but unable to collect enough of the kumiz the sultan had been drinking to study, he hadn't been able to say for sure. The phial inside the doll was opened and the few drops of liquid inside tested and confirmed as showing properties of hemlock, the symptoms of which correlated with those Baybars had exhibited on death. Khadir's mysterious disappearance and the emergence of the poison and the doll seemed to leave no doubt in the minds of the Mamluk court. Baybars had been murdered by his soothsayer.

Kalawun alone believed, beyond almost any shadow of doubt, that this wasn't so. Each time he saw Baraka, he was reminded of the expression on his face and the dead voice he had spoken in whilst he watched his father die in agony. For him, it was Baraka who had placed the poison in the sultan's drink on the night of the eclipse, when Khadir was already lying cold in his chambers. He was plagued too by other thoughts, more terrible than this: thoughts of his daughter and her demise, so similar, it seemed, to Baybars's death. Khadir had admitted his part in that, but he had also told Kalawun that he had been planning to poison him. The commander guessed that Khadir's plan had been thwarted by Baraka, who must have taken the poison. But how would the youth have known to look inside the doll, unless he had seen it before?

Kalawun had tried, as carefully and calmly as he could, to confront Baraka and attempt to draw the truth out of him. But the prince was unwilling to talk and Kalawun worried about pushing him. No one else knew that Baybars wanted Salamish to take his place, and so, as had been proclaimed, Baraka ascended the throne, inheriting control of the Eastern world, from Alexandria to Aleppo. Without a royal decree, signed by Baybars, Kalawun was powerless to stop it. The only comfort he had received was the declaration by the chief of staff that as Baraka was too young to rule, he and the empire would be guided by a regent until he turned eighteen. As Baybars's closest lieutenant and Baraka's father-in-law, Kalawun was the natural selection for the title. But this was cold comfort when faced with the grim possibility that the sour-faced youth, now occupying the throne, may have killed both Baybars and Aisha.

Kalawun felt someone beside him and looked down to see Khalil. He forced a smile and pushed back his young son's hair, which fell obstinately back into the boy's eyes. He was only thirteen but starting to shoot up rapidly in height. Kalawun guessed that he would be taller than him when fully grown.

"Ali wants to know when we get to eat, Father," Khalil murmured in his serious tone.

"Does he now?" asked Kalawun, keeping his voice low and looking over at his eldest son, who was watching the chief of staff drone on, with a bored, slightly amused expression on his face, arms crossed idly. "Go and tell your brother to bide his patience. And to speak for himself next time." When his son didn't move, he frowned. "Was there something else?"

Khalil fidgeted uncomfortably and shot a look at his brother. "Ali told me he saw Khadir."

"What?" said Kalawun, shock tightening the skin at the back of his neck.

"He said Khadir's ghost is here. He's watching us all through the walls like he used to, haunting us."

Kalawun let out a quick breath, then put his arm around his son's shoulders and gave him a rough squeeze. "Your brother was teasing you. Khadir is long gone."

"Are you sure?"

"I am. Now go." He gave a small smile, this time not forced, as he watched Khalil return to his brother and thump him on the arm.

Ali glanced over at Kalawun and grinned, then returned to his regard of the chief of staff with an obviously feigned expression of interest on his face. Whilst Ali couldn't have been more unlike his sober young brother in looks and temperament, he was the spitting image of Aisha, a slightly older, male version, that grin of his a comfort and a challenge. Kalawun thought, momentarily, how good a leader he would make one day: commander of a regiment or perhaps governor of a city. Then, as his eyes moved back to the scowling, baleful youth on the throne, he was filled with clarity and an enormous sense of defiance, purer, lighter than his anger and fears. He wasn't helpless. On the contrary, as regent he had more power than he'd ever had before. All he had to do was find an opportunity, and seize it. The dynasty of the Mamluks had been born in insurrection. Baybars himself had killed two sultans before securing the throne.

Never had such thoughts of rebellion entered Kalawun's head. He had been content in his position all this time under Baybars. But now, staring up at the throne as that gold circlet was placed upon Baraka's head, he knew what he had to do.

On the other side of the throne room, Nasir saw a smile raise the corner of Kalawun's mouth and wondered what it meant.

He had spent years studying that face, getting to know its expressions as one might a landscape and its changing, yet familiar seasons. Usually he could tell, just by looking, what the commander was thinking. But the smile seemed odd and out of place to him, knowing, as he did, what was currently on Kalawun's mind. Two days ago, the commander had confided in him his private belief that Baraka had killed Baybars. Nasir had been surprised by the suggestion, but had fairly readily accepted the fact that it could well be true. After all, he knew how easy it was to deceive people. He had been deceiving everyone around him, including earnest, *principled* Kalawun for years.

PART THREE

✠

36

Outside Bordeaux, The Kingdom of France

24 APRIL A.D. 1288

The hunt lanced through the forest, driving through the undergrowth, with twigs and branches whipping back and snapping. Storms had swept through the region the night before, and the trail was boggy, clods of mud kicked up under the fierce tattoo of hooves. Damp rose in gossamer mist between the trees, and the rich winter's mulch, rotting on the floor, gave off a dark, moldy smell. Sunlight pressed through breaks in the thick leaves, catching in the dew, turning spiders' webs to fragile strings of pearls and the grass in the clearings to shimmering satin. Snatches of sky appeared in the canopy, blue and brilliant. It was early, and the last vestiges of dawn's crispness clung to the air, soon to be burned away by the sun.

Near the head of the company rode an impressively tall, athletic-looking man. His sleek black hair was covered with an emerald-colored cap and his matching hunting tunic was brocaded with twisting gold flowers. Although almost fifty, he was still youthfully handsome. The slight droop in one of his eyelids, his father's defect, was the only blemish to speak of, and even this lent his face a certain distinctive appeal. Oblivious to the courtiers and squires who cantered on the trail before and behind him, Edward I, king of England, was wholly intent on the chase. Up ahead, not too distant now, came the baying of the scout dogs. The bellow of horns answered the dogs' cries as the hunting party crashed toward their quarry.

Edward felt a satisfied thrill as he saw the wolf for the first time. They had been tracking it for several hours, and he would have been disappointed had it been another of the half-starved creatures they had cornered the previous day. This one was a brute, all hunched blackness and muscle as it streaked ahead through the brush. The scout dogs were called to heel with sharp whistles from the pages, and now the mastiffs, ears flat on their square heads, were loosed at Edward's command. They pursued the wolf relentlessly for a few hundred yards before a dog at the head of the pack leapt forward. Its powerful jaws opened and came down on the wolf's neck, sinking into flesh and muscle with crushing force. The wolf let out a howled cry and crashed to the ground, tumbling over and over with the mastiff in a knotted barrage of snarls and fur. The other dogs moved in as the wolf fought vainly, and together they pinned it, biting and tearing, whilst the hunting party pulled up around them, the flanks of their coursers dark with sweat. The huntsmen moved in and whipped the mastiffs away brutally before the wolf was torn apart. Edward jumped gracefully from his saddle. The rest of the party was gathered in behind him now, silent but for the stamping hooves and the low, snorting growls of the dogs as they were chained.

Edward drew his sword. The wolf lay on its side, panting. As Edward approached, it tried to rise and feebly bared its teeth, but it was too weak to support itself and its head flopped back down uselessly. There were red rents in its neck and stomach, and a rank smell of sweat and urine came off it. It stared up at Edward with muddy yellow eyes. The king raised his sword and stabbed down through its heart. There was a cheer as blood spurted up, staining Edward's blade. Withdrawing it, he took the cloth that one of his squires passed to him and cleaned the sword brusquely. Squires collected the dead wolf, which would be skinned for its pelt, its carcass fed to the dogs, whilst the rest of the hunting party dismounted and passed around skins of wine, congratulating one another on the kill. Edward joined them, now relaxed, easing off his gloves.

One man, standing apart from the main company, his face sickly pale and filmed with sweat, reached for a skin as it was passed to him.

Edward's eyes flicked in his direction, mid-conversation, and he held up his hand. "Water for him."

The courtier didn't hesitate, but handed the wine on to someone else. The pale man watched it go with a bitter look.

"I would recommend a purge, de Lyons," said Edward, moving over to him.

"My liege," murmured Garin, inclining his head. His stomach heaved and twisted violently as he caught sight of the wolf being strung up on a pole by the squires, its matted fur lathered with blood and saliva.

"Or," continued Edward, "if a vomit doesn't work, might I suggest you consider drinking a little less at supper." His voice hadn't changed in pitch or tempo, but beneath that poised tone was an edge of steel.

Garin met the king's gray eyes, then looked away. He was forty-one years old, yet still, with just a few chosen words, Edward could make him feel as if he were thirteen. "My liege," he muttered again.

The king moved off to speak with one of his French vassals, leaving Garin standing there alone and shivering in the muggy air.

Usually, he managed to conceal the symptoms of a night's drunkenness from the king; he wasn't often called upon before mid-morning, and by then he would be over the worst of the shakes and sweats. Today, however, Edward had insisted that all of his advisors accompany him and his vassals on the hunt, giving him a chance to talk over his plans for the coming month. Garin too had been summoned to attend, even though he wasn't exactly an advisor, at least not in any official sense of the word. Indeed, after nigh on twenty-eight years in the king's employ, he still wasn't sure what his position was, or where he fitted in the complex hierarchy of the royal household. Neither, for that matter, were any of Edward's other staff, which was unfortunate for Garin as the lack of definition made them wary of him and he had always found himself to be something of a loner in the bustling life at court. He resented this segregation and simultaneously acknowledged that it was necessary. For some of the things he had to do for the king, he couldn't be seen to hold a formal position. Existing outside the restraining ring of bureaucracy imposed upon the other royal officials made his work that much easier to accomplish. Caught between the legal and illegal worlds, he lived a strange half life where he was neither one thing nor the other, a state exacerbated by his almost constant drinking.

When he thought these days about what he had become, Garin viewed his life with a certain bemused detachment, like a man who has, at some point, taken a wrong turning but is fairly sure that he will join the road he is supposed to be on anytime now. But he had been thinking this ever since he had returned from the Holy Land, eleven years ago, and still that road had not materialized. He could have left: disappeared one night with a stack of coins from Edward's coffers, fled to another kingdom far from the king's reach, started anew. But fear and indecision and hope had made him stay. In Edward's employ, he had purpose and status, however notorious; he was paid, not as well as he would like, but enough to live on, and he continued to believe, despite all evidence to the contrary, that Edward would eventually reward him for his faithful service. He also had a sense of belonging in the royal household, which was, in some ways, like being in a family, and this was important since his mother, Cecilia, had passed away five years earlier, leaving him alone. Edward had taken back the estate in Rochester, somehow, after blinding Garin with legalities and technicalities, managing to draw the remainder of the de Lyons' dwindled fortune into his own treasury, ensuring that Garin would never see a penny of his inheritance.

As the hunting party finished off their wine and mounted up, two squires carrying the wolf, lolling from side to side on its pole, Garin pulled himself weakly into his saddle, thinking how much better he would feel when he had a drop of wine inside him. Sobriety was not a comfortable state these days, and his thoughts always tended to the past and to gloom whenever he was sweating out the previous day's consumption. His spirits lifted briefly at the thought of the unfinished jug in his bedchamber, as the party moved off through the forest, heading back to Bordeaux.

Almost an hour later, they passed out of the forest reserve and into the fields and vineyards that spread out from the city in a patchwork of greens and yellows, cleaved by the blue Garonne, which flowed through Bordeaux and on to the sea. Farmers worked the russet soil, tending new crops. Grapes, still sour and young, clung to the vines. The dawn crispness had gone, burned off by the day's metallic heat. For Garin, there was something unequivocally English about the scene, despite the southern warmth and the ripening grapes and the neat little bastide towns that were scattered about the landscape, many of them built by Edward. The king had spent the past two years in Gascony, working tirelessly to create new settlements and to unite squabbling feudal lords in his French duchy, a territory attained by his great-grandfather, which had subsequently passed from his father, Henry III, to him. Bordeaux was Edward's capital, and the life he had made for himself and his family here was a comfortable one.

Riding swiftly through the city and up to the castle that perched arrogantly over the town and the lily-logged river, the hunting party clattered into the courtyard, the guards at the gatehouse saluting briskly. Considering that most of the royal court had been with Edward on the hunt, the yard was surprisingly busy. Outside the stables were around fourteen horses, with several young men loitering close by, squires perhaps. Garin noted that the beasts' trappings were of colors and styles he didn't recognize, but more curious than this were the squires themselves, who were distinctly foreign in appearance, with olive skin and colored turbans wound around their heads.

Edward too had seen them. As he dismounted, pulling off his cap and pushing a hand through his sweat-damp hair, he began to walk in their direction, an inquiring look on his face. Before he could reach the foreigners, however, he was greeted by his steward, who came quickly out of the main entrance to meet him.

"My lord, was your morning successful?"

Edward didn't answer. "We have guests?" Behind him, the rest of the hunting party were climbing from their saddles. The dogs, barking loudly, were led to the kennels.

"They arrived shortly after you left, my liege." The steward had to raise his voice over the dogs' din and looked pained to do so. "They are waiting in the reception room."

"Who are they?"

"A Mongolian embassy, my liege, under the authority of a man named Rabban Sauma, ambassador of the ilkhan, Arghun."

Garin, handing his reins to a page, listened interestedly to this. The last news they had received from Mongolia was that after Abaga, ilkhan of Persia, had died, and his brother had taken the throne, only to be murdered by his generals when he converted to Islam. Arghun, one of Abaga's sons, had been elected in his place, but so far, they had heard nothing from him.

"Take me to him," said Edward at once. He beckoned to several advisors, who fell into step behind him as he shrugged off his riding cloak and entered the castle with the steward. The wolf was taken away to be skinned and cut up for the dogs.

Garin followed Edward at a discreet distance, curious to know what the Mongol ambassador was doing so far from home.

In a bright, oak-beamed room at one end of the castle, a group was gathered. Several of them looked Western in origin, but more were foreign. As Garin entered the chamber, a little way behind the king and his advisors, his gaze fell on one figure at their center, a rotund, beaming man of middle years who wore an elegantly embroidered white and jade cloak, which contrasted starkly with his tanned face. His white turban was decorated with a plump, glossy sapphire, embedded in gold, and his mustache drooped sleek and black down his jawline, framing an oiled beard. He looked richly exotic standing in the center of the bare stone chamber. A thin, anemic-looking man stood to his right, staring contemptuously about.

"My liege," said the steward. "I present Ambassador ..."

The rotund man's beam widened. Before the steward had finished speaking, he was moving toward Edward. "Your Majesty," he said expansively, bowing low, "blessings upon you. I am Rabban Sauma, ambassador of his highness, the esteemed ilkhan of Persia." He spoke French slowly, stiltedly.

Edward accepted the greeting graciously. "Welcome to my court, Ambassador. Can I have my servants bring you anything? Food? Wine?"

Rabban frowned delicately and gestured to a man standing close by, who spoke quickly to him in a guttural language. Rabban smiled again and shook his head. He answered the man beside him, who at once translated his words to Edward.

"Thank you for your kind hospitality, my lord. Some food and something sweet to drink would be most welcome, for myself and my men."

"We will break our fast together," replied Edward. He nodded to his steward, who bowed and swept out of the room.

"My liege," Garin heard one of the advisors murmur. "Might it be prudent to ask the ambassador why he has come, before you break bread with him?"

The ambassador, oblivious to this exchange, had wandered over to one of the high windows where Bordeaux and the surrounding sunlit fields were framed. "Beautiful," he said in French, pointing to it. "Very beautiful." He lapsed back into his native tongue, the translator echoing him in a stuttering stream. "I have come from Paris. Paris too is beautiful, but in a manmade way. I marveled at the splendor of its university, the elegance of its architecture, the chapels." Rabban's eyes widened with delight. "You have seen Sainte-Chapelle, Your Majesty?"

Edward waited for the translator to catch up. "I have."

Rabban didn't seem to notice the sour note in Edward's tone. "King Philippe himself showed me this wondrous place. A fragment from the very crown of Christ, I saw there, conveyed by King Louis, and afterwards I took Mass with Philippe's court. It is a day I shall forever cherish."

Garin, standing behind and a little to the right of the king, saw Edward's jaw pulse at the mention of the king of France. Edward had begun his sojourn in Gascony with a visit to Paris to pay homage to the new king, an intense young man, whose subjects had already named him *le Bel*, "the Fair," on account of his legendary good looks. There had been an immediate sense of rivalry between the two men on that first meeting. Partly, Garin had thought, this was because Edward disliked being Philippe's vassal and Philippe disliked having an English monarch ruling territory in his kingdom; but possibly more, he had guessed shrewdly, because Philippe reminded Edward of himself years ago: young, ambitious and handsome, a rising star, whose light threatened to outshine that of the celebrated English king, hero of the Crusades and scourge of the Welsh. Edward didn't like sharing glory.

Edward's jaw tightened further when Rabban gestured to the thin, anemic man in his party. "This is Gobert de Helleville, Your Majesty. The generous King Philippe named him as ambassador. He is to return with me to the ilkhan's court to express the king's wish for lasting friendship and interest in a continuing alliance between our peoples."

Gobert inclined his head stiffly to Edward. He looked anything but pleased at the prospect of returning to Persia with Rabban.

"On what matter did you parley with King Philippe?" inquired Edward, ignoring Gobert.

"The same matter that brought me here, Your Majesty." Rabban's childlike excitement was replaced by somber poise. "The same matter that took me first to Rome to speak with the pope, only to find that he had died and no man had yet been elected in his place."

Edward nodded. "We have recently been informed of his successor, who has taken the name Nicholas IV. But what, exactly, is this matter, Ambassador?"

"The matter of a new Crusade, Your Majesty."

Edward listened closely as Rabban continued.

"Although His Highness, the ilkhan, is a Buddhist, he, like many others in his court, has a great liking of the Christians. His dearest friend, and mine, a Nestorian Christian like myself, has been elevated to the position of patriarch in Iraq. The ilkhan has long harbored a wish to take back the Christians' holy places from the Muslims, a wish shared by his close friend, the patriarch. To this end, he has sent me here to ask the kings and clergy of the West for their support. He will pledge his own men and money to this cause if the rulers of the West will do the same. Your Majesty," he said intently, "you once formed an alliance with his father, Ilkhan Abaga, against the Mamluks. Will you do so again? Will you commit to a Crusade?"

There was silence in the throne room. Edward was staring thoughtfully at Rabban. His advisors were looking at one another questioningly. The tension was broken by the footfalls of servants, who filed in bearing trays laden with cold meats, cheeses and hunks of warm bread.

"Wait," said Edward, as the servants crossed to a large trestle by the windows to set down the trays. "Bring food to my solar. The others can eat here." He looked to Rabban. "Will you speak with me alone?"

"Of course, Your Majesty."

Several of Edward's and Rabban's advisors tried to interrupt, looking affronted that they would be excluded from such an important discussion. But neither man backed down. Followed by the translator and servants bearing food, the two of them left the chamber.

Garin waited until they had gone then headed up to his room, leaving the advisors talking animatedly and indignantly amongst themselves. He entered, and sweeping the drapes across the window, he wondered what the outcome of the meeting would be. He knew full well that Edward's desire to take the Cross and return to Outremer at the head of an avenging army was far from dead. But, thus far, the king's hopes of achieving this had been forced to one side by events closer to home.

Twelve years ago, the king had publicly announced his decision to tackle the increasing threat posed by the prince of Wales and launched an invasion into the wild, mountainous north. After leading a rebellion, Llewelyn of Gwynedd was finally brought down and the fractured territories of northern and southern Wales were subsumed under Edward's judicial control. Should anyone dare protest, Llewelyn's severed head, bound in iron and stuck on a stake outside the Tower of London, was a grisly reminder of the price of treason.

Edward had an almost obsessive need for control, and to that end he desired the creation of an orderly kingdom with established borders, all fully under his dominion. After taking Wales, he commanded the building of several impressive castles to guard his new kingdom and to maintain his hold, before leaving for Gascony to organize his French territory. Both tasks he had undertaken with the same ruthless, single-minded intensity with which he tackled everything. Garin knew that victory in the Eastern world never strayed far from his thoughts. But Ireland and Scotland had not yet been brought to heel, and with the death of King Hugh of Cyprus, four years earlier, the promise of a military base for a Crusade had vanished.

When news of that death had come, Garin had felt a burden lift, for he had never told Edward about the plot he and Hugh had formulated to steal the Black Stone. On the return journey he had won back a portion of the money Hugh had given to him and sold his sword in a French port for more. The rest, he explained to a furious Edward, had been stolen from him, along with the funds he had managed to secure from the Anima Templi. He had fervently hoped this last lie would prevent Edward from sending him back to the Holy Land to threaten the Brethren into bending to his will, which he was terrified the king would do if he discovered Garin had disobeyed him. But even though he escaped with only a vicious, humiliating beating for his gross negligence, he had always worried that King Hugh might one day speak of the failed plan and his own involvement.

Garin found the unfinished jug of wine placed beneath his bed and drank, only savoring the warm sharpness when he had finished it and could feel it flowing through him, smoothing the harsh edges of the world. Kicking off his mud-stained boots, he lay back on his narrow bed and stared at the ceiling, trying to decide what the king would do with such a bold proposition from the Mongols.

He didn't have long to wait for an answer.

Two hours later, having dozed off and woken with a foul taste in his mouth and a beast of an appetite growling in his stomach, Garin was on his way to the kitchens when a servant found him and told him he had been summoned to Edward's solar.

Garin found the king alone, sitting at his desk, his slender fingers laced together and a pensive expression on his face. There was a letter before him.

"Shut the door." Edward watched Garin come forward. "I have an assignment for you. This letter is for the pope. I want you to travel to Rome immediately to deliver it."

Garin was surprised and displeased by the announcement, but he kept his feelings from showing, not wanting to reveal them to Edward, who always managed to exploit a person's emotions. Instead, he kept his face carefully blank, feeling more himself now than he had earlier, with last night's drink sour in his blood. He had been caught off guard this morning. He wouldn't be again. "Might I ask what the letter contains, my lord?"

"You may," replied Edward after a pause. He leaned back in his chair. "It entreats the pope to begin gathering support for a Crusade. It asks him to send legates out around the West to kings and princes, imploring them and their citizens to join in their support of a new war to take back Jerusalem, to begin anew our fight for the Holy Land and birthplace of Christ."

Garin had heard such speeches before. Mostly, that was all they remained; high rhetoric spoken with grave severity and deep enthusiasm, and all ultimately flowing out into an oblivious silence. The rulers of the West were too preoccupied with what was happening in their own kingdoms to listen to such war cries. Crusades had become expensive and outdated. Edward was different; he meant what he said. But, still, Garin couldn't see many other leaders heeding such a call. "You plan to take the Cross, my lord?"

"Eventually, yes. But in the meantime I do not want to lose the support of the Mongol Empire. Their proposition is an interesting and welcome one, if not particularly timely. For now, I will show my support of them and their plan by these means. King Philippe has apparently sent a similar request to Pope Nicholas." Edward's lip twisted ever so delicately. "I hear the pope is an advocate of the Crusade, and as he is new he will no doubt want to make an impression. I believe he will listen to our requests. In the meantime, I will return to England as planned. My work here is almost done."

Garin knew there was more. "Can I ask why you aren't sending a royal messenger with this, my lord? It isn't exactly sensitive information."

"I want you to do something else for me."

Garin waited.

"When you've delivered this to Rome, I want you to journey to Outremer and meet with William Campbell."

This time, Garin was unable to keep his emotions hidden; they flashed across his face, hateful, ugly.

Edward noted the change, but continued without comment. "I have plans, as you know, when I return to England, plans which, for now, keep me from launching a Crusade." He folded the letter and took a red candle from his desk, burning weakly in the sunlit room. He dribbled wax onto the join, then ground his signet ring into it, sealing the letter with his mark. "I am going to need all the funds I can lay my hands on if I am to go after Scotland."

Garin felt the softness of the wine drain away from him, rendering the world once more stark and harsh as Edward handed him the scroll. When he had left the Holy Land eleven years ago, he had made a promise never to return. "The Anima Templi were reluctant to offer funds to us before," he said in a low voice. "It took me a long time to persuade them to part with their gold the last time I was there."

"And a short time to lose that gold once you had it," said Edward harshly. He watched Garin hang his head and nodded, satisfied by his shame. "I do not care how difficult it proves. Whatever persuasions or threats you employed then obviously worked. Use them again now. Return to me with the money I need and perhaps I will find myself able to forgive your past blunders."

Garin said nothing. The thought of going back, of seeing Will, was like falling down inside.

37

The Citadel, Cairo

31 AUGUST A.D. 1288

Kalawun felt the dull ache in his forehead build to a burrowing pain as the voices around him grew more aggressive. He rubbed at his brow in slow circles, his fingers slick with sweat. The sun was going down, flooding the sky with a hundred shades of crimson and gold, but the heat in the air was still merciless, refusing to dissipate as the afternoon had worn on, clogging the atmosphere, shortening tempers.

"My lord?" There was a long pause. "My Lord Sultan?"

Kalawun raised his head, hearing the second address. He saw a young commander staring at him impatiently. "Yes, Amir Dawud?" he said tiredly.

"I said, the time to act is surely now. We know the ilkhan sent an embassy to the West to ask for support for a Crusade. We cannot let these powers ally themselves. Together, with fresh forces from their lands, the Franks and the Mongols could defeat us."

Some governors in the throne room were nodding. Others looked unconvinced.

"I grow weary of this debate," murmured Kalawun after a moment. "It has been a long day. Let us return to the matter tomorrow when sleep has refreshed us. Perhaps then a decision can be reached."

"That is what you said at the last council," growled another amir, "and still nothing is decided."

"You will show our sultan the respect he deserves when you speak to him, Amir Ahmed."

The men looked to the source of the clear, cold voice. Prince al-Ashraf Khalil was on his feet, erect and stiff. His brown hair had fallen into one of his eyes, but the other was fixed intently on the amir who had spoken.

Ahmed glanced at Kalawun. He bowed his head. "I am sorry, my Lord Sultan. My prince," he added courteously to Khalil.

Kalawun waved a hand at Khalil. "Sit, my son. The amir is correct and I understand his frustrations."

Some of the men looked surprised. They watched as he rose tiredly from his throne and stepped down from the dais to where they were seated on a large rug, around low tables laid with drinks and the remains of food. His broad figure was still powerfully muscled, but he seemed, to those who had known him longest, a little stooped these days. He was in his mid-sixties and his hair was streaked with waves of silver, his worn, tanned skin wrinkled around his eyes.

When he was among them, Kalawun spoke again. "We have been having this debate for years, more years than many of you here will know. Each time it is the same. Word comes that the Mongols and the Franks are going to join forces and invade us, attack our citizens, raid our lands. People get afraid, restless." Kalawun was pacing now, clenching a fist as he spoke. "They want to do something quickly to stop it from happening." He paused. The young amirs who had spoken were nodding vigorously. "But word always comes," finished Kalawun. "And the outcome is always the same. People forget that." He shook his head as he surveyed them. "The Franks in the West have no real desire for Crusade. All sources indicate thus and have done for decades. They will not join with the Mongols."

"What if they did, my lord?" asked one commander. "Let us say an alliance was forged. What then?"

"We would know about it months in advance and could act accordingly," responded Kalawun. "Think how long it would take the Franks to muster any truly effective force. As it stands, we have far greater capabilities in terms of strength and resources. We are safe."

"The men who were attacked by the Knights of St. John in their raids weren't safe, my lord," countered Dawud.

"We dealt with the Hospitallers," said an older commander, whose face was carved with scars, coming to Kalawun's defense. "The Knights of St. John paid for their attacks on our forces. We took the last of their inland fortresses in retaliation."

Dawud leaned forward, his face passionate. "We took their fortress, but not their lives. We let them go free to Acre, where they will no doubt be very useful in any further aggression against us."

"We have a truce with the Franks, Amir, unless you have forgotten," said the scarred commander in a rough yet patient voice. "At present, we have no quarrel with their forces and they have none with ours. Our primary threat comes from the Mongols, and even they do not pose the danger they once did. Why do you think they have sought out the Franks to make an alliance? They know they cannot defeat us alone. Each time they tried we pushed them back beyond the Euphrates. They grow weaker with every battle they lose."

Kalawun was nodding. "The Franks cannot win a war against us; neither can the Mongols. We are in a stalemate."

"We cannot vanquish the Mongols on their own ground, I agree," said Dawud, frustrated. "But we *can* tackle the Franks. They will no longer give us any problems at all if we drive them from Palestine for good!"

"You are not listening to me, Amir," said Kalawun in a tight voice. "We move on the Franks and the rules of the game change. The Mongols could take that opportunity to attack us from the rear. A siege on Acre will be long and costly, in terms of both money and men, and there is no guarantee we would take it." His brow furrowed as he saw the doubt in their eyes. "You are young, many of you, and so I will forgive your ignorance, this once. My predecessor, Sultan Baybars, tried five times to take the city of Acre. Do you know how many times he succeeded? Well?" he demanded into their silence.

"None," murmured Dawud.

Kalawun cupped a hand around his ear, emphasizing his point. "I didn't hear you."

"He never succeeded, my lord," said Dawud grudgingly.

"And do you not think if I break the peace treaty that I myself signed with the Temple, the merchants and the nobles at Acre, a peace to last a decade, that they will rethink any decision to join forces with the Mongols? If we attack Acre and they repel us, they will know we are a serious threat and will look to safeguard themselves. As you have said, a united Frankish and Mongol force could damage us." Kalawun's voice was harsh. "Do you suppose we want to push them into each other's arms out of necessity?" No one spoke. Kalawun shook his head angrily. "This meeting is ended. You are dismissed." He turned his back as they began to file out of the throne room. Ascending the dais to his throne, he sat with a wince as the attendants came forward to clear the plates and goblets. One man remained in the chamber.

"Thank you for your support," said Kalawun, rubbing at his brow again as the tall youth climbed the steps.

"You will always have my support, Father," said Khalil coolly.

Kalawun glanced at him. "But you do not agree with me?"

"You know I don't."

"Even after all you just heard me say?"

"I know we can beat the Franks, Father," said Khalil earnestly. "With enough men and engines. I have studied plans of the city. It has weaknesses. The Franks are nowhere near as strong as they were when Sultan Baybars tried to attack them. They are disorganized and fragmented."

"The city walls are still as strong," said Kalawun placidly. "That hasn't changed."

"Why is it so personal to you, Father?" demanded Khalil, surprising Kalawun with the force of his tone. "You have always defended them!" The prince stalked back down the dais steps and crossed to the window. As he stood there, a breath of wind lifted his hair.

Kalawun saw his fiercely knotted brow and felt a heavy weariness drag him down. Khalil always appeared to him like a scholar or a mullah, with his searching gaze and his quiet, aloof manner. But, in truth, he was a warrior, through and through, and, at twenty-four, a military strategist the like of which Baybars would have been proud.

Baybars.

Often these days Kalawun's thoughts were drawn back to his old comrade. Perhaps because he now understood, all too well, the difficulties his predecessor had faced in this court on this very same subject. The difference was, Baybars had had no desire for friendship with the Franks; he had wanted them gone as much as his men had; he just believed the Mongols to pose the greater threat. As it had happened, the threat, for Baybars, had been much closer to home.

Kalawun felt a slight shiver run through him as he watched Khalil. It was ironic. He had spent all those years trying to make Baraka Khan into a better man, a lover of peace, only to have his own son grow up to be a military genius.

It wasn't even that Khalil was possessed of any mindless, fanatical hatred toward the Franks. He just had a disturbingly matter-of-fact belief that they had no right to be here and should be removed. Sometimes, alone at night, unable to sleep, Kalawun wondered if he were being punished for his deception of Baybars and his heirs. But he tried to ignore such thoughts. He had deceived Baybars for the good of his own people as well as the Franks. As for Baraka, well, he had dealt with him as fairly as he could.

Baraka Khan was granted only two years on the throne of Egypt, making no accomplishments in that time, before Kalawun, having built enough support amongst the men of the army, threatened him with a coup d'état and marched on Cairo at the head of his Syrian troops. Baraka, finding little support from his own men and fearing for his life, fled with his mother, Nizam, leaving his infant brother, Salamish, as heir to the throne. Several months later, Kalawun gently deposed the child and was proclaimed sultan, inheriting all the lands Baybars had spent his years in power taking. He could have pursued Baraka, brought him into custody, interrogated him, but he let him go. He no longer had the stomach for a confrontation. Baybars was dead and so was Aisha. Nothing he did to Baraka would ever bring them back, and he had found the whole affair simply too painful to relive. Other factors in his unwillingness to confront the past were the deaths of Ali and Ishandiyar. His eldest son, strong, capable Ali, had succumbed to a fever and Ishandiyar had been stabbed in an alley in Cairo shortly after the Mamluk Army returned from Damascus, following Baybars's death. The murderer hadn't been caught. The fresh tide of grief had overwhelmed thoughts of revenge, and in the end, Kalawun had allowed himself to let it go. He had safeguarded the throne and his people. He would live with what he had lost for that.

But even with his best efforts, liasing in secret with the Anima Templi under William Campbell, peace had not been an easy thing to achieve. Kalawun had come to see it as a living, breathing thing. Peace was mutable, unreliable, meaning different things to different people and having unexpected effects. Between the Muslims and Christians it was still weak and untried; a child that needed to be protected. Despite this, much of Kalawun's reign had been calm and prosperous; trade had boomed, and although it remained impossible to secure any kind of peace with the Mongols, who were actively aggressive, the conflicts with them, although brutal, had been short-lived. Another treaty had been created to replace the truce signed by Edward and Baybars, mostly thanks to the Anima Templi, specifically Campbell, who had persuaded the grand master of the Temple to assert the proposition over the rest of Acre's leaders.

But his men weren't happy. And neither was his son.

Kalawun moved his gaze from Khalil as he heard a knock. Nasir was in the entrance, rapping his knuckles on the open door. He had a scroll in his other hand. Kalawun beckoned to him. "Come in."

Nasir entered, nodding in greeting to Khalil, who smiled. Kalawun felt an unwelcome twinge of jealousy; Nasir and Khalil had grown close in the past few years, since Nasir had returned to the citadel. But, despite his envy of their closeness, he was glad of the good relationship his son and his oldest comrade had. It was further cement to the bonds of friendship reestablished between himself and Nasir, which, several years ago, had seemed irrevocably broken.

Following Baybars's death, the Syrian officer had withdrawn into himself, becoming distracted and angry. Kalawun put it down to his ordeal as a prisoner of the Assassins and made concessions for his friend. But as the months went on and Nasir's dark moods grew worse, erupting into open insubordination, Kalawun found it harder and harder to excuse his behavior. Eventually, saddened, but having run out of ideas and patience, he sent Nasir to a garrison in a Syrian border town, hoping that time away from the hustle of court would temper him. It worked. Six years ago, Mongols captured the town and Nasir returned, a quieter, calmer man. It took some time, but Kalawun drew him back into his trust and into his life. Slowly, their friendship was rebuilt and Nasir once again became his closest confidant. Kalawun had even chosen to name his newborn son after the officer.

"The monthly reports from Damascus and Aleppo have arrived, my lord," said Nasir, heading up to the throne and offering Kalawun the scroll. "Your advisors have read through them. Apparently there is little to speak of."

"That is what I like to hear," murmured Kalawun, rising and taking the scroll.

"How did the council go?"

"I believe I managed to draw some of the men around to my point of view in the end."

There was a deliberate sigh from over by the window. Nasir and Kalawun looked at Khalil.

"If you have something to say, Khalil, then say it," said Kalawun. "You can always speak your mind to me, you know that."

"You put yourself at risk, Father, with your continued insistence on ignoring the problem of the Franks. And they are a problem, no matter what you say, if only because so many of your own people want them gone. I fear for your safety," Khalil added, quietly. "For your position."

"Let me and my guards worry about that," replied Kalawun gruffly.

"But I—"

"Listen to your father, my prince," said Nasir. "He knows what he is doing."

Kalawun gave Nasir a grateful look.

Khalil lowered his gaze. "I am sorry, Father."

Kalawun went to him and put a hand on his shoulder. "Come, let us take supper together; we can talk more then. Did you need to see me for anything else?" he asked Nasir.

"No, my lord."

Kalawun nodded to him and headed for the doors. Khalil shrugged away from his father's hand, but consented to walk at his side.

After they had gone, Nasir returned to his own chambers to organize some papers he had collected with the purchase of a new batch of slaves, mostly Mongols, for Kalawun's Mansuriyya regiment, now the Mamluk Royal Guard.

He was going through the list of slaves, checking the details the trader had written and deciding what Arabic names these boys would take, when there was a knock at his door. He crossed to it, muttering distractedly, and opened it to find a servant outside. "Yes?"

The servant passed him a scroll. "This arrived, sir."

"From whom?"

"I do not know, sir. It was left at the gates with instructions to pass it to you."

Nasir took the scroll and closed the door. Frowning, he returned to the window, where the last of the day's light was still strong enough to read by, and unfurled it. It took him several minutes to read, and by the end his hand, clutching it tightly, was white and trembling. When he had finished, he screwed it up fiercely and tossed it away, sending it skittering across the tiles. Putting his palms on the window ledge, Nasir hung his head. When he raised it, he caught sight of himself in the beaten mirror hanging on his wall. Pale, sweating, he looked as if he had just seen a ghost. Which, in some senses, he had.

Thirty years ago, Nasir's life, already blighted by conflict, had been thrown into turmoil with the fall of Baghdad to the Mongol forces. In the chaos, slave traders had captured him and torn him from his brother, his only surviving family. Nasir had been enslaved in the Mamluk Army, aged nineteen. He spent his first year in Cairo planning his escape. But not knowing where his brother was, or even if Kaysan were still alive, he didn't know where he could run to, and crucifixion remained an effective deterrent, always prevalent in his deserter's mind. Instead, he had thrown himself into his training, realizing that the more he did to distinguish himself the greater the power and, thus, freedom he would gain. Under Kalawun, he had advanced quickly and was eventually, the irony bitter within him, assigned to purchase slaves and train them for the army. It always amazed Nasir how quickly these children were assimilated into life within the rigid Mamluk regime, how rapidly they were indoctrinated, all senses of their past erased, forgotten; families, beliefs, gone in months. He guessed their young age must help this process, for he himself had been fully aware of who he was and what he believed in when he had been enslaved, and no amount of instruction had ever taught him otherwise.

He was an Ismaili Shia, born in northern Syria, where he had lived with his family until he was ten, when his village was brutally attacked by a mob of Nubuwwiyya: Sunni vigilantes who had been organized to cleanse the region of Shias, whom they proclaimed heretics. Kaysan, four years his senior, had taken him into the Jabal Bahra Mountains, fleeing the raid. They returned the next morning to find their family and everyone else butchered, the mutilated corpses strewn across the churned up earth. Stumbling out of the smoking ruins, the two boys had lived in the wild for almost a month until a Syrian Christian merchant, passing through the area with a trade caravan, had found them. The man took them into his care, where, in exchange for food and clothing, they looked after his camels. Nasir had taken well to life on the road, but Kaysan resented the menial work and was sullen and insolent, until the merchant thrust a sword into his hand and promoted him to guard duty. The eight years they spent on the road traveling between Aleppo, Baghdad and Damascus, whilst not enough to erase from the brothers' minds the tragedy that had set them on this course, had nonetheless been mostly good. But then the Mongols had attacked Baghdad and everything changed.

It had taken years, but in the end Nasir had come to accept his fate under the dominion of the Sunni Mamluks. He felt like a tiger that has had its teeth pulled and its claws blunted. In his heart, he was still wild, but seeing the futility, he had ceased flinging himself against the bars of his cage and had lain down, broken.

Turning from the window, he looked at the screwed up letter on the tiles. Slowly, he went to it and bent down. Picking it up, he opened it out, the creases crackling apart. Nasir's eyes drifted over the words and returned fearfully, yet with an almost indiscernible sense of hope, long forgotten, to the name scrawled untidily in red ink at the bottom.

Angelo Vitturi.

38

The Sands, Acre

20 OCTOBER A.D. 1288

Will lay back on the warm sand, propping himself up on his elbows. The glare was in his eyes and he could only see the outlines of the two figures down at the water's edge. Behind him, beyond the swelling dunes where the sand was fine and light as sugar, cypress trees flanked the beach. All morning, the sky had been a stunning, endless blue, but a bank of slate-gray clouds was starting to build in the south, creeping up behind the humped shadow of Mount Carmel. The sea glittered, rows of white waves chasing one another in their race for the shore. Will watched the two figures jumping them, heard laughter, felt contentment suffuse him, making him drowsy.

His eyes were closed and he was starting to drift when he heard the laughter again, this time closer. He opened his eyes, too late, as a shock of water splashed across his neck and chest. He sat up with a gasp and saw a grinning face and a flash of gold that was gone in an instant.

"Right," he said, pushing himself to his feet.

His attacker shrieked, half in fear, half in triumph. Picking up her skirts, her long legs took her racing away across the sand, diamond glints of water dripping from her hands.

Will caught her at the shore. Grabbing her around the waist, he hauled her screaming into the air. Throwing her over his shoulder, he waded into the foaming water, soaking his linen hose.

"No! *Don't!*"

"Did you say something?" He waded forward, the water sloshing up to his knees. The rushing hiss of the green waves was loud around them.

"I'm sorry!" shouted his attacker, yelling now, helpless with laughter.

"I can't hear you."

"Father!"

Will chuckled and headed for the shore, where he swung his daughter down into the shallows. She was breathing rapidly, her face flushed. She slapped his arm and grinned. Together, they walked back up the beach, hands entwined.

"Can we do this again soon, Father?"

Will glanced at his daughter and smiled. "I'm sure we can."

Her hand squeezed tighter and she stopped abruptly. "I wish we could do more."

Will halted too. Only a short while ago, it seemed, he would have crouched down to talk to her. Now though, she was already at his chest in height, and growing fast. Instead, he put a finger to her pointed chin and tipped it gently up until her eyes were fixed on his. They were navy blue, the color of a stormy spring sea. "You understand why, don't you, Rose?"

"Because of the Temple," she said quietly, her eyes flicking away.

"I would see you every single day if I could," Will murmured. "But I can't." He put his hands on her shoulders. "What I can promise is to try and make each day we spend together as perfect as this one."

"Do you swear?" Rose asked him, her eyes narrowing seriously.

Now Will did lower himself. Dropping to one knee, he put a hand over his heart. "I swear."

A smile flickered at the corner of her mouth. "I accept your oath."

"Will."

Will and Rose turned at the call to see Elwen a short distance up the beach by their clothes and the basket of food they had brought. With one hand she shielded her eyes from the sun; the other was pointing toward the cypress trees. Will saw a rider dressed in white, moving down onto the dunes. There was a flash of red on the man's chest, and Will felt his breath catch in his throat as he saw the splayed cross. He stood, then realized that he knew the rider. Relieved, he took Rose's hand and jogged to Elwen as the Templar made a beeline for them.

"It's all right," Will called. "It's only Robert."

Elwen rolled her eyes as he approached. "I can see that." Her skirts were damp from where she had been jumping the waves with her daughter, and they swished heavily around her ankles. She cast a tall, graceful silhouette in the sunlight. Elwen's beauty, when she was younger, had a purity and softness to it. Now it had power. At forty-one, her face was fuller, stronger, the lines more assured, more defined, and her hair was a darker, richer shade of gold. "Look at you both. You're wet through."

"It's Father's fault," said Rose immediately.

"It usually is," replied Elwen.

Robert dismounted and led his horse toward them. "Afternoon," he called, nodding to Elwen and flashing a grin at Rose, who blushed furiously and turned away, intently studying something in the sand at her feet.

"Is something wrong?" Will asked, heading to meet him.

"No. But the grand master is looking for you. I thought I'd better warn you in case someone else came searching for you on his behalf." He glanced at Elwen and Rose.

"Thank you," said Will gratefully.

"Thank Simon. He told me where I'd find you." Robert scanned the beach. "Beautiful, isn't it? I don't know why I don't come down here myself." He looked back at Will. "Oh, that's right, because you work me too damn hard."

"I can work you a lot harder if I've a mind to. Give me a moment." Will walked back to where Elwen was struggling to get Rose into a cap.

She looked sideways at him, ignoring the protests of her daughter. "What's the matter?"

"I have to get back. I'm sorry."

Elwen shook her head. "Don't be. It's been a lovely day." She nodded south to where the clouds were building. "It looks like it might storm soon anyway. Rose, please!" she said, scraping Rose's gold hair back from her face, sticky with sea salt.

"It itches!" complained Rose.

"I seem to remember you very rarely wore yours," Will told Elwen.

Rose shot Elwen a defiant look.

"Thank you very much," murmured Elwen to Will. She sighed and looked at her daughter. "All right, you can keep it off until we're at the city." Rose skipped triumphantly up the beach, her long hair flying, whilst Elwen gathered the supplies and Will shook sand from his surcoat and mantle. "When will we see you again?" Elwen asked him, as they headed toward Robert, leaving the glittering sea behind them.

"Soon."

Elwen said nothing for a few moments, then she smiled. "Catarina came to the house yesterday with her new baby. Rose spent the whole day pretending to be her mother." Elwen was laughing. "I wish you could have seen her. She was so solemn!"

Will glanced at her, hearing something sad in her laugh. "You don't ever wish that we'd had more?" He stopped when she didn't answer. "Do you?"

"No," replied Elwen, after a pause. She raised a cool hand to his cheek. "No," she repeated, firmer now. "Having you and Rose in my life is enough for me. More than enough."

The four of them walked together along a dusty track between the cypress trees, Robert leading his horse, until they reached Acre's vast walls. Once through Patriarch's Gate, they separated, Elwen and Rose heading for the Venetian quarter, Will and Robert veering toward the Temple.

After kissing his wife and daughter good-bye, Will shrugged on his mantle and surcoat. "Any idea why de Beaujeu wants to see me?" he asked Robert, his manner now businesslike.

Robert shook his head. "But I do know the Venetian consul was at the preceptory this morning, meeting with the grand master."

Will frowned speculatively. "Was anyone else in the meeting?"

"The seneschal was with de Beaujeu in his chambers, but he was dismissed when the consul arrived. That was how I heard. He was quite annoyed."

"No doubt," said Will, smiling wryly. The seneschal certainly hadn't mellowed with age. If anything he had grown more cantankerous than ever, but although Will didn't like to admit it, he had found the rigid old man to be an invaluable aid, especially in the early years of his leadership over the Anima Templi.

In time, even the seneschal hadn't been able to deny the reasons why Everard had picked Will to be his replacement. Not only did he have a personal relationship with Kalawun, an alliance which had truly borne fruit now Kalawun was sultan, but as a commander he worked closely with Guillaume de Beaujeu, who, whilst still unaware of the existence of the secret circle within his midst, relied on Will heavily. The other members of the Brethren liked his easy yet earnest style of leadership, and two new additions to their number, after the deaths of two of the older knights, had proved popular. The first was Robert de Paris, and the second, elected five years ago, Hugues de Pairaud, Will and Robert's childhood comrade, the visitor of the order, who had spent a year in the Holy Land before returning to Paris.

In the decade since Everard had passed on, there had been few great changes or difficulties facing either the Soul of the Temple or Outremer itself. But there had been many little problems, some of which might have threatened to swell into much larger troubles had it not been for the ceaseless peacekeeping mission undertaken by the Brethren. That said, the air of calm that generally pervaded the Crusader capital these days wasn't solely due to the efforts of the Anima Templi. Three years ago, Charles d'Anjou had died, never having taken up his seat in Acre, which Count Roger had held until Charles had called him back to Sicily, where he faced a rising rebellion against his rule. The king had passed on, leaving his progeny in the middle of a bloody struggle, and in their search for a replacement, the High Court in Acre had looked instead to Henry II, the heir of Hugh of Cyprus. The fourteen-year-old king had arrived in Acre two years earlier, where he had been received with great joy, which had grown even greater when the youth sailed back to Cyprus after his coronation, leaving a capable bailli in his place and Acre's resident rulers free to do as they pleased.

"Your girls are looking well."

Will looked at Robert.

The knight shook his head. "I cannot believe how fast Rose is growing."

"Hmmm," muttered Will darkly. "Too fast."

"What?" said Robert, laughing at the pointed stare Will gave him.

"You know what."

Up ahead, a small company of men appeared from a side street, walking purposefully. Most of them wore the plain, simple garments of servants, but one, who strode before them, was clad in an elegant black cloak, ornately embroidered. He wore a cowl over his head, but as he glanced down the street, Will caught a flash of metal and realized that the man was wearing a mask. It was fitted close to his skull, with black slits for eyes and mouth.

"I cannot help it if your daughter has an eye for me," Robert was saying. He lifted his shoulders in a shrug. "What can I say?"

"I think nothing would be best," said Will, distracted momentarily by the man in black. Masks were not uncommon and were often used to conceal the disfigurements of diseases such as leprosy, but he had only ever seen them made of cloth or leather. This one was fashioned out of silver. It was almost beautiful, if eerily expressionless.

"Shall I inform the seneschal that you're meeting with the grand master?"

As the masked man and his entourage crossed the street and moved on, Will looked at Robert. "No, I'll tell him myself. I have a few matters I need to discuss with him anyway."

"He really does respect you, you know."

"He keeps it well hidden," replied Will gruffly, although he smiled to himself as they walked the streets toward the Temple.

Once in the preceptory, he went straight to the grand master's palace, but was told that the master was in the gardens, inspecting the season's harvest. Will found him walking between rows of date palms and peach trees in the torpid shade of the preceptory's orchard, where huge black bees droned sluggishly around the fruit. There were sergeants in the orchards, gathering peaches in woven baskets.

The grand master saw Will approaching and greeted him with a brisk nod. "Ah, Commander." The years had been kind to Guillaume, and despite the gray in his hair, he still looked hale and spry. His eyes were a brilliant shade of turquoise against his sun-browned skin. He tossed Will a peach. "Better than last season, don't you think?"

Will tested the gold-flushed fruit in his hand. It was soft and warm like skin. "It has been a good year."

Guillaume strode out from under the shade of the branches and into the sunlight, his mantle sweeping the grass. "Walk with me." Will stepped in beside him, and together they moved out of the orchard, heading for the vegetable plots and storehouses. "Tell me what you know of the situation in Tripoli," said Guillaume, as they moved alongside rows of fragrant herbs.

Will glanced at him, wondering where this conversation was headed. He thought for a moment. "I know there has been a problem over the rule of the county since its lord, Bohemond, died last year." When Guillaume didn't respond, Will continued, sensing the grand master's expectancy. "Bohemond was succeeded by his sister, Lucia, who arrived from Apulia several months ago to take up her position, but was refused. After Bohemond died, the nobles and merchant families of the County of Tripoli chose to reject his line in favor of a new commune with an elected bailli that would govern itself autonomous of sovereign power."

Guillaume nodded. "As it stands, this issue might have been resolvable with the appropriate diplomatic interventions, only the Commune of Tripoli, in their infinite wisdom, decided to solicit the Genoese doge for protection, in case Princess Lucia decided to fight her corner. The doge sent a representative with five war galleys to their aid, but what the fools in the commune were not expecting was that the Genoese might have their own agenda. In return for protection, the doge's representative demanded that the republic be entitled to a greater proportion of the city than that which they already owned. More streets, more housing, larger space in the markets and the harbor." Guillaume's voice was dour.

Will knew most of this, but kept quiet, seeing that the grand master wanted to talk.

"Myself and the grand masters of the Knights of St. John and the Teutonics have attempted to persuade the commune to acknowledge Lucia as their ruler. The Venetians are particularly affected by Genoa's demands and personally asked for my support, but the commune refused to listen to our counsel." Guillaume looked at Will. "This is a serious situation, one that must be handled with care and consideration. We know, all too well, how easy it is to spark a conflagration between our communities."

Will nodded. Tripoli, which lay one hundred miles north of Acre, was the second largest city still held by the Franks, making it of vital importance to merchants and citizens alike.

"The Venetian consul came to see me today," continued Guillaume. "There have been a number of proposals put forward by the Venetian community, both here and in Tripoli. The consul has invited me to a meeting next week where it is hoped a course of action can be decided upon." Guillaume paused by a bush of strong-smelling coriander and pulled off a couple of dry leaves. He rolled them between his thumb and forefinger and sniffed. "I would like you to join me, Commander."

THE VENETIAN QUARTER, ACRE, 25 OCTOBER A.D. 1288

The council chambers inside the grand palazzo were steadily filling. Men, whose sumptuous clothing brazenly announced their wealth, filed in, taking up positions along rows of benches set before a dais. These were some of the most powerful men in Outremer, all of them Venetian merchants, whose houses dominated a multitude of industries within the trading world: silver, gold, timber, wool, spices and slaves.

Will followed the grand master into the ornate chamber, with its sweeping domed ceiling and mosaic-patterned floor. On the dais were seven seats, for the moment empty. Will realized that they were heading for them as Guillaume climbed the dais steps. He sat beside the grand master, feeling exposed on the raised platform in front of the growing audience. A few minutes later, the Venetian consul entered the chamber with four men and hurried up to the dais. The last few stragglers were admitted as he ascended. The consul appeared to be afflicted with a mild fever, for his skin was pale and he had a bright red nose, which he immediately wiped with a square of silk. The doors shut with a resounding echo, and the four men the consul had entered with, advisors Will guessed, took up their places on the dais.

"Welcome," said the consul in nasal Italian. As he spoke, one of the advisors leaned close to Guillaume and Will and translated the words in a faint whisper. "Most of you will have attended at least one meeting on the issue of Tripoli. Here, today, we will make a decision on how we should proceed. I have invited the grand master of the Temple, our staunchest friend, to enter this discussion in the hope that a fresh viewpoint may help us to find the answer we seek." The consul inclined his head to Guillaume, who smiled courteously at the assembled merchants. "I feel that we must set aside our differences of opinion in this matter," continued the consul, looking at the company, "in favor of a swift solution."

As the consul introduced his advisors, the translator whispering on, Will let his gaze wander over the crowd. It came to rest on a familiar face in the second row of benches: Andreas di Paolo, Elwen's master, and Rose's godfather. Andreas caught his eye and nodded.

After the introductions, the floor was opened and the meeting began.

A corpulent man with a high voice was the first to rise. "Lord Consul, do we have any further news from Tripoli? The last we heard was that the commune had contacted Princess Lucia here in Acre, stating that they would accept her as ruler if she would accept their authority within the county."

"We do," answered the consul. "It appears the commune is having doubts over its decision to involve Genoa in the dispute, which is unsurprising considering the state's outrageous demands for hegemony." A murmur of angry voices whispered around the chamber in agreement. The consul continued above them. "Princess Lucia, we have been informed, has accepted the commune's terms and has been recognized by them as rightful ruler of the County of Tripoli."

The angry mutters turned into a chorus of pleased surprise.

"Wait, please, gentlemen," said the consul, raising a hand to quiet them. "That is, unfortunately, not the end of the matter. Lucia, understandably, given her precarious position, contacted the Genoese representative sent by the doge after speaking with the commune." He paused and sneezed violently three times, before blowing his nose into the silk cloth. "The representative met with her in Acre last week, whereupon the princess told him that she would agree both to confirm the authority of the commune and the privileges demanded by the Genoese. The representative agreed to these terms. Thus, Lucia will shortly be named countess of Tripoli and the Genoese have been given want they want."

The murmurs of satisfaction vanished in a melee of raised voices. Some men stood.

"This is preposterous, Lord Consul!"

"Tripoli is the only port other than Acre and Tyre that we still have full access to. We cannot let the Genoese monopolize such a strategic base."

"If Genoa dominates Tripoli, Venice will be finished in Outremer! They have already seized control of the Byzantine trade routes out of Mongolia."

"This is not in dispute," countered the consul. He had to shout to be heard. "Of course Genoa cannot be allowed to take control of Tripoli, marginalizing our ability to trade freely and fairly in the city. We wanted Lucia as ruler, but not at this cost. The question is what do we do? The princess, the commune and the Genoese are now all in agreement. We cannot fight them on this issue. They stand united."

"Send ships," suggested one merchant. "Blockade the harbor until the Genoese back down from their demands."

"That will hurt our trade as much as theirs," complained another.

"What about the High Court, Lord Consul?" asked Andreas, rising. "Will they not intervene in this matter?"

"No," replied the consul bitterly. "They will not."

"There is another option."

Will looked to the source of the voice, which was oddly sibilant. His eyes fell on a figure dressed in an embroidered black cloak, standing near the back of the chamber. Will was drawn instantly to his face, or lack thereof, for instead of a face he had a silver mask. It was the man he had seen in the street with the entourage of servants, a week ago.

"Speak, Benito," said the consul, gesturing to him.

The man in the mask seemed to survey the chamber. "There is, I believe, one man who can help us. Sultan Kalawun."

A few people began talking over him at this, but others, Will noticed, were nodding.

"It has happened before that the Mamluks have been asked to intervene in our affairs, and in this case it will be in their best interests to do so. If Genoa controls Tripoli, they will dominate Eastern trade and that will affect the Mamluks as much as it will affect us. Sultan Kalawun has no personal quarrel with the Genoese or the commune and may be better suited to negotiating with them."

"You have presented this case before, Benito," said one merchant, rising. "But it is still unclear to me why the Genoese and the Commune of Tripoli would listen to the Egyptian sultan any more than they will listen to us."

"That is simply answered," replied Benito. "Sultan Kalawun can blockade Genoese trade in and out of Egypt. Genoa will lose more than she will gain should that happen."

One of the advisors leaned over and whispered something to the consul, who nodded. Around the chamber, voices were echoing again. But Will could see that there was support for Benito's suggestion. He wondered why the man wore the mask, but guessed, noting the thick black gloves on his hands, that his first assumption was probably correct, and that it concealed the blemishes of some disease.

The meeting continued for a while longer, with other ideas pushed forward, none of which generated much enthusiasm from the consul or the gathering. The grand master spoke only briefly, and in the end, the discussion returned to Benito's proposal.

"Who would we send?" asked one merchant. "Who would be the best person to approach the sultan?"

At this, Benito rose again. "My Lord Consul, as you know, I have had dealings with the Mamluks. I know Cairo well and would be happy to travel there as envoy for you."

Again, Will saw an advisor murmur something to the consul.

For a few moments, the consul said nothing, but he wiped his nose thoughtfully. "Very well. I propose that a delegation is sent to Sultan Kalawun, asking him to intervene. Hopefully, his mere involvement will be enough to cause the Genoese to back down, without any sanctions having to be put in place. I accept your proposal, Benito. You will travel to Cairo to meet with the sultan, bearing a letter from me explaining the situation and asking for his help." He scanned the chamber. "Are there any objections?" There were a few protests from some of the gathering, but those in agreement far outnumbered the dissenters. "That is settled then," said the consul, rising.

"My Lord Consul," interrupted Guillaume, "if I may add one change to the proposal?"

There was a pause, as the translator repeated his question.

"Of course, my lord," said the consul, nodding for Guillaume to continue.

"I propose that my man, here, goes with this delegation."

As Guillaume spoke in a calm, assured tone, Will suddenly understood why he had been invited. The grand master must have guessed, presumably from his discussion with the consul, that this would be the outcome of the meeting and had wanted him there for this very purpose. Guillaume wasn't going to let the Venetians have free reign on such a sensitive issue.

"My Lord Consul, I must protest," said Benito, before the consul could speak. "The grand master's offer, while appreciated, is unnecessary. As I said, I have worked closely with the Mamluks. A stranger might upset the delicate relationship I have formed with them."

"My man has liaised directly with Sultan Kalawun on my behalf in the past," said Guillaume smoothly. He looked to the consul. "And presents an unbiased voice in this matter."

"But I—"

"The knight will go with you, Benito," said the consul, interrupting the masked man. He crumpled the silk cloth in his hand and rose. "I would think you would be glad to have a Templar Knight accompany you. The roads are not without danger."

With that, the council was brought to a close. Will couldn't see the expression on Benito's face, but he had the impression that it wasn't a happy one. He sympathized. A journey to Cairo was the last thing he'd had planned.

THE SINAI DESERT, EGYPT, 6 NOVEMBER A.D. 1288

Will shifted uncomfortably in his saddle and took the reins in one hand to flex the other, which was cramped and aching. The sun was going down, and his shadow stretched long beside him, swaying in time with the horse. He glanced over his shoulder to see the rest of the company a little way behind, five squires on their packhorses, the sturdy beasts loaded with supplies, two guards sent along by the consul and, in the middle, Benito. This was how it had been for much of the journey. Benito and his attendants kept their distance, eating, sleeping, even riding apart from Will, and he had hardly spoken to any of them since they left Acre, ten days ago. For Will, this had been just fine; he hadn't been in the mood to make polite conversation.

He understood why de Beaujeu had wanted someone to accompany the Venetian to Kalawun's court, and he knew why de Beaujeu had picked him for the task. But over the past few years, he had grown used to spending most of his time in Acre, and he hated being away from Rose and Elwen. It made him feel restless and sort of prickly inside, as if the thread that connected the three of them were being pulled too taut. Displeased though he was to be on the assignment, however, he was glad to have the chance to talk to Kalawun. There had been rumors of unrest in the Mamluk court, murmurs of dissension over some of the sultan's policies, namely his leniency toward the Franks, and Will could use this opportunity to gauge the significance of this.

He turned back to the road ahead, but before he did so, his gaze locked briefly on Benito. There was no way of knowing through the blankness of that mask whether the merchant was looking at him. But somehow, Will felt he was. He had felt it all the way through the desert, like an itching sensation at the back of his neck. His speculations that Benito was afflicted with some disease seemed confirmed one evening when Benito had taken off his black gloves to pick up a bowl of soup. Will had stared out of the corner of his eye at the misshapen claws that had been revealed, the skin shriveled and knotted.

After another mile, the Venetian called a halt, suggesting they make camp by a series of low, jagged rocks, which lay off the track they were following. The squires dismounted when they reached the area, but before Will could climb out of the saddle, Benito hailed him. "We need more water, Commander." His voice came out with a whispery lisp through the mask. Benito jerked his head eastward. The sun caught in the metal, making it flare like fire for a second. "There's a well the Bedouin use about two miles from here."

"The Bedouin aren't usually amenable to people trespassing on their land," replied Will.

"They are amenable enough if you offer them money. I've used the well without any trouble in the past."

Will was silent for a few moments. "Why do you need me to go?"

"Just because I've not had any trouble before doesn't mean I'm going to be reckless." Benito cocked his head. "Didn't the consul say I should be glad a Templar was coming with me?" Will had the impression that the man might be smiling. "Isn't it your job, Commander, to guard Christian travelers on the road? Unless I am mistaken, that is the reason the Temple was founded."

Will wanted to refuse, but thought it petty to do so, and so the two of them set off across the desert, leaving the squires making camp. They had been easy on the horses for the last leg of the day's journey, and the beasts still had some pace left in them. As they rode, Will kept his eyes alert and his hand never strayed far from the pommel of his sword. The sun was almost down, and his shadow was now spindly and elongated, racing ahead. Benito rode a straight course, seeming to know exactly where he was going.

If it had been any darker, Will doubted he would have seen the well at all, for the stones were almost the same brown-pink color as the desert. They approached cautiously, but the sweeping sands were empty in every direction, the view halted only, here and there, by distant rock formations.

"Looks like it might be free today," Will said to Benito, who didn't answer. Swinging himself down from his saddle, Will walked over. The rim of the well was crumbled and fell away into black. On the other side, he found a wooden pail, half-buried in sand. It was bleached gray, the wood brittle, and a frayed old rope was curled around it like a dead snake. Will picked it up and tested it. A few hanks of hemp came away in his hand, but the central core of the rope held fast. One end was tied to an iron ring, fixed to the side of the well.

"Is there water?" Benito asked, setting down the skins he had brought.

Will leaned over and peered in. "I'm not sure." His voice stretched down the hole, diminishing. "Only one way to find out." Knotting the free end of the rope to the bucket, he swung it over the side and let it sink out of sight. He let out the slack on the rope, bit by bit, waiting for contact. Something, movement perhaps, made him glance up. On the ground was a shadow, coming at him; an arm raised, something tapering from a closed fist.

Will's head whipped around in time to see Benito advancing on him, a dagger in his hand. He dropped the rope and managed to half turn his body, ducking away from the arcing blade. The Venetian shouted in rage as the dagger sliced into air, inches from Will's shoulder. Will snatched at the man's wrist and caught it, digging his fingers into the flesh, pressing down for all he was worth. Benito yelled again, this time in pain, his limp fingers releasing the blade, which skittered into the well after the bucket. Letting go of Benito's wrist, Will went for his sword, but the Venetian moved quickly, shoving him viciously in the chest. Will went backward, hard. As his lower back connected with the lip of the well, he felt himself lift, begin to keel. Reaching desperately out, he clutched at Benito. His fingers caught the man's cloak, pulling him forward. His other hand immediately reached for better purchase and found the rim of the mask, which jutted up over Benito's skull. For one infinitesimal second, Will hung there, suspended. Safe. Then there was a *snap* as the leather strap around Benito's skull broke against the pressure and the mask came away in Will's hand. The Venetian stumbled forward with a grunt, knocking into him and pushing him those last few inches to send him toppling over the edge. Will felt warm metal clutched in his hand, felt space, sickening, inevitable, at his back. He saw a deformed face before him. Then it was gone, along with the rest of the world, as he fell into darkness.

The Venetian ran to his horse. The other beast he slapped hard on the rump, sending it galloping away. He mounted and rode back to their camp, the early evening air surprisingly cool on his bare, shriveled skin. "Pack up!" he shouted to the startled squires as he galloped into the camp. "Quickly!"

"What happened?" asked one of the guards, running over.

"Bandits. They killed the Templar. We leave now!"

The squires needed no further encouragement. Within ten minutes, they were mounted and riding out into the dusk, the two guards watching behind them for an unseen foe.

THE SINAI DESERT, EGYPT, 6 NOVEMBER A.D. 1288

There was darkness and there was cold. Bitter, merciless cold. Water seeped into him from somewhere. Every part of him was frozen, his limbs locked and solid like ice, like stone. His bones ached with it. When he tried to move, even the tiniest motion would awaken a pain deep within. Like a monster, this pain would rise and scream inside him, terrifying, overwhelming in its intensity. Far above, he could see a circle of sky, scattered with stars. He drifted in and out of consciousness.

Sometimes, Will was back in Acre; other times he was falling again. But always, in dream or when awake, there was a face. One half of it was blistered and hairless, wrinkled and mushy like rotten fruit. The other half was startlingly whole, and shockingly familiar. Still handsome, still cold and arrogant, that half was the face of Angelo Vitturi.

39

The Docks, Acre

13 NOVEMBER A.D. 1288

G arin's eyes fluttered open. Sunlight stabbed down into them and he winced, throwing an arm over his face. The movement made his head throb. A sloshing, creaking sound filled his ears. The bright light was blocked out by a shadow. He blinked up at the hulking silhouette.

"Didn't you hear me?" came a gruff voice. "I said we're here."

"Bertrand?" murmured Garin. The shadow didn't respond, but moved off, dropping out of the sun, which blinded Garin again. He sat up, wiping his mouth. He had drooled and his dark blond beard, which was long and tangled, was soggy. Dazedly, his head pounding, he looked around, the sleep gradually fading and reality seeping in, juddering, discordant. The man he had called Bertrand was clambering up to the quarterdeck and wasn't Bertrand at all. He had been dreaming again, dreaming he was back in Outremer, somewhere in the desert, looking for something he had forgotten. Something important? There was a forlorn crying sound whirling above him, faint, now close by, now faint again. It was a familiar sound, but one he hadn't heard in weeks. It was . . . gulls. Garin frowned and, gripping the side of the boat, pulled himself up. And there it was. Unchanged, unwelcome, unbearable. Acre. Those immense, arrogant walls encircling over 120,000 inhabitants, all pressed in together with their filth and their excrement, their sins and secrets; whores, knights, cutthroats, priests, lunatics and kings. God, how he hated it.

Having staggered to where his pack was stuffed against the side of the boat,

Garin picked it up and made his way unsteadily to the gangplanks, which had been thrown onto the harbor wall. A few of the crew nodded or called farewell, but he didn't notice. There was warmth in the sun, but he was freezing. Half-walking, half-stumbling across the dockside, he headed toward the iron gates that would take him inside. The smell from a heap of fish guts rotting in the sun turned his stomach, and he leaned up against a wall and dry-retched, his eyes smarting. He needed food. He hadn't eaten properly in weeks, and his stomach was sore and bloated from all the beer he'd been drinking on board the ship. He dropped his pack, then crouched down and dug inside, looking for the skin of wine he had saved. He found it with relief. A square of parchment was dislodged and came partially out with it. Garin stared at it balefully. It was the second letter he had to deliver.

Pope Nicholas had been delighted with Edward's promise that he would take the Cross when able. He had been planning to begin discussions about the Crusades with his advisors in the papal court and believed the pledges of Philippe and Edward to this cause would go a long way to convincing them to support the launch of a new holy war. He told Garin to inform Edward that he intended to send legates out around the West to call upon the citizens to take the cross for the liberation of Jerusalem. Eyes shining, Nicholas talked of how it would be like Clermont, two hundred years earlier, when Pope Urban II led the first call to arms for the holy mission and the first pilgrims set out for the East, his words ringing in their ears, sweet with the promise of absolution, a cloth cross in their hands.

Garin scowled and jammed the parchment back into the bag. The delivery of the second letter could wait. He couldn't bear the thought of seeing Will sober. He put the skin to his lips. It tipped back and back. A few drops splashed onto his tongue. He cursed and threw it aside. Standing, Garin swung his pack over his shoulder and looked around. His eyes came to rest on the row of taverns that bordered the waterfront. He lurched toward them, passing a few scrawny whores haunting the dockside, none of whom were desperate enough to call to him as he shambled past.

FUSTAT MISR, CAIRO, 13 NOVEMBER A.D. 1288

The two men headed through the twisted alleys, shadowed by the buildings that hemmed them on all sides, a labyrinth of dusty facades lined with barred windows and low doorways. Smells of meat and spices lingered in the warm air; a baby cried and a woman shouted.

"Where are we going?" murmured one of the men, his voice muffled through his kaffiyeh.

"It's not far now," replied the other, leading them into a tighter, darker set of alleys and finally through a doorway covered by a cloth that swung limply closed behind them.

Inside, a few lamps burned, giving off an oily smell. Men sat at tables playing chess, clay jugs and wooden bowls set beside them. One, lounging against the back wall, nodded as they crossed to a table away from the other occupants. He disappeared through a door and came out a moment later carrying a jug and two wooden bowls that he set on the table.

"It's wine," murmured Nasir, peering into the jug as the man left them.

"I'm not asking you to drink it," responded Angelo, his Arabic smooth and precise. He poured wine into the bowls and slid one across the table to Nasir.

"Baybars closed the taverns years ago." Nasir looked around the room at the other men who were drinking. He wondered how many were Muslim.

"Sultan Baybars has been gone for a long time." Angelo picked up the bowl in both hands and lifted it to his face. "Things have changed." He slurped at the wine, some of which drizzled down his chin.

Nasir watched, unable to look away, as that ravaged mouth worked against the bowl. Angelo had a strip of cloth covering half his face, tied at the back of his head, but the scars beneath became visible whenever he talked or moved, the cloth lifting to reveal the blistered skin. "What happened to you?" he whispered, unable to contain the question any longer.

Angelo set the bowl down and looked at him. "The Temple tried to kill me. They failed, mostly."

Nasir shook his head questioningly.

"The day you came to me in Acre," said Angelo flatly. "It happened that night."

Nasir recalled the day, eleven years ago, when Kalawun sent him to warn Will that Baybars was coming for him. He had instead gone straight to Angelo to tell the Venetian that Campbell had ruined their plans and saved the Stone. He demanded his promised reward: he had kept his end of the bargain, and even though the Venetian's designs had failed, he saw no reason for him not to receive it. But Angelo refused him. It hadn't worked; his business was still in jeopardy. There was no reward. In that moment, all Nasir's plans had crumbled. The shock was overwhelming. Everything he had done to try to secure his freedom and to rebuild his shattered life had been in vain. Something died in him then. Hope, for so long the only thing that had sustained him, at last had withered inside.

"I went after the grand master, to limit the damage done," continued Angelo, not noticing the bitter look on Nasir's face. He wrapped his gloved hands around the bowl. "I failed, and when my father and the other men we were working with met that night in an abandoned church, de Beaujeu came for us." He lifted the bowl to his lips, but paused. "My father's death saved me. Part of the building collapsed in the fire, killing him and the others, but opening a hole in the wall. I escaped."

"You stayed in Acre?"

Angelo set the bowl to his lips and drank. "Only until my wounds healed. The grand master had seized my family's house and wealth." Angelo shook his head. "We lost our empire in the East that night, an empire four generations had built. I returned to Venice, where my family had fled, and set about rebuilding what we had lost. I came back two years ago to restore our business here. This is where the wealth lies. Confined to the West, a slave trader cannot survive. I cannot sell Christians to Christians. I need Mongols, Turks, Arabs. It is the way of it, as you know," he added, noting Nasir's expression. "Now," he said curtly, "did you do as I asked in my letter?"

Nasir felt anger lance through him. "Why did you come to me, after all this time?" he demanded. A few of the tavern's occupants looked around, then returned to their games of chess. "You had no right!" hissed Nasir. "I should have gone to Sultan Kalawun when your letter came."

Angelo stared at him, surprised by the outburst. Then he laughed. It was a mocking sound. "But you wouldn't, would you, Nasir? How could you, without implicating yourself? Your fate at Kalawun's hands would be worse than mine."

"You promised me freedom. I lost my brother because of you."

"Freedom?" countered Angelo, sharply. "*That* you could have gained any time you wanted. You did not need me."

"I needed money."

"Money you could have stolen from your masters' coffers. Be honest, Nasir," growled Angelo. "Why did you stay? Will you not answer?" He leaned forward. "Then I shall tell you. You stayed because you are afraid of freedom."

Nasir fell silent at these words. To Kalawun and everyone around him, he was a loyal Mamluk and a faithful Sunni, but in his heart he was neither, and he had resented every day, every *second* he had been forced to pretend otherwise in this desperate parody of a life. But much as he despised them, the Mamluks were the closest thing to family he had left.

It was a fact that had rung all too true when he had discovered that Kaysan was dead, killed by Ishandiyar on Kalawun's orders. Raging with grief, Nasir had avenged his brother with the murder of the amir, but it had been a hollow victory. He had thought for a time of taking Kalawun's life, but had been afraid that to kill his master would ruin his chance for freedom. Even then, fury and anguish still raw inside him, he had known that this was an excuse. He was afraid to kill Kalawun not because he might not escape, but because then he would have to. When freed, animals bred in captivity most often died in the wild, unable to survive alone, unable to fend for themselves. After so many years, Nasir's prison had become his home. Angelo was right; he had simply been too scared to leave its walls. "Then why should I help you?" he muttered, pushing the bowl of wine away, untouched. "When there is obviously nothing you can offer me?"

"How about your life?" responded Angelo.

"What do you mean?"

"We worked together well enough for years, when my family supplied you boys for the Mansuriyya regiment. I do not want to have to threaten you, Nasir. But I shall if you force me to."

"Threaten me how?" murmured Nasir, his hand moving to his sword.

"I wouldn't need to lift a finger," said Angelo, his one dark eye, not covered by the cloth, following the movement. "Kalawun would do the deed for me were he to discover your betrayal." His voice dropped to a whisper. "How you worked with me to ensure the theft of the Black Stone, betraying your own faith. How you wrote to Kaysan and persuaded him to take the knights into Mecca."

"You forced me to do this! You told me you would kill my brother if I did not do as you asked!"

"I found Kaysan for you, Nasir. You owed me. One year it took me, after you begged me to search for him, not knowing if he was alive or dead."

Nasir was nodding furiously. "And in return I agreed to only buy slaves for the Mamluk Army from your family. We both got something we wanted. It was a deal."

"Sometimes, in business, deals change," said Angelo carelessly.

"Not in my business," said Nasir coldly, drawing his sword and rising. Behind him he heard the scraping of chairs, as a couple of the men in the tavern stood. Nasir glanced around to see that the man who had served them had taken up from somewhere a large club bristling with vicious-looking spikes.

"Sit, Nasir," said Angelo, not taking his eyes off the Syrian. "You won't leave here alive if you strike me. I still have friends in this city."

Nasir, breathing fast with pent-up rage, seated himself, but placed his sword on the table between them. The man set down the club.

Angelo leaned back against the wall. "If everything had gone as planned, my father would still be alive, this peace between our nations would be ended, and my household would dominate the Eastern slave trade. You would have been given your money, would have deserted with supplies and a new identity and gone to live with your brother as you planned. Fate dealt us both a heavy blow. But why should we surrender to its whim? I'm offering you another chance. It isn't too late, Nasir. And if you have done what I asked in my letter, you will believe this too." He paused. "Did you do it?"

Nasir paused, recalling that fragile feeling of hope, a feeling he had thought long since dead, when he read Angelo's letter. He had done what the Venetian had asked, despite his anger and misgivings. He had done it because even now, after so many years in slavery, after the loss of his brother and his faith, freedom remained a possibility, however distant, a possibility that the man in front of him could still perhaps deliver. He met Angelo's hard gaze. "Yes," he murmured. "I created the reports and made sure Kalawun received them."

The good half of Angelo's mouth lifted in a smile. "So," said Angelo, sitting forward, "Kalawun now believes the Franks in Tripoli, led by the Genoese, are working against him? Good. I will go to the citadel tomorrow and request an audience with the sultan. I am going to need you to help me persuade him."

"Persuade him to do what? Your letter wasn't clear."

"Together, Nasir, we are going to make certain that when Sultan Kalawun is finished with Tripoli and its citizens, there won't be enough left to fill this bowl." Picking up his wine, Angelo drained it in one go. "And then, perhaps, we will both get what we want."

THE VENETIAN QUARTER, ACRE, 13 NOVEMBER A.D. 1288

Garin jolted awake, feeling disorientated. The day had faded into a pale twilight. He struggled to sit up as he saw a girl standing in front of him. She had a small, serious face and searching eyes. Her cheeks were flushed, as if she had been running, and a wisp of gold hair floated across her cheek, escaped from her coif. She tugged it impatiently behind her ear, not taking her eyes off him, and said something in a language he didn't know. Italian?

Garin looked around dazedly. He was propped up against a wall in a dusty street, with no idea of how he had come to be there. "I'm sorry, I..." His voice was rough and he had to clear his throat.

"You speak English," said the girl.

This time he understood. Garin nodded. "Who are you?"

"I live here," replied the girl tautly, pointing.

Following her finger, Garin saw a blue door set into the wall of the house beside him, and all at once his memory came back to him, and he knew why he had come.

"Who are you?" she asked him.

"Rose!"

The girl looked around and Garin saw a slender woman hurrying down the street, a basket in each hand. "I told you not to run ahead," she called, sounding exasperated. She glanced warily at Garin and handed the girl one of the baskets. "Come inside."

"Elwen."

Elwen turned back, staring down at the man she had thought was a beggar. At first, she could see nothing familiar about him at all and her name on his lips seemed incomprehensible. His hair and beard were long and matted, his lips yellowed and scabbed. His clothes were stained, and a smell of ale and sea and desperation drifted from him. Then she met his dark blue eyes.

As Elwen drew a sharp intake of breath, Garin knew she had recognized him. He struggled to his feet.

"Go inside, Rose," said Elwen, her voice strained.

"But, Mother," began the girl, in protest.

"Now!" snapped Elwen, turning on her.

The girl looked startled at her tone, then angrily turned on her heel and pushed open the door.

"What are you doing here?" murmured Elwen, staring at Garin in shocked disbelief.

"I'm on an important assignment for the king," said Garin, trying to draw himself up. He was aware that his voice sounded a little slurred, and he tried to speak clearer. "I've come from the pope in Rome. King Edward wishes to launch a new Crusade."

Elwen lowered her voice further. "No," she said, shaking her head, "what are you doing *here*, outside my home?"

Garin looked to the door the girl had disappeared through. It was ajar, and he thought he saw movement in the shadows beyond. "She's your daughter?" he asked, looking back at Elwen. "You're still with Campbell?"

"Yes," replied Elwen sharply, clutching her basket to her.

Garin stared at the door. "Her name's Rose, is it then? Hello, Rosie," he called, seeing the shadows shift again.

"Leave her alone, Garin," said Elwen forcefully. She crossed to the door and stood protectively in front of it. "We don't want you in our life, neither of us."

She looked as if she might say something further, then stepped into the house and was gone.

"Wait," called Garin, as the door slammed. He stood there in the street, dazed. After a moment, he picked up his pack and moved off. When he was almost out of sight of the building, he stopped and looked back. Elwen's voice echoed in his mind. *We don't want you in our life, neither of us.* There was something odd in what she had said. It jarred in him. *Neither of us.*

40

The Citadel, Cairo

14 NOVEMBER A.D. 1288

"Lord Sultan," said Angelo. "Thank you for granting me an audience." His eyes flicked to Nasir, who stood on the lower steps of the dais with several other men. The Syrian didn't meet his gaze, but stared rigidly ahead.

"You explained to my advisors that you had come on a matter of urgency." Kalawun studied Angelo, his expression intent, but not unkind. "What has happened to you?" He gestured to his face.

"A fire, my lord," replied Angelo, absently touching the cloth that concealed the worst of his burns. He felt naked without his mask, but only Nasir knew him here. "It happened a long time ago and isn't why I have come."

"Why have you come, sir . . . ?" Kalawun glanced inquiringly at the attendant who stood to Angelo's side.

"Benito, my lord," the attendant reminded him, "his name is Benito di Ottavio."

"I was sent here by the Venetian consul in Acre, my lord. We have been experiencing difficulties over the recent shift in power in Tripoli."

Kalawun nodded. "The last report I received from my advisors said that the Genoese had become involved."

"That is correct, my lord. The Genoese made certain demands in return for their support of the commune. The princess Lucia has just been named ruler and has reaffirmed these privileges. The Genoese now have superior control in the county and over the port. Both my fellow Venetians and myself are obviously aggrieved by this turn of events, but all of us, including Egypt, stand to be affected. If Genoa dominates trade in Tripoli, she will dominate the East. We will all be at her mercy."

"This is grave news. But what is Venice is looking for from me?"

"The consul entreats you to intervene, my lord." From his bag Angelo withdrew the scroll, marked with the consul's seal, aware of the armed guards that stood around the throne room, their eyes following his every move. The attendant who had shown Angelo in took the scroll and conveyed it to the sultan. "The consul believes," Angelo continued, "that your involvement may diffuse the situation before it becomes violent."

Kalawun glanced up as he took the scroll, hearing something in the Venetian's voice. "You do not share his opinion?"

"I believe the situation will become violent whether you intervene or not, my lord. The Genoese have become increasingly aggressive, ever since they were ejected from Acre by my people following the War of St. Sabas. After their alliance with the Byzantine Empire they took control of the Black Sea shipping routes and now command trade coming out of the Mongol Empire. With this new hold over the County of Tripoli, their power grows even more formidable. But their ambitions do not stop there. In his letter, the consul speaks of the Genoese exerting themselves over Tripoli to the detriment of other nations. What he does not mention is that Genoa has plans beyond those borders, plans that extend to your territory." Every man in the chamber was watching Angelo closely now.

"What plans?"

"The Genoese intend to attack Alexandria, my lord, to seize control of the trade routes in and out of Egypt. To this end they have been building a fleet of warships in secret. This fleet, my sources tell me, is almost complete. The Commune of Tripoli is in full support of this plan and has been conscripting soldiers for some months."

The men on the dais began muttering agitatedly. One of them, a tall young man with a solemn face and a flop of brown hair, was frowning intently. Nasir was still looking straight ahead.

"Silence," called Kalawun. He stared at the Venetian. "I do not see how the Genoese, even with the help of the commune, could hope to take Alexandria, let alone hold it. Unless the republic plans to send its entire army across the sea, all reports would indicate that the Genoese do not have numbers anywhere near significant enough to mount such an attack."

"The Genoese have had strong relations with the Mongols this past decade, my lord, since they took control of the Black Sea trade. The Mongols, as I'm sure you are aware, are looking for an alliance with the Franks. I believe the Genoese will seek to exploit this. Allied with the Mongols, this fleet could take and hold Alexandria. Perhaps," added Angelo gravely, "even Cairo itself."

Kalawun was silent. One of the men behind him went to speak in the pause, but the sultan cut across him. "Why doesn't the consul tell me this?" he demanded of Angelo, holding up the scroll. "Does he know of these plans?"

"Undoubtedly, my lord, but I expect he worried that instead of intervening diplomatically, you would attack Tripoli."

"He is using me?" murmured Kalawun.

"Yes, my lord."

"And you are not afraid that I will attack Tripoli, Benito di Ottavio?"

"On the contrary, my lord, I urge you to do so. The Genoese will not listen to reason or diplomacy. I can lose business in Tripoli and survive, but I cannot lose the business I have had with Egypt."

"And what business is that?"

"I am a slave trader. I have had contracts with the Mamluks before. The Genoese threaten to destroy all that I have spent my life working for. Their main base in the East now lies in Tripoli. With that base destroyed, they will no longer pose a danger to our communities. It is a drastic measure, but the people of Tripoli have chosen to harbor the Genoese whilst they build their war fleet. They will have to face the consequences."

Kalawun sat back in his throne, looking grim. "If I attack Tripoli, I will break the truce I made with the Christians."

"This aggressive action against you countermands that truce, my lord," responded Angelo swiftly.

"Do not tell me my business," growled Kalawun, rising from his throne. "I am well aware of the legalities of my own treaty."

"Of course, my Lord Sultan, forgive me," said Angelo, bowing his head humbly. As he did so, he gave Nasir a sharp glance.

"It is true, my lord," said Nasir, after a pause. He looked at Kalawun. "If the Franks are planning an attack against you, then the treaty becomes null and void."

"My lord, I must speak up," said one of the men beside Nasir. He thrust a hand at Angelo. "What this man says is in accordance with recent reports we have received. We knew the Franks were building these ships. Now we know why."

"Amir Dawud," began Kalawun.

"We were afraid that the Mongols and the Franks might make a new alliance," said another man, before the sultan could continue. "This is the proof that our fears were not unfounded. We must take action."

Kalawun's face was hard. His hand curled around the consul's scroll, crushing it. "Why have you told me this?" he said suddenly, his eyes on Angelo.

"As I explained, my lord, what the Genoese are planning affects us all, they must be stopped for the good of—"

"No," interrupted Kalawun, "what is the real reason you are here? What will this deal do for you? Why are you the only merchant who has come forth to tell me this? You are certainly not the only one affected."

"It is true, my lord, I am looking for something in return for this information. As I said, I have worked with the Mamluks before. I would like to negotiate a new slave contract."

"If I attack Tripoli, I will have slaves for free."

"I realize this, my lord, which is why I am prepared to help your army enter Tripoli. I have associates in the city. They will be able to open the gates for you, countering the need for a lengthy, costly siege. In return, I ask only for ten percent of the citizens you capture."

"As far as I'm aware, as a Westerner you are bound by a law that forbids you from selling Christians as slaves. You are asking me for Muslims?" Kalawun asked in an ominous tone.

"No, my lord, only Westerners. But I do not need to sell them to their own kind. I also seek a contract with the Mongols, many of whom would gladly buy Christians from me."

Kalawun said nothing for some time. Finally, he raised his head. "Leave me, all of you. I need to think."

Angelo went to say something further, then felt the warning hand of the attendant on his arm. Giving Nasir one last look, he allowed himself to be led from the throne room. The rest of the men headed out, their expressions grim.

Khalil, who hadn't spoken throughout the discussion, lingered on the dais. "You must do this, my lord." Kalawun turned to him. "You must," repeated Khalil firmly. "Your generals are dissatisfied as it is. You have so far refused to comment on the reports we have received regarding these ships the Genoese are building. But you cannot ignore this. This news will inflame your men. They will demand that we tackle the Franks before they become a danger to us. Remember what happened to your predecessors. They were killed because those around them were unhappy with their decisions." Khalil crossed to him. "Do not give your men the same excuse."

Kalawun's brow furrowed. "Why does peace take so much work? Why does war so often seem the natural state?"

"Because we are not meant to have peace with the Christians," responded Khalil. "They are the infidel. The Franks invaded our lands, destroyed our mosques and massacred our people. They do not want peace with us. They want our territory, our wealth. Will you let them have it?" When Kalawun hung his head, Khalil's eyes narrowed. "You embarrass me, Father," he said frigidly, turning on his heel and striding from the room.

Kalawun felt as though he had been struck.

"He does not mean that, my lord."

Kalawun glanced around to see Nasir still standing there. "Yes, he does."

"He is right about one thing though. This news will inflame your court."

"Perhaps if I negotiate with the Franks at Acre I can . . ."

"There may be no time for that, my lord. The reports we received indicate that this fleet is almost complete. Also, there is no telling that the Franks at Acre will listen to our accusations."

"Then I do not have a choice," murmured Kalawun, tossing the crumpled scroll away. "Do I?"

"No, my lord," replied Nasir, his eyes on the sultan's weary face, "I do not think you do."

THE SINAI DESERT, EGYPT, 31 DECEMBER A.D. 1288

Will moaned as the walls pressed in around him. There was a feeling of suffocation, of panic. He tried to cry out, but just the faintest rasp of breath came. There were things crawling over him and pinching, seeking things burrowing into him. A harrowing light was beating down, the stone walls tunneling and intensifying it. Far above, a glowing eye cast its white-hot glare upon him. Soon, he prayed, soon it would go again and then the dark would come, and then the cold. For now, though, all he could do was lie twisted, caught in its merciless sight, his head raging with fever. And wait, and pray. But with every prayer the light became brighter and hotter, until every part of him felt as though it were burning, his face and hands blistering away, blood and fat sizzling and spitting, bones appearing in his fingers, charring, crumbling into ash.

Will came awake, gasping painfully for breath. After a few moments, staring at the heavy white cloth above him, his heart shuddered down to a brisk trot. He looked around as the tent flaps parted and a man entered. After all this time in his care, Will still didn't know his name, but called him what the others in the camp did: the sheikh, which meant leader.

The sheikh nodded to Will. "How is feeling?" Like everyone Will had heard speaking in the tribe, his Arabic was more basic and laconic than the speech of those in Acre or other cities. A few of them were deaf and mute, and as a community they seemed to rely more on unspoken understanding, a mixture of intuition and signals.

"Better," replied Will. "It feels stronger." He studied his right leg, which was bound with hemp to three strips of wood. One, wider and thicker than the others, was strapped to the back of his calf and lower thigh, above the knee join, and the other two were fixed to either side. "I want to try to walk today."

"Too soon, I think," responded the sheikh.

Frustration rose easily into Will's tone. "I've told you, I must get to Cairo."

"Seven days," stated the sheikh calmly. "You have more strength then."

Desperate, Will put his hand inside the collar of the coarse white tunic he had been dressed in. He pulled out the chain with the gold ring and the St. George pendant, forcing aside the loss he felt giving them up. "Take these."

The sheikh made a pushing motion with his hand. "No, I do not want."

"You saved my life."

The sheikh drew in a breath then seated himself smoothly on the mat beside Will, long legs crossed. "Would you leave wounded man to die in desert?"

"No, but ..."

"And would you save him for riches? For reward?"

"No."

"Then why you expect such of me? I do not want payment for saving your life, Christian. I am nomad, not mercenary. My people live hard life, but we do not thieve." The sheikh gave a brief chuckle. "And if we leave you in well and you die, when water comes back it is poisoned. It good for us all that you saved. You lucky well is dry this season and that when my people passed they heard your cries."

"I did not mean to insult you." Will pulled the chain over his head and held it out. "But I'm going to need a camel to get to Cairo. So, please, take this as payment."

"Why so important?" asked the sheikh after a moment. "Your heat." He patted his forehead and Will knew he meant fever. "It only just gone. You still weak, your leg unmended."

Will looked to where his belongings had been stacked neatly on the sand. His falchion was in its scabbard beside the clothes he had been wearing when the Bedouin had pulled him, delirious and ranting, from the well, covered in mud and blood and insects. His leg had been broken in two places, the bone protruding, splintered, from the side of his knee. Maggots oozed, white and fat, in the wound. His fingertips had been torn and crusted with blood where he had used them to try to climb the sheer walls. He remembered these things in bright bursts, both awake and in his dreams, but after the Bedouin brought him back to their camp where, between them, the sheikh and two other men had broken his leg again to set it in place, he recalled little. He didn't know how long he had been in the camp, but guessed it was at least a month. He feared it was longer.

The sheikh followed Will's gaze and frowned as his eyes alighted on the silver mask next to Will's sword and the silver-handled dagger Angelo had dropped into the well. The Bedouin seemed suspicious of the mask. Some of them, Will had noticed, made a gesture with their fingers toward it. He had sometimes wondered if they could sense the evil of the man who had worn it and were protecting themselves. "I fear something bad could happen if I don't get to Cairo," Will told the sheikh. "The man who pushed me into the well, he wanted me dead for a reason. Not just revenge, I think," he murmured, his gaze flicking back to the mask. "Maybe something bad has already happened, maybe I'm too late. But either way I cannot stay."

After a pause, the sheikh rose to his feet and crossed to Will's belongings. Crouching, he picked up the dagger and returned. Will flinched as the sheikh bent over him, but felt relief wash through him as the man deftly cut through the hemp ropes that bound the strips of wood. The sheikh closed Will's hand over the ring and the pendant. "These are no use to me." He stood. "I cannot give you camel, but one of my people will see you safe to Cairo. Now." He held out his hand. "We see if you can walk."

THE VENETIAN QUARTER, ACRE, 5 JANUARY A.D. 1289

It was raining as Garin loitered in an alley off Silk Street. His woolen cloak was sodden, his hood hanging limp in front of his face. Sniffing wetly, he pushed it back, eyeing the men and women who were hurrying home from a day's work. He didn't have long to wait. As Elwen moved past him, ducking her head to avoid the streams of water pouring from the eaves, Garin left the alley. He meant to call out, to stop her. But now the moment had come, he couldn't bring himself to do it. Instead, he followed her, feeling furtive and on edge.

For weeks now, he had been watching her, haunting the alleys around Silk

Street and her house, lingering in the marketplace where she would come to buy food. It had become an obsession, growing more intense with each week that passed. At first, after he saw her on the day he arrived in Acre, he was irritated by her manner toward him, but his mind soon after had turned moodily to the thought of meeting Will. It was three days before he had been able to muster the resolve to go to the Temple. Having been told that Commander Campbell was away on business and wouldn't be back for some time, Garin trudged back to his lodgings near the harbor, where he familiarized himself with the dockside taverns and brothels. It was during this hazy, fitful time that he had begun to think about Elwen, and what she had said.

One muggy afternoon, thrusting listlessly into some despondent whore, he found himself searching for images and thoughts that would bring the act to a swift conclusion, when, to his faint surprise, he conjured Elwen. With the picture of her reclining beneath him behind his closed eyes, the finale proved much more satisfying than the start. But after he was done, the image would not be forgotten, and Garin's thoughts settled and fixed on her. The day after, he kept his first watch on her house and followed when she and her daughter left for market. The girl, Rose, had skipped along the street beside her, occasionally waving at people she seemed to know. That evening, brooding over a bottle, Garin started to wonder. The golden-haired girl looked like Elwen, without a doubt, but there was nothing of Will's darkness in the child. He guessed she couldn't be more than twelve and did the sums, did them till his head ached. And he thought of the look on Elwen's face when she had seen him; the way she hurried her daughter inside; the words she had spoken. *Leave her alone, Garin. We don't want you in our life, neither of us.* Not "any of us," not "Will and I." But *neither of us.* Her and Rose? His mind rolled over the possibilities, gray and ghostly at first, yet brighter, stronger with each day he saw Elwen and her daughter, his eyes sunken from drink and lack of sleep. Until, finally, he was convinced.

The rain pelted his head as he hastened behind her, splashing through the mud. It was the first time he had been sober in weeks and he was feeling the affects. He hadn't wanted to be drunk for this, in fact he had even been to a barber's and had his hair and beard trimmed. But although he no longer looked like a beggar, he felt like one. The words he had prepared in his mind sounded wheedling, pleading, and he wished now, as he pursued Elwen onto the street where she lived, almost slipping in the wet, that he'd had a cup or two to steady him. She was nearly at the blue door. In a moment she would disappear inside and those questions would go round and round in his head again tonight, unanswered.

"Elwen!"

She turned quickly, her face gleaming with rain in the gray light. Her eyes locked on his and widened a little. But there was no real shock or surprise in her face, only an agitated resignation, as if she had known this moment would come, and dreaded it.

"Wait," he called, as she reached for the door. Garin sprinted down the street, now committed and impatient, catching her arm before she could go inside.

"I told you to leave me alone," said Elwen, shaking her head and sending drops of rain flying from her coif, which was plastered to her head. The material had turned transparent in the wet, and beneath it he could see her hair, coiled and twisted. "I've nothing to say to you."

"Well, I have something to say to you. That day, Elwen, when you came to me at the palace, when we ..."

Elwen looked mortified. "Don't, Garin, please!" she begged, before he could finish. "I can't bear it." She tried to draw her arm from his. "Please, just leave."

"You never told Will, did you?" Garin said, his tone hardening. He found himself annoyed by her distress. She had come to him! "You never told him that you lay with me." His fingers pinched into her arm and he drew her toward him, anger getting the better of him. "Did you tell him about Rose? Does he know about her?"

The blood drained from Elwen's face as Garin spoke her daughter's name. Then she raised her hand and slapped his face, hard. In surprise, he let go, and she pulled away, grasping her wrist where he had bruised her. Color sprang back into her cheeks, red and livid. "Don't *ever* talk about my daughter," she said in a steel voice. "I don't want you near her, I don't want you speaking to her. Do you hear me? Not ever!" Garin stood there blinking at her. Elwen faltered, her shoulders slumping. "What we did was a mistake, a mistake I've regretted every day since. I'm sorry I came to you, but I cannot change what happened. I love Will and we're happy. I'm not what you are looking for, Garin. I hope you find it. I do. But it isn't me." She reached for the door and pushed it open.

"She's mine, isn't she?" shouted Garin, behind her. "That's why you don't want me near you both! She's my daughter!" As the door banged shut, he stepped back into the street, rain dripping from his hood to trickle down his cheeks. His words hung in the wet air. He was about to go to the door, planning to hammer on it until she opened it, when he saw movement in one of the upstairs windows. He looked up, rain falling into his eyes, and saw Rose standing there staring down at him, holding back a curtain. Garin half raised his hand, then a shadow moved in behind her and the curtain was snatched shut. Stumbling backward, his feet sloshing in the mud, he lurched away.

41

Tripoli, The County of Tripoli

1 APRIL A.D. 1289

It was the thunder of God.

That's what the Mamluk soldiers called the sound made by the rocks hurled from the siege engines as they struck the city walls. Twenty-five *mandjaniks* lined up around the southeastern ramparts of Tripoli, the beams swinging up, one after the other, to fling their loads at the city. The Mamluk companies focused grimly on the backbreaking work from behind the safety of the buches: makeshift barriers of timbers lashed together to form a protective barricade. Sometimes, the engines would be loaded with barrels of naphtha, which would explode across the ramparts, torching structures and men, sending black smoke mushrooming into the blanched afternoon sky. Already, the Bishop's Tower and the Hospitallers' Tower were blackened and scarred. Inside the city, it was bedlam. No one had been prepared for the assault, even though they had been warned.

The month before, an envoy had arrived from Acre, on behalf of Grand Master de Beaujeu, to inform the city that Sultan Kalawun was leading his forces against them. But although officials in Tripoli had received reports that the Mamluks were on the move, no one, neither Princess Lucia, the Genoese or the commune, believed that they were the sultan's target, and the Temple's envoy was bluntly dismissed. The grand master, the officials haughtily claimed, was stirring up trouble for his own political ends. Kalawun was at peace with Tripoli. He had no reason to attack them! The Venetians were a little more circumspect. They trusted the grand master, and since their consul had heard no word from Benito di Ottavio, it was feared that the sultan might have made plans of his own. But, despite their apprehension, even they hadn't been fully prepared when, four days ago, the alarm had sounded around the walls.

Word had come before dawn from farmers in the surrounding countryside, fleeing before a vast, dark tide of men and machines. The Mamluks were coming. Tripoli's citizens were woken to the frenetic clanging of bells, too early to be for Prime. They watched in dread as the Mamluk force appeared and lined up outside their walls. That afternoon the siege had begun.

The southeastern walls were the weakest part of the fortifications, and it was here that the Mamluks were concentrating their efforts. After the initial confusion and panic, troops were armed and hastily positioned by the various communities: Templars, Hospitallers, Venetians, Genoese, Pisans, French. Houses were requisitioned and turned into guardposts, armories and stores. Huge sacks of sand, hauled from the beach, were lined up to counter the spread of fires as the naphtha barrels sailed over the walls and crashed down on rooftops in balls of flame. Mangonels and trebuchets were ranged along the ramparts. Some hadn't been used in years, the wood rotten, useless. These were taken down for the barricades being erected at the city gates, against the continuous booming punches of the Mamluks' massive battering ram. Crossbowmen took the place of the broken engines, their uniforms dusty, nostrils and mouths smoke-blackened.

That morning, troops on the walls, hunkered down against the volleys of arrows strafing up from the Mamluk lines, had watched, confused and troubled, as the great Venetian war galleys slowly turned and glided out of the harbor. The banners of San Marco caught and unfurled in the wind, fluttering smaller with every turn of the oars. The word went around quickly. Venetian officials had ordered the evacuation of their citizens. Venice was leaving. This started a general panic among the people of Tripoli, and since the morning, a growing number of citizens, carrying anything they could, had hastened down to the harbor, where now an almost continuous stream of galleys, fishing boats and merchants' vessels were sailing out. Others, who couldn't secure boats for themselves and their families, strapped children to their backs and swam desperately to the small island of Saint Thomas, which rose out of the sea just off the peninsula. Camps were being set up there, people said. Many more, however, stayed, trusting in God and the strength of their soldiers. They didn't know that in their midst an unseen threat was just waiting for an opportunity.

THE MAMLUK CAMP, OUTSIDE THE WALLS OF TRIPOLI,
1 APRIL A.D. 1289

Kalawun stood watching the stones fly up, one after the other, to smash against the walls. The sky was overcast, the air stagnant. Over the city hung a fog of dust and smoke. Once in a while, a stone would crash through a section of walkway and men would be crushed, or tossed from the walls. Kalawun wanted to turn around and escape the scene in the cover of his pavilion, to lie down and close his eyes against the pounding in his head and the pounding of the stones. But he made himself stay. His face pale, hands clenched at his sides, he fixed his eyes on the assault of Tripoli. It was his order that had brought this about. He wouldn't allow himself to hide from that. He would face it; the knowledge that this didn't have to be. He would suffer it; the seeping, choking guilt that every single man, woman and child that had died and was dying and would die inside those walls died because he had commanded it.

And he shouldn't have done so.

He should have done more to prevent this: should have opened diplomatic channels with Tripoli, or Acre; entered into negotiations; threatened action. But he hadn't. Instead, he had marched on Tripoli at the head of his army, not because it was the only option or because he believed it was right. He had done so because he was afraid. He was afraid of his men's response to his unwillingness to act, afraid of relinquishing his position or even his life, and he was afraid of losing the respect of his son. He had lost Ali and Aisha. He couldn't bear the thought of giving up Khalil. Tripoli was a trade-off; for the fall of the city, he would regain the approval of his court. But with every stone that was hurled against the walls, he felt the peace he had spent half his life struggling to build crumble a little more.

"My lord."

Kalawun turned to see his son approaching with Amir Dawud. Behind them strolled the Venetian, his gaze on the battered walls. As Benito di Ottavio turned, Kalawun saw that the good half of his face was eagerly expectant. He felt bitterness, sour and sick inside him, and focused instead on his son.

Khalil was clad in black brocaded robes, shot through with scarlet thread, a glittering coat of mail beneath. Under his arm he carried a silver helmet, and a saber hung from his sword belt at each hip. He looked every inch the warrior prince. "Nasir and his men are in place opposite the northeastern gate, my lord," he told Kalawun. "They are hidden and will not be seen until it is too late. Benito believes the signal will come soon. Most of the defenses are now concentrated in the southeastern quadrant. The city is suitably distracted by the bombardment."

Kalawun's eyes flicked to the Venetian and that self-satisfied expression. "If this plan fails, di Ottavio, I will hold you personally responsible for every man I lose."

Angelo Vitturi's composure didn't waver. "I promise you, my lord, you will be victorious. My men will obey my instructions."

There was a distant crack and a roar as the top section of the Bishop's Tower collapsed. A triumphant shout went up from the Mamluks around the *mandjanik* responsible for the stone that had caused the damage.

"We may not even need your men if this keeps up," murmured Kalawun.

Angelo's smile widened, the cloth that covered half his face stretching to reveal the riddle of scars beneath. "I may not be a general, my lord, but even I can see that it would take weeks to bring down those walls. With my help, you will take Tripoli in a day." He cocked his head. "I presume our deal still holds true?" Kalawun said nothing and Angelo's smile dropped away. "My lord? We had a contract." He flung a gloved hand east toward a line of scrubby hills. "I have forty wagons waiting to take slaves into Mongolia. I have arranged a buyer for them. Will you now renege on your promise?"

"No," said Kalawun. He had to force the words out. "Our deal is done." His gaze swept to Dawud. "I have a meeting with two of my governors, Amir. I will be in my tent. Have one of your men alert me when the signal comes." He headed for the red and gold pavilion, which rose majestically above the rest of the camp.

Khalil followed him. "My lord."

Kalawun didn't look at him. "What is it?"

"Father, wait." Khalil put his hand on Kalawun's arm as he entered the pavilion. "Please."

Kalawun stopped.

"I wanted to say," began Khalil. He looked away, then back at Kalawun. "I am proud of you," he finished. When Kalawun said nothing, he bowed. "I will take my place and await the signal."

"Be careful, Khalil," said Kalawun suddenly, planting a hand on his son's shoulder. He was about to say something further when he caught sight of three Mamluks standing at the foot of the royal dais. A fourth man was pinned between two of them, held by the upper arms. His nose was bloodied. Kalawun drew in a sharp breath.

"What is it, Father?" said Khalil, frowning at the prisoner.

Kalawun found his voice. "Nothing," he said quickly. "Go to your place." Leaving his son, he moved to the soldiers and their captive. "What is this?" he asked, forcing his gaze from the prisoner.

"My Lord Sultan," said the third Mamluk with a deep bow. He held a pack and a belt, from which hung a short sword. "We are here to see Amir Kamal. We were told that he would be meeting with you shortly." He looked at the captive. "We were patrolling the perimeter when we caught this man trying to enter our camp. He pretended to be one of us, but when asked he could not give the name of his superior. We think he is a spy, perhaps from the city. We have brought him to Amir Kamal for interrogation."

Kalawun paused, then strode toward the entrance to his private quarters. "Bring him."

The soldiers looked at one another uncertainly, but not daring to question the sultan, they hauled the prisoner after him.

Kalawun passed through an opening in the thick cloth. Several eunuchs were busy arranging the interior for his afternoon meal. He pointed to a couch. "Put him there."

The soldiers pushed the captive roughly down. "Shall we restrain him, my lord?" asked one.

"There is no need." Kalawun didn't take his eyes off the man. "Leave me. I will question him myself."

The soldiers bowed tentatively and backed away.

"And you," said Kalawun to the eunuchs and the third soldier, still carrying the prisoner's sword and pack. "Leave his things and go." He waited until they had left, then his face, which until now had been an expressionless mask, hardened. "Why did you come here?"

Will rose from the couch. "To stop you from making a terrible mistake. You have to call off this siege, my lord. Now."

Kalawun gave a bark of cold laughter. "Call off the siege?" His eyes narrowed. "And why should I when *your* people plot against me!" He raised his fist at Will. "Why didn't you warn me? Why didn't you tell me the Genoese were planning to attack Alexandria?"

"Because they weren't, my lord," replied Will roughly, wiping his bloodied nose. "Whatever Angelo told you was a lie."

"I know of no Angelo."

"Benito di Ottavio. That's what he is calling himself now. His real name is Angelo Vitturi. We thought he was dead, killed years ago on the grand master's orders. My lord," said Will, thrusting a hand toward the city beyond the tent, where the muffled thuds of the stones could be heard. "The man whose lies have brought you here is the very same man who was responsible for the attempted theft of the Black Stone."

"No," said Kalawun adamantly, "that isn't possible. No," he repeated loudly, holding up his hand as Will went to speak. "It wasn't just his word. I would not have come here on that alone. What do you take me for? I had reports! Reports that the Genoese were building a fleet, reports that suggested Tripoli was planning a war. My generals did not doubt it!" He walked away, shaking his head.

"Your generals didn't want to doubt it," answered Will sharply. He followed

Kalawun, moving a little stiffly. His injured leg still gave him pain, particularly when he rode for any length of time. The side of his knee was twisted where the bone had fractured, and scars made knobbly patterns across it. "Those reports? Could they have been faked?"

"What are you saying?" Kalawun faced him.

"You always knew there was a traitor in your midst. The man who wrote the coded letter to Kaysan? You never found out who he was."

"It was Khadir," snapped Kalawun, "I'm certain of it. He was once an Assassin, a Shia. He wanted the Christians gone from these lands. It was him."

"There was never any proof. You told me that yourself. You said—"

"Why didn't you come sooner?" Kalawun cut across him. "Why didn't you warn me that this Benito, or whoever he is, was lying? Why did his own people send him to me?"

"They didn't know he would do this. The Venetian consul agreed he should approach you last autumn to ask you to intervene in the conflict over Tripoli. Not with military action, but as an impartial negotiator. I was sent in this party, but I never made it to Cairo. Angelo tried to kill me. My life was saved, but I was wounded and it was weeks before I was able to follow." Kalawun was quiet, listening. "When I arrived in Cairo," continued Will, "I found that you had led your army into Palestine. I discovered through one of the citadel's servants that you were headed for Tripoli, and I sold what little I had on me in return for passage in a trade caravan traveling to Damascus. When I made it back to Acre, the grand master sent an envoy to Tripoli to warn them of your approach and sent a delegation to you in the hope of entering into negotiations. But the rulers of Tripoli wouldn't believe him and you wouldn't agree to see his man." Will watched Kalawun turn away. "We tried to stop this, my lord, believe me. But it seemed that ..." He frowned. "It seemed you wanted this."

"I didn't want it," replied Kalawun, looking back at him. "My men ..." He lifted a hand, then let it fall. "They needed this. I have held their reins too tightly for too long. Sooner or later, they would have turned on me. Sometimes, Campbell, I think we were born in the wrong time. I am no longer sure that peace between our faiths can ever work. You and I, we have given up so much for this cause and yet it seems we have hardly changed a thing. My own son ..." Kalawun exhaled wearily. "My own son wants the Franks gone."

"It has to work," answered Will. "Or this conflict will go on, and a thousand years from now both our peoples will still be dying. Stop the assault, my lord. Call your forces back. This battle threatens to destroy what we have given up so much for."

"I cannot. They are committed. I have lost men to this battle. If I call them back now, I might lose my position."

"And the people inside?" demanded Will. "What will they lose?"

Kalawun looked up as a blare of horns rose. "The signal." Snatching up Will's sword belt, he handed it to him. "Put this on," he added, passing him a helmet.

Strapping his falchion around his waist and pushing the helmet down over his head, Will followed Kalawun out of the royal pavilion and into the camp, where soldiers were hastening to mount horses.

"The arrow went up a moment ago, my Lord Sultan," called a Mamluk officer, hurrying toward Kalawun. "Officer Nasir's troops are on the move." He pointed north.

Will and Kalawun saw a company of fifty or so men, riding swiftly across the plain toward a gate in the northeastern walls.

"Dear God," murmured Will, stepping forward. Even at this distance, he could see that the gate was open. The *mandjaniks'* stones were still flying up against the southeastern walls. All of the focus of the city was fixed there. By the time anyone noticed the danger, the Mamluks would be inside. "You have to stop them," he urged Kalawun, as the officer turned away to help direct the men sprinting to their horses.

Kalawun didn't answer. His gaze had moved from the riders to a figure waiting nearby, watching the company approach the gate. Kalawun strode toward him. "Angelo Vitturi," he called out, his voice cutting across the shouts of the men and the blare of horns.

The figure turned, his one visible eye widening. But he recovered quickly. "Look, my lord. Your men will soon be inside."

"Why did you lie to me about the Genoese, Vitturi? Was it just for your slaves?"

"I'm sorry, my lord?" responded the Venetian, looking confused. "Why do you call me this name?" His eye flicked to the tall man beside the sultan, whose face was covered with a helmet. "What is this about?"

"You weren't the only one given a second chance at life," responded Will, staring at the Venetian through the slits in his visor. "The next time you push someone in a well, you might want to check it has water in it first."

Angelo let out a hiss of breath. He stumbled backward, away from Kalawun, who was advancing on him. In the distance, the riders, led by Nasir, reached the gate and funneled inside.

"Guards!" bellowed Kalawun. Despite the turmoil, four Mansuriyya warriors heard his call and came running. "Seize him!"

"Listen, my lord," shouted Angelo, as the Royal Guards took hold of his arms, pinning him. "I have done you a great service today, and tonight this camp will ring with praises for your name. Your position will be strengthened because of me." He was interrupted by a shout from a nearby officer.

Will and Kalawun looked up to see four flaming arrows shooting into the sky over the northeastern walls. The Mamluks were in. They had the gate. There was another cry of horns, and now lines of Mamluk cavalry, led by Amirs Dawud and Ahmed, swept out of the Mamluk encampment and across the plain.

"See!" shouted Angelo. "Your men have taken the city!"

"My lord," said Will urgently, "you have to stop this. Now!"

But Kalawun wasn't listening. "Who was it? Who were you working with? Which man betrayed me?"

Angelo fixed him with a belligerent stare. "Let me go and I will tell you."

Kalawun gestured to the Mansuriyya guards holding the Venetian. "Bring him here," he commanded, heading to one of the siege engines.

Will followed as Angelo was dragged, struggling and protesting, after the sultan. The first waves of cavalry were now halfway across the plain. A clanging of alarm bells rose from inside the city.

"Hold him down," said Kalawun, pointing to one of the stones in the pile beside the siege engine.

"My lord?" queried one of the Mansuriyya.

"Here," snapped Kalawun. "I want his neck on the block."

"No!" shouted Angelo, as the guards forced him down, pressing his chest onto the stone.

Kalawun held his saber in front of him. "Who was it?"

"Give me your word that you'll spare me," gasped Angelo.

Kalawun paused, then lowered the blade.

"It was Officer Nasir."

Kalawun's face seemed to sag at these words. All color went out of his cheeks. He took another step back and turned away. Then, all at once, his face twisted with fury. He spun round, raising the sword, and swung it down at Angelo's neck.

Angelo screamed as he saw the blade coming and tried to rise. As he lifted his head, the saber's edge sliced down into the bald and blistered half of his skull with a blunt *crack*. There was a burst of blood and Kalawun wrenched his sword free. Unbelievably, Angelo was still alive. A high, hideous scream was issuing from his open mouth and blood was pouring from the gaping wound in his head. Kalawun struck again, gasping with the effort. This time, he found the neck. But it took two more strokes before Angelo's head was completely severed and his gurgling scream was cut off.

The Mansuriyya had stepped away. Will stood there unable to take his eyes off Angelo's mangled skull. Kalawun's blue robe was blood-splattered and the blade of his saber was scarlet. Without saying a word, he pushed past Will and crossed to where several squires were waiting with horses, readied for battle. "What are you doing?" asked Will, following.

Still Kalawun didn't answer. Sheathing his sword without cleaning it, he took the reins of one of the horses.

"My Lord Sultan," said one of the squires, surprised. "Your horse is by the ..."

But Kalawun was pulling himself into the saddle. Will cursed and went to another of the beasts. The squire, seeing he was with the sultan, moved away uncertainly. As Kalawun galloped off, Will mounted. Jamming his heels into the flanks of the horse, he followed the sultan and the last waves of the cavalry, heading for the city gates.

By the time Will reached the city, most of the cavalry had disappeared inside. A bell was clanging frantically from the walls somewhere above, and he could see men running along the ramparts, shouting. A few arrows sailed down, not too far from him, and he ducked and urged the beast on faster, in through the gates, passing between the thick walls. Will's horse was jostled as he entered, a mass of mounted men before and around him. Then there was movement and space as the crush of men pressed on, fanning into the streets beyond the gatehouse, leaving fifty of their comrades to hold the gates. A few corpses littered the ground: bodies of Frankish soldiers. Already, Will could hear the sounds of fighting between the buildings ahead, as men around the city heeded the alarm. Word had gone up; the north gate had been breached, and the Franks were racing to meet their enemy.

Will rode in, cursing the helmet that restricted his vision, but not daring to remove it, as he searched for Kalawun, who had disappeared in the press of men. He clattered down a narrow street between a line of stores, glimpsed a child's face, white and staring, in a doorway, then saw a flash of blue ahead and forced his horse on, faster. He came out in a small square with a cistern at its center and saw Kalawun jumping from the saddle. There was a cluster of men beyond the cistern, one tall, slender figure issuing orders to the others. Leaving his horse, Kalawun marched across the square. The tall man turned. Will saw his face register surprise.

"My Lord Sultan?" he questioned, heading over.

"Do you know a man named Angelo Vitturi?" called Kalawun, his voice hoarse and harsh. He had drawn his saber, still red with Angelo's blood.

Nasir's eyes went to the blade, then back to Kalawun. "What has happened?"

Will, swinging himself down from the saddle, could discern the fear in his voice. He heard shouting from one of the streets leading off, followed by the clashing of swords echoing against the walls of the tightly packed buildings. Drawing his falchion, he hastened to Kalawun, who had halted and was facing Nasir. The sultan's face was filled up with rage and despair, and there was no room for mercy. Will knew then that the sultan wasn't going to listen until he had done what he had come here to do.

"Before I killed him," said Kalawun raggedly, staring at Nasir, "the Venetian said you had betrayed me, that you were working with him against me. Tell me this isn't true."

Nasir's lips pressed together. Finally, he spoke. "I cannot." His voice was thick with emotion. "I cannot tell you that."

Kalawun started to shake his head. "You wouldn't do this," he said firmly. "You wouldn't." He laughed. His eyes were bright and wide. "I know you, Nasir. By Allah, I *know* you!"

"You don't," said Nasir furiously. "Sunnis killed my family. How could I ever be one?" His voice was rising, as were the sounds of fighting in the streets beyond the square. Nasir flung up his hands. "You are deceived, Kalawun, you and all your men! You think you rule the world. But in truth you are slaves and always will be. None of you chose this life. You, me, we all came to it against our will, in chains. Our very name means *owned*! Freedom is an illusion for us. It is not real." Nasir's voice cracked. "I wanted ... *All* I wanted was to live with my brother, a life that I chose. The Venetian offered me that chance. I took it."

"I named my son after you," murmured Kalawun, his sword falling limp by his side. "I let you into my life!"

"And you killed my brother!" Nasir moved toward him, fists raised. "Kaysan was all I had left in this world. He was my family!"

"*I was your family!*" roared Kalawun, tossing aside his sword and grasping Nasir by the arms. He shook him violently. "I fed you! Clothed you! You were a brother, a *son* to me!"

Nasir made no effort to stop him, but hung slack in his grasp.

A group of men came riding into the square. Templars. One held up a bow and grasped an arrow from a quiver on his back. Will yelled a warning, half to Kalawun, half to the Templar. But the arrow was fitted, and fired.

Nasir lurched forward as the arrow thumped into the back of his neck, where there was no armor to protect him. Blood leaked from his mouth and his eyes widened up at Kalawun, who staggered back, still holding him. Nasir tried to form words, but couldn't.

Will ducked as an arrow came whizzing toward him; then he grabbed Kalawun's arm and hauled him away, leaving Nasir to sink to the ground. They dove into an alley as a company of Mamluks rode into the square in pursuit of the Templars.

All around the city, men were falling and dying. Within an hour, three more gates were taken and Mamluk soldiers poured in, pressing Tripoli's defenders back toward the sea. There was no halting this battle now. The conflict was harsh and swift. Any man found on the streets was put to the sword, and even those citizens who had fled to the island of St. Thomas were not spared the massacre. The Mamluk cavalry, having swept through the city in a bloody scythe, soon reached the water, where they drove their horses into the shallows, swimming across to the island, where, the madness of battle upon them, they butchered everyone they found. Princess Lucia and her court had left several hours before, sailing out of the harbor. Only her citizens were there to witness her city's fall.

Will managed to find horses and led Kalawun out of the city, seeing that any effort to halt the attack was futile. The only thing he could hope for was that the survivors would be spared.

Before they reached the camp, Kalawun reined in his horse and stared down at the dying city. "It's over," he murmured.

Will looked at him. "It doesn't have to be. Let your men have their spoils today, my lord, let them take Tripoli's wealth. But send the women and children to Acre. Offer a new truce to my people. They will accept. We cannot attack you; we do not have the strength. Everard de Troyes once told me that peace is sometimes bought with blood. Will the blood spilled today be enough to buy us this?"

Kalawun's face tightened, but he nodded. His gaze drifted back to the city, where black smoke was rising. He closed his eyes.

LOMBARDY, NORTHERN ITALY, 29 MAY A.D. 1289

A large throng had gathered in the fields, the numbers swelling as word went out. A legate of Rome had come, with a message from the pope. Children were hoisted onto the shoulders of fathers to get a better look as the legate stood on a specially erected platform, his loud voice booming across their heads.

The legate was a good speaker and the people were listening. He didn't talk about God's will or Christian duty, or even about absolution. Having faced many a bored and unresponsive crowd this past year, sent out on Pope Nicholas's orders, the legate had learned what the people wanted to hear. To the peasants, God happened in church, at mass, on feast days. But in the fields, carving another lean harvest out of this year's soil, in the streets of poor towns, begging for scraps, He didn't exist. The people didn't want to hear about His Holy Land, about Jerusalem and Acre; places that meant little to them, spoken on the lips of travelers, passing through. They wanted to hear what a Crusade would do for them. And so the legate told them.

He told the poor peasants of Lombardy and Tuscany that in the East there was a better life. In the East, men, landless men, could find themselves property and wealth, or even become the rulers of towns. There were hundreds of jobs for skilled workers, and even those without a trade could easily learn one there. It was a prosperous place, a place of riches and beauty. Truly, Outremer was the land of milk and honey. The legate's voice was earnest, passionate, but he spoke simply, in terms they understood. The peasants listened, borne up on his words and carried to a different world, a world of possibilities, of hope. All they had to do for it was take the Cross. There was very little fighting, the legate promised. They might be asked to help guard the walls at Acre or possibly act as auxiliary forces in a campaign if it became necessary. But ultimately, this was a small price to pay for their freedom.

That was the word Lombardy's peasants were left with as the legate and his advisors stepped down from the platform. Freedom. It was a tantalizing, intangible word that to most of them, throughout their lives, had been as far removed as the cities he had spoken of. Freedom was a word reserved for the richer classes, for the burghers and the clergy, kings and princes. The idea that such a thing could be easily found beyond the borders of their insular lives was seductive, beguiling. They massed together after the legate's speech, talking excitedly. Some of them dismissed his claims and took their children home, but many others congregated noisily to discuss what they had heard.

The legate patted his brow delicately with a cloth his servant handed to him and surveyed the gossiping crowd. "How his holiness ever hopes to form a new Crusade out of farmers and beggars I have no idea."

"I don't know, Brother," said his advisor, looking at the mob. "They seem fairly keen to me."

42

The Venetian Quarter, Acre

20 AUGUST A.D. 1290

There was a smile on Will's face as he strolled through the market, a smile of pure satisfaction. These were the best days, when he wasn't Sir William, or Commander Campbell, when he was simply Father, his daughter's warm hand threaded through his. Of course, he had to be careful and wore a kaffiyeh, which served to conceal his face, although he had never yet needed the disguise.

"Have you tried these, Father?"

Rose was tugging on his hand, angling toward a stall selling candies made of spun sugar, honey and spices. "What you mean," said Will, amused, "is that you want me to buy you one."

Rose shrugged nonchalantly, not willing to be caught out. "I just thought you might like to try them." But she shot him a swift, hopeful glance.

He chuckled and let her pull him toward the stall. The man behind it beamed at Rose and pointed to the candies, speaking the Venetian dialect. Will surveyed the bustling market as she answered him. Rarely had he seen the Venetian quarter so busy.

Since early August, trade caravans from Syria and Palestine had been rolling in through Acre's gates, flooding the markets with a glut of produce. The harvest in the Galilee had been one of the best in recent years and since the truce had been reestablished between Sultan Kalawun and Acre's rulers, trade had recommenced in a rush. After the unprovoked sack of Tripoli, the previous year Acre's citizens had waited in dread for the Mamluks to come for them. But when only straggling lines of refugees from the devastated city appeared, seeking sanctuary, they began to relax. Several months later, a delegation had ridden up from Cairo with a new offer of peace, which Acre's government had readily accepted.

With the arrival of the trade caravans, the city's population had swelled dramatically. No one could remember having seen it so crowded. The markets were mobbed with merchants: native Christians, Arabs, Turks, Greeks, bringing indigo from Iraq, swords from Damascus, iron from Beirut and glass from Egypt. The stalls in the Venetian, German and Pisan quarters were stacked with dyes, ivory, madder and olive oil; and goats and sheep packed into pens filled the blistering air with their frantic bleating. If this wasn't enough, earlier that week, twenty-five galleys from Italy had sailed into the harbor and the dockside taverns were now packed to bursting point with several thousand peasants from Lombardy and Tuscany, who had answered a call to Crusade. The government at Acre was not best pleased. Where, they demanded of the Crusaders' leaders, were they supposed to house these recruits, few of whom, it appeared, would be any use in the military whatsoever? But, despite their protests, room had been found, with men forced to sleep outside, on rooftops and in gardens, to many a welcome alternative in the stifling August heat.

"Can I have some money, Father?"

Will smiled at Rose and dug a hand into his pouch. He rarely had money himself, but Elwen had slipped a coin into his hand when he and Rose left the house. It was a ducat, one of the first of the new gold coins minted in Venice. It pleased him to do something so ordinary, yet so meaningful, as buy his daughter something she wanted. He was pulling out the coin when he heard shouting, rising above the noise of the crowds. Looking for the source, he saw four men dragging a fifth figure out of a building down a nearby side street. The man was fighting his captors wildly, but between them the four forced him to the ground, whereupon they began kicking and punching him savagely. A few people near Will tapped the shoulders of friends and pointed, but no one seemed willing to step in.

Hearing the man on the ground utter a strangled cry, Will handed Rose the ducat. "Wait here," he told her firmly, then hastened around the sweet stall. He sprinted down the side street and grabbed one of the attackers, who had just kicked the downed man in the head. Will hauled him roughly away, then barreled into one of the others, shoving him aside. The man grunted in surprise, then rounded on him. He growled something in Italian and, when Will didn't move, came at him, fists raised. His three companions stepped away from their victim and were now focused on Will. The smell of wine was strong on all of them. Will drew his falchion. The man faltered.

"Father!"

Will started at the cry and turned to see Rose, two candies wrapped in colored paper in her cupped hands. Her mouth formed a shocked oval at the sight of the sword in his hand and the four men advancing on him. Whilst Will was distracted, one of the men kicked the sword viciously out of his hand. As the falchion clattered away and Will shouted in pain and surprise, the man moved in. But his victory was short-lived when Will ducked his first clumsy punch and slammed a fist into his face, knocking his head back with the force of it and breaking his nose. Staggering away with a howl, the man caught in the legs of his victim, still lying facedown in the dust, and sprawled to the ground beside him. Will went for his falchion before any of the others could move. The man on the ground scrabbled backward, then got to his feet and fled with his companions as Will advanced. He watched them go, then sheathed his sword, gritting his teeth against the pain in his hand where the man had kicked him. Will bent down over their prostrate victim. "Stay there, Rose," he called over his shoulder, hearing light footfalls approaching. He turned the man over and heard a small gasp behind him as his face was revealed, slack, bleeding, and disagreeably familiar. It was Garin. Will glanced around. "Rose, I told you to . . ." He stopped, hearing a groan come from Garin.

Garin's eyes flickered, then opened. His pupils were glazed and unfocused. His beard was matted with blood where his lip had split. There was more of it in his hair from a cut on his scalp. "Get away from me!" he snarled. Will tugged down the front of the kaffiyeh so Garin could see his face, but the aggression didn't leave Garin's eyes as he recognized him. "What are you doing here?" he rasped, trying to sit.

"Get up," said Will bluntly, holding out his hand.

Garin muttered something obscene and pushed Will's hand away; then he seemed to see Rose for the first time. She was staring at him, the candies still clutched in her palms. Suddenly, his expression changed. He smiled, showing a row of bloodstained teeth that caused the girl to take an alarmed step back. "Beautiful Rose," he crooned, grasping Will's injured hand roughly and hauling himself up. "You grow bigger every time I see you." His words were slurred.

Will pulled away from Garin's painful grip. "You're drunk."

Garin put a hand over his heart and staggered back. "Never!" He rolled his eyes and then lurched forward, casting drops of blood across the ground as he swayed and leered at Rose. "I think your *father* might be a bit upset with me as usual," he said in a stage whisper. He laughed bitterly, then grew serious. "But you're not, are you, Rosie?"

Will stepped in front of his daughter. "Why did those men attack you?"

Garin let out a beleaguered sigh. "I expect because of these," he said thickly, holding out his palm to reveal two black dice. He chuckled as he tossed them to the ground. Both came up as sixes.

Will shook his head disgustedly. "Just go home, will you, and sleep this off."

"Home! Where the hell is home? I've got no home. Just a flea-ridden hovel." Garin thrust a hand in the direction of the docks. "It's madness down there. Those Lombards have taken over. Fights every night and the taverns crammed to the rafters with peasants. There's no room to swing a whore!" He threw back his head and cackled.

Will winced and put his hand on Rose's shoulder. "Perhaps you should think about going back to London then, as I've told you before."

Garin snarled at him. "Stop trying to save me, Saint William."

"Why are you still in Acre, Garin?" responded Will in a clenched voice. "It's not as if there's anything here for you."

"It's not *your* pissing city," Garin snapped back. "And besides, I've friends here. You, Elwen." He grinned. "Rosie."

"I'm not your friend," said Rose, her voice cool.

"Rose," murmured Will.

Garin grimaced. "Now, that's not nice. Rosie, sweetheart, did your father ever tell you we were friends when I was a Templar?" He leaned forward and poked Will in the chest. "I saved your life, Campbell. Three times!" He counted off on his fingers, not seeing the anger seeping into Will's eyes. "When Rook wanted to poison you in the brothel so he could go after the Book of the Grail and I drugged you instead. When we were at Antioch and the Mamluks were all over you. When you were in the desert and—" He clapped a hand over his mouth, his eyes going wide. "No, no, wait! That was someone else." Laughter burst out from between his fingers. It vanished quickly. He licked his split lip and spat blood on the ground forcefully.

"I won't pay Edward his money, Garin. Your decision to loiter around Acre without purpose isn't going to change my mind. Go back to your master and tell him." Will's gaze hardened. "Tell him he'll get nothing from me or the Anima Templi for his aggressions on Scotland." With that he started to walk away.

"Always the champion, aren't you? Always trying to save everyone!" shouted Garin, stumbling after him. "But you're as flawed and desperate as the rest of us. You pissing *hypocrite!*"

Will whirled on him, fury now taking him in its eager, scarlet grasp. "Stay the hell away from me."

"You took oaths, Will! Chastity, poverty, obedience. You knelt on the floor of the church in Paris and swore those vows to the Temple. How many have you kept? Chastity?" He laughed madly. "I think that one bolted from the stable a long time ago, didn't it? Poverty? Now you steal from the Temple's coffers to fund your own secret mission. Obedience? Well, we both know that's never been one of your strong points." Garin was raving now, spittle and blood flying from his mouth, along with the venom. "You're as much of a slut-swiving, oath-breaking, lying, cheating son of a whore as I am, and don't you *ever* forget it!"

That was it. Blind to all else, except the hateful man in front of him, a man he had once cried and laughed with, a man he had shared secrets with and whose life he too had saved, Will struck out savagely. His fist caught Garin squarely on his injured jaw, knocking loose a tooth. Garin reeled away, took a few staggering steps, then went down like a felled tree. A cloud of dust flew up around him as he struck the ground.

"I should have let them kill you," seethed Will, towering over him, ready to strike again.

"*Don't!*"

Will jerked around to see Rose. Her hands had flown to her face and she had dropped the candies. All the fury and hatred inside him drained from him at once, leaving him shocked and shaking.

As Garin looked up at Will, his dark blue eyes glinted in triumph. "See," he murmured thickly through a mouth full of blood, "you are like me."

Will didn't respond, but walked away, taking Rose by the arm.

Garin watched them through hooded eyes. Go home, Will had demanded. *Go home.* Will thought he still had a place back in London, a position and a home to go to. But, in truth, he had severed that tie a long time ago, sick of Edward's control over him, of all the years of false promises and insults and threats. Since then he had been filled with the possibility of hope, the possibility of a different life, of being a father to a child. That, more than anything, had cemented his decision to stay in Acre. Last year, some of the king's men had come looking for him, but he was forewarned and left the tavern he had been living in, where he made enough to eat and drink by gambling and stealing. He had gone into hiding, growing his beard long and full so that it covered his face, sleeping in shacks and hovels, moving from place to place, as nomadic as the desert tribes. Ironically, his years in service to Edward provided him with the skills he needed to keep hidden, and although he still feared the sound of footsteps in alleys behind him and the thought of a knife in the dark, he had managed to remain lost and anonymous, and out of Edward's reach.

Garin's gaze went to the candies Rose had dropped, which had rolled free of their colored wrappers. He crawled forward, grunting with the effort, and grasped one of them. It was warm and sticky from where it had rested in her hand. Slowly, he put the candy to his mouth and bit down. And the pain and the blood and the grit of the sugar and the street were all bound up in its aching sweetness.

"Father."

Will pulled his kaffiyeh up roughly as they moved back into the crowded marketplace.

"Father!" said Rose, sharply now.

Will halted. "What is it?"

"You're hurting my arm!"

Will stared into his daughter's scared and angry face and, at once, let go. "I'm sorry." He put his hands on her shoulders. "You shouldn't have had to see any of that."

Rose's expression changed as she looked at him, and now her fear was different, gentler: the fear of concern. "If Garin ever comes to the house, Mother always shouts at him and sends him away, and you get angry if we meet him in the street and he talks to you, even if he's courteous. Why?"

"I don't want him in my life, Rose. He did some things that deeply hurt your mother and me years ago, and although I've tried, I've found I cannot forgive him."

"But you were once friends? When you lived in England?"

"Yes. But things changed between us long ago. We're different people now." Will's voice roughened. "No matter what he says."

"Those things." Rose paused and pursed her lips, then met his eyes. "Those things he said about you, about you breaking your oaths. Did he mean them?"

Will exhaled wearily. "In some senses, yes. But not in the way that it sounded." He paused, unsure of what to say. He and Elwen had explained the Rule of the Temple to their daughter: how, as a knight, Will was forbidden from marrying or being with a woman, and how the Temple must never find out about them. But they had kept silent about Will's role in the Anima Templi. Rose was intelligent for her age, but she was still only twelve, and they didn't want to burden her with secrets. "Garin isn't a good man, Rose. Not anymore." He grasped her arms gently. "He isn't to be trusted. All right?"

Rose studied him with her intent gaze. "Is he going to stay here until you give him money?"

"I hope not."

"Why can you not give it to him if it will make him leave?"

"Because of what he will do with it." Will smiled tiredly at her inquiring frown. "Garin's master, King Edward, attacked Wales, where your mother was born, in order to secure more land for himself. It is rumored he has a similar desire to rule Ireland and Scotland. The king of the Scots died four years ago and his heir was his granddaughter. The last we heard was that Edward was planning to marry his son, Edward of Caernarvon, to the girl. The kings of England and Scotland have had good relations in the past, but I fear for the country with Edward's interference. There are men in Scotland who would, I believe, resist his rule, and I do not want to see what happened to Wales happen in my homeland. If I give Garin money, the king could use it to fund a war, as he has in the past."

"Are you worried for your sisters? For Ysenda and Ede?"

"For them and for the peace. And besides, I want you to see it one day, the place where I grew up. I don't want it spoiled."

Rose looked up at him as they started walking. "I want to see it too."

Will felt his daughter's small hand grasp his once more, but as they moved off through the marketplace a heaviness began to descend on his mind, weighing him down. The talk of his family was the cause. Those memories were still able to haunt.

There was his sister, Mary, whose death he had caused, the aftermath of which had seen his father enter the service of the Anima Templi and his mother and three surviving sisters enter a nunnery outside Edinburgh. There was his mother, with her distant eyes and faltering last kiss as his father took him away to join the Temple in London. And there, with a stab of raw grief, was James himself, with his crow-black hair and ink-stained hands, the man he had spent his whole life trying to live up to, forever seeking forgiveness for Mary's death, if no longer in this life, then in the next. These memories—the endings and the partings—were painful. But the others—the good memories before the deaths, before he left Scotland—were worse. The colors were faint now and some scenes were missing, but the laughter and the smell of summer gorse, and the shock of water against his legs as he waded into the loch—these things could pierce him. For years, he had kept them at bay, concentrating on his work and his duties, on his own family. Then, four months ago, the letter had come.

Opening it, he had scanned the unfamiliar handwriting, not really reading the words until he reached the name at the end. Ysenda Campbell. It was a name that had driven something blunt and brutal right through him. It was the name of his youngest sister, whom he hadn't seen or heard from since he was ten and she was an infant. It was a letter to inform him of the death of their mother, Isabel. She had died in her sleep from a sickness she had suffered with

for some time and had been buried in the chapel of the nunnery, where she had
remained since the day James and Will had left her. Reading his mother's name,
written in black, Will had seen her as he had for the last time, thirty-two years
earlier. She was standing outside the convent watching them ride away, a thin
woolen shawl wrapped around her shoulders, one hand pushing back her
springy red hair as the breeze lifted it. He had looked back after a little while to
see her still standing there, a figure who had once held and kissed him, laughed
with him, made indistinct by distance, a stranger on the hillside.

The letter bore news of another death too, but almost beside the point, as if
he should have known already. Their mother, Ysenda had written, had been ill
since the passing of their elder sister, Alycie. Will guessed the letter informing
him of that news must have gone missing. Or perhaps it had never been sent.
Now only Ede and Ysenda remained. The letter had been painfully impersonal,
as if the writing of it had been a duty, a burden even. In the lines, Will found a
sense of blame, a sense that Ysenda, who briefly mentioned her own children
without naming them, had never forgiven the brother and father who abandoned her and her mother, a sense that she wanted him to suffer. And suffer he
had. Isabel never even knew she had a grandchild. He had always been too
afraid to expose that secret in a letter.

"Father, what is that?"

Will glanced down, stirred from his thoughts. Rose was looking puzzled. He
looked around, realizing he could hear the clanging of a nearby bell. It was too
late to be for Nones and too early for Vespers. He was wondering how long it
had been ringing for, when the bell of San Marco joined it, sending a flock of
seabirds surging into the cobalt-blue sky. Other people were stopping now,
frowning up at San Marco's tower. Ahead came sounds of shouting. Five men
of the Venetian Guard rode into the square. A call went up.

"What are they saying, Rose?" asked Will.

"Erect the barricades," replied Rose, looking worried. "They're saying to
close the streets. There's fighting at the docks. Lots of men."

Within moments, stall holders were packing away their goods. Parents
grabbed the hands of children and hastened away, as the bells continued to re-
sound and more guards appeared. Moving in a frighteningly fast tide of people,
Will gripped Rose tightly and led her out of the marketplace. People were closing shutters, calling to friends and neighbors, rushing home.

When they reached Andreas's house, they found Elwen outside, talking worriedly with a neighbor. Her face filled with relief when she saw Will and Rose
running down the street.

"What is it?" she asked Will, pulling Rose to her gratefully.

"A riot by the sounds of it," Will panted. "I've got to get to the Temple. Go inside and lock the doors."

Elwen nodded and gave him a swift hug. "Be careful," she shouted, as he sprinted off.

THE DOCKS, ACRE, 20 AUGUST A.D. 1290

No one knew exactly how it started. Later, when the devastation was being cleared up and picked through, the bodies dumped onto the backs of carts, a rumor went around that a group of Lombardy Crusaders had heard that a Christian woman had been raped by two Muslims the night before. There were other explanations for the violence, most involving the heat and drink and poverty. But nothing—no reasons, no justifications—came close to excusing the mindless barbarity that began on the dockside and spread out through the city, like a rock dashed into a pool, the ripples of which grow wider and more far-reaching with every circle.

The temperature was scorching that afternoon, and the Italian peasants, who had been kicking their heels in the dockside taverns, were sunburned and hot-tempered. A company of men within the Lombardy group had been elected by the other peasants as unofficial spokespeople. The day before, these men had gone to complain to the Crusade's leaders, who had been put in place by the pope in Rome and included the dispossessed bishop of Tripoli. The tavern owners were demanding rent and they had no money for food. The bishop and the other nobles set in charge of the Crusade couldn't help: they hadn't been given funds themselves; there was nothing to offer the peasants. The bishop was particularly unhelpful, remarking sourly that if they wanted bed and board they should have thought twice about spending what little they had on drink and whores. The peasants had been turned away, sullen and bitter.

They had been promised a land of milk and honey, and indeed, they saw evidence of the East's affluence all around them: in the majestic buildings, the rich clothing of the locals; the markets overflowing with luxuries. But none of it was for them and no one wanted them here. Even the patriarch, the pope's representative in Acre, had been perplexed as to what to do with them. What the Christian leaders had looked for in a Crusade was well-trained soldiers under an efficient command, not an undisciplined rabble who didn't know the ways of the East. Local merchants, fishermen and customs officials complained that they now had to wade through a sea of half-conscious men, vomit and blood each morning on the docks. Tavern owners complained of nonpayment, of damage to goods and property and staff. Prostitutes had been beaten and abused, locals had been robbed, churches vandalized. The Italian peasants had abandoned their families and the fields, and had sailed into the unknown in hope of a better life. Instead, they had just found flies and unbearable heat and more poverty. They had come for a war; only no one seemed to be fighting one. And so, that afternoon, bored, hot and hungover, the peasants formed their own Crusade.

The first death occurred on the docks outside a tavern known as the Three Kings. Six men staggered out onto the harbor wall. They seemed to hang there for a moment, their faces flushed, before one of them shouted and pointed to two Arabs, leading camels loaded with panniers. With a united cry of excited fury, the six men rushed the Arabs, who stood stunned as they saw them coming. One of the Arabs was punched in the side of the head and went down, dropping the reins of the camel, which galloped off in fright across the dockside. The other man tried to run, but was leapt upon by two of the attackers. Fishermen and dockworkers watched on, hardly believing what they were seeing. Several locals tried to stop the assault, but two of the attackers had pulled planks of wood off a crate and were brandishing them like weapons. Someone hastened to the customs house to get help. But it was too late for the Arabs. By the time the punches and kicks ceased and the six staggered back, the two men had been beaten beyond recognition, their heads and faces a bloody pulp.

Other Lombardy Crusaders, comrades of the six, were now pouring out of the Three Kings at the commotion. They looked stunned to see their fellows soaked in blood. As their gazes alighted on the dead Arabs, a couple of them stumbled away, sickened. But one man cheered. It was a guttural, animal sound, which seemed to act as a signal to the rest of the pack, a signal that a line had been crossed and there was no going back. Other cries and shouts of triumph followed. And, just like that, a mob was formed.

"Kill all filthy Saracens!" shouted one man.

"Kill them! Kill them!" the chant went up.

The peasants set off across the dockside. Men, most of them Italian Crusaders, streamed out of inns to see what the commotion was. When they heard the calls, many fell into step beside their countrymen, exhilarated by the palpable fever coming off the growing crowd.

"What's happening?" called one man, rushing out of a tavern.

"A Crusade," someone shouted back. "We're going to kill the Saracens!"

"Then we'll get paid!" yelled someone else.

There was a loud cheer.

The man's eyes lit up with edgy excitement, and he raced back inside to tell his comrades, many of whom followed him.

Men joined because they didn't want to be left out; because someone said they were going to get paid; because they didn't have anything else to do. A roar went up, started by those near the front and cascading through the crowd.

"*Deus vult! Deus vult!*" God wills it! God wills it!

As they walked, men picked up rocks or stuffed rusted nails between their knuckles and swiped the air, grinning grimly to their companions. If their leaders wouldn't arm them, they would arm themselves. If they wouldn't pay them, they would pay themselves. Customs officials and guards had come out of their buildings at the alarm raised by the locals, but they weren't prepared for the fervent horde they met coming across the dockside.

"Mother of God," murmured one man. "We need more guards."

Another plucked up his courage. "Please!" he shouted to the crowd, holding up his hands. "Please! You must stop!"

The mob surged on, jeering at the officials, laughing as the men in their fine robes and oiled hair tried to halt them.

"Look at them!" scoffed one. "Dressed up like Saracens!"

"You must stop!" demanded the customs official.

Suddenly, a rock was loosed from somewhere within the crowd. It struck the official in the forehead. He went down hard. The mob halted, a ripple of unease shuddering through it. This man wasn't a Saracen; he was a Westerner, a Christian, like them, a man of power and importance.

Nothing happened.

There was no bolt from heaven to strike down the Crusader who had cast the stone. The other officials grabbed their bleeding comrade and pulled him back inside their building. Even the guards followed them.

Shouting wildly at the victory, the peasants moved on. They were invincible, unstoppable. Their newfound power was a drug, intoxicating them.

"How do we find the Saracens?" one man wanted to know.

"All Saracens have beards," answered another. "We kill anyone with a beard."

People nodded determinedly, glad to have a focus for their rage.

A shout rose. One of the peasants pointed. The massive iron gates that led into the city proper were being shut. Beyond lay the Pisan market. Traders were fleeing and a bell was clanging a warning, but, even so, the place was still crowded. Seeing the stalls piled high with fruits and porcelain, precious stones and silks, the peasants rushed forward. The Pisan guards made a last-ditch attempt to close the heavy barriers, but they were too late. The peasants threw themselves against the gates like a storm tide and forced them apart. At first, a trickle of men flowed out, brandishing their makeshift weapons warily. Then the dam burst and it became a flood.

Stalls were overturned as the peasants rushed in, buyers and sellers alike were shoved to the ground. A woman started to scream as her daughter was knocked over and trampled by men eager to get to the treasures on the stalls. One merchant, a Greek, tried to save his bag of money from two peasants who rushed him. Together, they forced him down. One stamped on his head repeatedly, whilst the other tore the bag from his hands. A Bedouin woman's veil was torn off and she was spat at, her husband's face raked open by a set of nails jammed between one man's knuckles. A Syrian Christian selling dates was picked up by five men and hauled, shouting and struggling, to a bakery. One man ripped off the turban the Syrian wore and tied it tightly around his neck.

"Kill the Saracen!" another screeched.

A third climbed up and looped the other end around the bakery's iron sign. Together, the men hoisted him and hung him from the sign. The Christian dangled there, kicking and choking, before going limp.

On the other side of the marketplace, three men broke into an Arab bookshop, where, after butchering the owner, they found two Arab women cowering in the back. One of the women tried to fight them off with a club, but her attackers wrestled it from her and beat her to death with it. The other woman was held down and violated. And the same scenes were repeated all across the square.

The Crusaders swarmed over the market like locusts over a field of corn. Rubies and sapphires, gold and food were stuffed into tunics and sacks. Windows were broken, fires started in houses and shops, and the chaos spread as the locusts finished their feast and moved on into the city. There were several thousand of them, a mélange of death and destruction. They rampaged through the streets, a river that had broken its banks, slipping off into tributaries to avoid the barricades that were being erected. Fights broke out between city guards and the Crusaders, but, as yet, although the bells were ringing the alarm, an effective force hadn't been raised to counter them. Any man with a beard the Crusaders found was killed, but as many Christians and Jews had beards, it wasn't only Muslims who died.

The Knights of the Temple and Hospital rode into the streets to halt the massacre, soon followed by more city guards and the Teutonics. Muslims were ushered into the safety of the Temple or let into churches and private houses. Mosques weren't considered safe, since the Crusaders had managed to break into one and had massacred everyone they found inside, leaving the white marble walls and floors awash with blood. Little pockets of violence raged, city guards and locals joining forces to confront the mob. But the knights were moving steadily out around the city now, breaking down the peasants' resistance, and after an hour or so, the fighting slowed.

Finally, when it had visited terror on much of Acre, the mob broke up and scattered. Men tired and grew sober. Men, loaded down with too much loot, returned to the docks. Men woke as if from a dream to find blood on their hands and staggered from houses, sickened by their own actions, leaving little scarlet chambers of anguish all across the city. In just under two hours, the peasants' Crusade lurched to its conclusion. The knights set a curfew and roamed the streets as night fell. The rioters who were caught were rounded up and thrown in the city jails and the corpses were collected in carts. More than two hundred Italian Crusaders died in the riot. But over one thousand of Acre's citizens had perished. And the coming of night made the fires that much brighter and the bloodstains that much darker.

43

The Citadel, Cairo

7 SEPTEMBER A.D. 1290

The company rode in through the imposing arch of al-Mudarraj, into the courtyard of the citadel. The guards at the gates watched on with wary, hostile eyes as the seven riders dismounted. They were met by ten Mamluks of the Royal Guard and led through the vaulted marble passageways of the palace. Servants and soldiers stopped what they were doing and watched them stride past, their gazes curious, cautious. When they reached the double doors of the throne room, the company was told to wait. Two of the Mansuriyya disappeared inside. They were gone for less than a minute before the doors were opened again.

Will was the first to enter. Behind him came six Templars, hoods pulled back. Will felt exposed and uncomfortable in his uniform. He had only been to Cairo in secret, in disguise. To be here now on official business felt strange. He quickly assessed the cavernous chamber: elegant pillars marching down either

side of a central aisle; huge fans on the ceiling; slaves clad in white. As the Mansuriyya warriors led the company to a platform at the end of the chamber, Will's
gaze was drawn to five figures standing around one man seated on a gold throne.
He guessed they were generals or advisors, although one, a young man with a
mop of hair and an aloof expression, looked enough like the man on the throne
for him to think they were related. As he drew closer, he thought he had perhaps
seen him before, but his speculations were cut short as one of the Royal Guards
announced them.

Kalawun was staring at Will. There had been a look of surprised concern in
his face when Will entered, but that had been covered quickly. "Speak," he said
gruffly. "Why have you come?"

Will held out a scroll. "We have come on the orders of Grand Master de
Beaujeu, my Lord Sultan." The scroll was taken by one of the guards and conveyed to Kalawun, who opened it.

The chamber was silent as the sultan read. When he had finished, he looked
up. "I will speak with the Templar alone."

"My lord," began one of the men behind him.

"We will finish our discussion later, Amir," responded Kalawun brusquely.
"You are dismissed."

The man pursed his lips, but bowed. He and the other men on the dais
headed down to a side door.

"And you, Khalil," said Kalawun, gesturing to the young man with the mop
of hair.

"My lord, I …"

Kalawun looked at him sharply, silencing him with his stare.

With a stiff bow, the young man descended the dais. His gaze lingered on
Will for a second in a mixture of hostility and interest, before he pushed open
the door. The Mansuriyya soldiers were also reluctant to leave, but Kalawun
refused to listen to their careful protests, and they too were forced to head off,
along with the servants. The knights who had accompanied Will were escorted
out, and within moments, only Will and Kalawun remained.

Kalawun rose from his throne, the scroll gripped in his fist. He strode down
the steps, brandishing it at Will. "What happened?"

Will faltered. "I thought you would have known by now what—"

"I know *what* happened," Kalawun cut across him angrily. "Our people in
Acre told me. *Why?* Why did it happen?"

"We don't know for sure. A group of Italian peasants came on a Crusade,
sanctioned by the pope in Rome and supported by King Edward of England

and King Philippe of France. It's believed the violence started when some of these men heard a rumor that a Christian woman was raped by two Muslims."

"This is your excuse?" demanded Kalawun.

"No," said Will quickly, "of course not. There is no excuse for what happened in Acre. But you wanted a reason, an explanation." He shook his head. "It is the only one we have."

"Do you know," began Kalawun, his voice brittle with rage and emotion, "how difficult it was, after Tripoli, to halt the campaign against your people? It took months to convince my court that the Franks did not intend to attack us, that men within your forces had corrupted the information for their own ends. It took every ounce of strength left in me to persuade them that it would be in our best interests to renegotiate a truce with the Franks."

"With all due respect, my lord, Tripoli was an unprovoked attack. You and your forces had no just cause to besiege the city. You say it as though we were fortunate that you decided to spare Acre. You say it as though it were an indulgence on your part, rather than a legality bound by your own signature!"

"Legality matters little to my court when it comes to the Franks," countered Kalawun roughly. "Most of my men want you gone. They will accept any excuse for this." He pushed a hand through his silver hair. "And you have certainly given them one now." His eyes narrowed. "Over a thousand dead. Corpses left in the streets, unburied. Children orphaned. Homes and livelihoods destroyed. It was one of the most brutal assaults I have heard of in years. It wasn't trained warriors these animals attacked; it was booksellers, jewelers, bakers, fishermen, all of whom had lived peacefully among your people for decades. My spies tell me how men were stripped naked and carried through the streets to places where they could be strung up." Kalawun thrust out the scroll, now crumpled. "And your grand master thinks we will be placated by an *apology?*"

"It is little compensation I realize," said Will quietly, "but Christians and Jews were also killed in the massacre. The Italians were not under orders from any ruler in Acre. We did not even want them in the city."

"No? It wasn't so long ago that your own grand master was seeking a war with my people."

"Not anymore, my lord, and even those of our leaders who would still welcome a Crusade did not want this. These men weren't trained soldiers, sent to fortify our strongholds and augment our forces. They were half-starved peasants, enticed with the usual promises of wealth and absolution, noncombatants with no understanding of Outremer and her people. We tried to stop them, believe me. Many Muslims were slain, yes. But more were saved by the quick actions of our people."

Kalawun shook his head. "That logic will not penetrate the fury of my court, Campbell. My people demand retribution for this. It has been all I can do to stop them taking up arms under their own volition and heading north for blood."

"We have worked hard, Kalawun, together and separately, to maintain the peace between our people. I know that fragile balance we created faltered with Tripoli. But I'm begging you again: do not let the mindless actions of a few dictate the future of many." Will held Kalawun's tense gaze. "Do not allow your court's need for vengeance to destroy what we have built. Do not let our own sacrifices for this cause be in vain."

"What have we built, Campbell?" said Kalawun tiredly. "Can it even be measured anymore? Is it worth all of this? Any of it?"

"You know it is," responded Will, "or you wouldn't have called your forces to heel after Tripoli." He sighed roughly, wishing, as he often did these days, that Everard were here. It was exhausting, trying to hold the world together, when all it seemed to want to do was spin out of control. "You wouldn't have worked so damn hard to keep the peace. You would have just let it end. Lesser men would have," he added. "When you met my father and agreed to this alliance, against the knowledge of Baybars, against the knowledge of your family and your people, you didn't do so because it would be easy. You did so because you believed, as he did, as I do, that our people can benefit from peace."

Kalawun closed his eyes as Will's words penetrated his rage, breaking it down, turning it into weary confusion. Was this true? Had he done the right thing by his people, by his family? With so many of his men telling him, day after day, year after year, that he must confront the Franks, he had started to forget why he'd fought so hard against that counsel; he had begun to lose his convictions.

"You believe," continued Will, "that Christians and Muslims and Jews do not have to be at war with one another, that, in many senses, we are all the same and that when we fight, it is against our own siblings that we raise arms. We are all children of God. You know this."

Kalawun's eyes opened as something awakened within him at this. It was anger, bright and sharp. But it wasn't directed at the Christians; it was directed at his own people, at the men who had made him doubt himself, who had shaken his faith. *Do not let our own sacrifices for this cause be in vain.* He had given up too much to turn his back on everything he had been working toward now, when it mattered most. He had lost so much in pursuit of the cause, to give up the cause itself would render his entire life meaningless. No. He had to believe that he had been guided to this end for a reason. He had to believe that God had a purpose for him, that he was right. "I'll need compensation," he murmured, looking at Will. "It is the only way I will be able to hold my generals in check and retain my position."

"We expected this. As well as sending me to convey his deep regret and a personal apology for the atrocity, Grand Master de Beaujeu wanted me to ask for your terms of reparation."

"I want the ringleaders of the violence arrested and sent to me for trial," said Kalawun. He paused. "And I want one Venetian sequin for every citizen in Acre."

Will frowned. "That's over one hundred and twenty thousand gold pieces, my lord."

Kalawun nodded. "It will make a statement. A statement my people will heed. I'll play my part, Campbell. Now you play yours. Go to your grand master and persuade Acre to agree to these terms and I will hold my people back."

In the tight gap between the wall of the servants' passage and the throne room, Khalil watched his father and the Templar shake hands. His whole body was humming with suppressed energy, which, as yet, hadn't transformed itself into any coherent emotion. He was still reeling.

As he had left the throne room, Khalil had realized where he had seen the Templar before. It was at the siege of Tripoli, in his father's pavilion. Something, curiosity or rebellion, had made him turn aside outside and squeeze into the gap in the wall, which Khadir had always used to spy on the court. He hadn't liked the feeling of spying on his father. But, as soon as Kalawun and the Templar began to speak, this compunction vanished.

Khalil stood in stunned silence as the knight's footsteps receded. Through the crack in the wall, he watched his father wearily ascend the dais and sit slumped in his throne. All at once a stranger to him.

THE CHURCH OF ST. CROSS, 23 SEPTEMBER A.D. 1290

Guillaume de Beaujeu was red in the face from shouting and his eyes were blazing. He stood behind the altar, his gaze raking the assembly. The Church of St. Cross was packed. Lawyers from the High Court, legates and bishops, the patriarch, the grand masters of the military orders, princes, consuls and merchants had crowded in, jamming the aisles. On the platform with Guillaume were Grand Commander Theobald Gaudin, Marshal Peter de Sevrey and the sene-. schal, along with several high-ranking commanders, including Will. The council had been going for less than half an hour and tempers were already fraying. The atmosphere was hostile, and Guillaume was struggling to make himself heard.

"You must understand that Sultan Kalawun has every right to attack us," he was bellowing. "We aren't pandering to his wishes with this offer, we are bargaining for our survival!"

"We shouldn't treat with the infidel!" shouted one merchant, but his words were drowned out by others, not quite as fanatical, but nonetheless adamant.

"The men of Lombardy and Tuscany were not acting under the orders of any man here, Master Templar," called a haughty voice from the side of the aisle, rising above the others. It was the bishop of Tripoli. "Why should we be made to pay for something that was no fault of our own? One hundred and twenty thousand sequins? It is an absurd amount of money."

Guillaume's eyes fixed on him. "I would think, Bishop, that you more than most would understand the price we will pay for inaction at this juncture. You saw your own city destroyed by Kalawun's troops. Will you stand by and witness the same fate befall Acre?" He swept the agitated gathering with his stare. "Will you let your arrogance kill us all? No, we did not order the Lombards to commit the atrocities, but it was our pope who sent them here and our people who were put in charge. If we will not take responsibility for the actions of our citizens, who will?" His eyes flicked back to the bishop, who scowled.

Will gripped his sword, his heart thumping, as the crowd churned with agitation. He couldn't believe that they were arguing so stubbornly against the grand master's proposal, not with what was at stake.

"I agree with what you say, Master de Beaujeu," came a croaking voice from a wintry, white-haired man with a stooped back. His voice was so frail that those near the back couldn't hear him and began shouting over him, until they were quieted by their fellows. He was Nicholas de Hanape, the patriarch of Jerusalem. "I agree that we must take responsibility for the outrage that has happened here." He looked around the church. "Good Christians died too in this mindless slaughter, and nothing can excuse it." He peered up at Guillaume. "But the sultan of Egypt asks too much. We have imprisoned some of the men who were believed to have carried out the attacks, but the trials against them are still continuing as far as I am aware. The atrocity happened on our own soil and we must be the ones to dispense justice. In Egypt, any man we send would face execution, regardless of his guilt or innocence."

"They face execution here also, Nicholas," said Theobald Gaudin sternly, beside Will.

"Only when their guilt has been ascertained," responded the patriarch. He shook his head. "And the monies the sultan asks for are simply too high."

"With respect, what price would you put on the lives of those slaughtered?" demanded Guillaume.

Will found himself nodding vigorously, as if to lend credence to the grand master's words.

The patriarch, however, wouldn't back down. "There is no price high enough to compensate for those deaths, Master Templar, as we both know. The sultan knows it also. The money we give to him would most likely be used to fund a war against us in the future. We should not arm him out of our own pockets. Let us find another solution." He spread his hands. "Perhaps if we send him the Muslims from our jails?"

"Kalawun has given us his terms," said Guillaume firmly. "We not do have time to barter with him. We are in no position to negotiate."

"What about Kabul?" It was an official from the High Court who had spoken. A few people turned to look at him, but his gaze was fixed on Guillaume. "What about the atrocities the Mamluks committed in their attack on the village? Men butchered? Women and children defiled?"

"That's right!" someone else interrupted. "Hundreds of Christians were killed then and the Mamluks placated us with a few bags of gold!"

Guillaume threw up his hands as others nodded and called out in agreement. "Are you not listening? What happened in the past is irrelevant. Unless we give in to Kalawun's demands, the Mamluk Army will march on us and Acre will face destruction!"

The crowd was pushing forward now, fists clenched and lifted as men tried to make themselves heard. Will tensed even more, seeing the sea of angry, resentful faces swelling in front of him. He looked at the grand master, who stepped forward to meet them, hands raised behind the altar like a desperate priest trying to save his congregation. There was irony, Will realized, in the fact that the one man now trying to safeguard the city had put it in such grave danger only thirteen years before. But Guillaume de Beaujeu was no longer the same man who had tried to steal the Black Stone in an attempt to launch a new Crusade. He had seen the error of his judgment the day he learned of the plot's failure; had almost died because of it.

In the years since, he had learned to be a diplomat as well as a general. It had not come easy, and his passion and ambitions could still run away with him, but he solved more disputes than he started and he'd learned to listen as well as to lead. He had lost some of that fiery, unpredictable energy and had become more measured in his dealings. Guillaume wanted Acre to survive, wanted Christendom to maintain its hold in the Holy Land, and Will's relationship with Kalawun offered him a chance to work toward this, without violence. The fleet he'd had built, years ago had never been sent to blockade Egypt, the ships instead used to transfer goods and pilgrims. But very few people were aware of this change in the grand master and that was apparent now, as the men in the church harangued and challenged him.

"Listen to him, god damn you," Will murmured beneath his breath.

Then, within the turmoil, one clear voice was lifted louder than the others. "Master de Beaujeu is right," said a stocky, broad-chested man, nodding brusquely to Guillaume. "We should accept Kalawun's terms. It is a small sum to pay for our continued existence."

The church went quiet.

Will looked in astonishment at the man who had spoken in Guillaume's defense. It was the last person he had ever expected to do so. It was Jean de Villiers, grand master of the Knights of St. John. The Temple and the Hospital had been bitter rivals for decades. If there were two opposing sides, they would be on them. Like the Genoese and the Venetians, theirs was a hatred ingrained in the fabric of their communities, inherent in their histories, caused by competition and feuds not forgotten. Will stared out at the crowd, holding his breath in the silence, certain the fact that the two grand masters were in agreement would make a difference to the outcome of the council. But although many people were visibly surprised, tempers, he soon realized, were running too high to be extinguished, even by this unexpected turn of events.

"How will we find the funds?" asked one of the magistrates. "Our citizens will not pay them. Whose coffers will be drained?"

This question resulted in a barrage of shouting as everyone tried to make himself heard.

"Acre's walls can withstand an attack! Let the Saracens dash themselves upon our ramparts in vain!"

"Do not give in to their demands!"

"No fortress, no city can withstand a prolonged attack indefinitely," countered Guillaume. "We have weaknesses. We are not invincible." His voice was becoming hoarse with the effort. "Western forces took this city from the Arabs two centuries ago! How complacent you have become to forget this. And complacent without reason. Tripoli, Antioch, Edessa, Caesarea, Jerusalem." He punched a fist into his palm as he named each city. "All of them gone, fallen to the Muslims. Acre is our last stronghold, by God!" he roared, as they tried to argue over him. "If we lose it, we will lose the Holy Land!"

"The West will not forsake us," barked the bishop of Tripoli, turning to the crowd in defiance of Guillaume. "Do not listen to the Templars. If the Saracens come, our people will send men and arms to aid us. The Church of Rome will not let the Holy Land fall to the infidel. And neither," he said harshly, looking back at Guillaume, "will our God."

Guillaume's eyes flashed. "There is a time for faith, Bishop, and a time for action. It would be a foolish man who stood on a battlefield and faced an army with a Bible in his hands. We are here to do the bidding of our Lord Almighty, but it is through deeds, as well as piety, that we serve Him. We cannot hold back the Saracens with prayers alone. Even if the West were to send aid, it would not come in time should the Saracens move against us. And it was the West, brothers, who sent us the very men who may have sealed our doom. Why do you think only shepherds and farmers came on this Crusade? Because no one else would!" His voice cracked across them. "The West no longer cares, embroiled as it is in its own wars and politics. We stand alone, Brothers!"

"We aren't your brothers," shouted someone near the back. It was a Teutonic Knight. "We weren't your brothers when you made certain King Hugh of Cyprus was removed from the throne and that your cousin d'Anjou succeeded him, an action which caused a civil war in this city. You did it for your own sake, for the sake of the Temple, without regard for anyone else. You and every grand master before you have been at the heart of every political problem in this kingdom! You've started wars to fill your coffers and fulfil your own agendas! Why should we listen to you now?"

Guillaume took a step back at the wave of accord that washed through the crowd at this, their cries almost seeming to slam into him physically. He opened his mouth, but no words came.

Will could stand it no longer. Rage exploded inside him, sending him striding to the edge of the dais. "You are fools, every one of you! I have been to Cairo. I've seen the fury in the eyes of the Muslims. If you do not accept these demands, I swear by God there will be war, and we will fall!" He felt a hand on his arm, drawing him back. It was Theobald Gaudin.

"This isn't your place, Commander," Theobald warned, his voice lost in the rising tumult.

"They have to listen!" Will told him, flinging a hand at the fraught crowd.

Guillaume was stepping forward again, calling for them to heed him.

Someone threw an apple at the dais. It missed Guillaume, but the *thwack* of it against the back wall of the church was enough of a signal for Theobald Gaudin. He let go of Will and drew his sword. "We need to leave, my lord," he shouted to Guillaume. "This is out of hand."

"You're a traitor to your own kind, de Beaujeu!" someone yelled.

Now Will also drew his sword. Things had gone beyond reason. Next it might be a rock or a dagger thrown. Between them, he and Theobald hustled the grand master down from the dais. As the crowd surged toward them, unwilling to part, the rest of the Templars unsheathed their blades. This provoked a chorus of jeers and shouts.

"The Templars are better Saracens than they are Christians!"

"They should have crescents on their mantles, not crosses!"

"Traitors!" A shout went up. "Traitors!"

But the crowd parted reluctantly before the blades, and the knights forced their way out, the scornful shouts following them through the doors and into the gray, windy afternoon, where they went swiftly to their horses. The other knights began to mount, but Guillaume hung back, clutching hold of Will.

"Is this what we have come to?" he demanded, his eyes feverish. "All those who died protecting Christendom's dream, and now, after two hundred years, we throw it all away for the sake of one gold coin each?" He gripped Will's shoulder hard. "Did they sacrifice themselves for this? Your father? Our brothers? Did our people drown in the blood of Jerusalem for nothing?" He hung his head, seeming barely able to hold it up. "How the knights of the First Crusade, how our *founders* must be turning in their graves! How God must turn from us, our greed, our vanity. Two hundred years and this is how it is to end? Not on a battlefield, with soldiers against soldiers. But with the senseless slaughter of innocents in their homes, in peacetime, by a group of ignorant, starving peasants who came here looking for a better life?" He laughed. It was a broken sound. "Is this truly how it ends?"

Will didn't speak. Wasn't this how most wars ended, and started? Only the pages of history books and men who wanted to be heroes remembered the blazing banners and noble warriors who had gone before. The people faced a different reality. The songs and the stories spoke of bright helmets and swords, brothers in arms and God and glory. They didn't speak of the silent millions who faced brutal, anonymous death. After two hundred years of slaughter on both sides, to Will it made a perverse sense if this was how it was to end.

"Dear God, save us," groaned Guillaume, almost dropping to his knees. Behind them, the cries of the crowd, now spilling out of the church, stung their ears. Theobald and Peter went toward the grand master.

Will grasped Guillaume to stop him from falling. For a moment, he cursed

Everard for dying, for putting him in this position and leaving him. But then he felt Guillaume's hands clutching his own and sensed the strength in his own arms. He was the head of the Anima Templi. He was a husband and a father. "It isn't over yet, my lord," he said sharply, moving his head to force the grand master to meet his gaze. "It isn't over yet."

44

The Citadel, Cairo

20 OCTOBER A.D. 1290

Kalawun pushed his way through the doors and lurched into the garden. The sunlight flared in his vision. He put a hand over his eyes as he headed deeper into the grounds, past spindly trunked palms and garish flowers. He followed a water channel cut through the stone walkway that led him to the center of the gardens, where a pool lay, inky in the shade, filled with slow-moving fish. Kalawun sat heavily on one of the stone benches around the pool and put his throbbing head in his hands. His skin felt dry and cold. A plug of nausea clogged up his airway, and he had to fight away an urge to vomit. The sickness used to be worse in the mornings, but now he seemed to feel it right through the day. The medicine his physician had given him wasn't working. It hadn't been working for months.

"My lord?" There was the sound of hurried footsteps. "My Lord Sultan?"

Kalawun sat up, grimacing with pain, and saw Khalil appear through the trees. His son's face was grim, and for one terrible moment, Kalawun found himself wishing that Khalil not Ali had succumbed to that fever. Ali had been fair and honorable and filled with a sense of joy in life; he might have believed in the cause. Khalil was surrounded with a cold wall of faith and duty that Kalawun had never been able to penetrate. He wondered if he should have looked for another successor when Ali died. But these were desolate thoughts. Kalawun let out a hiss of breath and squeezed his eyes shut. He loved Khalil. He still had hope that they could find a common ground.

"What is wrong, my lord?" said Khalil, heading over. "Why did you leave the council? The men are keen to receive the order for war." He gritted his teeth. "How dare the Franks refuse your terms! They will pay dear for this."

"I needed time to think, Khalil. I needed air."

"Time to think about what?" murmured Khalil, standing in front of him. When Kalawun didn't answer, he gestured to the palace, stark and white behind them. "The men are waiting, my lord." Still, Kalawun said nothing. "Father, please," said Khalil, frustrated, "why do you not answer?"

Kalawun met his stony gaze. "I have made my decision," he said quietly.

"Then let us announce it. We have much to prepare and little time." Khalil turned toward the palace, but halted when Kalawun didn't rise.

Kalawun looked up at his son, wincing at the stabbing sensation between his eyes as the light hit them. "I will not declare war on the Franks."

Khalil said nothing for a moment, confusion turning to anger across his face. "In Allah's name, why would you do this? The Franks have refused your terms of reparation for the atrocity at Acre. They have ignored your ultimatum. You have to attack them!"

"Do not forget to whom you are speaking, Khalil," responded Kalawun sharply. "I am sultan and my word is law."

"The court will not let you do this," said Khalil, pacing ferociously. "They will not accept this decision. The Franks slaughtered Muslims in the hundreds, breaking the treaty. Your men will demand that we now take action!"

"I listened to others when it came to Tripoli and I have regretted that action every day since. I will not make the same mistake again." Kalawun rose with effort and walked around the pool. He looked to the sky, then laughed forlornly. "I miss Nasir." He looked at his son. "Do you think that strange? He betrayed me terribly and yet I miss him. I do not think I would have killed him had he survived Tripoli. I do not think I would have been able to bring myself to do it. I have seen so many die around me. Aisha, Ishandiyar, Ali, Baybars, Nasir. Sometimes, I wonder why I am still here. Perhaps Allah has forgotten me, Khalil?"

Khalil wasn't listening. He had stopped pacing and had gone still. "You will lead your people to war, Father. You will march on Acre and destroy the Franks' last base."

Kalawun's brow knotted as he turned to his son.

"You will do it," murmured Khalil, "because it is necessary and because it is the right thing, the *only* thing, to do. You will do it because your people demand it and because the Franks deserve it. And you will do it because if you do not, I will tell the men in that council chamber that you are a traitor."

"What?"

"I heard you!" shouted Khalil, emotion rushing back into his voice as his father stared at him aghast. "When the Christians came here, I hid and I watched

you! I heard you talking to the Templar ... heard him speak of how you had
been working together all these years, working against Baybars, against our
people. Against *me*!" He was striding again now, his hands flying as he spoke.
"I kept it secret all these weeks, knowing that your life would be in danger were
I to reveal it to anyone. I kept it hidden because I wanted to give you a chance
to do what is right by your people. But now I see I have no choice." His voice
cracked and almost broke. "You are giving me no choice!"

"You are threatening me?" whispered Kalawun, jarred to his core.

Khalil took a step toward him, then stopped. "You have been bewitched,
father. How could you work with the Western invaders? With a *Templar*? These
people murder us, defile our temples and assault our cities. They have been doing so for two hundred years. The only reason this knight wants peace with you
is because he and his kind want to retain a position in the Holy Land that they
can strike at us from. If we give them long enough, they will regroup and try to
take what Baybars and his predecessors managed to rip from their grasp." Khalil
shook his head slowly. "Somehow, you have lost sight of this truth, Father. You
have lost your way."

"Why can we not have peace with these people?" demanded Kalawun, going
to his son and grasping his shoulders. "*Why?* We trade with one another, share
ideas and inventions; much of what is sacred to us is also sacred to them. Why
do we have to be enemies? I know this is not the Franks' land; I know their
people came to take it by force. But is it ours? I was a slave, Khalil, born hundreds of miles from here. It is any more my land than Franks' who have been
here for generations? Ourselves and the Christians have been in this war for so
long we have forgotten why we are fighting it!"

"We fight because we have to, because if we don't the Franks will take our
lands and our livelihoods. It does not matter where you came from, where any
of us came from. As Sultan of Egypt and Syria you now have a duty to your
people, *Muslim* people, to defend them from harm." Khalil pulled away from
him. "And you will do your duty."

Kalawun stared into his son's unyielding gaze for a long, aching moment.
Then at last, numb and defeated, he followed Khalil out of the gardens and
back into the palace. His head pulsing, he stood before his court and, in a voice
as faint as a breeze, declared war on the Franks. And the solid, unified cheer that
erupted around the throne room following his words was a hammer to his
heart.

As soon as it was done, preparations were set in motion. The generals wanted
to discuss the strategy of the campaign, but Kalawun postponed any further
discussion until tomorrow. Leaving the throne room buzzing with anticipation,

he retired to his quarters, avoiding his son's gaze as he swept out. Once in his chambers, he dismissed his servants and went to his desk. Snatching up parchment and a quill, he sat down to write. Two days after he had been given notification that Acre's rulers had refused his demands, he had received a message from Will, begging for more time to persuade the government. The grand master, he said, had written to the visitor of the order in Paris, summoning extra funds. Guillaume de Beaujeu planned to pay the sultan out of the Temple's coffers if the government wouldn't listen. They just needed more time. But time was one thing Kalawun could no longer give them. *If you do not want to see my army on your horizon,* he scribbled furiously, *you will convince your government to change its mind.*

By the time he had finished writing, the pain in his head was so bad he could hardly see.

AL-SALIHIYYA, EGYPT, 10 NOVEMBER A.D. 1290

"How is he?"

"Not good. I have given him drugs to ease his suffering, but there is nothing more I can do. I fear it will not be long now."

The voices were soft, apologetic. Kalawun heard them as if in a dream, unreal and distant. He felt cocooned by the warmth of his bed, by the opiates drifting through his system. He knew he should be concerned by the voices and by what they were saying, but he felt just a pleasant, warm detachment. The pain had receded, chased away by the drugs. It was now a point of crimson brightness in his mind. He could sense it, but he was removed from it. He felt a shift on the bed beside him. A cool hand was placed on his brow.

"Father? Can you hear me?"

Kalawun wanted to stay in the velvet darkness, but as well as the pain, he could sense other things, worry and purpose, crouching nearby, and these were closer, demanding his attention. His eyes slid open and pain took a step nearer. Even though his quarters were only lit by two low-burning braziers, the dull glow still hurt him. Khalil was sitting beside him on the bed, his face shadowed.

"I'm dying." It was more of a statement than a question, but Kalawun still felt numb as he said the words.

Khalil looked away. "Yes." His voice was strained.

Kalawun lifted his hand weakly and raised it to his son's face. His skin felt smooth. It still had youth to grace it. "Will you do something for me?"

Khalil put his hand over his father's. "If I can."

"Do not attack the Franks. Give them a chance to make amends. Show mercy."

Khalil tensed. "We are committed."

"No, there is still time. We do not have to give the order for war."

"You already have given it. You summoned the troops, built siege engines."

Khalil stared at him. "We are in al-Salihiyya, Father. We are about to cross the Sinai."

Kalawun's gaze drifted past him, and now he saw that what he had thought were the walls of his palace quarters were in fact the cloth sides of his pavilion. And it all came back to him.

The last three weeks had passed in a blur of activity as the generals worked ceaselessly to ready the army for war. Kalawun's heart was not in it, and every order for provisions and armaments that he signed, every messenger he sent out, he did so unwillingly, as all the while he waited for Will to respond to his letter. But the generals were impatient, wanting to march on Acre before the winter rains set in across the Palestinian hinterland. Once they made their camp outside Acre's walls, they could summon more troops from Aleppo and Damascus. The harvests were in; the towns well stocked. It was, they had said, a good time to leave.

"We have to turn back," said Kalawun, his fingers moving to tighten around his son's. "I haven't given them enough time. Campbell will persuade them."

Khalil pulled his hand from his father's grip. "Campbell?" he demanded. "The Templar?"

"The Franks will agree to our demands. He will persuade them."

"No, he won't," said Khalil bluntly, rising.

"I wrote to him," said Kalawun, struggling to sit up. "I told him that we were coming, that he needed to convince his government to concede."

"I know."

Kalawun's brow furrowed. "What do ...?"

"I am not a fool, Father," snapped Khalil, rounding on him. "I made sure to intercept any message you sent out after you had given the order. I know you only gave it because of my threat."

Kalawun closed his eyes.

"I destroyed it," continued Khalil, looking at him. "The Franks will not pay because they do not know that we are coming for them. And by the time they do, it will be too late."

"Why?"

"Because I had to." Khalil sat beside his father again and took his hand.

Kalawun tried to turn away from him, but he was too weak. "When you die, Father, I want our people to remember your name with honor. I want them to know that you loved them, that you never faltered in that love and that you would always do what was right by them. I will see that your name lives on in history, that our people remember you well."

"It is because I loved them that I did this," whispered Kalawun. "Can you not see that?"

"I know you believe this," said Khalil quietly. "But it is a delusion. Father..." He swallowed back his emotion and made himself look upon his father's gray, desolate face. "It does not matter what you and a handful of Christians believe. The very fact that this Templar would have to convince his own government to make reparations for the atrocity in Acre shows that his people are no more willing to engage in this foolish peace than your own are. Ideals will not safeguard us, not while our enemy remains in these lands to threaten us. Only a heavy hand and an iron sword will protect them from the Western invaders."

Kalawun let his head fall back onto the pillow. "Nasir was right," he breathed. "We are all slaves. Slaves to duty, to faith, to revenge. I do not want to be a slave anymore, Khalil, a slave or a warrior." He closed his eyes.

Khalil was speaking again, earnestly, passionately, but Kalawun blocked out the sound.

Behind his eyelids, he sought that softness, turning away from the sharpness of fear and disappointment and regret. He ran from them, retreating inside himself, seeking solace and comfort. Allah had not forgotten him. He could feel the moment descending on him, filling him with perfect calm.

And somewhere in that deep dark, that fathomless space inside him, Kalawun found what he was looking for in the smiling faces of Aisha and Ali, whom he summoned with his last breath to come forward and take him into Paradise.

Khalil sat beside his father for some time after his chest had ceased to rise and fall. A charcoal in one of the braziers split with a hissing crack and sparks fizzled in the air, brief and bright. Khalil leaned over and whispered the Shahada in Kalawun's ear. After it was done, he stayed there for a while, smelling the sweet oil in his father's hair. Then, his grief done, he rose. Outside, the army awaited their new general. But they would not be marching this dawn. Kalawun had believed the army would not be needed, that in the end peace would prevail, and the generals had believed that they couldn't delay if they were to avoid the harshest months of winter. Because of these things, they had too few troops and not enough siege engines. Khalil knew they would need every possible resource if they had a hope of taking Acre, and not just Acre, but every last castle and town where the Franks still resided. No, he wouldn't march his men yet. They would wait out the winter here and gather more forces. Then, one final push, one final, massive push, and it would be over. Zengi, Nureddin, Saladin, Ayyub, Baybars: he would follow in their footsteps and finish what those before him had started. It was time to end the Crusades.

45

The Venetian Quarter, Acre

30 MARCH A.D. 1291

"I wish you would listen."

Elwen, packing silk sheets into a chest, paused to look at Will. "I am listening. But you haven't changed my mind. I'm not leaving."

Will left the window and crossed to her. "I'm serious, Elwen."

She shook her head as she pulled the cover from Andreas and Besina's bed. "So am I."

Will felt his frustration grow as he saw the resolve in her face. He knew that he wasn't going to be able to persuade her and was irritated both by her unwillingness to listen and his own inability to convince her. "Think about Rose," he said after a moment. "Think about our daughter."

"I am," replied Elwen, folding the sheet. "Andreas's physician believes she is too weak to travel. We shouldn't risk it, he said, and I agree."

"How much safer will she be here?" Will pushed a hand through his hair. "When they come, I'm not going to be able to protect you, either of you."

Elwen placed the sheet on top of the others in the chest and went to him, cupping his cheek with her hand. "We have more than a thousand knights to protect us. Acre is strong, Will. Have faith."

"Since the ships have been carrying citizens to Cyprus, our forces have dwindled to fewer than twenty thousand fighting men. You know the Mamluks outnumber us."

Elwen frowned at him. "What would you have me do? Take our daughter on a ship for months on rough seas without a physician or proper supplies, or keep her here until she is well enough to leave? Besides," she added brusquely, "I'm not going without you, and as you're not prepared to leave, neither am I."

"I have a duty to this city, Elwen. I have to stay."

"And as your wife I have a duty to you."

There was a knock at the door. It opened and Catarina appeared. She smiled at Will, then went to Elwen and spoke softly in Italian. Will, watching them, was struck by the memory of Elwen ushering Catarina out after the girl had caught them kissing. It didn't seem possible that fifteen years had passed since that day, but the evidence was in front of him in the faces of Catarina, now a grown woman, and Elwen, the mother of his child. It gave him a sense of sadness, but he couldn't quite say why.

"Rose is awake," Elwen told him. "I'll check on her."

When they had gone, Will went to the window and looked out. Two men stood in the street below talking, cloaks pulled tight around their shoulders. It had been a brutal winter, and even now, this far into spring, the air was still chilly. For weeks, sleet and rain had whipped the coastline mercilessly, and March brought strong winds that sent ragged clouds to cast huge shadows across the plains, churned to an icy sludge outside Acre's walls. Sickness blighted the city and surrounding settlements, with one particularly virulent fever killing over one hundred children. Rose had come down with it last month, and for several weeks, Will and Elwen thought they had lost her. Those nights had been some of the worst of Will's life; awake and pacing his quarters in the Temple, imagining his daughter lying not half a mile away, shaking and sweating. The pure, maddening fear of it; not being able to be there, or help her, not knowing whether a message would be waiting for him at the gate when he went down for Matins, telling him she was dead. But she was strong and had survived the worst of it. Now Rose was on the mend and the weather was becoming milder, but rather than bringing relief these warmer, drier days and lighter nights held a growing sense of menace. The mud on the roads was drying, hardening, able to take the weight of an army. If Will closed his eyes, he fancied he could hear them: the stamp of thousands of booted feet; the jangle of bridles and chain mail; the rumble of the siege engines' wheels, the thudding drums.

Behind him, the door creaked as it opened.

"How is she?" asked Will, turning. He expected to see Elwen, but it was Andreas who was standing in the doorway. Will nodded to him, feeling awkward in the mercer's private room. Over the years, he and Andreas had learned to get along, but they had never become close. They only had Elwen in common and were both too protective of their respective roles in her life to ever be able to feel truly comfortable with one another. Will gestured to the door. "Do you want me to wait outside?" He spoke in Arabic; the one language they shared.

Andreas waved a hand and crossed to his desk, which was empty save for a stack of papers. "No, no. Stay." He rifled through the papers, then glanced up and gave the bare room a brief inspection. "It isn't as if it will be mine for much longer. Have you seen Rose?"

"Not yet. I'll go up before I leave. Elwen thought it best not to tire her out."

Andreas grunted and went back to his study of the papers. "I take it you have talked to Elwen? Tried to persuade her?"

"Short of knocking her unconscious and throwing her onto your ship, Andreas, I've tried everything I can think of."

Andreas smiled slightly. "She is headstrong for certain. I cannot convince her either." He sobered. "She stays because of you, you know."

"I realize that. But she does so also out of fear for Rose, as does your physician I'm told."

"It isn't an agreeable choice to make, certainly. But it is surely safer to brave the sea than to stay and await what is coming for Acre? People are saying Sultan Khalil has two hundred thousand men. I am not a soldier, but even I can see that we will be hard-pressed to survive an assault by such a number." Andreas shook his head when Will didn't answer. "Well, Commander, it may not be a comfortable situation you are faced with, but one thing you can be sure of is that you have a fiercely loyal woman for a wife."

"Too loyal," responded Will. "I don't want her to give up her life for me. She has no need to stay."

"Love is foolish that way." Andreas gathered the papers. "As I have told you, I have a good friend who will take Elwen and Rose out of the city on his ship. He is ready to leave and will do so if it the assault goes ill for our forces, although I think, like many in the city, he is hopeful our walls will hold. As long as they get to the harbor, they will be safe. He will bring them to Venice and I will take care of them until you send word. I know that when the assault comes you will be engaged elsewhere, Commander. But make sure they get to the harbor in time." There were footfalls in the passage and Andreas fell silent as Elwen entered.

She smiled at the two of them a little quizzically, then looked to Will. "I've told Rose that you'll come up."

Will nodded to Andreas, then followed her up the winding stair to the servants' quarters.

Rose was swaddled in a large woolen blanket. He felt his heart wrench as he saw how ashen her skin was. Her golden hair, splayed on the pillow, was dull and limp. He had hoped she would be looking better by now. "Rose," he murmured, crouching by the narrow bed.

Rose's eyes were half-open. "Father," she whispered, struggling to sit.

Will put his hand gently on her shoulder. "Don't try to move, my love. I just wanted to give my beautiful girl a kiss. Then I want you to go back to sleep. You need your rest."

"Tell Catarina not to go," said Rose in a small voice. "I don't want her to."

Will stroked her hair. "You'll see her again soon, when you're well. But the more you rest and sleep, the faster that will happen."

"Do you promise?"

Will smiled and put his hand over his heart. "I swear."

The corner of Rose's mouth turned up. "I accept your oath."

Will stayed there, stroking her hair, until her eyelids smoothed shut and her breaths evened out. His legs throbbed uncomfortably from the crouch, but still he didn't move. Presently, he felt Elwen's hand on his shoulder.

"You should get back to the preceptory. You'll be needed there."

Will leaned forward and planted a soft kiss on his daughter's cheek, then stood. On the landing outside he caught Elwen's arm as she went to descend the stairs. "Andreas has a friend who has agreed to take you out of the city if the defenses are breached."

"I know."

"If that happens, I want you and Rose to leave with him, even if I cannot. Do you understand?"

Elwen looked away. "Yes," she murmured.

Will pulled her to him, wrapping her up in his arms.

Elwen closed her eyes. "I'm scared, Will."

"We're going to be all right. All of us."

They stayed there for a moment, neither wanting to relinquish their hold, then broke apart and headed downstairs, hands entwined. In the hallway, by a pile of sacks and chests, Catarina was waiting.

She came forward to take Elwen's hands. "Papa wants me to go to the ship with the first load. Giovanni and the children are waiting for me there." She frowned. "Won't you come with us?"

"I cannot," murmured Elwen.

Will, not understanding the words, but guessing the gist of the conversation, looked away as Catarina began to cry.

Elwen hugged her. "Rose and I will be fine, I promise. If the fight goes badly, I'll see you in Venice. If not, no doubt your father will want to return. Either way, this isn't good-bye."

Catarina sniffed, then kissed Elwen on both cheeks. She smiled past her to Will. "Good-bye, Weel," she said in English. "Make sure she safe."

Elwen stood close by Will as Catarina stepped outside and climbed into a wagon loaded with the di Paolo family's belongings. As the horses pulled off, Catarina lifted her hand.

"This house is going to feel strange with just me and Rose," sighed Elwen, as the wagon disappeared from view.

"I thought Andreas was leaving you with some staff."

"His guard, Piero, is staying, but it will not be the same." She shook her head. "I wish the Anima Templi had succeeded."

Will kissed her forehead rather than reply.

Three days ago he had called a meeting of the Brethren, a final gathering before the war was upon them, ordering them to collect any documents or monies relating to the Anima Templi. In truth, they owned very little as an order, their need for secrecy overriding the requirement for written records. The few documents they did have, guarded, along with their treasury, by the seneschal, were loaded into a crate in the seneschal's quarters. Will placed Everard's chronicle, taken from the locked chest in his dormitory, reluctantly alongside their other possessions. It might only be a book filled, for the most part, with the incoherent ramblings of an old man, but it had felt too much like a defeat. It was as though, by sending it away, he believed Acre would fall and that the Anima Templi's dream had ended.

"You should just burn it," the seneschal had said gruffly, seeing his reluctance to part with the tome.

"No," Will had replied quickly, "it's all we have left of ..." He went to say Everard, but then stopped himself, wary of showing weakness in front of the seneschal. "No," he repeated firmly. "We'll send them to Hugues de Pairaud in Paris as we agreed. Have your squires load it onto the ship."

The seneschal nodded grudgingly. "As you wish."

After that, Will had gone in person to speak with several of their contacts, including Elias, to persuade them to leave the city. The rabbi had laughed good-naturedly and told him that he would go nowhere whilst there was still a chance that peace would prevail. There was a confidence in the old man's voice and manner that had offered Will a sense of hope.

Now, as he turned to Elwen, he tried to convey that same optimism. "Maybe we still can succeed," he said, taking her hand. But inside, a voice told him that his words were only to comfort her. He did not believe them himself.

Squeezing her hand, he stepped out into the street. He had only gone a few paces when he turned back. Elwen stood on the step, shivering in the cold wind, her eyes pale and bright in the weak sun, watching him go. The sight of her caused a rush of emotion to surge through him and he strode back to her and drew her into his arms. She laughed in surprise, then fell silent. Will felt her hands grip his back fiercely. They stayed there for a long moment, just holding on. "I love you," he murmured into her hair.

Finally, they pulled apart and Will headed for the preceptory, leaving the Venetian quarter behind him.

People loitered in the streets, talking, their faces all cast with the same grim expressions. Others were loading belongings onto carts or slinging panniers over the backs of mules and camels, heading for the harbor. All around the city, people were leaving. But too few and too slowly for Will's liking. Many simply did not believe that Acre's walls could be breached, having lived through Baybars's attacks, and some still had faith in the ability of Acre's government to negotiate with the Mamluks. Will knew different.

On receiving the devastating news of Kalawun's death, which had hit Will hard, Guillaume de Beaujeu sent an envoy to the new sultan, al-Ashraf Khalil, to attempt to enter into fresh negotiations. Will was ill with a sickness of the stomach and was excused from going. This was fortunate for him indeed for the two knights the grand master sent never returned. Instead, a letter came to Guillaume from Sultan Khalil himself advising them not to send any more messages or offer any gifts, for he would not receive them. *We are coming into your regions,* the letter had stated, *to right the wrongs that have been done.*

Following that letter, reports had begun to filter into Acre from the Franks' spies that Sultan Khalil was organizing an army, the like of which hadn't been seen since the dawn of the Crusades. Every Mamluk was being consigned, as well as all auxiliary troops. The amirs of Hamah and Damascus were raising their own forces, and many thousands of ordinary Muslim men from across Egypt, Palestine, Lebanon and Syria—retired soldiers, farmers, laborers, zealous youths—were coming forward, on hearing the calls to war in the mosques, to pledge themselves to the battle. It was a jihad of terrifying proportions. Further reports came down from Lebanon of trees being felled for siege engines. It was rumored that Khalil had ordered the building of one hundred engines, some of which were the largest ever constructed. One *mandjanik,* called the Furious, took the entire population of Damascus to move out of the city through mud and snow. Now these men and their engines were coming for the Christians. The cold and the rain that hampered their marches in the early part of the month had died away, and this massive force would reach Acre's walls in a matter of days.

Every Western man of fighting age left in Outremer had been called to arms to defend Acre, many soldiers being withdrawn from garrisons in the few Frank-ish-held settlements left along the coast, leaving these strongholds with little or no protection. Acre was the Crusaders' last bastion of strength, and every able hand was needed to secure her. For the first time in decades, Acre's divided communities stood united. The Templars and the Hospitallers worked with the Teutonics to ready the defenses. The French regiment, posted by the late French King, Louis IX, which included more than one hundred crossbowmen, liaised with the royal garrison left by King Henry II of Cyprus and the English order of St. Thomas. The Pisans and the Venetians joined together to build great mangonels for the siege, and all the mercenaries and guard forces of the merchant states and other quarters were drawn up and armed. Whatever happened now, Acre was ready for a fight.

As Will wandered through the city streets, he could feel this air of determination. Beneath the fear and worry, there was a sense of defiance. It was visible in the faces of the merchants who nailed planks of wood over windows of their stores, refusing to leave, visible in the lines of women and girls, hauling sacks of grain into guardhouses around the walls. It was visible in the fiery glow of smithies, where the clang of iron on iron was like a drumbeat through the days, and in the stables, where farriers nailed fresh shoes on horses. And it was visible in the mangonels and trebuchets, hauled by teams of oxen to the walls, where torches flared every evening, flickering across the shadows of twenty thousand waiting soldiers.

Will, climbing the hill of Montjoie, which straddled the Venetian and Genoese quarters, halted and looked out across Acre. His gaze moved over the jumbled labyrinth of streets, carved into quarters by walls and gates. He picked out the spires of churches and the domes of mosques, the windswept docks and the iron chain raised across the harbor. He looked north to the grand enclosure of the Knights of St. John with its large infirmary and behind it to the moat that separated the city from the suburb of Montmusart. His gaze moved on, over the rooftops of homes and workshops and the towers of the leper hospital of the Order of St. Lazarus. Beyond Montmusart was a double wall lined with towers that marched all the way around the city on the landward side, encircling the peninsular Acre lay on in a giant girdle of stone. Will looked to the Jewish and Arab quarters, the Italian markets, the cathedral and the royal palace. He stood there for some time, a lone figure in his white mantle that was snatched at by the wind, his black hair whipping in his eyes, beard flecked with the first signs of gray around his mouth. He looked to it all, taking in the silence, the calm before the storm. And as he did so, he felt that sense of defiance swell and rise in him.

When Guillaume's envoy had failed to return, Will immediately commanded the rest of the Brethren to summon the aid of all their contacts in the city. Through Muslims in Acre, who believed in the cause and who stood to lose as much as the Christians should the city fall, they sent messages to Khalil and his generals. In these messages, which he wrote personally, Will begged the sultan to reconsider, citing his friendship with Kalawun and the peace their people had enjoyed for years. He offered money, new trade agreements, the release of Muslim prisoners. But he knew, even before they were sent, that there would be no response to his pleas, seeing in his words the desperation, painfully aware of his own impotence in the face of the coming storm. He had been trying to hold back the sea for years, but it had been slipping past him. He had blocked up the holes in the dam he had created as they appeared, but now the holes were too wide and the flood too big for him to halt. He had two choices left. He could let himself be washed away, or he could turn and face it with force. The Anima Templi had done all they could. Whatever the future might hold, for the moment he couldn't be the head of the Brethren. He had a duty to the people of this city, the Temple, to his friends, his wife and his child; a duty to protect them. And he would, with his last breath if necessary. The defiance inside him hardened, became steel.

Now he had to fight. He had to be the man the Temple had trained him to be.

THE GATE OF ST. LAZARUS, 15 APRIL A.D. 1291

The moonlight shone on the men's faces as they waited in the outer enceinte, the breaths of their horses fogging the air. The blue light bathed the channel that ran between the inner and outer walls in an eerie glow. The whole area was littered with debris: huge boulders, heaps of rubble, arrows.

Will looked over the heads of the assembled knights to where Guillaume de Beaujeu was talking with two men by the Gate of St. Lazarus that led back into the city. All three were dressed for battle, but the grand master cut the most imposing figure. His surcoat and mantle drew in tight over his knee-length hauberk, then flowed out around the chausses that covered his legs. Chain-mail gauntlets shielded his hands and a hood of mail protected his head and neck. Under one arm, he carried a helmet crowned with a snowy plume of eagles' feathers, the tips of which had been stained red with henna, so they looked as though they had been dipped in blood. A broad-bladed sword hung from his belt. With him were a Swiss nobleman called Othon de Grandson in command of the English Order of St. Thomas and the master of the leper Order of St. Lazarus. Will glanced around, hearing Robert sigh impatiently. He could feel the strain in the other men around him, as they waited for battle, but for the most part they sat still and silent by the gate in the outer walls, holding in that tension as they were trained to do. When they were ready, they would unleash it on their enemies.

Shortly, Guillaume broke away from his discussion and returned to the Templars. Othon moved over to the soldiers of St. Thomas, and after sending two of his men back through the Gate of St. Lazarus, the master of the lepers took up position at the head of his foot soldiers, who waited some distance from the other troops. In total, this force, made up of cavalry and infantry, numbered almost three hundred.

Guillaume was helped into his saddle by two of his pages, both of them straining with the weight of him and all his bulky battle-gear. The whole of the northwest side of the suburb of Montmusart had been entrusted to the defense of the Temple, and the men now worked in shifts from makeshift barracks in stables and houses, running supplies and messages between Montmusart and the preceptory. As the pages moved off, the knights crossed themselves and pushed down visors. Moving into formation, they faced the outer gate. The grand master was in front with Theobald Gaudin and Will. Zaccaria was behind with Robert and the gonfanier: the banner-bearer, who held aloft the Temple's piebald flag.

The seconds went by and Will felt his heart begin to speed with anticipation. Inside his helmet, his breaths echoed, while the world outside remained strangely muffled. He gripped his shield, which was bright white in the moon's bleaching luminescence, and the strap tightened around his taut muscles. A signal was given and five men of the Order of St. Lazarus moved to the gates and, together, heaved up the great wooden bar and dragged them open. There was a ponderous clanking sound as the iron portcullis was winched up and the drawbridge beyond was let down. Will flexed his jaw, which was locked and tight, and fixed his gaze on the strip of sky growing wider ahead. The bridge descended slowly, the freshly oiled winches and pulleys working almost soundlessly. Outside, the rushing of the sea grew louder and the wind stronger, streaming in through the gates. It smelled of salt and mud, and it smelled of men; the thick, permeating reek made by many men in a confined area, composed of layer upon layer of odors: animal and human dung, sweat and metal, lamp oil and burning wood, spices, cooked meat and incense. The bridge thudded into place across the narrow trench of the fosse that circled the outer walls. What lay beyond filled Will's view.

Stretched some distance behind the siege lines, formed of wooden barriers and wicker screens, was the Mamluk encampment. Will knew that it was several camps, each governed by different leaders, but the sea of tents was so enormous, covering an area much farther than his eyes could see, that it was almost impossible to tell where one camp started and another ended. The tents, vivid colors by day, were all the same gauzy gray in the moonlight, the grander ones housing amirs. Between them and the siege lines stood the engines. Some were small, only ten to twenty feet in height, fitted with javelins that were aimed at the ramparts and the tower platforms. Others were larger, for stones and naphtha pots, and four of them were gigantic. These monsters, placed at intervals around Acre's walls, rose into the nighttime sky, their frames white and skeletal, the beams, for now, motionless. One, a short distance to the right, was the Furious, transported from Damascus. It was manned by men under the command of the amir of Hamah, whose camp covered a wide area adjacent to the shore, directly in front of the knights. For the past ten days, the Furious had lived up to its name.

On the fifth of April, the Mamluk Army had come, like a vast black sea, swelling to fill the horizon. The last refugees, many of them native Christians from the outlying settlements, fled in through Acre's gates, bringing stories of burning villages and slaughter. On arriving, Sultan Khalil made his camp on a small hill, northeast of the city, where the Templars owned a vineyard. His royal pavilion, bloody scarlet in color, was set up facing Acre, and the army was moved swiftly into position, until it stretched around the outer walls from the shore on the northwest edge of the peninsula to the shore on the southeast. Tents were erected, latrines and ditches dug, engines constructed, stones emptied from carts beside the *mandjaniks*. At points during the day, the army stopped its work for prayers, and the Crusaders, watching their progress from Acre's ramparts, listened in silence to the Muslims' ululating calls. The next day, the siege against Acre had begun.

Each dawn since, a deep-voiced drum would announce a fresh assault and a day of bombardment would begin. Mamluk archers loosed swarms of arrows against the Franks on the ramparts, whilst boulders were hurled continuously against the towers. Out in the harbor, ships carried women and children, the elderly and the sick across the sea to Cyprus, and safety. But many more stayed, those who were hopeful and those who couldn't afford passage. Will had been back to Elwen to beg her to leave, but still she refused, and day by day, the Mamluks drew closer to the walls, soldiers picking up the wooden screens and inching them forward, dragging the enormous engines. The Christians attempted to repel these advances, their own engines catapulting stones down from the tower platforms. But the screens were protected by buches, the bundles of wood lashed together and stacked up to form a protective layer, and most stones simply bounced off this thick wall and dropped harmlessly into the fosse. The Franks launched several valiant attacks from the sea, one mangonel on board a Venetian ship afflicting severe damage to the right flank of the Mamluk Army. The day after, three Pisan ships attacked the camp of Hamah with stones flung from their trebuchets, but a storm blew up, forcing the Pisans to turn back and causing some soldiers to mutter that the Saracens were using sorcery against them. Now, after ten days of relentless assault, the Christians were starting to flag. They needed a victory.

Will loosened his sword in its scabbard as six men from the Order of St. Thomas hastened through the gate. Working quickly, they unrolled a large rectangle of cloth, several layers thick, across the drawbridge. When they were finished, Guillaume raised his mail-clad fist. Will pressed his knees into the flanks of his destrier and rode out beside the grand master and Theobald Gaudin. The hooves of their horses were muffled on the bridge, and the surging sea covered what little other noise they made. Straight ahead lay the barricades of the siege lines, with the monstrous shape of the Furious rising above. The grand master led the Templars off the bridge and onto the sandy ground, heading toward the engine. Behind him, Othon de Grandson led the Order of St. Thomas, and the leper foot soldiers left toward the siege lines that fronted the camp of Hamah, which was mostly populated by Syrian soldiers, augmented by Bedouin and a few hundred Mamluks.

Once off the bridge, the ground dipped down, obscuring most of the camp from view, until only the Furious was visible. The men moved quickly and quietly, footfalls and hooves smothered by the sand. To anyone looking down from the siege lines, the knights would have been instantly visible, but there were no sentries here. The Mamluks had come so close to the walls that they were well in range of the Crusaders' arrows, and any man showing himself over the barriers became a target. Besides, most of the camp was asleep. There was no action on their part at night, and they wouldn't expect such a bold move from the besieged and outnumbered Crusaders. The Mamluks had no idea that from out of gates all around the city, companies like this one, formed of Hospitallers, Teutonics, Pisans and Genoese, were making silent, creeping sorties on their sleeping camp.

Within moments, the Templars had reached the siege lines. Six sergeants ran up alongside the wooden barriers in front of the Furious, holding grapples, whilst the knights moved into position, nudging their well-trained horses with tiny movements of their knees and flicks of the reins. The moon gave off a deceptive light; there were no colors; shapes seemed to bleed into one another and shadows were razor sharp. But this blue half-light was about to change. Now they would turn night to day.

For a few seconds, nothing happened. Guillaume looked toward the ramparts high above them, the feathers of his helmet quivering in the breeze. Will, following his gaze, heard the distant click and thud of machinery and saw a tiny light appear in the sky. It curled up and seemed to hang suspended for a brief moment, then rushed to earth like a shooting star, growing larger as it came. Will suddenly realized that it was going to miss its target. Guillaume seemed to see this also, for he hissed a curse. Sure enough, the large pot, filled with flaming Greek fire, slammed down just feet from the buches surrounding the Furious, which it was supposed to have struck, setting them alight; a fire that would have quickly spread, destroying the protective wall and allowing the men to attack in the ensuing confusion. The pot shattered loudly, sending several Templar sergeants staggering back from the brief burst of fire, but on the sandy earth it had nothing to consume and although some of the sergeants ran forward, trying to kick the flaming substance toward the buches, it quickly guttered and went out. Guillaume rose in his saddle and went to lift his hand to signal to the men on the ramparts to fire again, but before his arm was even raised there was a shout from the other side of the barrier. Someone had heard the commotion.

"Now!" shouted Guillaume to the sergeants, who rushed back into position and launched their grapples into the air.

As the metal hooks fixed on the top of the wooden barriers, more shouts went up from the camp beyond. Together, the sergeants heaved on the grapple ropes and pulled down the barriers surrounding the Furious. The wooden walls thumped to the sand, crushing the buches. Into the breach rode the knights. Will was one of the first through, alongside Guillaume. The Syrian soldiers who manned the Furious were billeted close by and came racing toward the knights, weapons drawn. Other troops in the main camp, some distance beyond, were dashing from tents, half-dressed and half-asleep. Torches, thrust into low-burning fires, flared to life.

"Demolish the engine!" Guillaume roared at the sergeants, some of whom were wielding axes in preparation. "On!" he shouted to the knights. "Attack! Attack!"

As a small company of knights forked off to tackle the approaching Syrians, Guillaume led the rest on at a fierce charge across the open ground toward the Hamah camp. They stormed into the fringes of the camp, cutting a bloody swath through the first lines of soldiers, most of whom were still dazed from sleep. To their left, the soldiers of the Order of St. Thomas had pulled down more of the barriers and were converging on the Templars' position, led by Othon de Grandson. They shouted battle cries as they came.

As the bolt from a crossbow was launched at him, Will ducked and spurred his horse on. A man darted out of a tent in front of him, bare-chested, brandishing a sword. He slashed out, aiming for the destrier's neck. Will wrenched on the reins, turning the horse away at the last second, and hacked at the man with his falchion. The momentum carried the stout blade right through the Syrian's arm, taking it off at the wrist and sending the sword, with the man's hand still clamped around it, flying into the shadows. The Syrian screamed and dropped to his knees, clutching the gushing stump. Two more soldiers came at Will from the right, and using the horse like a weapon, Will wheeled the beast around so that it crashed into them, sending them sprawling. The horse reared up and stamped down with its iron-shod hooves, crushing and breaking limbs, as it was trained to do.

As more soldiers rushed out of tents to aid their comrades, Will found himself pinned in a circle with three other knights, lashing out with his sword, his shield arm throbbing with every bone-crushing thump as a blade struck the wood each time he deflected a blow. A sword scraped across his thigh, but skittered harmlessly off his chain mail; another tore through his mantle. He kept the horse moving, its armor deflecting the sword strokes. Sweat coursed down his cheeks inside his helmet, through the slit of which he could only see the faces of the Syrians in front of him. Guillaume and Robert were gone with the rest of the knights, farther into the camp, trying to buy the sergeants enough time to destroy the Furious. There were screams all around, the clash of iron on steel.

Will fought ruthlessly, methodically, pounding away at the men around him, his only aim to fell them before they killed the knights. These were not men anymore. In his sights, they were targets that had to be destroyed. Instinct had taken over from intellect, and remorse had vanished out of necessity. Now Will was a machine, fueled by a need to survive, by fear and adrenaline. He roared as he slammed down at them, the edge of his blade slicing through any area of exposed flesh it struck. The last man in front of him dropped, his unprotected skull cleaved down the middle, all the way to the nostrils. The way ahead was clear. Will pressed his horse forward. Up ahead there were fresh cries. Knights were shouting, calling out in panic. Something was wrong.

Guillaume and the others had driven deep into the camp, where the tents were crowded close together. But in the moon's deceptive light, they couldn't properly see the guy ropes. The legs of the charging horses caught in the taut hemp lines, sending beasts and knights sprawling. One horse crashed into a tent, pulling it down around it. The horse's rider fell sideways onto a sharpened tent spike that pierced through his neck. He lay there choking and convulsing, his leg crushed by his horse, as two Syrians fell on him and hacked him and the beast to death. Another knight, thrown from his horse, was staggering back from three advancing Mamluks, his ankle sprained from the fall, when he fell over one of the guy ropes and lurched backward into a cloth screen that had been erected around a latrine. The screen collapsed under his weight, and he smashed onto the boards covering the deep ditch that was filled with ten days' worth of excrement. The boards shattered beneath him, sending him plunging into the stinking filth. He struggled there for a moment, grasping desperately at the slimy sides of the pit, until three arrows thumped into him, one after the other, and he collapsed back into the ditch, the weight of his armor taking him under the sludge with a cry that cut off instantly.

More knights were going down, falling foul of the hidden ropes. The Syrians were massing, many having had time to put on helmets and grab shields and weapons. Guillaume, fighting his way savagely through a group of Mamluks who were threatening to surround him, roared the retreat. The Orders of St. Thomas and St. Lazarus rallying around them, the Templars, following their banner, swept out of the camp of Hamah as quickly as they had entered.

Will had turned his horse, preparing to join the retreat, when he saw another knight flung from his saddle and catapulted over the head of his horse as the beast tangled in the ropes. The helmet was dislodged from the knight's head in the fall. It was Robert. The other Templars were racing ahead, blind to his plight. A crowd of soldiers was charging up in their wake, baying for blood, enraged by the assault, seeking retribution for dead comrades.

Will kicked his horse toward Robert, ignoring a shout from Guillaume as he passed him. "Get up!" he yelled to the knight. *"Get up!"*

Robert, scrabbling for his fallen sword, raised his head at the call. Snatching a look behind him at the charging mass of soldiers, he pushed himself to his feet and, forgetting his sword, ran toward Will. Will steered the armored horse past him, straight at the Syrians, who scattered. Then he pulled the beast round in a tight arc and raced back to Robert. With a huge force of effort, the knight just managed to haul himself up behind Will. Grasping the saddle grimly with both hands and fighting for purchase, Robert lay across it, bouncing awkwardly about as Will carried them off, back to the siege lines, where the ground was littered with corpses. The Furious stood, undefeated. Without the fire to aid them and with too little time allowed, the sergeants had been able to do no more than scar its wooden sides.

The raiding party rode swiftly across the bridge and into the outer enceinte, archers on the ramparts firing down at the Syrians and Mamluks who followed them from the camp. When the last man limped in, the bridge was raised, the gates shut and barred. The wounded were helped or carried back through the Gate of St. Lazarus, where they were tended by physicians or priests. Some of the men had captured Mamluk drums and shields, which would be hung on the walls to demoralize the Muslims. But these tokens were small victories that had come at a high price. Of the 152 cavalry and foot soldiers of the Orders of St. Thomas and St. Lazarus who had entered the camp of Hamah, 27 hadn't returned. The Templars had lost four sergeants and eighteen knights, a terrible loss.

And at dawn, when word came to the Templars' camp that the other sorties sent out had suffered similar losses, morale sunk lower still.

46

The Docks, Acre

18 MAY A.D. 1291

G arin pushed through the crowds, ignoring the angry calls of those he forced his way past. One bulky woman with a beefy red face refused to be moved by him.

"Wait your turn," she said, wrinkling her nose as she looked him up and down; his worn, stained clothing, his glazed eyes.

Garin leaned toward her, lip curled in a snarl. "Move, you hag." He attempted to elbow his way past, then felt someone grab his cloak. Whipping around, he saw an old man.

"How dare you speak to my wife in this way!" exclaimed the man. "I've a mind to—!"

Garin punched him in the face, sending him rocking back. As the beefy-faced woman cried out and went to her husband's aid, Garin thrust past her and on through the press of bodies that packed the dockside.

It was approaching dawn, and the inky sea beyond the western mole reflected the first pale shades of morning. The calls of sailors echoed above the fretful murmuring of the restless throng, punctuated by the whimpering of infants. Most of the people on the harbor wall were women and children. There were few adult men, and those that were present were either very old or very rich. There was a sense of agitation, barely held in check. It was apparent in the panicked eyes of Acre's last refugees, who crammed together, jostling and shivering in the morning air, all waiting for a boat to take them to safety. The young men, soldiers and knights now joined by farmers and laborers, were behind them on the walls, still fighting for the city, but over the past month hope had dwindled.

After several more night sorties had attempted to breach the Mamluk camp, none of which had been successful, Acre's gates had been shut for the last time. Spirits lifted briefly when the young king of Cyprus and Jerusalem, Henry II, arrived by ship with two hundred cavalry and five hundred infantry. But when his attempts to negotiate with Sultan Khalil proved fruitless and the daily attacks continued without abate, the people's newfound optimism began to fade. Since then, two of Acre's twelve towers—the English Tower and the Tower of the Countess of Blois—had collapsed under the continuous bombardment, along with three sections of the outer wall, by the Gates of St. Anthony and St. Nicholas, and the King's Tower. Yesterday morning, the rulers of Acre, those who hadn't fled to Cyprus, had met in the council chambers of the royal palace and called for the final evacuation of the women and children.

After word had gone around, Acre's last citizens made their way down to the docks, carrying what possessions they could. Their numbers had been swelling since the previous afternoon, most of them queuing on the dockside, waiting through the night. A trickle of boats had pulled out of the harbor, crammed with people, most of whom had lost everything and had no idea what they would do for food or shelter when they reached whatever shore they were bound for. Many had lived their whole lives in Acre. Leaving husbands, fathers and sons on the walls to hold back the ravenous horde that was clawing its way, brick by brick, through the defenses, these wives, daughters and mothers climbed into the boats, some clutching babies. Looking around for friends or neighbors, seeking comfort, they found only strangers with the same dust-streaked, haunted faces as their own. Now, as the sky lightened, turning from gray-white to pale pink, shedding light over the harbor, it was painfully clear that there were simply too many people and not enough ships.

Garin, panting for breath, finally reached the harbor wall, where the first rows of women were being helped into a Venetian merchant vessel. Paying no attention to those who called to him to move back and to wait his turn, he wrestled his way to the front, knocking into a small child, who began to cry. "Hey!" he shouted to one of the crewmen. "You!"

The crewman scowled at him, reaching out to take a woman's arm as she stepped gingerly across the planks. "What do you want?" he said gruffly, his accent heavy and coarse.

"I need to get on your boat," Garin shouted over the child's wails.

The crewman laughed and turned to one of his fellows. Nodding his head toward Garin, he called to his comrade in Italian. Some of the women on the harbor wall, obviously Italians themselves, glanced at Garin and smirked; one giggled.

"I say you are funny-looking woman," the crewman repeated in scornful English for Garin's benefit. He started whistling a tune and helped another woman across.

Garin glared at him. "I've got money," he growled, reaching into the bag that was slung over his shoulder and pulling out a shabby drawstring pouch.

"Then go buy yourself some courage and get back to the walls where you belong."

The laughter and calls of agreement from the onlookers stung Garin's ears. Rage shuddered inside him, but he could see he was wasting his time. Shoving the pouch into his bag, he stared down the dockside to where several more boats were lined up along the wall. One, not too far away, had men on board. It was a small vessel, barely more than a pinnace, but there was still room for more. He guessed it was probably a carrier, taking its passengers out to one of the few remaining larger galleys moored in the outer harbor. Leaving the jeers behind him, Garin pushed his way toward it. There were more women here, lingering around the wall, looking hopefully at the boat, but several men were standing in front of it with swords drawn, watching the shifting crowds warily. As Garin approached, the crowd ahead of him parted and a stooped old man with white hair, dressed in a black robe, came into view. He was aided by two men clad in purple and gold silks, bishops by the look of them; they were dripping with jewels. Garin recognized the man in black as the patriarch of Jerusalem, Nicholas de Hanape. He hastened along the wall as the patriarch was assisted into the vessel. When Garin reached it, one of the guards halted him with a firm hand in the chest.

"Let me buy passage," Garin pleaded with the guard. "They're not letting any men on board the others. I'm wounded." He gestured vaguely to his leg. "I cannot fight."

"You're not getting on board," said the guard firmly.

"For Christ's sake, I'm begging you!"

The guard shook his head. "There's a Templar ship, the *Falcon*," he pointed along the dockside to where a large galley sat in the outer harbor, just off the crumbled eastern mole, alongside several others. "The captain's done away with his mantle and has commandeered it. He's accepting money for passage, so I've heard. But you're going to need a lot to persuade him."

"More than five gold?"

The guard arched an eyebrow. "Much more."

Leaving the guards to push the desperate crowds back as the half-empty pinnace, with the white-faced patriarch and bishops on board, pushed off from the wall, Garin forced his way through the crush. Heading back into the city, he jogged through the streets, his mind working furiously. A lot of the people he was passing were obviously poor folk, unable to afford passage in the earlier evacuations. It would be pointless, he knew, to rob any of them. He cursed himself savagely for leaving it so late.

He had been drinking himself into a stupor for the past few weeks in a vain attempt to block out the horrendous noise of the attack; the thuds and crashes of stones, the war drums and battle cries, the fevered prayers, clanging bells and screams. But he had dug in to wait it out, believing, as many had, that the walls would hold. Last night he had surfaced from a drunken haze in a subdued brothel in the Pisan quarter to discover that the call for a citywide evacuation had gone out. Sick to his stomach, he gathered his few belongings and, with thoughts of France, of building a new life, crowding up his mind, had made his way to the docks. It hadn't entered his head that he might not be able to leave.

Plumes of black smoke curled into the air from fires that burned untended. In the distance, Acre's walls were jagged and scarred. The crumbled remains of the English Tower, just a broken spur of stone, pointed like a thin finger into the dawn. Pigs and goats, masterless, crowded the alleys in frightened packs. Houses stood empty. As Garin stumbled through the streets, three carts trundled slowly by, piled high with bodies, some burned and blackened, others missing limbs. Streams of people were hastening past him in the opposite direction, all heading for the docks. One woman, her hair flying loose and disheveled around her face, shouted at two children to keep up. Both were crying.

The woman, who held a baby bundled in her arms, dashed back to them. "You have to walk faster," she snapped.

One, a small blond boy, cried harder. "I want Papa!"

The woman looked stricken for a moment, then crouched down. "Papa will follow us soon," she said gently. "But we've got to find a boat first." She kissed them both. "Now help Mama and be good boys."

Garin watched them head off, the two boys hurrying behind her. He thought of calling out to the woman, of telling her that it was no use; she was too late and all the boats would soon be gone. But before he could open his mouth, they disappeared in the throng. He stood there, staring after them, considering their fate. If the walls broke and the Saracens came through, the woman would most likely face rape and death. She was too old to be enslaved and wouldn't fetch a worthwhile sum in the markets. Her baby would be killed; it would die anyway without a mother to suckle it, and the boys would be taken as slaves. It would be the fate of thousands like them. Garin found little emotion in the thought, until his mind filled with an image of Rose.

He was almost certain she was still in the city. He had seen Elwen only two days ago, in a line of women hauling buckets of water and sand to help quell the fires, which sprang up daily as the Mamluks shot flaming arrows and Greek fire over the walls. She had been flushed and looked exhausted, dark circles under her eyes, her gown stained. She hadn't seen him, but he had watched her for a while. Will and Elwen had done everything they could to keep him out of their lives. But that hadn't stopped him believing that he was Rose's father, or hoping that, one day, he could prove it to her. He wasn't sure why he had this need; perhaps it was nothing more than spite, a simple wish to see Will suffer, as he himself had suffered. But he liked to think it was because he could love a child, and be loved in return.

Were Rose and Elwen still in Acre? Or had they found a boat? If they were here, Garin seriously doubted that Will, however occupied, would leave them without hope of escape. No doubt he had secured them passage, possibly even on board a Templar ship. An idea forming in his mind, Garin turned down one of the side streets, heading for the Venetian quarter.

TEMPLAR HEADQUARTERS, MONTMUSART, ACRE, 18 MAY A.D. 1291

Will rode swiftly through the ruined streets of Montmusart, steering his destrier around piles of rubble and the burned-out shells of houses. The dawn air was filled with smoke. He could feel it scratching at the back of his throat, taste it where it coated his lips in the same powdery gray dust that covered everything. Far above him, torches flared on the walls, the men on guard casting huge shadows as they passed through the pools of yellow light. Will rode on, through the camp of the Hospitallers, the knights in their black mantles with the splayed white cross moving ghostlike in the half-light. Wounded men huddled on the back of a cart as it bounced over the uneven ground on the way to the infirmary, past a train of slow-moving mules loaded down with arrows in bundles on their backs. All along the walls, he had passed similar scenes. Only the colors of uniforms and banners changed. The subdued sense of apprehension remained the same. The old songs of the West that soldiers had cheered themselves with during the eerily silent nights of the siege had stopped several days ago. There wasn't much to sing about anymore.

Mamluk sappers, known as *nakkabun,* had been busily undermining Acre's twelve towers over the past month, each mining team made up of one thousand men. Tunnels were dug from within the Mamluk camp all the way up to the walls, and when they arrived beneath the towers, a large cavern was excavated. The foundations were held up with timber, which was set alight, causing the tower wall to collapse into the cavern. Three days ago, after one such excavation, the whole outer face of the King's Tower had collapsed in on itself. The rubble had fallen into the fosse, making it impossible for the Mamluks to pass, but the Crusaders' relief was short-lived when they had awoken the next morning to find that the Mamluks had erected a giant cloth screen in the night, from behind which they were clearing a path through the debris. Arrows and stones were repelled by the screen, and the Christians on the walls could only look on as the Mamluks took the remaining section of the King's Tower.

When he reached the Templar headquarters, set up in a now abandoned church with a hole in the roof, Will dismounted. He handed the reins to a nearby squire. The area was still fairly quiet, the men catching as much rest as possible before the daily assault began. "Have you seen Simon Tanner?" he asked the squire.

"Last I saw him was in the stables by the hospital of St. Lazarus, Commander."

Will paused, torn by the choice, looking to the doors of the church, where two knights were posted on guard. The stables were at least five minutes away on foot and he didn't have that much time. Cursing, he strode to the church. The knights nodded respectfully to him as he pushed open the doors. Inside, he found Guillaume de Beaujeu and Peter de Sevrey bent over a drawing of the walls laid out on two barrels. Torchlight threw their silhouettes up the sides of the lofty chamber, the floor of which was littered with shards of stone.

Guillaume looked round. "Ah, Commander. That was quick. What news is there from King Henry's camp?"

"I didn't make it to the king's camp, my lord," replied Will. "Before I reached it, I was alerted by Teutonic Knights near the remains of the English Tower. The Mamluks are on the move."

De Sevrey frowned. "Already?" He gave a rough sigh. "The Saracens intend to wake us early today."

"You misunderstand me, Sir Marshal. They are all moving, every camp from the Patriarch's Tower to St. Anthony's Gate. The largest concentration of them is massing in front of the Accursed Tower."

"You are certain?" demanded Guillaume.

"I went onto the ramparts and saw it for myself. They obviously began moving during the night, under cover of darkness. They are almost up to the base of the walls."

"Have the other leaders been warned?" asked the marshal swiftly.

"Word was being sent out as I left. I expect the other camps will all know within the next few minutes."

"Wake the men, Peter," said Guillaume, turning to the marshal. "Tell them we are expecting an all-out assault. Gather them here immediately."

"My lord," said the marshal, bowing and moving out.

Guillaume, his face haggard in the torchlight, turned to Will. "This could be it, Commander," he said after a pause.

Will's jaw tightened. He nodded.

Guillaume looked to the chancel, where a silver crucifix, suspended above the altar, gleamed dully. His brow furrowed. "Will you pray with me, William?"

"My lord," said Will, hesitant, "I should go to the barracks. Help ready the men."

"Of course," said Guillaume, shaking his head. "Prepare yourself. We will pray with our brothers when you return."

Forcing himself to turn away from the grand master, Will hastened out of the church and into the streets, where the camp was already waking, word going around.

Will found Simon in the stables next to the Hospital of St. Lazarus, looking scared but grim, overseeing the saddling of the knights' destriers.

Simon looked relieved to see him. "Have you come for a horse?" He stuck a hand through his dusty hair. "People are saying there's going to be an attack, a bigger one than usual."

"I need to speak to you," said Will, steering him into the yard, away from the pages and grooms around the stalls.

"What is it?" asked Simon worriedly. He had lost weight over the past few weeks and his usually broad and ruddy face was hollow and pale. "Will? What's wrong?"

"I need you to do something for me."

"Anything."

"I need you to go to Elwen. I want you to make sure she and Rose get on board that ship. I told her to leave yesterday, but she said she had to pack some things. She promised to get to the harbor by this afternoon." Will paused, staring hard at Simon. "But I don't think we've got that long."

Simon looked shocked, but he nodded. "I will, of course. Although I don't reckon the stable master will be too happy with me leaving my post this minute."

"Tell him I've reassigned you."

"I'll come back as soon as she's on the ship." Simon went to head into the stables, then turned back and grasped Will's hand in both of his own, which were rough and callused. He squeezed hard. "God be with you," he said in a tight voice.

"And with you."

Will watched Simon go, before moving off. As he passed the Gate of St. Lazarus, his eyes caught sight of large black words that had been scratched in charcoal across the wood.

Non nobis, Domine, non nobis, sed nomini tuo da gloriam. Not unto us, O Lord, not unto us, but unto Thy name the glory.

He stood there for a moment, an image of his father clear and sharp in his mind.

Somewhere in the distance, beyond the walls, a drum began to pound.

THE VENETIAN QUARTER, ACRE, 18 MAY A.D. 1291

Garin reached the blue door and halted, straining for breath. He went to rub the sweat from his forehead and realized that his hand was trembling violently. The drink had soured in his system and was now a poison, working its way through him. If he had stopped to think, he could have looted one of the abandoned taverns, perhaps even found some coins, but all his thoughts had been fixed on getting here. He clenched his fist and banged on the painted wood. The sound echoed in the quiet street. A man pulling a handcart filled with pots and pans loped past. He glanced suspiciously at Garin and kept on going. Garin scowled after him, then heard a bolt slide back. Quickly, he smoothed his filthy hair and straightened his vomit-stained cloak. The door opened.

Rose appeared. Her hair was scraped back under a cap, and she wore a yellow and green traveling cloak over a white gown. She looked tired. As she saw Garin, she frowned. "What do you want?" she murmured, holding onto the door, not opening it any further.

"Rose, sweetheart," said Garin, trying his best to smile, "is your mother here?"

Rose didn't respond. Behind her, Garin heard rapid footfalls.

"Rose!" came a sharp call. "Why is the door open? Who's there?"

As Rose looked around at Elwen's voice, Garin pushed her inside as gently as he could and forced his way in, knowing that if Elwen locked him out, he wouldn't have another chance to get inside. He pushed it shut and shoved the bolt home. Rose stepped away, staring up at him as he loomed over her in the passage, where there was a stack of chests and a few sack bags. It looked as if they were about to leave.

"Get the hell out." Elwen was down the stairs and in the corridor, her gaze locked on him. Her face was fierce with anger in the glow of a lantern hanging from a hook in the passage. "Rose, come here." She went forward and put her hands on her daughter's shoulders, pulling her back. "I mean it, Garin. Leave."

Garin shook his head slowly. "I can't do that."

"Why?" Elwen's voice was still harsh, but Garin heard a note of fear slip into it.

"The boats aren't taking men unless they have money, and there aren't enough ships left for everyone." He shrugged. "I've got nowhere else to go."

"I can't help you."

"I think you can." Garin cocked his head to one side and studied her. He was feeling more confident now. "You owe me, Elwen." He smiled at Rose and gave her a wink as if this was a game.

"Our guard, Piero, will be back any minute," said Elwen.

Garin frowned and glanced at the door. "Is that so? Well, I suppose we shouldn't stand around here then. Upstairs," he said, walking toward them.

Elwen stepped in front of Rose and held her ground. "If Piero finds you here, he'll kill you. Just go." She lowered her voice. "Please, Garin. You're scaring my daughter."

Garin's eyes flared with anger. "*Our* daughter!" he hissed, taking hold of Elwen's arm and propelling her toward the stairs.

"Run, Rose!" shouted Elwen, struggling wildly in his grip, kicking out and hitting him with her free hand. "*Go!*" she screamed, turning to look at her daughter.

Rose staggered back a few steps, wide-eyed, then ran to the door at the end of the passage.

Garin's hand flew to his belt. His fingers curled around the dagger that was sheathed there and pulled it free. "Rose, sweetheart!" he shouted, twisting El-wen viciously around and putting the dagger to her throat. "If you run, I'll kill your mother."

Rose stopped dead. She spun around and cried out in horror as she saw the dagger at Elwen's neck. Outside in the distance, a deep-voiced drum began to sound, low and ominous.

"You bastard," murmured Elwen, going still and trembling against the blade.

Garin felt bile rise in his throat. Sweat dripped into his eyes and his hands shook. This wasn't what he had planned. This wasn't the way he wanted it. He needed to calm things down, but he couldn't do it here. He had to get them upstairs and then, somehow, get Elwen to listen to him. "Rosie," he called. "If you do as I say, everything will be fine. I want you to go upstairs for me."

Rose hesitated. She stood there breathing hard, looking from Garin to Elwen.

Garin frowned. He put his face closer to Elwen's. "Tell her to go upstairs," he breathed, his mouth hot against her ear, "or I swear I'll make her watch as I cut you."

Elwen felt her legs go weak. "Do as he says, Rose," she whispered.

Slowly, Rose walked toward the stairs and began to climb, not taking her eyes off Elwen, who followed, Garin pushing her forward, still holding the blade at her throat.

When they reached the first floor, Garin nodded to one of the doors. "What's in there?"

"Nothing," said Elwen. "That's Andreas's room. It's empty."

"Go in there, Rosie," he said calmly.

She pushed open the door and backed in, still staring at him. Andreas's chambers, with the solar leading into the bedroom, were cold and dark. Just a few items of furniture remained: a table and stool, and the large bed. The wind that blew in through the windows smelled of smoke; the bare boards creaked beneath their feet.

"Go and sit by the window, Rose." Garin took the knife away from Elwen's throat. "Go to her."

Released from his grasp, Elwen ran to Rose and wrapped her arms around her. "It's all right, my darling," she whispered into her hair. "It's going to be all right."

"Listen to your mother, Rose," said Garin absently, as he shut the door, pleased to find a large iron key in the lock.

"Garin, it's freezing," said Elwen, looking up at him. "Rose hasn't been well. She'll catch her death in here."

Garin paused, looking at the pale-faced, shivering girl. "Do you have blankets?" he asked Elwen.

"Downstairs, in one of the sacks in the hall. I can get them."

Garin's eyes narrowed. "I'll go." He wiggled the heavy key out of the lock and waved it at her. "Don't try anything foolish." He stared hard at her until he was satisfied that she knew he was serious, then headed out, sheathing the dagger and locking the door. He heard a muffled sob as he walked away and swore bitterly. No, this wasn't what he had planned at all. He went hurriedly down and searched through the sacks. He found one stuffed with blankets and linen, and was hefting it up when he heard noise through the door at the end of the passage, which he guessed led to a kitchen. Putting the sack down, he padded to it. He heard a man's voice call Elwen's name. The footfalls came closer.

Garin braced himself. As the door opened, he grabbed hold of it and slammed it into the startled-looking man who appeared behind it. The man staggered back, clutching his face, and barreled into a table, the legs of which screeched on the stone floor. Garin followed him swiftly and shoved him down onto it. The man was yelling now, but it was all in Italian and Garin couldn't understand him. Grabbing a fistful of the man's hair, he smashed his head on the wood, meaning to knock him unconscious. But the exertion brought a fresh wave of dizziness washing over him and the impact wasn't nearly as hard as he'd intended. The man cried out in pain, then launched himself into Garin. Ducking out of his grip, the man turned and punched him in the face, sending him reeling into the wall, knocking several pots off their hooks, which crashed down around him. Garin recovered and dove at him. The two of them wrestled together, lurching heavily around the kitchen, sending things flying. The man got away and drew a sword that was sheathed at his hip. He lunged at Garin, who sidestepped the blade, throwing his head back at the last minute to avoid its sweeping arc. Drawing his dagger, Garin darted through the man's defenses and plunged it in, sliding it expertly up between the man's ribs.

The man gave a cry. Garin wrenched the blade out, spun him around and sliced the dagger across his throat, severing the artery. The man slumped to the floor amidst the debris. Garin, panting and soaked in greasy sweat, looked down at him. Piero, he guessed, wiping the blade on his cloak and sheathing it with a forceful stab. He went to head out, but paused as something caught his eye. On a shelf was a row of jugs above pots of herbs and oil. Stepping over

Piero, Garin went to them. He felt relief go through him as he saw that they were filled with wine. Taking two, he went out into the passage and bundled the sack with the blankets under one arm. Grabbing the lantern off its hook, he climbed the stairs.

Elwen stared at him in shock as he entered. She was where he had left her, standing by the window, holding Rose to her. "What was happening? What was that noise?"

"Piero came home," muttered Garin, kicking the door closed. Putting the lantern and jugs on the table, he locked the door and stowed the key in the pouch at his belt.

"My God," whispered Elwen, staring at a smear of blood that glistened darkly on his cloak. "What did you do?" Her voice was numb, but her eyes were filling up with real fear now as she realized what he was capable of.

"Here," said Garin gruffly, looking away from her appalled stare. He threw her the sack. He pointed to Rose when Elwen didn't move. "She's cold, Elwen."

Moving slowly, her fingers rigid, clumsy, Elwen pulled two blankets from the sack as Garin perched on the edge of the table and drank greedily from the jug. Elwen, wrapping the blanket around Rose's shoulders, watched him. Through the fog of terror, she saw a chance, a small window of hope. If he continued to drink like this, he would become slower, weaker. She might be able to fight him, get past him. Holding onto that thought, feeling some of her strength come back to her, she pulled a blanket around her own shoulders.

Garin finished drinking, belched and put the empty jug on the table. He half-closed his eyes at the feeling of the alcohol coursing through him, soaking into every part of him, making his limbs heavy and solid. The fog in his brain cleared. "I'm sorry about Piero," he told Elwen, opening his eyes. "I wouldn't have killed him if he'd given me the choice."

"Why did you come here?" she asked him, her voice quiet. "The city is about to fall. You are putting all our lives at risk by keeping us here." She paused. "If you care so much about Rose, you wouldn't do this."

Garin sat forward, his eyes growing sharper. "It's because I care about her that I'm doing this. It isn't fair on her, not knowing who her real father is."

Rose stared at him belligerently from under the folds of the blanket. "I know who my father is," she said in a hard voice.

Garin shook his head. "No, sweetheart, I don't think you do."

Elwen closed her eyes. "Please, Garin. Don't do this. I'll give you whatever you want. Just don't do this to us." She took a step toward him. "We have money downstairs in one of the bags. Take it. We don't need it, we have a ship secured. If you go now you'll be able to buy yourself passage."

"You're trying to bribe me?" he demanded.

"No, I ..."

Garin pushed himself off the table and went toward her and Rose. Halting halfway as they cowered back against the wall, he thrust a finger at Elwen. "Who's going to take care of her, of you, when this is over?" The drink was in him now, building its fire. He was alive with emotion, blazing with it. "Will isn't going with you, is he? He'd rather stay here and play the hero than make sure his own wife and daughter are safe. He doesn't deserve you, Elwen, either of you. He never has."

"Will stays because he has a duty to do so."

"To the Temple?" demanded Garin, incredulously. "He doesn't even believe in the pissing Temple!"

"If he deserts the order, he deserts the Brethren, you know that. The Anima Templi cannot exist without the resources the Temple provides. If he leaves, he loses all chance for peace. I understand that. I *admire* him for that." Elwen's voice was hardening. "That is the difference between him and you, Garin. Will does what is best for everyone around him. You only do what's best for you, and damn the consequences!"

"So he's better than me, is he?"

"More than you'll ever know," she replied with a defiant laugh.

Garin shook his head. "If that is so, Elwen, why did you come to me that day? Answer me!" he shouted, as she turned away. "If Will is so damn good, why the hell did you spread your legs for me?"

"*Shut up!*" she screamed, whirling on him. "*Just shut up!*"

Rose had clapped her hands over her ears and was sliding down the wall. She squeezed her eyes shut. Neither Elwen nor Garin were looking at her; all their attention was focused on each other.

"That's why you're still here, isn't it? Why you haven't left yet? I'll bet Will secured you a ship weeks ago when the siege first started. You could have gone, but you stayed. You stayed because of guilt, because you couldn't bear to leave him here alone, knowing that you left him once, left him so utterly when you lay with me."

"No," Elwen said, shaking her head wildly. "No."

"Believe me, I know about guilt. I can recognize it when I see it." Garin went back to the table and lifted the other jug. He drank, only taking a few sips this time. He laughed. "We're all so guilty. You, me. Will. So damned and so guilty."

"We're nothing like you, Garin. You're weak and you're cruel, and you're nothing."

"Will killed his own sister."

"That was an accident."

"You slept with me."

"That was a mistake."

"And what about me?" yelled Garin, flinging the jug against the door. Rose screamed and Elwen flinched as it smashed, wine splashing across the boards and up the walls. "Aren't I entitled to make mistakes? Can't I be forgiven for the things that I have done?"

"You did them out of selfishness."

"You have no idea what I've been through." Garin jabbed a finger at his chest. "How I've suffered. I was thirteen when Edward found me and lured me into his service with promises to help my family. Do you know the things my uncle Jacques used to do to me? I used to bite my fingernails." He looked down at his dirty, ragged nails and snorted. "I still do. Jacques hated it. He saw it as a weakness. One day I forgot and did it in front of him. He shut my finger in the door of his solar, took the nail right off. But I still loved him, even after the beatings. All I wanted was to make him and my mother happy. Edward, I thought, could give me that, and so I agreed when he asked me to help take back the crown jewels."

Elwen had gone still. "What?"

Garin nodded at her expression. "It was me, Elwen, I betrayed the knights. I gave Edward's men the information they needed to mount the attack at Honfleur. I killed my uncle." He looked into her eyes. "I killed yours. Jacques and Owein died because of me."

Elwen had gone white.

Garin let out a shuddering breath. "I've never told anyone that before," he said a little wonderingly. "After it happened, I hated myself, hated what I had made possible. I would have gone back to London, grieved alone, only Rook, Edward's man, found me and told me that if I didn't keep working for them, didn't prove myself useful, he would rape and kill my mother. That much was true. And so I worked for Edward for years, using my position in the Temple to get him what he wanted."

"The Book of the Grail," breathed Elwen.

"Edward wanted to use it against the Temple, as evidence of heresy. He thought he could bribe the Anima Templi into giving him the money and resources he wanted when he became king. He was planning to expand his empire even when he was still a prince. He's always known what he wanted." Garin lifted his head, hearing the distant sound of drums and horns for the first time. He looked back at her. "Then I came here, to Outremer. I proved myself in battle, saved lives, knew what it was to be a knight, knew what it was to feel proud and good. I forgot Edward. I helped Will track down the Book of the Grail, and when Rook tried to stop us I killed him. But then I was imprisoned." He spoke bitterly. "I had tried so hard to make amends and still I was punished. It was Edward who got me out."

"You've been working for him ever since?"

Garin pressed his lips together. "For years. Killing and spying, all in his name." His brow creased as she turned away in shock and disgust. "But all that changed when I saw Rose." He crossed the room to her. "I swear it, Elwen. Something changed in me. When I saw it was possible for me to create life as well as destroy it." He put his hands on her shoulders and turned her to face him. "She's mine, isn't she? Just tell me that."

Elwen stared at the floor. "I don't know," she whispered.

"But there's a chance?" said Garin quickly. The tears that welled up and slipped from Elwen's eyes as she looked up at him were all the answer he needed. He smiled and exhaled deeply. "Let me come with you, Elwen, on board the ship." His hands, gripping her, were quivering with emotion. "Let me be a father, a husband even. Let me prove that I can be a better man, that I can make amends. Let Will look after the world and I swear I will look after you, both of you. I can do this. I can make you love me."

Elwen stared up at him. "You're a liar," she said in a voice as cold as the dawn. "A liar and a murderer. I could never love you."

Garin let out a breath, her words like a slap. Anger rushed into his face, coloring his cheeks. "Well, you loved me once," he snarled at her. "I was good enough for you then." Seizing her, he propelled her to the table. "I'm good enough for you now." He threw her down on the wood. Ignoring her terrified screams, he caught her hands, which clawed and scratched at his face, and forced them above her head, pinning them. "I'll *make* you love me again!" he gasped, grabbing hold of her gown and ripping it down, baring her breasts.

Suddenly, he felt fists pummelling at his back and legs. It didn't exactly hurt, but it was distracting. Turning with a snarl, he lashed out, blind with drink and fury. He caught Rose on the side of the face, sending her spinning. She fell to the floor and stayed there. Garin's vision slammed into focus as he saw her crumpled form. Letting go of Elwen, he dropped down beside her. "Rosie," he cried hoarsely. "Rosie! I'm sorry."

Elwen pushed herself off the table and launched herself at him, grabbing the empty jug. She slammed it down on his head and it shattered. Garin lurched forward on his hands next to Rose, who jolted awake. But even as Elwen, sobbing, her hands shaking madly, tugged at the pouch on his belt with the door key in it, Garin recovered and pushed himself to his feet. Forcing her off him, he shoved her away. She fell hard against the table, hitting her forehead on the corner of it as she went down. She slumped to the floor beside Rose, who cried out.

"Mama!"

"You think you're leaving?" roared Garin, his shame gone as suddenly as it had come. "Think you're leaving me? You're not going anywhere!" Seizing the lantern, he threw it against the door, where the wine had pooled. The glass smashed and oil spattered out. The flame fluttered, almost disappeared, then flared in the oil and wine.

Garin staggered back as Rose bent over Elwen. "Mama, wake up!"

The fire spread quickly, leaping into life across the boards, alive and hungry. Garin watched it, mesmerized.

Elwen stirred and woke, looking dazedly up at her daughter. Her cap had come off and her hair hung around her shoulders. A bruise was swelling on her forehead. "What ...?" she murmured, raising her hand to it. Suddenly, she sat up and looked aghast at the fire that was now burning merrily up the door, crackling and spitting into life with every patch of oil and wine it found. Garin stood there dazedly, a trickle of blood oozing from the back of his head where the bottle had cut him. "My God!" she shouted. "What have you done?"

He turned to look at her, his face slack and gray. "We're staying here now."

ST. ANTHONY'S GATE, ACRE, 18 MAY A.D. 1291

It was a scene from hell. Smoke billowed in black choking clouds as clay pots of Greek fire exploded across the street. Horses screamed and reared as their flesh burned, tossing riders into the boiling mass of men. One man, an English knight whose mount had been slain beneath him, burst into flames as one of the pots smashed against him, the fire setting his cloak alight. He thrashed blindly as the flames roared up around him and his face began to burn, his skin melting and running like tallow. The Mamluk lines were a seething wall of men and spears and shields, those in front forced forward, pushed by those behind. The first soldiers held tall shields, from behind which archers launched volleys of arrows into the Christians. Others threw javelins, and still the pots of Greek fire kept coming, until it seemed the whole world was burning.

Will was on his horse, alongside Guillaume de Beaujeu. His arms were throbbing and his mantle was torn and blackened, soaked in blood, his and others'. As another javelin was hurled at him, he lifted his shield to deflect it and crashed against the high back of his saddle with the impact. Robert and Zaccaria had been close by, but he could no longer see them through the smoke and bedlam all around him. He didn't know if they were alive. The sound of three hundred kettledrums rang insanely inside his helmet, along with the screams of the dying scattered all around him. The white cloaks of the Templars were joined by the black of the Hospitallers. Jean de Villiers was fighting valiantly beside Guillaume as if the two grand masters had been comrades in arms all their lives and there had never been an ounce of rivalry between them or their orders. The soldiers of Cyprus, under King Henry II, were there, surcoats flashing red and gold in the sunlight that appeared through breaks in the smoke as dawn broke.

Following the beating of the thunderous drum that had continued to reverberate as the Templars gathered outside the church, the Mamluks had launched their assault. They had come as a single, solid mass. Many had fallen, crushed beneath the stones slung from the city walls or burned alive in the boiling oil that was poured onto their ranks. But many more kept coming, striding over the dead. The clouds of arrows flying up at Acre's troops were simply too thick for the Christians to stand against, and within a short time, the Mamluks had taken the Accursed Tower. They poured in through the breach, pushing back the troops that tried to halt them, and entered the outer enceinte between the double walls. Some broke left and charged along the channel toward the Pisans' camp, where the siege engines of the Italians were doing terrible damage to the rest of the army outside the walls. Another company, made up of several thousand, surged right through the outer enceinte to St. Anthony's Gate. But the warning had gone up and the Templars and the Knights of St. John were there to meet them.

Time after time, the Mamluks in the front rows hefted their shields to move forward through the broken, burned gates, advancing inch by inch into the rock-strewn street. As they did so, Guillaume would let out a rallying cry and the knights would charge against them. But as soon as they came, the Mamluks would close ranks, so the knights dashed themselves against their impenetrable line. It was a hopeless struggle. The knights knew they couldn't hold this force back much longer. But every precious second they held on for meant another body on a boat, another wife or daughter spared. This kept them going, carried them through the pain and terror, made them hurl themselves against the Mamluk lines, bringing down swords and axe blades into the heads and throats and arms of their enemy. Some men fought on with arrows piercing their sides or appalling wounds that shook them with agony every movement they made. This was it. The final stand.

In their midst, Guillaume de Beaujeu, his helmet with its bloody feathers having been knocked from his head, was roaring like a lion. His blue eyes shone in the first rays of sun, his face and beard blackened with smoke and dust and blood. Because the call to arms had come so quickly, he'd not had time to don his chain-mail armor, only a light, plate hauberk that covered his shoulders and torso. He was crying out to God to give strength to their arms and hearts, shouting that all of Christendom was with them, that they would be remembered, that they would be honored on earth and in heaven, that angels would sing for them. And his words soared like fire into the knights' ears as they spurred their exhausted horses into the ranks, turning the world red with the cutting of their blades, turning the sting of metal across their skin to the kiss of God on their souls.

Smoke swirled, and the front lines of the Mamluks lifted their shields and began to march forward again, striding over the mutilated and burned corpses of comrades, Crusaders, horses.

Guillaume raised his sword to signal another charge. "To me!" he roared. *"To me!"*

At that moment, a javelin sailed out from the Mamluk lines.

It came like a bolt of black lightning, ripping through the smoke, flying straight at the grand master. Guillaume didn't see it coming. As his men thrust their spurs into their horses and surged forward, the head of the javelin slammed straight into Guillaume's side, just under his armpit, bared where he had raised his sword arm. The hauberk's plates didn't cover him there, and the javelin's point drove five inches under his skin. Guillaume was rammed back in his saddle. His broad-bladed sword fell from his fingers. In front of him, his men were crashing into the Mamluk lines. Through the mist of pain clouding his eyes, Guillaume saw two knights go down, their horses wheeling and falling, pierced with spears. With his free hand, he grasped the shaft of the javelin and, with a bellow of agony, wrenched it from his side. He slumped forward in his saddle, just as his men began to retreat from the Mamluk shield wall.

Will was the first to see him. "My lord!" He steered his horse over, pulling the destrier up sharp alongside the grand master, just managing to grab him before he slipped from the saddle. He saw blood drenching Guillaume's surcoat. "We've got to get you to the infirmary."

Guillaume's eyes flickered open. "No, William, I must lead the men."

"You cannot even ride, my lord."

Zaccaria and several others had seen him now and were racing over, along with the grand master of the Hospital. Behind them, the knights of King Henry hefted their shields against the arrows flying down around them.

"Take him to your preceptory," said Jean, looking from the grand master to Will. "Do what you can for him."

Zaccaria dismounted. "Bring me a shield!" he shouted to four sergeants.

Will and the Hospitaller grand master helped Guillaume down from his saddle and eased him onto the ground. Behind them, another charge was led by King Henry's knights.

"Jean," murmured Guillaume, grasping his arm.

"We will hold them for as long as possible," said Jean. "Take him," he said to Will, then mounted his horse and rode back to his men.

Zaccaria laid the tall shield the sergeants brought him next to Guillaume. Between them, Zaccaria and Will lifted the grand master onto it. The sergeants bore him up, straining at the weight, and Will motioned to Zaccaria and three other knights. "Come with me."

Zaccaria, his short white hair sooty, climbed into his saddle without a word. Will had the impression that the Sicilian would have followed the grand master's body whether he'd ordered him to or not. Leaving the remainder of their knights with the Hospitallers, under the command of Theobald Gaudin, who now took charge in Guillaume's place, Will led the knights away from St. Anthony's Gate and back through the streets. It was slow going, the sergeants struggling with Guillaume. All around the walls, the drums and horns continued to sound. As he rode slowly, in front of the sergeants, Will's mind was filled with the image of the Mamluk shield wall, their men dashing themselves uselessly upon it. Now he was out of the battle, able to think more clearly, he knew that it couldn't hold for much longer. The knights would either die there, one by one, or would be forced to retreat. It was only a matter of time. Will looked at the bloodied, half-unconscious form of the grand master; then, pulling his horse around, he rode back to Zaccaria. "Stay with the grand master. Get him to the preceptory."

Zaccaria studied Will. "Are you going somewhere, Commander?"

Will drew his horse to a stop beside Zaccaria, letting the others go on ahead. "The gate will not hold for much longer, we both know that," he said in a low voice. "Before it falls, before the Mamluks breach the city, I must make sure those I care about are safe. I know that you will take care of the grand master."

After a pause, Zaccaria gave a small nod. "Will we see you back at the preceptory, Commander?"

"If God will spare me."

With that, Will turned his horse and jabbed his spurs into its flanks, as behind him, the knights defending St. Anthony's Gate fell, one by one.

47

The Venetian Quarter, Acre

18 MAY A.D. 1291

E lwen leaned out of the window, gasping for air. Smoke surged around her, stinging her eyes and throat. Her fingers scrabbled at the outside of the house, trying to find purchase on the rough stones. There was none. The breeze prickled her skin, taunting her, just beyond reach. Beneath her, the wall fell sheer to the ground, thirty feet below. Her eyes searched the way down, looking for hope. At her feet, crouched below the window ledge and swaddled in the blankets, Rose began to cough harshly.

Elwen turned to the bed, where Garin was lying on his back. "You're going to have to help me," she called, holding her dress to her chest where he had ripped it. "Garin!"

His drunken gaze swiveled in her direction. His eyes and nose were red. "You'll break both your legs if you jump," he mumbled thickly.

"There's a ledge beneath this window. If you lower me down, I should be able to stand on it. If I jump from there, I might be all right. You can tie the blankets together and use them like a rope. If you lower Rose down part of the way, I can catch her."

Garin returned to his study of the ceiling.

"Garin, please! We're going to die in here!" Elwen looked to the door. In the solar, the fire had spread rapidly, blocking their escape. They had gone into the bedchamber, but now the smoke was working its way steadily through the gap beneath the door, even though she had plugged it with one of the blankets. She could hear the crackle of flames on the other side, could feel the pulsing heat through the wood.

"We're going to die anyway," said Garin. "Don't you hear the horns? They are sounding a retreat. I expect the Mamluks have breached the walls. We'll never find a ship in time."

"I told you! We have a ship."

"I don't."

"You can come with us." Elwen crossed to the bed. "We'll take you to Venice. Just help me get us out."

Garin stared morosely up at her. "You don't mean that."

"I do, I swear."

He pushed himself up, swiping at his dripping nose. His eyes were bloodshot and heavy-lidded. He grasped her arm and pulled her to him. "Tell me you love me then."

Elwen glanced at Rose, sitting huddled in the blankets beneath the window, coughing abrasively. Taking in a thin breath, she looked back at Garin. Her eyes lowered. "I love you," she murmured.

Garin hissed and let go of her arm. "You lie," he snarled. "You say it to save yourself."

"God, please, Garin!" she cried. "If you want me to suffer for what I've done to you, then leave me here. But I'm begging you, spare my daughter. Help me get her out!" When Garin didn't respond, Elwen went back to the window, her thoughts muddled with fear and panic. She didn't know what to do. They could stay here and choke or burn to death, or she could try to let Rose out of the window, maybe jump down after her. But what if Garin was right, what if the Mamluks had entered the city? Would they even make it to the docks? This was her fault. Her daughter was going to die. And it was her fault. Clasping her hand over her mouth, Elwen let out a hoarse sob. Her eyes, blinded by tears from the smoke, closed and she sunk down beneath the window ledge next to Rose, who was choking and retching, her face clenched in pain. Beyond the chamber, the crackle of the flames grew louder, and the door began to blacken and blister. Elwen drew her daughter into her arms and wept into her hair. "I'm so very sorry, my beautiful girl. I should have taken you away when I had the chance."

"Don't cry, Mama," said Rose, sobbing herself. Her hands came out from under the blankets and her arms went around Elwen's neck.

"I love your father so much, Rose, as much as I love you, with every last breath. I didn't want to leave him. I didn't ever want to leave him. Now he's out there fighting for us and I betrayed him so terribly. I was in pain and I was angry. I thought I wanted him to suffer too. But I didn't." Elwen's body shook. She squeezed her eyes shut against the awful pain that assailed her, inside and out. "Oh God, forgive me." Flames began to lick around the edges of the door. "Please, sweet Jesus, forgive me. Just let me see him one last time, just let me see him!"

Garin sat up groggily, Elwen's anguish puncturing his intoxicated haze. He leaned over and began to cough. His instinct for survival was pushing through the drink now, sobering him. That blank, emotionless stupor was fading, replaced by a terrible pounding in his head and an even more terrible sinking sensation that dragged at the very core of him. He felt ragged, soaked through and sickened by the depth of the bitterness and hatred inside him. Wiping his eyes, he could just make out Elwen and Rose through the pall of smoke, clinging desperately to each other. The door burst into fire, and they cried out as heat swept into the room from the inferno beyond. Garin shielded his face with his arm. Was this hell? Was this where it ended? Staring at Rose, he recalled how much joy he had received in the simple pleasure of watching her play, all those times he had spied on her, imagining that one day she would come running to him, thread her hand through his and smile. He remembered how it had felt to be good, making his mother proud, fighting for Christendom, rescuing Elwen from Bertrand and Amaury, even though it had been a charade. As the smoke billowed, he pushed himself from the bed and stumbled to Rose. Reaching down, he dragged her from Elwen's arms. She was limp and unmoving. Elwen cried out as her daughter was wrenched from her. Garin drew the blanket around Rose, covering her head and face, and bundled her over his shoulder. "I'll come back for you," he rasped at Elwen.

Elwen stared up at him. "Get her out, Garin," she breathed. "Just get Rose out."

Garin turned and ran toward the fire. He staggered back as the heat hit him, then let loose a harsh cry and barreled through it.

As he disappeared into the flames, Elwen slumped to the floor, too weak from the smoke in her lungs to hold herself up any longer. "I love you, Will Campbell," she breathed, putting her wet cheek to the warm boards. She closed her eyes, willing the words to travel whatever distance was between them, for him to hear them wherever he was. "I love you."

Simon, red-faced and panting, was approaching the house when he saw the flames darting from the upstairs windows. He halted. The Venetian quarter was well out of range of the Mamluks' siege engines, and he couldn't understand why the building, so far from the battle, was burning. The front door burst open and a figure came rushing out. It was a man and he was screaming. His hair and clothes were burning. He carried something over his shoulder in a smoldering blanket that he dropped to the ground outside. Simon shouted as he saw a body roll out of the blanket, and he raced the last few yards down the sunlit street.

It had taken him much longer than expected to get here. By the time he had found the stable master in order to excuse himself, the knights were already leaving for St. Anthony's Gate. It was some distance from the city walls to the Venetian quarter on foot and this, coupled with the barricades and guard posts he'd had to negotiate his way around, meant that more than an hour had passed since Will had ordered him to Elwen's.

Grabbing the smoking blanket off the prostrate figure in the street, whom he realized with a jolt of horror was Rose, Simon went after the burning man. His nostrils filling with the meaty, acrid stink of burning flesh and hair, he threw the blanket over the man and tackled him to the floor. Dropping to his knees, his large hands thumping down, scorched by the heat, Simon beat out the fire. When the flames had been quelled, he tore the blanket off and turned over the body, dreading what he might find. Even though most of his blond hair and beard had been burned away and his face and neck were horribly blistered, Garin was still recognizable. Simon sat back on his heels, confounded. As Garin groaned, his scalded lips opening and closing, Simon got to his feet. Forcing his gaze away, he ran to where Rose was lying in the street. The fire was now chasing itself up the side of the building to the roof.

Rose's face was stained with smoke and her hair was lank with sweat. One of her hands and part of her arm had been badly burned by the fire, the skin shriveled and raw. Her eyes were closed, her mouth slack.

"Dear God," murmured Simon, kneeling beside her and taking her good hand in his. "Rose, can you hear me? Rose?"

"Is she alive? Tell me she's alive."

Simon looked around. Garin had somehow dragged himself to his feet and was stumbling over. His arms reached out as he saw Rose and he let out a howl. "Oh God, no!" He pushed past Simon and threw himself down beside Rose, draping his burned body over hers. "Rosie!" he cried, in a ravaged voice. His head jerked round at the stunned groom. "Simon, do something," he begged. "Bring her back!"

"What happened?" demanded Simon. "Where's Elwen?"

Garin looked from Rose's limp body to the blazing house. "I tried to save them," he whispered. "I tried."

"Jesus," said Simon, staring up at the house. "Where is she?" he growled. "What room?"

But Garin had draped himself back over Rose. "I never meant to hurt you, my baby," he babbled madly. "I never meant to hurt you."

Leaving him, Simon ran to the front door. He stepped inside and was struck by a wall of heat. Shielding his face, he inched forward into the thick gray clouds that were spewing out. He could hardly see a thing. He heard a roaring sound, and as he passed the foot of the stairs, he saw the fire raging above him in the gallery, devouring the walls, boiling and rippling across the ceiling. He could hear timbers spitting and groaning, and guessed that he didn't have long. At the end of the passage was a door. Clamping his hand over his mouth and nose, Simon shouldered it open and lurched into a kitchen hazy with smoke. The place was a mess. He went forward a few feet and stumbled over something on the floor. Looking down, he saw a man lying in a pool of blood. His throat had been cut. Backing away, feeling his eyes begin to smart, Simon returned to the passage. Steeling himself, he began to climb the stairs.

Heat beat down on him like a fist from the inferno above. It forced him back, making him shout with pain and frustration. Sweat welled up and dripped down his face. He tried again, but he was choking now, faint and blind with smoke. He couldn't go on. Dropping to his knees, Simon clawed his way along the passage, out into the blessed air. He lay there gasping, until his eyes cleared and he realized that although Rose was still lying where he had left her, Garin had gone. As he crawled to her, through the tatters of smoke now drifting out across the street, he saw a rider in white coming toward him.

Will dismounted as he saw Simon crawling from the burning house. He sprinted to him, then staggered to a stop as he saw the body of his daughter, lying motionless in the street. His throat, his mouth, every part of him slammed shut at the sight of her. Terror clogged him up like cement, hardening to stone inside him. His whole being went rigid as his mind first tried to make sense of, then tried to deny, what he was seeing.

"Will!" croaked Simon, scrabbling to his feet.

Will stared dumbly at him. Then his eyes moved past him to the burning house, and now the terror was liquid, flowing through him in a freezing, rushing torrent. "Elwen!" he shouted, running to the door.

Simon went after him. "Will, no!" he shouted hoarsely. "You'll never get in." He grabbed hold of his mantle.

Will fought him savagely, yelling Elwen's name. He landed a punch on Simon's chin, breaking his hold, then plunged headlong into the building, his mouth and eyes filling instantly with smoke. It was like being suffocated. Already, the stairs were burning. Will reached them and began to climb, now gasping Elwen's name. The heat from above was incredible. He held his arm over his face, grunting as his skin seared and tightened painfully. The hairs on the back of his hand frazzled and burned away. But still he climbed, one step, then another. Above him, there was a groan and a crack as a timber in the upstairs hall collapsed. Flames and sparks swept down toward him, and he threw himself down the stairs, collapsing in a heap at the bottom as embers rained down around him. He roared hoarsely in rage, picked himself up and tried again. But the fire was winning, the heat and the smoke now forcing him to his knees. And he hated it. Hated the bright and hungry flames. Hated his own weak flesh. Hated God for making him so feeble. There were other creaking, groaning sounds as more timbers began to disintergrate above him. Then, strong arms were grabbing him, pulling him out into air.

This time, his strength recovered, Simon clung to Will determinedly. The two men pulled and pushed against each other, panting and straining with the effort. But Will, already wounded and exhausted from battle, soon slumped in Simon's arms. He howled with frustration. As he went limp, Simon dragged him back, away from the door. Inside the house, one of the floors upstairs collapsed, sending flaming timbers crashing down into the hall and clouds of smoke gusting out. The building was now engulfed in flames. Nothing, no one, could stand that heat.

The realization hit Will like a hammer, knocking all feeling out of him with the shock of it. He took hold of Simon's tunic. "What happened?"

"I don't know," gasped Simon. "The house was on fire when I got here." He looked away, unable to meet Will's murderous stare. "I tried to go in and find Elwen, but I couldn't. Garin pulled Rose out." His eyes drifted to Rose's lifeless body. "But he was too late."

Will let go of Simon's tunic. "Garin?" he said numbly. "Garin was here?"

Simon dragged his hands through his hair. "I don't know what happened, Will. There was a man in the kitchen, murdered. Garin was hurt from the fire and crying over Rose. He was saying all these things."

"What things?"

"None of it made any sense." Simon sucked in a breath. "He said something about not meaning to have hurt her. He kept calling her his baby. He was raving mad, I swear."

Will stared down at Rose. "Where is he now?" His voice was glacial, devoid of emotion. All feeling had dammed inside him. There was a wall between him and his heart.

"He was gone by the time I came back out."

Will looked to the east as he heard the frantic sound of horns lifting on the wind. A bell began ringing, then another. "They're inside," he murmured detachedly. He knelt beside Rose and took her lifeless hand in his. Closing his eyes he put his lips to her fingertips, then placed her hand gently on her chest and turned to Simon. "Go to the preceptory. I want you to take . . ." He paused, a crack starting in the wall inside him, breaking through into his voice. He swallowed it back. "Take my daughter's body. Don't you leave her, Simon, do you understand me? Don't you dare leave her."

"Where are you going?"

"To find Garin."

"You don't even know where he is!" shouted Simon, as Will crossed to the destrier.

"Garin is a rat and this ship is sinking. He'll be wherever the best chance of escape is. He'll be at the harbor."

"You wife and daughter are dead," cried Simon in a strained voice, as Will kicked his spurs into the beast's flanks. "Killing Garin won't change that. Save yourself, I beg you. Come with me!"

But Will was gone, charging down the street in a cloud of dust and fury.

THE DOCKS, ACRE, 18 MAY A.D. 1291

The call of alarm had gone up. Bells and horns and trumpets sounded. The Mamluks had broken through.

They came on camels and horses, swords flashing in the morning light, their cloaks and armor a storm of shimmering color. They came in a hail of arrows and fire, and the deafening rhythm of the kettledrums. They came on foot with mace and axe, and burning torches that they tossed onto rooftops and at the base of siege engines. They came with two centuries of slaughter and oppression in their minds, and a call for vengeance in their hearts that, for some, in the madness of battle, turned into a vicious lust for blood and butchery.

After a brief, bitter struggle, St. Anthony's Gate finally fell, the remaining Templars and Hospitallers, along with King Henry's soldiers, retreating before the surging Mamluks, now pouring through in their thousands. Jean de Villiers was wounded. Some of his knights carried him down to the last Hospitaller ship in the harbor, whilst others retreated to their fortress. On the walls, the Franks' great mangonels were burning. The Mamluks had stormed the Pisans' camp, slaughtering any man they found and, from there, entered the German quarter garrisoned by the Teutonics, where the killing continued. On the seaward side, by the Tower of the Legate, another breach soon appeared, and although the crossbowmen left to the city by King Louis and the English knights under Othon de Grandson fought the Mamluks ruthlessly, it wasn't long before they too had to retreat, leaving dead and dying comrades behind them.

Down on the harbor, it was chaos. The last few boats were being filled, and more were sailing out when the bells began to sound. Soldiers, fleeing the battle, rode down to the docks to alert all those still there that the city had fallen. They shouted to the milling, frightened women to get back inside their houses, to hide and wait out the violence. But their words were soon lost in shouts and cries of terror as those at the back began to force their way forward, trying to get to the last boats. A stampede began. Women and children screamed as they were pushed from the wall and went toppling into the water. Sailors on the boats managed to reach down and haul some of them on board, and a few women, those able to swim, plunged in to pull children back to the wall. But many more drowned in the deep water, mothers flailing and splashing, screaming for their babies as they went under. The patriarch of Jerusalem, Nicholas de Hanape, who had been waiting in the pinnace for the ships ahead to move out through the chain, had ordered the crew of the little vessel to row back to shore, much to the protests of the bishops with him. "We can save some of them," he had croaked in his aged voice. "We have to save some."

There were more people in the water now, swimming out to the retreating boats. Some of them reached the patriarch's vessel, and Nicholas himself bent over to offer his hand to help them in. But soon there were too many of them.

"Away!" shouted one of the bishops to the men at the oars. "Away!"

But the terrified refugees were scrabbling into the back of the boat or clinging desperately to the sides, not heeding the bishop's calls. One of the crewmen got pushed into the water and lost an oar. The boat began to tip with so many people hanging onto it. One of the bishops snatched an oar and began battering at their heads and hands, trying to fend them off. He was purple-faced and screaming, his eyes wild. But although some of the people he struck relinquished their hold and slipped down under the water, knuckles shattered, skulls cracked, it was too late for the pinnace. After a few moments, it lurched to the right and water gushed over the sides, and a moment after that it rolled over, tossing everyone on board into the water, trapping some of them beneath it. Nicholas de Hanape flailed and gasped for a short while, before the dark water closed over his head. The last thing he saw was Acre's skyline lit up in flames and a seething mass of citizens left behind on the dockside.

Into this turmoil rode Will. He cantered through the city gates onto the harbor wall, people scattering before him. He forced his horse on through the crush, not heeding the calls of panic all around him. His eyes roved, searching for Garin. Simon had said he had been hurt. He couldn't have gone far. The crowds at the back, near the rows of ramshackle taverns and warehouses, were thinning. People, realizing that they wouldn't make it out by boat, were heading back into the city, looking for places to hide. The fate of Tripoli was still fresh in their minds. There, the rape and slaughter had mostly been confined to the streets. Those who remained inside until the soldiers were brought to heel and the bloodlust dissipated were spared death. For many, hope now lay in the mercy of the Mamluks.

Will steered his horse through the fleeing mob, wheeling the beast to check behind him and across the water. The bay was filled with ships, all sailing out. Starting to worry that he had been wrong and that Garin hadn't come here, he began calling to people, asking if they had seen a man who had been burned. Most people rushed past, ignoring him, but one elderly man pointed east along the docks. Will saw a line of figures scrambling along the eastern mole toward a Templar ship moored in the outer harbor. One, a lone man, was at the back, stumbling along. Digging his spurs into his horse, Will cantered across the harbor to the point where the mole stretched out from the shore. The mole, bitten by the windswept sea, was ancient and crumbled, some sections so eroded that the sea washed across them. Leaving his horse on the harbor, Will raced along the mole, splashing through the blue water that rushed and dragged over the stones. To his left, the open sea churned, deep and dark; to his right, the outer harbor was calm and green. His feet slipped and slid on the slimy stones, threatening to plunge him into the black, rolling waves. "Garin!" he shouted, as he gained on the figure. He was gratified to see the man jerk around at the call.

Garin's face was badly burned, and he clutched his hands to his chest as if they pained him. His tunic had been incinerated; just a few ragged scraps of it still fluttered about his chest, and some of the material had been burned into his skin in black, scorched patches. He took a few stuttering steps back as he saw Will, then turned and ran, following the line of women, all heading for the Templar ship with its renegade captain. Will went after him, leaping from one exposed rock to the next. Garin, throwing a glance over his shoulder, saw that he wasn't going to make it. He turned and drew his dagger as Will wrenched free his sword.

The two of them staggered to a halt, the hungry sea gnawing the rocks between them.

Garin's face was clenched with pain, but his expression, although defiant, held a look of resignation. "Let us do what must be done then," he called, his voice thick with pain and drink.

Will felt a decade's worth of hatred explode inside him at the sight of Garin. "What did you do? What did you do to my daughter?"

"It's always *yours*, isn't it," Garin shouted back. "Your wife, your daughter, your place in the Temple."

"*What did you do?*"

Garin stepped back as Will came forward. "But Rose wasn't your daughter." Will stopped, his sword frozen in midair. "Oh, Elwen said she didn't know for sure. But I knew." Garin jabbed at his chest. "I *knew* she was mine."

"You're lying. Why are you saying this?"

"Because it's the truth and there's no one else to tell it to you now. You need to know what I've lost. You need to understand." Will was shaking his head. "Why do you think you spent all those years in her bed and she only bore you one child?" demanded Garin. "It doesn't make sense, does it?"

"Elwen would never ... she would never ..." But the words gummed up in Will's mouth and he found he couldn't say them. Behind them in the city, something exploded, sending a shower of rock and flames into the sky. Screams drifted from the harbor. Neither of them looked around. "When?" said Will frigidly. "When did it happen?"

"Before you went to Mecca. Elwen came to me. There was no seduction, no pursuit on my part. She came to me."

"And you took her," breathed Will.

"Why do you think you can have everything?" Garin shouted suddenly. "What makes you so much better than everyone else? So much more worthy? You had a place in the Temple, but that wasn't enough, was it? You had to have more, so when Everard recruited you, you forsook your oaths and joined the Brethren. But even that wasn't enough. You deceived the Brethren to go after Baybars, betrayed the grand master when he tried to take the Black Stone, even after he made you commander, then you deceived everyone to be with a woman you treated like a whore!"

Will was staring at him, hardly hearing all the words. "How do you know of the Stone?"

"Elwen told me about it. She was scared for you." Garin nodded as Will's face filled up with shock and pain. "She did love you, I won't deny that. She only lay with me once. But that was no excuse for what she did, shutting me out of Rose's life like I was nothing, like I had no right to know my own child! God *damn* her!" He thrust the dagger toward Will. "I could have taken care of them. You wouldn't have given them a real life, a good life."

Will threw back his head and laughed, tears of rage and grief and disbelief burning from his eyes. "And you would have?" he seethed. "You? Garin de Lyons? Too feeble to stand up to his uncle, too weak to fend off Rook, too foolish to make a life for himself, too useless to be anything but a drunken whoreson. You're envious of everything I have, Garin. You always have been, ever since we were children, and so you took it from me." Will strode toward him. "You took the Book of the Grail. You took my virtue in that brothel. You took my wife and my child."

"No, Will," said Garin in a low voice, standing his ground. "I took much more than that."

Will halted.

"Did you ever wonder why you were saved in the desert when the Bedouin caught you? Did you ever wonder who stayed that man's hand?" Garin frowned and looked down into the water that washed around his feet. "Because I wondered myself, for years afterwards, why I spared you, why I shouted at Bertrand to leave you be. I'm still not sure why I did. Perhaps some old reflex of loyalty." He looked back at Will. "Or perhaps it was because I didn't want you to die not knowing the face of your betrayer. In my mind, when I killed you, you always knew it was me. You were always looking right into my eyes when it happened." Garin laughed a little. "You see, Will, I do have some honor, which is why I want you to know that Rook was never my master. He was as much of a puppet as I was. It was always Edward pulling the strings." Garin laughed again, harder and bitter. "And I dangled limply in his grip, whilst all my dreams faded and died around me, and all yours came true. Yes, Will, I am envious of your life, a life where forgiveness and hope have always existed, a life where all men aren't brutal and cruel, a life filled with things you chose, not things forced upon you. Do you know, the only time I felt truly free was when Everard had me imprisoned? When I came to Acre to get Edward his money and I found out about the Black Stone and your involvement, I knew he could use it to his advantage and so I went after it myself. I had been Edward's puppet for so long that I danced to his tune even when he wasn't controlling me. Then I saw Rose and his hold on me broke."

Will was stunned into total silence. He felt crushed by the revelations, by the depth of Garin's betrayal, felt his whole world starting to crack under the enormous weight of it. The emotionless wall that had slammed up inside him at the sight of his daughter's body was ripped down in the turmoil inside him and he gave a strangled roar of anguish.

As Will came the last few feet toward him, Garin flung the dagger into the waves. "You know what it feels like now, don't you?" he cried. "You know how I've felt my whole life! Used and betrayed!" Dropping to his knees, the water spraying up around him, he spread his arms wide. His blistered lips cracked apart in a smile. "Now you understand."

"Get up!" Will yelled at him, flicking the sword at his throat. "Get up, you *bastard*!"

"It's over, Will. Don't you see? It's over for both of us. We've lost everything. All we can do is die!"

"Get up!"

"Do it. I want it over. I want it ended."

Will grabbed Garin's tattered tunic. His tears and his spit spattered Garin's face as he screamed at him. The sea washed around them, soaking them, its salt in their mouths.

Garin caught hold of Will's wrist. "Do it!" he yelled, turning the sword toward him. *"Do it!"*

Suddenly, Will pulled himself free. Then, still clutching his sword, he began to walk away.

Garin stared after him, slack-jawed. "Where are you going?" he shouted, struggling to his feet. "Finish it!" He stood there, his legs weak as he watched Will go; then he turned and began to walk, slowly at first, then faster, the Templar ship filling his vision. Over the lashing of the waves, he didn't hear the footsteps charging up behind him.

Garin felt a pain in his back, a sensation like being struck, then a searing agony that ripped right through him, turning his insides to liquid fire. Looking down, he saw a sword point protruding from his stomach. Then it was gone, wrenched back through him, twisting as it went, splaying him apart inside, splicing organs and muscles with one silver stroke. He half-turned, then fell to his knees. Clutching the ragged hole in his stomach, he collapsed sideways onto the rocks and rolled onto his back, arching and squirming. Looking up, through the blinding pain, he saw Will standing above him like some avenging angel, dressed in white, his sword drenched in blood, the sun and the city on fire blazing behind him. He opened his mouth to draw in a breath, but it filled with seawater as a wave curled over him. He went with it, tumbling off the mole into the deep green water of the harbor. For a few moments, he hung there, buoyed up by the waves, then slowly, struggling weakly, he went under. As he sank, Garin saw Will on the surface watching him, his form rippling, distorted. Then the sea filled his lungs and he was dragged down into blackness.

Will made it to the end of the mole and halfway across the harbor, before he slumped to his knees, his father's sword clattering down beside him. Bending over, he vomited onto the stone, ignoring the people who raced past him, still trying to get to the boats, still trying to find safety. His bile was black with the smoke he had inhaled in the battle, but it felt like all the poison inside him was coming out, as if, unable to stomach Garin's words, they was pouring back out of him; the ugly truth. For it was true. He could feel it. It all made a horrible, dreadful sense. He was a fool, a blind fool. He had wasted his life in pursuit of a dream. Now that dream was burning up around him and he had been left with nothing. His father, Everard, Kalawun, all were gone, along with all hope for peace. He could have lived with that, could have lived with Garin's betrayal even, if only his wife and daughter had been spared. But they were gone too, turned to ashes along with everything else.

Suddenly, he threw back his head and roared at the sky. *"What more do you want from me, you bastard?"* he screamed at God, whom he could feel watching him emotionlessly from somewhere in that endless blue, like a cat with a mouse it has played with and now grown bored of. *"What more?"*

"Sir William?"

Will, swaying on his hands, spittle trailing from his mouth, stared up at the voice. A stooped, bearded man was in front of him, bending down toward him. It was the old rabbi, Everard's friend. "Elias," he said thickly.

"Are you hurt?" questioned the old man, offering his hand. "Let me help you."

Will sat back on his heels. "No," he breathed, pushing away Elias's hand. "No." He got to his feet with effort and picked up his sword.

"We came from the Jewish quarter, looking for a ship, but there are none," said Elias, gesturing anxiously to a group of people huddled together behind him; there were a few men, but most of them were women and children. "What can we do?"

"I don't know," said Will, wiping his mouth with the back of his hand. "I don't know."

Screams sounded from the city gates. Mamluk riders were storming onto the harbor, cutting through the last citizens gathered there. In desperation, people started throwing themselves into the water, trying to get away from the soldiers and their blades. Elias clutched Will's arm. Will saw a child go down, trampled by the Mamluks' horses, saw a sword plunge into the belly of a pregnant woman, saw an old woman's skull crushed by a spiked mace. Then he saw the men and women in front of him, wailing and crying and clinging to one another, smelled urine as children wet themselves, felt Elias's hand clamped in terror around his arm. And something stirred in him, firing his deadened senses. "That way," he said to Elias, pointing across the harbor to the entrance of the underground tunnel that ran under the city to the preceptory. "Go!" he urged the rabbi, thrusting him forward. Will strode to the group of Jews. "Move!" he shouted at them.

Confused and terror-stricken, they needed little encouragement. Will herded them across the harbor wall, driving them on like sheep. As they saw the group, a few Mamluks broke off and thundered toward them. Will went to meet the Mamluks, swinging his sword, two-handed, through the neck of one of the horses. He slashed through the back legs of another, crippling it, then stabbed down into the throat of its fallen rider. "Go!" he yelled at the fleeing citizens, ducking as an arrow shot past him. Another struck his back, but bounced off his chain mail. The entrance to the tunnel loomed up ahead. Most of the Mamluks were busy with the slaughter of the stampeding crowds around the gates. Will fought off another soldier, then led the frightened group into the tunnel. Knights were there, guarding the entrance. They ushered Will and the citizens through.

It wasn't until they climbed up into the preceptory's sunlit courtyard, twenty minutes later, that Will realized just how many he had managed to save. There was around sixty of them, all white-faced and shaking, but all alive. And they weren't the only survivors. The Temple, whose indomitable walls had shut out the world for so long, had opened its gates to Acre's citizens. Men and women, rich and poor, they thronged the courtyard in a fretful mass. There were thousands of them.

"Will!"

He looked around as his name was called, but couldn't see anyone he recognized.

"Will!"

He turned in a circle, staring about him, until he saw someone pushing through the crowds to his right. It was Simon. In his arms was a girl. Her gold hair hung loose around her shoulders; her face was sooty, eyes blinking bewilderedly around her. It was Rose. She cried out as she saw him and stretched out her arms, one of which was blistered and red. Will rushed to her, sweeping her up.

"She woke after you'd gone," Simon was saying. "I was carrying her and she started speaking. Gave me the fright of my life!"

But Will wasn't listening. Holding his daughter to him, feeling her body shuddering with grief against his, he sank to the ground.

48

The Temple, Acre

The tunnel was dark and dank. The splashing of feet through the water-logged ground echoed off the walls, along with the whisper of many breaths and the muffled crying of children. Torchlight flickered agitatedly in the air, which smelled of salt and dampness. Over two hundred people moved in the pool of light. Many were dazed, some were quietly weeping, others were grim and silent.

At the head strode Theobald Gaudin with several officials and the seneschal. Behind them, twelve sergeants pulled handcarts filled with the Temple's treasury and the order's documents. Coins, holy relics, jewels, golden chalices, rings and books—all were stacked into the carts. Following the treasury were forty-two knights, twenty-seven sergeants and a few priests. Bringing up the rear were over one hundred of Acre's refugees. In this group, Will walked in silence, staring rigidly ahead. To his left was Robert, a freshly stitched scar carving a line across his forehead. To his right was Simon. The groom's broad face was white, but he moved staunchly at Will's side, glancing at him every so often, then around at Rose, walking behind with Elias, clutching the rabbi's hand and staring after her father. Her burned arm had been treated with a poultice and bandaged with fresh linen, but her face was smudged with dirt and she still wore the singed traveling cloak she had been wearing when Garin pulled her from the house. She had hardly spoken a word since then.

Will saw Simon's expression and, reading his thoughts, glanced back at Rose. He met her stunned eyes briefly, then fixed his eyes forward. It would change, he knew, in time. But after the overwhelming relief of finding Rose alive, he had discovered that when he now looked at her all he saw was Elwen, her beautiful face a screaming mask of fear and agony as she burned alive, over and over, in his mind. The image threatened to tear him apart, and there had simply been too much to do for him to be able to let it. And so, his grief locked inside him, he had left his daughter in Elias's care and battled on, hardly eating or sleeping.

It was seven days since Acre had fallen. The Crusaders' capital was gone and with it the dream of a Christian Holy Land. The slaughter, which had begun as the Mamluks stormed through breaches in the walls, had continued for the rest of that day, and by the time the sun set, a shroud of black smoke hung over the city and the streets were littered with the dead. Acre had become a charnel house, a stinking open grave filled with children, lying twisted and bloodied, men hacked down as they ran, women viciously raped then disemboweled or beheaded. All along the walls and outside the gates and entrances of towers, the corpses of knights and soldiers lay sprawled across one another, along with many Mamluk, Bedouin and Syrian troops. Banners and flags, some still clutched by their bearers, fluttered limply over the piles of dead. Here and there, the wounded groaned and stirred, trying to pull themselves through the quagmire of blood and death before the Mamluk patrols came.

As evening had fallen on the first day, carrion birds gathered in the skies, as through the smoking ruins, survivors flitted, trying to find somewhere to hide from the roaming soldiers. Sultan Khalil had managed to bring most of his army to order, but some men, mercenaries and undisciplined marauders, were still crazed from the killing, and for them the rape and the butchery continued. Others sought plunder, and palazzos, churches and stores were raided for treasure. As Khalil set up his headquarters in the royal palace and his generals moved to rein in their men, squadrons were sent out to round up the survivors. Only wealthy men or those of rank were spared the sword. The women and children were taken as slaves, gathered up in their thousands. Only three buildings withstood these systematic raids: the strongholds of the Hospitallers, the Teutonics and the Templars, all of which were crammed with refugees.

The sounds of killing had carried on into the night. Will, standing at the window in the grand master's chambers, listened to them grimly for a time, before he heard Zaccaria move behind him and a priest begin to mutter, and turned to see the grand master drag in his last breath. Guillaume hadn't spoken since he had been brought into his solar, still bleeding profusely from his wound, except to ask how the city was faring. When Theobald Gaudin told him it was lost, the grand master sunk back onto his pillows. A silent tear slipped from the corner of his eye as he lay there, hearing the massacre continuing beyond the walls. Guillaume de Beaujeu was buried the next morning in the preceptory's orchard. Zaccaria wasn't at his funeral. After the grand master's passing, he led a small company of knights, including some Hospitallers who had taken refuge in the preceptory, out of the gates. According to the only survivor, they stormed several Mamluk companies, killing many, Zaccaria and the Templars yelling the grand master's name as they cut a brutal path through the soldiers.

A day after this, the fortresses of the Hospitallers and Teutonics had capitulated, the knights on the ramparts observing the *nakkabun* being drawn up, ready to begin mining the walls. They appealed to Khalil for amnesty and the sultan agreed. The Temple held out, with some of the refugees within its walls being taken each night through the underground tunnel to ships returning from Cyprus. The Mamluks had no way of stopping these evacuations. They had no ships of their own, and the Franks' vessels, safely at anchor in the bay, were armed with trebuchets that would sling stones at any Mamluk patrols that ventured onto the harbor. Unable to counter them, Khalil pulled most of his forces back from the docks, unconcerned by the escape of a few hundred civilians. Inside the preceptory, the evacuations were happening all too slowly. They had nowhere near enough provisions for this many people, and with the death of the grand master creating a general sense of despair, the Templars finally agreed to surrender. Before they sent word to Khalil, Marshal Peter de Sevrey ordered Theobald Gaudin to leave with the order's treasury on the one Templar ship that remained in the harbor.

As the knights approached the entrance to the tunnel, the gate was opened. Some of the men went ahead to secure the harbor wall. The few Mamluks on patrol there were killed, quickly and quietly, and the sergeants began to move out, hauling the handcarts across toward the mole, followed by the refugees. In the bay, the lanterns on the Templar galley, which was called the *Phoenix*, glowed like tiny beacons, guiding them. Whilst the other knights filed out, swords drawn, Will paused in the entrance.

The seneschal was standing there with several men who had helped convey the treasury. His hard gaze turned on Will. "What are you waiting for, Commander?"

"Come with us," murmured Will.

The seneschal jerked his head at the men. "Start making your way back," he ordered them. When they were out of earshot, he looked at Will. "My place is here, with the marshal and the others."

"You'll be killed or imprisoned."

"I am old," said the seneschal gruffly, "and I have lived most of my life in this city. I would call nowhere else home. My time has passed. Yours has not. You still have work to do."

"It is over," said Will flatly. "We have lost the Holy Land. The Anima Templi no longer has a purpose."

The seneschal's eyes narrowed. "You are wrong," he replied sternly. "We may have lost our base in the East, but that is only land, mere sand and stone. We are more than that. The Temple still exists, and without a master it is rud-

derless. This is a dangerous time. Now, more than ever, you must work to safeguard the order from those who would seek to use its resources for their own
ends. You must work to preserve the peace and the aims of the Brethren, if not
in Outremer then in the West, for its kingdoms are as war-torn as this one.
There are men on those thrones, Commander, unscrupulous men, hungry for
power, who would jeopardize entire nations to satisfy their desire for supremacy. It will be your task, as it was here, to preserve the balance and to safeguard
those of all races and faiths who would be destroyed by the greed and ignorance
of others." The seneschal's voice was rough. "That is your purpose and that is
why it was made certain that you and Robert de Paris were on this ship. Others
stayed behind in your place, Campbell. Do not let our sacrifice be in vain." He
took hold of the gate. "Now, go."

Leaving the seneschal in the tunnel to haul the gate closed behind him, Will
stepped out into the cool night air. The rush of the waves was loud in his ears.

OUTSIDE THE WALLS OF THE TEMPLE, ACRE, 28 MAY A.D. 1291

Sultan al-Ashraf Khalil stood in silence and watched as the lines of captives were
led out of the ruins of the Temple. The evening sun cast a ruddy light over the
crumbled walls, which had been undermined and had collapsed that afternoon.
Into the breach, two thousand Mamluks had ridden into battle with the last
remaining knights and soldiers inside. But the walls had been destabilized by
the mining, and half of the landward side of the fortifications came down in a
roar of dust and stone, crushing Christians and Muslims alike beneath the piles
of rubble. It wasn't supposed to have been this way, but negotiations with the
Templars had broken down and Khalil had decided to force his way into the
compound.

With the fall of the Temple, the battle was ended. Acre, first captured by the
Crusaders two hundred years ago, was back in Muslim hands. Khalil had sent
one of his generals down to Tyre to see that it too was taken, although from the
reports sent back it seemed few citizens were there to witness its demise, for
many had put to sea, seeing the vast pall of smoke rising from Acre on the horizon. Sidon, Beirut and Haifa, the Franks' last strongholds, would soon share
Acre's fate and then, at last, it would be over. No more would the Western invaders hold sway in Palestine; no more would they threaten them or take their
lands, turning mosques into churches and Muslim citizens into slaves. Khalil
was a conqueror, victorious. The men of his army praised him as a hero, as van-
quisher of the infidel, as God's own sword. Khalil accepted their praise without

comment. In the days to come he would receive it with gratitude and with pride, for he was glad that it had finally ended and that he had done what he had set out to do. Now that the Western Christians were gone, the Mamluks could turn their full attention to the Mongols without worry that the two forces would ally. Khalil had followed in the footsteps of Baybars and Saladin, excising the last of the poison from the wound first carved by the Franks two centuries before. He had liberated his people. It was over. It was finally over.

But in the grave that was Acre, in the bloody streets that stank of death, it was hard to be glad. And so, al-Ashraf Khalil turned from the trudging lines of captives and walked grimly away from the ruins of the Temple, his face lit by the setting sun.

THE *PHOENIX*, THE MEDITERRANEAN, 30 MAY A.D. 1291

Will stood on the deck of the *Phoenix*, the blue sea stretching before him. Behind him men, women and children huddled on the decks. After days of silence, the murmur of conversation had begun again. People had started to eat, to tend to wounds and comfort their neighbors, and the atmosphere, although still subdued, had lifted a little. It was, Will knew, the way of things. Despite what they had been through, they had survived. The only thing they could do now was to go on surviving, to go on living, no matter what they had lost. He looked down at his open palm, at the gold ring lying in it, remembering Elwen's cool skin as she had placed it on his finger, pushing it gently over the ridge of his knuckle. He had worn it thereafter on the chain with the St. George pendant. The pain, both of her passing and her betrayal, was deep within him. He could feel the enormity of it, struggling to break free and engulf him. But he hadn't let it. He couldn't.

Three days ago, he had sat with Rose at the stern, ignoring the curious glances of some of the knights, and asked her to tell him what had happened at the house. It took his daughter a long time to say the words, and they were torturous for her to utter, even the parts she hadn't understood. But keeping his tone calm and composed, Will eventually coaxed the truth out of her. Now he knew the extent of Garin's treachery, from the attack on Honfleur to the attempted taking of the Black Stone. But, more than that, he knew the face of his enemy.

Garin had been a pawn, a weak, controlled pawn. It was King Edward who was the real traitor, the wolf in the fold and instigator of all his woes. He had been their guardian. He had become their enemy.

The seneschal was right. The Anima Templi's work was not finished, not by a long way. He was its head, and as all those before him, he had a duty to defend it from harm. That was why Everard had chosen him. He would make certain the Brethren would go on. But, in order to do that, *he* had to go on. Lifting the gold ring to his lips, Will kissed the cool metal tenderly, then flung it to the sea. It went spinning over and over, flashing in the light, before it hit the water and disappeared beneath the waves. Will felt someone move up alongside him.

"Rose is awake," said Simon, resting his arms on the side of the galley. "She's down in the hold asking for you."

"I'll be there in a moment."

Simon nodded and clasped his shoulder before moving off.

Will drew in a breath, and with it his determination strengthened. He still had Rose. Whether she was his daughter or not, he loved her. He had Simon and Robert, and somewhere, back in Scotland, he had family. The crumpled letter from his sister, Ysenda, was folded in his pouch, salvaged from the preceptory. He was not alone. His mind filling with memories of moors and rain, Will turned his back on the East and looked west toward home. Toward revenge.

Author's Note

I endeavored to stay as close to the history as possible in the writing of this novel, but as history doesn't always work as neatly or conveniently as one might like I've inevitably had to apply a certain amount of artistic license. Dates, in particular, can often prove problematic as you try to weave a fictional story and characters through real events in the narrative, and sometimes it becomes necessary for details to be tweaked for the sake of the plot and ease of reading. For instance, by this point in the Templars' history the office of seneschal had been abandoned, but as the duties of this post were taken over by an official who, along with Theobald Gaudin, was also entitled grand commander, I have resurrected it to avoid unnecessary confusion. The town of al-Bira was attacked by the Mongols in the winter of 1275 and the siege was actually raised before Baybars' force reached it. King Hugh III initially retired to Tyre after leaving Acre rather than going straight to Cyprus, and it would have taken a little longer than I have described for news to reach the city that Charles d'Anjou had bought the rights to the throne of Jerusalem. The Islamic month of Muharram occurred in June of 1277 rather than April, and Tripoli, which was besieged at the end of March 1289, in reality took almost a month to fall to Kalawun's forces.

My version of Baybars' demise is fictitious; Baraka Khan couldn't have poisoned his father, for he remained in Cairo when Baybars left on the Anatolian campaign, but the sultan's death has nonetheless been the subject of much speculation. Several chroniclers believe Baybars died after drinking poisoned kumiz. These accounts suggest that astrologers warned him of a lunar eclipse that would herald the death of a king and that to safeguard himself he decided to poison another ruler, an Ayyubid prince who had aided him against the Mongols at Albistan, but who thereafter had displeased him. The accounts vary in detail, but tend to agree that Baybars drank the poisoned cup he had prepared for the prince by mistake. Other sources say he died from a wound sustained on campaign, others still that he succumbed to a sickness. Whatever happened, Baybars did not die instantly, but after thirteen days of ill health. For those who wish to discover more information on historical events detailed in the narrative, I have enclosed a bibliography for further reading.

The fall of Acre in 1291 to the Muslim forces under Sultan al-Ashraf Khalil heralded the ending of the Crusades first preached by Pope Urban II in France two hundred years earlier. Theobald Gaudin, the Temple's grand commander, led the knights who sailed with him out of Acre down the coast to their stronghold at Sidon, where he was elected grand master. Here, the surviving Templars remained for a month, but were forced to withdraw when the Mamluks arrived. Gaudin sailed for Cyprus with the Order's treasury, leaving only a small group of knights based on an island two miles off the coast. The Templars would maintain a garrison here for twelve years, but the remaining Frankish settlements in the Holy Land would be captured by the Mamluks over the following months.

Acre was virtually abandoned and left in ruins for years, while many of the citizens who survived the siege disappeared into the prisons, labor camps and harems of the Mamluks. Some captives, including knights from the military orders, were ransomed, others converted to Islam. Decades later, a Western pilgrim in the Holy Land saw Templars working as woodcutters near the Dead Sea.

Sultan Khalil did not long survive his victory over the Franks. At the end of 1293 he was assassinated by his own generals, shortly after proclaiming a jihad against the Mongols. He was succeeded by his brother, Kalawun's young son, al-Nasir Muhammad. The Mamluk Sultanate continued to hold sway in the Middle East until it was overthrown by the Ottoman Turks in 1517.

In the West, desire to win back territory lost to the Muslim forces didn't die immediately with the fall of Acre, but although later planned Crusades to recapture the Holy Land proved unsuccessful the echoes of this bloody period in the world's history would resonate painfully on both sides of the sea for centuries to come. We are still feeling those echoes today.

—Robyn Young
Brighton, March 2007

Character List

(* denotes real figures from history)

*ABAGA: Mongol ilkhan of Persia (1265–1282)
AISHA: daughter of Kalawun, married to Baraka Khan
*AL-ASHRAF KHALIL: son of Kalawun; sultan of Egypt and Syria (1290–1293)
ALESSANDRO: Knight Templar, personal guard to Guillaume de Beaujeu
AMAURY: royal guard under Hugh III
ANDREAS DI PAOLO: Venetian silk merchant
ANGELO VITTURI: Venetian slave trader, son of Venerio
*ARGHUN: son of Abaga, installed as ilkhan in 1284
*ARMAND DE PÉRIGORD: grand master of the Temple (1232–1244)
*AS-SALIH ALI: son of Kalawun

*BALIAN OF IBELIN: Hugh III's bailli in Acre
*BARAKA KHAN: son of Baybars, married to Aisha; sultan of Egypt and Syria (1277–1279)
*BAYBARS BUNDUKDARI: sultan of Egypt and Syria (1260–1277)
BERTRAND: royal guard under Hugh III

CARLO: Knight Templar, personal guard to Guillaume de Beaujeu
CATARINA: daughter of Andreas
CECELIA DE LYONS: mother of Garin
*CHARLES D'ANJOU: brother of Louis IX; king of Sicily and Naples (1266–1285), king of Jerusalem (1277–1285)
CONRADT VON BREMEN: German horse dealer

DAWUD: Mamluk amir

*EDWARD I: king of England (1272–1307)
ELIAS: rabbi and bookseller
ELWEN: Will's lover
EVERARD DE TROYES: Templar priest and head of the Anima Templi

FATIMA: wife of Baybars, mother of Salamish
FRANCESCO: Knight Templar, personal guard to Guillaume de Beaujeu

GARIN DE LYONS: former Knight Templar in the service of Edward I
*GÉRARD DE RIDEFORT: grand master of the Temple (1185–1189)
*GREGORY X: Pope (1271–1276)
GUIDO SORANZO: Genoese shipbuilder
*GUILLAUME DE BEAUJEU: grand master of the Temple (1273–1291)
GUY: royal advisor to Hugh III

HASAN: former comrade of Everard de Troyes, died in Paris in 1266
*HENRY II: son of Hugh III; king of Cyprus (1285–1324), king of Jerusalem (1286–1291)
*HUGH III: king of Cyprus (1267–1284), king of Jerusalem (1269–1277)
*HUGUES DE PAIRAUD: visitor of the Temple, based in Paris

IDRIS: a Syrian Assassin
ISABEL: Will's mother
ISHANDIYAR: Mamluk amir

JACQUES DE LYONS: Knight Templar and uncle of Garin, former member of the Anima Templi, died at Honfleur in 1260
JAMES CAMPBELL: Knight Templar and father of Will, former member of the Anima Templi, died at Safed in 1266
*JEAN DE VILLIERS: Grand Master of the Hospital (1284–1293)

*KALAWUN AL-ALFI: Mamluk amir, Baybars's chief lieutenant and father-in-law to Baraka Khan; sultan of Egypt and Syria (1280–1290)
KAYSAN: a mercenary, hired to protect pilgrims in Arabia
*KHADIR: Baybars's soothsayer

*LOUIS IX: king of France (1226–1270)
LUCA: Genoese boy, brother of Marco
*LUCIA: countess of Tripoli

MAHMUD: Mamluk amir
MARCO: Genoese man, brother of Luca
*MARIA OF ANTIOCH: cousin of Hugh III and claimant to Jerusalem
MARY: Will's sister, died in Scotland when they were children
MICHAEL PISANI: Pisan arms merchant

NASIR: Kalawun's comrade and officer in the Mansuriyya
*NICHOLAS IV: pope (1288–1292)
*NICHOLAS DE HANAPE: patriarch of Jerusalem
NIZAM: wife of Baybars, mother of Baraka Khan

OMAR: former comrade of Baybars, died in an attack by Assassins in 1271

OWEIN AP GWYN: uncle of Elwen and Will's former master, died at Honfleur in 1260

*****PETER DE SEVREY:** marshal of the Temple

*****PHILIPPE IV:** king of France (1285–1314)

*****RABBAN SAUMA:** ambassador to Ilkhan Arghun

RENAUD DE TOURS: French armorer

ROBERT DE PARIS: Knight Templar

*****ROBERT DE SABLÉ:** grand master of the Temple (1191–1193)

*****ROGER DE SAN SEVERINO:** Charles d'Anjou's bailli in Acre

ROOK: formerly in the service of Edward I, was killed by Garin in 1268

ROSE: daughter of Will and Elwen

*****SALAMISH:** son of Baybars

SCLAVO: Genoese landlord

SENESCHAL, THE: official of the Temple and member of the Anima Templi

SIMON TANNER: Templar sergeant

*****TATAWUN:** Mongol commander

*****THEOBALD GAUDIN:** grand commander of the Temple

USAMAH: Mamluk amir

VELASCO: Templar priest and member of the Anima Templi

VENERIO VITTURI: Venetian slave trader, father of Angelo

WILL CAMPELL: commander in the Knights Templar and member of the Anima Templi

YSENDA: Will's youngest sister

YUSUF: Mamluk amir

ZACCARIA: Knight Templar, personal guard to Guillaume de Beaujeu

Glossary

ACRE: a city on the coast of Palestine, conquered by the Arabs in AD 640. It was captured by the Crusaders in the early twelfth century and became the principal port of the new Latin Kingdom of Jerusalem. Acre was ruled by a king, but by the mid-thirteenth century royal authority was disputed by the local Frankish nobles and from this time the city, with its twenty-seven separate quarters, was largely governed oligarchically.

AMIR: Arabic for *commander*, also used as a title for some rulers.

ANIMA TEMPLI: Latin for "Soul of the Temple." A fictional group within the Knights Templar founded by Grand Master Robert de Sablé in 1191 in the aftermath of the Battle of Hattin to protect the Temple from corruption. It is formed of twelve Brethren, drawn from the order's ranks, with a Guardian to mediate during disputes, and is dedicated to achieving reconciliation among the Christian, Muslim and Jewish faiths.

ASSASSINS: an extremist sect founded in Persia in the eleventh century. The Assassins were adherents of the Ismaili division of the Shia Muslim faith and, over the following years, spread to several countries, including Syria. Here, under their most famous leader, Sinan, "the Old Man of the Mountain," they formed an independent state, where they retained control until they were eventually subsumed into the Mamluk territories controlled by Baybars.

AYYUBIDS: dynastic rulers of Egypt and Syria during the twelfth and thirteenth centuries, responsible for the creation of the Mamluk (slave) army. Saladin was of this line and during his reign the Ayyubids achieved the height of their power. The last Ayyubid was Turanshah, who was killed by Baybars under the orders of the Mamluk commander Aibek, ending the Ayyubid dynasty and beginning the reign of the Mamluks.

BAILLI: the representative of a king or other ruler.

BERNARD DE CLAIRVAUX, ST.: (1090–1153) abbot and founder of the Cistercian monastery at Clairvaux in France. An early supporter of the Templars, Bernard aided the order in the creation of their Rule.

BEZANT: a gold coin of the medieval period, first minted in Byzantium.

BLACK STONE: in Arabic "al-Hajar al-Aswad," a sacred relic set in the eastern corner of the Ka'ba in Mecca, held in place by a silver band and kissed or touched by Muslims during the rites of pilgrimage. In 929, the Karmatians (Ismaili Shias) took possession of the Black Stone and carried it out of Mecca, effectively holding it ransom until its restoration twenty-two years later.

CRUSADES: a European movement of the medieval period, spurred by economic, religious and political ideals. The First Crusade was preached in 1095 by Pope Urban II at Clermont in France. The call to Crusade came initially as a response to appeals from the Greek emperor in Byzantium whose domains were being invaded by the Seljuk Turks, who had captured Jerusalem in 1071. The Roman and Greek Orthodox Churches had been divided since 1054 and Urban saw in this plea the chance to reunite the two Churches and, in so doing, gain Catholicism a firmer hold over the Eastern world. Urban's goal was achieved only briefly and imperfectly in the wake of the Fourth Crusade of 1204. Over two centuries, more than eleven Crusades to the Holy Land were launched from Europe's shores.

DESTRIER: Old French for *war horse.*

ENCEINTE: fortifications enclosing a castle.

FALCHION: a short sword with a curved edge, primarily used by infantry.

FRANKS: in the Middle East the term Franks (*al-Firinjah*) referred to Western Christians. In the West it was the name of the Germanic tribe that conquered Gaul in the sixth century, which thereafter became known as France.

GRAIL ROMANCE: a popular cycle of romances prevalent during the twelfth and thirteenth centuries, the first of which was *Joseph d'Arimathie* written by Robert de Borron at the end of the twelfth century. From this time, the Grail, the concept of which is thought to be derived from pre-Christian mythology, was Christianized and adopted into the Arthurian legend, made famous by the twelfth-century French poet Chrétien de Troyes, whose work influenced later writers such as Malory and Tennyson. The following century saw many more takes on the Grail theme, including Wolfram von Eschenbach's *Parzival,* which inspired Wagner's opera. Romances were courtly stories, usually composed in verse in the vernacular, that combined historical, mythical and religious themes.

GRAND MASTER: head of a military order. The grand master of the Templars was elected for life by a council of Templar officials and until the end of the Crusades was based at the Order's headquarters in Palestine.

GREAVES: armor worn to protect the shins.

GREEK FIRE: invented in Byzantium in the seventh century, Greek fire was a mixture of pitch, sulfur and naphtha that was used in warfare to set fire to ships and fortifications.

HAJJ: the annual pilgrimage to Mecca that Muslims are required to make at least once in their lives, during Dhu al-Hijja, the twelfth month of the Islamic calendar (a lunar calendar, meaning months aren't static). Another pilgrimage, known as the Umra, can be made at any time.

HAUBERK: a shirt of mail or scale armor.

JIHAD: meaning "to strive," *jihad* can be interpreted in both a physical and spiritual sense. In the physical it means holy war in the defense of and for the spread of Islam; in the spiritual it is the inner struggle of individual Muslims against worldly temptations.

KA'BA: meaning "cube" in Arabic, a stone building situated in the center of the Great Mosque in Mecca, toward which Muslims face during prayer. It is believed to have been a pre-Islamic holy place for Arabian tribes, but later became central to Muslim worship when Muhammad set the Black Stone into the eastern corner of the shrine and rededicated it to Islam. Muslim tradition states that it was built by Adam, then rebuilt by

Abraham and Ishmael. It is Islam's holiest shrine, around which Muslims circle during pilgrimage.

KAFFIYEH: head scarf worn by Arab men.

KINGDOM OF JERUSALEM: the Latin Kingdom of Jerusalem was founded in 1099, following the capture of Jerusalem by the First Crusade. Its first ruler was Godfrey de Bouillon, a Frankish count. Jerusalem itself became the new Crusader capital, but it was lost and regained several times over the following two centuries until it was finally reclaimed by the Muslims in 1244, whereupon the city of Acre became the Crusaders' capital. Three other states were formed by the Western invaders during the early Crusades: the Principality of Antioch and the Counties of Edessa and Tripoli. Edessa was lost in 1144, captured by the Seljuk leader Zengi. The Principality of Antioch fell to Baybars in 1268, Tripoli fell in 1289, and Acre, the last principal city held by the Crusaders, fell in 1291, signaling the end of the Kingdom of Jerusalem and of Western power in the Middle East.

KNIGHTS OF ST. JOHN: Order founded in the late eleventh century that takes its name from the hospital of St. John the Baptist in Jerusalem, where it had its first headquarters. Also known as the Hospitallers, their initial brief was the care of Christian pilgrims, but after the First Crusade their objectives changed dramatically. They retained their hospitals, but their primary preoccupation became the building and the defense of their castles in the Holy Land, recruitment of knights and the acquisition of land and property. They enjoyed similar power and status as the Templars and the orders were often rivals. After the end of the Crusades, the Knights of St. John moved their headquarters to Rhodes, then later to Malta, where they became known as the Knights of Malta.

KNIGHTS TEMPLAR: Order of knights formed early in the twelfth century, after the First Crusade. Established by Hugues de Payns, who traveled to Jerusalem with eight fellow French knights, the order was named after the Temple of Solomon, upon the site of which they had their first headquarters. The Templars, who were formally recognized in 1128 at the Council of Troyes, followed both a religious rule and a strict military code. Their initial raison d'être was to protect Christian pilgrims in the Holy Land; however, they far exceeded this early brief in their military and mercantile endeavors both in the Middle East and throughout Europe, where they rose to become one of the wealthiest and most powerful organizations of their day. There were three separate classes within the order: sergeants, priests and knights, but only knights, who took the three monastic vows of chastity, poverty and obedience, were permitted to wear the distinctive white habits that bore a splayed red cross.

MADRASAH: a religious school dedicated to the study of Islamic law.

MAMLUKS: from the Arabic, meaning "slave," the name was given to the royal bodyguard, mainly of Turkish descent, bought and raised by the Ayyubid sultans of Egypt into a standing army of devout Muslim warriors. Known in their day as "the Templars of Islam," the Mamluks achieved ascendancy in 1250 when they assassinated Sultan Turanshah, a nephew of Saladin, and took control of Egypt. Under Baybars, the Mamluk Empire grew to encompass Egypt and Syria, and they were ultimately responsible for removing Frankish influence in the Middle East. After the end of the Crusades in 1291, the Mamluks' reign continued until they were overthrown by the Ottoman Turks in 1517.

MARITIME REPUBLICS: Italian mercantile city-states of Venice, Genoa and Pisa.

MARSHAL: in the Templar hierarchy, the chief military official.

MECCA: a city in Saudi Arabia. Birthplace of Muhammad and the holy city of Islam.

MONGOLS: nomadic tribespeople who lived around the steppes of eastern Asia until the late twelfth century when they were united under Genghis Khan, who established his capital at Karakorum and set out on a series of massive conquests. When Genghis Khan died, his empire extended across Asia, Persia, southern Russia and China. The Mongols' first great defeat came at the hands of Baybars and Kutuz at Ayn Jalut in 1260, and their empire began a gradual decline in the fourteenth century.

OUTREMER: French word meaning "overseas," referring to the Holy Land.

PALFREY: a light horse used for normal riding.

PARLEY: a discussion to debate points of a dispute, most commonly the terms of a truce.

PRECEPTORY: Latin name for the administrative houses of military orders, which would have been like manors, with domestic quarters, workshops and usually a chapel.

RICHARD THE LIONHEART: (1157–99) son of Henry II and Eleanor of Aquitaine, Richard ruled as king of England from 1189 to his death in 1199, but spent very little time in the kingdom. Along with Frederick Barbarossa and Philip II of France, he led the Third Crusade to recapture Jerusalem, which had fallen to Saladin.

RULE, THE: the Rule of the Temple was drawn up in 1129, with the aid of St. Bernard de Clairvaux, at the Council of Troyes, where the Temple was formally recognized. It was written as part religious rule, part military code, and set out how members of the order should live and conduct themselves during their daily lives and during combat. The Rule was added to over the years and by the thirteenth century there were over six hundred clauses, some more serious than others, the breaching of which would mean expulsion for the offender.

SALADIN: (1138–1193) of Kurdish origin, he became sultan of Egypt and Syria in 1173, after winning several power struggles. Saladin led his army against the Crusaders at Hattin and dealt the Franks a devastating blow. He reclaimed most of the Kingdom of Jerusalem created by the Christians during the First Crusade, leading to the launch of the Third Crusade, which saw him pitted against Richard the Lionheart. Saladin was a hero throughout the Islamic East, but was also admired, and feared, by the Crusaders for his courage and gallantry.

SALAT: ritual prayer carried out by Muslims five times a day.

SARACEN: in the medieval period, a term used by Europeans for all Arabs and Muslims.

SENESCHAL: the steward or chief official of an estate. In the Temple's hierarchy, the seneschal held one of the highest positions.

SEQUIN: Venetian gold coin.

SIEGE ENGINE: any machine used to attack fortifications during sieges such as mangonels (Arabic: *mandjaniks*), trebuchets and espringales (Arabic: *'arradas*).

SHIA AND SUNNI MUSLIMS: two branches of Islam formed in the schism that arose after the death of Muhammad over the question of who should be his successor. The Sunnis, forming the majority, believed that no one could truly succeed Muhammad and appointed a caliph as leader of the Muslim community. Sunnis revere the first four caliphs appointed after Muhammad's death, whose example they follow as the custom (*sunna*) that all Muslims should follow. Shias hold as their figure of authority only the *imam,* the fourth caliph, whom they consider heir of the Prophet, descended from the bloodline of Ali, Muhammad's son-in-law. Shias reject the first three caliphs and the traditions of Sunni belief.

SURCOAT: a long linen or silk sleeveless garment, usually worn over mail or armor.

TAKE THE CROSS: to go on Crusade, a term derived from the cloth crosses that were handed out to those who pledged to become Crusaders.

TEUTONIC KNIGHTS: military order of knights, similar to the Templars and the Hospitallers, originating in Germany. The Teutonics were founded in 1198 and during their time in the Holy Land were responsible for guarding the area northeast of Acre. By the mid-thirteenth century they had conquered Prussia, which later became their base.

VAMBRACES: armor worn to protect the forearms.

VELLUM: parchment used for writing, most commonly taken from the skin of a calf.

VISITOR: a post within the Temple's hierarchy created in the thirteenth century. The visitor, who was second only to the grand master, was the overlord of all the Temple's possessions in the West.

Select Bibliography

Acre 1291: Bloody Sunset of the Crusader States. David Nicolle. Osprey Publishing, 2005.

The Cross and the Crescent: A History of the Crusades. Malcolm Billings. BBC Publications, 1987.

A History of Business in Medieval Europe: 1200–1550. Edwin S. Hunt and James M. Murray. Cambridge University Press, 1999.

A History of Medieval Life: A Guide to Life From 1000 to 1500 AD. David Nicolle. Chancellor Press, 2000.

A History of the Crusades (3 volumes). Steven Runciman. Cambridge University Press, 1954.

The Illustrated Encyclopedia of Medieval Civilization. Aryeh Grabois. Octopus, 1980.

The Knights Templar: A New History. Helen Nicholson. Sutton Publishing, 2001.

The Life and Times of Edward I. John Chancellor. Weidenfeld & Nicolson, 1981.

The Lion of Egypt: Sultan Baybars I and the Near East in the 13th Century. Peter Thorau. Trans: P. M. Holt. Longman Group UK, 1987.

One Thousand Roads to Mecca. Ed: Michael Wolfe. Grove Press, 1997.

Power and Profit: The Merchant in Medieval Europe. Peter Spufford. Thames & Hudson, 2002.

The Templar of Tyre: Part III of the "Deeds of the Cypriots" (Crusade Texts in Translation). Paul Crawford. Ashgate Publishing, 2003.

The Templars. Piers Paul Read. Weidenfeld & Nicolson, 1999.

The Templars and the Assassins: The Militia of Heaven. James Wasserman. Inner Traditions, 2001.

The Times Atlas of European History. 2nd Edition. Times Books, 1998.

The Trial of the Templars. Malcolm Barber. Cambridge University Press, 1978.

The Wars of the Crusades: 1096–1291. Terence Wise. Osprey Publishing, 1978.

The World's Religions. Ninian Smart. Cambridge University Press, 1989.

TURN THE PAGE FOR A SNEAK PEEK
OF THE FINAL BOOK IN
THE BRETHREN TRILOGY . . .

THE FALL OF THE TEMPLARS

After two hundred years, the Crusades are over.
Leaving the Christian Empire in the East in ruins, Will
Campbell and the survivors return to the West, to find a
continent in shock over the loss of the Holy Land. Will, his
grief still raw, has only one thing on his mind: Revenge.

After years of political plotting, King Edward I finally has
Scotland in his sights, and as the English army marches
north, Will is forced to make a decision that will change
his life forever. But with all his thoughts bent on defeating
his enemy, he does not realize that an even more ominous
threat is growing.

For there is a warrior king on the throne of France, whose
desire for supremacy knows no bounds, and who will stop
at nothing to fulfill his twisted ambitions.

The fight for the Holy Land has ended.
The Temple's last battle has just begun.

AVAILABLE FROM DUTTON IN JANUARY 2009

Prologue

As the young man knelt, the iron cold of the floor seeped through the thin material of his hose. He felt the stone, hard and unyielding, bruising him, but the discomfort was reassuring; the flagstones beneath him were the only thing in the chamber that felt solid. A fog of incense hung in shifting layers, stinging his eyes. It was a bitter smell that reminded him of burning leaves. He didn't know what it was, but it wasn't the serene frankincense that always welcomed him into church. Around him, shadows stole across the walls, nebulous and unfamiliar, as figures passed by candles that sputtered in holders on the ground, placed so far apart that the quivering points of fire cast little real light and served only to blind and disorient him further. A few yards away to his left the floor was spattered with a substance that gleamed wetly. Here, in this dimness, it looked almost black, but in daylight the young man knew it would be a bright, shocking red. He could still smell its sharp, metallic odor, even over the pungent incense, and he swallowed tightly, a plug of nausea clogging his throat.

This wasn't what he had expected. Part of him was glad of that; he may not have gone through with it had he known what would be asked of him this night. The only things that kept him here, doing as he was bid, were the presence of the men in the shadows and the fear of what would happen if he refused. But he didn't want to show weakness. He wanted to do this right, despite his trepidation, and so he stared straight ahead, his chest, bare and pale, thrust forward, hands, slick with sweat, clasped tightly behind his back.

Now the men had stopped moving and the chamber had fallen silent again; he could hear faint birdsong coming through the high windows, all covered with heavy black cloth. It must be almost dawn.

There was movement to his left. He saw a figure approaching and his stomach churned with apprehension. It was a man dressed in a shimmering cloak sewn from hundreds of overlapping circles of silk, all different shades of blue and pink: cobalt, sapphire, rose, violet. Here and there the material was shot through with silver thread that glistened whenever the candlelight caught it, the overall effect creating the impression that he was clad in the scales of a fish. The young man knew the figure was male, for he had spoken often during the ceremony, guiding him, commanding him, but so far his face had been concealed by a cowl, fashioned from the same material as the cloak, that hung down almost to his chest. It was surprising he could even see to walk. Under the cowl, his head appeared oddly misshapen and his voice, when he spoke, came out muffled and deep.

"You have chosen the path and it was wisely chosen. You have sworn the oaths and stood fast in the face of temptation and dread. Now is the final test and the most perilous. But obey me as you have pledged and all will be well." The figure paused. "Will you obey me now and always?"

"I will," breathed the young man.

"Then prove it!" snapped the figure, whipping back the cowl and dropping to a crouch before the young man, who recoiled from the grinning skull that was revealed, the candles on the floor up-lighting it, making the bone that much yellower and the huge, hollow eye sockets that much blacker.

Even though he knew it was just a mask, even though he caught a glimpse of dark human eyes through the sockets of the skull, his terror didn't dissipate, and when a small gold cross was drawn from the folds of the fish-scale cloak and held in front of him, his heart seemed fit to explode in his chest.

"Spit on it."

"W . . . what?"

"Denounce its power over you. Prove you are loyal to me alone, that you speak as one with your brothers."

The young man's eyes darted left and right as the men moved out of the shadows. They too wore masks; blood red with the image of a white stag's head painted on the front of each.

"Spit!" came the command again.

Feeling the men crowding in around him, blocking out the frail candlelight, the young man leaned forward over the proffered cross. He collected saliva in his dry mouth with difficulty. Closing his eyes, he spat.

THE **BRETHREN** TRILOGY
NEARS ITS THRILLING CONCLUSION . . .

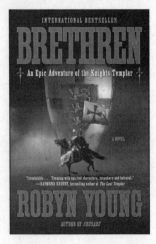

ISBN 978-0-452-28833-1

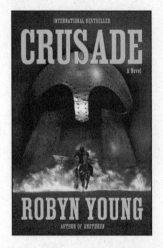

ISBN 978-0-452-28960-4

LOOK FOR

THE FALL OF THE TEMPLARS
IN JANUARY 2009 FROM DUTTON

www.robynyoung.com

Available wherever books are sold.

Plume
A member of Penguin Group (USA) Inc.
www.penguin.com

Giles tried to sit up, but could only just raise his head off the pillow; enough to see a framed picture on the wall of Adolf Hitler giving him a Nazi salute.

'How many of our boys survived?'

'Only a handful. The lads took the colonel's words to heart. "We will all sacrifice our lives before Rommel books a suite at the Majestic Hotel".'

'Did anyone else from our platoon make it?'

'You, me and—'

'Don't tell me, Fisher?'

'No. Because if they'd sent him to Weinsberg, I'd have asked for a transfer to Colditz.'

Giles lay still, staring up at the ceiling. 'So how do we escape?'

'I wondered how long it would be before you asked that.'

'And what's the answer?'

'Not a chance while your leg's still in plaster, and even after that it won't be easy, but I've got a plan.'

'Of course you have.'

'The plan's not the problem,' said Bates. 'The problem is the escape committee. They control the waiting list, and you're at the back of the queue.'

'How do I get to the front?'

'It's like any queue in England, you just have to wait your turn . . . unless—'

'Unless?'

'Unless Brigadier Turnbull, the senior ranking officer, thinks there's a good reason why you should be moved up the queue.'

'Like what?'

'If you can speak fluent German, it's a bonus.'

20

THE FIRST THING Giles saw was his right leg hitched to a pulley and encased in plaster.

He could dimly remember a long journey, during which the pain had become almost unbearable, and he had assumed he would die long before they got him to a hospital. And he would never forget the operation, but then how could he, when they'd run out of anaesthetic moments before the doctor made the first incision?

He turned his head very slowly to the left and saw a window with three bars across it, then to the right; that's when he saw him.

'No, not you,' Giles said. 'For a moment I thought I'd escaped and gone to heaven.'

'Not yet,' said Bates. 'First you have to do a spell in purgatory.'

'For how long?'

'At least until your leg's mended, possibly longer.'

'Are we back in England?' Giles asked hopefully.

'I wish,' said Bates. 'No, we're in Germany, Weinsberg PoW camp, which is where we all ended up after being taken prisoner.'

GILES BARRINGTON

1941–1942